The *Wonderful* Professor *Wolgath*

∞

A Novel
by Alexis Rhae

Neck Reigned Publishing, LLC
Florence, Alabama

In the interest of realistic portrayal, certain historical figures and places are encountered or mentioned by name in this novel. However this is a work of fiction that is the product of the author's imagination based on the author's historical studies. The dialogue and events in this novel, while based on the author's research, are fictional and should not be regarded as fact.

Thank You

My God, my heavenly Father, I give You great thanks. I prayed that You would take this book in Your hands and direct the future of this manuscript as You pleased. You have answered my prayer! I praise You for that in Your greatness You saw fit to lead me toward this day; a day I could not see. Jesus Christ, only begotten Son of my Father, I give You humble thanks. You have seen fit to grant me mercy and grace by Your salvation as I walk through the years of my learning until I can be completed in the sight of heaven. Wisdom I give you loving thanks, for even in my imperfection You have been willing to touch my spirit. I am overcome by Your presence and overjoyed in Your love.

Thank you Terry for your belief and care. Thank you for nurturing this dream and the maturity you have watched me grow into. I am so glad that God saw fit to keep my writing back so that you could be the one to lift it up.

With all my love,

Alexis

To the Readers

The following is a fictional tale about a man and his loved ones and how it came to be that they journeyed across an ocean. His is a voyage born of misfortune that does not end when he finds himself thrust into a new land. It is only through each of the characters' hope by faith in God and love for one another that the sinister and even circumstantial calamities they face are overcome.

At the time when I wrote this book, I poured more of my heart into it than I had into any other piece I had ever published before it. It is a real representation of the mind of a young lady seeking Christ in an imaginary landscape of her own making. There was not much more to me yet than that. It is a reflection of my Christian imagination held out in simple offering for you to see. I sincerely hope that in reading this work you will be encouraged to remember where you have been and consider who you might be in Christ.

Thank you for reading,

Alexis

Part I

Earnest Sentiment

Chapter 1

*T*here are few sights in this world so pitiful, so effective at the thumping of one's heartstrings, as that of a fine dog watching his affectionate master reach for his hat and coat by the door. So it was that the Great Dane raised his head as Lucius Wolgath slipped one arm into its sleeve. He stood firmly facing away from the drooping animal, who was at present only perplexed by his actions.

"I'll not do it this time, Commodore."

The Great Dane emitted a confused whine.

"Because whenever I do, you get your hopes up."

Commodore moaned a sorrowful moan.

"And then you make that sound as though you cannot understand why I'm doing my best to hurt your feelings."

Commodore came to his feet and nudged Wolgath's legs. The man sighed the long-suffering sigh of one thoroughly annoyed with a certain routine. He faced the dog as he buttoned the cloth buttons of his long coat and peered down over the gold rims of his spectacles.

"Then I turn around, and you become indignant and flounce off."

Commodore sneezed.

"Well there's no need to be terse."

The dog grunted, clearly fed up with his master's lack of interest in his feelings. He turned to wander in the direction of the bedroom.

"I told you!"

A heavy bark sounded from the hall. Lucius grinned as he set his tricorn hat atop his head and started out the door. Sunlight lit his face, casting radiant glares from the gold rims of the glasses perched on his shapely nose. He stood reveling in the bright, crisp air of that January afternoon.

Wolgath was handsome enough, as opinions go, according to the fashionable expectations of the women of the day. He was of slight build, neither weighty nor muscular. His hair and beard were of pale golden curls. It was a soft shade that bespoke an even softer demeanor. He possessed simple blue eyes set above high cheekbones. The chin was angular with a small cleft. His hands seemed uncommonly large, though they expressed the lithe dexterity of a musician. Due to a healthy enjoyment of being out of doors, Lucius' face, neck, and hands bore more color than was to be desired. Thankfully his many other pleasing qualities warranted overlooking such a defect.

Lucius lived on a single floor of a three story stone building within sight of the village at Penn and Tyler's Green in Buckinghamshire just twenty-five miles from London. The floor he rented happened to be the third one and his front door happened to be on the side of it, accessible only by a set of wooden stairs. It was from this height that Lucius had a very clear view of the village and the nearest border of the Condreve estate, where he would be dining that very evening. From there his gaze rose to encompass the familiar faces of the Chiltern Hills, still flecked with light snow.

He had chosen his residence primarily for its location. The hamlet was securely set between London and the University of Cambridge, giving him just enough access to both. During the week he would stay at his college at the generous insistence of one of his professors, but at week's end he would retreat to the quiet of the Green.

The damp ground shifted beneath his feet as he made his way along the narrow road, a consequence of the melted snow of yesterday. The brisk air left a biting chill on his cheeks and hands. Still, he was not a man to accept the bad without remembering the good.

Cold hands…muddy shoes…Familiar. Reminds me that I'm home.

He was just turning a corner in the village when he spied a man he recognized on the uncrowded street ahead.

"Rodney!"

The man acknowledged him with a bob of his head as he approached.

"Lucius."

The man who spoke was Rodney Dushaw, a fellow student of Wolgath's at Cambridge. Though he was a younger man of twenty-one, Dushaw bore the sour disposition of an old miser. His hair was so brown it might be called black. His plain gray eyes reflected nothing. His build was slightly heavier than that of Wolgath, and he was a good three inches shorter. His clothing, in contrast to Wolgath's, was of the finest material, produced in London by one of the best tailors ever to carry a thimble.

Lucius did not notice the difference in character or clothing, though Dushaw certainly did. To his credit, he managed to keep his gray eyes expressionless as they roved over Lucius' wool coat, sheepskin trousers, thin stockings, and muddy shoes.

"What brings you from Cambridge, Rodney?" Wolgath wondered pleasantly.

Dushaw buried his hands in his pockets. "Nothing important. Just supper at Mr. Condreve's estate."

"Lawrence Condreve?"

"Yes, I see you've heard of him. His annual contributions to the college are quite considerable. I understand it's his daughter's birthday, and they've invited several people from Cambridge to their little party."

"I'm going there myself!" Lucius smiled happily.

Rodney blinked and recovered. "How-unexpected. I take it you know his daughter?"

"No. I've been a guest of Mr. Condreve's for tea two or three times, but I've never had the pleasure of meeting his wife and daughter. You?"

"Well, you know I-" Rodney broke off and tilted his head to observe a stray cat sauntering across the road. "Makes it terribly annoying to find a proper gift, wouldn't you say?"

Lucius was stricken at this. He chewed his lip and immediately began ferreting around in his pockets, checking each not once but twice.

"May one ask the reason for this sudden agitation?" Rodney inquired, though he could well guess the answer.

"I forgot to purchase a gift."

"That's the very crux of the reason we're going in the first place!"

At long last Lucius produced two silver shillings and three copper ha'pennies.

"There. What shall I buy?"

"Sadly, I haven't a clue."

"You must have *some* notion of what a young lady should like for a present. You must have *some* experience to draw from."

Dushaw's gaze narrowed a fraction. "Isn't this cutting things a bit close? Buying the gift on the way to the celebration, I mean."

Lucius studied the scarred face of his pocket watch. "You're right, Rodney, but that's an understatement considering how late we're going to be already."

"True," Dushaw agreed with an elevated eyebrow. "More like cropping it to the ground."

Lucius brushed by him, going only a few steps before pausing at the window of a shop. The creaking sign read *Bolton's Beauties*. The spotted glass provided passers-by with a view of dusty bottles, weathered books, and a moldy hat, all arranged on a length of faded brown velvet.

Dushaw's nostrils flared with distaste. "Surely there is someplace better to shop in this…town."

Lucius glanced to him with a knowing smile as he stooped by the window. This was ironic, for, outside the realms of his expertise, Lucius rarely knew anything.

"You ought to have more appreciation for the diamond in the rough, Rodney. You never know when you're going to find it." With that he straightened and slipped inside the shop.

Rodney bent at once to see what it was that had caught the other man's attention. A small stand of hooks in the casement held several battered bracelets. On one solitary hook, there was suspended a silk ribbon necklace of a delicate shade of pink. Hanging from the necklace was a brilliant black and white cameo pendant. A rough hand lifted the necklace from its place, and Lucius soon exited the establishment, drawing the strings of a small white silk pouch.

"There, you see," he triumphed as they set off once more. "I even have change." He flipped a solitary coin into the air, caught it, and nestled it within his waistcoat pocket.

"Capital." Now that Wolgath was feeling cheery again, Rodney was slipping into a dark mood. The man had a never-ending supply of good humor that always managed to crawl under Rodney's skin in a most annoying way. "Why did you agree to come to this little soiree anyway?"

This gave Lucius brief pause. "What a question to ask."

"A legitimate one," Rodney added, "since you don't even know the girl."

"Neither do you," Lucius countered innocently.

Rodney's cheeks colored. "I know her father."

"So do I. I met him at Cambridge some six months ago."

"I met him at a meeting of the Royal Society!"

Lucius chuckled with genuine humor. "Calm down, Dushaw. My, my, everything's a competition to you isn't it?"

Rodney averted his eyes, aggravated that his emotions might be so simple to read.

"It doesn't matter who has more reason to be attending this party. Let us go and enjoy ourselves."

Rodney scowled.

Lucius began walking swiftly again. "We've been invited; we ought to go. It's called common courtesy."

"Huh," Rodney muttered darkly. "So that's what replaced your common sense."

The stone drive leading up to the Condreve manor was curved and short, contrary to most popular styles of the day. The house was flanked by equal clumps of maple trees and guarded by a single row of expertly manicured hedges. They seemed to Lucius to be like leafy soldiers standing at attention before their charge; Lissome Ground, the palace Condreve.

A line of carriages rose up the drive along one side all the way to the steps. Lucius reached the threshold first and looked down at Rodney as he raised a hand to the heavy brass knocker. Before he ever grasped the thing, the door was flung open quite suddenly by Eshton, the butler. He was outfitted in splendid regalia for the occasion. Lucius' gaze leapt to the ever-present powdered wig. Eshton had gone to great lengths for his appearance, giving his wig-and, inadvertently, his shoulders-a heavy dusting of powder and even applying a bit of cosmetic to his nose and cheeks.

"Ah, Mssr. Wolgath." Eshton sniffed and bowed.

"Good evening, Eshton."

Rodney shrugged up beside Lucius, and the butler squinted.

"And Mr.…sir. Won't you please come in?"

Eshton stepped aside to allow them entrance.

"It's Dushaw," Rodney snapped as the butler was closing the door.

"Of course. Mr. Rodney Dushaw. Do forgive me, sir," he finished with a low bow and an astoundingly insincere smile. "The Condreves are expecting you both. Please, this way."

Eshton guided the men down a long hallway. It was a corridor Lucius had been down once before when Lawrence Condreve had invited him to see his study. As they passed that very room, Lucius looked through the open door to a painting on the wall above Lawrence's massive desk. It depicted a very young woman with auburn hair in a rosey pink dress. The bodice and sleeves of the dress were covered in lace and ribbons. In one hand she held the long stem of a white rose. Her head was turned slightly, though her eyes faced straight ahead. The artist seemed to have captured the woman's very intelligence in that gaze. Lucius had been very taken with the image and very curious when he learned that the woman was Lawrence's daughter. He knew that the Condreves had commissioned the painting to be done by Mr. Gainsborough after seeing his work of the Countess Howe. Gainsborough was a great master, to be sure, but Lucius had long wondered whether his vision of Ms. Condreve was true or kind.

Once they had passed by the study, Lucius' attention veered to the butler as he led the way. He watched Eshton's rigid military movements with almost childish curiosity. Eventually they came to a spacious formal drawing room on the left. Once they had reached their destination, Eshton bowed and turned away.

The room was lavish, decorated with plush chairs, loveseats, and settees arranged throughout. A breathtaking ornate fireplace dominated the far wall. In one corner a young lady sat dabbling at the keys of a smart piano forte, and had attracted quite a group of listeners. The remainder of the guests seemed to be milling about in flocks of threes and fours. Every so often some courageous soul would break from a cluster to cross the room and join another. A servant dressed to match Eshton flitted from group to group offering refreshments from a tray. He looked very much like a bee moving from flower to flower. With the ladies' dresses ranging from turquoise to scarlet to gold, the gathering did give off the illusion of a field of wild flowers swaying to and fro with the breeze.

Lucius spied Lawrence almost at once. He stood close to the fireplace amid a clump of guests. Smiling, he started toward his friend.

"Mr. Walgoth!"

Lucius visibly cringed at this shrill call.

Rodney placed an almost sympathetic hand on his shoulder. "Tough luck Lucius, old boy," he tittered and headed toward the fireplace.

"Lousy deserter." Even as he mumbled this, Lucius set a polite smile firmly in place. He turned to meet the blond wisp of a girl scampering his way. "Ms. Winslett. How good it is to see you."

The freckled nose wrinkled as she burst into giggles. "It is good to see you as well, Mr. Walgoth."

"Thank you," he replied. "But the name's Wolgath, Ms. Winslett."

The girl's green eyes grew wide and her red lips bunched in embarrassment.

"Perhaps," he was swift to add, "you should simply call me Lucius."

"Oh!" She beamed at him with teeth most dull. "And you shall call me Tabitha?"

"Of course."

At this the young Ms. Winslett exploded into such a fit of nervous laughter that she was forced to retreat. Lucius chuckled and shook his head as he watched her go.

"I believe you may have just blown the dam, sir."

Wolgath turned to see another young woman standing behind him. She was grinning like an older sister who has just caught her brother in the cake cupboard before dinner.

"Fortunately I know how to swim," Lucius said smoothly.

"That was very kind of you."

He sobered at the compliment. "'Twas not kindness. She's a pleasant girl, if a little …overenthusiastic."

The lady gave a deep nod of agreement. "You are a guest at my birthday party, but I do not believe we have met." She extended one delicate hand. "I am Alexcena Condreve."

"Of course!" Lucius took her hand in his own. "I recognize you from your painting."

It was as if the image had stepped down from the mantel and wandered through the hall to join them. Her chocolate brown hair hung in shining, meticulous waves on her shoulders. In several places this color was highlighted by bright strands of copper. Her complexion was creamy, her cheeks tinged pink. Her soft lips were stained a velvet red, though the color was her own. Her starched dress was pale and edged with tiny blue satin rosettes. Frail bits of lace lined the hem, collar, and cuffs. The bodice fit her form with a flattering modesty. The simple gold earrings and bracelet she wore were very fine. The inviting hazel eyes radiated intelligence and seemed to hint of the depth of her spirit. The more he studied the elegant lines of her face, the more he came to decide that the portrait had not done her the slightest justice.

"-afraid the painting was not a *true* likeness," she was saying meekly.

"No, indeed," Lucius agreed. "I am Lucius Wolgath."

She curtsied to his bow and each dropped their hands. "My father has told me much of you."

"Has he?" Lucius grinned. "I must assure you, none of it is true."

She laughed, an airy sound that drifted lightly away. "Surely you place more faith in your reputation than that, sir."

"Only in the classroom, Ms. Condreve."

"Because no one will listen to him anywhere else," Rodney added, appearing close beside the two.

Alexcena looked to the rug. Lucius smiled and gestured toward her.

"Rodney," he said cheerfully, "may I present Ms. Condreve?"

"No need, Lucius." Rodney reached for the lady's hand, and a color grew in her cheeks as his lips brushed her knuckles. "We have already met."

Alexcena gave a brief turn of her mouth and quickly withdrew her hand. "Mr. Dushaw."

"I was not aware the two of you were acquainted," Lucius went on, oblivious to Alexcena's discomfiture.

"Yes, I ought to have said something sooner." Rodney paused to sip from a glass of punch he had pinched from a passing tray. "Ms. Condreve and I have known one another for some time." He gave her an oily smile.

She looked to Lucius. "We met at a party my father once held."

"You must have been out of town for that one, Lucius," Rodney commented lazily.

"No, I've only known Lawrence about six months. I'm not really one for parties anyway." As soon as the words left his mouth, Lucius froze, realizing he must sound rude.

Alexcena smiled, the smooth lines of her countenance relaxing somewhat. "Me too." Then, lowering her voice to a conspiring tone, she leaned closer to Lucius. "I always feel surrounded, like a fox in his burrow."

"Precisely!" Lucius chimed. "And you always end up standing by someone whose name you can't remember."

"Then they refuse to start a conversation-"

"Probably because they've forgotten your name."

"-and then they expect you to say something, but you can't."

"Because you're still trying to remember their name!"

Lucius pursed his lips to stifle a laugh, and Alexcena covered hers with one delicate hand.

"Mr. Dushaw seems to have slipped away," she said after a moment. "Why don't you come and greet my parents, Mr. Wolgath."

"Do I remember their names?"

Alexcena clamped her mouth shut, her eyes alight.

"Well, no matter." Lucius bowed once more. "Lead the way, fair lady."

They threaded their way to the fireplace. Cecelia Condreve sat in a straight backed chair and Lawrence stood close beside her. Lucius made a swift study of his friend, whom he had not seen for some weeks. He found Lawrence looking pleased and content. His powdered wig, fashionable attire, and broad smile all helped to make him seem younger than his true years, although none of these aspects could hide his true size. His waistcoat was pulled tight over his thick padding, and Lucius noted that it appeared to have extended further over his belt even since he had met him. Cecelia was a different figure entirely. Even seated as she was, it was obvious that she was a tall, reedy sort of woman. Her skin seemed paper thin and her silver hair was dull, but the happiness in her expression gave light to her features. Lucius thought that in her youth she would have been quite striking.

Lawrence beamed with recognition when the two approached. "Ah!" he grunted merrily. "Wolgath arrives! You've met Alexcena, now you must meet my wife, Cecelia."

The lady bobbed her head and Lucius gave a deep bow. "It is a great pleasure to finally meet you, Mrs. Condreve. And a most joyous occasion, I might add."

Lawrence turned his generous smiles to his daughter. "Yes, indeed. It's not every day a young lady becomes nineteen years of age."

Lucius raised a finger expressively. "Which reminds me!" He reached gingerly into his pocket and withdrew the silken pouch. He held it out at arm's length to Alexcena.

Her gaze registered surprise and delight. She accepted it and fumbled with the drawstrings. "Mr. Wolgath, thank you. It's beautiful."

"That's the first time I've ever been thanked before the gift was opened."

Lawrence chuckled. "I wonder if she'll react the same way to whatever is inside."

She gave the strings an impatient tug. They all heard a light snap, and a button from her glove flew high in the air. She bit her lip at the ludicrous faux pas, but Lucius caught the object easily. He then motioned for her to continue. Alexcena slipped her slim fingers into the bag, and Lucius was delighted by the enchantment that crossed her features as she studied the cameo.

"It is *beautiful*, Mr. Wolgath."

Lucius clasped his hands behind his back. "Perfect."

The two ladies began inspecting the necklace more closely, momentarily paying the men no mind. Condreve nodded to the young man.

"Well done, Lucius."

"It is most charming, Professor."

"Oh, I'm not a professor just yet, ma'am," Lucius hurried to correct Mrs. Condreve. "Not for several months more."

Lawrence gave his shoulder a hearty pat-causing his knees to buckle-before turning to address the other guests. "Shall we adjourn to the dining room?"

Condreve's booming proclamation was met with scores of agreement, and everyone began trickling through a second door to another part of the house. The last to leave was Rodney Dushaw. He knocked off the remainder of his punch as he watched his fellow student's retreating back.

"Yes, Lucius," he mumbled in a tainted tone. "Well done."

Dinner was anything but a simple affair. A fleet of servants-one to every two guests-were stationed around the walls of the room. Entertainment was provided by a stuffy gentleman playing the water glasses in a discrete corner. The ringing tones resounded about the room in a soft background to the steady chatter of those in attendance. The place settings alone were enough to undermine Lucius' confidence. He could not recall ever having seen so many utensils. Fingerbowls, the latest trend to sweep from London through the neighboring towns, were also set before each seat. The formal table easily sat the twenty or so people in attendance with Lawrence at its head, Cecelia at the opposite end, and Alexcena squarely in the middle. The Condreves did not approve of the new fashion of promiscuous seating, which placed gentlemen and ladies alternating all around the table. So it was that the men lined the right and ladies occupied the left. Lucius could not have been more pleased to find himself placed directly across from Alexcena, despite the fact that Miss Tabitha Winslett was seated at Alexcena's side with her mother, Deborah Winslett beside her. Her father, who Lucius had not been formally introduced to, sat across from his daughter at Lucius' left. Rodney was placed on his right.

"I'm so glad to see other families upholding a traditional seating arrangement," Deborah commented vaguely. It was all the prompting Tabitha needed.

"Oh yes, indeed. Quite scandalous! You know I flatly refused to participate in it at Lillian Crawler's party two weeks past. She looked down her nose at me-bit miffed I should think-but it's not as if she had arranged anything at all well for that night. Everyone just wandered about everywhere and was expected to just *blend* into their seats. Of course with so many young men in attendance at a party with so many young ladies, I suppose it was inevitable that some let propriety slide. At least that's what I told Mimi. You know Mimi Harper, Alexcena? I told her it was bound to happen. Then, I was told later, that Carter and Bartholum Doyle-have you met them Alexcena? They're both horrid, though Bartholum is sort of easy on the eyes if you tilt your gaze to the left just a bit. Anyway, they waited until after supper when everyone was out in the gardens and snuck down into the valley of the ha-ha. Then as soon as Lillian's guests started walking about its edge, they would reach up and grab their ank-er, excuse me, their *shoes*. Billy Weston almost gave them what-for for grasping his fiance's shoe, but then he was too hysterical when he saw Sophia Johnston beating Carter senseless with her hat for the same offense. Then-"

Deborah laid a hand on her daughter's arm. "Tabitha, do take a breath. Try some of your soup."

Lucius had been so fascinated by Tabitha's inane talent for chatter that he had failed to notice the arrival of a bowl of steaming asparagus soup at his place. He gave his head a shake and glanced around to see if anyone had noticed his ungainly staring. Or rather, if Alexcena had noticed. She was watching Tabitha, one hand pressing her napkin to her mouth, her eyes ablaze with merriment at the girl's never-ending dirge.

"Something catch your eye, Lucius?"

"Uh-what?" He flipped his focus to Rodney seated at his right. "Ah, no, thanks," he stammered. He was quite perplexed by Rodney's apparent irritation.

"Then stuff them back into their sockets, why don't you."

"Oh." Lucius sheepishly lifted his spoon to sample his soup. Still his gaze trailed up to Alexcena.

"-dreadful thing for someone to do at a party," she was saying to Tabitha. "I shall certainly think twice before approaching the edge of a ha-ha. Wouldn't you, Mr. Wolgath?"

Lucius gulped and his collar visibly bobbed. "Forgive my ignorance, Ms. Condreve, but what exactly is a ha-ha?"

"It's a…trench of sorts with a supporting wall on one side. People place them around their gardens to keep out deer, livestock, raccoons, and the like."

"Acting as a barrier while still preserving the view."

"Exactly."

"Marvelous idea. I am not familiar with it. I can't say as I've spent much time in the English countryside before the past year."

"Where do you live now?"

Lucius paused, wondering if she was truly speaking to him. When Alexcena's eyebrows rose, he took heart and went on. "I reside here in Penn. I was staying at the dorms in Cambridge before that, but now that my professorship is in sight, I decided that after a lifetime of boisterous cities I wanted a change."

"You mean some quiet."

Lucius was taken aback and pleased by her light teasing.

"He means boredom," Rodney interrupted. "He locks himself in that rickety old boarding house and sleeps the weekends away." He paused to drink from his glass. "Meanwhile he could be enjoying the pleasures of Cambridge with the rest of us. Go on, tell Ms. Condreve about your rickety old boarding house."

Lucius blinked in mild surprise at Rodney's comments. Still he looked to Alexcena and cleared his throat. "It's…rickety."

He was vastly relieved when she started laughing.

"A boarding house?" Tabitha squeaked. "How very quaint! I had no idea you resided in such a humble dwelling, Mr. Lucius." She drew out the first syllable of his name with a great flourish and glanced about as though hoping someone would raise an eyebrow at her familiarity. "It is so funny you should bring this up, because I have a friend who has a cousin that-"

"Tabitha, do take a drink," her mother chided from beside her. "I am sure you are quite flushed. When we arrive home you must lie down at once. I'll not take no for an answer."

Tabitha's jaw twitched shut and she reached for her glass. "Of course, Mother."

Ordinarily, Wolgath would have given the younger girl an encouraging glance. As it happened, Alexcena placed a hand on her arm and helpfully offered a change of topic.

"What exactly are you studying at Cambridge, Mr. Wolgath?"

"I plan to become a professor of science."

"A professor! That is most ambitious. What field of science do you intend to teach?"

Lucius smiled, more than a little embarrassed by her praise. "I should like to be a professor of chemistry, although, I am just as qualified in botany. I may just do both. I was quite fond of collecting various plants and insects when I was a boy. I suppose I never grew out of it."

"Come now, Lucius," Rodney interjected, "these fine ladies have no desire to speak of insects at all, much less on an occasion such as this." He raised his glass to Alexcena.

She gave an obligatory dip of her head and said nothing more.

"From whence did you come to Cambridge, er, Wolgath?"

This question was directed from his left, and for the first time Lucius took notice of Tabitha's father. The man was already dipping his head for another swallow of soup.

"Forgive our questioning, Mr. Wolgath," Deborah apologized for her husband. "You are quite a new face for us hereabouts, and we can't help but notice that you do not speak to anyone much outside of church."

Mr. Winslett chuckled as he raised his head. "Forgive my *wife*, Mr. Wolgath," he said with a happy wink. "She carries a long-held notion that anyone who does not talk as much or more than she at tea parties and dinners and afternoons-out must be odd and therefore, interesting."

"Oh, Harrison, really!" Deborah scoffed, though she smiled endearingly at him.

Lucius, being confused by their banter, chose to answer the gentleman's first comment. "I was born in Town and lived there until the age of ten. From then on I lived in Austria. I have quite a lot of family there."

"Austria. So that's where the name Wolgath arises from?"

"No, sir." Lucius took another sip of soup. "My grandparents were from Germany."

"Ah, so it is German then?"

"No, sir. It's Romanian, from my father's side."

"So your mother is German?"

"Italian actually."

Mr. Winslett-Harrison-gave up questioning Lucius' heritage after that and went back to his first course. As he had given his rather curious answers, Lucius had also been aware of the fact that Rodney was speaking to Alexcena. His words were mumbled in such a confidence that Lucius could not make them out as he was talking himself. His gaze drifted to Alexcena to see what she might say in return. If he did not know better (and it must be known that Lucius Wolgath usually did not) he might have guessed that Alexcena seemed bored. He struggled for something to say. No one should ever be unhappy on their own birthday afterall.

Then he was out of time. She looked to him and he had not yet found a single word to utter. He felt his breath quicken with a sudden nerve. The anxiety passed when the lady raised her glass a fraction of an inch toward him and grinned.

Chapter 2

January 24, 1764

Tick, tick, tick, tick.

Lucius buried his face in his pillow, willing the rhythmic noise of the clock to cease. A muffled thumping drew his gaze to the side of the bed, where he saw Commodore watching him intently. His tail beat the rug in time with the clock.

"You do realize that I do not have classes until tomorrow," he argued. "There is no reason for me to be up at this hour."

The animal gave him a you-humans-are-so-lazy moan and left the room.

Lucius rolled over to take a look at the grandfather clock at the foot of his bed. He saw nothing but a blur of color and reached for his spectacles. He was shocked to find that it was actually eight in the morning and determined to rise. His Bible lay sprawled across the pillow beside him. The bedside candle had burned low during the night.

Must stop doing that. Going to burn the house down one of these days.

Lucius Wolgath had always been an avid student of Scripture. Even before his baptism, which had been at a young age, he could remember his parents reading to him the stories of the holy Bible. He recalled his mother softly repeating the letters of Paul and Peter and his father passionately reciting stories of the battles of Saul and David in the Old Testament. Just the night before he had read of Saul's searches in vain for David in the wilderness and how God had delivered the King into David's hand.

All this he remembered as he dressed and went to meet Commodore in the hall moments later.

"How's my boy today?"

The dog leapt up, his paws landing on Lucius' chest. Lucius staggered and rubbed his companion with vigor behind each ear. This earned him a lick across the face and foggy glasses.

"You should have been there last night my friend," he said as he set to preparing breakfast in his modest kitchen. "The party went very well."

He was describing bits and pieces in great detail to his Great Dane when there was a knock at the door. He answered it to find a young woman before him. She was thin with a long face that was not quite pretty and simple attire. She carried a large metal jug balanced atop her head with one hand.

"Milk, sir?"

Lucius raised a critical brow. "How long since it came from its source?"

"Two days, sir, but it's fresh as they come." She lowered the jug for his inspection.

The milk was thick, its color a dull shade of pale yellow. A skin of foam floated along the top. Lucius wrinkled his nose.

"No."

"But, sir-"

"Thank you, but I only buy my milk direct from the cow. Good day." He closed the door and the lady left, muttering as she went. He turned to Commodore. "I believe the milk maids of London are beginning to branch out."

He soon sat down to a solitary meal of tough beef and yesterday's bread. *Far cry from last night's fare...and last night's company.*

Rodney had pretty well kept silent throughout the remainder of the party and had taken his leave of the place very early. Lucius could tell that he was irritated, but he hadn't the faintest idea what about.

Alexcena didn't seem to notice. She was busy, of course, with so many guests...don't remember if she said anything at all to him last night at supper...

Lucius popped the table with his hand. "That's it!"

Commodore raised his head.

"That's it!" he exclaimed again. "I can't believe I didn't think of it before. I forgot to buy tea! I knew I forgot something yesterday."

Commodore lowered his head in discouragement as Lucius reached for his coat moments later. He was pleasantly surprised when he was allowed to follow along.

Lucius thought again of how much he enjoyed his walks through the village of Penn and Tyler's Green. The contrast between them and the close streets of Cambridge was uncanny and remarkable. The air was lighter, even sweeter, and he found himself falling in love with his most recent home all over again. His tender thoughts ebbed somewhat when he stepped in an ankle-deep puddle.

Once within the paths of Penn, he ducked around back of a particular stone house. A wicker fence surrounded the garden. Glancing to see that he was not watched, Lucius pointed ominously to Commodore.

"Tarry."

The animal sat obediently without a sound, and Lucius slipped through the flimsy gate. He passed over the steps to the back door in a single stride. The wide threshold provided cover against prying eyes. A boy answered his knock.

Lucius grinned down at him. "Good morning, young sir."

"Hello." Without further communication the boy turned away. "Mother, Mr. Wolgath's here!"

"I'm comin', I'm comin'. No need to shout." A haunchy woman in a drab dress, cap, and apron appeared in the doorway. "You'll wake the whole house and then wish you'd kept quiet you will. Mornin' Mr. Wolgath."

"Good day, Mrs. Strumble." Lucius beamed. He made an elegant leg, but Mrs. Strumble waved the gesture away.

"Don't you be makin' that fuss for the likes o' me. Go on, how was the party then?"

"Delightful."

Greed lent a keen glint to her eye. "What did they serve?"

"The last course was venison."

Mrs. Strumble gasped and fanned herself with one hand. Then she leaned forward to confide in a surreptitious tone, "I had a taste of venison once."

"I could hardly believe my eyes when I saw it." Lucius straightened. "Have you filled my order?"

She leaned back and smirked. "Don't I always?" She produced a small brown pouch from her apron pocket and passed it to him.

Lucius peered inside to inspect the withered tea leaves. He was thoroughly disgruntled with purchasing leaves that had been used and dried again. Still they were less than half the price of fresh leaves, which were ludicrously expensive. He passed his coins to Mrs. Strumble.

She took them, though she seemed to be watching him with speculation. "It's been almost two weeks now since I seen you, Mr. Wolgath. You wouldn't be going to anyone else for your tea, now would you?"

Lucius raised an eyebrow. "My dear Mrs. Strumble, where else would I go? You just be sure you don't get caught doing this."

"Well thank you indeed, Mr. Wolgath."

He dipped his head. "I bid you good day, ma'am."

"Indeed 'tis!" Her thin lips spread in a wide grin as she produced a tattered book from her pocket. "Harry got me a new Grub Street penny book and the missus is goin' out."

"How fortunate for you."

She nodded. "By noontide I'll be sittin' by the fire and fillin' me head with the story as I turn the roast."

That's good I suppose, Lucius later thought as he turned out onto the main road with Commodore in tow. *Though it is Grub Street, and its writers are known for being untalented and gruesome…I remember a time when reading was not quite so proficient in England…*

This line of thought was broken when Commodore let out a gruff moan. Lucius glanced down to see him hurrying into an alley, his nose to the ground. Aggravated, he stood watching, his hands on his hips.

"I'm not waiting for you!"

With that he turned and found himself entangled in the wide skirts and slim arms of a young lady. They had run aground of one another and now each had a firm hold on the other's elbows. They performed a sort of spinning dance in an attempt to keep their balance.

"Do forgive me-" Wolgath began, but his voice broke off when he realized that he was holding Alexcena Condreve.

She was busily brushing her skirts with one hand. "No, no, it was all my fault-" She too stopped speaking when she raised her eyes. "Lucius." He released her arms and she folded her hands in a prim pose. "Mr. Wolgath."

"Ms. Condreve." Lucius quickly regained his composure and made a polite smile. "It is good to see you again."

"And you," she smiled up at him in return.

They stood in awkward silence for a moment before both saw that they had dropped something; she her reticule, and Lucius his tea leaves. Despite her protest, Wolgath bent to retrieve both. He knelt and as he was handing her the purse, he saw that she was wearing the cameo necklace.

"Thank you."

Their fingers touched as she accepted the bag and Lucius swallowed convulsively. They created an interesting spectacle. He remained kneeling, their hands remained touching. It was not until a passing child giggled at the sight of them that Lucius came to his senses and his feet.

"I was-"

"Of what age are you, Mr. Wolgath?"

Truthfully, he was glad for the interruption, for he had begun the sentence without first considering how it would end, but Alexcena's cheeks glowed a regretful pink.

"Forgive me, it was an impertinent question." She turned her eyes to the ground.

Lucius raised an eyebrow and grinned none the less. "Yes, it was. Although, as wisdom cannot be attained without some experience, knowledge cannot be attained without questions."

When Alexcena looked up, her eyes were glinting most curiously. "You are a surprising man, Mr. Wolgath."

Lucius, having nothing more to say, felt a retreat was in order. "I bid you good day, Ms. Condreve." As he passed, he whispered, "I'm twenty-six."

Lucius walked on, carrying with him the treasure of her compliment. He went two full blocks before he realized he was traveling in the direction opposite his destination. Alexcena walked even farther.

Rodney Dushaw was not at all fond of his father's home. Although he had grown up at Cedar Heights, the dilapidated mansion now reeked of rotting wood, cheap whiskey, and stale memories. Most of the servants had left long ago with hopes of a better existence-perhaps in prison. Many of the rest had been sold to supplement the Dushaws' failing fortune.

Rodney did not bother with the rusting knocker, but strode directly into the household. A grating cough led him to the front parlor where his father lay sprawled on a faded sofa. The man was unshaven and overweight, and Rodney's lip curled with disgust at the sight of him.

Randolph Dushaw grunted a harsh chuckle. "Why Rodney! Come to laugh at the old man?"

"A lazy old pauper is nothing to laugh at," he replied stiffly. "Unless of course you're not related."

Randolph's answering laugh seemed to stick in his throat, for he coughed yet again. "So," he went on conversationally, "what have you brought me? Food? Ale? A daughter-in-law with a fat dowry?"

"None of the above." Rodney collapsed into a sagging armchair. He tilted his head in thought. "But there is one girl."

Randolph straightened, suddenly serious.

"Don't break out the scotch yet."

"Too late. Is she fair to the eye?"

Rodney merely smirked. "One of the fairest I've seen, but she's also quite sharp. She would not grow dull with time, of that I'm certain."

"So snatch her up!"

Rodney' features hardened a fraction. "I have a new impediment there. *Wolgath.*"

"Who?"

"Lucius Wolgath." He ground out the name.

"Is he that foppish simpleton in your college?"

"Lucius is smart enough, he just has no sense."

"The way you talk you're twice as clever as Wolgath ever was, though I have yet to see the evidence of that." He ignored the vicious glance his son gave him. "He oughtn't be a problem for you."

"They've spoken once and already she prefers him to me." Rodney got to his feet and began to pace the creaking floor. "It won't be so easy to woo her, either."

"I don't see why not."

"I told you," Rodney grumbled. "Alexcena Condreve is different. She's intelligent."

"She's a woman!" Randolph scoffed. "Find out what she likes and use it. A woman's mind is like a jewelry box. The lock might seem complex, but if you find the correct key-"

"It's not so simple. It's not just her I must consider. Her father's opinion of me is also important. And *he* treats Wolgath like a son!" He paused and gave his head a shake. "Lucius is the problem here."

"Then get him out of the way!"

For some reason this statement, even coming from his father, was startling to Rodney. He swallowed and began to pace once more. "No," he mumbled. "No, that would just arouse suspicion."

"That wasn't what I meant, you dolt." Randolph scratched his whiskers. "But if you did it right-"

"You're daft old man!" Rodney snapped. "I'll think of something."

"Well the quicker you think, the more inheritance you'll have," Dushaw coughed hoarsely. "I'd get to it if I were you, boy!"

"If you were me we wouldn't be having this discussion."

He kept his final thought to himself, knowing his father would never acknowledge the truth of it. *For I would not have gambled the estate away.*

Chapter 3

February 2, 1764

"Mr. Wolgath, you lost count!"

Lucius nearly grinned at the earnest expression of Armina Reagan. The girl's otherwise adorable features were marred by a frustrated scowl as she tried to make sense of the abacus. Her tiny chin was thrust forward in determination against the struggle.

"So I did." He quickly repositioned the beads to show the correct calculation. "Very astute of you to notice, Ms. Reagan."

Lucius had been well aware of the count all along. After almost four years of mathematical study at Cambridge, he could keep track of simple arithmetic in his sleep. He had discovered, however, as he tutored Armina that making little slips on purpose allowed him to gage just how much the child was truly taking in. It was a way to check her without testing her, since she tended to be so anxious about exams.

"I've finished my essay, Mr. Wolgath."

Lucius turned to Armina's older brother Phinnaeus. The boy's book was closed and he lounged back in his chair. An innocent smile lurked about his mouth.

"All right," Lucius smiled with equal innocence. "Allow me to take a look." He held out his hand.

The boy adopted an air of shock. "Mr. Wolgath, I'm affronted! You don't trust me?"

"Not a wit."

Phinnaeus frowned in defeat and produced two scant pages from within the book.

"This will never do," Lucius murmured as he perused the papers. "You have three spelling errors in the first paragraph alone."

"I'll rewrite that page on a new sheet then."

"One page and a half is hardly long enough to qualify as an essay," Wolgath went on. "Especially when the script is an inch tall."

Phinnaeus accepted the pages with a huff. "You'll never give me any slack will you, Mr. Wolgath?"

"How long have I been your tutor?" He allowed a bit of a grin to cross him then, but quickly replaced it with a stern frown. "I'll expect a proper draft of that essay next week."

"Yes, sir."

Lucius rose and reached for his coat. "With that children, I leave you to your work."

He paused at the door to retrieve an oblong rectangular box. He stepped out into a mild drizzle and pulled his collar tighter about his neck. As he made his way around the house to the connecting stables, he could not help thinking that this would make the ride from Cambridge to Penn miserable. *It's a far sight better than being too dry, though,* he amended. *I'd rather have rain in my hair than dust in my throat.* He wasn't entirely certain if he believed that, but for the moment he was willing to stick to it.

He met Tim Reagan, the rotund owner of the establishment, in his usual seat by the entrance of the stables whittling at a stick of wood. He sat back when he caught sight of Lucius and grunted.

"Afternoon, Mr. Wolgath."

"Mr. Reagan," Lucius tipped his hat.

"How's them kids of mine?"

"Obstinate as ever."

Tim gave a gleeful guffaw, which died down into a gruff cough as he reached around for his pipe. "I got Ms. Maeva ready for you." He jerked his head toward a palomino mare several feet away. She was saddled and bridled, her reins thrown over a hitching post.

"Thank you, Mr. Tim. Say-" He paused half way to the animal. "Who uses Maeva during the week?"

"Whatever paying customer what wants her," Reagan replied. "But she'll be yours every weekend so long as you keep tutorin' them kids."

Lucius lifted the reins. "Until next week then, Mr. Tim."

Rather than heading toward Penn right away, Lucius turned toward the market, where venders of every sort shouted their wares.

"We'll get some vittles while we're here, eh Maeva?"

Produce was better in Penn, he knew, but he also knew that his pantry was bare, and it would be well into the evening before he arrived home. He took careful stock of the coins in his pocket and purchased one smoked perch, a small package of flour, and some vegetables. He was just paying for these vegetables when the merchant said,

"Fancy a plum, sir?"

Lucius's mouth watered at the thought of fresh fruit, but he hesitated when he saw the shrunken specimen. "It's bruised," he observed. "And rather…filthy."

His stomach gave a flip as the man calmly popped the plum into his mouth. He rolled it around a bit, spat it back into his palm, and held it out again.

"Clean as a queen's glove!"

Lucius suppressed a shudder and shook his head. "Another time, thank you."

The ride to Tyler's Green was not so unpleasant as he assumed it would be. The drizzle broke off just before he left, and the sun showed its face between the clouds for an hour before deciding to drop out of sight. He rode Maeva home, balancing the box filled with his purchases and various odds and ends, which he had collected for a special project. Commodore was waiting beneath the coffee table when he arrived home.

"Hello, old boy."

Commodore barely raised his head beneath the confines of the table.

"I've a surprise for you."

This seemed to intrigue him, and he emerged from his little hovel to stare perplexedly at his master.

Lucius slung his coat over one of the dining table chairs and deposited the groceries in their proper places. Moving to the desk, he rummaged around for his hand tools. He set the tools and the box by the door and went to work. Commodore merely turned his head to follow his movements.

"You just give me an hour," Lucius told him, "and I'll show you my idea."

Wolgath opened the door a fraction and set it securely against his shoulder. He then lifted a sturdy hand saw and set to his task. For the next hour the dank evening air rang with the hushed rasping of the saw and the sharp raps of a tack hammer. Sawdust fluttered about the threshold, stirred by the night breeze. Commodore remained motionless, fixated on his master's movements and grunting expectantly at intervals.

"Nearly done, nearly done," Lucius assured him with only mild aggravation. "Got to get you out of the house more. You're beginning to sound like an old nag."

He was greatly startled when a creaking female voice replied, "My word, Mr. Wolgath!"

He raised a skeptical brow to Commodore. The dog yelped and Lucius turned to see the scant form of his landlady close by the open door.

"Oh, Mrs. Petlam…er." He scrambled up to bow with the hammer still clutched in one hand. "Good evening. I didn't expect the pleasure-"

"Is that you making all that clatter?" Mrs. Petlam demanded. "What 'ave you done to my door?!"

"Oh, well, er-" Lucius stood back and gestured toward the contraption now mounted to the bottom half of the door. "It's an invention of mine. For my dog."

The right hand corner of the planks had been removed and the cutout piece reattached by a hinge at the top. A tight cord was nailed to the end of the cutout closest to the floor. This cord traced its way up the planks to thread through two pulleys secured to the left of the cutout. The end was knotted to form a loop which hung loosely about one foot from the floor.

"Commodore, hither!"

Lucius slipped the toe of his shoe through the loop and tugged gently. The cutout sprang up on its hinge, and Commodore slipped through the new opening.

"My goodness!" Mrs. Petlam yipped when the wood sprang up.

"It's his own little door, see?" Lucius let the thing fall and Commodore happily nosed his way back through.

Mrs. Petlam looked at him uncertainly from the corner of her eye. "Uh-huuuh."

Lucius wondered just how eccentric the woman imagined he was and how long it would be before she thought him just plain crazy. But this was coming from a woman who soaked her hair in rosemary tea once a week and called her garden patch "the minikin promenade."

"You won't be much longer, I hope," she went on. "I do have other tenants who like their sleep."

"I'm finished now, ma'am," he replied easily. "I do apologize for the inconvenience."

"Uh-huuuh." She eyed the little door with open suspicion. "I almost forgot, this came for you today." She produced a sealed note from her apron. "It's an invite to that town dance over at the commons next week. Whole building got them."

"Thank you."

The lady left and Lucius flipped the missive onto the table with minimal concern.

"They shouldn't have bothered," he commented to Commodore as he gathered his tools. "More than likely won't go. Those parties are always so crowded. I can count my acquaintances on one hand, and I never know who to speak to…" *Only who I would like to speak to.*

Chapter 4

February 11, 1764

Lucius tugged at the stiff collar of his suit and sighed, wondering how it was that he had managed to talk himself into attending another party. This latest event was a dance for the entire hamlet, held in the common building. The building was nothing more than a large square and not nearly large enough to accommodate the quantity of those who had turned out for the evening. It seemed that at every moment someone was apologizing for bumping into some gentleman or trodding on a lady's dress. He had put off going to the point of rudeness, and the place was horribly crowded when he arrived. From the moment he entered the door, it was all Lucius could do to make his way to the back wall, where a buffet of edibles and a low rafter provided him with some cover. Even there it seemed he was not safe.

"Oh, Mr. Lucius! Lucius!"

The din of the merry dance was not enough to mask the voice of Tabitha Winslett as it projected across the room. She was waving rather enthusiastically as well. Smiling slightly Lucius raised a hand, and the girl hurried by the dancing couples to his side. He had to admit, she did appear quite pretty in her satin gown. Her hair had been swept up atop her head with a large red rose pinned beside it. Unfortunately, Tabitha's curls had been too much for the little pins, who seemed to be throwing themselves overboard with every turn of her head. The rose was steadily sliding toward her left ear.

"Tabitha." Lucius bowed as low as he might in the small space afforded them. "It is good to see you again. I trust you are well."

"Am I! Oh, I mean I am, thank you," she babbled.

Lucius smiled indulgingly. "Are you enjoying your evening?"

"Oh, tremendolously!" she burst. "And it has given me a proper excuse to wear my new gown."

"Yes, indeed." Lucius did not bother to correct her pronunciation of the word 'tremendously.' The girl seemed to be content, and he could not bear to upset her innocent happiness. "Beautiful. And your hair looks nice, as well. Very…curly."

"Do you think so? I refuse to let my maid touch it. The woman is atrocious with it! I much prefer to do it myself."

"So I see."

She hesitated and seemed to be deciding something. She played with a bit of ribbon at her cuff. "Perhaps we could dance together?"

Lucius became fearful at this. "I must decline," he hurried to say. "I have never learned to dance, you see. Not properly anyway."

"Oh." Tabitha's eyes began to water then and there.

"But the moment I learn, you shall be the first young lady I ask," he added swiftly.

She beamed. Not two seconds passed before her gaze veered to the surrounding crowd. "Mimi's arrived. You remember Mimi Harper? I must go and greet her. Mimi!" Two more pins hit the floor as she turned to hurry away.

Lucius shook his head. He was very fond of the sweetness in the girl. *Perhaps one day that sweetness will outweigh her spontaneity.*

"Lucius!"

Wolgath bent beneath the weight of Lawrence Condreve's meaty hand as it landed on his shoulder. He gestured to the jovial atmosphere about them. "Having a good time?"

"I suppose so, sir," Lucius replied as he straightened his glasses. "I'm not acquainted with many of those here."

"And yet you ignore those you do know."

Wolgath focused his gaze over Lawrence's shoulder to see Alexcena and her mother. Cecelia was in a gown of wine red. Alexcena was resplendent in pure white. The dress was simple enough, enhanced only by fine black lace covering the stomacher and black piping at the cuffs and shoulders. The décolletage was wide, though not low. She wore black lace mitt gloves and pearl earrings. Resting about her neck was a strand of impossibly small seed pearls.

"Ms. Condreve!" Lucius suppressed his enthusiasm and shifted his gaze away. "Mrs. Condreve! Forgive me, I meant no disrespect-"

"I'm sure my father was only teasing, Mr. Wolgath," Alexcena was quick to reassure him.

"I see," Lucius grinned through his embarrassment. He swallowed and turned his eyes away from the young woman, even as he said, "You look lovely, Ms. Condreve."

She smiled, a touch of color rising in her cheeks. "Thank you."

"I am absolutely parched, Lawrence," Cecelia said from somewhere beside them.

Lucius managed to turn his back to Alexcena and offer the lady his arm. "I should be happy to escort you to the buffet, madam."

Alexcena stared after them as the pair moved away. Lawrence wore a perceptive smile as he studied his daughter.

"You're quite taken with him, aren't you?"

"Father!" she gasped. "No one speaks of such things."

"Nonsense. You ladies speak of this sort of thing all the time. You just assume that we men cannot hear you."

"Don't fool yourself into thinking men don't produce their share of chatter. You're liable to be struck down by lightening."

"Don't think I don't realize you're trying to change the subject. So?"

She fiddled with the lace of one mitt. "He is a most…intriguing man."

Condreve chuckled. "He most certainly is."

"Who might that be?"

"Ah, Harrison!" Lawrence turned to grasp the hand of the gentleman who had approached. "Good to see you."

"Lawrence. Ms. Condreve." He bowed regally.

"Are Mrs. and Ms. Winslett about?"

Alexcena perked up. "Oh, yes, I've been looking for Tabitha."

"They're both about somewhere. Well, and here's Mrs. Condreve."

"Good evening, Harry."

"I had no idea we had the pleasure, Mr. Winslett."

"The pleasure's all mine." Harrison's gaze rose to Lucius. "I don't believe I've met-"

"Lucius Wolgath, sir. We met at Ms. Condreve's birthday dinner."

Harrison blinked rapidly. "Ah, yes! The rickety old boarding house, eh?"

"Quite so, sir."

"Glad you made it out to join us!"

"Rickety?" Lawrence wondered aloud as he threw quite a curious look Wolgath's way. "I had no idea your living arrangements were… undesirable."

Lucius began tugging at his left cuff, unnerved by the scrutiny of the older gentlemen. "It is by choice, I assure you, sir. Such an arrangement has inabled me to invest funds elsewhere. The boarding house is temporary and the state of it is sound."

"So there's no chance of it falling down then?" Harrison winked.

Lucius shrugged with a sheepish grin. "I do tend to step lightly."

"I've noticed you do the same with your peers, as well as your professors," Lawrence remarked with good humor. "Though to be fair I suppose regular confrontations might cause you to step harder with temper, and then you would have a very undesirable living arrangement."

The three elder adults seemed to think this terribly merry and laughed aloud. This left Alexcena and Lucius just outside their little circle.

"Such modesty, Mr. Wolgath."

"I should prefer the term meek."

"Every time someone makes a compliment to your character you deny it," she commented further. "I begin to wonder if you're hiding something."

"I confess that I am one of God's more transparent creations," he replied. His words were earnest, though the smile still lurked about his lips. "I learned very quickly as a boy that I have no talent for hiding anything, be it from my parents, my brother, boys at school… I was always easily found out." He suddenly became aware that she was watching him with intensity. The happy light of her countenance had become a poignant glow of what he could almost call appreciation. What would warrant such feelings in her towards him, he could not say.

"Which is why," he went on, "I am not known for my prowess at the gambling table."

The brightness of her look was shaded then, and she took on a mischievous expression. "Oh no? What are you known for at the gambling table?"

He let out a breath of relief. "Nothing. I don't gamble."

"Admirable. What are you known for doing?"

"Some would say not much of anything. Nothing other than work anyway." He felt himself grow easier when she began to laugh.

"Do you not have anything you do to relax? Is there nothing you simply enjoy?"

"You are full of questions, Ms. Condreve."

"What was it you said to me?" She cleared her throat and straightened her shoulders. "As wisdom cannot be attained without some experience, knowledge cannot be attained without questions."

He blinked, more than a little surprised that she had mimicked his words with such accuracy.

"-so I ask, what do you enjoy in the rare moments when you are *not* working?"

Lucius opened his mouth, but something in her words made him pause. His own words flitted through his mind. *Knowledge… attained… questions… Her questions aren't just for me, they're about me. Could it be possible that she is trying to form a knowledge of me? That she could be-*

"Ms. Condreve, may I be so bold as to take this dance?"

Lucius' thought broke and he saw that a young man had approached. Though Lucius had seen him about the village, he could not recall the man's name. Alexcena hesitated, smiled, and offered her hand.

"You may, Mr. Williamson."

She dipped her head to Lucius and followed Williamson to the center of the floor.

Lucius was infinitely glad for the interruption. He straightened the tight stock of his collar and clasped his hands behind his back. He observed the couples as they moved across the floor. One half of his mind timed their movements to the beat of the music; one, two and three, four and one, two and three. The other half of his brain struggled with another topic.

Lucius had courted only two women in his relatively short life. The first was a young lady in Austria, who had proved to be ridiculous. The second had lived in Cambridge. She had tired of Lucius' busy schedule after just three weeks. Two other ladies had flirted almost shamelessly with him in the last year. The first had lost interest when another young bachelor had proposed. The second was Tabitha Winslett.

As Lucius watched the dancers, he compared Alexcena to each of the women in his limited experience. Like all the others, she was a Christian, and a true Christian at that. She was certainly *not* ridiculous. She knew his tendencies for work and yet she seemed to express a desire to know him better. She conducted herself with ladylike propriety and decorum. Her kind and personable nature was endearing and confusing. Such qualities made it difficult indeed for him to discern her true opinion of him. This coupled with the restrained passion he had witnessed in her left him unsure of himself. He could not recall another woman in his acquaintance who had demonstrated such dimension of spirit.

Behind him Harrison Winslett had moved away, and Lawrence and Cecelia stood back to watch the guests.

"Where is Alexcena gone to?" Lawrence wondered.

"There." Cecelia gestured. "She is dancing with Mr. Williamson."

"Williamson?" The old man's gaze swiveled across the crowd until he caught sight of Lucius some feet away from them. "And there's Wolgath," he sighed. "You know for all that man's brilliance, I do wonder about him sometimes."

"Lawrence, what a thing to say," Cecelia scoffed.

Even as they spoke, the music ended, and Williamson deposited Alexcena at Lucius' side once more.

"He's a perfectly nice gentleman," Cecelia went on.

"Nice, yes," Lawrence conceded, "but he can be somewhat simple when it comes to some of the most obvious things."

Cecelia's mouth slid into a knowing smile. "For instance-"

Lawrence shook his head. "I fail to see how the man can miss the perfect opportunity when it is standing right next to him."

"He's a man, isn't he?"

"Cecelia, if I didn't know you better, I'd think you serious and take offense to that remark."

"I'm shocked that you have forgotten your own style of courtship so easily."

He chuckled. "Yes, yes. How did you describe it again?"

"Clumsy at best."

"And victorious in the end."

"Mm," Cecelia agreed. "I wrapped you around my little finger, and then you wrapped me around yours."

Lucius clapped along with everyone else as the music ended. He saw Alexcena turn to him. She moved forward, but Williamson was right behind her. She paused to say something to him. The man looked perplexed, but he merely bowed and turned away. Alexcena faced Lucius once more.

"Have you had time enough to consider my question, Mr. Wolgath?"

"I-" Lucius paused. "Forgive me, I seem to have forgotten the question."

"Why, Lucius," a bland voice sounded behind them. "Certainly you don't expect Ms. Condreve to repeat herself."

"Rodney."

"Mr. Dushaw," Alexcena murmured. "I was not aware that you were here."

"Well, I spent the last few days in London," he explained. "I was riding through on my way back to Cambridge when I heard that your little town was having a gathering of sorts." He looked out over the crowd with something akin to both curiosity and pity. He abruptly turned back to Alexcena. "I thought I'd stop in and offer my hand."

Lucius' head snapped around to Rodney, whose expressionless eyes remained on the lady. He found that his heart beat quicker for the space of several seconds.

A surreptitious grin spread across Rodney's mouth. "For a dance, of course." He bowed low to her and held up one arm.

Alexcena's eyes widened perceptibly. "Oh, but-" She turned to Lucius.

Wolgath was always amazed that at that moment he knew precisely what to do without hesitation. Rodney was straightening just as Lucius took hold of Alexcena's hand.

"Unfortunately, Rodney, I have just claimed the next dance."

"Yes!" Alexcena exclaimed. "And I have just agreed. You understand, Mr. Dushaw?"

Rodney's mouth smoothed into a thin line. "Another time then."

Alexcena threaded her way through the people of Penn. Lucius followed stupidly. His skin had grown cold and he suspected it was also very pale. He licked his lips.

"Forgive me, Ms. Condreve," he stammered. "I don't know what came over me."

"And I can't thank you enough."

"Really?" He cleared his throat. "I must warn you, there's a fatal flaw in this impulse."

She faced him. "You don't know the dance?"

Lucius swallowed. "Two fatal flaws."

She smiled and he was dimly aware of the music starting up again. "It's not so difficult as all that. You look like you've just been set adrift at sea."

"It's not just the dance that has me nervous."

Taking this revelation in stride, Alexcena raised his hands. "Here. Move with me."

So he did. Lucius allowed her to lead him across the floor. He recalled the count he had kept earlier with the musicians and kept his eyes on the dancers around them, copying their moves as best he could. Soon he had fallen into step with them.

"Are you all right?"

"Yes," he replied with pleasant surprise. "I simply applied basic principles of music theory to-whoa!"

Suddenly he was on his knees, grasping Alexcena by her forearms. She had landed sitting on the floor, her cheeks a brilliant crimson. The dancers around them halted altogether. The musicians, to their credit, never faltered.

"I beg your pardon, Mr. Wolgath. I slipped in something. I just couldn't stop myself, I-" Alexcena babbled.

"Not at all." Lucius cleared his throat. "Are you all right?" He rose and helped her to her feet.

"What is it people say… Merely my pride."

The villagers around them seemed to lose interest and resumed their dance.

"And look at this." Alexcena spread her snowy skirt to display a wide orange stain near her hem. "I suppose that's the punishment for wearing white. It always seems to attract spots."

"Ms. Condreve," Rodney appeared at their side again, a look of mild concern on his dreary face. "Are you quite unharmed?"

She sighed. "Quite, thank you."

"Well then, in that case-"

"I see mother and father are heading for the door. It has been a most pleasurable evening, but I fear I must be going."

Rodney's eyes narrowed a fraction, and then relaxed. "Indeed."

Lucius raised a hand in parting to her parents where they stood across the room. "I'll see you soon then." He turned to her. "Good evening, Ms. Condreve."

"Mr. Wolgath. Mr. Dushaw." She curtsied deeply to them both.

Lucius watched her go, feeling a great deal more composed now that he had managed to survive the dance and escape total humiliation. He turned to his friend.

"So what were you doing in London, Rodney?"

Dushaw cut his eyes to Lucius and then away. "See you at school, Wolgath."

Chapter 5

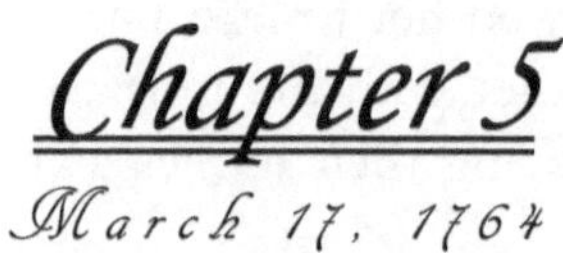

March 17, 1764

Lucius drew one last note to the tip of his bow as it crossed the string of his violin. His eyes remained closed in appreciation until he heard the reluctant applause of the children. He smiled and bobbed his head to his audience.

"That was wonderful, Mr. Wolgath!" Mrs. Millby came forward to say.

Edna Millby was the proprietor of a small orphanage adjacent to the newly constructed poorhouse in Penn.

"What was it, Mr. Wolgath?" The inquiry was made by a small boy about six years of age.

Lucius was drawing breath to answer when an older boy in the back of the room spoke for him. "It was somethin' very slow written by someone wot was really old. Play something' we can dance to can't you?"

Lucius sighed. "It would serve you right if I played nothing but concertos, lad." Never the less, he struck up a wild jig. The bow leapt across the strings of the violin. The younger children were soon up and hoping around the room. They laughed and shouted and waved their little arms madly. The older ones stood to the side, laughing and clapping at the antics of the small ones. Lucius' fingers bounced nimbly from string to string. He grinned with satisfaction at the pleasure written across the tiny faces and in the eyes that had already witnessed hardships he could not imagine.

One hour later he was returning his instrument to its case. Mrs. Millby had sent the youngest children to nap and the older ones to doing such useful chores as sweeping, dusting, and the like. Lucius smiled as the lady approached him.

"Thank you so much, Mr. Wolgath," she said brightly. "The children absolutely adored it."

Lucius flexed the fingers of his left hand and grimaced. "Once I left off playing operetta scores anyway. But it was my pleasure," he declared, rising to his feet. "You're doing a wonderful thing here, Mrs. Millby."

The lady sobered. "I do what I can, but this is a small house. I can only keep so many."

"Something perplexes me," he admitted. "The children, they all have the letter *P* sewn twice into their sleeves."

"*P* for poor, *P* for Penn. They do the same to those in the poor house. And now will you answer a question for me?"

"Of course."

"Why did you volunteer to help me?"

"A friend told me I was working too hard," Lucius explained, grinning at a child as she passed. "I'm not really helping, just…entertaining."

"You're a fine gentleman, Mr. Wolgath."

Lucius was now scrutinizing his pocket watch. "You must excuse me, Mrs. Millby, but I am meeting a friend for supper."

"My, you must have a great many acquaintances, Mr. Wolgath."

"Not at all, and the few that I have mean all the more to me."

At that same instant not so many miles away, Lawrence Condreve also happened to be looking at his watch. He stood in the foyer pretending to straighten his coat for the third time. The tall and imposing form of Eshton came to the top of the stairs and descended. He drew himself up before his employer and sniffed.

"Madam Condreve wishes to know if you intend to wear the grey suit, sir."

Lawrence stared for moment, and then lifted the flaps of his coat.

"No, Eshton, I believe I shall remain in the blue one."

"Yes, sir." Eshton bowed and turned away.

"Eshton?" he called as an afterthought. The butler faced him. "What does it matter which suit I'm wearing?"

"I believe Madam Condreve is attempting to coordinate her garb to your own, sir."

Lawrence nodded.

"Also, she mentioned something about the grey washing out the color of your hair."

"Hm," Lawrence grunted. "You can hardly see my hair as it is."

"I believe she said that as well, sir."

"Make sure she knows we're going to be very late for our dinner with the Nettles, please."

"Yes, sir."

"The Nettles?"

Lawrence turned to face his daughter as she came into the foyer. "Hello, Alexcena."

"I thought you were meeting Lucius…Wolgath today."

"Are you short of breath, Alexcena? I thought I noted a pause in your voice just now."

She dipped her head in embarrassment. "Not at all, Father."

Lawrence grinned. "You're correct, by the way. I had completely forgotten my engagement with Lucius." He glanced to his watch once more. "I can't very well send your mother to the Nettles on her own. She and Mrs. Nettles would start talking and we would never see her again. You'll just have to meet with young Mr. Lucius for me."

The girl was positively dumbfounded. "Wh-me?"

"I could send a courier, I suppose."

"No," she replied quickly. "No. That would be even more rude, to forget him and then send an impersonal note."

"What are you waiting for then?" Condreve chuckled and waved at the stairs. "Go pinch your cheeks and smooth your hair. You don't want to be too late, do you?"

Alexcena whirled about. She passed her mother at the top of the stairs in a flurry of skirts.

"See you this afternoon, Mother!"

Cecelia raised an eyebrow to her husband.

"Lawrence," she said, slowly moving down the steps, "I have never known you to forget an appointment."

"Rather fortuitous, wouldn't you say, m'dear?"

Cecelia shook her head wearily. "Do try not to push them, Lawrence. You're liable to set poor Mr. Wolgath running for his life."

Alexcena did not have long to wait once she arrived at the small coffee house. She had spent ten full minutes debating her gown and fussing with her curling tresses at the armoire door, but lack of time and patience had forced her to deem herself presentable. She sat at a small round table in the center of the rectangular room brushing at imaginary wrinkles in her skirt. The establishment was quite charming; one that she frequented in fact. So anxious was she that she could not bring herself to enjoy it. It was a small, fleeting relief to her nerves when Lucius did appear at the door. He stood clutching a long wooden box and speaking easily to the owner of the coffee house.

Alexcena came to her feet, raising a hand so as to catch the man's eye. "Mr. Wolgath-ow!"

In raising her hand, she inadvertently knocked a tray from the hands of a passing steward. The heavy goblets he was balancing then toppled to the floor. The wide room was instantly-and jarringly-thrown into silence.

"Sir!" Alexcena exclaimed in surprised remorse. "Please forgive me, I-"

"Not a problem, ma'am," the man insisted, though it was obvious that he was annoyed. "Believe me, it happens all the time." Bowing, he turned to go and promptly slipped in the puddle of refreshment. The unfortunate man fell flat on his back, and the entire scene was punctuated by the smack of the tray landing squarely on his chest.

"Please allow me." Lucius swooped in to help the steward to his feet. "Are you injured?"

The man made a hoarse grunting noise and stalked away without another word. Talk at the surrounding tables began to resume.

When Lucius looked to Alexcena she was blushing mightily. He charmed her with a smile, but for a moment he could not bring himself to speak. She was lovely indeed, though her countenance was frozen in blank astonishment.

"Ms. Condreve," he said at last. She curtsied and he bowed low over her hand.

"Hello, Mr. Wolgath."

Lucius moved to pull her chair out as she spoke.

"I must apologize. I know you were expecting my father. Unfortunately another matter diverted his time. He sent me in his place." Shy as a young girl, she watched him as he sat across from her.

"I see that."

Despite his calm manner, a mild, instinctive panic had descended over Lucius. His conscious mind was piqued by the chance to spend some time with Alexcena uninterrupted and relatively unobserved. A blessing of the most unexpected, and therefore the sweetest, kind. Yet still he felt his mouth dry and his palms grow moist by the same phantom anxiety that had come over him the night of the dance. He had no idea how to react to such a bright woman.

Alexcena did not notice his hesitancy, for she had her own awkwardness to deal with. "I hope you are not disappointed."

"On the contrary," Lucius insisted. "This will give the two of us an opportunity to talk a little more. It was rather difficult to have a quiet chat when last I saw you."

"At the dance, yes," she agreed. "It was so very close and noisy in there."

"Everyone was obliged to shout at everyone else."

An older woman appeared to set a porcelain coffee service before them. Lucius was confused until Alexcena said, "I requested the coffee. I hope you do not mind."

He smiled easily. "Not at all."

He set to preparing his cup. Lucius Wolgath had a most peculiar way of preparing both his tea and coffee, and Alexcena watched his movements with open fascination.

Taking a chunk of sugar with the tongs, he placed it in his palm and pressed the piece between both his large hands. He ground the compressed sugar over his cup until it was broken up completely. Then he dusted his hands and fingers over the cup to be sure that every granule had fallen from them. Next, he took the tiny pitcher of cream in one hand and his teaspoon in the other. With measured movements he poured cream slowly into the spoon. He then poured the cream into the coffee, stirred it twice clockwise, and repeated this process. After this was done, he set the pitcher down, lifted his cup, and drank.

He raised one eyebrow, watching Alexcena over the rim. She realized at once that she must have a blank look on her face. Giving her head a little shake, she lifted her own spoon.

"Well, it's relatively quiet here," Lucius went on after a prolonged silence. "We can have a true conversation."

Alexcena watched him through her dark lashes. "A more intimate conversation."

Lucius was taking another sip. He felt his eyes widen and spluttered a bit of the coffee. Alexcena determined to change the subject to a less complicated topic.

"What are you carrying in your case?"

"My violin," he answered. "I have a great love for music."

"No doubt you can read sheet music."

"Certainly."

She wrinkled the bridge of her nose and quirked a smile. "I'm envious. Although I enjoy music, I have never had much of an aptitude for *making* it."

"Do you play, Ms. Condreve?"

"My mother had her heart set that I would learn the piano forte'. That was fine with me until I sat down to try." Her cheeks colored. "The idea of it was appealing enough, but when I tried the keys, my coordination was lacking. I can play with one hand tolerably so long as the other is not moving. I can play one part of a two part song only if I have memorized all the notes first." She shrugged. "Five years of lessons, and I doubt I can play more than three pieces."

"I'm sorry to hear it."

Alexcena almost winced. "That I cannot play?"

"That you were forced to keep at it." He was encouraged by the soft glow of pleasure that spread across her face. "Music is a wonderful thing for a child to learn and experience, but after practicing for years with minimal improvement..."

"That's what I said. Sometimes I think the blessing of opportunity is wasted without the blessing of talent."

"Especially if there is no ambition."

"Especially."

Lucius cleared his throat after a suspended silence. "So…what do you enjoy doing?"

"I do love to read," she replied wistfully. "Poetry, mostly."

"I confess, I cannot abide poetry. Although I think perhaps that I haven't found the right poet yet."

"I've recently read some of James Thomson's works. Do you know him?"

"No, I can't say that I do."

"He wrote poetry."

"What else do you like to read?"

The lady hesitated and leaned forward a fraction. "May I have your confidence, Mr. Wolgath?"

"Certainly."

"I have become quite addicted to the literature of Grub Street."

Lucius let out a chuckle and Alexcena joined him. "Forgive me," he breathed, "but I never would have taken you for a Grub Street reader, Ms. Condreve."

"I know!" she giggled. "It's fraught with bland stuff and shabby publishing, but if one is willing to sift through it, it is possible to find a truly unique story. My mother and I are always trading up penny novels."

"And your father?"

"He shakes his head and sighs. I'm afraid he agrees with Misters Swift and Pope, that Grub Street is a threat to both literature and good taste."

She said this with an air so similar to her father's that Lucius had to laugh again.

"I do love a good play, too," she added.

"We have something in common there," Lucius replied. "I have been fortunate enough in recent years to be able to witness several plays in London. My family attended many when I was a boy."

Alexcena smiled in appreciation. "I've heard it said that London is a different city at night. That an entirely different population arises with the moon. I cannot ever seem to sleep soundly when my family is there. I think I have a hidden fear that some calamity will befall us in the dark."

"Yes, I had heard from your father that you have a second residence there. Do you stay there often?"

Alexcena shook her head. "My parents are there more often than I. I prefer the open air of the country, and, as I said, there are so many people in Town."

"And sometimes those people find their way into London's surrounding hamlets."

Alexcena's attention immediately shifted to the man now standing close behind Lucius.

"For why else would Lucius Wolgath be sitting here in the quiet of Penn?"

She quirked an eyebrow at the man's intrusion. Lucius turned to him as well and leapt to his feet.

"Leopold!"

"Hello, Lucius."

To Alexcena's great surprise, the two embraced warmly, slapping one another's backs and shaking hands.

"What on earth are you doing here?"

"I came to collect all that money you owe me."

"I paid every cent of that back when we were boys."

"Ah, but you forgot the matter of the interest!"

The two shared a good laugh over this, and Alexcena took the opportunity to study the newcomer. He was several inches taller than Lucius and easily twice as strong with a full barrel chest and thick limbs. His eyes were a light hazel, while his hair was a rich wealth of brown reaching well below his collar. Deep wrinkles born of laughter and sunlight ran close to his eyes and mouth. The shaven cheeks were covered with pock scars. He presented a dashing picture in a great coat and boots. A thick crossbelt was strapped over his chest. By the look of him Alexcena would not have been the least bit surprised if it held a sheathed dagger beneath his coat. She could just perceive the butt of a pistol at his waist.

"Ms. Condreve," Lucius said suddenly. "This is my older brother, Leopold Wolgath. Leo, may I present Alexcena Condreve?"

"Indeed!" He grinned winningly and kissed the top of her hand.

Alexcena could not help thinking that a handsome smile was a family trait among the Wolgaths. In fact it seemed to be the only trait the brothers shared at all. "It's a pleasure to meet you, sir."

"Likewise."

Leo helped himself to a chair. Lucius sat as well and the three of them spent the next hour in pleasant conversation. Alexcena often laughed softly at the antics of the siblings. When the coffee was finished, she excused herself, saying, "You must play for me soon, Mr. Wolgath."

Both men stood and bowed as she left.

"So tell me, Lucius." Leo crossed his arms and studied his brother as he watched Alexcena's retreating back. "Am I invited?"

"To what?" His gaze did not shift.

"To the wedding."

"Whose wedding?"

Leo laughed, a great booming sound. "Why, baby brother, you're thicker than I thought."

Lucius finally seemed to catch on and said quietly, "Am I so obvious?"

Leo guffawed again, slapping his thigh. "No, but I dare say she is!"

"Alexcena?" Lucius perked up and looked to the door, although she was already long gone.

"Sometimes Lucius," Leo said easily, "I think you've been alone far too long."

Lucius turned a skeptical eye. "I'm not alone, I have-" He fished for a name, and would have said 'Commodore,' but decided against it when he thought of how his brother would laugh. "Friends."

Leo chuckled. "Uh-huh."

"Well look at you!" Lucius argued. "You don't even have a home. All you do is travel the continent living on wild game and amazing grace."

"That's different," Leo scoffed. "I'm suited to this sort of thing. You're more of a social chap, but you've grown more and more secluded ever since you started at Cambridge." Leo saw what only a brother could see beneath Lucius' optimistic attitude. These last few years were beginning to weigh heavily on him. "Look, you've played the part of a dedicated scholar for a long time, but that's about to come to an end."

"I've thought the same thing. That's why I came to Penn, seeking a quieter life in a new society-"

"And look what a terrific opportunity this society has offered up."

Lucius nodded. "She's a fine young lady. A devout Christian, smart, caring, gentle, humorous-"

"And let us not forget attractive." Leo leaned forward with a creak of his chair, looking Lucius squarely in the eye. "As your brother, I'm telling you, take the initiative and run."

"Run, eh?"

Leo grinned and sat back. "Head long into the wind."

Chapter 6

June 24, 1764

"Three months." Randolph Dushaw shook his head and sighed pityingly.

"It's maddening!" Rodney ranted. "They're sickeningly perfect together. College benefits…dinner parties. My subterfuge is no match for Wolgath's stupidity. I suppose she finds it endearing."

"That does not help your argument a wit."

"Lucius is so thick, I don't even think he's tried to make his overture to her yet."

Randolph let out a long, low chuckle. "Then what are you worried about?"

"You've not seen them," Rodney ground out through gritted teeth. "They're becoming…close."

Randolph assumed a doubtful look to his sour face but said nothing more.

An old dish rag of a woman entered bearing a plate of smoked fish. The set of her eyes and mouth was similar indeed to that of the poor creature she set before her master.

Randolph grimaced. "What is this supposed to be?"

"Fish, sir," the woman croaked. "Fresh from the Thames this morning."

"Well, get rid of it!" he barked. "And bring me back some pork while you're at it!"

"That's all the meat there is just now, sir."

Randolph deigned to come to his feet and glower. "How did you let that happen?"

"Tweren't me, sir," she went on doggedly. "That was all the meat I could afford with what you gave me for market."

Randolph pointed a trembling finger at his plate. "*Fish*," he snapped, "is the food of peasants and whelps! The next time I see fish in my home again, you'll be using your own pay to buy me some decent meat! Am I quite understood?"

The cook's countenance never changed even as she bore these complaints. She waited until her employer was seated and then headed out of the room. Halfway to the door, however, she returned.

"There's one more thing, sir."

"What?"

She paused a moment, and seemed to be gathering her nerve. Then she straightened her sagging shoulders and lifted her chin. "I quit, sir."

Randolph was altogether unperturbed. "Fine."

"My sister's found me a position with her employer, and I'm going to take it, sir."

"Be gone. It'll spare me this horrid mess that you call cooking."

"You owe me two weeks pay, but I'll not return for it. You can keep your money for all I care, sir. I want no more of it."

He twisted in his chair to look at her at last. "Have you anything else to say?"

"Just one more thing, sir."

The woman stepped forward. She tore her greasy apron from her waist, tossed it down by his chair, and left without another word or even a glance at Rodney. Randolph lifted his utensils and set about devouring the meal.

She might have said 'I poisoned the trout' for all he cares, Rodney thought dully. *He'd probably wolf it down all the more quickly if she had.*

"Any relationship can be crushed," Randolph went on, as though he had never been interrupted. "You simply require the correct vice."

Rodney ran a hand through his thick hair. "I think Lawrence is trying to encourage the two of them together. I think they're speaking at church when I'm not there."

"Typical," his father replied around a forkful of fish. "I suppose they've been passing notes about you as well."

Rodney scowled. "We're not children, Father."

"You're certainly behaving like one. You've got to think bigger; do more than just make Wolgath appear stupid."

"You're right about that. He does that well enough himself."

"What you've got to do is ruin his chances. Make him unweddible!"

Rodney savored the idea that suddenly began forming in his crafty mind. "Yes. Unweddible."

"That is unless you'd like to consider my original plan."

One glance at his father, and Rodney realized the gruesome truth of what he meant. He shook his head. "No. I'll do this my way."

Chapter 7

June 29, 1764

In a perspective, no projective…In a projective *space, two triangles are axle…axially… perspective axially if and only if…they are…Let's see, Pythagoras said…or was it Desargues? Yes, Desargues…Two triangles are in perspective centrally if and only if…the axles…*

Lucius ceased scribbling and sighed.

I've known this theorem forwards and backwards and sideways for months…Why can't I find it now?

He was seated in one of the many study halls of the campus of Cambridge University. The room was dusky and dark, much like his gray mood. Whispers and shuffled footsteps echoed around the wide hall. Lamplight flickered between the bookshelves all around him, barely illuminating the pages of his notes. Lucius readjusted his glasses and began flipping through the sheaves.

I must have it somewhere…Why would I? It's been in my head for so long…Ah, here…

"Is that M-Mr. Wolgath?"

He raised his head to squint at the man approaching. When recognition dawned he rose at once. "Mr. Priestly." They bowed to one another. "I'm honored you remember me, sir."

Joseph Priestly happened to be one of the more learned scientists of the day. The gentleman spoke of science in ways Lucius had never heard of before. Soon after any scholar spoke to him the stutter was easily forgotten.

"It isn't often I give a l-lecture and a student starts adding his own thoughts in al-long with his questions."

Lucius was instantly sheepish. "I do apologize about that."

"It's q-quite all right. I was r-rather anxious when I was asked to g-give that lecture. Y-your challenges succeeded in p-putting me at ease somewhat."

"I must admit I was so carried away by some of your thoughts on airs that I quite forgot myself."

"You're not yourself tod-day either, or else you have m-my pity," the man murmured. "You look as though you slept on this v-very floor last night rather than your own be-bed."

Wolgath shrugged. "I didn't sleep much at all last night I'm afraid."

"And the n-night before?"

Lucius blew out a great puff of air.

Priestly raised an eyebrow.

"I seem to be…um…losing my focus," Lucius explained. "I'm having to work harder to keep up."

"So you're slowing down t-to a more human level of int-telligence, then?" Priestly grinned, though Lucius was not amused. "You seem to have the unhappy t-talent of pushing yourself t-too hard. The weekend is c-coming up. Why don't you simply enjoy yours-s-self for a few days? L-let your mind breathe."

Lucius smiled and bit back a sigh as Priestly walked away. He began to wonder if he shouldn't accept the man's advice. He knew very well what his problem was. It was a problem that could not be solved by simply changing the variables of a compound in his chemistry studies. This was not like adding integers and picking at equations in a mathematics lecture. This would not be as straightforward as collecting a sample for his botany observations. This was something entirely different, because Alexcena was entirely different.

How to begin; this was the great question. He had avoided returning to Penn the previous week so that he might have more time to consider his tactics. Alexcena was surprisingly, pleasantly, unpredictable. There was no possible way for him to consider his responses in advance when there was little or no chance of correctly guessing her reaction.

You ought to be accustomed to dealing with unexpected reactions.

All at once Lucius smiled to himself. "Yes."

You're a scientist. You've carried out your share of experiments. This is no different. Ample information has been gathered, you need only begin.

He rose and hurried to stack his papers. He would need to leave right away if he was to reach Penn and Tyler's Green by nightfall. The streets of Cambridge were not overly crowded, and he reached Reagan's stables in no time at all. Tim Reagan sat out front smoking his habitual pipe.

"Wolgath," he grunted. "Missed you last week." He snorted and swiped a hand across his bulbous nose. "Maeva'll be ready in no time for ye." Reagan whistled and Lucius saw a man dart through the wide stable door.

"I wondered if you had a curricle available as well."

Tim squinted and shrugged. "Aye. But our arrangement is for Maeva. The curric'le cost you."

"I figured as much." Lucius passed him the coins.

Tim bit one of the pieces, spat, and disappeared into the stable. Moments later he immerged leading the mare hitched to a modest, two-wheeled conveyance.

"Thank you, Mr. Tim," Lucius called as he pulled himself up into the seat.

He felt a thin sense of relief, and even hummed quietly to himself most of the way to the hostler's stable at Penn. In the failing light he saw a shadowy figure approach and tossed him the reins.

"You're awfully trusting with these."

"I'd know your scraggly head anywhere," Lucius replied as he descended to shake hands with his brother. "What are you still doing in Penn?"

Leopold grinned and gripped Lucius's hand. "Landed a job with the hostler here abouts. Got to build the funds a bit, you know."

"Where are you off to next?"

"Spain is looking nice nowadays. Just have to wait and see how long I stay here."

"You're welcome to my house whenever you like."

"Careful," Leo warned. "I'm likely to take you up on that before long." He jerked his thumb back toward the barn. "These aren't exactly fancy accommodations I'm in now."

"Say no more. Commodore will be glad for the company when I don't take him to Cambridge with me."

Leo gave his brother a questioning glance at that. "I notice I didn't see you here last week."

"I was, uh…" Lucius broke off and attempted a chuckle. "I was having difficulty with a-project."

Leo blinked and then looked sly. "I know what you're thinking of. Or rather *who* you're thinking of. What's the matter?" he laughed. "Lost your nerve before the relationship's even begun?"

Lucius batted his brother's arm. "Leave off with that. I've decided how to approach her."

"Just remember to keep your wits about you. This isn't like one of your science projects you can control and study."

Lucius blinked. "I don't see why not."

This set Leopold laughing again. "Ah, Lucius! We're talking about a woman. They're perilous, shifty, emotional creatures, and if you let the wrong one get hold of you, they're liable to change you forever."

"I wouldn't call Alexcena perilous," Lucius argued weakly.

Leo opened his mouth to retort, but both men were distracted by a sudden movement nearby. A young lady-who before had been approaching them-had turned abruptly and was walking in the opposite direction. Her blond curls bounced wildly against her neck.

"Tabitha!"

The girl hesitated and faced them.

Lucius was smiling kindly. "What a pleasure it is to see you again."

She licked her lips. "H-hello, Lucius." She bobbed a nervous curtsy to his bow. Her jaw was working oddly, and one hand strayed up behind her back to twirl a loose lock of hair. The soft young eyes darted over his shoulder to Leo.

Lucius stepped aside. "Allow me to introduce my brother Leopold."

"A man who needs no introduction," Leo added as he bent to kiss Tabitha's hand.

"How do you do?" Tabitha raised one eyebrow with evident curiosity. Lucius failed to notice this, but Leo certainly did not.

"I do very well. Better than most, I'd say."

"Oh? Are you wealthy then, sir?"

"Only in spirit, miss," he snickered at her blunt question.

Tabitha sniffed, taking in the rough appearance and cool demeanor of the man. Leo simply smiled under her scrutiny.

"Well," she said after a moment. "I must-must be off now." She grasped two great handfuls of her skirts. "Good day, Lucius. Sir." She left with a curtsy and a flounce of her curls.

"Odd," Lucius remarked as he watched her go. "That is the first time I have ever spoken with her that she didn't laugh."

Leo was leaning back, the better to see over Lucius' shoulder. "Who was that?"

"Tabitha. Tabitha Winslett. Odd little thing, is she not?"

"You're one to talk."

Lucius glanced over and saw the direction of his brother's gaze. "What's gotten into you?"

Leo didn't seem to hear the question. "What's she like?"

"Well-"

"Never mind." He waved a hand and set to unhitching Maeva from the curricle. "I shall soon find out."

"Would you like me to put in a good word for you?"

"Now that's all I need. My baby brother embellishing my reputation." He shook his head gravely. "No thanks, mate. I'll do well enough on my own."

"Now remember," Lucius warned mockingly, "she's a woman. They're perilous, emotional-"

"Yea, yea." Leo gave his brother a shove. "Off with you. You've your own safety to worry about."

Chapter 8
June 29, 1764

Lucius reached the drive leading up to the Lissome Ground altogether too quickly and sighed. His brother had quite effectively managed to complicate the whole situation for him once again. Lucius recalled images of pleasant conversations he had shared with Alexcena over the last several weeks. They had cultivated such a charming friendship, and he was about to bring that friendship to the brink. He imagined the noble gladiator standing before Rome's powerful emperor, waiting silently for his ruler's thumb to turn up, and praying fervently that it would not point down.

He paced the end of the drive three times before finally making his way toward the house. The shrubs seemed to mock him with their military precision. The sight of them made him feel unkempt. He paused to brush at the light dust the road had left on his trousers and coat. Then he painstakingly lifted the brass ring and knocked.

The door was answered by Eshton, who admitted him at once. "Mr. Wolgath. A pleasure to see you again, sir."

"Afternoon, Eshton." He could not help but pass a furtive glance about the foyer. "Are the Condreves at home?"

"Yes, sir. I believe Mr. Condreve is in his study. Shall I show you in?"

"Are Mrs. and Ms. Condreve in?"

"In the parlor, sir. Shall I announce you?"

"That'll be fine, Eshton. That is if they're not busy."

"Follow me, sir."

Lucius allowed himself to be led to one of the more spacious parlors, although he knew very well where it was. They paused outside the door and Eshton straightened his collar. Lucius reached up self-consciously to do the same.

"Please wait here." Eshton stepped just inside the room. "Mr. Lucius Wolgath, Madam."

At some signal from Mrs. Condreve, Eshton dipped his head and gestured for Lucius to enter. The two ladies were seated at ends of a plush davenport. Cecelia greeted him with a demure smile and a nod. Alexcena beamed. She sat on the sofa's edge, her back erect, her hands folded in the proper pose. Her dark hair was swept up with a single lock resting gracefully across one shoulder. Belatedly, Lucius thought to remove his hat and bow.

"Good day, ladies."

"Good day, Mr. Wolgath. Shall I call for my husband to join us?"

Lucius fingered the edge of his tricorn hat. "I do not wish to disturb him. This is merely a social call."

"Please be seated," Alexcena invited.

He lowered himself into an armchair some seven feet away from the ladies. Failing sunlight flooded the room through a row of tall windows behind him, throwing him into shadow while brilliantly reflecting the ladies.

Cecelia gestured to the windows. "We were just discussing how warm it has become out of doors."

"Yes?"

"The chill has quite left the air, and the garden is already enjoying the change," she went on. "It is perfect weather for a stroll."

Lucius unconsciously leapt to his feet. "I'd love to."

Alexcena rose as well. "Go for a walk?"

"Yes, indeed."

"Then I shall join you. You won't mind, Mother?"

"You're welcome to join us, Mrs. Condreve."

"No, you two go along. I shall observe the sunset through the glass from here."

"Then it's settled."

"After you, Ms. Condreve."

Cecelia watched them go with some mild surprise. The entire exchange had lasted all of thirty seconds.

The sun seemed to watch the two of them as it peaked over the distant hills. It was already part of the way through its setting, but as Mrs. Condreve had said, the air was comfortable about them. They moved in silence for several minutes; Alexcena attempting to appear nonchalant and Lucius fidgeting with his hat in his left hand.

"I feel obligated to tell you, Ms. Condreve," he began at last, "that I did not come here to see your father."

"Yes, I know."

Lucius blinked. "Or your mother."

She giggled slightly. "I assumed as much."

Lucius cleared his throat and plunged doggedly on. "It is my intention, that is, if I may be so bold as to inquire-"

Alexcena stopped and watched him through her hazel green eyes. He broke off, searching for an appropriate phrase. The corners of her small mouth turned up just enough to form a becoming smile. Encouraged, he began again.

"It is my wish to spend a great deal more time in your company in the future, and I wondered if perhaps you would like to spend more time with me."

So it was done. Their budding friendship now lay at her feet. It was honest and simple. Fitting, since he would have no extravagances or luxuries to offer her as of yet. He let out a slow breath and waited, though not for long.

"I believe I would, Mr. Wolgath."

Lucius blinked again. "Really? You're under no obligation."

She laughed quietly at this. "It is an honor, Mr. Wolgath. I'm so very pleased that you asked."

He could not stop the smile that came to him. "Oh?"

She said nothing, but threaded her arm through his elbow. They started down the path once more.

"Very well, then," Lucius murmured, resting his hand over her own.

Lawrence was on his way to the parlor when he met his wife in the hall.

"Is someone here, m'dear? I thought I heard Eshton at the door an hour ago."

Cecelia snickered and patted her husband's arm. "Oh, yes. Someone is here. He's coming out of the garden with Alexcena now."

"Who-"

He broke off at the sound of approaching footsteps and muffled voices. He visibly relaxed when he saw Lucius leading his daughter around the corner.

"Wolgath!" he exclaimeded merrily. "We weren't expecting you tonight."

"I didn't wish to disturb you, sir," Lucius said easily. "I was just taking my leave, but there is something I would like to ask you before I go."

"Yes?"

"Might I have the pleasure of calling on your daughter tomorrow morning?"

"Oh!" Lawrence looked from Lucius to Cecelia and back. "Certainly! Certainly, m'boy!" He shook Lucius' hand with vigor. "You're always welcome. Always!"

"Uh…Thank you," Lucius stammered and released his hand. "I shall head for home then. Good night."

"Good night," the Condreves answered in unison. They remained as they were in the hall until they heard the door closing and Eshton walking away.

"So." Alexcena faced her parents, her hands innocently clasped behind her back. "What do you think of him?"

"Alexcena," her mother sighed. "Sometimes you are incorrigible."

Lawrence drew himself up with a measure of dignity. "She has it from my side of the family."

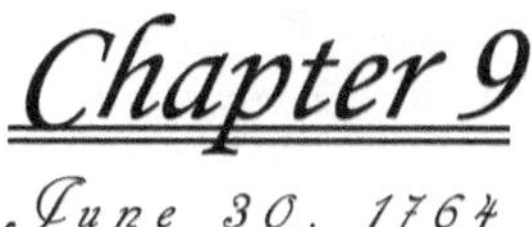

Chapter 9

June 30, 1764

"Lydia!" Alexcena called as she breezed into the bed chamber.

"Yes, miss?"

She was quite shocked, and even gave a start when the maid appeared in the door of her dressing room. Sighing, she made a valiant attempt to calm down.

"Lydia, will you please help me to change?"

"Of course, miss."

Alecena followed her into the spacious dressing room. She had fidgeted all through breakfast, and then determined to start getting ready immediately. Lucius had said he would come in the morning, but not when.

"I laid these out for you, miss," Lydia was saying. "Which would you like?"

The doors of the large armoire were opened wide, and three dresses were laid out on a small sofa nearby. She studied them and fingered the sleeve of the one closest to her. Somehow they all looked the same.

"Um…"

Lydia sensed her plight, and lifted one gown. "I would say this one, if you ask me, miss. The color accentuates your eyes, and it's simply made, so it's good for any activity."

Alexcena let her shoulders slump and gave the woman a smile. "Thank you, Lydia. I suppose I'm a bit edgy."

Lydia set to unfastening the buttons at Alexcena's back. "It's perfectly natural. Mr. Wolgath is a handsome man, and a kind one at that."

"He certainly is," Alexcena sighed. "I don't know why I'm so anxious. I'm usually not this way around Lucius."

"You'll be more yourself once he arrives and the two of you start talking. You're just nervous because you don't know when he's coming, so no matter when he arrives, it'll surprise you."

Alexcena blinked and looked to the woman. "My goodness," she murmured. "You're right."

Lydia smiled and slipped the chosen gown over Alexcena's head. "Don't forget, miss, I have three sisters, all married. I've seen my share of couples in love. I've seen the both of you on nights when Mr. Wolgath has come by. You have similar souls, the two of you. That's a rare thing indeed, something you'll want to hang onto the rest of your days."

"Oh, Lydia," Alexcena muttered in mock frustration. "You manage to calm me down and then you stir me up again."

Lucius stood in the foyer, his hat in hand, his heart in his throat. He rubbed his chin absently, wondering just what had possessed him to do this. His brother's words came unbidden to his mind. *She's a woman. They're perilous, shifty, emotional creatures.*

He pushed the warning from his thoughts. He tapped the top of his hat and expelled a great puff of air. *The difficult part is done. This ought to be no problem.* It oughtn't to be, but it was. He paced to the bottom of the stairs and back toward the door. He was walking toward the stairs again when Alexcena appeared at the top.

"Good morning, Mr. Wolgath."

She was halfway down the steps before Lucius could force himself to reply. "Good morning. Ho-how are you?"

"Very well, thank you…You?"

"The same." A pause. "I had toast for breakfast."

"We had pancakes and some sausage."

"That sounds delicious."

"It was, but I'm more partial to bacon myself."

"Oh? I eat either one."

"Oh?"

Lucius gave himself a mental blow. How had he managed to drive them into this vein; 'I had toast' indeed. Had he bothered to watch her more closely, he might have seen that she was not at all put off by this odd conversation. In fact she was glad to be discussing something as simple as toast.

"I put too much sugar in my coffee," she commented.

"Yes?"

"Yes. I normally do not take it sweet, but I did this morning."

Lucius tried to laugh and ended up clearing his throat.

"How do you take your coffee?"

"The same way I take my tea," he replied. "Unless I'm feeling irritable. Then I take it black."

She grinned kindly. "I cannot imagine that happening often."

"You've never seen me before my coffee."

Alexcena tittered and then clamped her lips shut. If she hadn't, she would have giggled like an idiot.

"Here you are, miss." Lydia appeared quite suddenly bearing Alexcena's cloak. "I saw Mr. Wolgath's cart and thought you might need this."

"I had intended to take you for a ride about the Green, if you would like."

"That sounds lovely," she said even as she donned the cloak. "I didn't know you owned a curricle."

"I don't," Lucius said as he held the door for her. "I rented it for a few days."

Alexcena descended the steps and could not resist stroking the palomino's nose when she reached the curricle.

"That's Maeva," he told her.

"Is she yours?"

"No, I don't own a horse at the moment. She belongs to a stable in Cambridge. The proprietor allows me to use her on the weekends in exchange for tutoring his son and daughter."

They moved to one side of the buggy and Lucius faltered over how to help her up. He thought to grasp her waist and lift her up but wondered if she would take offense. Failing that he offered his hand and she managed easily enough. He came up beside her and took hold of the reins.

"Now, where shall we go?"

Alexcena looked him straight in the eye to answer. "Anywhere."

Leopold was given Sunday to himself from the stables, and so it was that he made his way to Lucius' boarding house that Saturday night. After a full week of smelling nothing but horses, he was very much looking forward to a night away from the stables. It wasn't until he scaled the stairs to the third floor and found the door locked that he realized he had no key. Lucius hadn't thought of it, and he had neglected to ask.

A movement far below caught his attention. Commodore peered up at him expectantly from his little door. He slipped through, as if in illustration.

Leo raised an eyebrow. "Yea, well I'm afraid it's not that easy for those of us with wide shoulders."

Commodore snorted and darted back inside the house.

Leo looked casually about before pulling a formidable knife from its sheath under his coat. He deftly worked the blade into the crevice of the door and its frame even with the lock. In a thrice the door was open, allowing him to stroll nonchalantly in.

Commodore sat before the door, eagerly waiting for the first familiar face to come inside. So it was that when the unsuspecting Leo opened the door, he pounced.

"Whoa!"

Leo fell back against the door as Commodore threw his head against his knees and grunted.

"Nice to see you as well, old boy," he said, scratching lustily at the blue-gray ears presented to him.

He moved toward the kitchen only to be butted by Commodore again, this time from the back. He caught his balance and turned to the animal.

"Can I help you with something?"

Commodore moaned piteously.

"What is it you want? Entrée?"

The dog yelped and his large tongue lulled out one side of his mouth.

Leo searched the cupboards and came up with some salted pork. He tossed several pieces to the dog and took the rest for himself.

"I wonder where that master of yours has got to."

He tried to pretend he was worried about his younger brother, but he could only grin, knowing that it was far from true. He was going to take great pleasure in ribbing him if he had managed to draw up the courage to approach Ms. Condreve. Of course if he had not been able to do it, he would be obliged to jerk him up by the collar and order him to man up about it.

He dropped down on the sofa with a chuckle, remembering the last time he had approached a woman. Commodore settled himself on the rug, and Leo reached down to rub his head.

"Gabriella Montescu," he recalled.

Ms. Montescu was a heavyset young lady of twenty-three, nearly ten years his junior. He had met her in Italy just over a year ago. What with her contagious laugh, agile mind, and impossibly long lashes, he found that he could not resist. He had approached the house confidently with flowers in one hand and his hat in the other. He ended up fleeing the property without even seeing Gabriella, and closely pursued by her mother, two brothers, and the family goat. A year had passed, and he found that he could not quite bring himself to laugh at the image of round Mrs. Montescu waving a rolling pen and shouting in rapid Italian.

"Well, perhaps Lucius had a better reception than I. What d'you think?"

Commodore rolled over for Leo to scratch his lean belly. He was doing just that when Lucius came in. Leo sat up straight.

"Well?"

Lucius was grinning from ear to ear. He removed his hat and tossed it smoothly into a nearby armchair. "I hope you won't be needing me for anything tomorrow after church."

Leo cocked an eyebrow. "I take it you have plans?"

Lucius made no reply, but sauntered off toward the bedroom without a backward glance.

Leo looked to Commodore and shook his head. "It's lucky for you I'm unattached or you'd go hungry."

A face materialized unexpectedly in his mind. A smooth, young face wreathed in wild blond curls.

Chapter 10

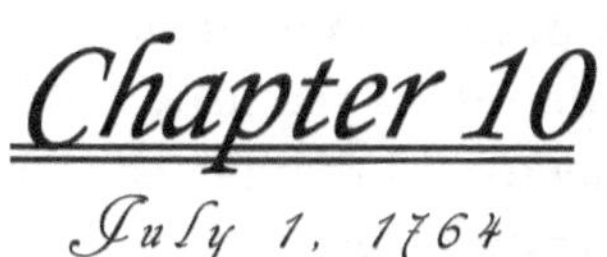

July 1, 1764

"Good afternoon, Lucius!" Lawrence waved him into the cozy breakfast room. The table-which would only accommodate six people at best-was laid with a beautiful spread of fruit, cheeses, cold cuts of meat, and tantalizing sweet rolls.

"I hope you don't think us odd, but since we could convince no one else to join us after church, we decided to use this table rather than the large dining room."

"Not at all," Lucius replied. His eyes slid toward Alexcena and then back to her parents.

"-that you've brought, Mr. Wolgath?" Cecelia was saying.

He hesitated to answer as he took his seat. He smiled with pleasure in spite of his embarrassment. "My violin. I seem to remember promising to play for you all sometime," he answered, at last allowing his attention to rest on Alexcena. "I hope you don't think me presumptuous."

"Of course not, we'd love to hear it."

"You ought to have brought it last week. You're too bashful, m'boy!" Lawrence chortled. "After all, you're practically family already."

A clatter of glass drew everyone's attention to Alexcena. She had her glass set up right almost before anyone realized that it had fallen. The look on her face was so comically calm that Wolgath had to cover his mouth to hide his mirth. Alexcena waved an approaching servant away and placed her napkin over the stain on the tablecloth. Without further adieu, Lawrence asked a blessing and the meal was underway. Alexcena was first to speak.

"How were your lectures this week, Mr. Wolgath?"

"Long. Sometimes I wonder just how long this last six months is going to be."

"Come now," Cecelia smiled kindly. "They cannot be any worse than the years you've spent at Cambridge before."

"But this is his *last* year, m'dear," Lawrence interjected. "The toughest one, especially for someone with his agenda."

"And it will only get tougher," Lucius grimaced. "I only hope I survive the tripos."

Alexcena looked up from her plate. "The tripos?"

"It's a series of three final exams at the end of the graduating year."

"Those who pass are called Wranglers," Lawrence added. "The student with the highest score is pronounced 'Senior Wrangler.' The one with the next highest after him is dubbed 'Second Wrangler' and so on."

"Wait," Cecelia interjected, "I thought the tripos were the examinations for mathematics. I understood you to be a scholar of chemistry, Mr. Wolgath."

He sighed forlornly. "I was feeling rather ambitious when I came to Cambridge. I wanted to make chemistry my career. I signed on for a botany course because it was something I enjoyed and the math because it was something I was very good at."

Lawrence gapped at him. "Are you telling me you're studying

mathematics at Cambridge University because you assumed it would be easy?"

"Much to my chagrin, I have found that the chemistry has become much more natural to me. I take comfort in the fact that a certain degree of mathematics was required along with all this chemistry in order for me to earn my professorship."

Lawrence still stared at him. "Well," he said at last, "that's some comfort since you'll be making your living from it."

"I just had a terrible thought," Alexcena said after a lull in the conversation. "What do they call the wrangler with the lowest score? It's not Last Wrangler is it? That would be awful!"

Lucius could not help but laugh as he spooned fresh fruit compote onto his plate. "It's worse, I'm afraid." He held the silver utensil aloft for her to see. "They call him the Wooden Spoon."

Alexcena's mouth fell open just a bit, and then she chewed her lip to hide a sudden bought of laughter. "That's...dreadful."

"They actually present the poor fellow with a wooden spoon too, if you can believe that."

"I must say," Lawrence commented thoughtfully, "I've seen plenty of men that were grateful for that wooden spoon, because they had been convinced that they would not pass at all."

"I can't say it would be much of a relief," Lucius replied, "but if it were between that and failing, I would be swift to accept the title of Wooden Spoon."

"What made you want to attend Cambridge?" Alexcena asked him.

Lucius took on a wistful look and fiddled with his fork. "I always wanted to learn. When I was a boy that was what it was about; the learning. I wanted to know everything. To this day I greatly respect and desire knowledge. I've hoped to become a professor for a very long time, and I think it's because I want to show others that there are significant reasons for us to learn what we're learning, to study what we're studying. I chose Cambridge mainly because it's one of the finest universities in the world, coupled with the fact that it's so close to London, where I lived out most of my childhood."

Alexcena looked on in quiet appreciation as Lucius finished his explanation. Suddenly the wistful look left his face. He made a little smile down at his plate, but somehow she knew it was for her.

"Speaking of London, Lucius," Condreve said, "has Alexcena told you?"

He looked up and she explained. "We'll be going to our house in Town on Tuesday."

"That sounds enjoyable," he replied noncommittally. "How long will you be staying?"

"A few weeks at least," Cecelia said. "A few weeks may be all that some of us can stand."

Alexcena looked appalled at this. "I never said a word!"

"Something you will learn very quickly about my daughter, Mr. Wolgath," Cecelia continued. "She hates Town."

"Yes, she mentioned something of that before."

"It is not only London," Alexcena defended. "It's large cities in general."

"Society will never forgive you for that, I'm afraid," her father warned. "It seems to thrive on them."

"Yes, yes. And society will never forgive me for choosing to marry so late in life either, but that does not concern me in the least." She lifted her shoulders with an air of confidence. "I have all the society I want right here."

Lucius raised an eyebrow and caught her glance. At that moment she realized how that must have sounded and was swift to amend.

"Right here at Penn and Tyler's Green."

"Well, this society wants entertainment." Lawrence came to his feet as the servants began clearing away the plates. "Shall we go to the music room?"

Moments later the Condreves watched eagerly as Lucius lifted his violin from its padded box. He was shy beneath their gazes, as he was with almost every audience. He plucked a few strings and tweaked a few knobs before raising his bow.

"Now, what to play…"

"Do you know any hymns?"

"Do you know anything fast?"

"Play something we haven't heard before."

The requests flew at him, and Lucius latched onto the third. "Here's one you may not know," he grinned. There was an unmistakable twinkle to his eye as he struck up a rather slow rendition of "Greensleeves."

"No!" Alexcena cried in mock terror, though her plea was quite serious. "Anything but that!"

Lucius complied with a chuckle, and played one of his personal favorites. The 'concert' lasted half an hour before Lucius voluntarily set the instrument aside.

"Mr. Condreve, may I speak with you?"

"Certainly." The men moved to the far corner of the room while the ladies remained seated and chattering. "What's on your mind, m'boy?"

"I would like your permission to visit Ms. Condreve while you're all in London next week. May I have it?"

Lucius would not have pegged Lawrence as the cruel type of man that would force a good man to wait with a sour look of disapproval masking his mirth, but evidently he was.

"You may."

Lucius let out a breath, making Lawrence laugh. "Thank you, sir. I would also ask your confidence. I would like to surprise her." As he spoke he looked to the object of his affections far across the room and smiled.

"You have it. Is there anything else you would like to ask me?"

"May I take your daughter for a walk?"

Lawrence laughed again and clapped Lucius soundly on the shoulder. "Perhaps you ought to simply take some of these questions to the lady in the future, hm? Save some time."

"But you make for such good practice."

When Lawrence caught his breath again he shook his head. "I think Lucius that if you would take a moment and look at her, you would realize that she is just as smitten as you are."

So it was that the pair went for a walk that slow Sunday afternoon. They followed a worn footpath that snaked its way around the fields of Penn. Lucius was only slightly surprised to find himself at ease as he strode beside the lady.

"I'm afraid I've not done much traveling," Alexcena commented as they went. "I've never been outside the country."

"Never?"

"No, I've barely seen the country itself."

"Perhaps we should remedy that."

"I fear I am just as content to walk these same paths time after time."

A distant sound reached them before he could say anything further. A bark. It sounded again just as Lucius caught sight of two familiar figures moving across the Green in their direction.

"Commodore!" Lucius chuckled. "And Leo. What a surprise." He raised his arm in greeting even as Commodore bounded in circles about his knees. "Hello, boy. Leo, what brings you out here?"

"My Sundays are my own," he replied jovially and grasped his brother's hand. "Commodore insisted we go for a walk."

"He's quite persistent isn't he?" He turned to say something to Alexcena, but she wasn't there.

Leo cleared his throat. "Ahem. Lucius."

Lucius followed his gaze. Alexcena stood several feet away pressed against the trunk of a tall tree. Her complexion was white as a winter moon. Her fists were knotted around great handfuls of her skirts. Her round eyes were fastened on Commodore.

He sat not three feet from her. He seemed to be studying her with something akin to both curiosity and arrogance.

"Alexcena?" Lucius moved to her side and took her elbow. The slim arm trembled beneath his touch.

With visible effort, Alexcena drew a shuddering breath and answered. "Do you know the term phobia, Mr. Wolgath?"

"Yes. A phobia is an irrational aversion or fear to something otherwise seen as harmless or-" He glanced from her to his dog and back. "Oh."

Commodore emitted a low grunt and Alexcena sucked a gasp of air through her teeth.

"Why don't Commodore and I just move along?" Leo took hold of the dog and gave him a tug. "Come, boy."

"Hike," Lucius supplied.

Commodore came to his feet with a snort that carried such an air of snobbery, it would have offended King George himself.

"Nice to see you again!" Leo called as the pair moved away.

Lucius turned a worried eye to the lady. "Alexcena?"

She laid one hand at her collar and moved unconsciously closer to Lucius. His concern was so great that he failed to feel this motion, which came as naturally as it was ignored.

"Come." Raising his free hand to gently rest about her shoulder, he led her to a stone bench a short distance away.

She was scarcely aware of their movements as she worked to calm her breathing. She sat and he remained half leaning above her. The distress he felt for her nerves was plain to see in his kind face and she regretted it with the whole of her heart.

"Do forgive me," she began lamely.

"Nonsense. Are you better now?"

"Quite, thank you." She moved her wide skirts so as to make room for him on the bench. "What was that you said as Mr. Wolgath was trying to move the dog away?"

"Hike. It's one of his commands," he explained. "One of Commodore's commands, I mean. Hike means go, tarry for stay, hither to come, and entrée to eat. You'd be surprised how often those words come up in regular conversation."

"Goodness. How ever did you teach him all of that?"

He grinned roguishly. "Don't forget, Ms. Condreve, I am studying to be a teacher."

Chapter 11
July 13, 1764

"Do join us, Alexcena."

The young lady turned from the window to her mother as she donned her cloak and hat. Her father was close at hand, fiddling with the gold buttons of his waistcoat.

"Where are you off to?"

"We're heading over to visit with our friend, Mr. Whitesley."

Alexcena wrinkled her nose. She remembered Whitesley well in all his foppish finery. The man never failed to wax poetic about his wide-ranging collection of fine china and crystals. She secretly suspected that he did this only to improve his popularity with the ladies-at least that's what she hoped.

"I think I'll stay here."

"Now Alexcena." Her father tsk-tsked wearily. "You cannot keep inside for the whole of our stay in London."

Her mother agreed. "As nice as our townhouse is, you really must get out more."

"If you would allow yourself to, you might find that you actually enjoy London at times."

She bit back a sigh characteristic of one who is badgered by either parents or well-meaning compatriots. "Very well. I shall keep that in mind and leave word if I decide to go anywhere."

Lawrence patted her hand not unkindly. "Just beware of where you go alone, hm?"

Once her family had gone, Alexcena turned back to the window to observe the movements of the city on that sunny afternoon in July. It never ceased to amaze her just how many people there were traipsing the streets in this, the hub of England, and she shuddered to see them jostling and hurrying without a glance at anyone. She hated to think what aspects of city life would cause a person to be so withdrawn.

"Begging your pardon, Ms. Condreve." Eshton bowed low and awaited acknowledgement.

"Yes?"

"There is a gentleman arrived to see you. Shall I show him in?"

Alexcena considered. Good manners won out and she rose to smooth her gown. "Yes, Eshton. Return in a few moments to see about tea, if you please."

"Of course."

Alexcena turned her back to the door and tucked an errant wisp of hair back behind one ear. Feeling weighed down by all the close confines of the city, she was in no mood to entertain. Still it was beneath her breeding to intentionally turn someone away without a compelling reason. So it was that she stood facing the window and recalling the proverb of the wise woman and her household when Eshton returned.

"Mr. Lucius Wolgath."

Alexcena was ever grateful that she was facing away from the door that day. Her mouth fell open for a full three seconds and a hot color rose in her cheeks. With some great effort, she managed to school her features and slowly turned to her guest.

He stood there, hat in hand, with a hidden smile lighting his blue eyes. "Good afternoon my-that is, Ms. Condreve." He bowed.

"Mr. Wolgath." She fluttered and held out her hand. To her delight, he took it after only a slight hesitation.

"I hope I find you well," he said formally. "I know you are not overly fond of the city."

A stupid giggle escaped her lips and her hand flew to her mouth to stop it. She never forgave herself for that in future musings. Lucius seemed to enjoy it, which made the slip all the more embarrassing.

"What has brought you to Town?"

His thumb stroked her knuckles. "I heard somewhere that a family in my acquaintance would be staying here."

She smiled. "Would you care to sit down?"

"Actually, I have come for a different reason. Do you know the Hawthorne Tea Garden?"

"No, I can't say that I do."

"It is quite brilliant this time of year," he went on. "I could not let you leave without seeing it. May I have the pleasure of escorting you?"

Before she could reply, Eshton appeared in the doorway. It did not escape her notice that Lucius maintained his light hold of her hand, despite the man's appearance.

"Shall I bring in refreshment, Ms. Condreve?"

"That won't be necessary. Mr. Wolgath has just invited me out to see the Hawthorne Tea Garden. Would you please inform my parents of my whereabouts when they return?"

"Of course, ma'am."

To his credit, Lucius did a masterful job of quelling his inward excitement. He waited patiently for Alexcena to gather her wrap and hat, and offered her his arm as they left. The Hawthorne Tea Garden was a mere four blocks away and they covered the distance easily. Lucius found himself torn between wishing the streets were not so crowded and being thankful that they were. It was a convenient excuse to keep Alexcena close the entire way.

Though Hawthorne was certainly smaller than Vauxhall or some of the other more popular gardens, it boasted a fine array of entertainments. Rectangular in shape and lined on three sides by shop buildings, it seemed an oasis of green against the shadowed hues of the city. Rows of thin trees lined the paths. To one side a clever café owner had set several tables and chairs on the lawn at the rear of his establishment, offering a wide array of refreshment to the visitors. Opposite him a small acting troupe had set a puppet stage and put on regular shows for the children. The far end of the garden was kept carefully clear and served as a bowling green. Close by the gate a pantomimer entertained patrons as they arrived. Two musicians strolled the grounds at intervals, filling the atmosphere with merry tunes for their listeners.

Lucius could not recall spending a happier afternoon. Alexcena was beautiful in her cream colored skirt and embroidered stomacher. He was hard pressed to recall knowing anyone with tastes so suited to his own. He would scarcely think of a comment before she voiced it herself.

The sun was well into its setting before the pair reluctantly took their leave. Lawrence and Cecelia were waiting for them when they arrived. They had just reached the stairs of the stoop when Lawrence opened the door.

"Lucius! Fancy seeing you here, m'boy."

"Good evening, sir." He bowed. "I hope you don't mind my stealing away with Ms. Condreve for the afternoon."

"Not at all. Not at all."

"Then I hope you'll accept another invitation. To a play tomorrow night."

Alexcena smiled at this.

"With your permission, Lawrence, I shall secure us a box."

"We would be delighted."

"Wonderful. I'll see you then, sir." He bowed to Alexcena. "Good night, Ms. Condreve."

"Good night."

He made his way to the road and could not resist one final glance behind. Alexcena stood illuminated in the doorway. She raised her finger tips to her lips and slowly shut the door.

Chapter 12
October 12, 1764

Lucius spurred Maeva to a brisk pace as they neared Lissome Ground. He had spent more time than ever with Alexcena in London, but his studies at Cambridge had allowed him precious few days at a time in Town. It had been more than a week since last he saw her, and he was overjoyed to receive a note from Lawrence only yesterday saying that they had returned to Penn.

As always, Eshton met him at the door.

"Good day, Mr. Wolgath," he said, reaching to accept Lucius' hat.

"Hello, Eshton. I assume the family is at home."

"Indeed, sir, and entertaining a guest in the upstairs salon."

Wolgath hesitated. "Oh. Perhaps I should wait to-"

"On the contrary, sir." Eshton managed to snatch his coat very politely from his shoulders. "I believe your visit will be much appreciated. If you'll follow me."

The butler's uncharacteristic assertiveness peaked Lucius' interest mightily. Facing the prospect of a visit with Alexcena, he managed to set his suspicion aside. He straightened his cravat as he followed him up the stairs, matching the butler's brisk pace. His misgivings rose once more as soon as he entered the salon.

Lawrence stood at the wide fireplace. He smiled and said nothing; the silence of the chatty man spoke volumes. Cecelia sat on a wide settee with a look of pleasant propriety frozen on her face, an unopened book on her lap. Her expression softened for an instant when she caught sight of him. A little apart from them, Alexcena was seated in a plush chair. Looming not so far from her was Rodney Dushaw. She seemed immensely preoccupied with her hands while he stood watching her.

Lucius took in the scene and his brow furrowed as his gaze lingered on Alexcena and Rodney. He smoothed his countenance and turned mechanically to husband and wife.

"Good day, Lawrence, Mrs. Condreve."

"Lucius."

Cecelia raised a hand and the young man bowed low over it.

"What brings you by?" Lawrence wondered.

"I received your note that you had all arrived from London. I thought I'd ask the pleasure of your company."

"Mr. Dushaw said the very same... With the exception of the note, of course."

"Please sit down, Mr. Wolgath." Alexcena indicated a seat near her own and opposite Rodney. She did not smile, but her eyes widened with appreciation.

Rodney looked him up and down with a pinched expression, which he did not bother to mask. "Wolgath."

"Rodney, what an unexpected pleasure."

The two men bowed and Lucius took the indicated seat. Alexcena went back to studying her nails. Lucius was by now more aware of her discomfiture in the presence of his fellow student. He could not say exactly what had passed between the two to warrant such feelings on her part, but the knowledge had made him somewhat wary. Silence reigned over the room. Cecelia had left her seat to discuss something with her husband in the book she was reading, leaving the younger people to converse together.

Lucius cleared his throat. "So what brings you to Penn, Rodney?"

"Like you, I heard that the Condreves had returned. And I am so fond of the scenery at Lissome Ground."

"Yes. The grounds of Tyler's Green, the Chiltern Hills. It can all be quite-" Lucius faltered when he realized that Rodney was openly staring at Alexcena. "Stunning."

When the lady did not look up, Rodney turned his attention away. "Haven't seen much of you, Wolgath, since you made that junket to London."

"I've been deep in studies I'm afraid."

A queer grin lit Rodney's face. "Remind me why it was that you went."

"I-" Alexcena chose that moment to look at him and he lost his nerve. "I don't believe I ever told you why it was that I went," he replied with a shrug. "But while I was there, I did make my way to the Royal Exchange to see about a horse."

"Really?"

"It's high time I purchase my own mount."

"Mare or stud?"

This was said very casually. Alexcena's brows rose in mild shock.

Lucius cast a brief glance to her. "Perhaps," he said to Rodney, "we ought not to discuss such things before Ms. Condreve."

Rodney chuckled more to cover his aggravation than anything else. His attempt to draw Lucius into unsavory conversation had not worked, so he would try another tact.

"Forgive me, Ms. Alexcena," he said. "I do so love discussing horseflesh, I fear I forget myself."

"Indeed, Mr. Dushaw."

"I entreat you, Ms. Alexcena, you must address me by my Christian name. I assure you it is quite proper when two people have known one another as long as we have. You agree, don't you, Lucius?"

Wolgath shifted in his seat. "I would not presume to tell a true lady such as Ms. Condreve what is proper."

"And what of that lady friend of yours, Ms. Winslett?"

Lucius struggled for a reply.

"I understand you and she have taken advantage of such propriety and come to a first name basis."

"I'm sure Mr. Wolgath would never intentionally take advantage of anything," Alexcena commented distractedly. "And I pray that you remember it is not only himself, but my cousin you are speaking of."

"I quite agree," Rodney jeered, ignoring her second comment. "But one must admit, when a man is in the throes of youthful infatuation, it is difficult to keep some of the rules of society and remain in check, or so I've heard."

Lucius felt his neck burn with embarrassment. In contrast Alexcena was strangely pale. *What can Rodney be thinking? There can be no excuse for such behavior.* He cleared his throat and replied in a rigid rasp, "I have never entertained such thoughts of that young lady."

"Not openly anyway."

"Alexcena?"

"Yes, Mother?"

"Where is that exotic field reference I saw you with yesterday?"

"I think I left it in father's study. Shall I fetch it?"

"No need, dear."

Her parents left arm-in-arm and Eshton appeared to station himself by the door as a silent sentinel.

Rodney dropped onto a lavish davenport and leaned lazily back.

"Your mother seems to enjoy a great deal of reading."

"As a scholar I should think you would find that admirable, Mr. Dushaw. Do you not enjoy reading?"

"Not particularly. I read only to obtain facts. Cold, hard facts. Intelligence is man's greatest weapon."

"Yes, I have long known you to be fond of things that are cold and hard."

Rodney blinked and chuckled gamely.

At that moment Lawrence reappeared at the door. "I nearly forgot, Dushaw, I recently acquired a set of fourteenth century atlases. Would you care to peruse them?"

Rodney would rather give up his left front tooth than leave Lucius and Alexcena alone together, but hers was not the only opinion he needed to secure. He rose and took his leave to follow the man.

Lucius watched him go. "I must apologize," he said solemnly. "I had no intention of bringing up such subjects in your presence." He turned to her, and was astonished at the change in her appearance. The set of her shoulders was a good deal more relaxed, and a pleased smile smoothed her features.

"It was not you who brought them up." She rose and moved to share his wide seat.

"Well," he mumbled, feeling a need to defend his colleague. "I'm sure Rodney meant nothing by what he said."

"His barbed comments would make any other man livid."

"I hold strongly to my belief in giving the benefit of the doubt. If I were to make an offhanded comment and have it misconstrued I would hope for the same."

To his utter and everlasting shock, Alexcena leaned toward him to place a sweet kiss on his cheek.

"That's noble of you."

"I'm sorry, what were we speaking of?"

Amusement caused Alexcena to smile. "That you're a good man." The smile wavered momentarily, and when she spoke, her words were a mere breath against his cheek. "A wonderful man."

"Well, I-uh-" His voice seemed to shudder. His keen senses were very aware of her nearness. At that moment she looked fragile, even fearful. Words failed him, and he felt a distinct desire to reassure her. A need to hold her so that she would know there was nothing to fear. He needed to tell her quite urgently that as long as they two carried breath in their lungs he would be there with her.

He raised a hand to caress her shoulder. "I-"

Footsteps sounded on the threshold. Someone appeared in the doorway and Lucius found himself standing a full three feet away from the seat they shared.

"Lucius and I have been talking, Father," Alexcena commented quickly.

Lawrence, realizing something had passed between the pair, tried in vain to mask his awkwardness. "That's…nice. I came to let the two of you know that Mr. Dushaw has taken his leave."

"And I must as well!" Lucius said, altogether too loudly.

"You're going?"

"I'm afraid I must." *I seem to be having some trouble keeping my distance from your daughter.*

Lawrence looked more than a little confused. "But you'll be here for dinner tomorrow?"

"Absolutely." In his haste to gain the door, he became entangled in a small table and paused to steady it.

"Come early," Alexcena called. "We'll have tea."

At last he reached the door and faced the pair of them. "As you wish." He bowed and slipped out of the room.

Lawrence turned in puzzlement to his daughter. "That was the fastest exit I have ever witnessed a man make without actually running."

Startled by a resounding thud from the floor above her, Tabitha Winslett jabbed her dainty finger with her embroidery needle and gave a yip.

"Are you all right, dear?" her mother asked from across the room.

Tabitha stuck her fingertip between her lips. Her mother never looked up from her paper. "I'm fine, Mama."

Another thump sounded from upstairs. The chandelier trembled.

Deborah Winslett sighed. "I do wish those brothers of yours would learn to be more quiet."

Harrison Winslett came to his feet with a resigned grunt. "I'll go see to them."

A maid passed him as he left the room. She approached her mistress bearing a rectangular silver tray.

"A letter for you, ma'am."

Tabitha dully lifted her needle to resume her embroidery as her mother broke the seal.

"A note from your Aunt Cecelia."

"Oh?"

"They're all doing well," Deborah went on after a pause. "Your cousin has been seeing that young man, Mr. Wolgath, a great deal."

Tabitha nearly stabbed herself again. "Lucius?"

Her mother was surprised by her distressed tone. She put down the letter. "Now, dear. You're not still carrying feelings for him are you?" Her daughter's stricken look was answer enough. "Tabitha, you can't let yourself be upset by this."

"But she knew," Tabitha uttered with a passion. "She knew I wanted his attention! She knew I tried to cap-"

"Capture him?"

Tabitha straightened her shoulders and raised a hand to smooth her curls. "I was going to say 'captivate' him."

"But that's the point, dear," her mother said gently. "A woman is not to pursue, but to *be* pursued. Mr. Wolgath cannot have missed the signs you have given him, but neither has he followed them."

The words were like a death knell to her heart.

"A man cannot be forced to love, and you will only bring more hurt on yourself if you continue to try him."

Tabitha hung her head. All at once she finally realized the truth of all these months she had spent dreaming of her future. It was a life she would never have. She swallowed her tears and came to her feet, still clutching her embroidery in one hand. She moved by her mother to leave the room.

"Are you all right, dear?"

Slowly she turned with a wooden smile. Her mother had already returned to her paper.

"I'm fine, mother."

"Hm?" Deborah Winslett's focus remained on the coarse paper in her hands.

Tabitha's smile shrank. "I said I'm fine."

Chapter 13

January 8, 1765

Lucius suppressed a yawn and peered drearily down at the dingy reference book. His back ached from hours of leaning over in study. His head throbbed with the effort of retaining information. Every muscle in his body seemed to have hardened in the last hour. He tried to move about, but with every motion his arms, legs, and back cried out in protest. All of his senses seemed dim, much like the light in the narrow coffee house where he sat. He had come to the place to escape the throngs of young men now filling the study halls of Cambridge, all desperately trying to prepare for the exams beginning just two days hence.

Two days. Lucius shuddered and concentrated harder on the blurred words that marched across the pages before him. He dared not let himself remember that the day after tomorrow he would face his masters in disputation. The reminder only served to break him out in a cold sweat.

"Another cup, sir?"

Lucius did not even look at the woman who asked, but held out his mug so that she might fill it from the tin kettle she carried. "Yes, thank you."

He added no cream or sugar to the steaming liquid, but simply drank in half the contents before setting it aside again. He straightened his back and removed his glasses. He was in the midst of polishing them on his sleeve when another woman approached his table.

"Lucius?"

He looked up. The figure before him was hazy and dull, but familiar all the same. Still he raised his spectacles to his eyes to be sure that he was not imagining the recognition.

"Alexcena." A measure of relief flooded through his weary form as he rose and accepted her outstretched hands. "What are you doing in Cambridge?"

"We came to see you," she smiled warmly. "Well, I came to see you, anyway." She gestured behind him, and Lucius caught sight of Lawrence over his shoulder. He was speaking to a group of gentlemen at another table. He raised a hand and nodded to Lucius but did not approach.

The lady leaned forward to say in a conspiratle whisper, "Father was coming this way on business, and I followed along with him. I know ladies are not generally encouraged to seek out their beaux, but-"

"Balderdash!" Lucius exclaimed in earnest. "I'm delighted that you've come, honestly." He flashed her the most reassuring smile he could muster.

"I know you're studying hard," Alexcena went on quietly, "but I wanted to see if there was anything I could do to help."

"Please, sit down."

She slid into the bench across from him and he reclaimed his seat as well. For a long moment they said nothing at all. They simply stared at one another.

"Are you well, Lucius?"

"Well enough."

She seemed doubtful. "You don't look yourself."

He opened his mouth to protest, hesitated, and shrugged with a sheepish grin. "I have never felt less like myself."

Alexcena bit her lip, clearly trying not to smile at that.

Lucius felt himself beginning to chuckle when he saw that look. "You truly want to help me, don't you?" He lifted one of the six or so books before him and passed it to her. "Here. Ask me anything."

She accepted it and skimmed the page. "This theorem states that in projective space two triangles are in perspective axially if…what?"

"If and only if they are in perspective centrally. The Desargues' Theorem."

"And why is this theorem important?"

"Because…it is the only theorem of projective space that holds true in all planes. Correct?"

"I don't know, I made that question up."

Lucius smiled. "All right. Let's try another one."

"Gerard Desargues-"

"Desargues?"

Lucius' smile faded when he caught sight of Rodney Dushaw approaching their table. He swiped the large book from Alexcena's hands. "Surely you've not asked Ms. Condreve to do your research for you, Lucius."

Wolgath cleared his throat. "Good afternoon, Rodney."

"Wolgath." He idly turned a few pages in the book before smiling wolfishly down at the lady. "And good afternoon to you, Ms. condreve. We seem to possess a happy talent for being at all the same places at once."

"I wouldn't say that."

"Wouldn't you?"

"Goodness, no." She tugged at her cuffs to smooth her sleeves, refusing to look at him. "I see a great deal more of Lucius than I ever have of you."

"Indeed." His smooth gray eyes flitted to Wolgath. "So it's Lucius now, eh?"

Ignoring the jibe, he noted the heavy bags beneath Dushaw's eyes. "How goes the studying, Rodney?"

"Fine. I'm doing quite well on my own. It's obvious at times like this why they do not admit women to Cambridge, or any university for that matter. No true lady ought to be subjected to such pressures. Their minds are far too genteel for strenuous exercises."

At this Alexcena's gaze snapped up to Rodney and then Lucius. Both failed to notice.

"So how goes *your* studying, Lucius?" Rodney continued on. "I suppose that's a silly question. By the look of you things are going quite well." He gave a dry laugh and flipped through a few pages of the reference once more.

Lucius cleared his throat again and tugged at his collar. "I really do need to get back to it."

"I'm sure you do. So I'll just escort Ms. Condreve up the road for a nice bite to eat."

In his somewhat exhausted state, Lucius was in no position to make a sound judgment, but that was just what he attempted. Alexcena was watching him closely, and he mistook the puzzlement in her eyes for an inward struggle of whether to stay or go on her part. His shoulders slumped a bit, and he mumbled, "You may do as you like, of course, Ms. Condreve. You needn't stay on my account."

"Because those dusty old books are too taxing on my delicate sensibilities?"

He looked to her, perplexed by these words, but she had already rounded on Rodney.

"My thanks to you all the same, sir, but I would much rather stay here." She seized another volume and opened it at random.

A scowl flashed across Rodney's countenance for a mere instant and was gone. He clamped the book he held shut and tucked it under his arm.

"Just the one I've been looking for," he muttered and stalked away.

Lucius glanced after him.

Alexcena waited until Dushaw was out the door before she spoke. "Why didn't you say something?"

"Beg pardon?" Lucius couldn't quite comprehend the flabbergasted and almost hurt look on her face.

"He took your book. Why didn't you say something?"

"It's not my book," Lucius returned. "It belongs to the college."

"That man showed a total lack of common courtesy toward you, not to mention what he implied about me, and you said nothing."

Wolgath made the grave mistake of asking, "What did he insinuate about you?"

Alexcena's mouth worked for a few seconds before she could reply. "That I shouldn't be helping you study. That as a woman I am not *capable* of helping you study."

Lucius shook his head. "But you are helping me. Why are you getting so upset about this?"

"I worry about you with the likes of him. Why do you refuse to defend yourself?"

He sighed, though it sounded more similar to a groan. "Even if Rodney did mean to be impolite in what he said, I just didn't see a need-"

"Then why did you refuse to defend me?" One slender eyebrow slid up on Alexcena's forehead. She looked sorrowful indeed. "You really would have allowed me to go with him?"

If that's what you wanted. He leaned back from the table. "You know I would have."

She did not exactly flinch, but her bottom lip quivered and she swallowed hard. "Forgive me, sir," she said calmly and rose from the bench. "I should not have interrupted your work." She dropped a curtsy and was gone.

Belatedly Lucius rose as well and watched as she joined her father. Lawrence, looking more than a little confused, nodded and took his daughter's arm. When they were lost from view, Lucius allowed himself to fall back onto the bench, wondering just where the conversation had gone awry.

Why do you refuse to defend yourself? Why did you refuse to defend me? More importantly why had she let such a little thing bother her? What was it he said...*True ladies' minds are far too genteel for strenuous exercises.*

The full import of these words came to him then, and he let his head droop limply in his hand.

"Another cup?"

Mute, he looked up, and the woman held out the tin kettle.

"Another cup, sir?"

"Please." Lucius set the mug before her and looked to his books. "Keep it full."

Chapter 14

January 8 and 10, 1765

Lucius let the heavy brass knocker fall without hesitation. The noise was stark against the relative quiet of the night. He shifted from one foot to the other as he waited for the door to be answered. Twice he considered walking away altogether, but he knew with staunch certainty that all would be lost if he did.

The door was answered by Eshton, as always. He sniffed and bowed. "Good evening, Mr. Wolgath."

"Hello, Eshton," Lucius greeted as he moved across the threshold.

The butler shut the door on the chilly night. "May I take your coat and your, er, basket, sir?"

Lucius held the small vessel with unwarranted care in both his large hands. "It's fine, thank you. Is Ms. Condreve about?"

"In the garden, sir."

"The garden?"

"Yes, sir. Her parents retired, but Ms. Condreve claimed that she was not at all drowsy."

"I see."

"Shall I escort you there?"

"With your permission, Eshton, I believe I know the way."

For the very first time since Wolgath had known him, Eshton's features stretched into a sincere look of pleasure, though it was not quite a smile.

"Yes, sir."

He found her seated on a bench close by the house, wrapped in a rich brown cloak. The light of the full moon made her skin seem ethereal against the dark tresses of her hair. She was a spectral being amid the remains of a dormant winter garden. He closed the door silently and still managed to startle her as he approached. She leapt to her feet in fright, though she recognized him at once.

"M-Mr. Wolgath."

He bowed low. "Ms. Condreve. I do hope you'll forgive the late hour. It could not be helped."

"Hm." She swallowed and exhaled a light breath of steam.

They were silent for a few minutes and Lucius felt his heart pounding in his ears. He indicated the bench with his basket. "I apologize. I did not mean to frighten you from your seat."

"Will you join me?"

He was vastly relieved when she gestured to the place beside herself. He settled down on the bench.

"I've made this for you." He passed her the basket and watched as she lifted the cloth to find a short cake. "It's a recipe of my own invention."

With great care she broke off a bit of the corner. The cake was so moist and soft that it fell apart in her very fingers. Catching the bits with both hands, she tilted her chin upward and allowed them to fall into her mouth. Her lips became coated with crumbs and her fingers sticky with honey. When she brought her chin down, she could not help laughing.

"Do you like it?" Lucius inquired hopefully.

"Yes," she giggled, trying to catch her breath. "It's very good."

They sat for a time breaking off hunks of the cake and attempting in vain to bring them to their mouths before they crumbled.

"I was not aware," she remarked, "that you were so fond of cooking. Or so good at it."

"A necessary skill for a bachelor without a housekeeper I'm afraid. As for being good at it, cooking is a modest form of chemistry. I suppose it comes more naturally to me than some men."

"Than most men." She grinned to herself. "I'm a fair cook."

"You cook? I thought your family retained one."

"We do, but I've asked if I could help her out on occasion. I think it's a very good skill to have."

Lucius nodded. He sighed and looked out at the garden surrounding them.

"I came to tell you how sorry I am for everything that was said earlier today."

She shook her head. "I overreacted. And I questioned your judgment."

"You're not to blame here. I was so caught up in my own distress that I allowed a man to offend you without so much as a wave of my hand." He gently lifted her hand in his own. "A man can mock me and that's fine, but to think of a man intentionally insulting you…I pledge myself here and now to uphold your honor from this day forward."

Alexcena could not help but smile. Relief and contentment swept through her being and shown from every feature of her face. Lucius saw it, and he was captivated.

"Marry me."

The words were spoken so quietly that he barely heard them himself. To Alexcena they were loud as a symphony. A great blast of crescendoed noise in a clammer of discordant keys. She leapt to her feet, her voice failing momentarily and then growing shrill.

"But you can't just-I mean-"

She backed away and then stepped forward again. Lucius watched her with the utmost curiosity. He, unlike Alexcena, was unsurprised by his own words. It was only a matter of time before the idea occurred to them. He had not meant to speak what he thought, but he was not at all sorry that he had.

"Mr. Wolgath," she said with a shiver. "There is a certain order as to how these things are to be done."

Setting aside the cake, he came to his feet before her.

She faltered again. "You-you cannot simply ask and have done with it! There is to be planning and hints and nerves and-"

"Is this your answer?"

"No, it's-"

"Then what is your reply?"

She blinked dumbly. "To what?"

Very slowly, as if in a dream, Lucius took her cold hands in his own. "Will you have me, Alexcena Condreve?"

For a suspended moment she could say nothing at all. Then she licked her lips. "You seem awfully spontaneous tonight, Lucius."

"It has been a trying day," he replied conversationally.

Her fingers flexed and tightened around his own. "I will have you, my most wonderful Mr. Wolgath."

Lucius leaned in at last to kiss the woman he loved so dearly. She felt his hands fall limp and released them to place her arms about his neck. She was dimly aware of his broad hands encircling her waist. So, Alexcena found herself deep in the arms of the man she had loved so long. When he pulled away, she felt all air releasing from her lungs in a great flutter. In that instant her vision encompassed only his crystal blue eyes, perfect in their intensity, timeless in the love they held. He on the other hand, was careful to take in every line and curve of her face. Every exquisite feature preserved in his memory. He could only smile at the happiness welling up within himself and lightly traced the smooth skin of her lips with his thumb. Those round, red lips stretched into a sparing smile.

"My darling bride to be," he chuckled. "My brother will give a good laugh to hear it."

"A laugh?" she smiled. "Will he not be happy to have me as a sister?"

"Certainly. It was he who warned me that it would come to this, and he was right. You are a perilous creature."

Laughter flowed from her then in a stream of gladness. "Perilous? And why should he think me perilous?"

"Oh, he thinks that of all women," Lucius replied matter-of-factly.

"The mystery of his being a bachelor deepens."

They shared a laugh over this and clasped themselves in each others' arms again. Lucius found that he was pleasantly surprised by it all.

"I never thought it would be like this."

"What?"

"This warmth, this happiness. It seems that it will last for as long as we endure."

She sobered somewhat. "Do you want to be happy with me, Lucius? Forever?"

He stroked her hair and seemed to ponder the question, though his answer was clear. "Forever. I will keep you with me forever."

Forever. He shifted on the hard bench where he sat waiting for the voices to die down, and it seemed to have taken forever. Lucius fingered the cuffs of his sleeves and glanced around at the men assembled all around him. The hall was long, but the thirty or so men there seemed to crowd close to one particular door to his left, all awaiting the same thing.

His hand lingered over his right sleeve. Inside there was tucked a pale silken handkerchief; a token of encouragement from Alexcena the night before. His heart soared to think of all that had happened the night before, only to be brought down by the crescendo of voices from within the ominous room.

Just as quickly as the voices rose, they died out and were lost in silence. This was followed by a round of strained applause and the door was opened. A pale gentleman emerged. He stood stock still just passed the threshold for a full minute. Two of his companions approached.

"Well, Smith?"

"How did it go?"

The man looked up. A fearful, almost astounded expression crossed his face. He opened his mouth to speak, but seemed only able to emit a strangled groan before turning swiftly down the hall.

"Lucius Wolgath."

The guttural call came from within the room. All eyes turned to him. Lucius absently gripped his right wrist one last time. Then he rose and slipped through the door to face his masters, knowing full well that the next hour would determine his future. He would quit the city of Cambridge for Penn that very afternoon eligible to become a professor, or…what? So much of his life had been devoted to this one moment, he could not truly say what he would do if it all came to naught. *But I shall know soon enough.*

Chapter 15

January 23, 1765

"You're dancing very well, Professor Wolgath."

"A student is only as skilled as his master. Generally."

Lucius could not help but marvel at the woman who was to be his bride. She radiated in a dress of kelly green satin, edged in white lace with a snowy fichu' tucked into the squared neckline. Her eyes appeared more green than hazel next to her dress, and the affect was quite appealing. Her glossy chocolate hair was swept up in an exquisite coiffure with a single ringlet trailing over one shoulder. He wondered fleetingly just how long her hair was. *I'll know soon, won't I?*

Alexcena in her turn was not paying quite as much attention to her birthday guests as she had the year before. As they made their round about the dance floor, she found herself studying the cut of his plain black suit and how it fit across his wide shoulders. She adored the way his moustache quirked over his lip when he smiled. His brilliant blond hair was always combed to perfection, and it looked so soft…

The music ended and the pair reluctantly released their hands to clap along with the rest. They found themselves on the edge of the floor and moved away by silent agreement as the quartet struck up a new score.

"I think you have truly outdone yourself this year," Lucius commented brightly. "I've never attended a pleasanter affair."

"But aren't you a little biased?"

Lucius did not reply right away, but enjoyed the laughter that played in her eyes. "All of Penn must be in attendance."

"To be honest, my mother embellished the guest list somewhat. I had no intention of inviting so many people."

"I hope you don't mind that I asked my brother along."

"No!" She laid a gentle hand on his forearm. "Never. I love your brother."

"Not too much, I hope."

She feigned a sigh. "Of course not. I hope he's enjoying himself."

He couldn't resist to brush her cheek with his knuckle before giving his wry reply. "Not to worry. He's in his element, I assure you."

"And I see he's been caught by the Winsletts," Alexcena bubbled. "Shall we go and rescue him?" She moved to go, but Lucius laid a hand on her shoulder.

"This is a rare moment," he murmured with all the manly suave he could muster. "We are in a crowded room of people and no one is clamoring for your attention just now. I'm certain the Winsletts are ample entertainment for my brother-and vice versa."

Leo smiled as he watched the couples swaying across the floor of the Condreves' somewhat modest ballroom. He had met more people in the last hour than he knew existed in all of Penn. He had danced with three passable young ladies-one of which had somehow managed to thoroughly stomp his foot through his heavy boot-and now stood sipping his second cup of an oddly fizzy punch. He was close by the long refreshment table scanning the many faces around him, nodding to those he recognized. He paused only when he caught sight of the slight figure of Tabitha Winslett. She was standing at the far end of the refreshment table, also fixated intently upon the dancers. Her dress was covered in countless flounces, and her flaxen ringlets were piled impossibly high atop her proud head. She gave the affect of a very young girl who had found her way into her mother's dressing closet. Leo set down his cup, and swaggered toward her.

"Are you enjoying the party, Tabitha?"

The girl turned, more than a little surprised to see Leopold Wolgath standing beside her. He smiled and she swallowed. "I-I suppose, I guess." She flipped open a bitty silk fan and attempted to hide behind it. "It's Ms. Winslett, sir."

"Would you care for a drink?"

"No." She said this with a dismissive air, in hopes that he would leave her be.

Leopold in his turn enjoyed the game inordinately, and relaxed against the table to stare at her over her own shoulder. A saucy half-grin crossed his features.

When she did not feel his gaze waver, she turned to face him again. Her eyes roved up and down his figure, taking in the weathered leather coat and cross belt. "Do you always dress in such-" She waved her hand, searching for a suitable term. "-getups?"

Leo gripped the collar of his coat and pulled it straight. "Don't you like me livery?"

Tabitha turned and began beating her fan fiercely. "Please go away. I have no desire to speak to you just now."

Leo followed her gaze just then and caught sight of Alexcena and his brother. "Oh, yes," he mumbled with ease. "S'pose you're too busy mourning to have a good time."

She glanced at him to discern his meaning only to be further incensed by his pleasant look.

"Would you care to dance?"

"It seems to be the only way I'm going to be rid of you."

Leo swallowed a chuckle, but just as he was about to lead her to the floor-

"Tabitha!" Deborah Winslett approached closely followed by Harrison and two young boys. "You need not be in such a hurry, dear. We have the whole night ahead of us."

"That anxious to see me, eh?" Leo murmured close beside her.

"Mama, this is Leopold Wolgath," Tabitha said smoothly. "This is my mother Deborah Winslett. I warn you, Mama, Mr. Wolgath seems to have trouble with our surname."

Leo hid his insulted pride at that remark by making a chivalrous bow to the lady. He could not entirely deny her daughter's accusation after all. "Enchanted to make your acquaintance, my lady."

"Well!" Deborah breathed and blinked rapidly over his attention.

Seeing her mother's pleasure, Tabitha thrust a hand between the two as Leo straightened. "And this is my father-"

"Harrison Winslett." The man thrust forth his arm and Leo received his hand. "Wolgath's brother, yes?"

"Indeed, sir."

Harrison to looked him up and down. "Not much of a resemblance though, is there?"

Leo laughed, a sound that seemed to echo all around them. "No, I'm afraid not, sir."

Tabitha took advantage of the distraction and threaded her arm through her mother's elbow. She muttered something and the pair wandered toward a gaggle of skirts against the far wall. Leo's gaze flitted after them.

"I understand you've met my daughter before."

Leo forced his attention back to Harrison. "I have, sir. She is a most captivating young lady."

Harrison shifted his stance. "Yes, but unfortunately I tend to think that's only because she always manages to draw attention to herself, sweet child that she is."

Leo sobered somewhat. He would have disagreed with the statement. Although she was eighteen at most-more likely seventeen-he had found qualities in her which were lacking in many of the women he had met over the years. She was self-possessed and aggressive in a way that he had never witnessed in the feminine sense. She was arrogant because she was young, a willing fighter when provoked. Her mind could be called quick; it wanted only a few more years exposure to adult sensibilities. If someone managed to get her away from the 'friends' of her youth-now currently babbling about nothing in high-pitched voices by the wall-she was sure to become a rare lady by his estimate.

"I tell you, Wolgath," Harrison sighed with a shake of his head. "Sometimes I think it would take a man aflame to handle my daughter and her gift for exuberance."

The two men chuckled. Leo had no argument with *that* statement.

"Daddy?" A little voice called from far below them. The men looked down to see the two boys watching them intently.

"Yes Ernst, what is it?"

The smallest boy replied, "Can we go and find Sam?"

"You'll have to ask Eshton about that."

Leo squatted down close to the two boys. "Who's Sam?"

The little one's eyes grew wide and round, but his voice never wavered. "Eshton's is his uncle. He stays with him a lot, and we're close to the same, almost the same age."

"Uh-huh," Leo said with understanding. "And how old does that make you? I'd say-" He squinted one eye to study the boy. "Seven."

Ernst's little face brightened and he giggled at some private joke.

"He's not even six yet," the taller boy scoffed. "And I'm nine."

"I am so almost, Tram!" Ernst stomped.

Harrison raised a warning brow. "Boys."

"So," Leo said smoothly. "Ernst and Tram." He held out his hand to shake. Ernst took it easily, but his brother was skeptical.

"It's Bertram," he asserted, timidly gripping Leo's palm. "Bertram Winslett."

Leo raised an eyebrow. "You're a lot like your sister, aren't you?"

Ernst giggled again and a flush of anger rose in Bertram. He turned to his father, "Dad, can we go to the conservatory?"

"I don't want you going alone."

"What's in the conservatory?" Leo wondered.

"A telescope!" Ernst raised his arms in excitement.

"That is impressive. Would you boys be willing to have me along? If that's all right with you, Mr. Winslett," Leo added as he stood.

Harrison chuckled. "You don't have children, do you, Mr. Wolgath?"

Leo quirked a wry smile. "No, sir, but as you recall I do have a younger brother."

Chapter 16

January 23, 1765

The evening wore on calmly enough. Everyone danced and ate and laughed together as they celebrated Alexcena's twentieth year, though to be fair, the atmosphere seemed more akin to a town dance than a birthday until about eight o'clock when Alexcena was prevailed upon to open her gifts. She resisted at first, blushing and raising her hand demurely. Despite her protests, a chair was brought forward and she was made to sit by the low table where the gifts were set. Lucius stood not so far away beside Lawrence. The men talked and smiled as they watched her tearing into the packages. When it came down to the last two, Lawrence presented a question.

"So which package is yours, Lucius?" He spoke quietly, so as not to be overheard.

Lucius merely raised an eyebrow. "Mine is not up there." He half turned away from Alexcena and produced a diamond ring from his breast pocket for Lawrence to see.

The man's chest, as well as his smile, swelled with emotion. "You'll announce it tonight, then?"

"In just a few moments."

Lawrence, of course, knew of the engagement. Lucius would have preferred to speak with him before hand, but the way the words slipped out that night, there was no opportunity. He and Alexcena had spoken with her parents as soon as they were able, and, as they expected, there had been no objection.

Lawrence slapped the man's shoulder and chuckled softly. "Well done, Wolgath."

After the last gift was opened, Alexcena came to her feet. "I must thank you all," she began. "Your presents were wonderful. I can't remember a better birthday." She turned warmly to Lucius, and he moved to her side. "And now, I have an announcement to make."

Lucius raised his voice to the crowd. "Ms. Condreve and her parents have consented that she shall be my bride!"

A murmur of slight shock ran through the guests, followed by calls of congratulations and applause.

Lucius took her hand and spoke loudly so as to be heard over the din. "I think there is still one gift to give."

Alexcena's smile never wavered, though her brows dropped in confusion. Lucius let her wonder for a fraction of a second before pulling the ring from his pocket. She had never been more shocked. She knew of course that he would give her a ring eventually. His proposal had been so impromptu that he did not yet have one to give. She never would have thought that he would do it in such a public way. Every eye in the room was on them she knew, and still she could not quell the tears rushing to her eyes. She clamped a hand over her mouth as the tears overflowed to spill down her ivory cheeks. Lucius was content and calm as he took her free hand and slipped the ring onto her delicate finger.

Once this was done, they were instantly crowded by women clamoring to see the ring and men wanting to shake Lucius' hand. No one appeared to notice as Tabitha Winslett fled the room in a flurry of skirts.

Leo was making his way back to the party when he saw her in the hall. She turned in the opposite direction, her movements jagged and sharp.

"Tabitha?" he called uncertainly.

She ignored him and ducked around the corner into a dark parlor. He followed. A deep concern had come to him the instant he had seen her. Even in the darkness, broken only by moonlight from a wide window, he could see that she was crying. She jumped when she saw him in the doorway.

"Leave me be!" she snapped.

"Tabitha-"

"I don't want to see anyone!"

He made a cautious step toward her. He held out his hands, as though he were dealing with a frightened animal. "What's wrong? You're not hurt, are you?"

"Now why would I be hurt?" she demanded, clearly exasperated. "It's not like someone assaulted me or something. Though he might as well have struck me."

This last bit slipped out involuntarily, but it was just enough for Leo to guess what was going on. "They've made their announcement, haven't they?"

Tabitha realized her blunder and abruptly changed the topic. "Why were you in the hall, anyway?"

"I was with your brothers in the conservatory. They've gone with Eshton now to play with his nephew." He moved more slowly toward her. "You cannot simply run and hide here."

"Why not?"

Despite this situation, the thought came to Leo that she made a very pretty image. The moonlight caught her teary eyes, and her blond hair seemed to glisten as it wound its way free of the pins. Fierce shadows accentuated her angular features.

"I'm upset!" she insisted. "I shouldn't be made to see anyone!"

"That's not the way life works. Sometimes it hurts at the most inconvenient times." He drew a handkerchief from his pocket and passed it to her. "The proper thing for you to do," he went on as she dried her face, "is to march back in there and congratulate them."

"B-but I can't!"

"You ought to. Lucius is a grown man, and though you would have swayed him, he has made his decision. There is nothing left for you to do but accept it."

Tabitha sniffed one final time and rubbed her eyes. She handed the handkerchief back and straightened her shoulders defiantly.

"If I were you, Tabitha," Leo commented as he tucked the cloth back into his coat, "I would take those pins out of my hair."

"What?" she blurted, scandalized.

"They're falling out anyway," he pointed out. "You're about to do something infinitely unpleasant. You may as well be somewhat comfortable."

Tabitha hesitated only an instant before tugging at the pins with both hands. She made quick work of it and gave her locks one final shake to put them in their place.

"There now. And where's that engaging smile we all know so well?"

She made a halfhearted effort at looking lighthearted.

Leo offered his elbow. "Now for the final touch. It wouldn't hurt to be on the arm of a handsome gent like me, now would it?"

With a flounce of her skirt, she sauntered by him and out the door. Leo straightened with a chuckle, thoroughly satisfied. He had prodded her temper just enough that she would hold herself upright until she reached home and the darkness of her own chamber. But he pitied her then.

Chapter 17

January 26, 1765

Rodney let the door of the London coffee house slam with ill-concealed belligerence. Several influential heads rose in his direction. Dushaw glared at the room in general, daring any of them to utter a word against him. With a sharp ache raging through his head and a dull fatigue hanging heavily on his shoulders, he was in no mood to be reproved.

He moved roughly through the tight tables to the far corner, hiding his headache from the light of the front windows within its shadows. The patrons slowly returned their attention to their own business as he dropped into the rickety chair. He rubbed his eyes warily, breathing deeply of the thick scents of roasted coffee beans, tallow candles, and tobacco. He resisted the urge to glare at the little tea maid when she came to his table-but only just. There was no one but himself to blame for his present state. He knew that and yet he ignored the fact in favor of a more enticing recipient for his foul mood.

Lucius Wolgath.

He expelled a great snort of derision at the very thought of him. The man never failed to outdo him, and his luck was unfathomable. That's just what it was; luck. Dushaw would never admit that Wolgath had the intelligence necessary to deliberately show him up. The latest incident was just another bead in a string of happy accidents in Wolgath's favor.

The memory of it flashed in Rodney's mind, that awful day at Cambridge last week when the graduates had been announced. His name had been among them, naturally, though it was several places behind Wolgath's. Lucius had finished Third Wrangler in the class. Rodney was just two places above the dreaded Wooden Spoon.

He willfully shoved the memory aside and reached for the coffee. The maid had placed it before him without a word, and he drank deeply of its dark, rejuvenating contents. His mind skipped ahead to the hours after this grave announcement.

Rodney, sick with resentment and shuddering to picture his father's reaction, had left immediately for the welcoming arms of London. He sought his refuge among the high society theaters, salons, and clubs for two days. Then he moved on to the lower society pubs, tea houses, and gaming tables. Now that his temper tantrum was cooling he was free to consider more rational vents for his irrational grudge. Wolgath's sudden fall from society's good graces came to mind.

He downed the remains of his scorching coffee and motioned the maid to bring more. He had thought to nab a Cambridge society paper that morning and now flipped it open crisply. *Of a certainty, there must be some dent in his reputation I've been overlooking. There's not a man on this earth who doesn't possess a few stones he doesn't want overturned. But I must be careful to conceal my probing, especially from Alexcena. It would all be for naught if I ruined my reputation along with his. I must focus on Wolgath, and once he is set aside, Alexcena will be free and vulnerable to the pursuit.*

Rodney smiled in pleasure to himself as he relished his strategy. His eyes flitted across the paper, only half absorbing the words while his mind roamed the walks of revenge. It was not until he turned to the second page that the periodical truly caught his attention. He froze, his cup raised almost to his lips, and reread the minute, insignificant heading before him;

ANNOUNCING THE BETROTHAL OF PROF. LUCIUS WOLGATH AND THE LADY, MS. ALEXCENA CONDREVE.

Below this were a few scant lines listing various details concerning the pair and their families, but Rodney could not bring himself to read further. The page trembled in his hand. With one fell stamp of the press his hopes were dashed on the rocks of truth. The very rocks he had intended to overturn had in that moment ruined all but his most desperate hopes. His jaw clenched and every spent muscle in his slim form seized at once. He managed to release the paper. It fell back onto the table. Rodney looked away, but even without the specter of the written announcement before him, he could not quell the surging panic that filled him.

After a suspended moment he realized just how ridiculous he must appear and set the cup in its saucer. He forced a breath through his lungs and rested his chin on his folded hands.

This situation is not without solution.

Breathe…in and out.

I cannot afford to give in to desperation.

In and out. His normally impassive brow darkened.

But I will have her, and I will be rid of him!

Chapter 18

February 23, 1765

He could not help it. Lucius simply could not restrain his hand as it strayed over to catch Alexcena's. It never ceased to amuse him how much smaller her hand seemed when it was inside his own. She squeezed his fingers gratefully, though her smiling eyes were trained on her parents as they walked several yards ahead of them. He became apprehensive as an afterthought, and loosened his hold. He knew of course that Lawrence and Cecelia would never say anything if they caught sight of this innocent gesture, but still…

Alexcena squeezed harder, refusing to let his hand drop, and a soft blush rose in her creamy cheeks.

Lucius shook his head with a chuckle. "If I didn't know you well enough, my dear, I'd say you must have been a headstrong child."

"I was," she replied, adding a musical laugh. "To a small degree, anyway. I've learned quite well how to temper it with sweetness." She flashed him a brilliant smile to match his own.

"Was that a warning?" he wondered aloud.

"Certainly not!" She feigned shock at his audacity. "Merely a keen observation of my childhood."

"I see."

"By the time I was seven I had calmed down a great deal."

"You make it sound as though you were difficult up until then."

"I think I was the first person to ever cause my mother to swoon."

Lucius erupted with such laughter that the lady of their topic turned to look at them with a skeptical brow. Alexcena giggled as Lucius worked to carefully school his features. When the scrutiny was lifted, he leaned down closer to his lady's ear.

"I would dearly love to hear *this* tale." *Almost as much as I love to watch you grow indignant.*

She did not disappoint. Her lower lip extended and her brow furrowed in an ill-concealed pout.

"To this day, I still don't think it was as serious as all that," she frowned. "Cook's granddaughter's cat had three kittens. We conspired together and she snuck one over to me when the little things were big enough. I thought that if Mother and Father saw what a well-behaved and civilized animal a cat can be they were sure to let me keep him."

"So you called them into the drawing room to introduce your new friend."

"On the contrary."

Something in her tone made him groan with apprehension.

"I didn't want to expose the little thing to the pressure of such a meeting. I thought it would be better if they met him on their own, so I sort of…set him loose."

"And where was he found?"

"My mother's handkerchief drawer."

Lucius raised a swift hand to suppress his laughter before he drew another gaze.

"Does that shock you?"

His amusement faded to a chuckle. "Not as much as I imagine you would like it to."

She giggled again. "You know me well. Sometimes it's like you've opened the door of my heart to see just what I'm feeling."

"Eshton gave me the key. He has keys for everything."

This time it was Alexcena's laughter that drew the stares from up ahead.

"You must think me terribly rude," he went on once she had caught her breath. "I use it every chance I get."

"Why would I mind that?" she asked kindly. "I love you."

Lucius paused and raised her hand to press his lips against it. "And I you, my dear."

Her contented expression slid into a more somber one. "When will we be married?"

It was a question he had grown accustomed to in the month since the announcement of their engagement. He smiled reassuringly.

"We've been through this. I have my professorship, but I must find a position and a place for us."

"Must it take so long?" she asked in a small voice.

"For some, yes."

"May I ask-" She moistened her lips and tried again. "May I ask why it is that you are so frightened by the prospect of not finding a position right away? I only wonder because, well, I know you do not actually have one now. As far as I know, you have not worked sense you began your studies at Cambridge. You must have funds from somewhere…" Her voice trailed away. "I'm sorry. That sounded as if I'm mistrusting you."

"Not at all," he replied easily. "It is a valid question, readily answered."

"Oh?"

"Leo and I received our inheritances a bit early," he began. "A large portion of them anyway. We were each given the sum of a generous living to accomplish certain plans that we had at the time. Leo, at age twenty was set on purchasing a military commission."

"The military?"

"Yes." Lucius smiled broadly at the multiple inquiries hidden behind the one. "Mother pleaded with him to wait a year and consider before he did it. Over the course of that year, his plans shifted from military to navy to owning a stable of no less than forty thoroughbred horses. I think he fancied raising Arabians to be specific. By the time that year was up, he had traveled the whole of the country and was keen on visiting others. He went to our parents to give them back the living."

"But why?"

"Guilt. He would not be using it as he had told them he would, and he felt he would be taking advantage if he kept it. But Father would hear none of it, insisting that it was his to use as he saw fit. So Leo made a compromise; he placed half the sum in trust, and used the other to finance his travels. Over the course of twelve years, that amount has dissolved, but as far as I know he still has not touched the rest."

Alexcena nodded. "So that explains Leopold… but not you."

"Ah, me!" He sighed dramatically and she giggled at that. "When my father offered Leo his living, he thought it only fair to make the same offer to me, though I was only fifteen."

"Ah, so he is five years older than you," she interrupted. "Somehow it seems like more."

"Was that in insult to him or flattery of me?"

"By the way, Lucius, when is your birthday?" He groaned, and she was surprised by his reaction. "What's the matter?" she coaxed.

"Haven't I told you already?"

"You certainly have not. Absent as I am, I never thought to ask."

"You're not absent." He stated this truth emphatically. Then he sighed in resignation. "It's in July."

"I missed it!" She was indeed distressed at that.

"It's not your fault. I didn't tell you."

"Why ever not?"

"Honestly? Your parents, as much as I love them, have a gift for planning overly-extravagant fetes. You mind them now, but imagine how you'll feel at my age!"

She smothered her mirth with one hand. "I will carry your secret to the grave."

"Thank you. Now would you like to hear the rest of my story?" She assented, and he picked up his tale once more. His voice took on a listless quality as he remembered. "Father asked me if I knew what I wanted. There was only one thing I wanted. He kept the living until I was accepted at the University years later. I have used it to fund my education-as well as everything else while I lived there." Lucius searched for the right explanation, and was vastly relieved when she seemed to understand.

"Education is expensive."

"I have kept my budget carefully planned out for the past several years, but my plans did not extend overly far beyond graduation. If I do not find work, I have nothing left to rely on."

She took in his worries, smiled, and calmly teased him. "So you spent your retirement in your twenties. Very irresponsible."

He chuckled and faced her squarely. "Dreadfully. Now do you see?"

"Yes..." she replied slowly. "I understand. I just think we ought to face the problem as one, that's all."

His vision was filled with her round hazel eyes and the smooth curves of her face. He swallowed convulsively and played with her small fingers in his hand.

"I'm just as impatient as you, you know." A half smile rose on one side of his mouth. "But then I know something you don't."

Her serious countenance became perplexed. "What is it?"

He bent to lean in closer then, and his grin was nothing short of a smirk. "There's a position open at one of the colleges. And I'm being considered."

The initial astonishment lasted only an instant, and then she beamed sweetly at him. "Really?! Well, that's-"

A cursory glance assured them that her parents had rounded a corner in the path ahead of them, and they met in a warm kiss. When they parted she was laughing again.

"I'm so happy, Lucius!"

"Not so fast," he murmured, fingering a curl that fluttered behind her ear. "I don't have the post yet, but it's promising."

She seemed not to notice his words. "Will we live in Cambridge?"

"Near Cambridge. One of us is not overly fond of city life, as I recall."

"I'm fond of a life with you," she crooned.

"And you shall have it." He chuckled as a small bit of the former enthusiasm seemed to drain from her. "Never fear. I won't keep you waiting too long. I'm terrified that any day now you'll finally take a good look at me and do an abrupt about-face." Though his tone was light, his apprehension was blatantly serious.

Alexcena looked at him for a hard moment. "Do you listen when I talk to you, Lucius? I mean really listen?"

He blinked, vastly taken aback by her question.

"How many times have I told you that you ought to have more confidence in yourself? You see yourself through a glass darkly, or you would have some inkling of what is so obvious to me." As she spoke, she calmly straightened the lapel of his coat and then took both his hands in her own.

Lucius shook his head hopelessly. "Have you ever considered spectacles?"

Alexcena could not help it. A smile tugged at her full mouth, and soon became a long trill of laughter. He joined in and drew her deep into his arms. They hurried to catch up to her parents after that but not before indulging in another smooth kiss.

Chapter 19

February 28, 1765

Lucius raised his hand to knock and invariably hesitated. Cowardly as it was, there was still a part of him that did not want to know. It was severely unorthodox that he had been called back for this meeting, and Lawrence was just as baffled as he was. This was cause for slight alarm given how involved the man was in the bureaucracy of Cambridge.

It was not until a passing student cleared his throat that Lucius realized he had been standing there for a full minute. He expelled a breath of frustration and straightened the lapel of his coat before drawing up the courage to knock.

"Enter."

The ominous command came from inside, and Lucius stepped tentatively over the threshold. Five gentlemen stood in the center of the long lecture hall, imposing in their scholar's robes and stiff powdered wigs. The men were deep in conversation and seemed not to notice his entrance. So he waited, shifting his weight and counting the many rows of raised seats lining the walls.

"Lucius Wolgath."

The cluster of professors was disbanded and one of the taller gentlemen was heading his way. Lucius recognized him as the Professor of Civil Law for the college.

"Professor Ridlington," Lucius managed to smile easily and bowed.

"I've heard quite a lot of you in the last week, Wolgath."

"Thank you, sir."

"I suppose you're feeling a bit nervous."

An embarrassingly shrill laugh escaped him. "I cannot deny that I'm apprehensive, sir."

"Not to worry, m'boy." Professor Ridlington gave Lucius a sound clap on the arm. "It'll all be over soon."

The man moved away, and Lucius was left recalling a particularly gruesome novel he had passed on reading recently. It was the story of a man who had engaged in an investment with two of his closest friends, who then conspired to kill him in order to claim his share of the profit. They called him into a "meeting" in order to accomplish the deed. He suppressed a shudder and attempted in vain to mill about inconspicuously as he waited for…what? Two of the gentlemen seemed to be arguing in the far corner while the rest moved about in effortless boredom.

Lucius thought he felt anxious, but it paled in comparison to the feeling that arose when Rodney Dushaw entered the room. He caught sight of him instantly, as the opening of the door seemed loud in the subdued space. Dushaw averted his gaze upon recognizing Wolgath. A cold shudder fluttered through Lucius' shoulders when Rodney was beckoned to the corner where the gentlemen stood arguing. Their whispers echoed sharply around the hall. After less than a minute, the conversation broke off and the Professors converged to take their seats at one end of the room. Only Professor Ridlington remained on his feet.

"Gentlemen," he said, addressing Wolgath and Dushaw. "I am not certain if you are both aware, but you have both been seriously considered for the same position here at one of Cambridge University's many colleges."

How was it that a man who had come so close to failing his exams was competing with him for the same job? Lucius' gaze leapt toward Rodney. The man stood tall and stiff with a brooding expression on his normally somber features.

"We have reviewed your records and discussed this among ourselves," the Professor went on casually. "We have determined that the two of you will dispute before a decision is made."

Lucius absorbed this. The procedure was completely unheard of. He nodded calmly. "Will we be disputing the Professor separately?" he asked.

"Oh, not at all. You'll be disputing each other."

Another anomaly. Lucius swallowed.

"Professor Watson holds the same position at another of the colleges, as I'm certain you know. He will be corroborating the accuracy of your statements.

Professor Watson had been one of those who stood arguing when Rodney entered. But Lucius had no time to consider this, because Professor Ridlington was indicating the stands on either side of himself.

"If you gentlemen are quite ready, let's begin."

Lucius moved forward on wooden legs. He had confidence in his disputation skills, but never before had he gone up against a fellow scholar. Memories of his previous spats with Rodney lingered in his mind as he stepped onto his platform. He was filled with foreboding and the sudden knowledge that Rodney would not argue fairly. He gripped the sides of his podium and faced his opponent.

Dispirited. Wholly dispirited.

Lucius lay in his flat staring glumly at the ceiling. No matter how hard he stared he could not see beyond the taunting smile of satisfaction Rodney had given him when the disputation was over. Nor could he ignore the Professors who shook their heads in his direction with such seeming sympathy. Even in the confines of his own home they pricked him.

I should move about. Find something for myself to do.

Lucius allowed one boot to slide over the edge of the long sofa and moved no further. He lay on his back with one arm thrown over his eyes, contemplating his future. It was several minutes before a muffled thud roused him. He turned his head to find Commodore sitting nose to nose with him by the sofa.

"May I help you with something?" Lucius sighed dismally.

The Great Dane moaned and smacked his chops.

"What would you suggest I do?" Lucius grumbled, allowing his animosity to get the better of him. "I've sent inquiries out everywhere. This was my best and *last* opportunity!"

Commodore yelped.

"Granted." Lucius pulled himself into a sitting position and scratched lustily behind the dog's ample ears. "You're right. It wasn't my last opportunity," he conceded. "But it was the last foreseeable one. I suppose this means I'll be lowering my expectations. Consider teaching simpler subjects in smaller schools. The living will be a good deal smaller too, though."

Commodore whimpered.

"She won't say anything, anyway."

Lucius could picture Alexcena's response. A bright smile and a cheery 'not to worry, Lucius.' He shifted restlessly at the thought. Then his mind wandered to a modest cottage just outside of Cambridge. It was not large, but it boasted two stories, a wide fireplace, a new Franklin stove, and all surrounded by rolling green for three miles in every direction. Lucius allowed the dream to fade. He had gone to see the house for himself only last week and assured the landlord that he could afford the rent when his new job started, having been assured of that himself. As it was now, his funds were very low and he could barely afford the rent in this small boarding house for much longer.

So it was that he had much to brood over. It was the knock at his door that brought him to his feet at last.

"Lucius?"

More knocks, but Lucius had already recognized the voice. He was on his feet and at the door in an instant. Even knowing the voice he was caught off guard by the loveliness of Alexcena. Her dark hair fell in loose waves about her shoulders. She wore a light sun hat made of a filmy material far too light to perform its function. The sun was high, its warm rays spilling down over her.

Lawrence Condreve stood to one side. He cleared his throat and prodded gently. "May we come in?"

"Yes!" Lucius moved swiftly out of the door. "Of course, please come in." He snatched a jacket from the rack by the door as he moved, hastily shoving his arms into the sleeves. "You'll have to forgive the untidiness."

'Untidy' was probably an understatement. Dishes from earlier that day were stacked haphazardly along the cabinets of the little kitchen. A half-full coffee pot sat cold on the stove. A blanket lay waded by the arm of the rumpled sofa. The floor boards were soiled in several places where Leo's muddy boots had made tracks the night before. A shirt and a pair of socks in sore need of mending lay strewn over one chair.

Lucius grabbed the blanket and hastily began folding it. "My brother's been staying with me, you know," he prattled on. "What with the two of us I'm afraid the mess just grows." He suddenly noticed that Lawrence was standing by the sofa while Alexcena had not moved more than three mincing steps into the room. At first he wondered if it was the mess that gave her pause, but then he caught sight of her face. He dropped the blanket and moved to stand by her.

"Are you all right?"

When she spoke her voice was tentative and pleading. "Do you think you could do something about…?" She waved vaguely.

As if in response to the gesture, Commodore got to his feet and cocked his head.

Lucius was appalled by his own carelessness. "Commodore, hike! Go on."

The Great Dane grumbled as he trotted down the hall.

"I am sorry for that," Lucius murmured. "Are you all right now?" He cupped her elbow and guided her to the nearest armchair.

"Perfectly," she smiled. Her voice carried a mere hint of its former desperation. "I'm certain I'll become better accustomed to-Oh!"

Lucius jumped back a step at her exclamation. His face was a cloud of worry. "What's happened?"

She giggled and held up a bobbin of thread. "I sat on a spool."

"O-oh." Heat rose in Lucius' cheeks. He hurried to gather the socks and shirt. He reached for the thread, but Alexcena was quicker.

"Would you like me to darn it?"

"What?"

"The socks." She held one of the offending articles up with an amused grin.

"Careful, Lucius," Lawrence put in from across the room. "She offered to do that for me once. I ended up walking around with a knot in my heel the size of my thumb."

Alexcena was already unwinding a length of thread, her brows knitted in consternation. "You might mention that I was ten years old at the time."

"I'll keep that in mind for future tellings."

Lucius could not help but chuckle at the pair of them. He set the shirt on the coffee table and sank into the matching armchair beside Alexcena.

"I assure you that my sewing skills have improved in the last decade," she commented.

"It doesn't bother me either way," Lucius grinned tenderly. "Those socks belong to my brother."

Lawrence laughed heartily over this. As they sat in companionable conversation, Lucius let his eyes hover over Alexcena's hands while she worked. Her deft, even movements formed a hypnotizing rhythm, and he found his troubled mood ebbing away as he watched. He was so relaxed in fact that he was not startled by the sudden entrance of his brother.

"I see we have company," Leo said enthusiastically when he caught sight of their guests. "Wish I'd thought to clean up a bit before I came home now," he added ruefully. "I would have sluiced off at the pump beforehand."

Leo was spattered with mud and dust. Bits of straw stood out from his hair and clothes at impossible angles. Lawrence ignored all of this and grasped the man's hand.

"Not at all, m'boy. How do you like working in the stable?"

"I think I preferred the gondola in Italy."

Lawrence chuckled and resumed his seat.

"How is your hand today?" Lucius wondered. He was referring to a nasty blister that had appeared on his brother's palm.

Leo examined it. "Still a bit tender. I could use another batch of that paste you concocted for me."

"I'll make you some more this afternoon." Lucius noticed Alexcena watching him with an upraised brow then. He loved to look at her when she was intrigued. "I am quite adept at forming curatives and herbal remedies," he explained.

"Are you really?"

He could only smile sheepishly.

Leo seemed to notice Alexcena for the first time when she spoke. (How he managed that, Lucius could not fathom.) "I beg your pardon. Good afternoon to you, Ms. Condreve."

"Good afternoon, Leopold," she replied warmly.

"May I ask what you're trying to do to my sock?"

"Ow!" At that precise moment, she jabbed herself with the needle. "Darn it."

"Well if you're trying to sew your hand into it, you need only say so. A demonstration is hardly necessary." He said this with mock severity and a roguish wink. Alexcena giggled.

Lucius was content to observe while his brother carried on with his banter. The more he talked the longer he delayed the dreadful news which Lucius had no desire to deliver. The distraction did not last nearly long enough. Leo was in deep description with Lawrence concerning his travels when it was suggested that they map out his routes.

"There are some charts at Lucius' desk," Leo stated and led the way to the bedroom.

Lucius sighed and rubbed the whiskers of his chin, trying to think how best to broach the subject.

"Do you want to tell me about it?" Alexcena murmured in the sudden stillness.

"What?" Lucius was taken off guard.

"Father said you had a meeting," she went on softly. "And I know they gave the position to someone else."

"How did you hear that?"

"I didn't. When we came in you didn't say anything about it, and so I knew."

He swallowed and looked away. So the blow had been given for him. He could not tell if this was favorable or not.

"I'm sorry for that, dear one."

"Sorry?" she echoed, bemused. "You had no control over it."

"So it would seem," he sighed and leaned back against the chair. "A professor without a position. It seems a contradiction of terms. This throws some larger problems into relief for us."

"Such as?"

"That was the last solid opening that I knew of. I've sent inquiries to everywhere I can think of, but they've all replied 'no' or not at all."

"So we'll keep looking," she replied, undaunted. "Though I do wish you would allow me to start planning our ceremony. These things generally take some time to arrange."

He looked to her then. "I may need to settle for something else. A lower position at a rudimentary school perhaps."

Her expression changed a little at that, and he thought she had understood until she replied.

"That's a fine start, but I am sorry. I know that's not where you want to be, Lucius."

"And we would need to wait even longer if I chose to do that."

The shock that registered on Alexcena's features was almost comical. Lucius nearly grimaced. *Perhaps she misunderstood after all.*

"On such a limited salary," he began slowly, "it would take quite a while for me to build the funds necessary to acquire a decent home. Housing in and around Cambridge can be quite outlandish."

"Lucius, you insult me," Alexcena pouted. "You think I don't realize that? That I would be turned away by the specter of adversity?"

"Not at all," he said calmly. "But I see no point in walking you through the adversities of a strained living when you are in a perfectly secure home now."

"Say you did find a place and we were married and some tragedy struck and you found yourself without a living. What then? Would you send me home to live with my parents for a few years until the hard times passed? A wife is a help-meet, Lucius. As I understand it one of the finer points of being married is that one no longer faces hardship alone. And you honestly think that if we were separated I wouldn't use every means available to reach you again?"

Her cheeks were pink after this emblazoned speech, and she seemed somewhat embarrassed. Lucius was caught once more by the sight of her. *I should've fought harder.*

"What do you mean?"

It took a moment for him to realize that he had voiced his thought. He gave his head a shake. "The meeting. The professors could not decide between myself and-the other. So they suggested that we dispute to determine who would be given the job."

Lawrence and Leo had wandered back into the room by the time he said this, the former looking troubled.

"Dispute? That's unconventional." He resumed his seat on the sofa. "Who was your opponent?"

Lucius had hoped to avoid giving this information, as he knew it would bring unnecessary hostility. Not that he didn't carry some of his own, but the facts could not be changed now.

"Rodney Dushaw."

Alexcena snapped around to face him again. Leo's mouth opened as if he would speak and then clamped shut. Only Lawrence replied.

"That man's only half as qualified as you," he frowned. "Was an explanation given for this decision?"

Lucius sank lower in his chair. "None except to say that he had won the dispute."

"And therefore the job," Leo tacked on darkly.

"Surely there has been some error," Lawrence went on. "I've yet to see you fail in a dispute, Lucius."

Wolgath let his head hang a little lower as a heavy silence fell on the room. Lawrence was the first to break it.

"I do hold a certain standing in Cambridge," he mused aloud. "I could speak to them if you like. Surely my reputation carries more weight than Dushaw's family name."

"No."

All three men turned to look at Alexcena. Lucius could not help but smile as she spoke his thoughts aloud.

"Lucius has already been humbled by this defeat. It would only bring him lower in their eyes if you attempted to take his living from another…even if it is Mr. Dushaw."

"Were you there before Rodney arrived today, Luc?" Leo asked.

"Yes."

"How did the Professors react when they saw him? Did he speak to any of them?"

His brow furrowed. He had not been concerned with remembering that portion of the incident. "Yes. Yes, some of the masters were in the far corner when he came in. They seemed to be arguing and one of them motioned him over." It was Professors Watson and Plumptre that he spoke to. Plumptre had been the one to deliver the questions of the disputation. Watson had been the first to defend Rodney's rebuttals.

"I'd very much like to know who these arguing professors were," Leo said all too casually.

Lucius caught the gleam in his brother's eye. "No," he snapped. "I'll not have you repeat your treatment of the Trobeson boys!"

"Who?" Alexcena asked.

"Some lads I grew up with," Lucius told her. "They used to steal my school books and put stones in my horse's shoe."

"Those boys had it coming to them," Leo scoffed. "And they're both clergymen now, thank you very much."

Lucius expelled a harsh breath and came to his feet. "No one is going to do anything about this. The decision is made. It's done." His weary gaze roamed toward Alexcena. "We shall just wait and see what happens next."

Chapter 20
March 1, 1765

Rodney stood in the wings and waited. He found a somewhat deserted alley in the midst of the Royal Exchange. He hid himself casually there, unseen by most, ignored by the rest. This suited his purpose perfectly. The cries of London rolled through the air, matching the cries of the gulls high above, and proclaiming the wares below. Fish, poultry, baked goods, semi-fresh vegetables, fabrics, tools, workmen, livestock. Every imaginable service and good could be found in this, the hub of the core of England. Thousands mobbed the streets of this clustered gathering of venders and shops nearly every day.

Rodney separated the individuals from the animal mob in his mind, considering them from the limited angles they offered. Despite his many faults, Dushaw possessed a terrific talent for judging people. His vision in this aspect seemed highly attuned to the set of a person's jaw, the rigid lines of the posture, the fleeting movements of their hands.

For more than an hour he watched, pensive and still, as they passed; old, young, short, thin, heavy, rustic, fair. His mind seldom wandered, but always to the same place. The spat with his father the night before had not been a pleasant one.

"I have a plan for ridding myself of Lucius, and failing that invoking jealousy on Alexcena's part."

"It's been months now," Randolph grumbled. "You brought him several pegs lower when you landed his professorship. What has it won you?"

"Some ready funds for one thing," Rodney retorted.

"Yes, but you're nowhere nearer to-"

"As I told you before," Rodney explained with failing patience, "it will take time to undo what's been done, but I now hold the advantage."

"Why don't you just give in and go for another girl? There are so many that would be so easy to snap up."

"I don't want just any girl with a banknote," Rodney fumed. "I don't just want a warm body to carry to parties for the rest of my natural life. I want the prestige. There is a certain respect attached to good names-"

"Don't pretend that you know more than I of the treachery of society! Even you cannot be so diluted." Randolph watched his son then from the corner of his eye. "Do you love her?"

Rodney blinked. "I would not call it-"

"What then?"

He floundered. "Affection."

"Well," Randolph snapped. "I suggest you get a hold on your *affection*, and pay attention to your actions. Though what makes you think you could be capable of succeeding I cannot fathom."

Rodney did not answer, but half turned away to the window and ground his teeth.

"You seem awfully confidant of yourself, boy!"

"Perhaps that is because I am a man, no longer a boy."

"The measure of a man is not in his height," his father commented soberly. "It's earned."

Rodney swallowed and looked to the floor. "Then I suppose it's a pity neither of us lived up to our height."

He waited for a rebuke, but none came. Then he spun on his heel to stalk from the house.

He turned from the memory and attempted to focus on the crowded street before him. It was not more than half an hour later when at last a smirk came to his lips, and he knew he had found just the one to suit his needs.

The woman was tall and spindly with a pleasant figure and squarish jaw. Her blond hair was shoved haphazardly up into a worn hat. Her furtive eyes were a rich brown. Her lips were full and red, offsetting her tiny nose. The skirt and blouse she wore were plain and half hidden by an oversized fawn coat, which was peppered with holes and tears. She carried an umbrella with the same affliction of tears. Her boots were scuffed and appeared more suited to the feet of a man. When she walked it was with long, self-assured strides. It was a wonder that she did not see the cart before she crossed its path.

The horse screeched in protest at the sudden jerk of his reins. The driver shouted something unintelligible-which was more than likely for the better-and shook a hand in the woman's direction. She never paused, and for that matter barely glanced at the man. Her chin tilted farther upward as she passed, dismissing the man's complaints.

Rodney moved forward as she approached. "Excuse me."

The woman never slowed, but rather turned to avoid him.

Rodney pursued at a brisk pace. "Excuse me!" He caught hold of her elbow.

She whirled about and Dushaw suddenly found the tip of the umbrella at his chest. She brandished the ridiculous thing like a sword. "What do you want?" she spat.

"I beg your pardon." He pushed the umbrella point aside with his index finger and coolly ran a hand through his hair. "My name is Dushaw. Professor Dushaw. I have a proposition for you."

"Not interested."

"You have no idea what it is yet."

"I don't care." She spun on her heel and started away again.

Again he took her elbow. "Now wait-"

The tip of the umbrella was jabbed at his chest. "I said I'm not interested. Now unhand me!"

"I'll pay you five shillings to listen to me," Dushaw said hurriedly, "and five guineas if you'll agree to it."

The umbrella lowered a fraction of an inch. "Where are the shillings?"

Dushaw shoved a hand into his pocket and produced them. "Anymore questions?" he asked, sliding the coins into her palm.

"Why did you pick me?"

"You seem the kind suited to it. I need someone who can act. I want you to play a part for, oh-" he feigned consideration, "two weeks at least. Once I've given you payment, you may leave without a backward glance."

"Five guineas doesn't seem like much of a payment for two-weeks-at-least of my life."

Rodney's shrewd eyes tightened. It was a gracious amount. "That was for agreeing to this. We will be discussing further payment."

"Who am I lying to?" This was said without so much as a batted eyelash.

Rodney released her arm. "My, my, how quickly we catch on," he sneered. "Pray, what is your name?"

The brown eyes flitted across his face. "Elida Morgan."

"Ms. Morgan." Rodney's teeth flashed in a grin that almost made the woman shudder. "I believe you shall do the job splendidly."

Chapter 21

March 20, 1765

March rolled slowly along. For Lucius the days seemed a bland blur. He fought his melancholy admirably, but the feeling was never far from his conscience. It was distinct in the early mornings, trenchant in the late nights, and always potent whenever he left Alexcena's presence. Though she would never admit to it-and he shied from bringing it up-there was a subtle change in her mood that plagued him. It was not so much impatience as it was resolve. She was resolved to wait through the unknown delay. He saw her as much as ever, venturing to the Lissome Ground nearly every day and meeting her in town most others. It was very easy to simply revel in her company and move his despairs to the back of his mind. Then, when he took his leave of her, the worries returned four fold. He would turn their visits over in his mind, and the differences in her attitude would stand out clearly. It was like seeing something first hand and then watching its reflection in a mirror, the glass etched with scratches and imperfections. At odd intervals her eyebrows would pucker. Her shoulders were rounded by some unseen weight. The soft timber of her voice had stiffened. They still shared the same affectionate touches when they managed to secure a moment of privacy, but the look that would come to her eyes always haunted him afterwards. It was like watching a tethered colt strain against its bond. He grimaced at the recollection.

The guilt would bother him then. Guilt for the self-imposed delay to their plans. He had taken a temporary job as a clerk to a lawyer's office, but it was not enough. What was worse, he knew that when-if-he found a position in a rudimentary school it would be much the same. He would rationalize his guilt with those facts, though they hardly made him feel better. How could he secure her happiness when he could scarcely afford his own?

Leo sensed his underlying mood despite any outward display of contentment, and made it his personal pursuit to minimize the dullness. He was an invariable light of sunshine, and Lucius could not help thinking that he would certainly have made a fortune as an entertainer if he chose.

The days wore on and he attempted to persevere against his dejection. Constant normality will eventually make anyone feel dull, and so there was no way to blunt the blow that was about to come to him.

He was working late one afternoon in the solicitor's office when the letter came by special courier. The paper was pale, heavy, and stiff. The seal was ornate in gold and crimson wax imprinted with the snarling face of what was either a lion or a gargoyle. The sharp hues of the wax made the thing look ablaze with flames. The address was simple;

Mr. Lucius Wolgath, Penn on the Green, c/o C.S. Solicitors, etc.

No return address.

His ever present curiosity took an instant hold. As carefully and casually as he could manage, Lucius leaned back in his chair. He strained to look into his employer's office through the adjoining door, which stood ajar. The man was sitting comfortably at his own desk. His head was thrown back in heavy slumber, his immaculately powdered wig only slightly askew.

Lucius sat up straight and snatched the dainty letter opener from the drawer. Inside he found one brief page of neatly choreographed script and a small packet. He unfolded the packet and skimmed over its contents; papers for sea passage aboard the vessel *Scarlet Pride*. Bemused and intrigued, he set these aside and lifted the letter. In retrospect only specific words seemed to stand out in his memory. He later wondered if he ever really read the entire missive at all. He caught only a handful of words before the intent was perfectly clear.

Prestigeous. Boarding school. Professors. Dire need. Ample compensation.

Lucius leapt to his feet, clutching the page in his hands. His chair fell back unnoticed. The commotion carried through the adjoining door and the dozing lawyer sat up with a boisterous snort. Lucius righted his chair and sat before the old man could notice. He folded the letter and packet back together and slipped them into his coat. He then faced the interminable task of containing his excitement for another two hours until he would be free to leave. He fought to control his hands as he scratched out what seemed like miles of transcriptions, not bothering to keep the smile from his face.

Alexcena was not home. She and her mother had gone to see a friend that afternoon, and so were not there when Lucius arrived. Unaware of this, he rapped enthusiastically on the door. He stood, hat in one hand, the letter in the other, when Eshton answered.

"Good afternoon, Professor."

"Eshton!" Lucius hastened by him and glanced eagerly around the wide foyer. "Where is Alexcena, today?"

"I'm afraid that Ms. Condreve is not in just now."

"Oh?" Before Lucius managed to look too crestfallen, Lawrence appeared from the front salon.

"Lucius!" he boomed with a jovial laugh. "What's the rush about? It's not as though you haven't seen her in five or six days."

Eshton murmured something that sounded suspiciously like 'hours' when Lawrence said this, but he then disappeared from the room and neither man noticed.

"Mr. Condreve, sir!" Lucius gripped the man's hand, another smile lighting his face. "I've just received the most extraordinary news."

"Well, you're not making me wait until the ladies return," Lawrence said, taking in his harried manner. "Come! Let's hear this news."

He led Lucius into the salon. Before he could offer him a seat or even sit himself, Lucius burst out, "It's about a position."

"A professor's position?"

"Yes!" Lucius held out the letter. "It's for a school that was just built in Eastbourne. Apparently the gentleman they hired for their chemistry department has declined after all and now they're desperate."

Lawrence's jaw jutted out in thought. "I wonder why he declined it."

"They didn't say." Lucius looked down at the letter stupidly and then back up at Lawrence. "I didn't think-but it doesn't matter much anyway. They've asked me to come and visit the school myself before I make up my mind. Though I don't see how I can refuse them at this point."

Condreve chuckled lightly and sank into the davenport. "Sometimes it's better to wait than to settle."

"Even if you find yourself mucking through an endless monotony of days and nights and hours..." Lucius let his voice trail. He was talking to himself more than Lawrence. He cleared his throat and began to pace a curving pattern around the room. "Do you have any notion as to when the ladies might return?" he asked more calmly.

"No, I can't say as I do."

Lucius nodded. *Of course.*

"They're visiting Ms. Lillian Crawler and Mrs. Crawler. I think Mr. and Mrs. Penn were to join them as well. You know how they can be when those ladies come together."

"Yes." Just short of Tabitha, there could not be two more chatty women then Lillian's mother, Mrs. Crawler, and Mrs. Penn. Unless it was Mimi Harper. "I suppose they'll be a while yet. I should get out of your way until then."

"Now you know you're in no one's way here, Lucius," Condreve replied, "but perhaps if you went home for an hour you'd calm down."

There was no small measure of concern in his voice, and Lucius knew he must look awful. "Perhaps you're right. I cannot fathom why I'm so anxious over this now. It is what Alexcena and I both want." He headed for the door. *A change of clothes, an hour to sit and calm my thoughts...This is sounding better by the minute.*

He was shocked by the appearance of Cecelia in the doorway just as he reached it.

"M-M-Mrs. Condreve." He cleared his throat once again and bowed.

"Hello, Lucius. We did not know you were here."

"Yes, well, it was an impromptu visit. Is Alexcena with you?"

"She's gone upstairs, I think."

"Why don't you go and find her, Lucius," Lawrence prompted. "I'll let Mrs. Condreve in on your news."

"Thank you, sir."

With a hasty bow, Lucius took the stairs two at a time and found Alexcena in one of the more private upstairs parlors. She was standing by the mantel with her back to the door when he caught sight of her. She turned at his approach. A becoming blush rose in her cheeks, and his worries abated in an instant.

"Lucius." She smiled.

"Good afternoon," he replied as he came into the room.

Her genuine pleasure betrayed her good manners, and she wrapped her arms securely around him once he was within reach. Lucius was taken aback, but the motion was so natural that he did not hesitate in returning it. He held her close, laying his cheek against her fragrant hair.

"I had some good news today," he murmured.

"And did you have a good day to go along with it?" She leaned back, but stayed within his grasp.

"Fair. And you?"

She opened her mouth, but then wrinkled her nose and thought better of it. He raised an eyebrow and she sighed. "I suppose you and Father noticed that we came home rather soon from our outing."

"To be honest I hadn't had time to consider it yet."

Alexcena toyed with one of the cloth buttons of his coat. "Mr. Dushaw was there."

"Dushaw?" Lucius felt his grip tighten marginally around her elbows. "Why was he there?"

"Mrs. Penn. He has a new acquaintance-a lady-who apparently knows Mrs. Penn. She invited them along."

"Did he speak to you?"

"Actually he didn't, but it was just horrible to watch him flaunting poor Ms. Morgan."

"His new acquaintance?"

She nodded. "Elida Morgan. I got the impression they hadn't known one another very long, but he treated her with such shameless familiarity. It must have been galling to her-or at least it ought to have been."

She moved away slowly and perched on the edge of a nearby settee. She brushed her hands smartly over her skirt, as if brushing away the memory. "Now you must tell me about your news. Has your landlady consented to have the roof repaired?"

Lucius tried in vain to conceal the grin that came to him. He tapped the envelope he still held against his fingers. "I received a letter today... from a school in Eastbourne."

Alexcena froze, her round eyes staring up at him.

"It seems they're desperate for a certain teacher," Lucius went on, enjoying the look. "A professor of science, no less."

"Truly?" Her earnest words drew him to kneel before her. Her eyes followed him the entire way. "Truly, Lucius?"

"They want me to come down and see the school for myself, and I expect they'll want an answer."

An excited twitter bubbled out of her.

"But this will be farther from here than we had planned," he admonished her seriously. "Farther from your friends and your parents than we expected."

"Not so far," she countered. "And you know I would only notice the distance if it were separating the two of us."

"It will for a little while," he replied. "I'm to go down and see the school. Of course I'll need to look for a more permanent residence while I'm there. I can't have my wife living in an inn or a boarding house for days on end while I try to find the perfect home."

"Though she would have willingly," she smirked. "You underestimate me too often, Professor Wolgath, and it's bound to catch up with you."

He leaned in to place a sweet peck on her nose. "I'm sorry you think so," he grinned.

Alexcena laughed and was cut short as he met her in another fond kiss. The future which awaited them had at last appeared on the horizon. Relief and contentment covered them like the welcome warmth of a winter flame.

Chapter 22

March 25 and 26, 1765

The days passed by more quickly than Alexcena would have thought possible. She warred within herself often on this account. As ecstatic as she was that her fiancé had at last found work-though it was not entirely confirmed as yet-she knew the coming separation would be difficult to say the least. Lucius had dinner with the Condreves nearly every night for the next five days. Tonight was no different except that Leo had joined them as well. The fact that Lucius was leaving the next morning lent a feeling of dreary excitement to the evening.

"As I understand it," Lucius said idly over a bowl of savory asparagus soup, "the *HMS Scarlet Pride* has been a cargo ship for years. The company that charters her is attempting to expand."

"I think they're just trying to add trading posts to their regular routes," Leo added. "Diverting down to Eastbourne adds several days to their trip to the Americas."

Alexcena looked up, her spoon clattering against her bowl. "The Americas?"

Leo suppressed a laugh, but could do nothing about the grin. "Sorry, Luc."

"Better be certain you're not asleep when they stop in Eastbourne, Lucius," Lawrence chuckled. He let his good humor die down into a cough at the sight of the scathing looks on the faces of his wife and daughter.

"Don't worry," Lucius said calmly. "My passage has only been paid as far as Eastbourne. They'll probably cast me over the railing to be sure they're rid of me."

Lawrence coughed again, but Cecelia and Alexcena appeared mortified.

"It's nothing to joke about," the latter complained. "You know I shall worry when you are away."

"Well then you can remember all the jokes I've made and know that no harm has come to me."

"That is the most wretchedly ridiculous sentiment I have ever had the inordinate misfortune to hear."

Even Cecelia was forced to purse her lips over that mouthful. Leo spluttered into his beaker mid-gulp and hastily wiped at his chin. Lawrence disappeared behind his own napkin.

Alexcena seemed not to notice their mirth at her expense. She watched Lucius carefully for a few moments. Then, seeming slighted, she returned to her soup. She fiddled with her spoon in her left hand and pretended to eat.

Lucius hefted a sigh. Then, masking a grin, he lifted his own spoon. "You've nothing to fear, my dear, although I believe I might."

She cut her eyes toward him with adamant curiosity.

"After all, if you're this concerned about my going to see the school, just imagine how overwrought you'll be when I actually do take their offer." As he spoke his hand stole under the table to nonchalantly stroke the top of Alexcena's. If she was startled by this, she gave no sign. "I may just need to consider a different line of work."

"I'd be happy to give you some advice, Lucius," the elder Wolgath pointed out. "I happen to be quite well versed in a plethora of occupations, hazardous and otherwise." He could not resist a jaunty wink in Alexcena's direction.

"Oh yes," Lucius murmured dully. "You're never-ending resume of work and hobbies you just happened to be compensated for."

Leo did not answer his brother's cheek, but leaned toward Lawrence. "Have you ever stretched a sheepskin drum?"

"I find it fascinating, Leo, that of all the places you've gone, of all the insane things you've tried, you've yet to find something that you genuinely love doing," Lucius smiled.

"That's not true."

"I mean something that holds you to a place."

"Very obtuse of you, baby brother," Leo chuckled smugly. "The *roaming* is what I love; the travel, the change, the countryside. And I find it *fascinating*, Lucius, that someone who is about to take a week long journey to do the work he loves is lecturing me about my traveling habits."

Lawrence leaned toward him and swallowed thoughtfully. "What exactly does one do with these sheepskin drums?"

"You'd be surprised how terrific the market is."

Banter traveled about the table. Lucius and Alexcena contributed as much as was necessary, all the while clasping one another's hands beneath the table. The Condreves insisted on conveying the Wolgaths to the port in London early the next morning. Leopold bowed gracefully out of the invitation, but they would not hear of it from Lucius. This made no difference, as he accepted readily. The closer he came to his departure, the longer his journey seemed. He knew of course that there was no proper way for him to take Alexcena along, but he was sorely tempted to try.

He found her in the east garden that day. He was just approaching the front steps of the manor when she emerged from the little gate to one side of the house. A gray cloak was fastened over her shoulders. What was that material? It changed from pale gray to satin white as she moved. It was as though the dawn clouds above had fallen to settle over her, and she smiled to him the smile of the sky that welcomes the sun.

He moved to her and they walked silently along the rocky path. It was several moments before she actually spoke.

"Three weeks."

Lucius puckered his eyebrows. "How do you figure that?"

"One week to arrive there," she explained, ticking the time off with her fingers. "One week to see the school, and one week to return. That's three at the least."

"Make that 'at the most.'" He snatched the fingers she had been counting with and tucked them into the crook of his arm. "Seven days is the maximum amount of time required to reach Eastbourne. More often the voyage is made in five. *Two* days is the amount of time I plan to give them while I'm there, and then five days back."

"Two days is an optimistic amount of time to find a suitable dwelling." She grinned and he knew that she was teasing.

"I thought about that," he smiled, knowing his next words would please her. "I think perhaps you ought to have more of a say in our home. And you said you would not mind a boarding house at first."

Alexcena whirled to face him, clinging excitedly to his arm. "Oh, Lucius, do you mean it?"

"Certainly."

They were around the back of the manor now, standing by a stone wall engulfed in ivy, now green at the first hints of spring. They were conveniently obscured from anyone's view, and he took advantage of this, reaching up to brush a curl of dark hair back over his fiancé's shoulder.

"If you wish, I will take you back with me on my next trip and we will find our home together."

Anticipation shone through the happiness in her eyes. "I do! Oh, I would love that, Lucius! Only I would need to find a suitable chaperone, though even then it might still be questioned-"

"Not if you went as my wife."

The change in her was quite comical. Her mouth clamped shut against the babble and she swallowed. Lucius raised an eyebrow.

"I don't know how long we'll have. Do you think there will be enough time for you to prepare?"

"Of course!" she bubbled more eagerly. "The most difficult part is done. We would need only two weeks or so to send invitations around, and-"

"The most difficult part?"

A sheepish blush rose in her cheeks. "I…may have commissioned my attire ahead of schedule."

"Ah, I see. Of a certainty that would take some time. Selecting the trimmings, the endless fittings." He moved impulsively, startling Alexcena and honestly surprising himself as well. He stretched his hands out beneath her cloak to encircle her waist and close the minute distance between them. "That poor seamstress has ruined her eyesight no doubt, fashioning a gown for such a slender model."

Alexcena made no reply, but released a breath against his chin. The air came as a fog in the chill of the morning. Lucius felt the cold no more as he pressed his kiss upon her. She returned it with a vibrant pressure. Neither one had any inkling as to how long they stood enjoying one another's warmth, lingering over this last private farewell. If they had carried even one true notion of the tragedy which was about to befall them, they might never have left the place.

As it was, the cry from the house startled them both.

"Alexcena, why don't you bring Mr. Wolgath in for coffee?"

The pair sprang apart. Lucius' glasses slid down his nose with the motion, and might have been dashed on the path if he hadn't managed to catch them. Alexcena only giggled.

"Yes, Mother!"

Lucius turned his incredulity to her. "How did she-"

"I don't know," Alexcena replied, still giggling. "And I flatly refuse to ask."

It was not until they were in the carriage that they truly spoke again. Her parents offered them as much privacy as was possible, facing away from the young couple and speaking only between themselves.

"I was not able to sleep very much last night," Lucius confessed. "I doubt if I'll have any true rest until I return."

"I had the strangest dream last night," Alexcena said, suddenly seeming listless. "I just remembered-" She broke off, pursing her lips.

"What was that?" he wondered, missing her discomfiture.

"I shouldn't have brought it up," she mumbled. "We were, the two of us, running along a beach. We were being chased by a dragon."

"A dragon?" Lucius pondered. "I should've liked to see that. I have always wondered as to the approximate wingspan needed for such a creature to achieve flight. In theory it ought to be based on the volume of the creature itself-"

"Lucius, we were separated," she interjected. "It came at us and you ran into the sea. Then I woke up."

Now he perceived the true anxiety in her look. He brushed his fingers lightly down her cheek. "That would never happen," he soothed. "I cannot swim."

The twenty-five mile journey to London seemed to have been made in half the time. It was mid afternoon when they found themselves moving sluggishly through the crowded streets of the great city. The Port of London was easy enough to find, the trickiest part was navigating one's way through the masses to get there. Lucius was the first to emerge from the coach and found himself facing a forest of a thousand masts rising up from the waters. The disjointed wharves extended eleven miles long; the *Scarlet Pride* could be anywhere.

"This will be like trying to fly a kite in a hurricane," Lawrence grunted as he too stepped down from the coach. "You stay here with the ladies, Lucius. I'll take Mills and see if we can't find some information." He motioned to the footman, who hurried to join him.

The driver busied himself with checking the horses while Lucius stood in the open door of the carriage. He stretched his legs experimentally. He could hear Alexcena chatting with her mother, but decided he would enjoy standing a few minutes longer. This particular wharf was not as crowded as most of the others, and he watched curiously as the people passed by, hearing snatches of conversation. At one point a man stopped quite close to him. He held the hand of a boy, no older than five, whose enormous eyes were turned toward the river.

"Father, why's it all curvy?"

"That's the Thames," his father said in explanation. "Come along now, we've got to find your uncle's boat."

"It's like a snake, Father." The boy wove his hand through the air in illustration.

"Yes," the man sighed indulgently. "All rivers bend."

"But this one is sooo curvy. Wouldn't ever'thin' here be easier if'n it was like...?" He shot his arm in a line through the air.

"Straight?"

"Mm, yes." The boy stomped and nodded. "Straighter! Can you make it straighter?"

The man seemed to roll his eyes. "We'll ask your mother about it, now come on Willey."

Lucius chuckled and Alexcena gave him a questioning look. "What is so funny?"

"Nothing," he gasped. "Only something that reminded me of myself, the child with the curiosity and the outrageous theories."

"Mother never did take to your theories."

Lucius jumped when his brother appeared through the throng to stand at his side.

"Leopold!"

He ignored him, propping his arms on the door of the carriage and speaking to the ladies inside. "I never will forget the time he tried to grow his own mushroom ring."

"All right, Leo."

"Whole house stank for a month."

"All right, Leo!"

"Careful," he warned. "You take that tone, and I might decide not to tell you where you're boat is docked."

"You know where it is?"

"Found it m'self an hour ago. You travel awfully slow, you know."

Lucius drew himself up. "I refused to have the ladies jostled."

"Uh-huh. And every other time we've journeyed together and you moved slow as paste, why was that?"

Lucius harrumphed at that, and the ladies giggled behind their ivory fans.

"Well, never mind," Leo went on. "I'm sure you'll travel much faster this time around."

Lucius grinned sheepishly. Before he could muster a suitable reply, he felt a familiar push against his knees. He looked down to see a disgruntled Great Dane at his feet.

"Commodore!"

The dog gave a huffy grunt as if to say, 'just because your conversation is taking place three feet above my head, that does not give you leave to exclude me.'

"My apologies, old boy. I didn't see you there." Lucius scratched heartily behind each of the animal's floppy ears.

"Forgive me, Ms. Condreve," Leo was saying into the coach. "Should I take him away?"

"No, no."

Cecelia touched her daughter's skirt anxiously. "Are you all right, dear?"

"Y-y-mm." Alexcena cleared her throat. "I suppose I shall need to become accustomed to this."

Lucius straightened. "He is harmless, I assure you."

He watched with an anxious eye as she moved toward the door and reached down with one hand. Commodore sat perfectly still as she patted his massive head. A few heavy seconds passed and his tongue lulled out to one side in approval. Alexcena shuddered and withdrew.

They called Lawrence and Mills back to them and followed Leo as he confidently led the way down the docks. The *Scarlet Pride* was an attractive vessel, Lucius was relieved to find. He had been dreading the sight of it, afraid that it would be some frail, oversized dingy, worn gray with age. He breathed an inward sigh when he took in its inviting appearance. Mills lifted his trunk from the carriage and hurried to deposit it on deck. Lucius turned to survey his family.

He went to Leo first, who was standing some feet away from the others with Commodore.

"Take care of this one while I'm gone," he said, lifting his chin to the dog.

"Did you mean him or me?" Leo wondered.

"Either way," Lucius replied as they grasped hands. "So long as my house is in one piece when I return."

Leo flashed him a brilliant and cunning smile. "Take care of yourself, brother."

Lucius nodded and moved back to the Condreves. Lawrence extended his hand.

"I suppose you'll want to be aboard now. Don't want them to pull out without you, eh?"

"Yes, sir."

The two men shook and Lucius kissed Cecelia's cheek. He looked to Alexcena, and suddenly they were struck dumb. Each of them tried to smile, but it was a formality. It was a bit late for him to start considering the dangers of sea-going now, but suddenly any number of scenarios swam in his head. Her thoughts were much the same. She flipped her gaze briefly to one side, and her eyes narrowed speculatively at the ship.

"Mr. Wolgath?"

Lucius was somewhat confused until his brother answered from the distance behind him.

"Leo, please." There was a smile in his voice, but his tone was deceptively low. Only Lucius seemed to notice this tell-tale sign of his discomfiture.

"Do you happen to know how old this vessel is? When it was built?"

Leo managed to cut his chuckle short. "The *Scarlet Pride* is as strong and as swift a vessel as they come. She could weather ten storms and not get so much as a splinter in her railing."

Alexcena nodded. "It's not her railing that I'm concerned about."

Lucius detected the true and uncertain fear in her voice. He reached for her hand. Even as he secured her grasp, her eyes remained on the ship. "There's nothing to fear," he assured her. "It's the sixties. They don't make ships the way they once did."

This seemed to comfort her, and she even offered him a slow smile.

"Wait for me?" He had not planned to say this, but his mouth acted of its own accord.

"Of course," Alexcena replied, "but only when forced. I may just run after you." As she spoke, she pulled the strings of her reticule and produced a small object from its depths. "Here. I want you to keep this while you're away." She dropped the thing into his hand and he recognized the cameo necklace at once. "The token of your fair lady," she said.

Lucius had no more words. He rested one hand on her cheek and planted a long, firm kiss on her forehead. Then he headed up the plank walk toward the ship. He was just about to board when she called out to him.

"Take care, Lucius!"

He looked back over the rims of his glasses at her. Her countenance flooded with color. He gave her one last dashing smile.

"Always."

Part II

The Waylaying Tempest

Chapter 1

March 26, 1765

*T*hat was the last Lucius saw of her face, an image destined to haunt him, but now, as he turned from the very soul his own needed most, his pains were smitten by the briny spray of the sea. He even dared to smile in the midst of his own brief sorrows. The hope of a future lay before him in a vast expanse of ocean waves backed by the firm soil of his country. So it was that he took his first innocent step away from England.

The polished deck moaned as he came aboard, although it was from the underlying currents rather than his weight. Every visible inch of the vessel gleamed in the low light of the evening sun. Men swarmed in a flurry of carefully mandated activities. All were clothed in roughly similar canvas trews and muslin shirts, giving them an air of uniformity. Some of the men, especially those scampering up the ratlines, wore their sleeves folded high up on their elbows, despite the blustering winds of the English coast. They responded like trained hounds to the rapt orders of the officers. Each and every movement was efficient and precise with not an ounce of effort wasted.

Lucius felt his fears of an ocean calamity waning as he watched. This was an able crew, not only seasoned by years of experience, but by years of voyaging *together*. Each man was as a piece in a kaleidoscope mirrored six times over by his shipmates. All fit together equally to form the mechanics of the fine vessel. Lucius' mind was put to ease by these routines of automatic rhythm. The timpani of this rhythm came from amidships where three men stood at the helm. One was dressed in the plain garb of his fellow sailors. The other two were dressed with far more formality, as befitting officers. Lucius approached them and was greeted by a pleasant glance from the shorter of the two.

"Gentlemen," he began with a dip of his head, "I am Lucius Wolgath."

"I see our seventh passenger has arrived, Mr. Sweney," the shorter man said. He offered a courtly bow. "Captain John Davidson, sir. And this is my first mate, Mr. Sweney."

"It is a pleasure to meet you both."

"The others have all arrived and consented to go below," the Captain explained. "Though you're most welcome to stay above, Professor."

"I think I should like to see my quarters."

"Of course, sir. Show the Professor to his cabin if you please, Mr.

Sweney."

"Aye, Captain Davy."

Davidson turned once again to grin at Lucius. "Welcome aboard the *Scarlet Pride*, sir."

Lucius found himself pondering the contrast of characteristics between the captain and his first mate. Sweney was a tall, heavy sort of man, though lithely proportioned by a lean diet and years of earnest sailing. His brow overshadowed his dull gaze. His massive arms always seemed to be pulled taught behind his back with his hands tightly clasped. The stern expression rarely left his face. He appeared more born to command than John Davidson (or Captain Davy as he was called by his men). The Captain was a good six inches shorter than Sweney and four inches shorter than Lucius himself. His hair had receded well back over his forehead. Craggy trenches born of sun and age lined his face at all angles. His legs and arms seemed almost too short for his long body. There was a thick paunch about his waist that could not quite be hidden by his fine frock coat. Though the Captain was a reasonable commander, he was stern by nature, in spite of the fact that he was wont to smile, even to his subordinates. Lucius wondered vaguely if Mr. Sweney had ever smiled in his life.

They were halfway down the stairs to the lower decks when the ship leaned quite suddenly to port. Sweney seemed not to feel the motion while Lucius hit the wall with a groan.

Sweney turned to him with knowing eyes. "You're going to have a rough time of it I see, Professor."

Lucius managed to move down the hall without stumbling again. His smile wavered when he caught a glimpse of his accommodations. There was no window, of course. The short bed was exactly five feet long, the width of the entire room, and wedged against the far wall. It was built securely in place with a raised board creating a border on the one exposed side, thus forming a box. Lucius immediately realized that there were going to be some problems with this, as he was a good five feet eleven inches in height. Though he had to admit this was better than the alternative; the room was only four feet deep. Above the bed was mounted a shelf, which was also of a box-like construction. The starboard wall had an empty wash stand and mirror bolted securely to its boards. A wide plank was chained horizontally to the port wall, and Wolgath would soon discover that this folded down to form a desk. It was mounted just high enough to provide space for his trunk to slide beneath it, leaving a two-foot square space empty in the center of the closet cabin.

"Are the accommodations to your liking?" Sweney wondered with a tinge of humor coming to his gray eyes.

"Yes," Wolgath said, finally regaining his composure enough to smile. "Yes, this will do just fine."

"Very well. I shall leave you to get settled, Professor." The man started to close the door, but turned with an afterthought. "The Captain has asked that the passengers dine with him this first night. His quarters are back down the hall and through the double doors to the right. The meal will be served at six."

"Then I shall be certain to attend."

The door shut. The ship pitched again and Lucius hit the wall. He grunted and attempted to suppress the queasy notion that had come to his stomach.

By six o'clock Lucius had learned to quell each burst of nausea that accompanied the motions of the ship. Unfortunately, as the day wore on into evening, the pitching became much more frequent. He drew himself upright outside the captain's double doors and fervently prayed for balance.

The cabin was large, but crowded. Several men milled about in easy conversation, including the Captain and First Mate Sweney. There was only one lady present. She stood to one side with two youngsters, whom Lucius assumed to be her children; a boy no more than eight years old and a girl not yet fourteen. She reminded him somewhat of Ms. Winslett in all her ridiculous lace and dark curls.

"Ah, the good Professor Wolgath," Captain Davy chimed as Lucius entered. "We were beginning to despair of your presence."

He gestured to the long table dominating the space. Normally it was laid with all manner of charts and logs, but tonight these were replaced by a fine tablecloth, porcelain, and gleaming silver. Everyone moved toward a chair. The Captain gallantly held the lady's out for her.

"Thank you indeed, Captain."

"You're servant, Mrs. Hatchens."

Mr. Sweney held the next seat out for Mrs. Hatchen's daughter, and the girl smirked unabashedly as she took it. Sweney harrumphed and moved away.

Lucius sat across from the boy between two of the three unknown men. Captain Davy took the head of the table with Sweney on his right and another unnamed officer on his left. He made some unseen signal, and the cook-a hideously overweight man dubbed "Gurt"- appeared bearing a covered silver tray. He set this in the center of the table and proceeded to bring in two more. Lucius watched with interest as the trays shifted every time the ship breached a wave. They all bowed their heads as Captain Davy asked the blessing. Gurt then removed the shining covers to reveal roasted pork, boiled vegetables, and steaming rolls. A bottle of wine was passed around, though the two younger guests were given water. The boy might have protested to this, but at a look from his mother he merely glared.

"I do hope you are all comfortable in your quarters," Captain Davy was saying. "You are the first passengers I have had aboard the *Scarlet Pride*. It has always been a cargo ship, you see, and this is something of an experiment."

Lucius soon discovered the identities of the other passengers. One was Harlan Pratt, who was going to America to survey a plot of land his father had recently purchased. Another was Thomas Gibbs, an agent of the company who owned the cargo below decks. The last was Smith Darlum, who sat directly beside Lucius. He was a rich young thrill-seeker traveling to America in search of Natives. He had a wild mop of fair hair, a wide jaw, and a mouth in need of a gag.

"Course I've read several books on the subject," he said knowingly, his pointed nose high in the air. "You being a professor-" He nudged Lucius' ribs none too gently. "-I'd guess you know what I'm talking about. Anyway when Harlan's old dad bought that spit of land over that way, I thought to meself, 'Here's your chance, Smith old boy!' So I offered meself as escort."

Lucius had been idly considering trying some boiled potatoes, but the ship pitched upward once again and he decided against it. Turning reluctantly to Smith, he said, "So you gentlemen are traveling together, then?"

"More like next to each other," Pratt sighed from two seats away. "I said it wasn't necessary."

Darlum was instantly affronted. "I couldn't let my cousin face the perils of America alone!" he cried.

"Though I know I could," Pratt murmured.

"You're cousins?" Wolgath asked in a strained voice. Anything to take his mind from the rolling of the deck.

"Only by birth," Harlan mumbled darkly.

Smith pointed across the table, though his focus was on Lucius. "Why, this man is the closest thing I have to a real brother! Poor sap that I am, I've got five sisters back home. But, oh, they were sorry to see old Smith leave!" He took a bite of pork, his lips smacking noisily. "Have you got family, Professor?"

"One brother, Leopold." He hesitated before adding, "And a fiancé."

Darlum nudged him again. "Ah, look at him blush now! Go on, what's her name?"

Lucius wished that he had not spoken, but it kept his mind from wandering to his stomach. "Alexcena Condreve."

"Pretty, eh?"

Thomas Gibbs spoke up, sparing Lucius the trouble of answering. "I've a wife myself. Her name is Lady." He spoke the name wistfully, but Smith broke his reverie with a raucous laugh.

"Lady?" he gasped out. "Is that her real name?"

Gibbs drew himself up with indignation. "Lady Ann Gibbs."

Smith guffawed. "It'd be a shame if you were ever knighted, sir. Then your poor wife would be Lady Lady Gibbs!" He seemed to think this terribly funny.

Mrs. Hatchens leaned over her son's head to speak quietly with Mr. Gibbs. The man smiled and nodded his appreciation.

Lucius lifted his utensil to sample some of the meat. The ship lurched again some seconds later, and he felt the bite plummet to his belly. He choked a bit and snatched up his wine. He caught his breath, but the room did not stop moving. The steady motions of the ship came all at once; side to side and up and down. He gripped the edge of the table, concentrating hard, as though he could halt the movements of the flute by sheer force of will.

"Are you all right, Professor?" the Captain wondered from two seats away.

"Mr. Pratt is not looking well either," Mrs. Hatchens commented.

Harlan Pratt did indeed appear pale. When Lucius looked to his hands, they were solid white. He opened his mouth to speak, but another dip in the vessel's motion caused a sharp intake of breath. In a thrice he was up and stumbling through the door. Wolgath regretted that he could make no apology, but the sudden overwhelming nausea that enveloped him had his mind-and mouth-otherwise preoccupied. Harlan Pratt was not two steps behind him.

Chapter 2

March 26, 1765

"Are you quite certain you wish to stay here, dear?"

Alexcena smiled to herself and turned from the bright window to face her mother, the fingers of her right hand still trailing over the filmy curtain.

"Of course, Mother."

They were standing in Alexcena's bedroom of their London home. She had made the decision to stay there the week before. Her father had given his assent, provided that his man Mills and a few others stayed with her in addition to the maid servants. These chosen men had come two days before to inform the regular housekeeper.

"I shall be just fine here," the young lady went on.

"But you hate Town so," Cecelia simpered. "Wouldn't you feel more at ease in your own home? In your own bed?"

"This is our home!" her daughter insisted merrily. "This is my bed!"

"That is not what I meant."

She had to admit that her mother did seem truly troubled. Being preoccupied as she was with her own misgivings, Alexcena was not entirely certain how to comfort her. Fortunately for the both of them, Lawrence appeared in the open doorway.

"She'll be just fine, Cecelia." He slid a comforting arm around his wife's shoulders and turned to her. "All I ask is that you do not venture out alone. Take someone with you when you leave the house."

"I wouldn't dream of going out otherwise."

He nodded his approval and looked to his wife. "We really ought to be going now. We'll be getting home long after dark as it is."

"I'll walk you out."

"Not at all," Lawrence waved his daughter's comment aside. "We certainly know the way." He gently pecked her creamy cheek. "We'll see you in a few weeks."

Cecelia wrapped her arms about her daughter. "Take care. Don't sit in this house worrying yourself to waning."

"I won't," Alexcena murmured, pulling back. "If I know you, you've already alerted every acquaintance you have in Town to my presence. I'm certain I shall have no end of visitors."

Cecelia ignored her skulking. "All's the better. These few days will go by quickly for you and you'll be thanking me."

"Of course, Mother."

There was a chorus of 'good-byes' and effusions of love, and all at once the Condreves were out the door. Alexcena was left alone amidst a strange silence, despite the flood of servants who had accompanied her. She folded her arms about her waist and stood still, unsure of what to do. She ran through all of her usual amusements in her mind, but none appealed. Her mind eventually trailed to Lucius, and she thought to write him a letter, but to what end? By the time it arrived he might very well be returning to her and never receive it.

So she stood, her arms crossed and toying with the lace fringe of her gown, when Lydia entered through the lavish dressing room.

"Do you care to take supper now, ma'am?"

Alexcena jumped and Lydia feigned ignorance.

"Cook's just finished a beautiful roast, and there's fresh boiled greens."

Alexcena calmed her breaths and sighed determinedly. "No. Thank you, Lydia."

"Very well, ma'am. I'll bring around a tray of snippets in a while," she added as she slipped out the door. "You never know when you might decide to feel peckish."

Alexcena smiled in spite of her heavy mood. This trait-the uncanny ability to lighten a dreary situation-was one that she particularly appreciated in Lydia. It was a trait she appreciated in Lucius as well.

She slumped down into a plush arm chair and reached for her Bible. Lifting the creaking cover, she flipped to Lamentations. It was one of her favorite books, and she knew the cadence would soothe her. She settled back to wait.

It was the noise that woke Lucius; the raucous, roaring, incessant rasp that seemed to be coming from all sides to crash down over his aching head in steady swells. Once the sound had him awake, the pains in his belly took hold, far outweighing the soreness in his temples. His arm moved instinctively over his stomach, but aside from that, he couldn't seem to move at all. Lightheaded and disoriented, he was only vaguely conscious enough to sense that he must have a fever. The ship rolled and his stomach lurched into his throat. He opened his eyes with the shock of the motion. A dim lantern had been set on the shelf of his little cabin. The glass of it obscured the meager flame, but even this was enough to set his head to throbbing sharply. Fighting the heaviness that had come to his limbs, Lucius threw one arm over his eyes and willed himself into unconsciousness.

This light torpor was broken by a pair of clammy hands on either side of his face. He knew not how long he slept, but it obviously was not long enough, for he still felt violently ill. He blinked furtively, hoping to see who it was standing over him while still avoiding the light.

"Professor Wolgath?" a bland voice rumbled. "You must try to eat something now."

One of the hands moved away and he caught sight of a saucer and spoon somewhere off to the side. He grew dizzy merely thinking of it.

Some foul odor found its way to his nose and he felt the acid surge again. He might have rolled away if not for his keen connection to the motions of the ship. He sidled back as best he could, his eyes tightly shut and one hand clamped over his mouth.

The rumbling voice sighed. "All right, Lucius."

A disembodied feeling of consciousness came to him then.

What have I done? I've just turned away help! *Why, why…Come back! Come back! Send him back! Send* anyone *back!*

He felt a sort of trembling in his lips and thought he must be mumbling.

This is madness…I am madness…Men are madness to refuse such help…To refuse the hand that feeds…The waters that sustain…

Somewhere in the midst of these silent ravings, his headache seemed to move to the back of his mind. The pain was still there, but now blunted by distance. Lucius cradled his head and drifted toward sleep.

<u>*Chapter 3*</u>

April 4, 1765

Alexcena smiled an odd smile. The corners of her round mouth pulled in, holding her laughter at the butler's startled expression in check.

The poor man had entered the back door of the kitchen, abruptly tugged his boots off and smacked them together. Clods of semi-firm ground skittered across the floor. He had noticed his mistress after the second smack and now stood half bowed, a boot in each hand, his arms spread wide, and a comical "oh" shape to his lips.

"Er, that is-Ms. Condreve."

"Good afternoon, Percyville."

Lydia's hands hesitated over the dough she was kneading. "Oh, for heaven's sake, Percyville!" she huffed. "Put your boots back on and sit down. You act like you've never seen a woman in the kitchen before."

The man straightened and donned his boots in a thrice, though he obstinately refused to sit in Alexcena's presence. "Forgive my awkwardness, Ms. Condreve. I was not expecting you."

"It's quite all right, Percyville," she replied when she trusted her voice. "I had forgotten that you have not been with us very long. I ought to have warned you that I sometimes find my way into the kitchen with Cook." She thought of the past two days spent in a nagging state of boredom and added, "You may as well expect to find me here again before we return to Penn."

"Yes, ma'am."

"What's this goin' on heah in my kitchen?!" the Cook blustered as she made her way in. "Mud on my flo'er and Ms. Condreve at my table and some I-don't-know-what in my oven."

"Ms. Condreve has put together a chocolate pudding," Lydia said. She sniffed in appreciation. "It smells heavenly."

"You're all welcome to some. It came out rather…large."

Lydia tittered, but only Alexcena seemed to notice. In mixing the ingredients of her pudding, she had inadvertently tripled part of the recipe. What was she to do but triple the rest of it?

"No, thankee, miss," the Cook grumbled as she bustled about. "Can't abide that stuff."

"Pudding?"

"Chocolate," she snapped. "Sets me teeth on edge. An' I think it agitates me rheumatiz too."

"I don't see how you get on without it," Lydia muttered. "I use it to cure everything! Aches, pains, colds, itchy throat, indigestion…"

"And an alcoholic drinks whiskey to cure his dizzy spells," Cook muttered sarcastically. "Chocolate don't help nothin'. A good swig o' tonic!" She squinted one eye and pounded one fist in her palm. "Now *that* cures what ails you!"

Alexcena was still hiding her giggles behind her handkerchief when Mills poked his head in the door.

"There's a gentleman here to see you, miss."

Alexcena's brow furrowed. "A gentleman?"

"Yes, ma'am," Mills assented reluctantly. "A Rodney Dushaw."

"Dushaw?!" She thought to mask her surprise too late. She folded her hands primly and said in a far calmer tone, "Are you quite certain?"

"Yes, ma'am."

Something between a sigh and a derisive huff escaped her as she came to her feet. "Very well. Percyville, will you accompany me, please?"

"Will ya be wanting tea, ma'am?" Cook wondered.

"No need," she replied stiffly. "Mr. Dushaw shan't be staying."

Alexcena had composed herself well enough to be polite, though she dared not smile. Rodney was awaiting her entrance with great expectation. He pounced, ignoring Percyville, who moved to a discrete corner of the room.

"Ms. Condreve, I do apologize. I was told that your entire family was staying in London.”

“Were you, Mr. Dushaw?”

“Yes. I came with the intent of speaking to your father. I had no idea that I would find you here by yourself.”

“Oh?” She was galled that he seemed unaware of her stiffness. He even had the audacity to snicker with that smug little lip of his.

“I suppose this must seem very untoward; a bachelor coming to a house where a young woman is known to be staying. Funny how these things turn out.”

“Mmm.” She stared at him blankly for a moment, and he seemed satisfied to stare sidelong at her. “Well, I’m certain that you would not wish to encroach upon my reputation any longer than you already have.”

Rodney’s eyes tightened almost imperceptibly. “Indeed not.” He bowed low. “I will be staying here in Town myself for a time. If you should desire anything at all, you need only send for me.”

“Nonsense.”

Rodney chuckled at that and set his hat on his head. “Your servant, ma’am.” He passed through the door, brushing dangerously close to her as he went.

Another quarter of an inch closer, she thought darkly, *and he surely would have felt the back of my hand…or perhaps the knuckle.*

The roll of the sea became a steady liturgy of aches and relief. The ship rolled one way and the nausea abated. It rolled another and the feeling returned full force. Wolgath’s entire body seemed hollow. Weakness seeped into every fiber of every muscle until he could no longer move. He spent more of his time conscious, though everyone around him seemed to assume he was still out cold. Voices reached him occasionally, but when he tried to answer, all he could manage was the curious trembling of his lips. Sometimes they moved of their own will, and he thought he must still be under the spell of the fever.

My body is rendered helpless…and so I must wait…

Time marched all around him, but seemed to halt at his door. His days consisted of wakefulness and his nights of a dull doze. No hint of daylight was able to penetrate the sealed walls of this floating wooden box, and so his hours melded together. He could speak to no one save the voices inside his head. He spent the majority of his reflections with Alexcena. Tracing the curves of her face with his fingertips. Stroking the full tresses of her hair. They had hours upon hours of conversations all filled with the things he wished to say and all serving to make him that much more miserable.

His prayers ran together into one endless conversation with the Lord. He soon found himself picking it up without hesitation each time he woke. Had his mild delirium abated long enough, he might have wondered as to his sanity. Even if he had been of a mind to question it, he could not deny the calm he felt as he carried out the one-sided dialogue. He did have the presence of mind enough to marvel at how easy it was to keep it going. It was during one of these long colloquies that he found himself reciting a familiar prayer. *...in the midst of the seas; and the floods compassed me about, all thy billows and thy waves passed over me. Then I said, I am cast out of thy sight; yet I will look again toward thy holy temple...* He was nearly through before he realized that the prayer he was recalling was that of Jonah.

Chapter 4
April 8, 1765

Wolgath awoke to the heavy sensation of utter exhaustion. He lay with his eyes closed for several minutes before he managed to draw up his lids. The cabin was all in shadow, the lantern having burned itself out. He blinked and winced at the grainy scratching in his eyes. From somewhere in the darkness he raised his hand up to rub the irritation away. The light sheets were damp, as well as his clothes. The realization that he was breathing through his mouth came dully. He clamped his jaw shut and attempted to ignore the horrid taste on his gummy tongue. It was then that he was assailed by the foul odor, suddenly overwhelming even to his dimmed senses. It was not surprising, given his ailment in the confined space, but pungent nonetheless. He sat up straight, one leg falling over the bed with a thud. It was sickening!

And something was missing. He heard the rush of waves. He felt the motions of the ship, and...nothing else. He slid his other leg over the bedside experimentally. The ship had not stopped he felt certain. The motions were too strong. Still the nausea was absent. He could have laughed with relief. He gripped the box bed and tried to pull himself up onto his feet.

Too much. The walls tilted crazily and he dropped back down. The sickness never came. It was replaced by a great weariness-and hunger. His appetite rumbled within him, and he was puzzled by the sound at first. Every other part of his body was too heavy, but his belly felt too empty.

The door opened, startling him where he sat. The cabin was flooded with dim light from the hall, silhouetting the large figure of Gurt, the ship's cook.

"Good morrow to ye," he growled in his rough voice. "Been comin' by every morning. This is the first time you been wakeful."

Gurt ambled in-filling the limited space-and sat atop Lucius' trunk. Wolgath wasn't paying particular attention to his words. His hollowed eyes were fixed on the beaker and bowl Gurt carried.

"You're hungry, are ye?" Gurt asked with a raised brow. "That's good."

He passed Lucius the bowl. It was filled with some sort of cool stock. He swallowed three mouthfuls in a wink.

"Careful now," Gurt laid one meaty finger on the edge of the bowl. "You'll want to go slow. Take some of this as well. But I warn ye, it ain't water."

Lucius accepted the beaker wearily and sniffed at its contents. As it was, anything which came from outside that little room was bound to smell good to him, so he turned it up. He stopped abruptly and nearly gagged. Gurt chuckled.

"What was that?" Lucius demanded when he had caught his breath. His voice escaped him in a feathery whisper.

"Lemon and olive juice. Old seafarer's remedy."

Lucius coughed and swallowed another mouthful of broth. "It's terrible!"

"Aye, and it'll curl the hair on your chest too." He eyed the younger man dubiously, as though he doubted there was any hair on his chest.

"You know, Samuel Johnson claims the cure for seasickness is to find a large tree and wrap your arms around it," Lucius replied sourly. His voice became stronger with every word.

Gurt grunted with scorn. "Yea, well the only tree you'll find around here is the mainmast, and it's covered in pitch up to your waist, so I wouldn't try that cure if I were you. I think you'll be fine in any case," he added as Lucius drained the contents of the bowl. "I'll alert Captain Davy that you're feelin' yourself again. He'll be wantin' to check in on ye I 'spect." The big man rose, taking the bowl and cup.

"Thank you, Gurt," Lucius thought to say just as the man was closing the door.

Left to himself, he attempted to stand once more. This time he succeeded, but only just. He lowered himself again. A change of clothes was definitely in order. Dressing was a chore, and took him the better part of half an hour. He felt around until he found his glasses where someone had kindly placed them on the shelf by the lantern. By this time he was waning and so he sat back on the bed. He felt himself dozing and made no attempt to struggle with it. This was the first restful sleep he experienced since his sickness began. He roused a few hours later when the door was opened again

"Professor Wolgath."

Lucius blinked rapidly in the sudden light and pushed himself up. Captain Davidson came in with Gurt close behind. "You're looking much better, sir."

"Thank you, Captain."

"You're the second passenger to recover from seasickness."

As the Captain spoke, Gurt leaned around him to hand Lucius another bowl of broth, this time accompanied by a scrap of bread. Lucius sipped it readily.

"Who else has been struck by this?" He started to say 'horrible malady,' but held that comment back. *Seasickness is not a disease,* he reminded himself. *I can blame only my own stomach for this.*

"First it was Mr. Pratt and yourself, then Ms. Delilah Hatchens came down with it."

"I'm grieved." Lucius' brow puckered in concern. "I do hope the child is all right."

"Oh, she came out of it last week. Right as rain now. I just hope Mr. Pratt is not far behind the both of you. Is something the matter, Professor?"

Lucius realized he had been staring oddly. "Forgive me. I was attempting to recall...I seem to remember you coming to see me with another man, Captain."

Davidson nodded. "That was Israel Granville. We lost our physician two voyages ago, you see and haven't replaced him. Granville is really the ship's carpenter, but he knows a thing or two about how to stop the bleeding."

Lucius swallowed nervously. "I see."

The men laughed then at his anxious look. "Come now, Professor," Davidson chuckled. "You've got your sea legs about you. It's on to new adventures from here!"

They left him to finish his broth. He nibbled experimentally at the bread, though he was already feeling much more like himself. He lounged about all morning, mostly mulling over vague memories he had while he was sick. The thing that puzzled him most was the dates. The Captain had said that Delilah Hatchens had recovered last week. That would mean that she had only been ill for a few days at most. To him it seemed that he had been ill a good deal longer, but then he had no idea as to what day it was. He dozed, still trying to figure it out.

Mr. Granville came to see him at two o'clock that afternoon. By then Lucius was feeling vital enough to walk around and in sore need of fresh air. With Granville close at hand, he exited the cabin, mounted the stairs, and emerged onto the main deck.

He took his first breath of clear oxygen gratefully; a thirsting man tasting his first swallow of cool water. The sun glinted merrily off his glasses from high above, and all around was blue. The white sails gleamed in the light as they billowed full with the wind.

Lucius and Granville slowly made their way to the tiller. Captain Davidson stood there speaking with Mr. Sweney while the helmsman stood at the wheel behind them. Sweney was the first to spot them.

"Professor, you must be feeling better."

"Indeed I am," Lucius smiled weakly. "Thank you."

"The air ought to do him good," Granville put in. "The fever's abated and he's kept his food down."

"That'll be all then, Israel."

"Aye, Cap'n Davy." Granville touched his knuckle to his forelock and moved away.

Lucius squinted as he watched him go. "I can't believe the brightness!"

"It tends to stay rather shadowed below decks," Sweney commented blandly.

"If this weather holds, we'll make port well ahead of schedule," Davidson added.

"Would you mind telling me, Captain," Lucius asked cautiously, "exactly how long was I ill?"

"I imagine the days ran together for you somewhat, eh?" Davidson turned to his first mate. "It's been about two weeks, wouldn't you say, Mr. Sweney?"

"Aye, sir. A few days less."

Lucius was puzzled. "Two weeks?" he said innocently. "Shouldn't we be in Eastbourne by now?"

It was a curious thing to watch as the smiles of the two men melted away into nothingness. They exchanged glances.

"Why should we be at Eastbourne?" Davidson wondered.

Lucius felt his heart's pace quicken. "That's where I'm going," he insisted. "That is where I was headed. My papers clearly stated Eastbourne."

Sweney stepped forward, his hands clasped tightly behind his back.

"Sir, are you quite yourself? This ship was never bound for Eastbourne."

"Yes it was." Lucius felt a bitter bile rising in his throat. His hands began to tremble in time with his heart. "Yes it was! You were to stop at Eastbourne-where I would disembark-and then…"

Comprehension dawned on them all, including the overcurious helmsman. The three sailors stared at Lucius with pronounced dread. Wolgath's eyes darted from one face to the next, and he had the sudden ridiculous urge to make a run for it. That would have been to no avail; he was trapped in a moving cage. A helpless mouse pinned by his tail for all the world to see.

"I am very sorry to be the one to tell you this, Professor," Mr. Sweney began carefully, "but the *Scarlet Pride* only had one destination, the Americas."

Lucius, whether to his credit or his doom, absorbed this blow incredibly well. He stared at Mr. Sweney, then Captain Davidson, and back again. His hand came up to grip the ratlines lashed to the railing at his side, but that was partly due to the dipping of the deck with the waves. The Professor blinked.

"Forgive me, sir. I want to be absolutely certain that we are quite clear," he said. "We are bound for the Colonies?"

"Yes."

"In America?"

"Quite so."

Wolgath swallowed. The two men waited, poised to offer their assistance should the Professor-for lack of a better phrase-lose his bond with sanity. But Lucius managed to hold his ground. "Well," he said curiously. "An expedition of that sort would require a proper set of boots. Would you gentlemen please excuse me while I look into the situation of my footwear?"

"Of-of course," the Captain was first to stutter.

"Thank you." Without a backward glance, Lucius spun on his heel and stalked away.

"We ought to have checked his forehead," Sweney said when he was gone. "The man still has fever."

Chapter 5
April 15, 1765

Alexcena had many more visitors than she expected. Her mother's friends refused to let her be alone. She made several calls in return, closely followed by Mills or Percyville. In truth she was glad for the company. The days wore on, but it seemed that the only time she had left to worry was just before she went to sleep at night. Even then she would not have called it worry. It was more like a reverie. She would summon all the feelings she remembered from being with Lucius and with them construct a new memory... afternoons on the Green, quiet mornings at Lissome Ground, even dinners at his table, always she remembered the sensations of contentment, simplicity, comfort. Life was straightforward with Lucius. No pretensions, no rigid etiquette, no false courtesy. He was a genuine man in a charlatan landscape. He did not even mind that she often fell all over herself within that landscape. He was just there to catch her.

Up until last night, anyway. She flinched, ashamed of the thought and aggravated by the recollections it brought.

She had been invited to a dinner party the previous evening. It was hosted by her father's aunt's sister-in-law; a matronly woman, widowed three times over and living in an extravagant house with three schnauzers. It promised to be a large party, but Alexcena thought it only polite that she go. Upon her arrival she spooked one of the carriage horses. The animal started and almost kicked back in Alexcena's direction. Thankfully, he did not, but she reacted reflexively, jumping back and promptly stumbling in the mire of the street. This was an omen as to just how low the evening would sink. She entered the party, spattered in mud from the knees down, to find that Rodney Dushaw had been invited along with his blond conquest, Elida Morgan.

Lady Elinor Elliot-Lawrence's aunt's sister-in-law-was determined that Alexcena should be clamped close to her side at all times since they were the only two "unattached" ladies there. She also kept Ms. Morgan close by, pronouncing her 'the best and most delightful of any of her young, unlearned acquaintances.' Alexcena did not see it. Not only that, but wherever Elida was, Rodney was close at hand. Still Alexcena made an effort at conversation with the young woman while suppressing her own discomfiture and diligently ignoring Rodney. He did his level best to force her to notice him. She could not help fantasizing that one of Lady Elliot's pesky little schnauzers would notice him with its teeth.

Alexcena shook her head, refusing to dwell on the most unpleasant evening of her London experience by far. She had just managed to thoroughly put it from her mind when she heard the housekeeper at the front door. Another well-meaning caller, no doubt. She welcomed the thought readily. A pleasant visit and a cup of coffee were just what she needed at present. What with Lucius being gone a few days longer than he had predicted, it was becoming difficult to keep herself distracted when she was alone.

It was bluntly disheartening to hear the maid at the parlor door saying-

"Rodney Dushaw to see you, ma'am."

Alexcena's eyes bulged momentarily. "What, I-"

"He claims he must speak to you as a matter of urgency, ma'am."

She digested this. "No. Please inform him that I am unavailable for visitors and send him away. *Far* away."

"Yes, ma'am."

Alexcena fell back against the deep armchair when she was left alone. The man was inescapable! *No,* she corrected. *I shall escape him well enough when I am married. He will not dare approach me then.* She toyed absently with her left hand, her fingertips caressing her engagement ring and tracing the space that would soon be covered by a second band.

"I came by reason of great importance, and I *will* not leave until I have spoken with her!"

Alexcena leapt to her feet just as Rodney darted around Mills and into the parlor.

"Sir!"

"Alexcena, I-"

Mills put a firm hand about Rodney's elbow. After a fleeting black look, Rodney turned his attention back to Alexcena.

"I have come to tell you that your trust is misplaced."

"Is this about Lucius?"

"I'm afraid so."

Alexcena's eyes narrowed coldly, and for an instant the room sparked with silent tension.

"Shall I show him out, ma'am?" Even as Mills voiced this question, he made a firm step toward the door.

"Not just yet." Alexcena tried in vain to smooth her features, now taught with fury, as she glared at her intruder. "Mr. Dushaw, allow me to make something perfectly clear to you once and for all. Whatever intentions you may entertain towards me, they are for naught. I am bound to Lucius Wolgath by love, and soon by marriage. I have tried to show my impartiality toward you and have never encouraged you. This fixation, which you have exhibited so shamelessly time and again is at an end. And now I will have Mills dismiss you, and if you ever attempt to approach me unaccompanied and unchaperoned again, my reactions will not be so discrete."

"I came to give you this."

She almost had her back completely turned when he blurted these words. He produced a folded square of paper from his pocket.

"You need not believe me, nor ever speak to me again if you wish." His voice was low, humbled. She saw now the dark smudges beneath his eyes. He shrugged limply. "Were you any other woman, I know you would hate me for sharing this. Justifiably so, but, pious as you are…" He shrugged again and offered the paper. "I cannot stand how this will hurt you, but you must know."

And Alexcena wavered. Against all reason, she took the page and moved close by the window to unfold it. A feminine script danced in neat lines across it.

"This is not Lucius' handwriting," she said dryly.

"It is not from him but to him."

My darling Wolgath.

The words made her breath catch. Her hands clutched the note convulsively. She took a moment to set these words and her emotions aside and read on;

Too long it has been since last we met at Cambridge. I regret that Rodney was with me then, and we could not share a more intimate rendezvous together.

The paragraph went on in this vein, so she skipped ahead.

It is torment awaiting your return, especially now that I cannot seem to rid myself our mutual friend, Mr. Dushaw. Even so, rest assured that I know your decision to be the right one. Taking the job in Eastbourne was infinitely kinder than taking the position at Cambridge. Your Alexcena will appreciate it in the end. This distance can only serve as a balm to her once we are gone.

She read no further. There was no need. Her thoughts swam incoherently. She wrenched her gaze from the page to stare out the window. An expression of most concentrated sorrow swept across her face.

"I found that on Elida's desk," Rodney murmured.

"Did you?" Her voice was calm and aloof.

"I approached her with it. She did not deny it. They plan to live together in Eastbourne."

"Really?"

"He sent her a message two days ago saying that the arrangements have all been made. Her trunks left this morning," he snorted.

Alexcena folded the paper, pinching each crease. When she faced him, it was with a look of cool anger. "When you say live together-"

"They intend to elope along the way to their new home," he explained. "Lucius apparently wanted a more lavish wedding, but Elida claims she would not hear of it in light of the two of us."

"And you believe her?"

"Quite frankly, no. I think-" He hesitated to clear his throat. "I wonder if she might be with child."

"Well that's a very nice little detail indeed!"

Rodney's eyes widened. Whatever reaction he had been expecting, this was not it.

Alexcena glowered with unrepentant ire. "This is the most outrageous, insidious, *loathsome* thing you have done thus far to come between us. Or I should say tried to do, because it will not work, *Mr.* Dushaw! Now take your imposter's letter and get out!"

He accepted the letter with a sigh. "Yes," he said resignedly. "I did not want to believe it at first either."

"Out!"

Mills reached out to lay hold of him again, but Rodney went quietly enough. He never looked back and Mills was close on his heels to see him out.

Alexcena felt herself floundering and fell back into her chair. Tremors wracked her body. The mask of anger fell away to reveal the true reaction; the fear. In all the time that Lucius spent at Cambridge, away from her, was it possible that he had met someone else? He said he had lost the position in Cambridge in an unheard of dispute. Then hadn't her father said that he had never known Lucius to fail in a dispute? The unthinkable possibilities rose up in her mind to overpower the memories of Lucius' promises and assurances of his devotion to her alone.

"And he did not argue," she mumbled.

She was speaking of Rodney. Not only did the meticulous man look disheveled and worn, but he also did not argue when she sent him out. He merely nodded at her expression of denial and left. He was not a man to take opposing views so lightly.

"What if…what if…"

Alexcena did not finish her sentence before the first sob overtook her.

Chapter 6
April 22, 1765

For days Alexcena moved through the house in subdued turmoil. Her body followed the motions while her thoughts wandered wildly. One moment she would be awash in a sea of worry, the next stranded on an isle of frustration. Why, oh why hadn't he taken her to Eastbourne! Why hadn't he elected to remain with her?

Now that Lucius' expected time of return was long past, it was impossible to ignore the doubts swarming about her mind. As it was she was not the only one with doubts. A note from her parents soon arrived, to which she responded that Lucius was only delayed. She thought perhaps that it was not a lie since it was possible.

Lydia noticed the change in her more than any of the others. There was a hesitant troubled look to her mistress' lively eyes that concerned her mightily. She had spent the last week attempting to cheer her, but now she sobered, wondering how best to combat the lady's melancholy. She could not help thinking that the best antidote was away in Eastbourne and had better return soon, and it please him (or so the saying goes).

In the six nights that passed after Rodney's visit, Alexcena rarely slept at all. She would retire early only to rise an hour later. Her restlessness was beginning to wear her nerves thin. Thoughts of Rodney and Elida did not do much to soothe them. She would rather think of anyone else in the world, but somehow the two of them always managed to press their way to the forefront of her thoughts just as soon as she would forget them.

She had received a note from Dushaw that afternoon-a message of apology and support-which only served to disturb her further. She gave herself an inward shake and perched in a stiff armchair with her Bible. *I'm working myself into a dither,* she thought sternly. *I refuse to think of Dushaw again tonight!*

There came a sharp thudding at the door. In the stillness of the house, she could hear it even in the upstairs parlor. It was less than a minute later when Lydia appeared in the hall.

"I beg your pardon, miss, but someone has come to see you."

"Me?" Alexcena replied dumbly.

Lydia seemed perturbed. "Yes. A young woman. I hope you don't mind, but I showed her in and led her to the drawing room. Poor thing is drenched through with the rain."

"Of course not." Alexcena was just as baffled as Lydia looked. She donned her robe as she came to her feet. "Why don't you come as well, Lydia. We'll find out the meaning of this."

"Yes, miss."

This visitor was close by the mantel in the drawing room as Lydia had said. Rain water ran down her skirts to pool around her shoes. Her blond hair coiled in damp locks around her shoulders. Alexcena could not restrain the little gasp that came to her when she saw the woman's face. It was Elida Morgan as she had never seen her. The woman's dress was faded with use. Her cloak was thin and her shoes awkward and scuffed. Her cheeks were flushed, and there was a pitiful pinched look to her features. Always before she had been in silks and satins with a distinct air of self-assurance. This was an Elida that Alexcena had never known.

"Ms. Condreve," she choked as Alexcena entered the room.

"El-Ms. Morgan." Alexcena blinked and attempted to smooth away her natural shock.

"No, no, Elida, please."

"Elida. May I ask what you're doing here?"

"I came to speak to you. I confess I have an awful story to tell."

Alexcena felt herself closing down. Her very heart fell under a sudden frost. Rodney had come to tell her of Elida's supposed treachery…and now Elida had come with her own tale.

Alexcena pulled her shoulders taught. "If you have something to say," she murmured, "please do so with dispatch."

"It's about your man, Mr. Wolgath."

"Professor Wolgath."

"Yes." Elida licked her lips. "You know that Rodney does not like him very much."

"Mr. Dushaw is entitled to his own opinion," Alexcena replied frigidly. "Though I fail to see why his poor view of my future husband should be of such urgent concern to me."

"But it should. I fear he is capable of more than you know."

Alexcena was unmoved by this warning. "I don't know what you mean."

"I came here to explain-" Elida broke off. Her bottom lip shuddered and she sniffed involuntarily. She hesitated, her eyes dropping to the polished coffee table standing between the two of them. "I had intended to make my own request first, but…I can't!" The words tore from her throat in a tormented whisper. A sob wracked her wretched frame.

Alexcena felt her resolve beginning to thaw, but still she was cautious. "What has happened, Elida?"

The woman raised her head to gaze squarely at Alexcena. "Professor Wolgath is not where you think he is."

"I don't see how. I saw him aboard the ship myself. He is bound for-"

"No!" Elida exclaimed. "He is still on that ship, but it was never bound for Eastbourne."

Confusion descended on Alexcena. She was expecting a blow of an entirely different form. She could only stare.

"Rodney wrote the letter Wolgath received. There was never any school. There was never any position. And now your professor is on his way to the Americas!"

Perplexity took hold, and Alexcena stared openly at the woman without really seeing her. "But…that's nowhere near Eastbourne."

"The *Scarlet Pride* was never going to Eastbourne. It was only going to America!"

Alexcena felt her hands curl into fists at her sides. She tried to make her mind work, to make her eyes focus, but she could not move passed it. She could not even speak.

Lydia spared no hesitation. She stepped forward, sliding slightly in front of Alexcena. "Are you suggesting that Mr. Dushaw tricked Mr. Lucius onto that ship knowing that it was headed halfway around the world?"

"He hired me to help him. I never knew, never dreamed…I was just supposed to play a part. A harmless farce!"

Elida's tortured voice drew Alexcena from her shock. "No farce is harmless," she replied softly.

"He hates Mr. Lucius that much does he?" Lydia snapped.

"He said that Wolgath stood in his way."

"Well if he did *hire* you," Lydia went on sarcastically, "how can we believe what you're saying to us now?"

"She's telling the truth." Alexcena was certain the moment Elida raised her head. The moment that woman dared to meet her gaze, she knew. The awful truth loomed before her, and she had only moments before the dawning would come.

"I don't know what Rodney will do when he finds out what I've done!" Elida was staring off to one side, her hand cupped against her temple.

"We will keep this quiet." Alexcena was pleasantly surprised that she managed to maintain a steady voice. The other two looked up as though they had forgotten her presence. "We will keep this quiet," she said again. The maid seemed rebellious. "Lydia, will you keep this confidence for me?"

"For *you*." She rounded on Elida. "Her discretion is more than you deserve, you know!"

"I know," Elida replied evenly, "but it is all I have to hope for."

Alexcena's vision began to cloud. There were only seconds left. "Elida, you will return to Rodney and behave no differently than you have thus far."

"Carry on the act?"

"Or do the honorable thing and tell him you're finished. I will be telling my parents and Lucius' brother what has happened, but no one else. The knowledge of your involvement will not go beyond the five of us."

"Thank you." Elida needed no further encouragement, and in an instant she was out the door.

"Lydia-" Only now did Alexcena's voice show the strain. "-call for the carriage and pack some things. We're returning to Penn."

"Yes, miss."

"Tell no one else what has happened," she called after her.

The room swam before her eyes. The specters of known and unknown alike towered as a great cloud before her. Was it possible, she wondered vaguely, to feel such a euphorium of relief and such fear all at once? Her doubts of Lucius' loyalty had vanished so that she could not fathom their very presence in the first place. Her Lucius, a betrayer capable of such treachery as that? Unthinkable! This left her with a wealth of hope and fresh love for her most wonderful Professor Wolgath. The only question that remained was this; would that hope be enough to quell the mighty fear and trepidation which would surely come after this last bout of confusion was passed?

Alexcena had no answer as she fell unconscious to the floor.

Chapter 7
April 23, 1765

It was the distant mumbling of voices which first reached her in the darkness. She struggled to concentrate and distinguished them as that of a man and woman, her mother and father. She also became aware of a presence close beside her, and a gentle breeze moved across her face. This feeling triggered a memory. She recalled standing in the garden at Lissome Ground. It was one of the last memories she had with Lucius. He held her so closely that the stark morning air had barely room to pass between them. That had been the last true goodbye.

Alexcena opened her weary eyes, and a single tear slipped passed her resolve to slide down her cheek.

"Oh, now miss," Lydia crooned. She was kneeling over the bed, fanning her mistress.

Alexcena knew at once that she had returned to Penn. Someone had carried her up to her room. Her cloak lay haphazardly across the foot of the bed. She still wore her robe and nightgown, but her feet were bare.

"Have you a headache?" Lydia asked fussily. "Shall I call for some tea?"

Alexcena brushed the moisture from her cheek and sat up. "No, thank you. I'm fine-I mean I *feel* fine anyway."

She moved slowly from the bed. Her body seemed fine, but her consciousness was not. It was as though every thought was sluggish, struggling to become oriented. The confusion was ebbing slowly, but for the moment she was still listless. Her wandering gaze honed in on the little table by her dressing room. There was a bit of something feathery and white there, which she could not fathom. She moved toward it mechanically, well aware of Lydia's troubled observance. She reached out to pick it up and inspect it further. *Oh, yes.* It was a snippet of the lace trimming to be used on her wedding dress. It was strange that so light an object could weigh so heavily in her palm.

All at once the confusion was gone and with clarity came a sudden stillness. Her mind was silent. It seemed to her as if she could feel time halt and the very seconds begin ticking again. It was the start of a journey. Each fleeting second pounded in her fluttering heart…and she had already lost so many.

Alexcena burst through the open door of the little sitting room adjacent to her own chamber. Her parents were stunned to silence by her sudden appearance, and Lydia hastened to follow. Alexcena ignored all three and went straight to the little writing desk.

"Alexcena, are you quite all right?"

She was already scribbling furiously at a scrap of paper. "As right as I can be, Mother."

"You've had a terrible shock, dear. We worried that-"

Alexcena was barely listening. She straightened and held the hasty note out to Lydia. "Have someone deliver this, please. They'll need to try Lucius' flat if he's not with the hostler."

"Yes, miss."

"Who's that?" Lawrence asked as Lydia scampered from the room.

"Leopold Wolgath," Alexcena replied. "I've asked him to come here. He should know what is going on."

Cecelia winced. "It's just dreadful!" she mumbled and clutched at her collar.

"I know, Mother."

"We don't know that it's true yet," Lawrence commented. "This Ms. Morgan is obviously not trustworthy."

"I agree." Alexcena recalled clearly the tortured look on Elida's features. "But I believe that she was telling the truth about this."

"I don't see how you can be so calm, Alexcena!" Cecelia moaned.

"There now," Lawrence soothed and produced a clean handkerchief for his wife. "Our daughter has never been given to rash reactions."

"But this is so-so-Oh!" Without further adieu, Cecelia fell into sobs. Lawrence drew her close and attempted to quiet her.

Lydia returned. She eyed her employers fearfully and then looked to her mistress. "The message is on its way."

"Excellent. Help me to dress, will you?"

"Yes, miss."

Alexcena was in truth very glad to leave her parents for the next few moments. She was not certain how she would explain what she intended, and her mother's obvious fear made it all the worse. She was painfully aware of each passing minute as she waited for Leo to arrive. It was an odd feeling, as though she had suddenly been pushed into a race and the deadline leered at her over the ever-shrinking gap.

They waited in the study. Lawrence stood by the window. Cecelia sat at his desk, still dabbing at her eyes periodically. Alexcena watched them with growing apprehension. Her nerves stretched tighter every moment. When Leo at last strode through the door, it seemed as if they were suddenly released. She leapt to her feet and smiled in weary relief.

"Leopold!"

"I came as soon as I-what's happened?" His anxiety overtook his manners. He looked to Alexcena. "You wrote that it was about Lucius, but-"

"He's on a ship bound for America," Lawrence declared, turning from the window.

"What? What about Eastbourne?" Leo's head whipped from one to the other of them in confusion.

"The ship did not stop there," Alexcena explained. "The *Scarlet Pride* was never going there."

"How could this have happened? I saw the passage papers myself!" Leo's voice rose unconsciously.

"A forgery."

Leo froze for a long moment. Alexcena was riveted on his face, willing him to come to the same determination as she. But he still did not fully understand.

"Do you mean to tell me," he said more quietly, "that Lucius was duped?"

"We all were," Lawrence sighed.

Leo rounded on him. "And who is responsible for this, as if I didn't know!"

"Rodney Dushaw," Lawrence confirmed. "He had an accomplice, that Ms. Morgan we've seen him with. She came to Alexcena last night to confess what she had done."

Leo scowled fiercely. "And where is Rodney now?"

"We believe he's still in London. I'll be going there myself to contact the authorities."

"No."

At Alexcena's single word, everyone turned to her in surprise.

"Alexcena!" Cecelia breathed.

"I gave Elida my word that no one would know of her involvement save for us."

"Then we'll leave her out of it," Leo replied stoically, "but we're going after Rodney."

"I don't think we should." She waited for this to sink in and braced herself to go on. "We have no proof whatsoever of his involvement except the word of one woman who is a known liar. Trying to have a well-known professor of Cambridge prosecuted on the sole testimony of an unknown woman will do us little good."

"Especially since women are not permitted to testify in court,"

Lawrence added.

"Precisely," Alexcena agreed. "All it will do is make Mr. Dushaw aware that we know what he has done. He concocted this scheme not only to get at Lucius, but to manipulate me, and I shudder to think what he is capable of next."

"We cannot sit idle," Leo almost snapped. "We'll all go mad!"

"That's not what I'm proposing at all." *Breathe.* "I want to go after Lucius."

Silence reigned. The Condreves displayed shock and confusion. Leo on the other hand gave her a look of approving admiration. It was all the encouragement she needed.

"When Lucius does land in America, he will not have any means by which to return. He will be stranded for months, maybe even years. If we prepare to leave immediately, we will only be four weeks behind him."

"What on earth are you saying, Alexcena?" Lawrence murmured, though he already knew.

"With Mr. Wolgath's help, I'm going after Lucius."

"B-but, the two of you?" Cecelia spluttered. "Your reputation! You-"

"I know, Mother. That is one of the foremost reasons why this must be kept quiet. No one must know where I have gone or who I am with."

"Oh, horrors!" Cecelia cried. "Heaven only knows the dangers you'll face when you arrive there! And how will you even know where you are going?"

"It will be simple enough to find out which port the *Scarlet Pride* was heading for."

"Any number of things could go wrong!" The poor woman flipped out her fan and began flapping it feverishly. "Oh, horrors!"

Alexcena looked to Leo. "Would you be willing to assist me on this journey, Mr. Wolgath?"

Leo flashed a delighted grin and gave her a regal bow. "Ms. Condreve, I'm your man. I'll be there every step of the way to see to your safety," he added for the benefit of her mother.

Alexcena turned to the only one left who had not reacted to her plan.

"Father," she began, "I have never consciously done anything reckless or dangerous in my life. Since I was a child I have done my level best to honor you both in deed and in heart. Please, Father, do not force me to go at this alone."

Lawrence remained silent and still. He appraised his daughter and then glanced at Leo before addressing her.

"You have never once given us cause to mistrust you, daughter. You have proven yourself a practical, thoughtful person. It is concern for your safety alone which gives me pause now, but it would seem that it has been spoken for. If you will give me your word that you will strive to be prudent on your journey, then I shall assist you in any way that I am able."

Tears filled Alexcena's eyes, and she could find no words to properly express the wealth of her gratitude. "Thank you, Father!"

Lawrence turned abruptly to Leo. "Sir, if my daughter were proposing to travel with anyone else, I would have refused her immediately."

Leo nodded somberly. The ever-present grin was absent for once. "I understand, sir."

Lawrence's gaze hardened. "Do you?"

Leo made no reply but raised his hand, offering it to the older man.

Lawrence accepted it. "That's done then. I admire you both for this. The courage you have shown today makes me glad to call you daughter-to call you family. I shall be sorry indeed to watch you go."

Alexcena crossed the room in an instant to throw her arms about her father. She would not be leaving for several days yet, but this was the true farewell with him. She remained locked against her father's chest until she saw Leo stepping out the door. She gently slipped away to follow. She longed to offer more comfort to her parents that day-and every day-but the seconds rolled on.

Lucius scrutinized his appearance in the little glass and shook his head. He seemed a mere shadow of himself in that dingy reflection. His eyes were dull and sunken behind his spectacles. He had lost weight, and it showed on his spindly form. The clothes on his back hung loose on his shoulders. His hair was the only aspect of his reflection that seemed familiar to him. It had been knotted and shaggy from two weeks of neglect, but Lucius had combed his close curls and trimmed his beard, which was a harrowing experience in itself being so far out to sea. His pallor was…well pallid. A fortnight of illness had sapped all pigment from him, and the following week spent almost entirely in his cabin had not done much toward recovering it. One cake of soap and a semi-fresh suit of clothes, and he was presentable.

Lucius left the cabin and somehow made his way to the officer's mess adjacent to the galley. Originally intended for the crew, it had been converted for passengers' use. Lucius had been dining either in his own cabin or the galley, so he had not yet visited this part of the ship. Mrs. Hatchens, her two children, and Mr. Gibbs were already assembled there. They stared openly when Lucius appeared in the door.

"Why, Mr. Wolgath," Mrs. Hatchens smiled at last. "Do join us."

He bowed. "I thank you." He took a seat across from the lady at the long table.

Silence reigned. Mrs. Hatchens and her daughter seemed pleasant enough, though the little boy eyed him warily. Gibbs nodded in his direction from a few seats away and then began to look very bored. The quiet was soon filled when Gurt burst through the door bearing three plates.

"Here ye go, ma'am," he said as he set the meal before the lady and her children. "I do 'pologize for the delay, but the gristle stuck to me pan. Now then, Mr. Gibbs-oh, and Professor Wolgath, sir. I'll be back in a tick with som'at for you gents." He disappeared and returned in a moment with two more plates.

"Thank you," Lucius said mechanically just before he noticed the round green thing Gurt dropped beside his platter. "What's this?"

"Lime."

Without so much as a warning, the burly cook produced a knife as long as a cutlass and slammed it down on the table. The lime fell in two halves.

"You look a mite scurvy-like to me," he said by way of explanation as he wiped the blade on his apron. "Eat up now."

Lucius swallowed and lifted his fork. His nerves had been stretched to the limit for a week now, and Gurt's knife-wielding had not been a help to them.

"You're not gonna get sick again, are you?"

"Matty!" Mrs. Hatchens *tsked* at her son and gave Lucius an apologetic look.

Lucius flashed a weak smile and turned to the little boy. "I won't if you won't, young man."

"We've all heard of your predicament," the woman remarked after a moment. "I'm plenty frightened going to America on purpose, but you don't seem worried at all."

"I don't intend to stay," Lucius told her. "I'll be there one day, maybe two. Just until I can find a ship heading back to England. In the end this will simply be a minor inconvenience and an adventure to laugh at in my old age."

Gibbs' head snapped up at that. He gave Lucius a queer look and returned to his meal. Mrs. Hatchens was somber for a moment and then her features lightened.

"How fortunate for you."

Lucius could not have missed the doubt in the expressions of his fellow passengers, but he dismissed it. He was assured of all that he had said to them. Everything would go exactly as he had said that it would, because it had to. If it didn't, he was fairly certain that he would go mad.

Chapter 8
April 28, 1765

The hem of Alexcena's skirt whispered against the carpet as she paced. This small sound was not nearly enough to fill the silence of the wide parlor. Her parents sat at one end of the room pretending to read and watching her anxiously.

The Condreves had come to their London home the day before. Leopold-who had arrived there two days prior-met them briefly to say that he had been unable to find a ship.

"Not one that I trust, anyway."

Lawrence had raised his brows at that. "Excuse me?"

"We could leave in the next hour if we chose. There are dozens of vessels willing to go if someone will pay their fees." Alexcena shifted forward eagerly, but Leo held up a hand. "It's not simply a matter of finding a crewed frigate. We will be at sea with these men-" His gaze narrowed meaningfully, and she dropped her eyes. "-for many weeks. I will not settle for sailing with anyone who is inexperienced, incompetent, or, worst of all, fool hardy. The crew is not the only matter to deal with here. They could be the best seamen since the Carnatic Wars, and it would not do us a bit of good if they sailed in a creaking tub that would sink halfway to America."

"Yes," Alexcena murmured. "Of course, you're right."

Leo laid a gentle hand on her arm. "I will find what we need."

He spent every waking moment on the wharves to no avail. Although he was clearly disgruntled, he seemed unsurprised by this turn of events. Alexcena, meanwhile, was quickly losing her sense of control. Frantic flutters assailed her chest at times, and she found that she had developed an odd habit of pulling at her fingers. By her third day in Town she was constantly fighting to hold her calm. Even when Leo did find a ship it would be longer still until she reached her destination. How was she to last seven full weeks at sea!?

Leo burst into the room, not bothering to wait for an announcement, and shouted, "I've done it!"

Alexcena felt relief sweep throughout her body in a surprisingly potent wave. She stared dumbly, allowing the tide of comfort to wash over her and completely cover the memory of the last three endless days.

"What news, m'boy?" Lawrence asked as he came to his feet.

"Forgive me," Leo pulled awkwardly at his collar. "Good evening Mr. Condreve, Mrs. Condreve, Ms. Condreve." He cleared his throat, reining his former excitement. "I have found us a ship!"

Alexcena sighed, breathing a word of thanks.

"A frigate called *Liberator,*" Leo went on. "She's captained by Sir William Loughdon."

Condreve's brow furrowed. "Seems I've heard the name."

"He was knighted in the court of King George II several years back. He heard stories of merchant ships being attacked by freebooters in the Caribbean seas. Off he goes; commissions a ship, hires a crew, and teaches himself to sail on the way down. It was quite a story at the time."

"Yes!" Lawrence declared. "I remember it clearly now. He stayed down there two years and didn't catch sight of a single pirate vessel."

"So they say. By the time he returned, he had lost the interest and support of the people."

"But he's willing to help us?" Alexcena interjected, growing harried.

"Reluctantly. Loughdon is a very gruff fellow." He cast a wry glance at her. "He has requested one hundred pounds pay for each of his men and one hundred fifty for himself. That comes to seven hundred and fifty, and he's also asking for a passenger fee."

Lawrence nodded curtly. "We have assured Alexcena that we will provide whatever sum is necessary to complete this venture."

"Good," Leo replied, "because that is exactly how much we're going to need."

"When do we leave?" the lady wondered.

"Two days."

The words echoed strangely in Alexcena's mind. *Two days.* The foremost rational part of her rejoiced at the prospect of departing so soon. A small, hidden corner of her mind moaned at the thought of the forty-eight hours that stretched before her. And how much more powerful would that underlying madness be when she was trapped aboard a frigate for seven weeks?

Lucius had always been a sociable man in close settings. True, he did not take much enjoyment from large parties or crowded dinner tables for he preferred a smaller circle of acquaintance. He had imagined just before coming to the *Scarlet Pride* that he might befriend a few of his fellow passengers, even in the short journey he was anticipating. It was odd even to him that he now preferred to spend his days alone.

He walked the decks aimlessly, feeling much like a wild bird that has been suddenly captured; confused and caged. The other passengers learned to ignore him to a degree, as it was obvious that conversation was not something he was overly interested in. The sailors merely nodded when he caught their eye, but then they treated all the voyagers this way. Captain Davy, unlike his subordinates, did try to strike up a dialogue with him, but soon gave up on each attempt.

So it was on one of many sleepless nights that Lucius found himself at the railing of the quarter deck watching the waves roll by. The line of the horizon was undefined, merged by the reflection of the night sky in the black sea. He drummed his fingers on the smooth wood and stared unseeing at the dark water, humming to himself.

"Professor Wolgath?"

"Oh!" Lucius turned abruptly. "Mrs. Hatchens! Good evening."

The rush of the water had covered the lady's approach. He did not notice her presence until she spoke close beside him.

"Forgive me, I couldn't help overhearing," the lady said by way of an apology. "Were you humming something?"

Lucius gave his head a little shake, struggling to remember the tune. "I was just recalling a song I know." He hummed a few bars, the fingers of his left hand moving again involuntarily. "I can't seem to remember it now."

She nodded. "That's an odd way of tapping to a song."

Lucius stupidly looked at his hand. "'Tis a reflex, I suppose. I play an instrument, the violin. My fingers are recalling their positions."

"I did not know you played."

"Yes." He flexed his digits and chuckled shortly. "Odd that my hand remembers the song better than I."

She nodded again, but Lucius was staring out to sea now.

"I do miss that-being able to make music. I chose not to bring my instrument along when I left because I was concerned about what the salty air would do to it. It's a good thing I didn't too. Heaven knows what state it would have been in by the time I finally arrive back in England."

"Perhaps you shall have the opportunity to play more in America."

"I'm not going to America."

Mrs. Hatchens bit her lip. His face had taken on some hard lines at this, and she was well aware that she had upset him.

"Not really anyway," Lucius amended when he saw her look. "To say that you're going somewhere implies that you're staying for a given length of time. I have no intention of doing so."

The lady was not certain how she should reply, for it was obvious to her that he was in some sort of denial. She was still debating within herself when Lucius interrupted her thoughts.

"Why is your family headed for the Colonies, Mrs. Hatchens?"

The woman smiled, glad that the younger man seemed inclined to talk for once. "We're going to join the rest of my family. My husband and my eldest son went ahead one year ago to find our land and build our new home. We are going to meet them there."

"One year?" Lucius raised his eyebrows. "That must have been difficult indeed to bear!"

"Yes," she replied in a placid tone. "We have been staying with my parents until such time as we could depart."

"I admire you, ma'am. I have been away from my Alexcena just over four weeks and already the feeling seems insufferable."

"Granted, however, our separation was by design, not mistake. And you will be returning soon, yes?"

Lucius was silent for so long that she began to wonder if the conversation was over. His hands gripped the railing convulsively as he continued to gaze at the sea.

"I have very little money with me," he murmured thickly. "Next to none. How will I return to England?"

His mood changed with no warning in the space of one breath. The instant this thought had formed on his lips, his mind turned from it, and he smiled graciously to his kind companion.

"I expect I shall find a way. Good evening, Mrs. Hatchens."

He bowed and strode away before she had time to reply. It occurred to him in a strangely detached way that perhaps this was why he had withdrawn into himself so deeply. If he did converse freely with any of the others on board, there was a good chance that they would press through his threadbare defense and force him to realize the truths he was so desperately trying to hide from. His predicament was far worse than he was able to admit.

Chapter 9
April 30, 1765

"You cannot keep at this."

Cecelia Condreve set the small tray down rather hard on the end table. Alexcena was curled up in the overstuffed chair beside it, her head resting in her palm. When her mother set the tray down, she looked up, startled from her doze.

Cecelia settled primly on the settee across from her. "You've not been eating enough, and I know you haven't slept in days."

Alexcena looked blankly down at the tray, and her stomach groaned at the sight of the bread and cuts of chicken in gravy on the plate. She lifted the fork and set to it without hesitation. Although Alexcena cut the habitual mincing bites expected of a lady, she took them as quickly as breath.

"Why don't you go and lie down for a bit?" Cecelia suggested. "The rest will do you good before you leave tomorrow."

"I can't," Alexcena replied as she smoothly buttered her bread. "Leopold has been arranging the remainder of the supplies all morning. I want to catch up to him and make sure he was able to secure all that we shall need."

"Leopold?"

"Hmmm." Alexcena swallowed a long drought of milk. Her mother was silent, and that fact alone was odd enough to make her look up. "What is it, Mother?"

Cecelia pouted, deliberated, and tilted her chin up. "I do not think you should be embarking on this venture."

Alexcena watched her with caution.

"If someone must go, then Mr. Leopold is more than capable of going himself. Your place is here at home!"

"I cannot do that, Mother."

"You should be here with your family as our daughter!" The passion and pleading alternately manipulated Cecelia's features.

Alexcena set the plate aside. She rose and moved to kneel by her mother's chair. "I will always be your daughter, but do not forget that I will become Lucius' wife as well."

Cecelia hesitated, taken aback by her manner. "So your duty, your loyalty; they fall to him now?"

Alexcena folded her hands in her lap. "In many ways...yes. In becoming his wife is it not right that he will also become the head of my household?" It was a simple question, full of meaning. She hoped against hope that her mother would understand.

Cecelia looked away and sighed. "We are women. We follow where our men lead."

Alexcena twitched a sheepish smile. "Yes."

"You have to go…don't you?"

"Yes." Alexcena felt all the conviction of her aching heart exposed in her look and voice.

Cecelia nodded and produced a handkerchief from her sleeve. She sniffed daintily and shuddered one last time as she dabbed her eyes. "Very well, daughter."

Rodney's lips spread into a malignant grin when he saw her leave the house. He was milling about in an alley angled across the street from the Condreve's London abode, as he had done several times since he learned of their hasty arrival. So it was that he saw Alexcena very clearly when she appeared on the doorstep, waved a tall groomsman away, and set off down the busy street.

He clamped his hat on his head and broke into a brisk pace, shadowing her movements. She was walking quickly, and he would need to be ahead of her. He managed to gain one block, and crossed the rutted road, throwing himself in her way. Alexcena had paused to look around. She stretched to see over the heads of the passers-by surrounding them, but when she turned Rodney was waiting. She rammed into his side with her shoulder and bounced back in shock.

"Goodness, I-" Her eyes focused and widened. "What are you doing here?"

Rodney smiled in genuine amusement at the astounded-indeed almost frightened-expression on her ivory features. "I have not left London since last you saw me here."

Her mouth worked as she struggled to collect herself. "Are you not needed at Cambridge, Professor?"

"The term has ended. I shall be returning there next month."

They stood in close proximity to one another on the crowded avenue. He inhaled appreciatively of her light perfume.

She moved her head in an odd way, as though it was all she could do to look at him without rolling her eyes. "Good *day*, sir."

She stepped around him, but he would not let her away so easily. In fact he rather enjoyed the challenge. He whirled after her and touched her wrist before she had scarcely taken a single step.

"How are you, Alexcena?" He carefully tempered his voice with concern. "I worry about you so since this calamity occurred."

She had faced him to jerk her hand away, though he had not grasped it. Now she cinched her teeth together. "Well enough."

"Poor, dear lady. This must be so hard for you to bear," Rodney said coolly. The predator luring his prey. "But you need not bear this alone."

"Do not concern yourself."

Not too strong now. "Very well. I can see that you are still deeply wounded by all that Lucius and Elida have done. I am a patient man, Ms. Condreve, and you are a rare lady. A sharper woman I have never met. When all of this initial astonishment has gone, I will be here…if you'll have me. I will be a willing savior to your mending heart."

"I'm afraid that position was filled long ago upon the tree," she replied evenly. "Besides it is plain to see that the only comfort you are capable of offering is a net of roses. It may break the fall, but it is laced with hidden thorns."

He blinked, momentarily befuddled. "On the contrary. Mine is a net of-hyacinths."

"But a net nonetheless," Alexcena retorted more coldly now. "And I refuse to be its catch." She turned abruptly, raising one arm in greeting, and leaving Rodney to flounder amid her scathing remarks. "Leopold!"

Rodney glared, scrutinizing the man who approached at her call. This Leopold was maybe ten years his senior and a good six inches taller. His rugged garb was accentuated sharply by the pistols at his waist and the wide belt crossing his chest. The firm muscles of his arms and torso pressed the sleeves of his coat and the fabric of his shirt. He was a man well prepared to defend himself and others as he saw fit.

Rodney swallowed against the anger that burned his throat, and managed to smooth his countenance into a more placid expression. Leopold's pleasure at his discomfiture was apparent, though not as apparent as the menacing glare about his eyes.

"Mr. Wolgath has been helping me extensively as of late."

Rodney flinched. "Wolgath?" he growled.

"Lucius' brother."

Leo was standing as close to Alexcena as her wide skirts would allow. The man was watching her, but Rodney had the distinct impression that he was looming toward him.

"Is everything all right, Ms. Condreve?"

"Forgive me," she replied. "I was just dealing with a minor problem."

"I should be more than happy to help you with it."

Leo's gaze flickered to Rodney with a sneer, and he seethed beneath it.

"Not necessary. Professor Dushaw and I were just saying good day."

They looked to him blankly. Rodney fought for a clever reply, but there was nothing he could do. He had been dismissed.

"Good day, then, Ms. Cond-"

The pair turned to go before he had even finished. Rodney knew with a sudden sickening clarity that it was over. The plotting, the scheming, even the success, had all come to naught. He had managed to cut in on the dance, but now the music had ended and his partner was leaving the floor with another. So Rodney did the unthinkable. He did what all men of his character do in some fashion or another when they finally realize that they have been overcome beyond retaliation. He went home to cower.

Chapter 10

April 30, 1765

Lucius' days-much like his view-were a relentless monotony. He wandered the deck, staring out at the rhythmic rise and fall of the waves surrounding them all, pulling his coat tighter about his gaunt frame against the stark winds. Every so often his fingers would trail down into his pocket to stroke the silk of Alexcena's cameo necklace. He kept it tied to the inside of his waistcoat, so great was his fear of losing it at sea. Every once in a while he would remove it so that he might look at it in the light, as though he would ever lose sight of its appearance in his mind. He was doing this very thing when Smith Darlum happened upon him that day.

"Professor!"

Lucius was amazed at the grating sound his own title made on the lips of this man. Darlum clapped him on the back and fell into step beside him. He was the only one on board who was not content to leave Lucius well enough alone. Ironically, he was also the only passenger on board whose presence Lucius could not stand.

"What are you at today, sir?"

Lucius glanced at him and then away. "I'm walking."

"You say that every day."

"Because it's true."

"Yea, but why not put some personality into it?" Darlum was often not satisfied with merely voicing a suggestion; he was given to demonstrations.

"'Taking a jolly old stroll about the deck.' Or how about, 'Treading the boards in boredom.' 'Ahoy there! Taking a turn about the *Pride*.' That last one was rather good wasn't it?"

"You ought to be a poet."

"Nay. I'm too impetuous for that scholarly stuff. Why've you always got your hand in your pocket?"

Lucius stopped midstride, visibly thrown by the question. He instantly yanked his hand out and clasped them both behind his back.

"You got some gold in there or something?"

"No, its-" Lucius was not certain what he had planned to say, and he was never forced to find out. In a flash Smith's hand was in and out of his pocket with the necklace.

"Ugh! What's this ragged ol' thing?"

"Stay there!"

"What?" Smith was completely perplexed by Lucius' sudden shout.

"Don't move, Darlum."

Wolgath's firm tone was enough to paralyze him on the spot. Only the man's eyes moved, flitting around in search of any impending danger. Without another word Lucius snatched the ribbon cameo from his grasp and stalked away.

"You're a weird one, aren't you, Professor?" Smith muttered at his retreating back.

"And a good day to you, Mr. Darlum!"

As he walked, he could not help but chuckle at the astounded expression that had come to Darlum as he stood there. It felt strange to laugh. The very sound of it coming from his own lips sounded foreign to him. He shook his head and smiled down at the cameo necklace in his palm. The distant, merry sound of fair Alexcena's laughter echoed in his memory.

"We have shared our humor, haven't we?" he sighed as he tucked the thing away.

"Professor Wolgath?"

Lucius looked up to see Captain Davy approaching him.

"I hope you haven't taken to talking to yourself, sir."

Lucius tweaked a smile. "Not quite."

"Just as well," Davidson shrugged. "Many's the time I found myself without company and tempted to do the same. I was told you wanted to see me?"

"Yes, I did. Thank you for taking the time to find me."

"Not a hard task."

Now that the opportunity had come for Lucius to broach his proposal, he found that he was intensely eager to do so. He determined to forego any inane banter. "I have a request to make of you, Captain, regarding my current predicament."

Davidson looked him up and down, and sighed. "I thought you might eventually. What have you to say, then, Professor?"

"I find myself in need of a return passage to England," Lucius declared. "Naturally, I do not have the funds for such a thing on hand. I was hoping that you would be willing to waive the cost of the voyage until we reach London. Do you intend to sail for England right away?"

"Yes, as a matter of fact," Davidson replied. "We'll be receiving a shipment of tobacco to transport back to England. We shan't stay more than three or four days in America, but I'm afraid I cannot help you in this respect."

Just as Wolgath's hopes began to rise, they again came crashing down. "You can't?"

"If I were to do this for you, others would surely follow. Travel is an expensive commodity these days, and I cannot afford to have my decks swamped by unfortunates. Also there is the Company to consider. My employers would not look kindly on my allowing free passage to anyone."

"But I'm not asking for free transportation at all!" Lucius insisted hurriedly. "All I am asking is that you wait to collect the money until I have reached England, just as you would any indentured servant."

Davidson was considering, and did not seem convinced.

"I think it only fair to mention that I am very close to certain wealthy citizens of the country," Lucius added. "They would be more than willing to make my speedy return worth your while." It sickened him to think of asking Lawrence for such assistance, but in light of what he faced it was of no consequence.

"Very well, Professor," Captain Davy said at last. "I have determined over the last few weeks that you are a trustworthy soul, expecting the same of others. If you don't mind my saying so, I believe that may be the very quality which has made it so easy for you to come into this mess."

"Yes, sir."

"I will personally guarantee you a place on board when we return. We'll look at this as a loan between the two of us. That way, I can show that you have paid in full in my ledgers, and you may pay me back as you are able."

Lucius felt almost weak with relief. His anxiety over this had been greater than he realized. "Thank you, Captain." He grasped the shorter man's hand and shook it with a vigor.

Davy chuckled again and laid his free hand on Lucius' shoulder. "My conscience would have plagued me if I'd left you behind anyhow."

Lucius turned to face the wind as Davidson moved away. Though he was hundreds of miles away, in that single moment he felt closer to England than he had in weeks.

Chapter 11

May 1, 1765

The day came at long last, but, as anxious as Alexcena was to leave, she was reluctant to be gone. It was her parents that worried her. Suddenly it was not their concerns that bothered her, but her own. Their unspoken thoughts, 'Will we ever see you again,' had been reversed in her mind; 'Will I ever see *you* again?' The frightening possibilities had always been there, of course, but they had been a mere footnote up until that morning. It seemed selfish of her to consider them only now, when the moment had come, and she grimaced with guilt as she faced her mother and father in the foyer.

Cecelia was looking bleary-eyed as she did so often these days. Her lower lip trembled and she pressed it tight against her teeth. Lawrence appeared downright murderous. His brow was dark and low, and his hands clenched convulsively at his sides. His features were sulled up as though he were concentrating with distinct intent.

Alexcena moved forward to embrace her mother. While Lawrence would accompany her to the wharves, Cecelia had elected to remain at the house. This was to be their good-bye.

"Are you certain, Alexcena?"

She closed her eyes and whispered, "Do not worry after me, Mother. Mr. Wolgath will be there to protect me." She straightened then and offered her smile.

Lawrence grunted. "He is a sturdy fellow, isn't he?"

"Mmm."

Cecelia sighed, still holding her daughter's hands. "I don't see how you'll get on. You can't be carrying more than three dresses with you." She was looking down at Alexcena's meager satchel.

"Two actually, but I shan't need more than that, and it will only make the traveling easier."

"Yes," Cecelia conceded, though she still looked doubtful. "Yes, of course."

A low rap sounded at the door behind them, and Claire-the little maid who was standing off to one side-hurried to answer it. Leo stood at the threshold with an authentic seaman's canvas bag slung over his shoulder and a broad grin.

"Morning all, ma'am," he greeted, bowing graciously to the ladies. "I hate to pop in in a rush, but the Captain was quite explicit about his time of departure. Is this yours, Alexcena?" He lifted the satchel without really waiting for her reply.

"Yes, thank you." She looked to her mother again, anxious to be done with the tearful adieu.

"Take care, my dear, and write me if you can."

Alexcena swallowed and reached for her once more. In the end Lawrence guided her to the door when her own tears had clouded her vision. The men occupied themselves in the carriage, allowing her time to collect herself before they reached the water's edge. She made dogged attempts to listen to their conversation.

"What is this ship like?" Lawrence inquired at one point.

"It's a smart little frigate," Leo replied. "Only two masts, but she boasts good speeds, and she's well armed. Twenty-five guns."

"Twenty-five?"

Leo smiled wryly then. "For just such an emergency." There was a pause, and he added, "She's a bit ragged 'round the edges, but she's sturdy where it counts. I'd bet my life on her."

"And the Captain?"

"He's a bit ragged 'round the edges too."

Alexcena pondered this last bit until they reached the wharf, but it was not until then that she truly understood what Leo was implying.

The *Liberator* was not a large vessel by any means, but that made her all the more conducive to their purpose. The sails were furled at the yardarms of two fine masts. Even from the shore, she could see that the boards of the hull and deck were worn to a uniform smoky gray with age. Men moved across her deck and rigging, not in a harried fashion, but rather in confident, coordinated steps. Even amid the activity, it was the figurehead of the vessel that caught her interest. An English soldier was depicted there with a large flag billowing out across his chest. The flag was exquisitely sculpted, seeming to roll in the very wind that blew across it. This was not the King's flag, however; it quite clearly showed a skull and crossbones.

"Strange," she murmured. "What flag is that?"

Leo followed her gaze. "That's the Jolly Roger," he explained. "Or a Jolly Roger as it were. Most pirates have their own version."

"Why should the captain want a pirate flag and not the Union Flag?"

"I asked Captain Loughdon about that when I hired him," he replied. "He said that it was to show the buccaneers that England would give as good as she got."

A deep-throated bark drew their attention. Alexcena grimaced painfully when she saw Commodore bounding toward them. She backed only a few steps away before her father caught her about the waist. Leo, on the other hand, stooped to meet the animal.

"Hello, there! How are you, good boy?"

He rubbed Commodore's ears and neck with a vigor. Commodore yelped gleefully and would have licked Leo across his face, but he pulled deftly out of reach.

Alexcena realized as she watched that her hands were gripping wildly at her skirts, as though gathering them to run. She relaxed them and licked her dry lips. "W-why did you bring him?"

"Lucius asked me to look after his dog," Leo answered without looking up. "I couldn't leave the poor brute behind. But he's a swell ol' thing, eh Commodore?"

"Surel-ely you don't intend to take him aboard," she said tentatively.

Leo heard the strange catch in her words and rose to face her. "Does he bother you so much?"

"They *all* do."

"Of course, I had forgotten."

It was obvious that he was anxious now, and Alexcena considered the predicament she had placed before him. He had given Lucius his word that he would care for the dog, and he would feel guilty if he left him behind. Then, too, he would sooner leave Commodore here than to have her feeling nervous or afraid in any way. She was certain of that as she studied his handsome face, now watching her with apprehension. Commodore sat behind him. One of his great ears was flipped at an odd angle. His tail thumped in perfect rhythm as he waited for them to work out their own silly problems. Harmless.

She stretched the corners of her mouth into a small, tight smile. "He's not really so bad, I'm sure," she demured. "I will need the practice after all if I am to be Lucius' wife."

Leo relaxed visibly, and that at least pleased her over the prospect of spending seven or more weeks at sea with a dog. Not to mention the return voyage.

"Now see here!" Lawrence snapped and pulled his daughter close to his side. He shook a severe finger at the younger man. "I trust you,

Wolgath, but you had best not allow this, or any beast, to come near my daughter. Understood?"

Leo made no answer, but silently offered his hand. Lawrence accepted it.

"I'm looking for the *Liberator*! Can anyone tell me where to find the *Liberator*! Halloo! the *Liberator*!"

"Who's that?" Leopold was instantly wary as he looked off down the way at the man who was so boisterously calling for their ship.

Alexcena and Lawrence turned in unison, and she recognized the man who was blundering his way along. "That's Uncle Harrison!"

"Harry?" Lawrence puzzled. "What on earth is he doing here? Harry!"

Harrison Winslett grinned and waved as he fought his way toward them. "Hew! Bit dangerous here abouts, isn't it? But thank the blue skies I found you!" he exclaimed, moping his forehead with his frilled cuff as he spoke.

"What are you doing here, Harrison?" Lawrence demanded, wholly unabashed.

"Well, I came to see Ms. Alexcena off, didn't I?"

Alexcena felt very nervous once again. Her uncle spoke as if this should be obvious. "But how did you know, Uncle?"

"Seems one of your men told one of our maids who mentioned it to Deborah who immediately asked Cecelia about it. Deborah in turn told me, because she is so terribly worried for you."

Leo raised an eyebrow. "Through the gnarled grapevine, eh?"

"Just so," he replied. "But I want you all to know that I am wholly ignorant as to the reasoning behind this junket. Cecelia impressed the need for secrecy quite clearly on Deborah-who in turn impressed it upon me. She did not reveal a single detail other than to say that you were going on a voyage that would take you away for some time. The whole situation goes against the grain for me-allowing my fair niece to travel unaccompanied-but I trust my brother-in-law's judgment enough not to stand in your way." He meant the last part as a joke, and bowed slightly in Lawrence's direction.

Alexcena rubbed her temples and breathed to calm her nerves. "Now that you know, Uncle, you will hold to our pact of discretion, won't you?"

"Indeed!" He held up one hand. "There'll not be one word from me."

"I do hate to break this up, but we really must be going." Leo's gaze was turned toward the *Liberator*. He did not look like he hated to go; in fact he seemed just as disgruntled as she was.

"You're going as well?"

All eyes turned to Harrison at this.

He pasted a grin on his face and half shrugged. "Right. Mum's the word. Farewell, young lady!" He bowed low over Alexcena's hand and retreated.

She smiled fleetingly and faced her father. Her heart twisted painfully at the sight of his brave face. Lawrence held out his arms and drew her close. She pressed her face against his shoulder, willing the tears to hold back.

"You take care now," he murmured into her hair.

She pulled back and was astonished that she was able to give him a smile. "I will."

Lawrence nodded, returning the sentiment. "There's something else."

He reached into his waistcoat and produced a letter. The paper was stiff and heavy. It seemed to hold several pages, for it was very thick. The entire outside was coated with a thin layer of tallow, thus protecting it from the elements. She accepted it curiously.

"I want you to deliver that to your Lucius when you find him. Alexcena, this is very important."

She raised her eyes.

Lawrence hooked one finger under her chin, and said quite seriously, "Under no circumstances are you to open it."

Her eyebrows puckered, but she nodded to assure him of her obedience. "Yes, Father." She felt the pressure of Leo's hand on her arm, and she took one tentative step away, though she was still watching her father with an almost frightened look.

He released her chin and offered another sad smile. "Farewell, daughter."

She nodded and allowed Leopold to steer her away.

Leo led the way up the plank walk to the deck, and Alexcena did her level best to ignore the sound of Commodore's paws as he ambled up behind her. They were within two steps of the deck when she could stand it no more. She moved past Leo in one long stride to stumble aboard. He grasped her forearms lightly to steady her.

"Whoa! Are you all right there?" he chuckled.

Commodore moved by them with an odd groan, as if to say, 'I had nothing whatsoever to do with *that*.'

Alexcena smoothed a loose bit of her hair and nodded. The challenges she knew she would face suddenly seemed overwhelming, but the seconds ticked by, and she was already that much closer to Lucius.

"That's the captain there." Leo gestured toward two men standing together on the quarter deck. "I'll introduce you." He snapped his fingers to Commodore. "Tarry!"

Ever obedient, the animal sat beside their bags.

Alexcena looked the two men up and down. One was lean, wearing an oiled long coat that billowed around him. His red hair was thinning and cropped very close to his scalp. The other was thickly built and slightly taller. He wore a carefully powdered wig beneath his tricorn hat. This alone caused her to assume that he was the senior officer, but she would soon learn that she was mistaken.

Leo paused a few feet from them and neither man showed a sign that they had seen them. Despite this, the lithe one spoke up.

"You're right on time, Mr. Wolgath."

His voice was a low rumble laced with a hint of menace. A tiger growling a warning to another creature that has dared to approach him.

"Might I introduce Ms. Alexcena Condreve?" Leo said. "The other financier of our voyage."

Captain Loughdon turned to her then. The heady breeze blew his coat out behind him. His ruffled shirt and gray breeches were obviously of rich quality, and his black knee boots gleamed brilliant in the light of the sun. A spyglass hung at his hip, somehow attached to the wide belt encircling his waist. Ironically, Sir William Loughdon resembled a pirate captain more than any seaman she had ever met.

She bobbed a curtsy. "'Tis a pleasure Captain Loughdon."

"Indeed." The man dipped his head in slim acknowledgement.

"It is our pleasure, ma'am," the bewigged man said more kindly and offered a gracious bow. "I am Lieutenant John Greyson, first mate aboard the *Liberator.*"

"How do you do, sir."

Greyson smiled at the both of them. The contrast was stark between this man and his captain.

"If there is nothing further," Loughdon turned on his heel back to the railing-clearly not allowing for anything further. "Have Mr. Marks show the passengers to their quarters, Lieutenant."

"Aye, sir."

Greyson produced a small silver whistle and piped out two shrill notes. A sprightly man with wild red hair and a pleasant look leapt up onto the deck to stand at attention.

"Show these good people below decks Mr. Marks."

"Aye, sir!"

Marks touched his forelock and led the way down to the main deck. He lifted their bags and patted Commodore's ears, as though it were the most natural thing in the world to have a dog on board. Alexcena glanced back at the surly Captain once more before they went below. The Lieutenant had moved closer to him and was speaking quietly, his kind expression now quite serious. Loughdon's languid features remained impassive and he raised one eyebrow. That seemed to end whatever comments the Lieutenant was making, but they were lost to sight then as she stepped below.

Marks let Leo's heavy seabag fall and opened two doors which faced each other in the shadowed hall. "That one there is yours, sir, and this one here is the lady's."

Alexcena slipped by him into the larger cabin. Inside she found two bunks stacked one atop the other, a writing table, and a small wash stand. Marks followed and set her satchel on the bed. Something odd caught her attention, but the little man hurried away before she could voice any question about it. Three large trunks were stacked to one side of the wide room.

"I'm glad to see they gave you the larger cabin," Leo said, leaning casually in her door. "Saves me the trouble of offering it to you."

"What do you make of this?" she pointed to the anonymous trunks.

Leo followed her direction and quirked an eyebrow. "Huh. Must be some extra uniforms or something. I think these cabins are just used for storage. They were awfully cluttered when Loughdon showed them to me."

"Hmmm." Alexcena's brow puckered. Somehow the explanation did not seem to cover it. She had an odd, uneasy feeling. Although she had felt much the same since she had determined to go to America.

"Would you like to come up and watch the launch?" Leo asked, seeming eager.

The sails had been loosed by the time they made their reappearance on deck. They stood at the railing off to one side as the men moved to and fro across the decks, puppets directed by the piping of Lieutenant Greyson's silver whistle. They made short work of the lines that held them to shore, and all too soon they were drifting slowly out of port. Alexcena gripped the railing as she watched the shoreline beginning to shrink in their wake. She felt silent tears rolling unbidden from her eyes to be blown across her cheeks by the sharp wind.

Leo leaned back against the railing beside her. To avoid embarrassment, he said nothing about her weeping, but offered her a handkerchief in mute understanding.

"And so we journey," he murmured somberly.

"Yes." Drying her eyes, she turned from the land to watch the movements of the ship with him. "So we do."

Chapter 12
May 1, 1765

Rodney had come to rely on gossip. His desire for Alexcena had created a thirst for knowing all that he was able about her movements. This thirst fueled his ambitious probing in discreet areas until he was well acquainted with the workings of the town of Penn and all that surrounded her. Until Luicus' recent departure, he had also made it a point to know his dealings as well; all the better to best him in some form or another. Fortunately for him the thread of gossip ran rampant in the hamlet. After months of keeping casual, covert tabs, it was only natural that information of Alexcena's chartered voyage would filter back to him.

The town common ground was his chief source of information. It was here that grooms and man servants, as well as the husbands and fathers of maids and housekeepers in the area, would gather while out on various errands. It was here that he heard snatches of a conversation between two men standing near a cart. One was the proprietor of a local bakery, while the other was a man he did not recognize.

"I'll wager that pretty sister of yours will be wanting some more sweet rolls soon, eh?"

"Nay, she's over in London for a few days. The Condreves are closing their London home for the season."

"Why's that, then?"

"They don't plan to use it."

"But I heard tell their daughter was staying there."

"She was 'til she left."

"Come back home has she?"

"No."

"Well, where's she got to then?"

The stranger cocked a brow. "You're eager as an old biddy with your questions."

The baker ignored his comment. "The lady has to be somewhere. If she's not at home and she's not run off and she's not in London then I ask you where is she?"

"She's gone out to sea, if you must know. Left early this morning."

"Why in blazes did she do that?"

"That's what makes it so funny, mate. No one knows. Her parents haven't told anyone, and obviously we can't ask, so we just have to wait and see who finally lets the cat out of the bag. Personally I think it has som'at to do with that professor of hers. You know he was supposed to have returned almost two weeks ago. He's been gone more than a full month now."

"You don't say…"

Rodney lost their words in the rush of his own thoughts after that. Alexcena gone? Where on earth would she *go?* His pulse thundered in his veins. Surely she was not fool enough to go looking for Lucius! *Even if she is it will do her no good, since he is not anywhere near where she thinks he is.* But had she truly gone to Eastbourne? If she had gone there to find him, she would naturally be making inquiries at the port. She was a clever woman. She would discover that the *Scarlet Pride* had never docked there, and where would that lead her? Inquiries about the ship? Questions about her intended destinations? Innocent answers as to those who had purchased passage aboard her?

Rodney was walking very fast along the rutted street. Now he halted at these sudden realizations. His squinty eyes narrowed.

No.

He could not allow such suspicions to go that far. He had to catch up to her-and catch her-long before she made any such conclusions.

Plans began running through his head like scenes in an elaborate play. He would go to his father, make use of certain connections of his to get moving. Elida Morgan had proven herself an invaluable actress. Perhaps he would employ her talents again. He had just the roll for her; the grieving widow. There would be no room left for doubt in Alexcena's mind this time!

These fresh schemes sent his diabolical mind into a near frenzy. The hope of even minute success was enough to push him to dire risks. The combination of fierce rivalry and rampant arrogance left no more room for gentlemanly intelligence. The fact that Alexcena was running *away* from him ought to have been enough to stop him.

The door of his father's manor gave easily before him. *Unlocked. Typical. Thoughtless.*

The house was still and dark. Most of the curtains remained closed even in the early afternoon. This gave Rodney pause. Also, no one had come at his approach. Randolph only kept two or three servants now-and they, bound by indenture contracts, were obligated to stay. No one seemed to have noticed his boisterous entrance. A tiny inkling of fear chilled him.

"Hello?"

He felt idiotic, standing in the foyer and yelling, but the fear was growing stronger.

"Father?"

He moved through the parlors and the dining room, pulling aside curtains as he went. The house remained dank and shadowed. The stairs groaned beneath his feet as he ascended to the second floor, still calling for the mansion's master. It was after the fifth shout, when he was walking into the study, that he allowed his voice to die on his lips.

Randolph Dushaw lay on the musty couch at the far end of the room. His feet were thrown up over one of the arms, as though he was dosing. One hand lay fisted upon his chest, while the other hung loosely over the carpet. The man's face was frozen forever in a derisive, aloof scowl, his eyes only half-closed. Not a breath moved in his chest.

Rodney stepped curiously forward, though he already realized that his father was dead. A victim to his violent consumption, no doubt.

He knelt by the sofa on trembling knees. He very deliberately lifted his father's arm to place it over his chest, crossing the other. He drew his hand down over his brow, closing his eyes forever. He stood then, looking down on this man who had always looked down on him. There were no more thoughts or plans or even fears of suspicion left in his mind. Without a word or a prayer, Rodney spun on his heel and quit the room, slamming the door securely behind him.

Chapter 13

May 1 and 2, 1765

Dawn melded slowly with the day. Its ebbing seemed lazy. The brilliant colors of the rising sun gave way to the cloudless, crystalline sky at their leisure, as though they had all the time in the world. The seconds ticked on.

Alexcena sat on a crate, leaning back against the wall of the quarter deck. Leopold had deposited her there while he roamed the ship. All things considered, he seemed to be enjoying himself. Even Commodore seemed content. He could not pass within three feet of a sailor without receiving a pat and a kind word. They were as happy as they could be, considering their mission. She, on the other hand, felt dull and depressed. Sailing held no measure of joy for her. The crew of the *Liberator* gave her a wide berth and surreptitious looks. Often they would salute her as they passed, never meeting her glance and looking away after a second or two. This obvious showing of respect was good for many reasons, but it was sure to make for a lonely voyage.

The sky filled her vision. The sun was bright and high above. She blinked and looked down at the deck instead. A light breeze ruffled the fringe of her shawl and she shivered involuntarily. She winced when Commodore barked from somewhere near the bow. The sudden sound made her realize that she had developed a dull headache. Probably from sitting and staring at the sky for so long.

She rose stiffly, deciding to slip below to lie down. She was suddenly very tired. As she went she felt the steady swaying of the deck almost for the first time. She had wondered if she would succumb to some measure of seasickness, but this concern seemed moot as she descended the narrow stairs without so much as a stumble. She reached out to the door of her cabin and froze.

A soft thud sounded from beyond the wood.

Alexcena sucked in a sharp breath. She leaned hesitantly closer, certain that she had imagined the noise, but turning her ear to the door all the same.

Another thump, this time followed by a low rustling.

Alexcena did not pause again. She hurried back up the stairs and caught sight of Leo by the far rail. He came at once when she waved to him. Concern grew more evident on his features the closer he came.

"What's happened?"

"I think there's someone in my room!" she hissed.

Wolgath's gaze moved to the stairway behind her. He gripped her arms to gently press her aside and started down them. She followed close at his heels. He listened for an instant before gripping the door knob. She could not be sure, but it looked as though his other hand had slipped casually beneath his coat-preparing to draw his pistol.

Leo flung the door aside. It slammed against the wall of the cabin with an almighty crash. He halted midstride.

"You?" he spluttered.

Alexcena strained to see around his impressive form. His wide shoulders dominated the narrow doorway.

"What are you doing here?"

This was a different voice. A woman's voice.

"What is the meaning of-" Leo broke off, unable to finish.

"You know," the haughty woman went on, "a gentleman would knock before entering a lady's chamber."

Something was terribly amiss. This was not merely the vocalization of a lady. This voice was familiar. Alexcena pressed closer to Leo, struggling to see, thinking she was mistaken. Not so. Her recognition was absolutely correct.

Tabitha Winslett stood in the center of the room, and she looked utterly ridiculous at that. As usual she was dressed in a heavily embroidered gown of expensive and gaudy material. Her curls were pinned into a tightly woven twist at the nape of her neck with two or three locks popping out at odd angles. Her fisted hands were propped on her hips. A scowl marred her prim features and her lower lip was jutted out in a sullen pout as she stared Leo down.

Alexcena could only stare, wide-eyed and confused. "Tabitha?"

Tabitha's gaze moved slowly to her cousin. "Good day, Alexcena."

"What on earth are you doing here?"

Tabitha seemed not to notice her sharp tone. "I could ask *him* the same thing." She glared at Leopold once more.

The man's face hardened. A fierce light came to his eyes. He whirled from the room, brushing by Alexcena to storm up the stairs.

"Ruffian," Tabitha murmured.

Alexcena stepped into the room, still watching the girl as though she might disappear at any moment. "Tabitha, what are you *doing* here?"

"I came to help you, obviously."

Alexcena looked just as confused as she felt, so the girl began to explain.

"I heard that you were leaving. I know that Lucius is not where he is supposed to be. I want to help you find him."

Alexcena could think of nothing at all to say. What could this girl possibly be thinking? She left the room without another word, intending to see how Leo would handle the situation. Tabitha followed several steps behind, but she ignored her. Leo stood at the mainmast talking excitedly with the First Mate and drawing several stares from nearby crewmen.

"I want to know how she got aboard!"

"She paid her passage, as you have."

"That's not possible!"

"It is entirely possible," Greyson insisted. He was very exasperated with Leo's ire.

"You had no right to allow it!"

"We had every right to allow it. I do not care for your attitude, sir. If something does not go according to your preference, you simply insist that it must be impossible. Do you realize that if we all went around doing that nothing would be possible? Horse shoes would last forever, no man would ever lose his hair, and Mondays would cease to exist!"

"Is that such a bad thing?"

"Yes, because somewhere out there is a man who makes his living selling horseshoes!"

"I demand to speak to the Captain," Leo growled.

"He's busy, I'm afraid."

Leo caught sight of Alexcena then and his gaze flitted to Tabitha close behind her. He pointed harshly, still speaking to the Lieutenant. "That woman-that child-is going back ashore!" he vowed. "I imagine the Captain might want to know about it before I toss her over the rail myself!"

The First Mate raised an eyebrow. Tabitha's jaw fell comically. "Sir!"

"Not a word from you," Leo snapped without looking at her. "If you don't take me to the Captain, I'll find him myself."

Greyson looked rebellious, but still led the way to the helm where his commander stood speaking to the helmsman. Leo strode ahead of the others.

"Loughdon!"

The man turned slowly, a bland look on his stern face. His keen eyes took in the four people before him. "I see no cause for alarm, Mr. Wolgath," he commented. "And you *will* address me as Captain."

"We are taking this girl back to England, *Captain*," Leo declared. "Turn the ship around."

Loughdon glanced at both ladies. "I see no reason to do that. She has paid her passage."

"The Captain had no choice," Tabitha added. Her voice had reached a brittle octave.

"I had every choice," Loughdon corrected her in the same monotone. "I chose to allow it. We will not turn back."

"But we hired this dingy!" Leo fumed, gesturing to Alexcena and himself.

Loughdon's eyes became narrow slits beside his nose. "You hired me, Mr. Wolgath, and I happen to have a ship and a crew. If we turn back now it will cause an unnecessary and lengthy delay. So unless you are suggesting that we set the lady adrift, you'll just have to make the best of it, sir."

Loughdon turned his back on them then, dismissing them. Leo stormed away. Alexcena would have followed, but Tabitha touched her arm.

"What's he doing here?" She tipped her head the way Leo had gone.

"Lucius is his brother!" Alexcena snapped. *Has the girl gone dimwitted?*

She brushed passed her to go down to the main deck. Leo was just emerging from below, dragging a trunk in each hand. Alexcena suddenly realized that they were the trunks from her cabin. They were Tabitha's trunks. When the sailor had showed her below, he had said 'the lady's room.' What he meant was 'the ladies' room.' Plural as well as possessive.

Leo dropped the trunks in front of Tabitha, who had followed Alexcena once again. The girl was stark white, but her hands remained balled in defiant fists.

"What d'you expect to do with those in America?" he demanded.

"A lady ought to be prepared for any occasion."

"You can't bring them."

"And what, pray do you expect me to do without them?"

"That's your problem," Leo scoffed. "I refuse to lug those things all about Creation just so you can change your skirts every afternoon for tea!"

"How dare you-you insolent cad!"

Leopold glared balefully. He lifted one trunk by its handle and swung it up to rest atop the railing.

For an instant Tabitha was mortified. "You can't! You wouldn't!"

"Wouldn't I? This is just one of a hundred things you should've thought of before you decided to manipulate your way onto our ship!"

Tabitha pursed her lips and crossed her arms. "Fine," she said at last. "I need a new set of luggage as it is. This will be a masterful excuse."

Alexcena's headache was now magnified three fold. She massaged her forehead with the heel of her hand as she considered how best to interrupt this scene before Leo truly did throw something over the side.

"Tabitha, do your parents know you're here?"

"I imagine they do now."

The trunk clattered to the deck and the two ladies jumped. Leo moved dangerously close to Tabitha.

"You selfish, haughty, spoiled little menace!" he thundered. "How could you do something so irresponsible and dense? You don't even know the full complexity of what is going on here!"

"I will not stand here and be shouted at like an errant child!"

"You *are* an errant child, and I'm sorely tempted to take a belt to you."

Just when Alexcena thought she could not be more shocked by her cousin's behavior, Tabitha raised a hand to strike the man. Leo rendered the offending wrist immobile in his iron grip.

"Try it, love."

Tabitha's eyes filled with true fear at the sheer sight of his fury. She steeled her countenance and attempted to yank free. He let her go as though he was disgusted even to have touched her. She retreated swiftly below decks. Captain Loughdon, languid as ever, chose that moment to descend and join them.

"I cannot ask you to be happy about this situation," he said more reasonably, "but I will ask that you treat the lady with respect at the very least."

"You might have warned us that she was here," Alexcena said, although he had clearly been speaking to Leo.

"You knew our circumstances were grave," that man added. "For all you knew she might have been a spy. Did it never occur to you to mention to us that a third passenger was on board?"

"I had no idea that Ms. Winslett had managed to keep her presence quiet for so long. I assumed that if there was a problem, one of you would come to me before we left port." A queer look came to him then as he eyed Leo. "Somehow, next to you, a silly little fluff of a woman does not seem like much of a threat." He turned to Alexcena then. "You're looking a bit off-color, Ms. Condreve. Please feel free to alert Lieutenant Greyson if either of you ladies should need anything."

It seemed odd that the Captain would make so cordial an offer after so much surliness. He realized what she did not, though to be fair the headache had dulled her senses. She was watching him go when she felt the first swell of nausea accompanied by the incessant rolling of the ship.

Chapter 14

May 2 through 10, 1765

Tabitha's eyes grew round with concern as she peered around the edge of the cabin door. Alexcena lay in bed as she had all night, covered in perspiration and restless with nausea. The only differences now were that she remained somewhat still and that there was someone beside her. The young girl watched as Leo soothed her cousin's face with a damp cloth. Alexcena raised a weak hand, her eyes remaining shut. Leo gently grasped her wrist and moved it back down to the bed. With a low moan, Alexcena twisted onto her side. Leo simply adjusted his position to hers and continued to bathe her face while brushing away her hair.

Tabitha was amazed by the tenderness of this rough man. As menacing as he was to her, he seemed the very essence of compassion to this ailing woman.

She smoothed her skirt and moved into the room. Leo glanced up and then away.

"I'm rather busy just now, Ms. Winslett." His words were harsh, a surprising contrast to his heartfelt expression.

"How is she?"

Wolgath sat back in his chair, the rag hanging limply from his hand. "You ought to know. You spent the night in here with her."

Tabitha said nothing to this acidic reply.

Leo sighed. "Much the same. I'm just trying to keep her comfortable now. I think that's about all we can do."

"Lt. Greyson said the same."

He was openly astonished at this, and somehow that pricked her. Here lay her only cousin in distress of illness. She could not be aware of such a thing and ignore the circumstance. She knew he thought her childish and irresponsible, but heartless? Surely she did not warrant such a hard opinion. Her chin wrinkled into a frown.

"I came here to help."

Leopold looked up as though he had already forgotten she was there. In that instant she saw the sincerity of his concern for Alexcena. The next second this worry was masked by an expression of indifference. She mistook it for doubt.

"You don't think I can handle it?" she demanded.

Leo shrugged. "Caring for someone besides yourself would be a new trick for you."

Tabitha bit back a snide reply. This man was certain to become more annoying by the day. She found herself wishing once again that she had known he would be here before she came. But would her position be any different if she had? She shoved the question away before she had time to consider the answer.

"She looks uncomfortable."

Leo nearly rolled his eyes. "Wouldn't you be?"

"Her gown ought to be changed."

He started and sat up straight, causing Tabitha to grin. "That would make her feel much better."

Leo opened his mouth to speak and simply rose instead. He glanced from the woman in the bed to the slight young lady before him. "Do you always implore cheap tactics to get your way?" he asked even as he turned for the door.

"They work very well in most cases."

"It's the weapon of the French, you know."

"*Bonsoir* then, Leopold."

He turned one last time at the door to give her a very serious look. "I'll be in to check on the both of you."

When the door was shut, Tabitha proceeded to care for her cousin without hesitation. It was true that she had never before performed the duties of a nurse, but she was confident that she would be able to keep Alexcena well enough. At least she thought she could…

A silent truce had fallen over Tabitha and Leopold. Over the next week she proved to be a competent nurse, which was a shocking revelation even to her. Leo was usually close at hand, hovering over her efforts. This fact alone seemed to spur her to greater lengths, even if her deep concern over Alexcena's descending condition had not. After the first several days he began to back down gradually. She hated admitting that this made her even more uncertain, but it did. With him there, he would readily stop her if she did something amiss. This was her first experience with an illness totally cut off from those she might have gone to for advice on the subject, and she could only do what she remembered others doing for her. It was nice when he was there and she had someone to rely on to guide her if she needed it, though it would have been galling if he had ever said anything.

Tabitha rolled her head to alleviate a crick in her neck and reached for the basin once more. A stiffness had settled into her muscles, which she attributed to constant correction of her equilibrium. It was not only this soreness that she was noticing. For the first time in her life she was truly tired. She had always been a vibrant person, unaccustomed to feeling exhausted upon awakening. What little sleep she managed to catch was less than restful. The wear on her trim figure became noticeable. Into the second week of the voyage her radiant complexion began to lack luster. Her hair, always glossy and smooth, was now a mass of stringy curls at her back. No matter which dress she donned, the skirt was always a crush of wrinkles. After only a few days at sea, she realized that it would be next to impossible to keep up her usual elaborate appearance. She settled for maintaining her strict posture, despite her fatigue, and determining to scowl daintily at anyone who said a word about her person. This was not likely to happen in any case, and she was mildly surprised at the amount of time and effort she reserved by bypassing this tedious habit of formal dress. She focused this newfound energy on caring for her cousin.

Another amazement for her was a sudden and nearly alarming fascination with domestic necessities. Tasks which she might have puckered her smart little nose at a fortnight before were now almost a source of entertainment for her. Laundry was the peak of the list simply because it was the most recurring one.

Alexcena had indeed traveled light, thus limiting her supply of clean clothing with every wash. The ship had a fair supply of linen, but she could not expect more than three sets of sheets as often as she was changing them. Learning to tend the laundry had been almost as much of an experience as the actual task.

Seeing this need, she had gone to find Leo on deck the second morning. He was near the stern and preoccupied with a length of thin rope. Tabitha made her way to him, and he greeted her before she could speak.

"What is it now?"

His eyes never left the line.

Tabitha blinked and swallowed her ire. "I've come across a problem. It's rather imperative, and I would like your instruction."

"I'm rather busy just this moment."

"You're splicing a spare rope."

He looked up blandly. "Is there a problem with Alexcena?"

"No. Not directly. She's much the same, but-"

"If the problem is not with Alexcena then the problem does not concern me."

Tabitha was stunned by his blatant rudeness, though she had ample reason not to be. "That's rather callous, sir."

"I suggest you listen to this here and now, Ms. Winslett." Leo rose to his full height as he spoke. "You signed yourself up for this trip. No one asked you to come and no one wanted you to come. You came on your own and now you're *on* your own. Anything-any nail you break, any barrette you lose-is entirely your fault and responsibility. So if the problem isn't with Alexcena and it's not with me, then I suggest you take it to the Captain." With that he resumed his seat and his splicing.

Tabitha absorbed all this calmly enough. "I see. Thank you for your time, Mr. Wolgath." The conversation was clearly over.

She emerged from below not five minutes later bearing a large knot of sheets. Leo saw her, as she knew he would. She marched by him without so much as a glance. Her focus was on the Captain where he stood on the forecastle deck.

"Captain Loughdon!" She called in her sweetest voice. "I wonder if you could-"

A rough hand was suddenly grasping the bundle she carried.

"What are you *doing?*" Leo hissed at her side.

"Going to someone who will help me with my problem!" she whispered back.

"That is *not* the sort of man you ask to do your laundry!" Leo argued. "I would have helped if I'd known it was something of this nature. You're going to make us both look incompetent."

"Don't you have a rope to splice?"

She took another step forward, but he smoothly snatched the bundle away.

"Is there a problem, Ms. Winslett?"

Tabitha turned to face the Captain and waved. "No, sir! My mistake!"

Leo was at the rail muttering darkly to himself when she joined him. "I'm going to teach you how to do this now, so don't be expecting me to wash for you day in and day out, all right?"

"Precisely what I was hoping for."

"I'm guessing you've never actually laundered anything before?"

She shook her head cheerfully. "No."

"Right. Well, there's only one way to milk a heifer and that's with a bucket. Why don't you go and find us one?"

So she learned to launder. She learned to scrub and scour. She learned to serve, and amidst all this, she learned the most unexpected thing of all; that in this droning domesticity, she could find a measure of enjoyment.

Chapter 15

May 13, 1765

Alexcena's memory came in distinct bursts of garish color. She remembered these images quite well, as they were accompanied by spikes of pain in her heavy head. Light had become a harsh enemy. It seemed that every time she opened her eyes, there was a face leaning over her. More often than not she recognized this face as that of Tabitha. Occasionally it would be the rougher countenance of Leopold. The worst moments were the few times she opened her eyes to see a stranger's concerned gaze. This was mortifying, and she would immediately turn away only to become ill from the motion. At one point a large, damp, round thing touched her cheek. She held out a hand toward it only to realize that it was Commodore. She nearly came out of the bed then and there, until she realized what a gut-wrenching mistake that would be. Mercifully her sickness was marked by prolonged unconsciousness. She had the impression that these spells lasted more than a day, and she was never awake for very long in between. Usually only long enough to be sick and roll over.

After nearly two weeks of constant nausea, headaches, and unconsciousness, it seemed odd indeed that she would simply awaken one morning and sit up. She did this quite without thinking. It was not until she stretched her weak arms upward and became lightheaded that she realized what ought to have been obvious. She no longer felt queasy. There was a frailty prominent in every limb. The awareness of the motions of the ship remained, and even then she could feel every slope of every wave. She waited anxiously, but her stomach did not turn with this action. Her head no longer ached.

Thinking this feeling of wellness might be fleeting, she began to take stock of herself. At first she did not recognize the white blouse she wore. It was so baggy and loose that it seemed more like a blanket around her shoulders. The sleeves were rolled up above her elbows. Her arms were thinner than she remembered, and she was sure the rest of her would be much the same.

"Hm."

The noise she made was not loud, but it was enough to wake the only other individual in the cabin. Commodore was lying in a lumpy blue-gray knot by the wall across from her. Now he came to his feet, cocking his head to one side with a puzzled groan.

Alexcena sucked in a startled breath. Commodore's head was now just at the foot of her bed, and since it was so low and he was so tall, the animal was at eye-level with her. She clutched the sheets and valiantly tried to think clearly over her thudding heart. Voices suddenly sounded in her mind.

"Do you know the term phobia, Mr. Wolgath?"

"He is harmless, I assure you."

She swallowed. These words brought on other, more tender memories, and so she was distracted as Commodore made his way around the bed. He sat down and his large head fell onto the sheets beside her. She snatched her hand away, but Commodore simply whimpered as if to say, 'I've missed you while you were sleeping and now you refuse me attention?'

Alexcena sighed, her pale hand still upraised. He *seemed* gentle enough, but somewhere in the back of her mind she knew that there were forty-some-odd formidable teeth behind those flabby jowls.

"Very well," she murmured.

The animal raised his head expectantly.

"Now I am going to try and become accustomed to you, but you mustn't startle me. I'm not very good at this."

If she didn't know better, she would say that Commodore shrugged. He shifted his weight and seemed to convey his thoughts with attitude. 'I knew the moment I saw you that you were a goldfish person.'

Alexcena reached tentatively forward. "Lucius trusts you. I can trust you." She said this mostly to reassure herself.

When her hand was almost to him, the Great Dane tilted his head into her palm and sighed. She sat perfectly still and then began to stroke his ear with her thumb. Commodore watched her through gray eyes that matched his coat. The fur was soft and pleasantly warm beneath her skin.

"Not so terrible," she managed.

Commodore's head tilted straight up with a whine that seemed more like a whistle. He trotted easily to the door so that his massive head was in the hall and emitted a low bark. The sound died away in the tight passage to be replaced by voices.

"How long ago did you leave her?"

"It can't be long. I was only asleep for an instant."

"You didn't even know you *were* asleep," Leo grumbled even as he appeared in the doorway. He patted the dog's shoulder and looked up. "Alexcena!"

Commodore gave a self-satisfied *harrumph* and returned to the wall by the foot of the bed to resume his nap. Alexcena smiled. Commodore could be quite amusing when she was able to allay her fears.

"You're awake," Leo mused as he crossed the room.

"I am," she replied unnecessarily.

Leo stood quite close to the bed, his arms akimbo and a broad smile lighting his features. "It does my heart well. Luc would never forgive me-and I in turn would never forgive Loughdon-if anything were to happen to such precious cargo."

She shared a chuckle with him over this and then noticed Tabitha standing in the corner. She smiled reassuringly to the girl, who was watching them with evident apprehension. Leo, on the other hand, had not yet seen her.

"Your nurse has been fairly loyal thus far," he commented, "but it is unfortunate that she was not here when you woke. Have you a need of anything at all?"

Tabitha moved to stand at the foot of the bed. Alexcena gave her a soft glance. Leo saw her now and looked repentant, but this vanished as he turned his attention back to Alexcena.

"Thank you both," she said complacently. "Some water would be nice."

Tabitha nearly tumbled over her ridiculous skirts in her rush to leave the room. Leo watched her go with the merest shake of his head. He seemed surprised indeed when he saw Alexcena's visible distress an instant later.

"Yes?"

"You've been hard with her?"

It was not truly a question, and he knew it. He let his arms fall loose.

"She deserves our hardness. Don't you agree?"

For the first time she perceived an uncertainty in his voice. She dipped her head.

"I suppose so."

She could not disagree, so what was she to do? Tabitha had put herself in the way of all this purposefully and must be expected to bear the result. She had been speechless with anger herself when she discovered her cousin was aboard, but it was difficult to remember that now.

"This is not our fault, Alexcena. None of it," Leo persisted. "She never should have been here in the first place."

She nodded. "But I'm glad now-for both our sakes-that she is."

A tinge of regret came to his features again, but it was contrasted by the grinding of his molars. "I will not feel guilty for this," he declared.

Alexcena watched him calmly. "I'm not asking you to."

The corner of his wide mouth twitched up into a grin. "You wouldn't, would you?"

A subdued thud drew their eyes to the door, where Tabitha appeared with a small cup and a bowl. She nearly fell forward on her way in, but managed to right herself with only a minimal amount of sloshing from the dishes.

"I'll leave you both to it then," Leo said abruptly, adding, "I am glad you're feeling better," as he made for the door.

Tabitha moved briskly, setting a small stool by the bed and passing the cup to Alexcena.

"I hope this is all right. The broth is only lukewarm, but Cook thought it might do you good."

Alexcena eyed the pale stock as she sipped her water. Her stomach growled. "It smells delicious to me." She tried to say this cheerfully, but her voice was paper thin. It came out sounding more exhausted than merry.

She had not realized how truly weak she was until she lifted the small cup. Even emptied it seemed heavy in her feeble grasp. The spoon trembled in her hand. Tabitha soon took over with a no-nonsense flip of her curls. Alexcena did not protest. Her cousin chattered along as she fed her. As was usual with Tabitha, the conversation was one-sided, but for once Alexcena did not mind.

"I have been learning so much about seafaring, and who knew there was so much to learn! I had no idea that there was so much involved with the steering and the navigating and the sailing. It's almost as though the men have their own language too with all of their own different names for things. Why I listened to them speak of the tiller, the rudder, and the helm for over a solid week before I realized they're all part of the steering of this large little vessel. Then there was the day I heard Mr. Marks saying that the upper yard had a small crack and I immediately started looking for a tear in one of the sails. Nearly volunteered my sewing needles before I realized he meant one of those cross timbers. I certainly felt silly, but why would you call those things 'yardarms' anyway? They're yards longer than anyone's actual arm."

"Perhaps because they hold up yards of canvas like arms."

Tabitha shook her head. "Honestly! I don't know how these men keep anything straight without writing it all down."

Alexcena smiled. "Tis fortunate you're not a sailor then."

Tabitha crossed her arms. "Tis fortunate I'm not a *man*. I'm too silly to be any good at it at all."

"I can't say that I've known too many women who would be good at it."

"Well," the younger lady shrugged. She had been joking up to that point, but suddenly she was very somber. "Sometimes I think I'm not doing so well as a lady, either."

Sorrow seeped into the girl's voice. Alexcena wanted desperately to reassure her, but she knew she couldn't. It would mean conveying a false impression and false encouragement. It was as though a tiny bit of Tabitha's childhood had just flecked away, and she was seeing her cousin mature slightly before her very eyes. A heavy silence passed, and Alexcena determined to ask the thing she had been wondering since she first laid eyes on her cousin in the cabin.

"Tabitha?" she murmured. "What are you hoping to accomplish by all this? Why are you here?"

"I-" She hesitated and straightened her shoulders. "Well, I-" She broke off again. She shifted awkwardly beneath Alexcena's gaze.

Alexcena leaned forward. "What is this about?" she coaxed, steeling herself for the answer. *What am I to do if she says that it's all for Lucius?*

A tortured look came over Tabitha's features. Her cheeks reddened and her voice escaped her in an almost panicked wail. "I-DON'T-KNOW!"

With that she buried her face in her hands and sobbed brokenly over the edge of Alexcena's bed.

Chapter 16
May 17, 1765

Alexcena woke to the sounds of a struggle. It seemed to be an intense one at that. She opened one eye experimentally and relaxed when she saw the cause of the noise.

Tabitha sat on the little stool before the wash stand, clutching the ivory handle of her brush as though it were a weapon. By the wild motions of her arms, she certainly seemed to be in the throes of battle. Her blonde tresses snapped and recoiled as she drug the brush down them. As Alexcena watched, the bristles of the brush became seriously lodged in her tangles. Tabitha allowed it to hang there and crossed her arms as though contemplating her next move, her lower lip pouting in frustration.

Alexcena sat up with a pronounced yawn. She thought it only fair now that she knew the noises were only Tabitha (who was scrambling to disentangle her brush). She stretched luxuriously, feeling the pull in every muscle. For four days since her illness had abated she had remained in bed, too weakened by the sickness to rise. Enough was enough. Her cousin had helped her so much in the last weeks, but now the need was reversed.

Swinging herself around beneath the sheet, Alexcena rose. Her legs felt brittle as kindling, but she kept her balance and moved smoothly across the room. Tabitha did not turn, but her reflection watched through the hazy looking glass with wide green eyes. Alexcena very carefully avoided her own image in that glass. She was certain to look as though she had passed through death and back. Instead she smiled reassuringly. It was amazing to watch Tabitha. One moment she looked her age, a young lady of wealth. The next instant she appeared to be no more than a frightened child.

"May I?"

Without waiting for a reply, Alexcena lifted the brush from Tabitha's hands. She took a thick curl and began smoothing its ends.

"I think if you try it this way," she commented casually, "working up from the tips, it might be easier."

Tabitha expelled a breath. "My hair is impossible."

"Not impossible," Alexcena coaxed. "Difficult. You just need to learn a trick or two to work with it."

"What tricks do you use?"

Alexcena blinked at her cousin's reflection. The girl's expression was eager this time. Alexcena floundered for a moment before she was able to answer.

"My hair is not nearly as curly as yours. I think if we plait it here and then twist the rest over it, the pins may be more secure."

"Yes?" Tabitha agreed. "It certainly sounds better than having pins fly out at every turn!"

Alexcena's gaze snapped up and she pursed her lips to keep from snickering, but Tabitha grinned at her.

"I'll bet no one thought I realized that did they? The only thing I didn't know about it was how to make them stop."

"I think we'll find a way. After all that's why you came isn't it?" she teased.

Tabitha snorted. "For all I know."

It surprised and almost pleased Alexcena that Tabitha was able to laugh over this. Part of her-the more serious part-worried for the future. It was one thing to be lost on board a relatively small ship, but it was quite another to be lost in the great land they were traveling to. Tabitha would soon realize in a very different way just how serious her life had become.

She twisted and smoothed and soon found that her cousin's coiffure was quite firmly in place. Tabitha turned her head and strained her gaze as though she might see it for herself.

"How is it?"

"Becoming," Alexcena affirmed. Her eyes strayed to the door as she spoke. She yearned for the golden warmth of sunshine. It seemed she had been locked in that dark little room for weeks, and of course, she had.

Tabitha echoed her thoughts. "We'll need to change those clothes of yours if we're going on deck."

"Hm?" She looked down at the wrinkled white shirt and rumpled navy skirt.

"I mean they're not really 'yours,' but-"

"What do you mean?"

Tabitha stopped short. "Didn't you notice? Well I had to put you in *something*, but you brought so few outfits and I was constantly washing them, but I still couldn't keep up. The skirt is mine-which explains why it's so very short on you-and the blouse is Leopold's."

"Leopold's?"

"Yes, although he probably doesn't call it a 'blouse' does he? I should hope not. Anyway your own clothes are clean now if you would like to change. I wouldn't dream of you going above deck in that state."

Alexcena looked down at herself again. If Tabitha hadn't said it, she never would have believed the skirt was hers. It was too plain. It had none of the usual flounces and bows her clothes always seemed to bear. She determined at that moment that she would find a way to speak to Tabitha about her clothing before that voyage was through.

Just moments later she was in her own smoke gray dress and they were emerging on deck to a crystal clear day on a cobalt sea. Alexcena closed her eyes and breathed deeply of the ocean wind. She could feel the eyes of the seamen on her, curious and wary of her condition. They reminded her dimly of her father, who always seemed to be almost fearful in the presence of any ailing woman. It was very different from Lucius' reactions. He was always worried, but eager to assist whenever he saw that she was in distress.

"Hike, Commodore!"

Her breath caught in her throat as the memories assailed her. It was as if she heard his voice near-by. Then she opened her eyes to see Leo off to the left. It was his voice she had heard, but in that moment her mind had believed differently. Quickly smoothing her features into a smile, she moved toward him. Tabitha went to Commodore.

"Up and walking," he said cheerily. "You're getting better by the day."

"Did you fear otherwise?"

"Not at all."

The pair turned to the railing. Alexcena leaned into the afternoon sun, inhaling the light breeze and squinting against the glare of the water. Leopold slumped lazily against the rail and watched the motions of the seamen on deck. He seemed content to remain in comfortable silence. Normally Alexcena would have been too, but after so many days of seeming isolation, she was in need of some companionship.

"Are you enjoying the voyage, Leo?"

He raised one dark eyebrow. "I think I preferred the livery in England."

"But you always said you like to travel."

"I love to travel-on foot. The sea is not my favorite landscape."

"Oh," she nodded. "I haven't really traveled enough to know what I like best."

Leo-no doubt unable to help himself-leaned closer to ask, "And how are you liking the ocean?"

Alexcena paled, and he had to choke back a laugh. She was soon laughing at herself anyway and he joined her.

"I'm sorry," he gasped out. "That shouldn't be funny at all."

"No, it's fine," she replied. She caught her breath and was sobered by her next thought. "This-this was never meant to be a pleasure journey in the first place."

She had a keen awareness of the sudden burning in her throat and the distinct prickling of moisture in her eyes. She became painfully conscious of the seconds rolling by just as she had before they left land. It was as though a clock was ticking loudly in her mind, drumming out the time until she would be reunited with Lucius. Each tick made her want to wince. The ship itself seemed to slow, though she was only partially paying attention. In that moment, if it had been at all conceivable, she would have gladly thrown herself from the deck and swam to Virginia.

Leo saved her contemplating the ridiculous notion. He twisted toward her. "So, Alexcena Condreve. That's quite a mouthful."

At first she struggled to comprehend. Then she smiled calmly. "So is Leopold Wolgath."

"That's why I like Leo better. Saves time when someone needs to talk to me in a hurry." He seemed to study her profile for a time and then shook his head. "Alexcena. There must be a way to shorten that."

She shrugged. She had honestly never considered such a thing, but now she was intrigued by the idea. "Alex?" she suggested.

Leo shook his head. "Too obvious. And too ordinary. Al?"

She wrinkled her nose. "Sounds too much like 'ale.'"

"That leaves us with Cena then."

"Why not just Ena?" She was pleased when he seemed to like the idea.

"Yes! It's simple enough, but with a unique flare."

She giggled. It was so much easier to talk about nothing than to dwell on the future when she was momentarily powerless in regards to her speed. She even teased Tabitha as the girl approached.

"I have been given a new name," she declared. "*Ena*. What do you think of it?"

Tabitha eyed Leo for an instant, but by the time this made Alexcena wonder, she was watching her again. "What made you think of that?"

Some of the easiness drained from Alexcena. "Well, it was Leo's idea, but I came up with the name. Do you like it?"

Tabitha seemed to be considering. "It's very lyrical," she began. "And very easy to pronounce if you are ever around small children. Of course when you have children of your own with Lucius they will call you 'mother' won't they?"

That did it. All simple thoughts flew from Alexcena's mind. She had been clinging to them since she had become more and more aware over the last four days. They had been like a warm quilt in winter, shielding her from relentless cold. In that moment the makeshift cover fell away, and she shivered.

Managing to put on a polite half-smile, she mumbled an excuse and hurried below decks before she could worry either one of them with her tears. Perhaps if she buried her face in the pillow for a few moments she might stave off the fears that assailed her. She let the door of the cabin fall shut behind her and was astounded to find that the bed was occupied. Commodore was stretched across it.

The burning in her throat rose, and she knew she could go no farther. She sank down to the floor, her hands clamped against her mouth to stifle the sound. Her eyes squeezed shut so hard her head hurt.

Commodore moved, but she did not notice until she felt him snort out a hot breath on her knees. She jumped and quieted immediately on finding his face so near her own. Then she found that she was shocked by her own reaction. She expected the cold grip of fear, but there was none. The animal's features were melancholy-an expression that was only enhanced by his gray coat. His pale eyes were deep and caring and suddenly very familiar. It was utterly ridiculous to see a bit of Lucius in this dog. She could not have explained it except to say it was a fleeting thing that she saw. A momentary connection with the gentle beast which calmed her troubled heart.

He whimpered and she sighed, offering up the smallest of smiles.

Chapter 17

Lucius was composing a letter, and he was vaguely surprised at the comfort this familiar task gave him. The husky *scratch, scratch, scratch* of quill tip against paper was calming as he wrote. The knees of his long legs crowded his elbows, and he was forced to steady the inkwell constantly as it moved with the waves. Despite these inconveniences, he smiled to himself as he continued;

> *My Alexcena, the depth of my despair at our forced separation is not merely unfathomable, but I may now take great comfort in knowing that I will be journeying to you within a matter of days. It is entirely possible that I will arrive before you ever receive this missive. I pray it is so, but if not, I beg you do not fret, for I am not far behind. Captain Davidson has proven a most compassionate man in agreeing to return me swiftly to England and to you.*

To be fair, it was in all likelihood the subject matter and not the actual writing which was encouraging to Lucius, but now he had come to the difficult portion of his letter. How would he mention the fact that the fee of passage-which was being waived now-would be required upon his arrival? He held no small measure of anxiety at the thought of asking the money of Lawrence. The man would help him in any way possible. If he were to know Lucius' thoughts, he would count out the coins in the blink of an eye and never require them back. Lucius would pay him back over time, whether his friend requested it of him or not, which he most certainly wouldn't, but it would take a great deal of time. *Such a sum!*

All this he was contemplating when a great cry from above stilled his every thought.

"Land, ho!"

Lucius heard the booming shout clearly even in his close little cabin. Still he did not allow himself to believe it until the call came a second time.

"Land, ho!"

Lucius leapt to his feet. Snatching his coat, he dashed out the door and up the stairs. He imagined that he could already smell the soil of firm, steady, unmoving earth.

Captain Davy stood in the bow with Mr. Sweney deep in conversation. Sailors moved swiftly across the decks and ratlines. The other passengers were all assembled at the port railing, staring expectantly at the faint dark line on the horizon. Gibbs seemed impassive as ever. Harlan Pratt looked relieved beyond measure. Smith Darlum was ecstatic and let out a good holler to be sure that no one doubted his enthusiasm. Mrs. Hatchens stood with an arm around each of her children, full tears of silent joy rolling down her cheeks. Her smile trembled just slightly.

Lucius moved to the railing, taking only cursory notice of the people he had spent the last nine weeks with. He gripped the wood and leaned as far out as he dared, drinking in the slight scent, which was so sweetly opposite that of salt. His eyes closed, a hundred images and memories filling his thoughts. Not the least of these were his last memories of Alexcena. He could not explain the measure of his relief. There was still another journey ahead of him. His return voyage would be every bit as long as his first, but somehow he felt as though he was escaping, at least for a time. The return seemed a lesser nightmare than the one he had just passed through. In his mind he reached for Alexcena. He murmured the words of reassurance he longed to give her, stroked her hair, and truly felt that his ordeal was nearly over.

The stiff wind that arose at that very moment ought to have been a clear warning against those optimisms. Any objective bystander who had bothered to pay the slightest attention would have seen this as the symbol of foreboding that it was. It was from that very moment on that nature itself seemed to declare war upon the insignificant Professor Wolgath.

Lucius leaned back, opening his eyes just as the sharp gust snatched Mrs. Hatchen's bonnet from her brow. He gallantly followed after it as it rolled along the weathered boards of the deck. He soon caught it, and she expressed her gratitude while she secured it more firmly beneath her chin. As she did this, something ominous caught her attention.

"Goodness."

At her indication Lucius grudgingly turned his back on land to see what she saw. A dark mass lined the horizon several leagues distant. At first it appeared very similar to the dark shape of the land behind them, except for one characteristic; this shape was larger, closer. As he watched, lightening flashed within the frothy, rolling clouds. Another fierce rush of wind racked the deck of the *Scarlet Pride*. This time the force was so great that every passenger bowed their shoulder against it.

"But we are headed in almost entirely the opposite direction," Lucius declared to no one in particular. "Surely such an atmospheric anomaly would not catch up to us."

Harlan swallowed visibly. "I've heard stories of storms like this at sea."

Smith pulled oddly at his collar. "But the land is right there! We'll make landfall long before that reaches us, eh?"

Again they were assaulted by a powerful gust.

"All hands on deck!"

They turned to see Captain Davy striding away from the bow and shouting orders. Sailors came like roaches from the woodwork, scuttling to do their captain's bidding. Lucius strode forward and caught Davidson's forearm.

"Surely you don't believe the storm will catch us?"

Davidson looked over his shoulder. The rolling clouds had already covered half the distance to the flute. The planes of his face were grave.

"It already has."

The passengers were immediately and indefinitely confined below decks. They were ushered swiftly to the mess hall by Mr. Granville, the carpenter, who assured them that there was absolutely no cause for alarm. He was not convincing. The Professor's former seasickness returned with all speed once they were below, though it did not come with nearly as much vigor as it had before. He endured it tolerably. He was not alone in this. As the waves grew in size and speed, the others seemed to steel themselves against rising sickness from the constant motion. Even roughhewn Smith Darlum held one hand tightly over his mouth. This rendered him speechless, to the immense relief of the other passengers. Lucius braced himself against the wall with each rise and fall of the floor. The room tilted crazily and often someone would fall into him. The noise of the raging wind and tumultuous thunder seemed to reach a fever pitch. Lucius was hard pressed to see how it could grow louder, but it did.

At one point water began to flood in beneath the door. Now the fearful souls were not only sick and sore, they were sodden. Mrs. Hatchens daughter was crying. Her son clung to her skirts. She held and patted them as best she could, though she herself appeared rather green. Harlan Pratt sat at one end of the room, his arms wrapped tightly about a large support brace. Darlum, Gibbs, and Gurt the cook, were all pressed against the opposite wall, doing their level best to stay put. The air in the cabin grew thick and hot, filled with terror as it was.

A single lantern was suspended from the ceiling. It swung madly back and forth until it finally flipped free of its hook and crashed to the floor, thus extinguishing the only source of light offered them. The darkness was instant, and a feminine scream wracked the nerves of the men.

Wolgath knew then that he could take no more. He swallowed his nausea and waited for the deck to level off as much as it was able. He began moving, slow as a crawl and three inches deep in sea water, making his way to the door. As it happened, the waves turned the ship in favor of this and catapulted him at the door. The thing swung open from the force of his slam, and the left side of his face began to sting. He scrambled up to press it shut once more. Turning, he saw the stairs to the main deck before him and plunged forward.

This was his fatal mistake. Oh! The nights he spent hereafter hoping that he had dreamed it! Praying that he was merely unconscious in his own little cabin, a victim still to the fever. He had not even been certain what he had planned to do once he reached the main deck, not that it really mattered long after that. Some part of him had succumbed to a mild, albeit powerful, sense of fear and spooked him into action. Now that the tortures of being below decks were gone, the more logical side of his brain twisted his motives into some desperate attempt to see how they fared up top. That was all. He was simply trying to determine if the storm was truly passing.

His eyes burned as the rain pelted his face behind his glasses, and he stood in the portal to the deck for some moments trying to orient himself. The dark shapes of sailors moved about everywhere, swarming the deck. The wind was savage indeed, tearing mercilessly at his clothes and hair. A tortured shout rose above the rest, carried by a monstrous gust. A great crack assailed his ears. He raised an arm to cover his face reflexively. Though the noise seemed to meld with the thunder of the gale, this new sound was clearly anything but natural. A mighty shudder rocked the ship, and when he lowered his arm he saw its cause. One of the aft yardarms had snapped almost entirely in half, and now lay at an angle at the base of the mast.

For an instant the storm was pushed to the back of Wolgath's mind. His thoughts turned to one pursuit; help. He had heard of the many dangers of the sea. It was possible, even likely, that some poor soul had been injured in this crippling of the *Scarlet Pride*. He could not turn from the situation.

He pushed himself forward, away from the stairs, to stagger across the deck. He was only part way into the melee when a massive swell surged upward. It seemed to come from the very depths of the murky ocean, the strongest they had seen yet. The vessel seemed to lift above the waters as it was born by this wicked thing. Lucius felt the deck rise quite suddenly beneath him until it was almost perpendicular. He could see nothing beyond the water and wind which assaulted him. All sense of equilibrium vanished, and he fell back. It seemed that he landed on his left side, though he could not even be certain of that meaningless fact. Something slammed into the young man's back. He had smashed against a group of barrels lashed to the deck by netting and rope. He had time to right himself, clinging desperately to the nets, just before the next wave came. This one did not rise below them, but above them. Lucius even fancied later that he had seen it as it towered over the deck for an instant and then crashed to meet it.

Lucius felt the water driving against him, harder than the rain ever had. Something snapped close by him. His feet were swept from beneath him, and then there was nothing but the sea.

Chapter 18

May 29, 1765

It is an appalling sensation indeed to awaken and find that you are unable to open your eyes. Even as Lucius strove to raise his lids, he could feel the salty grit that crusted his lashes. This mild struggle made him aware of other discomforts. His nose and throat burned like dry kindling. His limbs throbbed with ache. Something hard was pressed against his chest. Once this realization was processed, he was surprised to find that the same hard thing was pressing against his arms. Even more astonishing was the knowledge that it was not pressing him, but the other way around. Whatever this hard thing was, it was his own arms hugging it against his chest. He released it and rolled quite suddenly onto his back just as his eyes managed to open.

Glaring sunlight overwhelmed his vision. Lucius shielded his face with one hand while a few harsh coughs escaped him. A cool wind grazed his still damp form and he shivered. He rubbed his irritated eyes with the heels of his palms while his mind strained to adjust and recapture his more recent memories.

The *Scarlet Pride*. The storm. The deck. The mast. The waves. The ocean.

All at once Lucius became very aware of a devastatingly obvious fact. His hands fell to his sides. He reached out convulsively to grasp handfuls of the shifty turf surrounding him. He dug his fingers deep into the yielding sand.

He was on dry ground.

In that one sweet instant-though he was parched as ash-he would have been happy not to see a drop of water for a month. This sentiment did not last long after he attempted to lick his peeling lips. The soft lapping of gentle waters reached him, and he sat up, expecting to see naught but an ocean expanse.

He was in fact lying on the bank of a shallow stream. The sea was several yards distant on his right. What mercy was this! A quick taste of this calm rivulet revealed that it was indeed fresh water. Lucius drank and bathed his face in the tepid flow. Certainly his vision would clear once his eyes were freed of their crust. Not so. He was confused, and even worried, until he realized that his glasses were missing. He began to take further stock of himself. The pains in his muscles were already beginning to subside. His coat had stretched into some sort of a crooked shape, and most likely would never fit him quite right again. This was just as well since one sleeve was almost completely torn off.

The hard thing he had been clinging to was a barrel, which now lay on the bank beside him. No doubt this had been the very key to his survival when he was so mercilessly flung through the railing. Another such barrel, a crate, and various other pieces of debris lay scattered all around him. Lucius followed the line of the stream to the shore where it fed the sea.

Something somewhere in the back of his mind seemed off. Something about this whole scene was disconcerting-aside from the fact that he was a castaway in a foreign land. Lucius came to his feet, and knew all at once what was amiss.

There was no sign of the *Scarlet Pride*. There were no jolly boats. There was no sign of any human life anywhere abouts. Except for him. Every small detail of these circumstances suddenly came together, and the full import and significance of it all finally reached its mark. He was stranded in a wild land without so much as a stitch to his name aside from the threads on his back. It was entirely possible that he was the sole survivor of a tragic wreck at sea. The *Scarlet Pride*, his only chance at turning back to England and Alexcena, was lost to him.

Wolgath's hands trembled lightly. He reached up to entwine his fingers in his knotted curls. His eyes grew wide as they frantically searched the horizon and beach. There was not a single indication that anyone else had come ashore. Not even the animals were stirring. A garbled groan escaped his throat. He felt his heart twist as he pictured the faces of those on board. The Captain, the sailors, the passengers…the children. All lost to the deep.

He stumbled back in revulsion and fell onto his side. Suddenly his collar seemed utterly constricting. His breaths came in shallow drags. In the face of mortality, he had the presence of mind to take another look at himself. Aside from the missing glasses, ruined clothes, and a vague ache in his muscles there was nothing much the matter with him. He was whole and well and breathing, while all those poor people-

Lucius shut his mind on that particular despair. His situation was now more desperate than ever it had been before. If he was to have even a chance of making his way home-or surviving for that matter-he would need to be on his toes.

"Pray," he grunted between breaths. "Of course, I must pray."

So he did as he lay there face down on the damp, sandy ground. He prayed ardently for those aboard the doomed ship. He prayed for Alexcena, for her parents, and his brother. Last of all he prayed for himself. After several minutes he rose and turned his back on the sea.

Balance eluded him, and he stumbled aimlessly alongside the stream, concentrating on staying upright. His blurry vision did not help in the slightest. His sight was just clear enough that he was able to spot the bit of gold glinting in the sand. He bent down to retrieve it and found that it was his lost spectacles.

"Mercy of mercies!"

He set them atop his nose and looped the wire arms over his ears. One lens was cracked straight through. *Could be worse...*

"What's this then?"

Lucius gave a start at the first sound of these words and looked hastily around. A stubby, stick of an old man stood facing him from the opposite bank. His clothes and hair were bedraggled and dirty. In his arms was an age-old blunderbuss. He kept one eye squinted shut and the other glaring as he sighted the barrel on Luicus.

"Don't shoot!" Lucius exclaimed. "Hold fire, sir!"

"State your business."

"I-I just-"

"Where'd you come from?"

"I was on a ship," Lucius sputtered.

"Englisher, eh?"

The little man reminded him more and more of a snarling badger. He spat the word 'Englisher' as though it were a profanity. Lucius drew himself up indignantly. "Aye!"

"Of what party are ye?"

"Excuse me?"

"Whig or Tory ya ditherin' dandy. Whig or Tory?" He repeated them slowly so as to be sure that his prey would understand.

Lucius glared. "My politics are none of your affair."

The man chuckled bitterly. "Tory then."

"My ship wrecked off the coast," Wolgath explained desperately.

"An' you washed up here."

"Yes, yes," Lucius nodded. "Exactly! Can you help me?"

The man considered briefly and tightened his grip on the gun. "Listen up, Englisher," he barked. "Yore ship wrecked on my stretch o' the beach and I'm claimin' salvage. So anything you got in your pockets, you just throw down now and I'll let you leave in peace."

"What?!"

"That includes them fancy wire jobs you put on your face."

He reached up absently to touch the rim of his spectacles.

"Quick now!"

Lucius was torn between incredulity and absolute fear. "But I don't-I-" he stammered. "Show some decency, sir, I implore you!"

The grip on the blunderbuss shifted. The man slowly ran his tongue along his bottom lip as he considered. Lucius raised his brows and let his hands drop. At last his assailant would see reason.

"Fair enough," the man allowed. "You've had a hard day like as not. Least I can do is show ya a bit of kindness. So I'm givin' ya till the count of ten to high-tail it off my land."

Lucius was perplexed, convinced that he had misunderstood him. "Sir, I-"

"One."

"You can't possibly mean to use that!"

The stranger pulled the hammer of his bulbous weapon back. "I can only get high as six, Englisher, so you best start moving!...Two."

For a brief, insane instant that frivolous detail was appalling enough to give Lucius pause. "You can count no higher than six?"

The man snickered. "Care to find out yourself?"

By the time he got to *three* Lucius had decided that he did not care to find out. He turned on his heel and ran helter-skelter across the shore. His shoes were not at all conducive to the semi-firm ground. The scant trees and brush offered some cover, but he was not about to slow down. A low fence appeared several yards ahead. Lucius did not slow or even turn to avoid it. He grasped the rough wooden rail and used his momentum to vault-or fall-over it. Wolgath took the time to notice, as he was righting himself from this tumble, that he was not being pursued. This caused him to feel embarrassed about his hasty retreat, but he pressed on at a decent run.

Still he did not go for much longer. He was no athlete after all. He slowed and fell on all fours, gasping in great gulps of air. As his breathing slowed, he began to hear a new sound; laughter. It was then that he saw the buildings.

There were four of them in a wide clearing just up from the shore.

They were roughly constructed of curved cypress planks and thatched roofs. Dark smears of caulk sealed their walls against most of the elements. Light smoke wafted up from the brick chimneys. At the far end of the cluster of buildings two women stood by an open flame. One had a bundle of clothes clutched to her chest while the other was stirring something in a large cauldron.

The women eyed him suspiciously, nervously, as he rose to his feet. He nodded in respect and turned to the building emitting the most noise. The raucous guffaws and chatter labeled it clearly as a tavern. A plank was nailed above the door depicted a dog with a blindfold over his eyes. Lucius hesitated to straighten his coat, which was ridiculous since it was stretched almost completely out of shape.

Behind the door he found a flurry of merriment and activity. An array of men-and even a few women-sat around and on several crude tables scattered throughout the space. Three men stood at the short bar. In the midst of this scene, a long space had been cleared and a cluster of wooden pins set at one end. Two patrons were taking turns lobbing a weighty bowling ball at them while the others placed wagers on the outcome.

The din did not die down as Lucius appeared on the threshold. To his ears it multiplied in volume. Only the three men at the bar appeared to notice him. They merely stared, and for a moment Lucius stood unsure of what to do. The man in the middle raised his cup, and so Lucius moved forward. This man sported a long black beard and an oilskin coat. To his left was a heavier man in a weathered hat. The third was leaning back against the bar and wore a ragged apron over his clothes.

The one in the coat held out his hand. "Pardon the notion, but you look a mite lost."

Lucius grasped his hand and nodded. The other turned to the one in the apron. "Ale on me for the stranger."

"Water." The Professor's voice came as a rough croak. He cleared his throat. "Water, please."

The men stared at him briefly and chuckled. The man in the apron moved behind the bar to oblige.

"So where'd you come from?"

"England," Lucius rasped. "My ship wrecked off the coast last evening."

"A wreck?" The man turned to his companion. "Did you hear anythin' o' that?"

"Nay, not a word."

A beaker of water was set before Lucius, but upon seeing the cloudy looks of it, he was loath to touch it. "Where am I?" he said instead.

"Ye have landed in False Cape, Virginia."

The weathered hat trembled as the other man chuckled. "Better known as the graveyard of the Atlantic."

Lucius grimaced. "That explains the wreck, then."

"What do they call you?"

"Professor Wolgath."

"Professor he says!" The bearded man guffawed and slapped Lucius' back, nearly upsetting his already crooked glasses. "So what are you going to do in the great and vast America, Professor?"

Lucius could think of no other reply than the absolute truth. "I don't know."

"Well, you'll find your way. And you'll grow to like the place soon enough."

The weathered hat leaned forward again. "Good land hereabouts. We all grow to love it sooner rather than later."

Lucius raised a doubtful brow. "Forgive me if I do not readily believe you about that. This land has not received me well."

"Yea?" The first chuckled oddly. "How so?"

"Aside from being shipwrecked," Lucius said casually, lifting his beaker, "when I came awake this morning I was nearly shot by some lunatic."

The man stroked his whiskers. "Oh? Whereabouts was that?"

Lucius gestured vaguely. "Some distance that way by the stream."

"Shorter man? Gray hair?"

He swallowed his first and only sip from the cup. "Indeed. Threatened me with a blunderbuss for trespassing. I do hope he doesn't dwell alone. The man is obviously quite daft."

Without any sort of warning, a knife was slammed point-first into the wood of the bar beside Lucius' wrist. He glanced to the man in the long coat, whose nostrils were flaring mightily. His teeth were bared in a vicious snarl.

"That man is my brother!"

"Oh." Lucius felt the lump in his throat bob as the point of the knife rose up level with his nose.

Chapter 19
May 30, 1765

"Bit for a poor waif, ma'am? Bit for a poor waif?"

The boy worked to make his voice sound as small and slight as possible. He stood near the woman crushing his hat in his hands and watching her expectantly. By appearance he was no more than thirteen with smudged cheeks and tousled brown hair. His clothes were wrinkled and smeared, though not as filthy as some. His shoes were scuffed and poorly put together. Still, if one was able to see beyond this obvious exterior, there was a distinctly unobvious and unordinary glint in his green eyes.

The woman managed to perceive this light and glared. "Be off with you. Go on!"

The boy was not to be shooed. He held out his hat to collect. "Come now, ma'am. Bit for a poor waif?"

"I told you to get on!" She kicked a pebble or two at him. "Now go!"

He drew himself up to give a scornful sniff. "That was awfully rude."

The woman lifted the bucket of slop she carried and swung it toward him.

The boy danced back. "I'm goin'! I'm goin'!" He slipped through the fence and trudged down the road, donning his hat as he went. "Stubborn ol' bat."

This was not an unfamiliar scene in the life of this young boy. He spent his days romping about in search of what he fondly called 'donations.' He had been on his own now for the better part of six months. To ask him about it was to lift the cover of a great adventure novel, as he was not above embellishing the tale. Truth be known he had been staying with an elderly woman, serving as her helping hand quite against his will. She had always been a bit touchy, but by the time she ripened to the age of eighty-six, she had earned the title of cruel. She kept three cats, ten chickens, and a long, gnarled cane, all of which brought nothing but grief to the boy. So now he found himself on his own in the great American Colonies, and getting on well enough by his own measure. In any case he looked much better kept than the strange character he saw stumbling down the road toward him that day.

The man's coat drooped off his shoulders with one sleeve almost completely torn away. The glasses sat at a horrible angle across his angular nose. A crude strip of cloth was wrapped around one of his large hands.

He was clearly the worse for wear, but to the lad's semi-experienced eye, this was an opportunity. After all, how often did someone walk through the countryside wearing a waistcoat and spectacles?

The boy rushed to approach and fell in step alongside the man. "'scuse me, sir," he said, removing his hat once more. "Bit for a poor waif?"

The man did not seem to notice him and strode on.

The lad cleared his throat. "Sir?"

Nothing.

"Are you deaf, sir?"

The man brushed his blond hair from his forehead and kept walking.

The boy licked his lips and slid his nimble hand into the man's pocket as he kept pace with him.

"Oh, just take it!" Without warning the man wrenched the frock coat from his shoulders and let it fall at the thief's feet. "And good health! Even if I was deaf I would still be able to feel, wouldn't I?" he muttered as he trudged on.

The boy could not have been more shocked if the man had produced a fruit basket from his breast pocket. Quickly stemming his surprise, he rifled through the garment. This produced only a faded ribbon with a simple black and white pendant strung upon it.

"What's this?" he said brightly to himself.

The man, who was only a few yards distant, made an abrupt about-face and snatched the necklace away.

"Not that!" he growled. "Just the jacket." Whirling on his heel, he started away again.

The boy slipped into the coat, which smelled strongly of sea salt, and rolled up the sleeves. He did his best to straighten the collar, and began walking again. Perhaps this unfortunate stranger would be willing to give up more if he hung around long enough. Besides that, he was curious about the odd, stumbling man. He toyed with the buttons of his new oversized coat as he went. It was then that he noticed the initials stamped into the brass pieces.

"L W?" He ran to catch up to the man. "Who's L W?"

"I'm L W," the man sighed. "Now leave me alone."

"Someone's awful touchy," the boy murmured. "So what's your name?"

"Professor Lucius Wolgath."

"Wolgath?"

"Professor."

"Hm." Professor? He had never met a professor before. Not that he knew of anyway. "I'm Foley Conrad Princeton III." The man said nothing and Foley raised an eyebrow. "That's supposed to impress you, Professor."

Lucius snorted. "The only way you're going to impress me is if you produce some means of removing me from this miserable continent!" His voice crescendoed into a shout, though it was at no one in particular.

Foley was puzzled for a moment. "The sky is still up. The grass is still green. The ocean is still blue. What's the problem?"

"Ocean." Lucius stopped walking and stood still.

Foley theorized that the gentleman was either very angry or very ill, and either way he seemed on the verge of madness. The boy swallowed as he waited. When nothing happened, he determined to approach with all caution. Foley squinted up at him, but he did not stir. "Sir?"

"You're very philosophical for a young boy, aren't you?"

"Mr.-Professor Wolgath?"

At last Wolgath looked down at him. "I must find a ship."

Foley, sensing a fresh opportunity, drew himself up to his full height of four feet and three-quarter inches. "Right you are, sir! I happen to know the exact location of a little harbor not too far off."

Lucius eyed the small one before him. He was, naturally, suspicious of the boy. After all, his first act upon their meeting had been an attempt at thievery. Still, he was in desperate need of an ally in this untamed part of the world.

"How old are you?"

Foley hesitated. "Going on seventeen."

"If you intend on lying to me with every breath, I'll find the blessed port on my own." With that he started down the road again.

Foley shadowed him with a sigh. "Very well. It's fifteen."

"You're not a day older than twelve." He waved the little imp away, putting him from his mind as he did. He was most surprised when Foley appeared standing not an inch in front of him and scowling.

"I'm fourteen!" he declared emphatically. "Whether you believe it or not, that's the truth! And I can lead you to that harbor. At least I could have, and a lot faster than you could yourself I might add, Professor."

"And the fee?"

Foley blinked in confusion. He had not given the good Professor credit enough for that discernment.

"I assume you'll want something in return for this little excursion?" Lucius brushed by him once more. "Everyone wants something. Well I can't afford to go gallivanting hither and yon across America when I have a happy life waiting for me in England!" His voice rose to an agonized shout.

Foley watched curiously as he placed his hands on his head and then let them fall. The man's shoulders slumped with exhaustion-or perhaps defeat. The boy rushed to his side and stood with his arms akimbo.

"And so, sir?"

Lucius slowly shifted his gaze to look at the lad. "Can you truly do as you say boy?"

"Never fear that, sir."

"Well, we'll haggle a price out when we get there, then."

Foley grinned broadly and tugged at the collar of his "new" coat with a proud nod. "Right you are, sir! Foley'll have you there lock, stock, and barrel!"

The boy started off and Lucius quirked an eyebrow as he watched him go. "You'll forgive me if I doubt that, my boy."

Chapter 20
May 30, 1765

"How-much-"

Foley looked around in confusion. "What do you mean? I thought we were going to settle that when I got you there."

Lucius shook his aching head. He was following his guide up an intolerably steep hill, and now leaned against a tree by the path to catch his air. His breathing came in stiff gasps as he explained. "I was trying-to ask-how-much-farther?"

"Oh, that," Foley replied easily. "Another half an hour and we shall see white sails. So long as we keep the pace that is."

Lucius gave a mighty shove to push away from the tree. He quirked an eyebrow at the young opportunist. "I am a scholar. I never professed to be a frontiersman or a buckskin."

"I wouldn't exactly call this the frontier, Professor," Foley commented as they continued on. "Buckskin…Where'd you drag that up from?"

Lucius started to shrug and grinned sheepishly. "An old field journal."

"Well try to forget it," the boy advised. "That went out a while ago, and a slip like that is a sure sign you're not really American."

"That is if the slight accent doesn't tip anyone off," Lucius added ryely. "Anyway, I never professed to being American."

"I know, I know," Foley sighed. "You never professed to being anything but a professor, but I'm telling you now, Mr. Wolgath, you've come at a bad year. Being English over here doesn't make you noteworthy. At the moment it makes you lynch-worthy."

Lucius sighed. "Don't worry, lad. I'll watch how I step."

"Oh, I'm sure," Foley assured him. "I'm only afraid you're gonna take me down with you."

"How long did you say it was to the harbor?" Lucius inquired as they crested their hill.

"Half hour."

"Then why am I seeing mastheads?"

It was true enough. The land which stretched below them was a wide peninsula with a packed harbor on its eastern shore. The port was a mere ripple in a pond compared to the Port of London, but it was a soothing sight to Lucius' desperate heart.

"I wanted to give you a surprise," Foley said from somewhere behind him. "I knew we were this close, I just thought it'd be nice for you if-"

"Don't give it another thought," Lucius murmured. It was clear the boy was lying, but he wasn't really paying any attention to him anymore. Before him lay his escape, and it seemed that he needed only to reach out his hand to gain it.

He moved down the hill in long strides. Single-minded focus gave fresh wind to his lank sails, and the exertion of only moments ago was forgotten. He gained level ground and paused only when he reached the edge of the township. The first order of business was to find someone in charge. A harbormaster. But where? In a town so small, was it possible they didn't have one?

"Erum, Professor?"

Lucius looked down to see Foley at his side. The boy was holding his hat out expectantly.

"Where will the Harbormaster be?"

Foley blinked once. "I don't know. In the harbor, I guess."

Lucius shook his head. "Very perceptive of you." He moved on, barely giving the lad another look.

"Hold on there, Professor!" Foley scrambled to catch up. "You promised payment when I got you here, and I've got you here! What do I get, eh? You can't just-hey, Professor! Are you listening?"

While Foley babbled Lucius was fumbling with the pockets of his waistcoat. He finally yanked the top button free and tossed it to the boy.

"A button?" Foley exclaimed, stopping dead in his tracks. "One button!?"

"It's good brass," Lucius replied absently. "I was meticulous with my packing for this trip. I brought only my best," he sneered.

"I can't spend a button! What'd you expect me to do with this?"

"Wear it. Trade it off. Melt it down. It doesn't really matter because it's all I've got." He glanced over his shoulder and added, "Unless you want the actual garment as well. It would match your coat quite nicely."

Foley slowed his pace while the Professor continued on. He was studying the little brass piece when he had a sudden thought. He slipped the thing into the pocket of his trousers and hurried to catch the man once more.

"Wait a minute, Professor!"

"Now what?"

"I was just wondering," Foley began carefully, "how you intended to pay for your passage. Since you don't actually have any money, I mean."

Lucius was undaunted. "I can't pay anyone now. They will have to be gracious enough to wait until we reach England."

"I hate to have to tell you this-" Foley broke off in thought. "Actually I don't. Anyway, I hope you realize how difficult it's gonna be to get anyone to believe that you'll actually be able to pay when you reach England."

"I'll just have to convince them."

Foley raised his eyebrows and fell in step behind Lucius. He obviously doubted the man had any hope of success, but he would not miss the attempt for all the brass buttons in Virginia.

The small harbor did not seem to be very active, but that was to a man accustomed to the thriving Port of London. So it was relatively easy for Wolgath to underestimate the men there. The first ship at the wharf was a smart one-masted birth dubbed *The Courting Belle*. As sailors passed sacks of an unknown cargo from the wharf to others on deck, one man stood off to the side reading over a list. The fact that he could read at all marked him for leadership. Lucius moved toward this individual.

"Excuse me!"

"Keep those stacks straight there, Stevenson!" the man shouted without seeming to notice Lucius.

"Excuse me," Lucius said, closer now.

"Yes, I heard you the first time." At last the man turned to see who it was that wanted him. "My name is Moor, Captain of *The Courting Belle*."

"I'm Professor Lucius Wolgath."

"A professor?" The Captain turned his attention back to his men. "And is there something I can do for you? Though I must warn you that I am rather distracted just now."

"I am in need of assistance," Lucius told him. "I've been stranded here against my will."

"I don't know that I've ever met anyone who was stranded according to their will."

The Captain moved around the bow as he consulted his list. Lucius followed him and Foley trailed behind.

"I have a life and family waiting for me in England. I must get back to them or I could conceivably lose everything."

"You haven't even asked me where my ship is heading, Professor."

"So long as you're heading to Europe it doesn't matter. I don't care! Anything which puts me closer is a blessing."

Captain Moor raised an eyebrow and returned to his list. "We'll need these barrels over there, Daniels!"

"Aye, sir."

Lucius hesitated and looked expectantly at him. "I'm asking for your assistance. Begging it if I must."

Moor clenched his jaw and his countenance became grave. "I may be able to arrange something for you."

Lucius felt his shoulders sag with the warm weight of relief. A weary smile stretched across his worn features. "Thank you! You have my greatest-"

"I can assure you that the price will be fair, though the accommodations may be less than spacious."

Lucius nodded. "It does not matter. I will make sure you're paid as soon as we reach land."

It suddenly occurred to Lucius that if *The Courting Belle* was not heading directly to a port within easy reach of Penn and Tyler's Green, it would be difficult-one might even say impossible-to pay the Captain promptly. The man's next statement rendered this thought meaningless.

"I would ask for payment beforehand sir."

Lucius blinked. The smile on his face cracked. "What was that?"

"You can't expect me to cart you from here to Europe on good faith. Don't get me wrong, but I'll need more than that to fill my plate in the evening."

Lucius could not help but notice that the captain's tone was bland, almost as though he had expected this.

"I do have sympathy for your plight, sir. As much as I would like to, I cannot afford to give you a hand for nothing. An extra person on board means extra provisions and water for upwards of seven weeks. Can you provide that for yourself?"

Lucius twisted his hands so that his palms were out, a pleading gesture.

For one frantic instant he considered reasoning, begging, anything! His head drooped another inch toward his chest.

"No."

"Then there is only one more option I can offer you."

Wolgath's head snapped up excitedly. "Yes? What is it?"

Moor crossed his arms. "I can have you sign an indenture contract."

Lucius' jaw locked.

"When we make land," Moor went on. "You would stay aboard until someone offered to purchase you and your seven-year contract. Then you could work off your debt to them and be on your way."

"After being trapped in whatever port you drop me in for seven years?"

Moor shrugged and returned his focus to his lists. "You said you would take anything. So long as I was heading to Europe it did not matter."

"Perhaps that was a poor choice of words."

"So be it. I'm afraid there is nothing much more that I can do for you then, Professor. I bid you good day."

Moor stalked away, shouting to his deckhands and feeling rather heartless. But in these uncertain times, what could he do?

Lucius stared blankly after him. Another escape thwarted. Another flicker of hope snuffed out. He could not help but feel that he was standing in the middle of a sucking quagmire that pulled at his legs, threatening to cover his knees.

"Whoa."

Lucius heard Foley's voice dimly from somewhere at his side. His muscles were momentarily locked with tension. It was all he could do to murmur, "What?"

"I reckoned you would have taken him up on that," Foley replied, absently readjusting his hat as he spoke. "I mean I don't think anything's worth seven or eight or... twelve years of your life, but most disagree with me on that."

Lucius shook his head, now filled with images of his home, his brother, the Condreves, Alexcena. *Oh! Alexcena!*

"I cannot afford to lose seven years of my life. I've been gone too long now. Seven years is an eternity." His voice shuddered distinctly over these words.

The boy shrugged. "Yea... Three years is pretty long too."

Lucius missed this cryptic reply. He was already moving forward again on wooden legs. There were more sizable ships moored in close proximity thereabouts, several small crafts-presumably for fishing-and some forty random seamen wandering the banks. Lucius eyed these rough figures doubtfully at first. Then his hope swelled and he straightened his shoulders. He did not need forty; he needed only one. One man with means who believed in his story enough to afford him the mercy he was so desperate for.

"What 'er you doing now?" Foley called and half scrambled after him.

Lucius' determination would not allow his focus to drift, and so he did not look back, but merely replied, "I am doing what I must, boy!"

In the winter of 1765, the elected delegates of the American Colonies sent the Olive Branch Petition directly to their King and his parliament. Their illustrious and gracious monarch had the decency to restrain himself when he received it. He did not tear it apart. He did not burn it. As a matter of fact he did not even open it. He simply refused to acknowledge it. This was the colonists' last-stitch effort at establishing peace with their mother country, and their celebrated patriarch flung it in their faces.

Such was the reaction of every sailor on that stretch of bank to Lucius Wolgath's pleas. One man took pity, another took a swing. One would shrug away, another would laugh in his face. The replies were varied, but they could all be simplified into one lyrical phrase. *Not without the money, sonny.*

By the time the Professor made his way to the last berth, his story was well circulated. The burly captain held up a hand as he approached.

"I've already gotten the layout of your situation," he said sternly. "The answer's 'no.' I thought it only fair to tell you before you went through the whole thing again."

He moved away, leaving Lucius standing stock still in the road. A sick feeling twisted him inside. It was not a queasiness so much as an emptiness. A hollow exhaustion.

Some small part of his mind registered what his eyes were seeing. Foley was sitting comfortably at the base of a tree some five yards away munching noisily on a fresh apple. He started towards him, though he knew not why. What help could this boy provide? If he could he probably wouldn't anyway, but it was already a moot point to him.

"Hey, Professor."

"It's not like *you* have a ship!"

Foley turned his head. "Huh?"

Lucius ignored him and lengthened his strides. Foley leapt up behind him, but he did not notice. There was an audible whistling running through his head. His collar became too tight as his breathing accelerated. The land tapered before him into a point. He was surrounded on three sides by unforgiving ocean with only firm rejection spreading behind.

"Professor, where 'er you going?"

"Maybe I'll swim it," he said with dull ire. He was standing very close to the end of the peninsula, and even as he said this he slid one boot into the edge of the water. Logic won out and he spun on his heel. "Maybe I'll commission my own boat. To commandeer it would be much swifter, though."

Foley stood slack-jawed and watching as Lucius muttered to himself.

"Ridiculous. Send for help? Impossible. I'm cut off from all resources with not so much as a farthing to my name, and what do I do? What to do?"

Wolgath's eyes were unfocused and unseeing. As he talked his hand reached up to tug at his collar, which was constricting around his throat. A thread audibly popped, but it was not loud enough to be heard over the raspy ring in his head.

"Everything I've worked for. Everything I've come to care about." His other hand stretched out before him, reaching for what his mind saw. "I can almost see it. Like looking around a sharp corner. You know physically that it's there, but the wall is hiding it from you. You can't move, so you can't get to the wall to tear it down, but if you could get to it to tear it down it wouldn't matter because you could just move around it and there she'd be…"

He saw her clear as a crystal stream standing in the sun, her hair spilling down over her slim shoulders and a smile lighting her eyes. His arm fell to his side. He blinked and the memory vanished. A relief and a rending that she was gone again.

Foley shifted from foot to foot. "Professor? You're ripping your shirt." He indicated his collar.

"What does it matter?" Lucius' voice trembled with the gruff pain that wracked his mind. Very slowly he began to rip the coarse ruffles from around his throat. They fell to the ground in filmy strips. "What does any of it matter until I can return to England?"

He faced the ocean and all but fell to the ground. Foley stepped closer. The boy seemed afraid to touch him, or even speak to him, and soon moved away. Lucius sighed as his eyes roved over the desolate waves.

Chapter 21

May 30, 1765

Lucius drifted into a gray torpor. He sat there for days or hours or weeks, his mind a muddle of confused memories. Recollections of Alexcena, Leopold, his flat, Commodore, growing up, going to church; all walks of his life swirled and ebbed before his very eyes. Eventually he began to find his way through the jumble and his thoughts started to make sense again. It was as though he was stepping out of his life just for a moment to see it from a distance. It was odd at first because all that stood out from this new perspective were the good things. Perhaps this was because he was so desperate to regain them that he was momentarily transfixed by them. Hard as he had tried to keep them in mind while he had been at sea, somehow his predicament was always there to mar the comfort he sought. Now they shone clear and strong and he was able to remember all the important things which made up his purpose in life. And after all, this life was not meant to be about himself in the first place. A tiny piece of wisdom had been slipped into his palm, and the bulk of his despair lay in tatters at his sides. It was Wolgath's nature to face a situation, analyze it, at times even falter before it, and after careful consideration methodically solve the problem. This being the largest he had ever dealt with, the process took some considerable time.

He had been made to face this situation and had faltered. His faith waivered and he felt the full brunt of every horrible possibility on his shoulders. It was likely that he would never see his home and his family again. Having hope does not mean that one is safe from such misfortunes as this. Having faith does not necessarily make one's circumstances less tragic. But what Lucius had forgotten in that fateful hour was the assurance from God and Savior that even if the worst should happen, he had hope of security thereafter. He prayed that he might never forget again. He had felt the weight of hopelessness and knew with certainty that he could not bear the load.

Lucius rose. He had the odd feeling that his bones were creaking like so much old wood. The exhaustion was still there, but now his faculties at least were restored to him. He could not have been sitting on his own for more than one actual hour, he realized. By the looks of the sun it was mid-afternoon. Only five ships now were moored at the bank. Sailors still crowded around them. Gulls still cried overhead, and Foley was sitting under that same tree, now appearing to doze.

Lucius grimaced to himself and headed toward the boy. Foley cut his eyes toward him as he approached.

"May I?" he asked, gesturing toward the tree.

Foley appraised him for a moment and then nodded. "If you like."

Lucius plopped down beside him.

"Are you all right now, Professor?"

Lucius thought about this, and grinned weakly. "Scarred, but never better."

"That's good," Foley nodded. "You had me a little... *concerned*."

"Yes," Lucius replied. "I'm sorry about that."

"I've never seen anyone go mad before." The boy said this with a kind of awe, as though it was a fascinating concept.

Lucius chuckled. "It won't happen again, I assure you. I allowed my personal problems to get the better of me, that's all."

The boy nodded his understanding. They fell into silence while Lucius was wondering if he truly did understand. He was still wondering when his stomach gave an almighty growl. He held his arm against it to suppress it.

"Oh, I forgot I grabbed this for you, Professor." Foley produced a sizeable apple from his pocket. "I was about to give it to you earlier, but, well…"

Lucius accepted it suspiciously. He quirked an eyebrow at the boy. "Where did you get these, by the way?"

"I found them."

"You stole them?"

Foley bristled. "I didn't hop a single fence! They were by the side of the road. Besides, if they were gonna eat 'em, they would have made sure the tree grew so that they would all land on their side of the fence."

"A brilliant defence," Lucius said as he took a noisy bite from the apple. "But I'll not have you stealing. You ought to try asking. They might be more generous than you think."

Foley snorted. "You tried 'asking' about thirty times today and didn't find a single generous one in the whole bunch. No offense, but I'll stick with my method for now."

"Not if you want to stay near me you won't. I'm a little surprised you're still here anyway."

Foley shrugged with an offhanded grin. "Nowhere else to be."

"Oh?"

"Nope. Besides I'm enjoying watching you make an idiot of yourself in front of all these sailors."

Sudden ire flashed across Lucius' features and he glared. "Keep your mockery to yourself, boy, or I'll tow you back to your folks myself!"

"Sorry, Professor Wolgath." Normally Foley would have bucked at such a remark, but he was suddenly anxious. He was very happy being with the odd professor. He was funny without meaning to be, which Foley liked about him. Though he knew the professor could not make good on *that* particular threat, he still might send him away, and Foley did not want that. "Sorry, sir," he said again.

Lucius sighed heavily and leaned back against the tree trunk. He allowed his eyes to fall shut, considering. He had a general idea of how he wanted to proceed in dealing with the mammoth predicament he now found himself in. All he needed was a place to start.

"What'r you doing, Professor?" Foley chimed.

"Thinking," he replied dully, and then looked around at the boy. "I have made the largest decision. The hardest decision. I will work for one year-" His voice trembled despite his resolve. "-more if need be, and build up enough funds to travel back to England."

"I thought you had to get back right away."

"I do, but it is better to lose one year than to sign away seven."

"Yea," Foley nodded. "I wouldn't sign away anything either. I'm my own man!" He thumped his thin chest comically to emphasize that point.

Lucius eyed him beneath the rims of his glasses. "You're still a boy."

Foley leapt to his feet, his enthusiasm unphased. "I can help you."

"What do you mean?"

"I know this land," Foley explained. "You need a guide. Directionally and socially if you're gonna fit in. Face it, Professor, you won't last a week without someone helping you! ...sir."

Lucius raised an eyebrow. This boy was beginning to bear a striking resemblance to a stray cat. Endearing but annoying, and not leaving until he was ready to. "What of your family? Aren't you needed at home?"

"Don't have one."

"Home or family?"

"Both. Either. Doesn't matter," Foley stammered and flushed. "I want to go with you. Will you let me, Professor?"

Lucius pretended to ponder and bit into his apple again. "I don't know that I'm actually going anywhere."

"I would suggest Currituck." Foley turned to point over his shoulder. Lucius peered across the water at a long smudge on the horizon. "It's on the actual mainland and much larger than Knotts Isle, where we are now," Foley explained. "Bigger port, more opportunity."

"You mean more pockets to pick." Lucius rose so he could loom over the boy. If he was going to have him tag along, he wanted to make his next point adequately clear. "The first time I catch you stealing, I'll light up your scrawny hide, fourteen or not."

Foley simply grinned. "Yes, sir."

"The first time I catch you lying, I'm turning you in to a church orphanage."

Foley adjusted his cap. "Right you are, Professor. We best get to it if we're going to go now. It's a long walk up the river."

"Excuse me?"

"We gotta walk back up the river. The shortest place to cross the bay is three miles away."

Lucius stared incredulously. "But we just walked three miles to get here from that exact direction."

"Yep."

Lucius shook his head. His legs and the day's sunlight were sure to give out before they made the crossing.

"Isn't there some sort of ferry service?"

Foley's brow puckered. "Yea. There's one just over there, but-hang on, Professor! How are you gonna pay for that?"

Lucius gave the boy no heed as he strode toward the raft. A snaggle-toothed hermit of a man stood on the bank beside it. He was leaning against a pole and steadily chewing a brown hunk of something. Lucius approached with a determined lift in his chin.

The man nodded and spat in the sand. "How do?"

"We find ourselves in need of a way to cross to Currituck," Lucius declared.

"I got a way." The man kicked his raft fondly. "I'll take you both for four cents."

"Four?"

"Yea." He spat at the ground again. "Two apiece."

Lucius thought for a moment. He suddenly bent down and tore the copper buckle from his shoe. Foley looked on, shocked as ever by his strange behavior. Lucius offered the buckle to the ferryman.

"Will this do?"

"Well enough, thankee." He accepted it and bit the metal swiftly. "All aboard, then."

Lucius turned an amused eye to his little follower. "Wouldn't last one week, eh? I do possess some resourcefulness."

Foley shrugged. "Who'd 've thought it?"

Lucius had to grin forlornly at that. "You've never met my brother."

Chapter 22

May 30, 1765

At that moment Leopold was sitting on deck of the *Liberator* and wondering why in the world he hadn't used his gift for resourcefulness to come up with a means of getting Tabitha Winslett off the boat before they ever left port. Of course, he had not been aware of her presence when they left port, but he would not let himself off so easy. True, the girl had been a help with Alexcena, but more than that she had been a bother. Whatever assistance she gave was ultimately trumped by blunder. He taught her to handle her own laundry; she draped a set of sheets over the railing and they blew away. She mopped the floor of her cabin; she did it using vinegar and sea water. The room stank of pickled fish for several days, making Alexcena feel that much worse (he was certain) and not doing much good for the plank floor either. She had the cook teach her how to brew coffee; now she was bringing it up to the sailors on night watch. A lady of her station ought never to do something so base. A lady of her familial background ought to know her position and keep to it. In all fairness she was probably doing it to be nice, a new habit she seemed to be forming. Problem was that it would send the wrong message. The sailors might begin to relax with her. Worse still, they might get *familiar*. That would be the worst predicament thus far. It was certainly one he had no interest in dealing with. But he was already dealing with it. Just the thought of the possibility of such a thing was drawing him into a foul mood.

It was not the same with Alexcena. He had agreed to worrying about her from the start, knowing that he may never be called on to do that. Alexcena was as different from Tabitha as salt from pepper. She might fall into physical peril, but she would never deliberately, willingly, or stupidly put herself in a situation that would expose her to unnecessary danger. Especially *this* unnecessary danger.

He readjusted the Bible resting on his knees so that the moonlight fell directly onto the words. Even the improved light did no good. His concentration was broken by his own worrying. The glint of starlight reflecting on Tabitha's lustrous curls across the deck did not help his focus.

He grunted and turned his countenance to the sea. "Women."

Cliché as it was, he had to admit that it wasn't merely her presence that caused the issue, or issues as it were. If she were a man there would be almost no problem at all. The clumsiness would still be there. The naïveté, the arrogance, the pushiness, all would still be there, of course. It would be so much easier to deal with all of that if she were a boy. The conflict which plagued him most would disappear.

Tabitha chose that moment to twitter airily, and Leo looked around. She was talking to Lt. Greyson. He was laughing softly over his coffee mug as she spoke.

Leo turned back to the ocean. "So it starts."

He was so wrapped in his own aggravation that he did not hear the girl approaching just seconds later.

"Do you care for coffee, Mr. Wolgath?" She offered the kettle and produced a mug from her apron pocket. Where had she picked up an apron?

Leo grunted and blatantly readjusted his Book. He saw Tabitha's brow pucker, but she smoothed it quickly and poured a steaming stream of coffee into the mug. He was only slightly surprised when she settled herself on a crate by his feet to sip it slowly. Ladies like herself were supposed to take their coffee with cream and sugar, maybe even a splash of vanilla. Couldn't she do anything correctly?

"Alexcena is much improved," she began cheerily. "Her sleep is so much more easy now."

"So you decided to come on deck and play tea party?" Leo could not bring himself to hold this snide remark.

Tabitha raised an eyebrow. Her shoulders drew back by a fraction of an inch. "I am grateful to the sailors on board for giving us such an easy journey."

"They have had little to do with it," Leo returned. "Do they control the waves, or the winds? You gave them your gratitude when you gave them your money, so let that be an end to it."

"May I inquire as to why you are so offended by this?" she asked in what was obviously her best lady-to-servant voice.

"It's unseemly," Leo hissed. "A woman ought not to be cavorting on deck with seamen!"

She made a small, offended squeak, but he was passed caring. She had voiced the question, she could handle the answer.

"Serving coffee and giggling with the First Mate," he went on. "It will bring nothing but dishonor to your reputation and trouble to me. Call me insensible or insensitive if you like, but I don't really want that kind of trouble around."

Tabitha rose. "Since the start of this voyage I have done nothing but try to help. I've cared for Alexcena and I've tried to be respectful of you. Now I've simply attempted to show a little appreciation to these gentlemen and this is how you treat me?"

Leo suddenly found himself on his feet. His anger blazed, but he managed to keep his voice low. "You, young miss, are not even supposed to be here. Never think for one second that I owe you for anything. Maybe by society's thinkin' I am beneath you, but you have been nothing short of burdensome from the day you set foot on the *Liberator*. Don't delude yourself into thinking that you have ever been respectful of me. Your arrogance and sarcasm have cost me dearly in self-control."

He took a pause. Tabitha had not moved even to breathe throughout his unforgiving tirade. Her eyes glinted, and Leo thought for one petrified instant that she might burst into tears. Instead she raised a tremulous hand to smooth back a lock of hair and turned her gaze to the sea.

"That's too bad. I would have thought that you had grown accustomed to my presence by now." She broke off, clearing her throat. "I shall try harder to be of use in the future, certainly." With a sudden turn of her head, she grinned coolly at him. "Perhaps I'll join the men in the ratlines."

Her haughtiness only fueled the fire in him. "You think that's clever, do you?" He moved one step closer, looming over the lady. "Rest assured, Ms. Winslett, if you do so much as one more thing to disrupt this voyage, I'll set you adrift myself."

The grin on her pink lips wavered and held. "You cannot be rid of me so easily."

Leo couldn't help but smirk at the thought. "Try me."

"Is there something wrong, Ms. Winslett? Mr. Wolgath?" Lt. Greyson was suddenly close by them. He offered his hand to Tabitha, but she kept her own firmly clasped around her mug.

"No indeed, Lieutenant," Tabitha replied.

Leo worked to remove the glare from his face.

"I was just having a brief discussion with Mr. Wolgath," she went on, "but now I think I had best go and see about Alexcena. She does still need my help sometimes."

The Lieutenant nodded. "Of course. Shall I escort you to your cabin?"

Leo's scowl snapped back into place. "Oh, I think she knows the way by now, Greyson."

Greyson pursed his lips. Leo had been drawing similar expressions from the Captain as well as this man since his first spat with Tabitha. These shows of blatant animosity weren't likely to cease, so Leo only stared dully back.

"Do not trouble yourself, Lieutenant," Tabitha said sweetly. "I would not dream of drawing you from your duties. Good evening."

She walked off and Greyson moved away. Leo crossed his arms. She had given her adieu vaguely, but Leo was certain that no part of it was meant for him. He had become contemptible in her eyes. So be it. Probably the one man she ought to genuinely fear on board that ship, and she treated him with nothing more than aloof malice. He was reminded of her father's comment of so long ago as he lifted his Bible once more.

"And now I must agree," he muttered in the half light. "It would take a man aflame to handle that woman and her gift for exuberance!"

Chapter 23

May 31, 1765

Lucius awoke and gave an almighty sneeze. He sat up straight and was instantly, dizzyingly disoriented. Hay surrounded him in a layer one foot thick atop a plank floor. Stalks of it protruded from his clothes at all angles. His head felt as though it had swollen overnight. He breathed in through his mouth-since his nose was completely clogged-and felt motes of dust cling to his tongue.

"Ugh!"

He spat into the hay beside him and raised a hand to his aching head. Another sneeze erupted from his nose. He felt an urgent need to escape the clinging hay, but the wretched stuff seemed to be everywhere. He rose and began feverishly brushing it away from his clothes. This brought on a string of raucous sneezes.

A short pile of hay shivered in the far corner and Foley sat up beneath it.

"God bless you, Professor," he said cheerily.

Lucius eyed him almost darkly. "Thank you." And he sneezed again.

"You getting sick, Professor?"

Lucius massaged his forehead. Every sound seemed dull to his ears. "I think I've contracted a foul humor."

"Probably something in the hay," Foley commented matter-of-factly. He began picking the stalks from his own clothes one at a time.

Lucius dimly recalled the decision to slip into the barn last night. It had seemed like a good idea originally. Now it was simply a nuisance.

"Should've just slept under a tree," he mumbled.

"Not this close to the banks. You'd be liable to wake up with a snake up your sleeve."

Lucius suppressed a shudder and swallowed. "I'll have to keep that in mind."

He sneezed twice more while brushing frantically at his clothes. He was seized with a desperate need to be away from the all-too-sweet scent of hay.

"You'll just get dust in your eyes that way, Professor."

"Never you mind the motes in my eyes, boy!" Lucius snapped. "Let's get down from here before someone finds us."

They slipped down from the loft and out the door. Mercifully there seemed to be no one very close around, so they went unnoticed. The sun had just come fully over the tips of the trees lining a distant ridge. Lucius shielded his eyes against it. A light haze remained over the waking harbor of Currituck. The rays of the sun seemed to glint from every speck of dew, making the rooftops shimmer with golden light. Lucius was struck by the beauty of it, even through his cracked lenses. The feeling passed at once when he remembered where he was, leaving a bittersweet air behind.

"What do you want to do now, Professor?" Foley piped up after a moment.

"Just what I said I would," Wolgath replied with resolve. "I'm going to find work."

He started walking. Foley struggled to keep pace, taking two steps for each of his long strides. The boy said nothing as they went and Lucius threw him a sidelong glance.

"No suggestions? No impertinent warnings?"

Foley shook his head. "I like watching the way you do things, Professor."

Lucius snorted. "I'm just a big laugh to you. A walking, talking, amusing anecdote. The Cambridge idiot lost in a wild and unknown country."

"What's an antidote?"

"Anecdote. It's simply another word for 'joke.'"

"Oh. Yea, you're all of that, but I like you, Professor!" Foley gave him a jovial pat on the shoulder.

"Comforting if not terribly encouraging." Lucius paused and looked to the buildings surrounding them.

They had wandered into the city, away from the harbor, but Lucius had not paid much attention to the locality. The structures here were not as rough as they had been thus far. The streets between them seemed more organized. The blocks were more defined. If not for the differences in the abundance of trees and the surrounding foliage, he might have imagined himself in a small hamlet in England. The plants growing wild on the edges of the city were foreign to him. This detail was obvious thanks to his studies in botany.

"Where did you say we are?" he mumbled.

"Uh, Currituck of the colony of North Carolina."

"Odd name," Lucius commented. "I'd be petrified to attempt pronouncing it."

"It's an American native name."

"I see."

The town seemed to be coming alive now. Their morning meals complete, the colonists were beginning to emerge from their generally quiet homes. Lucius stood observing for several minutes while Foley lounged against the building behind them. He saw every sort of person he could possibly imagine there was. A young milk maid carried a yoke of pails over her shoulders. A blacksmith toted a barrel toward his forge. An old housewife snapped a clean sheet and strung it over her line. A merchant unlocked the door of his shop and greeted a passing couple. None of these ordinary townsfolk stood out to him, but the soldiers certainly did.

Red uniforms marched up and down the streets nearly as thick as the colonial citizens.

"Why are there so many English soldiers here?" Lucius asked.

Foley snorted indifferently. "I don't know. I hear talk, though. Most think they were sent to protect us from ourselves. The soldiers think they were sent to protect us from the frogs and the red skins and the smugglers."

"The Seven Years War ended over two years ago. Weren't they all relocated?"

"The French were…supposedly. The natives are still around, though. They're just a little more quiet than they used to be."

Lucius looked to him over his shoulder. "Are you always so offhanded with troubling revelations such as these?"

The boy shrugged. "They're only revelations to *you*. This stuff's all normal to me."

"Well, please try to remember in future that I wasn't born here."

"I wasn't either," Foley replied. "Learn to pay attention and maybe you'll catch on like I did."

"What did I tell you about keeping a civil tone in your head?"

Foley jabbed his hands in his pockets and dipped his head. "Sorry, sir."

"I'm going to ask one of the soldiers about finding work."

"Why ask them?" Foley puzzled. "They know about as much about

Currituck as you do, and what's worse they don't care."

"Wait for me here."

He did not delay to hear the boy's muttered reply. He strode across the street to the corner where three uniformed men stood conversing easily.

"Excuse me," Wolgath said as he approached. "I'm in need of assistance."

One of the three spared him a glance. "Not here to assist colonists. See your own authorities."

"Oh, I'm not a colonist. I'm an Englishman, lately of Penn and Tyler's Green."

The private turned to him again with a roll of his eyes. "You were in England, you came here, that makes you a colonist. So snap us a salute and get going."

By now the other two were looking at him as well. One held his musket cradled in his arms. Both eyed him with equal measures of distaste. Their blatant indifference pricked Wolgath's already sensitive temper.

"I am trying everything in my power to return to England. All I needed to ask was if you knew-"

"You can't be English," the first man jeered. "You obviously don't understand the language."

"Maybe you should try another," the second man suggested.

"He looks like a dandy. Let's try a dandy language. *Fait le nigaud comprend Français?*" he quoted in abominable French. The pair behind him snickered.

Lucius glared and then sighed, his shoulders slumping as his anger gave way. "*Parfaitement. Bon jour.*" With that he bowed and turned away. He was followed only by the soldiers' laughter as he went.

Foley, who had slipped down into a sitting position against the building, leapt to his feet as Wolgath approached. "Well?"

"Oh, they were charming," Lucius answered wryly.

"They always are. Care for a suggestion?" Lucius merely looked at him, so Foley went on. "Stick with the locals. Postmasters, pamphleteers, and tavern owners are your best bets."

"Why's that?"

"They always know everything that's going on. If anyone in town is looking to hire, they'll know about it."

Lucius nodded, already readjusting his plans by this new advice, but his attention was diverted just then by the pealing of church bells. The sound pulled him back to familiar places in his mind.

"Professor?" Foley tugged at his sleeve. "Come, Professor. The

Postmaster's office is over there."

Lucius was already moving, swiveling in the direction of the chiming bells. "No. There is something I need to do first."

Foley wrinkled his nose and hurried to follow. Wolgath's long strides were going to keep him on his toes; there was no questioning that.

Lucius rounded a corner, his eyes traveling up the whitewashed building to the steeple high above the churchyard. A middle-aged gentleman stood in the yard, tugging the rope of the impressive brass bell. As he watched the man stilled his bell and reentered the building, leaving the door ajar.

"A church?" Foley queried. "Why do you need to go to a church?"

"I don't *need* to go," Lucius replied as he strode on, "but it was a nice thought once it occurred to me."

He barely heard the boy as he grumbled, "The Postmaster was closer."

Inside the church seemed dark coming from the sunny street. Once Lucius' eyes had adjusted, it was more like stepping into a shady glen. The layout of it was similar to almost every Christian church in every country. This likeness sent a wave of tranquility through him, and he sighed. The warmth of it rushed over his shoulders and down his arms to make his very fingertips tingle.

Just in front of the pulpit a lady stood sweeping the wood floor. She seemed to be the only other soul in the place, though Lucius knew the man must be there as well. She looked up to smile as they came in and simply continued her work.

Lucius walked midway up the aisle and slipped into a pew. Foley flopped down beside him and grunted.

"Why are we here, Professor?" he whispered.

Lucius let his head lull back and his eyes fall closed. "Because it's comforting to me," he breathed. "Church is one of the most peaceful places on earth, even if one is convicted. If it's not, then something is truly out of place."

"I thought peaceful meant quiet," Foley commented, eyeing the woman and her broom. "Churches always have somebody preachin' or singin', and no matter which one they do, they always do it at the top of their voice."

The corner of Lucius' mouth twitched up in a grin. "That is not always the case."

The boy crossed his arms. "Well, churches still aren't quiet."

"Then why do you keep whispering?"

The boy had no answer, which made Lucius chuckle. Then he leaned forward, propping his elbows on his knees.

"Ah, Foley," he murmured.

"Yes, sir?"

"I was just thinking about my reaction to all this. I have a weak mind to be so overcome."

Foley patted his shoulder. "That's all right, Professor. It happens to the best of us."

"It was inexcusable." He shook his head slowly. "In my heart and in my head, I gave up. I nearly allowed the sorrows of this world to overtake me. In that hour, I succumbed. Of that I am desperately ashamed. I once was able to see the good and hope above everything."

Foley said nothing. He was puzzled, even outright confused, by the Professor's words. But he assumed it appropriate to keep his thoughts to himself sense Lucius wasn't really talking to him; his eyes were focused on something distant in the front of the church.

"My mind was shattered by this world," Wolgath went on, "and now I am left with the task of pulling the shards together once more. I fear they've scattered further than I ever intended to allow."

Silence reigned for several minutes until Foley said, "I'll bet that lady would loan you her broom if you asked her."

Lucius could not help laughing softly, both at his young companion and himself.

At that moment the man seen ringing the bell approached from a side door. He had a kindly demeanor and a portly look.

"Good day," he said as he positioned himself in the pew before them. "I'm Sheldon Grahme."

Lucius accepted his offered hand. "Lucius Wolgath, and this is Foley."

"Conrad Princeton III."

Grahme smiled. "I'm the preacher here in Currituck. I hope you don't mind me joining you. You seem to have come in for a purpose."

Foley expected Lucius to mention that he was looking for work. What he said next surprised him mightily.

"I came to apologize."

Grahme nodded in understanding.

Lucius' voice was quiet. Rough like a bush ravaged by drought and fire, but soft and frail as a budding stem. "I know it isn't Sunday, and I know I could have done this anywhere, but it seemed right for me to come here."

Grahme nodded easily and allowed Lucius to continue.

"I have been tried to the breaking, and I allowed the experience to tear me assunder. In my failure I have discovered my weakness. It humbles me."

"Then I would venture to say that it has fulfilled its purpose if one was intended."

The men were silent for several minutes and Foley squirmed on the pew. If churches were meant to be comforting, they would have cushions on all the benches!

"Will you be staying in town, Lucius?" Grahme wondered aloud.

"I'm not certain. I'm a traveler, and-" He waved a hand vaguely. "-this has all been a grand detour for me."

"If you've a need," the man began as he reached around on the pew, "you may have this."

He came up with a squat volume bound in tan leather. The stitches of the binding and all around the edges were fine and tiny. There were no words printed on the cover; no markings whatsoever in fact, but it was clearly a Bible.

"The citizens of Currituck are quite generous," Grahme said. "I commissioned these with a local printer and my wife stitches the covers."

Lucius could only stare at the Book for several seconds. When he looked up at the man, desire and hesitancy were evident in his blue eyes.

"You're more than welcome to it," the man said. "We have several, I assure you."

Lucius accepted it with scarcely a nod, his head bowed.

"Let us know if you need anything," Grahme said as he rose from his seat. "Enjoy your passage, Mr. Wolgath."

"I don't see why we stopped there," Foley huffed as they walked. "You didn't even get any information from him!"

Lucius was holding the Book very close to his face, flipping through the first few pages. "I received a wealth of information from him."

"I mean that we could use."

"I intend to use it." He cast the boy a sidelong glance. "Have you never read a Bible before?"

"I've never read anything before."

Lucius stopped in his tracks. "You cannot read?"

Foley shrugged. "Plenty of people older than me can't."

"Yes, but that's no reason for you not to know how." He snapped the Bible shut and strode on. "We shall work on that directly," he declared.

Foley was left standing in the road sporting a stunned expression. "Hold on there, Professor!" he cried as he ran to catch up. "What d'you mean we'll work on it?"

"Just what I said. I am a teacher by profession, you know."

Foley groaned in misery. "And here I thought I'd escaped school forever! You wouldn't deny a poor boy his dream, would you, Professor?"

Lucius grinned amusedly. "In years to come I dare say you'll thank me for the opportunity."

Foley grumbled something unintelligible.

"Think of it!" Lucius went on almost to himself. "You'll be in class by yourself. Not to mention receive the benefit of a second-hand Cambridge University education. That's practically unheard of in this part of the world."

"You sound like a tradesman."

A commotion just off the road ahead caused Lucius to pause, forgetting their conversation. Foley stopped beside him. They had determined to take the road that ran around behind the church when they left. Foley claimed that it would lead them to a cluster of inns and taverns, where they might glean the very information they needed. This road followed the outer edge of Currituck. A modest crowd had gathered in a field by the way just ahead. It was easy even for a stranger such as Lucius to see that these people were very agitated. Man and boy inched closer, straining to hear the words shouted by the men and encouraged by the women.

"Keep your crowns and your taxes!"

"Call back your dogs!"

"We'll not have their oppression here!"

"Or their stench!"

This comment was followed by a chorus of 'yeas', and as one the crowd hoisted something high above their heads. For one horrifying instant Lucius thought it was a body, but then he caught sight of the straw poking through the cuffs. An old bucket was perched as a head atop its shoulders. As he watched, the people produced a rope and slung the thing high on a nearby tree branch. A few enthusiastic young men even scaled the limbs to look down on the scene and cheer above the rest.

"What d'you think's happening, Professor?" Foley asked slowly.

Lucius shook his head, his eyes never leaving the drama before them. "I honestly don't know. It appears to be some sort of protest."

At that moment the effigy was raised by the rope around its 'neck.' A sign now covered his chest, and Lucius and Foley were just close enough to read it.

"Here hangs the glutton King George."

"His taxes he raised; his mouth he did gorge."

Someone then thought it good to set fire to the thing, and the crowd began to back away, the better to admire their ghastly handiwork.

"That's treasonous," Lucius murmured.

"Don't let them hear you say that, Professor!" Foley warned. "That's an awful lot of people…"

"Only twelve or so."

"It'd look like a lot more if they were coming at you instead of that King George scarecrow," Foley snorted.

Now that the crowd was farther apart it was easier to distinguish the individuals from the whole. Wolgath's gaze darted through the faces and back to the flaming symbol. "Rest assured gentlemen, I do believe you've killed him."

He had said 'gentlemen', but the more he looked, the more ladies he saw amongst them. Not all of these protestors were young as he would have assumed; rash, overgrown youngsters with nothing better to do or simply uncaring and rebellious. This group did not fit that profile in the slightest. These people seemed to range over all ages from twelve to ninety and nine. The old and wrinkled down to the young and pockmarked. These were individuals with purposes and responsibilities who did not have enough time in their lives for anything but the work essential to their households. They had little time to spare…but they were making time for this.

Lucius continued to study them for a time, but he stopped short when he saw one face in particular. His every muscle froze as his mind worked to comprehend what he was seeing. For unknown seconds, he could only stare.

Chapter 24

May 31, 1765

Lucius shuddered involuntarily. For the first time in the three days that he had spent in America, he recognized someone. Surely it was false! Surely it was not so! The longer he gazed the more certain he became.

"Oh, Lord," he murmured, "can this be so?"

Foley's brows puckered when he said this, but Lucius was too astonished to notice him. Even as he spoke the man had turned farther in their direction. He wore a hat of raccoon fur and a long coat that was bedraggled and dusty. He had been shouting just as loudly as the foremost members of the mob and louder than many of the rest. As he caught sight of Lucius, his voice dropped off, and his large mouth stretched into a grin. Even had the man not been so incessantly loud for several minutes before, it would be impossible to recognize him as anyone but Smith Darlum.

"Dr. Wolgath!" Darlum exclaimed as he came closer. He clapped Lucius soundly on both shoulders. "You're alive! You survived the undertow of the deep. You must be made of tougher stuff than you let on, man."

"I doubt that theory," Lucius replied absently. He glanced down furtively to catch Foley's reaction. This was mainly to reassure himself that he was not having a mental lapse and speaking to a mirage.

Darlum echoed his thoughts with, "I feel I'm speaking to a ghost, but you seem solid enough, and you have a little friend with you, eh?"

Lucius swallowed. "Yes, this is Foley."

"Conrad Princeton III," the boy finished.

"He's been helping me since I landed here."

"Pleasure to meet you, Mr. Conrad-Princeton." Smith reached down to tousle the boy's hair, upsetting his hat in the process. "Name's Smith Darlem. Most call me Darlum, the rest call me Smith."

Foley scowled and slapped his hat on his thigh, muttering something about 'Smittie.'

Lucius shook his head at Darlum's grin. "Smith," he breathed. "What are you doing here? What happened to the *Scarlet Pride*?"

"I could ask you the same thing. I'd like to know what happened back there! One minute you're moving up top to have a look about and the next thing you know we're limpin' to port and you've disappeared."

"Disappeared?" Foley puzzled.

"Vanished."

Lucius felt his head swimming as he recalled that horrible night, and, even worse, the next day when he was certain the ship had foundered.

"B-but the *Scarlet Pride*! It-"

Lucius broke off when he felt a tug at his sleeve. He looked down to see Foley eyeing the crowd. The group seemed to be a living entity all its own. Some twenty arms held fists, staves, and farm implements upraised.

Smith noticed them as well. "Fight on, chaps!" he shouted.

Lucius swallowed. "I think we had best move this discussion elsewhere."

"Right you are," Smith half-whispered. "They seem to be getting downright vicious."

"Um."

Smith turned to the road, brushing by the others. "Follow me then, boys."

Lucius let his shoulders droop. "A frightening alternative in its own right."

Darlum led them down the road to a two-story tavern and barber shop. Lucius followed behind him in a disbelieving stupor. Foley stomped along close at his side. It was not at all difficult to see that Smith had made a bad impression on him. Though, granted, he rarely seemed to make any impressions to the contrary.

Darlum burst through the tavern door ahead of them. "Table for three!"

A heavy man stood by the far wall polishing the globe of a lantern. He sneered at the sight of Smith. "Eh, eh, eh! Didn't I see you here this morning?"

Smith spread his hands. "What can I say? You're a lucky gent."

"Uh-huh. You still got coin?"

Darlum jangled his coat pocket and they claimed an empty table. Darlum ordered three plates of whatever might be hot. Lucius managed to hold his tongue until the proprietor brought their food, but then Smith cut him off.

"How did-"

"So, the imminent Dr. Wolgath." Smith sopped his bread in the steaming beef stew before him.

"Professor Wolgath."

"Ah, sorry. Professor." He shoved the morsel into his mouth and smacked as he spoke. "Master of the science of disappearing acts."

Foley nudged Wolgath. "How did you say you know him?" He eyed Smith warily.

"He was on board the ship that brought me here."

"An' we didn't have grub like this on board, I'll tell you!" he mumbled around a mouthful.

"You say that now," Foley grumbled. He lifted his spoon with the greatest reluctance. "I've swiped-I mean *swept* around this place before. I know what's in this soup!"

Smith paused, shrugged, and continued to pump his spoon.

Lucius brushed his bowl aside. The smell of it was suspicious enough to make him think twice. He laid both hands on the table and leaned forward.

"Smith!" he breathed. "What has become of the ship?"

"She's fine. Well, less than fine, but still afloat."

"And everyone aboard?"

"Safe as new kittens with their mam."

For the first time since his landing in America, Lucius Wolgath smiled his true smile. He vaguely recalled laughing with Foley and a few dim grins, but this was altogether different. This was a smile of contentment. There had been no more troubling thoughts in his mind than that of the unquestionable doom of those aboard the ship, aside from contemplating his own fate. Now this weight fell away. He removed his glasses and drew a hand over his face, savoring the shimmer of happiness he had been given.

"It was *you* everyone worried about," Smith went on. "No one realized you were gone until the storm was done, and we lowly passengers were allowed to come up again. It was the Captain who thought you might have slipped overboard."

Lucius raised an eyebrow. "He was correct."

"Not a revolutionary theory seeing as there were not many other places for you to go. But you survived! How did that happen? Bet that's a story."

Foley perked up at this. He was always one for a good tall tale and not above adding their plots to his own resume. Lucius did not give him very much to work with in this case.

"I was knocked off the side. I floated to shore."

The other two stared at him somewhat slack-jawed.

"But you swam it right?" Smith prompted. "Hand over fist."

"Sixteen foot waves," Foley threw in.

"All on your own muscle!"

"With nothing but the clothes on your back!"

Lucius quirked a sardonic look. "I don't really remember much. I was swept through the rail along with some debris. I managed to get my arms around a barrel and the current carried me to shore."

"Amazing!" Darlum exclaimed. "You might just be the only man alive to swim a mile while unconscious."

"Hm," Foley mused. "I wonder if people would pay money to see that."

"Not the kind of money I need," Lucius replied huffily, but even as he spoke, he was struck with a new thought. "Smith?"

"Hm?"

"Where did you say the *Scarlet Pride* was?"

"She stopped at a small port up the Virginia coast. That's where I got off, but Captain Davy wanted to take her on up to Williamsburg for proper repairs."

"Yes?"

"No."

"Excuse me?"

"I know what you're thinking, and I said 'no.' I'm sure Captain Davy would still be willing to make good on his promise to take you back, but he's got his own problems now. It's going to take months to patch up the *Scarlet Pride*. Months during which he will not be turning a profit to pay for said repatching. Not to mention the fact that he stands to lose his crew, who also won't be turning any profits during those months. Get me?"

Lucius groaned and cradled his forehead in his hand. "So it's about money. Again."

"Isn't it always?"

He was looking down and he found that he couldn't be certain whether it was Foley or Darlum who spoke. He wondered vaguely if it wasn't both of them.

The portly owner of the establishment was suddenly close by their table. "That's three helpings-whether they were eaten or not. That'll be six pence boys."

Smith grimaced and shoved his hand down into his pocket. "I've got three."

Lucius glanced at Foley, who glanced at the owner. The man's cheeks were becoming ruddy. He jabbed a finger at Darlum.

"You said you had coin when you walked in."

"Yea!" Foley scowled.

"Well I do, but I didn't reckon on these prices."

"Blame it on the Sugar Act."

"That's supposed to be repealed!"

"Rumor has it, but it ain't yet. So pay up."

Smith brought his hand up. "I've-I've got two cents!"

"You said three."

"At the time that was what I thought I had."

Lucius shook his head. "I've got something," he murmured.

"None o' that paper stuff."

Lucius tore one button from his waistcoat and added it to the coins. The proprietor grunted and accepted them.

"I best not see you boys in here again. Good afternoon to you."

Smith crossed his arms as the man ambled away. "Really knows how to sell his wares, don't he? So what's next for you then, Professor?" he asked as he came to his feet.

"I've got to find work," he answered automatically.

"What kind?" Smith continued as the three moved outside.

"Not certain."

"Any, uh-" Smith stroked his chin. "-thoughts?"

Suddenly Foley was in front of the two men, his fists clenched and his chin up. "Any work that we might find is ours!" he asserted.

Lucius had to admit that he was impressed with his little friend. It would have been several more minutes before he himself realized what Darlum was angling for. The other man raised his hands in defense.

"Settle down, little fellow," he chuckled. "Just making a conversation is all."

"You just worry about your own empty pockets," Foley muttered. "We'll worry about ours. Come on, Professor."

With that Foley strode on ahead of them, obviously expecting Lucius to follow, but something had just occurred to him. Why was it that Smith, the wealthy, self-proclaimed adventurer, was unable to afford a simple American meal? Lucius turned to him curiously.

"Why is it that you're down here while the *Scarlet Pride* is up in Williamsburg?"

"Oh, that. Well, I told you I hopped off before they actually headed on to Williamsburg." The man was trying in vain to seem casual. "And you know me. I'm the free-wheeling type."

"Where's your luggage then?"

Smith was stumped for a moment.

By now Foley had stopped to listen to this as well. "And how about the money?"

Lucius briefly wondered if Foley wasn't merely put out that Smith had no coin to steal.

"I was forced to leave the area in something of a hurry," Darlum finally said. "Then I ended up here."

Lucius crossed his arms. "Should we be afraid to be seen with you?"

"Well no one actually *followed* me!" he whined and rolled his eyes. "Brutes. If they're going to take their poker so seriously, they ought not to play."

"It's not their fault if you lost," Foley put in.

Darlum pretended not to hear, saying instead to Lucius, "Thanks to that lovely meal back there, I haven't two ha'pennies to make a whole. I may just be worse off than you now, eh, Professor?"

Lucius' brow darkened. "Do not flatter yourself, Darlum."

He must have appeared as irritated as he felt because Smith ducked his head and cleared his throat. "Er, yes, um… Anyway, to come out with it, I was hoping I might join the two of you since you seem to know where you're going."

Foley's eyes grew round in an interesting expression of fury and disbelief. Lucius noted this from his peripheral vision and kept his cracked lenses leveled at Smith. "I'm not sure that I trust you enough for that, Darlum."

"Trust!" He put on a mildly affronted look. "Why we've been thick as roses for neigh on two months now. Why shouldn't you trust me?"

Lucius chose to ignore the outrageous exaggeration, saying instead, "I just saw you egging on a mob committing treasonous acts in an open field."

"Oh, is that all!" Smith scoffed.

"How do I know you won't stir up trouble for us elsewhere?"

"But you have to understand the politics of it all, Wolgath. You may not realize this, but I have a brilliant political mind."

Lucius frowned. He was never one for politics and not too keen on getting his hands in them. Then there was the way Darlum waggled his eyebrows when he said the word. Politics by his definition would surely lean away from diplomacy and more toward bureaucracy. He pursed his lips and waited for Smith to explain himself more fully.

"See, our fine leaders back in England have seen fit over the last few years to pass a number of inordinately severe taxes and proclamations on our fair colonies."

Foley scuffed the toe of his shoe in the dirt. "Don't see why they had to," he huffed. "The soldiers always say it's for our own good."

"They do, eh?"

He shrugged. "That or that it's our own fault. The way it all makes everyone so furious it seems to me it'd be easier on everybody if they just left us alone."

"The colonies were never meant to support or govern themselves," Lucius commented, careful to keep his voice low.

"Ah!" Smith smiled. "But they can! These people are completely capable of supporting and maintaining their own lands. Certainly more than the men the crown has been sending over here, many of whom know nothing of the people or the land and couldn't care less."

"There are legal systems in place to allow people to deal with unjust governing," Lucius pressed. "They ought to be going through proper channels rather than waving their pitch forks."

"The legal systems that are run by men sent here by those in power who have decided that the unruly colonies must be regulated? That's half their problem. The rights of a colony and its citizens are very different from those of a shire."

Lucius narrowed his eyes, though now it was in confusion. "I don't see why they would be."

"But they are. You're thinking like a diplomat. Think like a king-and a foreign king at that." Straightening his shoulders and jutting his chin comically upward, Darlum gave an exaggerated impression of such a monarch. All he lacked was a flimsy paper crown. "My ancestors sent the ships, supplies, and men necessary to forge a beginning in that land. My soldiers have fought countless battles to hold that land. Its settlers have cried to me in the past for protection of that land. Now I find an amassed war debt in my country's lap, and those blooming colonists have not given us back a fraction of the cost of it. What am I to do?" Smith dropped the façade abruptly. "Taxes equal money. The American Colonies are currently paying more taxes than any other English province. In addition to that they essentially have no say over their own land. Because of this the colonials are beginning to revolt. Because of *that* England has determined it is necessary to install more soldiers and government officials to keep them in check. The resulting-and painfully obvious-problem is that it is costing them a great deal more to collect the taxes than the taxes are costing the colonists. The 'profits' trickle back to England, and Georgey suddenly realizes he has a situation. His chum Lord Greenville kicks up more taxes to balance his numbers, and the whole process begins again."

"A void." Lucius shook his head. "How is anyone supposed to make anything?"

"Exactly," Smith nodded. "But it's an equal road. If I was with them, I would have to agree. Why should the colonials have equal rights when the colonies were never meant to be 'shires' in the first place? Why shouldn't they pay for debts to fund the fighting for their half of the country on the other side of the world? They're fussing and causing trouble, why shouldn't they house the soldiers they're forcing us to send? You see it's quite easy to pass the line into their opinion given the right setting."

Lucius sighed in exasperation. "But aren't we them?"

"That depends on which side of the ocean you're on."

"You manipulate your ethics based on the company you keep and what part of the world you're in?" Lucius fumed. "That's egregious!"

"That's politics," Smith defended. "And it's kept me alive as long as I've been here."

"You mean all three days you've been here," Foley sneered.

"And you give this as an argument in favor of my trusting you?" Lucius demanded.

"You said you were worried about me causing trouble, but I would be more likely to keep you out of trouble. I can talk my way out of anything, and that's a fair defense for a man who doesn't know how to throw a decent punch."

Lucius clenched his jaws and his fists. He glanced down at Foley, who crossed his arms. Like himself, the boy seemed to be considering, but only just. He peered at Smith. "If you like talking so much, how can I be assured that you'll keep your tongue when necessary?"

"Because that's the other factor in a brilliant political argument; knowing when to keep your trap shut."

Lucius threw his hands up. "You're incorrigible!" With that he turned on his heel and stalked away.

"So I can come then?" Darlum shouted after him.

"You do what you like, Smith," he threw back over his shoulder, "but don't ever try to double talk me again!"

"Capitol!" Darlum clapped his hands together. "Looks like we get to be pals after all!" He tousled Foley's head again.

The poor, dumbstruck lad straightened his hat and hurried to catch up to Lucius. As much as he liked the Professor, he wondered vaguely if his company was worth time forced to be spent with Smith Darlum. Lucius was wondering the very same thing.

Chapter 25

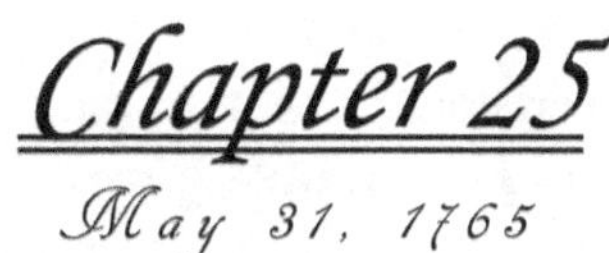

Lucius looked up from the pages of his Bible to cock one eyebrow. He sat surrounded by night and trees and doing his level best to read through cracked spectacles. In the end it did not matter because the other two could not seem to sleep and his peace was disturbed. He peered over the small fire at his compatriots where they lay across from one another in the forest grass.

Foley sat up on his elbows, Lucius' coat spread over his chest and legs. "You lied?"

Smith crossed his arms. "Well it's either that or I didn't know what I was talking about. I would rather admit to lying any day."

Lucius rolled his eyes. He had taken it upon himself to ignore Darlum whole-heartedly throughout the remainder of the afternoon. Foley was not capable of such discipline. Though, to be fair, he was only a boy.

"How about admitting that you were wrong?" Foley snapped. "You didn't think of that? You and your brilliant political mind." He stated that last part as a sarcastic afterthought under his breath, but Smith heard him none the less.

"You cannot blame me for stating the facts of our dire situation in this harsh land!" Smith shot back. "Is it not true that I lack a pillow beneath my fair head?"

Lucius wondered just how long they would go on if he remained silent and decided that he would rather not find out. "Neither of us has a bed to lie on either, Smith," he said blandly. "You are not the only man in this camp who suffers, so do quit proclaiming your hurts."

Smith sniffed and twitched his shoulders. "Well, I didn't say that I was. No need for you boys to both come at me. It's unfeeling."

"And if I had my violin I would play it for you."

That seemed to end the banter, and within minutes Darlum was snoring softly. Lucius had already returned to his reading, but Foley was restless. After a few minutes, he scooted closer to Lucius to ask, "How long is Smith going to stick with us?"

"I'll not hear any complaint about Smith," Lucius replied. "The complaints *from* Smith are bad enough."

Foley nodded in agreement. Lucius studied him in the darkness, this boy wrapped in his coat. His troubles were probably just as large as Wolgath's own. How was it that this boy was managing to cope all alone?

"How did you get here, Foley?"

"I came with you."

"No, I mean to America," Lucius explained. "You said you weren't born here."

The lad shook his head. "I was born in Wales. That's where my mother's from."

Hope sparked within Lucius. Perhaps this boy was just as lost as he was, placing him in the perfect position to help. "Your mother?" he prompted.

Foley nodded and watched the fire. "She was the most beautiful woman in the world. She died three years ago."

"I'm very sorry to hear that," Lucius murmured.

"Yea," Foley crossed his arms over his knees. Something changed in his voice when he spoke again. "She died saving us all."

"Saving you?"

"She gave her life on the high seas so that her family and a ship full of brave men and some women might be saved."

Lucius raised an eyebrow. "I fail to see how-"

"It was in the middle of a storm on the ocean that the leviathan found us. He rolled the ship back and forth and back with the humps of his wide back. Everyone clung to anything they could to stay aboard. Men were crying and women were sobbing, but my mother stepped forward. She opened her mouth to sing the song that would soothe the beast. When the leviathan paused she flung herself at it! The thing thrashed and she-"

"Stop right there," Lucius ground out. Foley glanced at him and flinched beneath his glare. "What did I tell you about lying, boy?"

Foley swallowed.

"Any more of that," Lucius added, "and I'll leave you alone with Smith."

"Sorry," Foley murmured as he ducked his head.

Lucius had just turned his hard gaze back to the Book when the boy spoke again.

"I had an uncle back in England," he said. "He used to tell amazing stories. He said I was good at it too. I wanted to be a storyteller one day."

"And your mother?" Lucius wondered.

"I was telling the truth when I said she died three years ago. She didn't survive the passage."

Lucius took this information casually. Foley was scowling into the flames. What a fascinating individual he was turning out to be. Seeing a small chip in the boy's tough pretext, Lucius determined to move in closer.

"If you're not in the mood for sleep," he said carefully, "perhaps we should start work on your lessons." Foley made a face, but Lucius spoke again before he had time to protest. "How good of a storyteller can you be if you can't read?"

Foley squinched his brows together. "What will you teach me with though?"

Lucius lifted the Bible. "The only book we have."

Foley's eyes grew round with obvious fear. "I can't read that! It's thicker than my whole head!"

"You're probably correct," Lucius chuckled. "But we'll use it to help you recognize letters and words and soon enough you'll be reading stories."

Foley seemed dubious, so Lucius chose a slightly different tact.

"Did you know the word 'leviathan' is in the Bible?"

"Huh?"

"See here. *Thou brakest the heads of the leviathan in pieces.* That is how that word looks on paper."

"What's this one?" Foley pointed a few lines down.

"That's 'day.' *The day is thine, the night also is thine. Thou has prepared the light and the sun.*"

Lucius looked to his little friend, who was staring at the page in consternation. Finally he shrugged and moved away.

"It all looks the same to me."

Lucius smiled. "You'll understand soon. I'll make sure you do."

"Yea," Foley yawned. "Guh' night, Professor."

Lucius lay back with the Bible pressed to his chest. His mouth quirked into a half-smile of pleasure. "Good night, Foley."

Chapter 26

June 1, 1765

"We-have asked-every bloomin' farmer-on this road!" Smith huffed. "I say we just push on to the next town!"

"More than a day away? What do you expect to do there that's any better than what we're doing now?"

Lucius shook his head as the pair bickered.

As he attempted to ignore Smith and Foley's squabbling, he seriously considered striking out on his own. They had set off down a southerly path from Currituck. Having found two farmers so far, they had begged work and found none. The locals whether Tory or Whig, did not seem overly eager to take in any man bearing an English accent. Either that or Smith Darlum's 'brilliant political mind' was making them leery.

"-what we've been doing!" Smith was saying. "We'll look for work with one small difference; we'll succeed. Business is always better in town! We never ought to have left Currituck in the first place."

"I'm glad you feel that way," Lucius interrupted loudly, causing the other two to stop short. "Since you have expressed your feelings so strongly, why don't you turn right around and march back." His eyes blazed behind his spectacles. Smith swallowed. Lucius breezed between the pair of them to stalk up the road. Seconds later he heard harried footsteps close behind. "If you'll remember, Darlum," he went on coldly, "we left Currituck just as much on your behalf as ours." A town of rioting colonists did not seem the best place for two Englishmen and a small boy to beg for work, and it was sure to be circulated that they had not one farthing to their names. What charity could they expect from the overtaxed citizens? The decision was unanimous.

"Right. I just don't see how we're going to get anywhere with all this walking," Darlum whined.

Foley rolled his eyes. "How else would you expect to get anywhere?"

"By the time we get there we'll be too tuckered out to work anyway. They won't give us a penny apiece for it, you mark my words!"

Lucius nodded calmly. "All right. We'll make a deal here and now." He halted and crossed his arms.

Smith spoke before he could. "I think we ought to pool any funds we make from here on out while we're together."

Foley's mouth fell open.

Lucius grinned serenely. "Why we can't do that. What if Foley and I were to earn less than you?"

"Yea," Foley smiled, having caught on.

Smith raised his hands defensively. "Oh, but I wouldn't-"

"No, no. Wouldn't be fair to you at all," Lucius continued as if he had not spoken. "From this point on we'll keep everything separate. Every man here earns what he works for. Every man supports his own weight. That way no one gets bogged down by the laziness or ineptitude of others. Do you agree, Mr. Princeton?"

Foley crossed his arms. "Yea!"

"And you, Mr. Darlum?"

Smith shook his head. "Nay."

The easy grin fell from Lucius' face. His features revealed the merest hint of his annoyance as he ground out his reply. "Overruled."

From that point on, Smith trailed along behind the other two in silence. The road twisted east, and soon they could see stretches of beach and ocean through the trees on their left. It was not until they broke into a small clearing that they encountered any other signs of human existence.

"A fence!" Foley cried as he ran ahead. "That means there's someone close around here!" He turned to face the two men.

Smith snorted. "Hardly. That fence could go on for miles."

Foley blushed in anger. "At least it's something!"

Smith opened his mouth again and Lucius started to shake his head, but neither of them ever finished. A sound had suddenly come to the hushed clearing, but it was obviously not a sound of the wood. It was an odd drumming, muffled but clearly drawing close. The three of them could feel the vibrations of it in the ground. Birds flew from the trees around them. Echoes bounced from the trunks behind them and then again from those before them, encompassing the small space in thrumming.

"What is it?" Smith wondered.

"*Where* is it?" Lucius countered.

Like the sudden rush of a wave coming over a rock, a herd of horses raced into view. Fifteen of them ranging from light bays to dark chestnuts, ran smoothly along the surf. Sand flew up to mingle with their streaming tails as they went. They seemed to be gone the instant they saw them. The stunned three remained silent long after the beating of their hooves died away. Foley was the first to break the silence.

"Whoa."

Lucius fell into a state of awe as he watched them go. Glistening and sinuous and ethereal, they left almost no trace at all of their presence. Lucius had to look at the tracks imprinted in the sand to assure himself that they had indeed been tangible. He remained silent in shock and wonder.

Smith cleared his throat. "I think we ought to follow the fence."

They set off, leaving the road to follow the edge of the fence. Lucius looked back just once more to see where the horses had been. The strange sight seemed to have shaken the others just as much as it had him, and they spoke not a word between them. Fortunately it was not long before they stepped clear of the forest to find a young man standing in the fenced-in field.

The man looked to be in his late teen years-only four or five years older than Foley. He was lanky and tan with his shirt sleeves rolled up nearly to his elbows. Sweat stains had soaked through his hat and clothes, evidence of the labor spent in the field where he stood. He watched them as they came closer to the fence with watery blue eyes and a bland expression.

"Güten tag."

Lucius and Foley stood up straight but Smith slouched against a fence post.

"Er, good afternoon," Lucius began. "Do you speak any English perchance?"

"Ja."

"Oh, very good." The lad said nothing further so Lucius continued. "We are travelers here looking for work. Are there any jobs about your farm that might need to be done?"

"Nein. No use have I for you," he replied in the same bland tone.

Foley huffed. Lucius nodded. Smith groaned audibly.

"But mein Fater-" The man pointed over his shoulder to a long barn in the distance. "Something he may have to do. Just up there."

Lucius let out a long breath in relief. "Thank you, indeed."

"Ja." The lad held out a hand. "Am Pater Braune."

They each introduced themselves and Pater Braune returned to his work as they made their way to the barn. The dirt path curved alongside the fence at a slight incline. Smith was only able to bite back his comments until they were about halfway to the building.

"Why didn't we just cut through the green? We look like fools taking the long way about it."

"Use your eyes, Smith," Lucius snapped. "These are not livestock farmers." He indicated the land, which was covered thickly in bright green, leafy stalks. Each stem was between two and three feet tall, and topped with tiny blue and white flowers. "That is a flax field. I don't believe they would be too quick to grant work to anyone who trampled a hundred or so of their good plants on the way up."

Smith clammed up, but Foley, was intrigued. "How'd you know it was flax, Professor?"

Lucius shrugged. "Botanist's reflexes. I recognized the plant from drawings."

"What's a botanist?" Foley stressed the vowels of the word, somehow refashioning it into 'bow-tan-est.'

"It just means that I studied plants at Cambridge," Lucius explained. "Do you know much about flax, Foley?"

"No, sir."

"It's quite a useful plant. This will be a good chance for you to learn about it."

"We hope," Smith added from behind.

Lucius shook his head. *If that man would spend as much time in sincere thought as he does talking, the world would be a much happier place.*

The doors of the barn were wide open, and three people stood in the yard. The first two that they noticed were the women out in front of the barn. The third was a man who came from inside the structure. This was obviously Pater's father. He bore the same bland expression and liquid eyes as his son. He approached calmly enough, though he placed his hands on his hips in a gesture of caution.

"Good afternoon," the Professor began uncertainly. "I'm Lucius Wolgath, and this is Smith Darlum and Foley."

"Conrad Pri-"

"We spoke with your son down the way. He informed us that we should come to you."

The man nodded once and offered his hand. "I own the farm. I'm Pater Braune."

"I-really?" The man merely blinked, so Lucius went on. "We are travelers looking for work. Do you have a need for any hired men?"

Pater brooded and stared them down for a slow moment. "Ja," he finally said. "Ja. We may be able to work you some. They are beginning to come in, my crops. Sometime is difficult to gather them all."

Lucius smiled in relief, but Darlum could not hold back his exclamation. "Amen!"

Pater raised an eyebrow at him, but continued to speak to Lucius. "I pay you some mit food, some mit money. We'll try a few days and see about longer. Ja?"

Foley's face split into a huge grin. Lucius nodded emphatically. "As you say, Mr. Braune." He bowed slightly.

"Güt." Pater grunted. "You are ready now to start?"

"Ja-er, yes. Yes, sir."

"Come." Pater led them back toward the barn and the two ladies. "My wife, Marget, and my eldest daughter, Tanya."

The ladies smiled graciously, and the three newcomers bobbed their heads in their direction.

"They do not speak your English yet," Braune added.

"What are they doing, sir?" Foley asked.

"Know you anything of flax, little man?" Braune inquired. He actually smiled when Foley shook his head. "They are scutching the flax."

Each of the women stood before a wooden contraption similar to a saw horse. A wooden arm was attached atop it with metal hinges. The arm rose and fell as they lifted the handle of it. They fed bundles of dried stems beneath it. The stems crunched and crackled as the arm fell to crush them.

"Those are flax breaks."

"Creative term for them," Smith mumbled.

Braune went on explaining to Foley. "The flax we dry and ret in the fields. Then, when all is ready, we gather and use the breaks. They break the stalks away from the fibers inside." He led them around the corner of the barn. Two small children stood at a makeshift table, their heads bent over their work. "My youngest," Braune confirmed. "Sara and Pater. They are cleaning the stalk pieces from the fibers by drawing through the hetchles."

What Braune called a 'hetchle' looked to be nothing more than a square board with nails hammered straight through it to form a crude comb. The children rotated around three different hetchles with nails of varying sizes from wide to very fine.

"I see," Lucius murmured as he took in the process. "They comb the fibers through three different sizes until they become supple."

When they had drawn the lock of fibers sufficiently through each hetchle, they laid it carefully in a wide square wheelbarrow and ran to grab the next bundle from the stacks their mother and sister left in a nearby wagon bed.

Braune looked to Lucius. "I think we leave the boy here while we go to fields. Ja?"

"All right, sir," Lucius agreed. Foley appeared slightly paranoid, but he attributed this to the fact that no one in this part of the farm spoke English. He was confident the boy would do fine…so long as he did not try to steal anything.

Braune gestured to Smith. "Go back out to Pater and do as he tells you."

Smith balked, probably at the thought of being directed by someone half his age, but at that same moment his stomach rumbled and he clamped his mouth shut. When he had disappeared around the side of the barn, Braune turned to lead Lucius in the opposite direction.

"You and myself, Mr. Wolgath, we will go to the north field."

Pater pronounced his name 'Volgat,' so a brief second actually passed before Lucius realized he meant him.

"After we hitch Juni to the wagon."

"Juni?" They rounded the wall of the barn where a young horse pranced inside a small coralle. "Oh."

"My horse, Juni," Pater said as he approached the enclosure. "He is many months broken, but still he likes some to show-off."

Lucius hurried to get the gate for Pater as he led the horse out. Juni trotted prettily enough, but every so often he would toss his head. The animal's sharp movements made Lucius anxious indeed as he fumbled with the straps of the wagon.

"Do not worry," Braune chuckled from the horse's other side. "Juni is a güt animal, just much too proud."

"But with pride comes 'temper," Lucius commented to himself. Juni wickered loudly and seemed to agree. Remembering Braune's promise of food as part of the payment, Lucius was able to allay his own fears and climb aboard the wagon. The thought of payment itself ought to have spurred him on all the more, for only with enough funds could he return to his home.

"We will be going to harvest the retted plants of the northern plot," Pater told him as he took up the reigns.

"If you don't mind my asking, sir, what do you mean by retted? Aren't the plants simply left to dry?"

"Yes, they are dried. After a few weeks we remove the seeds to be used for grain and for replanting. But then the plants are once again laid out for to rot with much moisture. Only then can the stem truly be separated from the fibers."

Lucius could see the field by then. The ground from fencerow to fencerow was carpeted in yellowed plants. Braune halted the cart alongside the open gate and they each began filling their arms with the stiff stalks. He spoke readily as they worked, which Lucius appreciated mightily. It helped both to satiate his curiosity and to pass the time.

"The women, they separate the fibers by line and tow," he explained. "Line fibers are long and fine. Used for linen and bedding and soft threads. The tow is short, suited for burlap and course materials or twine."

"You said you use some of the seeds for grain?"

"Ja, the seed can have many uses also. The oils pressed from them have many healthy properties."

"I've heard of the use of linseed oil by physicians," Lucius recalled.

"When the crop is planted for the seed, it is sewn thin and allowed to grow longer for a fuller harvest, but here, we grow for the fibers. We plant them thicker to yield thinner, straighter stems. Also, we harvest them earlier, when the plant still is green. It makes for finer threads, ja." The man nodded sagely, well satisfied with his work as he studied the plants in his arms.

"And you are doing well since you have come here?"

Pater considered the question and nodded. "Ja. We are keeping up. That first year was not so güt. A poor harvest. The plants have done well the last two, and with the boycotts, the industry has grown much this season."

Lucius' brow furrowed. "What boycotts do you mean?"

Pater did not look surprised, but merely shook his head. "You had not been here long, I knew. The colonies are so angered by their King, they are stopped purchasing many things from England."

"Such as fabric and thread," Lucius added.

"This is why, we hear, that so many shipping men are for us in that land," Braune explained. "Our business is hurt, so their business is hurt."

He laid his plants gingerly in the bed of the wagon in order to illustrate with his hands. "The King and his court, they see us as side to side." He held his hands straight up three inches apart. "But really we are meshed like this." He fit his fingers together one below the other not unlike the teeth of a pair of cogs.

"The taxes are affecting the money here," Lucius said thoughtfully, "and the money here affects the money there."

"So," Pater grunted as he bent to retrieve more flax. "It is as one economy, but soon now it will be two."

They had been at their gathering half an hour, and already Lucius' back ached fiercely. His hands were scratched by the stiff flax. A sheen of sweat covered his forehead, neck, and arms. He did not have high hopes for his muscles through the rest of that afternoon, but at least it was work. It was one tiny move closer to Alexcena, and if he could spend it in the pleasant company of this kindly farmer, the day was sure to pass easily enough.

At that moment Pater Braune (the younger) came running into view. Smith Darlum loped along behind. Lucius felt a cold lump form in his throat even before the younger man spoke. Pater stood very close to his father, speaking swiftly in their native tongue. Braune's expression grew harder with every syllable. He cut his eyes at Smith.

Lucius turned to face him. Darlum was doubled over, hands on his knees, and trying to catch his breath.

"What did you do?" Lucius whispered, and it was practically a growl.

"'S not-that-serious."

Lucius glanced at the Braunes. "Others seem to disagree."

Darlum straightened. "What can I say? I'm not cut out for this type of thing, you know."

"Do not say cut!"

Smith and Lucius looked around at Pater. The young man said something else in his own language, but his father interrupted him and they fell into conversation once more.

"What is that they're speaking?" Smith hissed at Lucius. "Dutch?"

"German."

"Um. Well, I guess it would sound just as bad in Dutch as it does now."

The son abruptly turned away to return to his work in the south field. The father calmly faced Darlum.

"You cut my plants?"

Smith held up a small, yet formidable blade.

Braune crossed his arms. "The flax fibers run from the flowers to the roots. That is why we pull plants up whole."

"You know, those roots are much stronger than they look. I-"

"My boy says you cut them six inches above ground."

Lucius looked to him with a disbelieving groan. "Smith!"

"When you cut my flax, you cut down on my profits. Short tow fibers are much less valuable than line fibers."

Darlum nodded. By his troubled expression, Lucius thought that perhaps he had begun to grasp the seriousness of his actions, just not quite enough.

"Apologize," he muttered.

"Oh, right. Sorry!" Smith babbled. "I am sorry about the flats."

"Flax."

"Right."

Braune's gaze roved over the both of them. Lucius thought not only of himself, but of Foley. This man had offered them a meal and coin, and there was the possibility of more work in the days to come. That possibility was shrinking fast. Was he willing to give up this opportunity for Smith Darlum?

Lucius bent and began to gather more flax stalks. Behind him the two men remained still, staring one another down.

"I'm going to leave you here with Mr. Wolgath," Braune determined.

Lucius wanted desperately to protest, but what could he say?

"I will go and help my son to pluck the plants while you men harvest this field. When the wagon you have filled, take it back around to the barn, and Mrs. Braune will direct you where to store it."

"Yes, sir."

"Thank you, sir."

Smith did not have the good sense to silence his wide mouth completely, but at least he waited until Braune was out of earshot.

"I say, these immigrant types do get touchy about their money problems, don't they?"

Lucius gritted his teeth as he lifted a large bundle of flax. "You're just as much an immigrant as they are."

Smith snorted. "Just because I 'migrated' here doesn't mean I intend to stay here. If this is how they treat their betters I shan't be staying long, I can tell you."

And how do you intend to attain passage back to England for nothing? Lucius kept this thought to himself. Darlum had not yet realized that by losing everything he had come over with, he had left himself just as stranded as Lucius. He ignored the man after that, allowing him to babble himself into relative silence. Fortunately, Darlum was not keen on one-sided conversations. He did make sure that he watched him from the corner of his eye. If Smith made another foul up, he could conceivably cost them all the job. How someone could mess up placing plants in the back of a wagon he could not be sure, but he did not want to find out.

While he kept an eye on Smith, he also tried to watch Juni. The horse had remained very still over the last hour, moving only as they led him through the various areas of the field. Lucius was beginning to relax for his sake, thinking that he must be calmer than he seemed at first. That was until he whinnied loudly and tossed his head. Smith was at the rear of the wagon, so Lucius let the stalks he held fall and moved toward the animal. By the time he turned, he realized what had made Juni sound off.

Braune's eldest daughter, Tanya, stood before him, offering a bit of sugar in her palm. She clucked her tongue and stroked his muzzle. As Lucius came to the gate he saw that her younger sister, Sara, was there as well.

Smith dropped to one knee by the little girl. She offered him a small cake wrapped in a checkered napkin. She then pointed back toward the barn, where her mother could still be seen working.

Tanya moved around the wagon, and Lucius saw that she carried a bucket of water. She offered him the dipper and a small, polite smile. Sara gave him his own cake and both girls watched curiously as the men inhaled their food. Eventually Sara tugged at her sister's sleeve to ask a question in German.

"Do you think she likes me?" Smith asked from the corner of his mouth as the sisters spoke. He indicated Tanya.

Lucius stiffened and truly wondered for Darlum's sanity. "If you try to find out, Smith, I'll kick you off this farm myself."

Smith merely chuckled and accepted another drink from Tanya. The polite smile vanished from the young lady's features as she caught his stare.

Lucius snatched the dipper from him. "Go check the horse." He kept his tone calm. The look on his face was ferocious enough to make his point.

Smith shrugged away. Lucius worked to soften his countenance as he turned back to the young ladies. He returned the ladle to Tanya, bowing low to them both. He only hoped that his overdone manners would be received as an adequate expression of apology. Sooner than he would have thought possible, he had much larger worries on his plate than just the good opinion of the Braune family.

Juni snorted and danced to one side, nearly tilting the wagon as he went. Lucius' head snapped around and he hurried to see what was happening.

Smith held Juni by the bridle. "Steady on there!" The horse whickered reluctantly.

"What did you do, Smith?"

"I calmed him down right enough."

Lucius raised one very sardonic eyebrow. "You also startled him."

"Well, he's fine now, isn't he?" Darlum retorted. "Don't see why everything has to be my fault."

There were, of course, several different replies which could be made to a statement such as that from the man. Rather than fan the flames, Lucius hauled himself up into the wagon, intending to throw the brake to keep it in place should the animal decide to move. It was then that he heard the sound that chilled his very blood.

"You're a good boy, aren't you?"

Smack!

The horse screamed. Before Lucius could turn, there was a great lurch as the wagon leapt into motion. He felt himself tumble back, rolling head first over the seat to land in a bed of dried flax. Juni careened down the road like a mad thing, the wagon crashing along behind him. Air whistled over the branches in the bed. Lucius felt himself leave the boards and tried to hang on as the thing bounced over ruts and rocks. His teeth rattled as he fought for control of his own movements, powerless compared to the gravity, the speed, and the animal itself.

After the first few harrowing minutes, he managed to turn over off of his back. Grasping the backboard of the seat for all he was worth, he pulled himself up onto his knees. Being able to see what was happening did not make him feel much better about his situation. Juni had left the road, favoring more open terrain, and he showed no indications of slowing his pace.

Gritting his teeth, Lucius flung a leg over the backboard and tumbled into the driver's seat. It was imperative-and obvious-that he must gain control. The reins dangled to one side, all but tangled around one hitching strap. Before he could change his mind, and knowing that his choices were limited, Lucius knelt low in the floor board. With one hand he grasped the seat. With the other he reached for the reins. His nose was just inches from the top of the spinning wheel. His ears were filled with the frantic, heaving breaths of the horse. He felt as if his arm was actually lengthened from the muscles of his shoulder to the very tips of his fingers with the stretch.

If the rock had been to the right rather than the left he never would have seen it. It made no difference in the end, for the wheel hit it in nearly that same instant. The entire left side of the cart lifted up and slammed down. Juni screamed and Lucius heard a faint *snap* as one side of the worn leather harness came apart. Juni stumbled and tried to pick up speed, but something looked wrong in his step. Suddenly the horse propelled himself into a leap over a ditch. Lucius had no preparation for that. The gap was small; in fact Lucius might have been able to jump the distance himself. Sitting as he was in the wagon, the stretch was altogether too wide.

The front wheels hit, and he wrenched one arm clinging to the seat. There was another pop and the harness broke free, as did the horse. Lucius was left in a broken wagon in a ditch watching Juni go and wondering what in the world he was going to do next.

Chapter 27
June 1, 1765

"You're awake."

Alexcena sucked in a breath and whirled to face the man who spoke so close behind her. "Captain Loughdon!"

"I apologize," the stern man conceded. "I've startled you."

She shook her head. "Not a difficult thing to accomplish, I'm afraid."

The Captain moved forward to join her at the rail of the *Liberator*. "I only expected to find my men at the helm."

"I-er-" Alexcena swallowed and laid her arms over the rail as they had been. "I don't sleep well lately," she admitted. "The closer we draw to America, the worse it becomes."

Silence reigned for many seconds. She was on the verge of returning to her cabin when Loughdon cleared his throat. He seemed to fight for the words as he spoke.

"You'll forgive me for saying so, Ms. Condreve, but I have found you to be an intelligent, right-minded, and hearty lady." She bit back an amused smile at his choice of words. He continued to watch the sea. "I've seen how Mr. Wolgath dotes on you, as though you're family already."

"In many ways we are."

He nodded. "That said, there is a question that must be asked, and I worry that no one will until the time is long past."

Confused and mildly intrigued, Alexcena steeled herself.

"What will you do when you realize that your Professor Wolgath is lost to you?"

She was not prepared enough for this. Rather than sadness, she felt anger flare within. "You are mistaken, Captain. I do have a measure of hope left for him." Her words were nearly sarcastic and sounded more rude than she meant for them to.

Loughdon merely pursed his lips. "My apologies."

She gripped the rail and faced the water. "This is, however, something I have considered."

"And?"

"I am not sure," she admitted, "how prepared a person can be for such as that."

"You recognize your strengths and shore up your weaknesses," he answered without hesitation. "You lean toward those better than yourself and away from those who only serve to undo each small success. You press on in prayer, in a search for understanding and knowledge and the wisdom to heed them both. One day you realize that you are no longer leaning on those around you and each day is a little more peaceful than the last."

Alexcena's eyes grew round and pooled with tears. She had not imagined that there could be such a depth of feeling in this man of few words. This was a speech born of painful experience.

"What was her name?" she whispered as the first tear slid down her cheek.

Loughdon let out a long breath before he answered. "I don't know."

She said nothing to this cryptic answer, but now that the subject had been broached, he seemed willing to give the story.

"We were two days east of St. Croix in the Caribbean. A schooner called *Maine Stream* was being attacked by pirate raiders. Just as we came abreast of the ship, I saw her. She was a small, frail thing in a blue dress with pale red hair. She could have been anyone; a farmer's daughter, a sailor's sister... a wife, a mother. I never knew because they shot her before we were able to board. I remember that man's face just as easily as I remember hers. It was I who shot him, but I made certain not to kill him. I wanted the courts to take care of that one."

"And did they?" She knew the answer long before she voiced the question.

"He made a deal with them. He signed a contract to become a privateer in the name of England and sailed away carrying letters of marque in his pocket. I could not handle that. The Lord above does not put anything before us that we cannot handle, but it was not He who did this. I could not force myself to fight for a government who contracts her enemies for unsavory work.”

“That’s why you left the South Seas,” Alexcena breathed.

“That’s why I no longer hunt for pirates.” He glanced at her, gauging her reaction. “That was my great loss. I was driven to fight for the protection of my fellow law-abiding men, and I was waved off like a worthless mutt at the end of the day.”

“The hound who flushes out the fox and then is forced to eat from the same plate.”

“You could say it that way. At the time it felt as though my portion had been given to the fox entirely. When I protested these proceedings I was told that this was a perfectly legal occurrence and I should mind my own business. Then I was threatened with the law and arrest if I interfered further.”

He grew silent for some time. At last Alexcena gathered the courage to ask, “Why are you telling me all of this, Captain Loughdon?”

He dropped his gaze. His rough thumb traced the grain of the wood in the rail. “Because I know what it’s like to have the objective of your life vanish before your very eyes. I’ve watched you, and I know that you have a far better chance of coping than I ever did. If you will prepare yourself for it.”

“Why is that?”

“You have your faith, and you have time to ready yourself.”

He looked at her with sharp blue eyes. They were every bit as hard as ice, but now they were just as transparent. Alexcena bowed her head beneath them.

“I will think on what you have said-if I am ever completely convinced that my Lucius is lost to me.”

Loughdon made no acknowledgement of this statement. Saying a brief goodnight, he bowed low and turned away. It was very likely, Alexcena mused, that he thought her in denial. In his mind he must have thought that she had pushed his advice away, but it was not she who ran before the conversation was over.

Chapter 28

June 1, 1765

Lucius determined to remain as he was until the pain came and he could readily assess his own limbs. He did not have long to wait. Soreness swelled in his left arm and lower right side. Everything ached to some degree, but it was his left arm that had kept him from flying free of the wagon and his right side that was bruised from flipping over the seat that were the worst of it. Sunlight glared across his glasses, making his head hurt. This pain was actually a relief, because it meant that they were still on his head. He had no concept of what he would do if he were to lose them, broken and battered though they were.

After several long minutes of stretching and flexing and finding no broken bones, Lucius rose into a sitting position, and tried to push himself up using the seat. The entire wagon had settled at a wild angle, and shifted when he moved. Gingerly lowering first one foot and then the other, Lucius made it to the ground and nearly fell over. His muscles trembled and he found that he needed to sit for a time before he could go anywhere. He laid his forehead in his palm.

"What is it that I have done to nature, who afflicts me!"

He tilted his head to study the wreckage. Bits of wood lay scattered by the ditch. Several large rocks jutted from the ground on either side of it. One axle was bent and useless. Seeing all of this and thinking of the crazed horse that had done it, a new perspective came to him.

It was not that nature afflicted him, but that God blessed him! In the weeks since he had first boarded the *Scarlet Pride*, he had passed through several life-threatening predicaments, and yet none had proven fatal or even serious. He marveled now at the ruined wagon. It was a testament to his blessings. How many men might have come through such as that without incurring a dangerous injury? He felt amused, and even a little crazy for feeling amused, but there was no denying the truth of it.

He considered his situation, wondering if there was any option other than returning to the Braune farm; one that would not involve so much walking. Since none was obvious, he came to his feet and started on his way. Stiffness was settling into his muscles, so he flexed them as he went, but still he did not feel bad. He was able to chuckle to himself when he thought of all that had happened, and he hoped that it was not a symptom of recurring madness. He offered a prayer of fervent thanks each time he paused to rest. Whether crazy or sane, he was still alive, and that alone made him more thankful than he had been in ages. He did worry as to Braune though. How would he ever make this right with him? Let alone his need for work, the man's wagon was destroyed and his horse missing.

Having stopped to rest several times along the way, it was two hours before he came within sight of the Braune farm. Fatigue weighed his long limbs down like lead. His steps were uneven and stumbling. It was nearly dark, with the sun setting behind him, and he squinted through the cracks of his glasses to see if anyone was outside.

A group of dark figures stood in a cluster, shadowed by the barn. Even in the failing light, it was plain to see that they were all men. They stood close in conversation, some with their shoulders hunched, as if in the midst of a hushed conspiracy. Lucius kept silent as he approached, since he recognized no one and none had noticed him. He had nearly gained the barn itself before one of them spoke up.

"Look, there!"

The men turned as one, and Lucius found himself pinned to the ground beneath seven glares. He froze and looked at each of them in turn. The last of this motley line was Pater Braune, the eldest son. Not a one of them spoke, so Lucius cleared his throat.

"I'm looking for Mr. Braune. Is he at home?"

"And would you be Lucius Wolgath?" one of them sneered.

Pater crossed his arms and replied before Lucius had a chance. "It is him."

Lucius glanced from one to the other of them again. He felt his nerves pull tight as he measured the hostility of this little crowd. At length one of them broke away and hurried into the barn. The others remained as they were, watching him.

"Braune says he hired you to work," one of them commented. "Where've you been?"

Wolgath's eyes widened. He gestured behind himself the way he had come. "I've been walking. The horse, Juni, he ran off with the wagon while I was in it. He went for quite a distance, but-"

"So where are they now?" someone else asked. "Juni and the buggy?"

"We searched for you for some time," murmured another, "without success."

"As I was reaching for the reins Juni went over a ditch. The harness broke, and I have no idea where he is now. I never saw him stop."

Their expressions remained fixed, their postures stiff.

"Didn't Smith tell you what happened?" he wondered cautiously. "Or Sara or Tanya?" They may not have believed Darlum, but surely they would have listened to Braune's own daughters!

"Tanya say you rode off mit my fater's horse," Pater replied harshly. "And that Darlum made winking eyes at her."

Lucius pulled back as though he had been shoved. These men were leading up to an accusation. Not only that, but they had made it clear that they saw no separation between Smith and himself. Heaven only knew what Smith had said or done since he had been gone.

Wolgath was in the midst of trying to put his thoughts into a coherent defense when Mr. Braune emerged from the barn. He was closely followed by Foley, Smith, and two others in guard behind them.

Lucius spoke to them all in an even tone. "If you men intend to impute me with something, I should like to know what it is."

Everyone looked to Braune, who was facing Lucius. "Is it not true that you drove my wagon from my farm?"

"It is *not* true." Lucius spared a glance at his companions. Smith bore a blackened eye and a repugnant expression. Foley looked willing for violence in his anger.

"I was borne from your farm by that wagon, but it was not at my own hand."

"My Tanya," Braune went on, "she says you slapped the reins and Juni bolted. It looks to her like you were making to steal my horse."

"Both of your daughters were at the rear of the wagon. How could they have seen me do anything with those reins?"

"They both heared you snap the horse."

Lucius leveled his gaze at Darlum. "And what does *Smith* say happened?" he asked menacingly. "He was there, standing even closer to me than your daughters. Have you not asked him what transpired?"

"I told them just what happened!" Smith asserted. "Juni was spooked. I saw him-"

"How could you?" Pater shouted. "Too busy you were eyeing my sister!"

Utterances of agreement sounded from the men around them. Braune raised a hand to quiet them. "He say that Juni spooked on his own, but if this is true then what heard my daughters when they say you slapped him?"

More agreement from their audience, presumably Braune's neighbors come to support him. Then again, they very well might have been intending to hunt Lucius down. What was the punishment for horse thieves according to Colonial law?

In an uncharacteristic wave of intuition, Lucius suddenly knew that any defense he might offer was worthless. Their opinions of him had been tainted by Smith's actions. Anything he said would be refuted, and would only serve to anger these agitated men further.

"I think you gentlemen have made your verdict perfectly clear, whether you believe this was all an accident or not." This statement was met with blank stares, so he went on. "The sensible solution before us is that my friends and I take our leave. The wagon is some distance back that direction, and, the good Lord willing, so is your horse."

Foley took one step forward to join Lucius. Lucius stepped back, preparing to go.

"We're not in the habit of allowing horse thieves to take their leaves," someone interjected.

"I did not steal anything," Lucius informed them as a whole. "If I had, I would not have been stupid enough to return. That said, I concede that it was in part by my folly that the animal escaped." *I never should have allowed Smith anywhere near him.* "I am sorry for the loss of this animal and the damage done to the wagon, but I am in no position to make restitution for these things."

"Braune," someone said. "What do you think?"

Braune shook his head forlornly. "His story I think is plausible, but genuine? I don't know."

"Mel?" another asked. "You're the closest we come to a lawyer around here. What do you think?"

An older man, obviously Mel, crossed his arms. "The law is very plain concerning matters such as this, but I think there is enough doubt here to warrant a lighter consequence. None of us wants to live wondering if we've executed the wrong fellow."

Lucius felt his mouth go dry. Smith visibly paled. "Ex-execute?" he stuttered.

"-execute them both, we'll always wonder which was the true guilty one. No, I vote for the less severe answer. Let them work until they have sufficiently compensated for both animal and buggy. Without pay, of course."

Lucius expelled a breath. It was as though someone had punched him in the chest. His thoughts jumbled together. How was he to get away if he was not allowed to earn an income? The reality and seeming finality of Mel's judgment nearly sent him reeling. In the end it was Braune who saved them.

"Let them go."

The men stared at him and one or two let out a protest. Foley's jaw fell and Smith clasped his hands above his head in victory. Wolgath collapsed to one knee, partially from fatigue, mostly from relief.

"Take your friends and go," Braune told him. "The horse will be caught. The wagon I will repair."

Foley was suddenly at Lucius' side, tugging at his arm. The boy was desperate to get away before anyone chose to argue the point. Smith strode by them as Lucius came to his feet. He knew the others were waiting, but he could not leave the situation thus. He moved forward to look Pater Braune square in the eye. Braune stared back with his watery gaze.

Lucius drew a long breath. "I want you to know that I am sorry for this. Please believe that I would not willingly leave you in this way were I given a choice."

"The choice is mine," Braune shrugged. "It is my decision that you go."

"And so we will."

Lucius bowed and followed slowly after the other two. His side ached abominably and the muscles of his legs trembled with each step. He hoped that Foley had some idea of where he was headed. He led the way down the road. Smith hovered between the two of them, unsure of where to stand.

By the time the sun had truly set, Lucius was fairly certain they were past the line of Braune's property. He turned from the road, breaking loudly into the tall grass of a meadow to their right. In the center of the neverending meadow was an ancient tree. He made for it, not caring whether or not the others followed. In any case they did. He could hear them crashing along behind him. He fell onto his back at the base of the tree. Moss covered the gnarled roots and formed a soft enough bed for one so exhausted.

Foley sat on one of the great roots. Darlum sprawled in the grass.

"Smith?" Lucius called, though he kept his eyes shut. "You had better not be here when I wake."

Smith sat up on his elbows, his outrage evident. "Me? Why?"

"We have come to the parting of our ways, Darlum," Lucius explained. "I would be remiss if I allowed you to believe that I ever had any desire to lay eyes on you again."

Though Lucius could not see it, Foley smiled as he leaned back against the tree.

Smith sniffed and lifted his chin high in the air. "Capitol," he snapped. "The two of you were beginning to slow me down anyway."

With that he stretched out on his back and was soon heard snoring. Lucius slipped into a dreamless sleep of exhaustion, and when he awoke in the morning Smith was gone, not having made a single sound to signal his departure.

Chapter 29

June 6, 1765

"Tell me truly, Ena,"

Alexcena sat back from the trunk and looked to her cousin. "Yes?"

Tabitha was pacing up and down the little hallway outside their cabin with a large book balanced atop her head. She tilted her chin ever so slightly and caught the volume as it slid off.

"Will something as silly as this really make me less clumsy?"

Alexcena had only mentioned the theory in passing to Tabitha. She had descended below deck sometime later to find her testing it.

She shrugged. "I've known ladies who attested to it strongly, but I tried it almost every day for six months straight and I'm clumsy as a kitten in a pond sometimes." She quirked a smile and shook her head. "Most of the time."

Tabitha stepped through the narrow doorway and perched on the bed. "You cannot find the hankies?" she asked, drawing her cousin's attention back to the trunk.

"No," Alexcena pouted. "I can't find anything in this box of fluff." She flicked one of the many ruffled skirts therein. "Heaven only knows where my own handkerchief went."

Tabitha knelt beside her and plunged her arms elbow deep in the silk and lace to help. This was the opportunity her cousin had been waiting for.

"Why must fashion be so difficult for us ladies?" she sighed.

"Heaven only knows that too."

"Don't get me wrong," Alexcena went on. "I like a lot of ribbons and bows now and again. It's just that there are times when it would be so much more convenient if our wardrobes were more conducive to function. I mean how many times have you seen me trip on my hem at parties?"

Tabitha giggled. "Probably just as many times as you've seen me do it."

"No! Far more."

Tabitha suddenly yanked a sleek case from the depths of the trunk. "Finally."

She offered it and Alexcena unbuttoned the clasp to borrow one of the neatly folded white squares from within.

"Next to none of these will do in America."

She looked up at Tabitha's quiet words. The younger girl was fingering the lace edging on the end of one sleeve. "That was silly of me, wasn't it, Ena?"

Though Tabitha smiled, her eyes were glossy, and Alexcena had not an inkling of what to say. She laid a hand on Tabitha's forearm and nodded. Though Alexcena did not know it, her own strength radiated from her gaze and the girl was comforted.

"Ms. Condreve? Ms. Winslett?"

Both ladies looked to the door, more than a little startled to see Lt. Greyson standing there. Clearing his throat, the man bowed low, and the ladies scrambled up to stand side by side before the trunk, effectively hiding its frilly contents with their skirts. Well, more Tabitha's than Alexcena's.

"The Captain would like a word with you both," Greyson explained. "He has called for Mr. Wolgath as well."

Alexcena flinched. Would she ever be accustomed to hearing that name while Lucius remained lost? Each time she heard those all-too-familiar syllables, it was as though a pin pricked her chest, prodding her wounded heart.

"Thank you indeed, Lieutenant," Tabitha said graciously. She lifted one foot beneath her skirt to kick the trunk behind her. There was a dull thud as the lid of the trunk fell shut behind them.

Greyson ducked from the door, and Alexcena followed her cousin out. When they reached Loughdon's office they found Leo already present and standing by one wall. He grinned, and Alexcena noticed a trace of something different in his expression. *Energy? Excitement?* Loughdon was seated behind his modest desk where Greyson had come to stand at his right side. Made alert by Leo's visage, Alexcena studied both men. Greyson seemed hopeful, perhaps even pleased. Loughdon was as stern and impassive as ever. He motioned for the ladies to each have a seat before his desk. He spoke quite briskly once they were settled.

"My men have spotted land."

Alexcena felt her eyes widen with the shock of such a stark statement. Her lips parted in awe. Land meant America; America meant Lucius. She turned to Leo, who only smiled wider. This bared his white teeth, making him seem almost fierce in the low light of the cabin.

"We will make landfall sometime after midnight, and you will all disembark early tomorrow morning."

Alexcena's hands began to tremble in her lap. She clasped them together and pursed her lips. She was in great danger of screaming her joys aloud. Though she remained silent, her eyes spoke volumes.

Tabitha let out a titter. "America?" she smiled breathlessly. "We're in America?"

"You are *near* America, Ms. Winslett," Loughdon replied. "There is a vast difference. You will all be allowed to leave once the ship has docked securely. Before you all leave to prepare, there is something else I should like to discuss with you." He folded his hands before him, growing more serious, if that were possible. "The *Liberator* will be leaving in two days for the Caribbean islands."

"The Caribbean?" Alexcena interrupted before she could stop herself. "But I thought you said-"

"I said that I no longer hunted for pirates, Ms. Condreve," Loughdon replied swiftly. "I never said I refused to sail their territory. Like everyone else in this world, I must maintain a profitable income and the trade commerce between the colonies and the islands continues to grow. We will be stocking up on cargo to be sold in Charleston, South Carolina. The ship will dock there in early September. I want you all to know that, should you have need of our services again, you may meet us there."

"If that is the case," Leo answered, "we will be sure to be there before you."

Loughdon gave a quick jerk of his head in acknowledgement. With that he returned to the charts covering his desk, signaling that the meeting was over.

Greyson led the three passengers from the room. Alexcena went only a few steps before leaning against the wall of the cramped hallway. Leo hovered beside her while the other two made for the upper deck.

"Leopold," she murmured.

He turned to face her, one rough hand coming up to her elbow. "What is it?"

Her voice barely escaped as a whisper. "Is it real?" She had meant to say 'really true,' but her throat constricted and she could not manage that much.

Leo smiled gently in understanding. "You will be in Williamsburg by morning."

A thrill raced through her, and she gave a small laugh as the first few tears rolled down her cheeks. "Virginia. At last!"

"At long last," Leo chuckled.

"On land by morning, in Lucius' arms by the evening."

She could picture it easily. She was no longer standing in the hall, she was on a starlit path, surrounded by the alien buildings of a strange town. Lucius was there just as she had last seen him. His wide hands grasped her arms with gentle pressure. He might not kiss her, not right away at least. She imagined that he would want to look, as she would. To see all that memory might have smoothed over in the past weeks.

Her hand gripped Leo's forearm absently. She was not looking at him, but beyond him with an unseeing gaze. For several seconds she was completely lost in her dream.

"Ena," Leo called softly.

He sounded so distant, but she managed to drag herself back to the present to listen to him. His gaze was almost troubled now.

"You must know, it may take several days for us to find him," he said slowly. "Maybe... longer."

Alexcena considered this, and the corners of her mouth turned up pleasantly. "Even so." He was obviously unconvinced by her serene statement, so she felt obliged to explain. "I am closer to him than I have been in months. The burden of distance is all but gone. For weeks now I thought that my pain would only heighten when this moment came, but I was wrong. I have been granted peace beyond measure." Another laugh escaped her as Leo's worry remained unchanged. "Besides," she told him, "I have you here. Your presence is a wonderful comfort to me."

Leo nodded and finally fell into a smile. He drew her closer and she set her chin on his shoulder. His arms encircled her, and she pressed her own around his back. A sigh born of happiness untold rose within her chest. Feeling protected and completely at ease, she would have gladly stayed just as she was until they set foot in America.

The pair eventually parted and ventured up to the railing together. It seemed that everyone aboard had stepped onto the deck to catch a glimpse of the first land they had seen in seven weeks. Even Commodore was amongst them, sitting between two sailors with his thick muzzle poked through the posts of the railing.

When Leo and Alexcena passed out into the sunshine they caught sight of Tabitha and Greyson standing close beside one another some distance away. Greyson was murmuring low to her, his back facing them. Tabitha's expression was shadowed by her parasol, but they soon heard her voice pealing gently in response.

Alexcena's hand was looped around Leo's arm, and she felt it flex as his own curled into a fist.

"What's that about?" he rumbled.

Alexcena raised her other hand to his shoulder. "Come," she said, "let's go to the rail."

Leo turned, albeit reluctantly, to show her the horizon. She glanced back once to see Greyson lift Tabitha's slim hand to his lips. She dipped her head and Greyson bowed simply before moving away.

"There it is," Leo said as they reached the rail.

Alexcena was not certain what she had expected to see, but she thought perhaps that it was more than this. The line of the horizon was darkened and slightly thicker, but aside from that it was not much different from the way it had looked since she had left England.

"It's not much to look at yet," Leo commented.

Alexcena shook her head slowly. "You're wrong," she whispered. "It's everything to look at."

Part III

The Path Persevered

Chapter 1

June 6, 1765

*H*unger was a distressing experience for Lucius Wolgath. He could safely say that it was one of the most uncomfortable sensations he had suffered in quite some time (his seasickness notwithstanding). His stomach was already shrunken from the meager meals he had taken in America thus far. Those had been few and far between, but now he was coming into a third day without any sustenance at all. There had been little food to be had along the road since they had made their anxious escape from the Braune farm. Even the forest had failed to offer them much of anything. Without weapon or trap they had no hope of catching any meat.

So it was that he blundered along beside Foley, barely aware of his companion or his surroundings. Mind numbing fatigue seemed to have seeped into the very marrow of Wolgath's bones. There were times when it even overpowered the hunger. The emptiness in him was poignant and painful, affecting his worn body in strange ways. At first his senses of smell and taste seemed oddly heightened by the absence of food. By the third day, the weariness had dulled any consciousness he had left. Foley seemed well enough, and Lucius noted somewhere in the back of his mind that this probably would not have affected him so strongly had he not lost so much weight on board the *Scarlet Pride*. What few stores of fat his body once carried were long gone, and his muscles moaned in protest with each step he took.

Every so often Foley would touch his arm to steady him. On occasion the boy would strike up a string of chatter. He mentioned that the next town that he knew of was Edenton, though he had never been there. This minute crumb of information was all that Lucius gleaned from all of Foley's talk during that long day. He was in a terrible state for listening, much less conversing. Foley was not bothered by his silence. The boy seemed to perceive the extreme concentration he was exerting simply to walk and remain awake…and move.

Without warning Lucius' right foot twisted out from beneath him. He fell to his knee, but managed to stay up straight. His vision tilted dizzyingly for an instant. Foley grabbed his shoulder somewhat belatedly.

"Professor!" he exclaimed.

Lucius made some rapid blinks in an attempt to clear his hazy head. "S'fine," he mumbled. "I just stepped in something I suspect." He shifted his weight and tried to push himself up on his left leg. He tilted sideways, but did not rise at all. "Why don't we sit down for a bit," he suggested before Foley could notice his distress. "Over here."

Lucius half crawled, half rolled onto the grassy embankment beside the worn path. (He flatly refused to call it a road. At times it was as narrow as his very shoes and almost seemed to disappear altogether.)

"Don't worry, Professor," Foley said as he flopped down beside him. "We'll be in Edenton long before nightfall."

"I don't worry for that," Lucius replied, and it was true. He was more concerned about starving. "I'm just…not feeling…very well at the moment." He let his head lull to one side so he could look at the boy. "What about you? Are you feeling all right?"

"Right enough, sir. Takes more than hunger to rattle me." He thumped his chest hard to give credence to the statement.

Lucius ignored the arrogance of his comment and said, "You speak as though you've been in this situation before."

Foley shrugged and pulled absently at the blades of grass around them.

"You know eventually I am going to expect you to explain to me how you came to be on your own here."

Foley gave no answer, and Lucius turned his attention to the sky above. It was odd to watch the clouds from behind his broken glasses. Their white expanses were marred by the hairline cracks that ran through the middle of each lens. He had become so accustomed to this over the past several days that he no longer noticed the fractures regularly. Now he traced them with his eyes back and forth, back and forth. The affect was hypnotic. He never felt himself drifting into a heady sleep.

He was unceremoniously jarred awake by Foley some hours later. "Professor! Professor!" the boy hissed somewhere close to Wolgath's face. He had a firm grasp on his sleeve with both hands, and was shaking him so hard that his glasses fell sideways. "Professor!"

Lucius opened one eye and then the other. It was almost dusk, and Foley's features were shadowed as he leaned close over him. He did not need to see his nervous expression to know that the boy was frightened.

"What is it? What's the matter?"

"Something's happening." Foley pointed back over his shoulder. "There, see?"

Lucius could hear them now. A hush of angry voices drifting up from the south. He slowly came to his feet and peered in the direction of the disconcerting sound. Beyond the grassy knoll where the pair stood, the road was flanked by thick groves of trees. Some forty yards distant, the path turned, obstructing it from view beyond the curve. The voices seemed to be moving along this path, and they were clearly coming closer. Lucius felt a twinge of anxiety deep in his chest.

"Come on."

He led Foley into the trees just as the first few travelers came into view around the bend. The first and foremost among them was a stout little man in a suit and tricorn hat. He seemed to be the object of their anger. He was moving backwards away from the rest as they stalked him. Both of his trembling hands were raised in the time-honored gesture of peace…or pleading.

"Let's not be hasty about this men, I-"

"We've heard all ye have to say!" someone shouted. "We aim to listen no more!"

A chorus of agreement followed from the small assembly.

"What are they doing, Professor?" Foley whispered.

Lucius eyed the crowd. It was comprised of ten or so individuals, mostly men, but also a few women. Their appearances varied from bedraggled and threadbare to starched and embroidered. Though smaller than the crowd they had witnessed in Currituck, this one still reminded Lucius of that incident. The difference was that these people were not venting their aggravations on a patchwork likeness.

"I'm not sure what's happening, Foley," Lucius murmured. "Let's move a bit closer."

He crouched and slipped forward under the dense shade of the trees. Foley moved along beside him, and Lucius worried briefly over the noise made by their shoes on the forest floor. As it was the clatter from the people was sufficient to cover their approach. When Lucius judged that they were close enough to hear and see all, he squatted down to listen.

"This has gone on long enough!"

"We've said it time and again. The time for talkin' is passed us now!"

The crowd nodded and hollered. A few even shook their fists at the man. He raised his arms higher to gain their attention.

"Gentlemen, gentlemen, please! I know you have grievances, and rightly so."

"And we women, too!" a feminine voice assorted. "Don't credit only the men. When you tax our fellas you tax us!"

"Aye!"

"When you tax our sugar and our flour and our *marriages*-"

"Aye! Aye!"

"-you tax us!"

"Ladies, please," the man tried again. "I have no quarrel with you or your men! I'm just a clerk."

"The Tories sent you here!"

The man seemed to rally himself at that. "Now just a moment. I was born in Georgia. I've lived in the Carolinas since I was four years of age. I know many of you by name, and you accuse me of being a British subversive?"

A few faces in the crowd appeared repentant, but this vanished when another, finely dressed man spoke up.

"If the Tories do not trust you to do their bidding, then why would they send you with this announcement?" he sneered. "You say you're not for the Tories, so why is it that you agree to do their will?"

"AYE!"

"I must feed my family!" the man protested. "I'm a clerk in the colony's capital. When someone walks into the office and tells me I must do this and that-at gun point!-I do it. I'm not proud of it and I do not enjoy it. The Stamp Act will affect me just as it affects any of you."

"But to carry it out as you have," the well-dressed man commented with a shake of his head. "Such an action suggests that you *agree* with the taxes."

"I have carried out nothing. All I have done is announce its passage to your town!"

The crowd advanced. The failing light seemed to enhance their fierce glares. Some grinned with wicked glee as the man trembled before them.

Lucius could watch no more. Whether his judgment was impaired by hunger, or he was moved by the Holy Spirit Himself, he could never say. He simply straightened and moved forward through the trees. Foley called out to him in a hoarse whisper, but he ignored him. Just as the crowd had said, this was a time for action. The time for listening was passed.

He emerged on the road even with their proposed victim, several feet away from the bend. At first none noticed him. He drew a great breath to say, "I ask you this, men!"

As one the people froze and turned their heads to look at him. There was an odd contrast between them, as they stood poised to snatch the shaking man while Lucius was slumped with his arms limp at his sides. He certainly did not look the part of a worthy opponent.

"You say he advocates England's taxes by announcing them to you," Lucius continued. "But then do you not all advocate these same taxes by paying them?"

There was a stunned silence followed by a grumbling among them. The clerk was looking to Lucius with something akin to awe.

"This man does the work of the Redcoats!" someone insisted, pointing at the clerk. "And he does it without protest!"

Before the mob could agree, Wolgath said, "You know this? Did any of you think to question him before you cornered him with your threats?"

The clerk took this invitation readily. "It wasn't hard to convince us in any case," the clerk piped up, drawing the attention back to himself. "They called half a dozen of us in and said that there was a new proclamation to give. They said we were to announce the passage of the Act and all that it stood for. Then we were to go to the offices of the Crown that were to enforce it in each town. If there was no such office yet established, we were to tell the people that Dr. Houston would be appointing someone to send directly. My fellow clerks and I argued the point. We *argued* it!" He smacked a fist down in his palm. "That's when the soldiers were called in to threaten us with arrest. We were not to be bothered with enforcing it in any way, because they did *not* trust us with that. We were to declare it and move on. Never in my wildest imaginings did I think that my fellow Americans would attempt to hang me for that!"

Murmurs ran through the crowd. "No one said anything of a hanging," someone complained sulkily.

"What did you intend then?" Lucius wondered aloud. "This man appears to be in agreement with all of you concerning the Act. Does that make him worthy of punishment?"

"But he still agreed to do it!" a man shouted. "I'll bet he's no more willing to fight for our rights than that yellow-back Houston!"

"That may be," Lucius replied, "but cowardice and disagreements aside, he has broken no law and, regarding this, he certainly has done nothing worthy of death. Are you all prepared to commit a blatant murder? To take the life that stands before you now?" None was able to answer. "If you lay a hand on this man, I charge that you all will be every bit as guilty as you imagine him to be."

The silence was brooding. The clerk raised his eyebrows, but Lucius did not notice. He was staring hard at the crowd. Ten pairs of eyes stared back in astonishment. The full import of his actions came to him as he took in the faces of the people from the brawny men to the petite women. The hands that had reached for the clerk in their craving for what they saw as justice might just as easily reach for his own neck at any time. In the same moment he registered this, he knew that the knowledge made no difference. Had he done nothing, he would bear the guilt of this man's torment as much as the rest.

"What do you say to that?" he muttered.

Very few looked rebellious. A handful turned and walked away. None spoke a word. The clerk moved to stand beside Lucius. Looking to the rest, he said, "We'll take our leave now. You'll not have to suffer me in your town again. I bid you good day, *sirs*."

With a click of his heels, he bowed and turned away. Lucius followed close at his side. They were several paces along the road when he heard Foley slip from the trees to scurry after them. He glanced back only once to see the people dispersing around the bend. His gaze quavered just then, and his entire body seemed to tilt. This must have been an illusion, however, because the other two failed to notice.

"How in the world did you manage that?" the clerk whispered furtively from the corner of his mouth, as though still fearful of those behind them.

Lucius gave a tiny shake of his head. "I haven't the faintest idea."

That said, he collapsed, fainting dead away as he went down.

<u>Chapter 2</u>

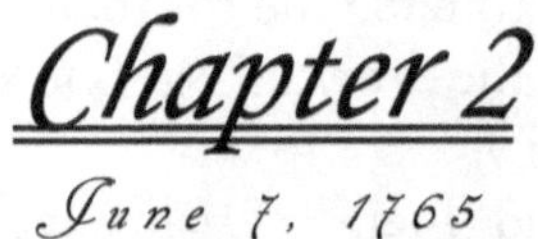

June 7, 1765

Land. Firm, unmoving, green, glorious, beautiful, bountiful *land*.

Alexcena looked down at her feet and smiled at the dirt beneath them; the very soil that was the land of Virginia. It was not quite dawn, and dew glistened on patches of grass all around her in a dazzling spectacle. She extended one foot just far enough that she could trace a pattern in the sandy terrain with the toe of her shoe.

Then something went wrong. The ground pitched at an insane angle. She felt herself beginning to fall. Luckily a pair of stalwart arms was close enough to catch her.

"Whoa, there!" Leo said as he held her. "Looks like you haven't unpacked your land legs yet."

Alexcena stifled a small giggle and straightened. "Sorry about that."

"No problem," he replied as he released her. "We'll just have to see if we can find them for you."

Commodore bounded by them in great bumbling strides. He ran in a few wide circles, barking huskily, and then plopped down facing them. His tongue lulled to one side, like the pleased grin of one who has found something grand.

She raised an eyebrow to him. "At least one of us remembered his land legs."

"And his hind legs."

She nearly laughed out loud and Leo chuckled at her. "I beg your pardon," she gasped, "I'm just so elated about finally being here."

"All I ask is that you keep in mind that we may still have a long way to go yet," Leo admonished her. "Virginia is a very large place, I'm told, and America is even larger."

Alexcena cleared her throat. "Yes, you're quite right. Have you decided how we are going to proceed with this search?"

"First thing, we've got to find a nice lodging somewhere. Williamsburg is greatly inhabited, so at least that oughtn't be too difficult. Then, when the sun is up, we'll start asking about the ship."

Alexcena nodded. She could well imagine herself pacing the floor of whatever room Leo found for them, just waiting for the sun to rise. She was not tired in the slightest, despite the hour. At that moment she felt capable of traversing the entire colony with the knowledge that Lucius might be staying in the very same city…on the very same street.

"Where has Tabitha got to?" she asked, partly from impatience and partly to distract herself.

Leo turned to look back up the gangplank of the wharf. Alexcena followed his gaze. Tabitha stood at the rail of the *Liberator* deep in conversation with Captain Loughdon. As they watched, Tabitha passed a small pouch to the man. Leo crossed his arms, and Alexcena did not need to look at him to see the anger now evident on his features. She winced at the thought as Tabitha moved calmly down the planks toward them. The constant conflict between Lucius' brother and her cousin was beginning to weigh on her.

"Making more deals with the Captain now, are you, Ms. Winslett?"

She gave a dainty almost-shrug and sniffed in his direction. "A private arrangement."

Alexcena's eyes darted to Leo. The man's jaw was set and his countenance was darkened.

"Right. Let's get this conversation out of the way here and now," he said flatly. "I am in command of this search. You're allowed along *so long* as you follow my directions to the letter. No assuming, no disobeying, and if you whine at all, you'll be solely responsible for the actions that follow. Is that all ringing clear in that curly head of yours?"

Whether to her credit or her shame, Tabitha bore his determined stare with only the merest tremor of her lip. "Perfectly."

With that she moved away and busied herself with smoothing her skirt and straightening her sleeves. Alexcena slipped her hand through Leo's elbow and he curled his arm up to support her. As usual he kept a suspicious eye on Tabitha.

"I don't think I like her," he rumbled.

Alexcena suppressed a sigh and looked to her cousin. She was going to tire of this quickly, and her nerves were strained as it was. "Which way to the inn?"

A familiar, easy grin returned to Leo. "Who knows? Shall we find out?"

Alexcena allowed him to pull her along. Her balance returned easily as she matched his pace, but still she clung to his arm. She had envisioned something akin to running through the streets and crying Lucius' name with all her might until he appeared before her. Now she merely wanted to blend into the shadows surrounding them. Her heart was beating at twice its normal speed and the buildings loomed, dark and unwelcoming, over them. In that moment every rumor and story she had been told of America since she was a girl welled up in her excited mind. The wild and fearsome land was said to be full of untamed creatures and dangerous men. A person could be lost in such a wilderness and not meet another for weeks. And yet she had come. What was she compared to the wilds of the New World? The daughter of a fine, wealthy family, how could one such as her expect to withstand the trials she would surely face?

Alexcena raised her other hand to rest in the crook of Leopold's arm and shrank closer to his side. It was comforting to know that he stood straight and tall beside her. A formidable force against any threat.

"I have your bag for you, Ena."

She jumped when Tabitha spoke very close at her other side.

"Thank you." She accepted the bag and released Leo's arm so she could slip the strap over her head and one shoulder. Her eyes continued to search the streets as a mouse watches for the hawk, but at the same time an odd thought occurred to her.

"Tabitha, where are your trunks?"

"On board the *Liberator.*"

She glanced down and saw that Tabitha too carried a simple sack, though it was bulging much larger than her own.

"I gave Captain Loughdon a little compensation in return for keeping them in trust for me."

For some reason this gave Alexcena a smile. Leo had told her that he would not be carting that luggage all across Virginia, and Tabitha had formulated her own solution. Alexcena turned slightly to catch his reaction, but he seemed not to be paying them any attention.

Hours later Tabitha said, "I think you had better stop, Alexcena."

She paused amidst her pacing to look at Tabitha.

"I'm afraid the carpet will not be able to withstand your footprints," she smiled. "It hasn't seen so much traffic in a year."

Alexcena looked down at the threadbare rug and continued to walk the length of the floor. Nine steps forward, nine steps back. With each footfall her self control stretched a little thinner.

Leo had managed to find them a fine boarding house at the edge of Williamsburg just one block from the wharves. Thankfully, the proprietor did not mind dogs, so Commodore was able to remain with them. Leo had deposited the ladies in a room across the hall from his own, promising to wake them in three hours time when he would leave to begin the search. Tabitha had fallen asleep the instant she laid across the bed. Alexcena had not even been able to sit down. Three hours and twelve minutes later, Tabitha had awakened and moved to the window seat. There she curled her knees up to her chest and watched her cousin pace.

Alexcena could feel herself slowly coming undone. Her entire body was tense and the muscles of her face were pulled into a tight expression of apprehension. She felt herself pulling at her fingers again.

"Ena, calm down."

She shook her head. "Don't you realize how long it has taken us to arrive here? In this very room? And Lucius could be-"

"Anywhere," Tabitha declared. "Anywhere within a hundred miles or more of this place. We will know nothing until Leopold finds the ship."

Alexcena shook her head again. She could not seem to absorb the sense in Tabitha's words. Fortunately for her, the young lady was not about to give in so easily.

"What does He say of worry?"

Somehow Alexcena did not have to ask to know of whom she spoke. The words came to her frantic mind in a thrice and brought it to a halt. *Ye cannot by worry add one inch to your stature...*

Her fevered thoughts calmed just long enough for her natural practicality to regain control of her senses. All at once she was ashamed and more than slightly fatigued. She moved to a plush armchair in the corner and slowly lowered herself into its welcoming seat.

The knock sounded on the door just seconds later and nearly brought her to her feet again, but it was Tabitha who went to answer it.

"Mr. Wolgath."

"What?!" Alexcena leapt up.

"Calm down," Tabitha told her. "It is only Leopold."

She forced herself to relax. Commodore rushed in to sit beside her. It was almost as if he could feel her tension. He leaned his warm shoulder against her skirt in comfort.

Leo remained on the threshold and bowed to them both. "Ladies. I came to tell you that I'll be going into the harbor. Our proprietor has assured me that if you need anything at all throughout the morning you have but to ask. Is everything all right in here?"

"I-I have a need," Alexcena replied, her voice a mere whisper. She waited until his eyes were on her to continue. "I need to come with you."

Leo's brow furrowed. "That's probably not the best course right now. I have no idea what these docks are like. There is no guarantee I'll even be able to find the *Scarlet Pride* today. There's no guarantee she's even here."

Alexcena pursed her lips and hoped the man would understand. "I did not come all this way to see a boarding house."

He looked her up and down and nodded. "Right." Then his gaze swiveled to Tabitha. "And I suppose you'll want to come too then. You seem to be making a career of following her around."

Chapter 3

June 7, 1765

The harbor at Williamsburg was a bustling hub of noise and activity, and seemed to be a city in and of itself. After asking some hasty directions from a fishmonger and a clerk, Leo managed to catch sight of the Harbormaster's office. The door of the building stood wide open and men poured to and fro over its threshold. He had never seen such varying diversity amongst a throng, and even noted a pair of well-dressed dark-skinned men at one point.

A strange and interesting place, this America.

He kept Tabitha in front of him and Alexcena at his elbow. Very few men looked their way, and as soon as they caught sight of Leo looming over the pair they turned abruptly. For that he was glad, though still very leery.

They passed through the open door, commanding Commodore to 'tarry' outside. The animal had kept very close to them since they left their rooms that morning, and it was plain to see that he was not pleased at this, but there he waited. They came into a wide room packed with people examining maps and lists and advertisements posted on nearly every wall. He moved the ladies to the side, where an older man graciously vacated a bench. It was then he spied the gold lettering above a side door; *Harbormaster*.

"I'm going to leave the two of you here for a few minutes," he said above the din. "If anyone gets too close, just scream."

Alexcena nodded. Tabitha gave an odd titter and coughed to try and hide it. Leo pursed his lips as he turned away.

The door to the Harbormaster's office was impossibly packed with men. Several were yelling. A few were waving sheaves of paper. One man sat behind a desk looking very exasperated and scribbling away with his quill pen. It was only a few seconds before Leo realized that he would stand in the little room for an hour and wait longer still to speak to the man in charge. Rather than try to press his way through that lot, he backed slightly away and looked around the wide room once more. For the first time he noticed a narrow hall off to the left. It was half hidden in a recessed portion of one wall, and though there were several individuals moving freely through it, it seemed much more likely that he would be able to speak to someone in that direction.

There were rooms on either side of him as he moved down the corridor, but the doors remained firmly closed. He had determined to try knocking vigorously on each and every one of them, but when he reached the end the hall opened up into a small office. A gentleman stood behind a desk grumbling to a man beside him and barking orders to a young clerk, who was dashing back and forth between the desk and a long row of drawers bearing bundles of paperwork.

"-go and tell him I refuse to accept that shipment," the gentleman was saying.

"Yes, sir."

"Go and tell him he can try another port, because we're not buying it, and no merchant worth his bones around here will take it either."

"Aye, sir," the other man replied even as he turned and hurried for the door.

"And tell him he can blame his captain if he likes, because every single crate was ruined by sea water!"

Leo had to sidestep in order to avoid being run over by the man as he rushed to do his master's bidding.

"And what is it that I can do for you, sir?"

Leo's head whipped back toward the gentleman when he spoke. He did not sound as though he cared to help him at all. He wore a carefully powdered wig and a finely tailored suit. He was not the Harbormaster, but he was just as certainly in charge of something pertaining to the port. Leo moved closer to the desk, straightening his shoulders as he went.

"I have journeyed a very long way," he began, "searching for a man sent here from England."

The man behind the desk slumped back down into his seat. "I'm not in the business of finding men. We have nothing to do with passenger manifests in this office. You'll have to go elsewhere."

"I'm not here to ask you for any manifest," Leo replied evenly. "I know very well what ship he was on. I need only find out where that ship is moored now."

"Well, that's a bit easier." The man passed a hand over his face and glanced at his clerk. The younger man was rifling through a drawer frantically, and his master sighed, exasperated with his slow progress. He turned back to Leo. "For what reason should I help you with this, hm? I know nothing about you. You have presented me with no identification. Why should I give you the information you desire?"

Leo licked his lips and calmed the tension that came to him. To everything there is a time and a season, and this was the time for great tact and patience. "There is no reason. I'm just hoping you understand that I mean no harm to the man I seek or to you. I am only trying to find someone who was lost to me. I took a chance down this hall because I could not speak with the Harbormaster himself, and now I am taking the chance that you, as a gentleman, will assist another."

The man watched, pensive throughout this monologue. When it was done he broke into a throaty chuckle. "What? You're not trying to sell me something? Not going to offer a bribe?"

Leo worked to keep his face impassive. "I do not sacrifice my principles so easily. It would take much more than sarcasm from a stranger."

This made the man chuckle all the more. "I must-" he gasped out. "I must tell you that I stand aghast. Look here!" he called to his clerk. "Here stands a man of integrity. Take note, they're one in one hundred these days."

Leopold's eyebrows rose slightly as he watched the man pull a ledger from within the desk.

"I am no gentleman, as you say," the man said as he filed by page after page, "but I will tell you what you need to know. Which ship is it, now?"

"The *Scarlet Pride* of England."

"She may have sailed from England, but she was built here." He turned ahead two pages and then back three more. "Ah. The ship is here-"

Leo felt a tremor run through his entire frame at those words.

"-but there was not a single passenger aboard her when she docked here."

Leo's muscles locked in place, and he could not manage to keep the emotion from his voice as he murmured, "How can that be?"

"Just a moment now." The gentleman's lips moved as he read further in the record. "The *Scarlet Pride* docked at Smithfield before she ever came here. It was there that her passengers and cargo must have come ashore. She's been here for repairs ever since. Unless the person you're searching for is a sailor, Smithfield is where you must go next."

"Where is that?"

"Just across the bay and a short distance southward. A ferry ride and a good day's walk should put you there, if you hurry."

Leo nodded, his mind already reeling with plans. "Thank you for your help, sir."

"My pleasure." The man rose to bow before him. "Good luck to you, sir."

Leopold was already at the door, hurrying down the hall to gather the ladies.

Chapter 4

June 7, 1765

Lucius awoke to a choking, sour scent that oppressed his nostrils forcefully. He had smelled alcohol before; ale, punch, whiskey. Even if he had not tasted it, he would certainly recognize it. This was so much stronger. So much *thicker*. Without opening his weary eyes, he let his lips fall apart. Drawing a breath through his mouth, he was amazed to find that the air was heavy with a taste that was much the same as the smell.

Lucius dully cleared his throat as he sat up. He was in a stiff little bed which was set in the corner of a dimly lit room. The only immediate source of light came from the crack beneath the only door. Moisture shimmered as it dripped down the rough stone walls. Barrels and casks of every size lined the floor in tall stacks. Dust motes floated down from above as the inhabitants of the place roamed the upper floor. He began to see more light filtering through the spaces between the boards of the ceiling.

As the haze of sleep began to leave him, he tried desperately to remember how he had come to the place. There was Foley, as always. Odd that he had known the boy but eight days and already he seemed a normality in his life. He recalled woods, and people, and the clerk. Of course, the clerk! He then imagined a vague recollection of a wagon, but it was doubtful at best. So how had he come to this bed in a room full of rancid wheat and liquor?

He did not so much as rise from the bed, but rather rolled from it onto his feet. Whoever it was that had deposited him there had not bothered to remove his shoes or even his glasses. Really that was all for the better since it spared him the worry of searching for them. He climbed the short steps to the door and pushed it open.

"Hey, Professor!"

Lucius squinted through the light to see Foley waving a spoon at him. The boy was seated at a small table amongst five other empty ones. Before him was a plate of boiled potatoes, cheese, and a crust of bread. The meal was plain at best, but the scent stretched across the room to make Lucius' mouth water.

"Come on, sit down," Foley said excitedly.

Lucius obeyed without a word. His muscles were stiff and surely sore, but he was so drawn of hunger that he could feel none of it.

"I thought you were never going to wake up, sir," Foley rambled on. "Did you have a good sleep?"

"Hardly." Unconsciousness is not to be confused with relaxing, blissful sleep. He did not feel the least bit rested.

"Oh, here." Foley shoved the platter across the table.

Lucius felt his hand shoot toward the utensil. He paused to look at the boy. "You, uh-"

Foley waved the comment away. "S'my third plate."

Lucius fell on the food like a ravening wolf. He swallowed half of one potato in two bites before he was able to force himself to move slower. To chew. All the while his eyes roved about the place. The shutters were drawn, but he could see that it was black as pitch beyond them. There seemed to be no one else moving about the place.

"So tell me," he finally said to Foley. "How exactly did we come to be where we are?"

"The clerk. Dewitt was his name."

"Was his name?" For a moment Lucius went back to the harrowing scene in the woods and the menacing crowd.

Foley nodded. "He had to leave after he brought us here."

"He left?"

"That's what I said isn't it?"

Wolgath's gaze narrowed and he pointed a finger at the boy. "Watch yourself."

Foley dipped his head. "Sorry…Anyway, you fell out and he says to me, 'Wait here, I'll get my carriage.' Well, I didn't believe he was coming back, and I was just trying to figure out what I was gonna do when here he comes around the corner driving a wagon. Then he tossed you up in it and drove us here."

"Where is here?" Lucius' gaze bounced furtively back and forth. "Surely he didn't leave us in Edenton."

Foley shook his head. "Nah, we're a good way off from there. You were out for a long time, Professor. Mr. Dewitt says he knows the owner of this place. He paid for us to stay four days with breakfast and dinner every day. He even left you a clean shirt and a razor and stuff."

"What?"

Foley pointed to the chair on his left, and there Lucius saw a sack. Inside was a complete change of clothes along with a razor, cake of soap, scissors, a needle, and thread for patchwork.

Lucius sat holding the sack and feeling stunned. He was troubled that the clerk was already gone, but also glad, because in that instant he could not think of a single thing to say to the man.

"Huh."

"Why are you surprised, Professor?"

"His generosity is-" He broke off and shook his head. "Well it's remarkable."

"But you saved him, Professor," Foley replied. "Hanged, drawn-and-quartered, tar-and-feathered; whatever it was they were gonna do, you stopped 'em cold. For that you deserve this and more."

"You pretend to know my worth young Foley?"

The boy shrugged and leaned back in his chair. "I just think everyone should get what they earn. You deserve a rest, Professor."

"I deserve nothing."

All I ask is forgiveness and grace of God so that I may continue to try and become better than I am in His sight. He did not attempt to explain such feeling to Foley. He feared he was still too lightheaded to answer the many comments the thought would spark.

Lucius smiled wanly and continued to eat in slow, deliberate movements. The hour was nearly dawn. After he had finished his meal, his dish was taken by a thick man in a stained apron who spoke not a word. He told Foley they would catch a few hours sleep before emerging to explore their new surroundings. He managed to beg a mirror from the surly cook along with a bowl of water. Even with such meager implements, he was able to give his hair and beard a sufficient trim and clean himself up. It was a wonderful thing to feel *clean* as he slid beneath the covers of the stiff little bed.

At eight o'clock that morning, they stepped from the inn. Lucius peered through the glaring sunlight at the bustling town before him.

"Where did you say we are?"

"Bath," Foley replied. "Mr. Dewitt said he was leery of Windsor, so he brought us here."

Lucius raised an eyebrow. "I've seen Bath. This is not it."

"It's the colony's capital."

At least that bodes well. To someone accustomed to the architecture and civility of London and Cambridge, the North Carolina settlement of Bath was not overly impressive by any means. Though even Lucius would readily admit that it was far finer and more prosperous than any town they had yet passed through. Where there was business, there was employment.

"Let's walk," Lucius said as he surveyed the congested street.

Foley stumbled along behind him, avoiding the people as best he could for fear that the Professor would accuse him of stealing again. "What are you looking for, Professor?"

"I'm not entirely sure at this point," he said as they paused at a corner. "I'm really just trying to get my bearings." He glanced down at the boy and saw that his shoulders were drooping low. "You may return to the inn if you like. I'll be back later."

"Thanks," Foley said hesitantly. "You're not tired anymore?"

"Not in the slightest. I've a full belly and a few hours good rest in an actual bed. Go on with you now."

"All right. Bye, sir."

As Lucius watched him go, he could not help adding, "Remember what I told you of stealing!"

Foley nodded and flitted back to the inn with one last wave.

Lucius wove his way through the city in and amongst the wide, dusty streets. He passed by many shops and offices of all sizes and trades. The farther he went the more surprised he was by the extent of the business there. This was no mere town; it fully deserved the title of city. He was shocked-and strangely comforted-by the number of people he observed. Several even nodded or smiled in his direction. Thus far, Lucius had felt isolated indeed, and the feeling was only heightened by the seemingly low population of America. The atmosphere of the city of Bath with its smiling faces and roar of chatter put him at ease almost completely. And he did not see so much as three redcoat soldiers in the place.

His body and stamina being in the state that they were, he did not walk all that far before determining to head back to the inn. Once there he would begin inquiring as to work in the area. He seemed to have come to the edge of the town anyway. The amount of passers-by had dwindled out the closer he came to the end of that particular road. He quickly bypassed a colorful cart on the corner where a merchant was speaking kindly to a woman and her daughter.

"Just take half a teaspoon of this powdered toad with your tea, and you needn't worry about the pox again."

The woman nodded and took the glass jar the man offered. The little girl made a face, and Lucius could not help but agree with her. He cringed at the thought of *that* medieval cure, and turned away. *They would likely be better off with leeches than that concoction.*

After that Lucius slipped down a side road and nearly got turned around. He had just determined to ask someone the way when one shop in particular drew his attention. The face of the building bore one door and a single wide window. Inside this window there were between twenty and thirty books stacked in columns of varying heights. Atop a few of these columns stood handwritten signs; "philosophy," "history," "science," "religious reference."

Without another thought, Lucius stepped through the door of the shop. He was greeted by an older woman behind a plain desk.

"Good afternoon. Welcome to the library."

For an instant Lucius stared, dumbfounded. "You have a library?"

"Yes indeed," she chuckled. "The first in all of North Carolina."

"Fascinating," Lucius murmured as his gaze roved over case upon case of volumes. "And what is your policy for lending out?"

"A simple deposit of the value of the book. We allow them out for exactly three weeks."

Lucius felt his enthusiasm wilt somewhat and it must have shown on his countenance, because the lady added, "Our policy is strict, but you are welcome to look as long as you wish, sir."

Wolgath smiled and bowed to her before disappearing into the shelves. He spent nearly an hour perusing the titles, occasionally flipping through a familiar one. He might have stayed longer if he had not opened one in particular.

Desargues' theorem of given projective space.

The page disappeared from view as memory assailed him. Lucius suddenly saw a little coffee shop. Though ill-lit at the time, it was brightened in his mind's eye by the presence of one familiar face.

"This theorem states that in projective space two triangles are in perspective axially if … what?" Alexcena had asked him. *"And why is this theorem important?"*

"Because it is the only theorem of projective space that holds true in all planes."

"I don't know. I made that question up."

Her laughter echoed in his mind, and it pained him to hear it. Here he was dawdling away in a library while she awaited his return. Or, worse yet, while she forgot him a little more with each passing day.

He snapped the book shut and slid it back into place. He was allowing himself to become distracted, and that was a blunder he could not afford. After politely inquiring about the inn from the lady behind the desk, he quit the shop and stalked away in the direction she had pointed him.

When he arrived the dining room was deserted, as it had been that morning. He saw that one door to the left was standing open, and when he poked his head through, he found another dining area with a bar along one wall. A young lady stood behind it polishing a glass with a rag. She appeared to be several years younger than Lucius, with fiery red curls and a stern expression.

"Afternoon gent," she said without looking up. "Have a sit down."

Lucius took the first chair he saw. He was suddenly very tired again.

"What'll you be havin' now?"

There was a strange lilt to her words that hinted of something foreign. Perhaps Scotland or Ireland. *That would certainly explain her hair.*

"I just put in a new tap if'n ye'd care to try some," she was saying.

"No, thank you," Lucius replied. "I have a room here already. I just came back for a rest."

"Aye." A grin came to her full mouth, and she set her hands on her hips. "I recognize ye now. Ye're the fella they brought in with the little man last night."

Assuming she meant Foley, Lucius nodded. "Indeed, ma'am."

"That man, Dewitt, he told us about yer situation. Said ye've got no cash to speak of, eh?"

Lucius cleared his throat and nodded cautiously. How much did this woman know? Surely Dewitt was not so stupid as to reveal the circumstances of their meeting. He had not been in America terribly long, but he was certain the territory had its share of gossips like any other place. A story like that could easily be misconstrued. As it stood, he was becoming more and more inclined to agree with the arguments of the colonials, but as he had seen with the clerk, it might be difficult to convince them of that if ever they were roused against him.

His fears were somewhat allayed when the woman spoke again.

"As much as Mr. Dewitt paid us to be keepin' ye here, I reckon I can spare ye a drink. What'll ye have?"

Lucius shrugged. "It's a bit early in the day for pickeling."

She patted the bar with her palm. "Come on up here, an' I'll pour ye a cider. It's not really cider, mind ye though," she explained as Lucius moved forward. "It's just apple juice with a bit o' cinnamon."

She set the glass of amber liquid before him and Lucius took a sip. The juice was surprisingly cool with a very pleasing flavor.

"How do ye like it?"

Lucius took a longer drought before answering. "It's very good."

She seemed satisfied and returned to polishing glasses with her rag. "We were full to the brim last night when ye came," she told him, "but we'll be able to move ye up out o' the cellar today. Had several men leave this morning."

"Whatever room you have is fine," he assured her. "I'm just happy to be in out of the elements."

A sudden thought seemed to occur to her, and she abruptly asked, "Would ye like to see a paper, sir?"

Lucius hesitated for a moment before he realized she must mean a newspaper. "Do you have one?"

She nodded and reached beneath the counter. "Someone left it here last night. Ye've obviously been traveling a good while, I thought ye might like a look at it."

"Yes, ma'am," he answered. "My thanks to you."

The first thing he noticed about the paper was the bold, black border around the edge of the print. Traditionally a thick line such as that on a paper was a sign of great mourning in the area. When he turned the page, he understood. A skull and crossbones was depicted there with the caption, "O! The wretched Stamp of George!" beneath it.

He raised an eyebrow. "The Stamp Act seems to be on everyone's mind."

The stern look returned to the maid. "And why shouldna it be? It's one o' the worst in a long line of atrocities put to us from over there."

"But it's not even a new act," Lucius commented. "It was passed in March, four months ago."

"Aye," she replied cheekily, "but no one bothered to tell *us* 'til now.

The day we were informed, we were all expected to start payin'."

Lucius shook his head slightly. From what he was hearing, the Crown was handling the situation very poorly. It was too bad that none of the King's parliament possessed the sight necessary to see what was going on across the way. The bigger problem was that a clear vision of what was happening would probably cause them to spur the colonies that much harder.

Before the conversation could move any further, a large man in a greasy apron came in. Lucius recognized him as the same man who had taken his plate much earlier that morning. He seemed not to notice Lucius, and immediatly rounded on the girl.

"What did I tell you about them two rooms on the left?" he demanded gruffly.

"The payment ran out," was her reply.

"I tol' you to hold 'em and I would take up the pay," he growled.

She glared bravely up at him. "I checked the ledgers this morning and there's not a farthing recorded for those rooms."

"I don't need any ledger to keep my business straight. It's all right here." He tapped his temple with one finger. "A good woman doesn't bother with numbers. She does as she's told. Now get back there and finish them dishes!"

Lucius glanced from one to the other of them. The young lady stood scowling at the man-who was easily a foot taller and three times as heavy as she-for a full minute before making a slow turn to leave the room. The big man then leaned one elbow on the counter and sighed in the direction the girl had gone.

"That un's got the temper of a wildcat in her, I'll tell you."

"She seems nice enough," Lucius replied carefully.

The man looked at him for the first time and shook his head. "Depends on who you ask. I saw her crack a man's hand with a fire iron in here one night just a'cause he paid her a compliment. I'da laid into her about that long before now if it wasn't for her father."

"She's not your daughter then?"

He shook his head and looked as though he were grateful for the fact. "Uh-uh. Her father's my business partner. He owns this place and I run it for him."

"Surely her father would speak to her if she were to get out of hand."

"I doubt that," the man said. "He's in prison. He'll be tied up there for the next few years."

The man chuckled, but Lucius found no humor in the situation. He returned to his paper casually and began reading the advertisements listed there. He had never had much of an ability at determining an individual's character, but he was certain that he would rather ask the young lady's opinion about finding work than this man.

Chapter 5

June 8, 1765

Never has there come to this land a man that regretted his farewell as I have. Never has there been a one more ashamed of the ignorance he suffered by his own shrugging smile. Never has there been a man in America with more lost to him than I.

Lucius paused in his musings, suddenly wondering if such thoughts were born of either vanity or selfishness. The question passed and he carried on with the letter.

If by chance or blessing this letter finds you waiting, I ask only that you will wait a while longer, and I will come to you.

A vision of Alexcena came to mind and watched him with ill-concealed pain and reproof. He could well predict what she would have said had he proposed such a situation before he left. Something along the lines of 'you doubt my love so much?' But that was months ago, and he was well aware that in the months to come a rule-driven society would force her to move on for the sake of her own prosperity and preservation. Even now at the thought of it, he knew he would never begrudge her that, though he would just as certainly begrudge himself black and blue.

Lucius blinked his eyes open, and the memory of Alexcena was replaced by a dim view of a dark ceiling. He had taken to composing these late-night missives to her in his head, hoping to land on the perfect words to say before he was given the opportunity to put pen to paper. After all opportunity seemed a fickle thing for him lately.

Feeling depressed, Lucius rolled over and managed to find sleep just before the early morning hours. He slept a good while into the day and woke to find Foley alone in the dining room except for the young lady he had met the day before.

"Morning, Professor!" the boy beamed.

"Good morning, Foley, and to you, ma'am."

The young woman leaned against her broom and cocked an eyebrow. "When ye say 'ma'am' round here, people think ye're referring to an old fishwife," she told him blandly. "I hate fish and I ain't ever been married. I'm Victoria Smythers."

Lucius nodded. "I do beg your pardon then, Ms. Smythers." He bowed low, thus missing the odd look she gave him for that display.

It was not until he bowed that he noticed just how filthy the floor was. Crumbs and bottles and splatters were spread far and wide across it. When he straightened he saw that the tables were not in much better shape.

"What happened here?" he asked as he slipped into a seat beside Foley.

"It's like this nearly every morning," Victoria explained. "It's not a rowdy group that comes in here at night mind ye, but it's a messy one. By mornin' every man's either gone early before his wifey knows what happened to him, or he's sleepin' off his excesses upstairs."

"Oh," Lucius mumbled. "I see what you mean. That's rather… uncouth."

"That's why me dad put those rooms up there," the girl went on unabashedly. "He said he felt guilty given the lad's naught but headaches to remember their fun by. Figured the least he could do was offer them a hiding place so's they could sleep it away before they went home to face their wives."

Foley chuckled, but he pulled up short when Lucius scowled darkly in his direction.

"That was not amusing," he snapped.

Foley looked embarrassed, but Victoria merely shrugged.

"This was a respectable place," she told them. "Before me dad partnered with me uncle ten or more years back. Now our reputation is somewhat…"

"Fermented?"

She grinned. "So ye might say."

While she continued to clean, Lucius turned his attention to Foley. He set his Bible on the table. He did have an obligation to keep after all.

"I thought since we had the opportunity to experience some quiet under an actual roof that we would get a good start on your lessons."

Foley almost rolled his eyes, but instead crossed his arms and leaned forward.

Lucius allowed his posture to go unchecked. He was confident-if naive-that the boy would appreciate the idea once he grew accustomed to it.

"First and foremost for you, my boy, is letter recognition," he began. "Each letter represents a sound and each group of sounds makes up a word."

"Yea… so what's what?"

"You'll curb that attitude of yours or I'll show you what's what, boy," Lucius warned. It was plain to see what sort of pupil Foley was going to be. "Letters are learned in a certain order, but for our purposes I'm going to point them out and see what you recognize easily." He lifted the cover of the Bible.

"Ye're teaching 'im to read?"

Lucius glanced at Victoria. The girl stood staring at them oddly, her broom poised over a mound of crumbs and dust.

Lucius cleared his throat. "Yes, Ms. Smythers. I am."

"But-" She glanced to the boy and back at him. "I thought ye-that the boy-had no money to speak of between ya?"

"That's true," Lucius replied. He was deeply puzzled by Victoria's surprise. "It is my pleasure to teach him."

She stared at him as though she had never seen another human being before. Lucius only wished that his spectacles were not cracked so that he could study her expression better. It was rather difficult to do that with one eye seeing double through a crack.

"Vicky! Oy, Vicky!" A deep voice rumbled from the back room.

Victoria cringed angrily and looked to her uncle as he shuffled through the door bearing a large crate in his thick arms. "I've asked ye not to call me that."

"I could call ya a different name if you like," he sneered. "*Stubborn* and *Stupid* and *Shrew* come to mind."

Victoria crossed her arms, allowing the broomstick to fall against a nearby chair. Foley jumped at the clatter it made, and Lucius leaned back from the table. Victoria's burly uncle seemed to think her ire was terribly humorous. He laughed aloud at them all.

"Awe, quit your sulkin' and get to workin'. There's coffee to brew and brews to unpack." He patted the crate and turned from the room.

Lucius raised an eyebrow at Victoria who stared after her uncle for a long moment before moving toward the counter. He felt almost guilty as he watched her, wondering what he could say to her.

Foley grunted unabashedly. "Why do you stay here, Victoria?"

"Foley-" Lucius began, but she interrupted.

"Where else have I to go?" she said evenly. "With me dad in prison, I'm the only one around to keep Uncle honest."

Lucius nodded. "It's better with your father here?"

She hesitated and smiled oddly. "Yea. They drink together all mornin' and forget about me. They can't yell at someone they forgot."

Victoria's words stayed with Lucius long after she had left the room. Even as he roamed the streets a few hours later, he continued to ponder them. *Where else have I to go?* she had said. He found himself in a similar predicament. The difference was that he was in a strange land with nowhere to go while she was anchored to her home with no hope. But Lucius had gone further. Though he moved in small, halting steps, he was searching for ways to travel on, and he would continue to travel until he found profitable work. On the other hand, Victoria was fettered to one place. What was the difference that held her captive?

He caught sight of a stump beside the quiet road and slumped down onto it.

Anchored with no hope... "The hope?" he wondered aloud. Could that truly be all that differed between them?

A mighty *crack* rent the air. Lucius leapt to his feet, effectively wrenched from his musings. He had been sitting quite close to a bend in the path, his back turned the way he had come. Now he saw that a large wagon, pulled by an ambling mule and driven by a middle-aged gentleman, had come into view. The crack he had heard a mere second before came from the right rear wheel of the conveyance.

For a moment Lucius worried that the gentleman might be hurt, but he jumped spryly from his seat and raced around to the broken hub.

"Awe!" the man half-shouted at the thing. "Of all the blundering bifowacks!" With that he threw his hands up and strode to the edge of the grass where he promptly fell to his seat. "I may as well proclaim ruin now and save time!" He propped his face on one meaty fist and watched as his mule began to graze at the grass close by the road.

Lucius observed all of this in stunned silence. After a few moments and, fearing for the man's mental state, he approached in caution.

"Are you all right, sir?"

The man grunted. "Yea. It's the wagon that has expired."

Seeing as he did seem all right, Lucius moved by him to take a look at the wheel.

"Don't bother!" the man called.

Lucius raised an eyebrow at him as he knelt by the cart. "It may be repairable yet."

"Doesn't matter if it is," the man persisted. "My business is failed. Finished. That wagon is no more good to me than that stump yonder! Good for nought but a place to sit."

"Perhaps-"

"Ch!" the man spat at the ground near his feet. "It's done! ...I'm done."

In that instance, Lucius felt a wave of compassion for the pitiful individual. Here was yet another without hope. Had he not experienced such desperation and loss ten days gone? He moved to sit casually beside the man.

"What is-er, was-your business, if I may ask?"

The man held his reply at first. He stroked his jaw, seeming lost in his thoughts until he spoke. "I sell elixirs...tonics, remedies, herbs, and a full array of curatives for the common household." He leaned close, as though imparting a great secret. "I even sent away to England for a full array of patent cures; Daffy's Elixir, Sir Walter Raleigh's Cordial, you name it. O' course that was some time ago, before all the trouble sprung up twixt them and us."

Lucius raised a quizzical brow. He knew the curatives well. He had been taught by a prominent professor in his studies of botany who had vehemently admonished his students against such patent cures. *"Those men are salesmen, not physicians,"* he would say. *"You can't trust your life to the stuff they bottle up. You men have knowledge enough now even to brew up your own cures, and I'd trust any one of you, even in your inexperience, before I should* ever *go to one of them!"*

Lucius shook his head, for the man was still speaking while he had drifted.

"-shipments plenty hard to come by," he was commenting. "The last six months I been trying my hand at things myself."

"Mixing your own concoctions?"

"Yea," he grunted with dark amusement. "My granny had some horse-sense with this, and she taught me a few things years back. And I got some recipes from, you know-" He dropped his voice to a rough whisper. "-them natives."

"I see." Lucius had no knowledge of the native medicinal practices, but somehow he had the feeling that their notions of experience would be much more reliable than this gentleman's guesswork.

The man babbled on about different remedies he had heard his grandmother speak of but had not been able to duplicate himself. The conversation was drawing up many far away memories for Lucius.

Formulas ran rampant through his head.

"Would you mind," he began, effectively cutting off the man's chatter, "if I were to have a look at your set up?"

The man nearly chuckled. "I just all but outright told you that I'm making it all up from memory, and you're actually interested in it?"

Lucius could not help but grin. "Not at all, but I think I may be able to help you."

"Help me, eh?" the man snorted. "Hardly."

But Lucius was already on his feet and moving toward the wagon.

"I told ya, there's no point!" the man called. "Don't matter how much fertillizer you put on a stick, ain't nothing gonna grow!"

Lucius threw back the patchwork flap of the cart. Vague sunshine filtered down through the colorful cover. A mess was illuminated in the hazy light before him. Narrow tables with hutches of shelves and tiny drawers had been secured to the floor on three sides, creating a small walkway in the center of the wagon. Bundles of greenery and herbs dangled from the supports above. Bottles and corks were strewn all around. Packages and papers and quill pens littered the tabletops, and a distinctly sour smell filled the air.

Picking his way through the implements, Lucius reached the far table where there sat a mortar and pestle. A compound was already in the mix there. He lifted the bowl to sniff experimentally at its gray contents. He dipped his finger into the grainy mix and touched it to his tongue. He held the flavor there for a mere second before promptly spitting it away.

"Hey, there!" the man exclaimed behind him.

"Do you have any catmint?"

"Of course, but-"

"It cuts down the bitterness of the earthnut."

The man handed him a packet wordlessly. He seemed more curious now and inclined to shut his mouth. Lucius muttered as he worked, grinding various ingredients into a finer, smoother powder than before. *Difficult to approximate the components without knowing exactly how much he began with…Had far too much coltsfoot, but how to counter it?* He vaguely rifled through some of the bottles stacked close by while still pulverizing the compound with one hand. *Ah, feverfew, and…sumac? It's no wonder no one has ever purchased from him twice.*

By this time, his new acquaintance was growing fidgety. "Now see here, what is this about? Not that I don't appreciate the effort, mister, but I do have to try and sell whatever that is that you're mixing there."

"I'm attempting to make your cure slightly more palatable. In the event that someone should happen to purchase something from you, you certainly don't want them to gag on it."

"Aye, but how did you even know what was in there? How do you know you didn't just turn a cure into arsenic by mixing in all that extra stuff?"

Lucius shrugged and set the mortar and pestle aside. "There's small chance of that, unless you had something poisonous in there to begin with. Earthnut, coltsfoot; perfect combination for stomach ailments. The catmint softens the flavor, and the dandelion roots will help to counter the overabundance of coltsfoot."

Lucius blinked in the gloom when his explanation was complete. The other man was staring at him in a peculiar way, causing him to feel self-conscious. He fiddled with his cuffs and cleared his throat.

"Does that sound correct to you?" he asked slowly. "I've studied all of these remedies before, but it has been some time since I put the knowledge to productive use."

"Yea," the man grunted. He adjusted his hat and turned his gaze around the cart.

"I'll be going then I suppose," Lucius declared, beginning to feel truly embarrassed. "I'm afraid I can't help with the wheel, but I'll be staying in town if you have need of my assistance."

"Passing through?"

Lucius avoided long explanations by saying that he was looking for work in the area. The man grunted again as Lucius ducked out of his cart. He hastened away, mentally chiding himself as he strode back through town. *Dolt…haven't time to spare for this…Revisiting memories of useless studies will do me no good here!*

He passed through several small shops and one office without much success in securing even a menial position. Alexcena was never far from his pondering that afternoon. Throughout each discouraging interview he forced himself to think of her simple reaction. To recall just how she *had* reacted all those times he had tried and failed to gain teaching posts back home. It was painful now-exceedingly so-to think of her, but the pain spurred him on.

It wasn't until well past noon that his spirits were lifted. A local livery was willing to take on an extra hand. The proprietor stressed that he could only keep him on temporarily; perhaps only for a few weeks. This did not dampen Lucius' enthusiasm in the slightest. That would be two more weeks of room and board. Plenty of time to arrange something else permanently.

After bailing hay and filling troughs for four exhausting hours, Lucius was dismissed for the evening. This came just after sunset. He half-stumbled the two blocks to the inn, his arms and back throbbing the entire way. *Will I have no memories of this land that are not marred by an aching body?*

The inn sounded crowded enough as he drew close beside it. He did not relish wading through the mass of patrons inside, and so he leaned back against the wall of the building next door to rest. His eyes fell closed of their own will. Try as he might, he could not seem to open them. *Perhaps I'll just sleep here.*

Obviously this was not a serious thought, but he soon found his eyes opening for a different reason aside from his own needs.

He was standing across from a side door, which he happened to know led out the back of the kitchen. This door was flung open quite suddenly, and a rectangle of light fell into the alley. The doorway was filled by Victoria and her hulking uncle.

"-dun told ya to behave time and again Vicky!"

"Ye oughtta be telling' those friends of yers to behave, hadn't ye now?" Victoria snapped. Her eyes flared almost as bright as her hair. "They're probably stealing us blind as we speak! All because ye-"

"Don't you go on talkin' about stuff you can't un'erstand!" he countered, wagging a finger at her. "Even if such a thing were true, it's nothing compared to the abuses you give 'em."

She set her hands on her hips. "Those so-called abuses are naught compared to the insults they've thrown at me."

"I'm apt to take a mind to tell your father on you," her uncle glared wrathfully. "This place'll run plum ragged if you don't ease up."

"This place was running right enough until yer friends found out about it."

Up to this point, Lucius had been watching quietly enough from the shadowed wall, but that changed when the man raised a hand to her. He did not bring it down, and Victoria barely flinched at the thought, but the threat was enough. Lucius stepped forward.

"Leave her be, sir!"

Both players in the drama turned in astonishment. After a few unflattering seconds, recognition dawned on the both of them. The large man sneered, but managed to keep the anger from his voice.

"Ah, leave it alone, mister."

"Wolgath. Whatever wrong she has done, you may be assured that the lady acted in self-defense."

"See here!" the man growled. "She's the maid; he's the customer. She is to treat him well and fulfill his needs while he's here."

"But not to prostrate herself before him."

Lucius spoke calmly enough, but his declaration was met with a hot scowl. Even in the half-light, he could see his opponent's face growing ruddy. His hands balled into fists, but Lucius remained unperturbed.

"Uncle," Victoria said suddenly. She waited until he looked her in the eye to continue. "I'm not sorry for what I've done, but I'll guarantee ye it won't happen again tonight. Is that good enough for ye?"

The man looked from one to the other of them and then toward the door of the inn. He shook his head and seemed to decide that he didn't care enough to deal with either of them. He moved inside, leaving the both of them behind. Victoria stared with great round eyes at Lucius. He was uncomfortable under her scrutiny.

"You needn't have agreed to that," he said.

The girl came out of her trance then. She cocked her head to one side. "He would'a beat ye to a bloody pulp."

"I was trying to think of something."

She shrugged. "I only agreed to *behave* for tonight anyway. Tomorrow I'll be after them with the frying pan."

She slipped inside without another word, and Lucius shook his head at the enigma before him.

Chapter 6

June 8, 1765

The seconds rolled on in oozing droves. Alexcena had trained herself quite efficiently in the art of losing track of time while on board the *Liberator*. If she could pass through one second without thinking of it, she knew she could last a minute. If she could last one minute, she could last an hour. The hours would multiply into days; the days into weeks. So much practice aboard a floating box had made this process easy, almost reflexive. Now she found herself concentrating again on the smallest elements of time simply to pass through them. This made them seem twice as long, but she was having trouble regaining her fragile sense of stability and self-control. Analyzing time at least gave her something to contemplate aside from… him.

Tabitha seemed to be having difficulty adjusting as well. She was quieter than normal and walked close at her cousin's side, as though she was afraid. Alexcena wondered if all the stories of savagery in the colonies, which they had all been exposed to, had finally begun to occur to her. Leo was working to remain cheerful, but it was obvious that he was not lighthearted. She was grateful to him and understood what he was trying not to show. After all, none of them was lighthearted about their mission. Except perhaps for Commodore. He was obviously thrilled with the new sights and scents that surrounded them, bounding away at times only to sniff and return. Since he was the most animated of the four, she determined to follow his lead and attempted to focus her senses on their surroundings.

They were on the move. Leo was leading the way, naturally, though she knew not where. He hired a man with a boat to take them across the sound of the bay at Williamsburg. The land on the other side was also Virginia, they were told, though it was vastly different from colonial Williamsburg. This was the wilderness she had been expecting to find all along. A long stretch of sandy ground marked by the lines of the tide led to a wall of thick trunks and brush. With the afternoon sun casting shadows from the trees, it seemed as though the forest was a solid thing, and she wondered vaguely how they would ever penetrate it. That was until Commodore leapt from the boat as it was pulled into the sand. He ran forward, his ears flying out behind him, and slipped into the darkness of the woods without a moment's hesitation.

Leo too had jumped from the skiff, and was reaching for her. She stood and allowed him to lift her out onto the shore, all the while keeping her eyes on the spot where the animal had disappeared.

"-watch it!"

She heard a light thrashing in the water and saw from the corner of her eye that Tabitha was on solid ground.

"Well, there's no need to snap at me," the girl was saying as she watched Leo with large eyes. "It wasn't intentional, you know."

Leo's jaw tensed. "Just-pay more attention, all right?" He turned from her to compensate the man that had brought them and then stepped up beside Alexcena, holding her bag out to her. "Ena?"

"Commodore went in there," she said uneasily as she accepted the satchel. Some of her anxiety filtered into her voice unbidden.

"Don't worry," Leo told her easily. "We shan't be going in there. Commodore!" He let out a shrill whistle. "Hither, boy!"

In an instant Commodore's large head appeared in the same spot where he had entered the forest, and he ran to sit before them. Alexcena let out the breath she was holding.

"Good boy."

Now that Commodore was in sight, she realized just how awful the thought of losing him had become. "He'll come every time you call him, won't he?"

"Every time. Come on, boy!"

They began walking along the beach parallel to the trees.

"If he wasn't so well-trained," Leo went on, "I never would have brought him."

"But, what would you have done with him?"

He shrugged and grinned. "Probably would have left him with your parents. It almost would have been worth it just to see if he found his way into your mother's handkerchief drawer. Like that kitten of yours."

Alexcena clamped a hand to her mouth. Her cheeks flushed red and hot. Then she began to chuckle. The laughter bubbled up from inside her and she couldn't quite figure out how to stop it. Leo's shoulders shook with mirth as well.

"Lucius told you-about that?" she giggled.

Leo nodded, his smile wide. "I hope I haven't offended you, but I couldn't resist."

"No, not at all." All at once the laughter became tears, and she worked to keep her face smooth. "I'm glad to know that he speaks fondly of me."

Leo nodded and sobered somewhat.

Several moments of silence passed, broken only when Tabitha finally piped up from behind them.

"Does either of you know where we are going?" she asked. Leo glanced over his shoulder at her, and she added sheepishly, "I mean, I was only wondering if there was a general plan in place."

"We're going to follow the coast," Leo replied, still facing forward as he walked. "The gentleman I spoke with at the harbor in Williamsburg told me that the *Scarlet Pride* stopped in a place called Smithfield to unload her cargo and that the passengers got off there as well. That is where we're headed. There is not enough day left for us to arrive there tonight, so we'll make camp an hour before sunset."

"Camp?" Tabitha echoed behind them.

Leo stopped short and twisted to look at her. "That's only if you want somewhere to sleep, of course. You're welcome to continue on as you please."

Tabitha appeared stricken. "On the ground!?" she shrilled.

Oh, dear... Alexcena turned from them both and moved a few steps away. She hoped the incident would not last long or else she might be forced to abandon them both. She was just wondering whether sanity was more important than safety when Tabitha's haughty voice broke the pause.

"All right. All right, I can do that."

"Good," Leo replied falsely.

"Good."

Alexcena faced them once again. Tabitha was looking uncertain, though not nearly as uncertain as Alexcena was for her. "Shall we continue on?"

They looked at her as though they had forgotten she was there. Leo strode in front with Alexcena, Tabitha, and Commodore following. The seconds trailed behind them.

Chapter 7

June 9, 1765

Lucius all but fell into the chair beside Foley and moaned at the pain it caused him. His back ached as it never had before.

"You look sick, Professor," the boy commented.

"Not sick," he replied. "Hurting. I'm not accustomed to the sort of work I'm doing these days."

The boy nodded. "Figured. Is it all that bad, though?"

The pain invaded Lucius' thoughts again at the question. "My back is pleading for mercy."

Foley shook his head in sympathy, then drew up straight with a self-satisfied grin. "You'll be happy to know that I have earned a few pence as well, sir." He dug deep into the pocket of Lucius' old coat and produced four pennies. "I carried water for an old lady, and I helped deliver an order from the mercantile, and I would have made more, but I flatly refuse to shake the head off a chicken."

Lucius raised an eyebrow, but let the comment pass without question. As they spoke, he looked around the dining room, which was deserted as usual that morning. All at once he realized just how bright the sun seemed as it streamed through the windows. He leapt to his feet in shock.

"What's wrong, Professor?"

"I overslept!" he exclaimed almost to himself. "I'm late. Oh, why didn't someone wake me?!"

"Professor, calm down," Foley cried. He tugged at Lucius' sleeve to keep him from dashing away. "It's Sunday!"

Sunday? The week had been so long and arduous that the very concept seemed foreign. "It is," he acknowledged, "and no one will be working today."

"Of course not. It's against the law."

Lucius sat down numbly. The idea of rest was so wonderfully inviting, but a large part of him wished that he would be able to work. It would have meant one more day's worth of wages. *No,* he thought to himself with stern determination. *This day has a purpose.*

"I'll need to find a church to attend," he commented.

"That might be kinda hard," Foley mumbled. "They rang the bells more than half an hour ago."

Lucius furrowed his brow. "I slept later than I thought."

The inn remained quiet and quite vacant throughout the morning. Even Victoria did not seem to be in the place, yet it was clean and straightened. Lucius concluded that she must have been there that morning. She appeared around noon, offering to fix the both of them dinner. Oddly enough, she was not the only individual to appear close around that time. Lucius was shocked when a familiar man walked through the front door and pointed directly at him.

"You, there!"

Lucius cocked an eyebrow. "Me?"

"Robert Mandrake!" Victoria exclaimed from the kitchen doorway. "What ar' ye doin' here?"

"I'm not here to sell anything," the man whined and gestured to Lucius again. "I'm just here to talk to him."

Foley leaned in to whisper, "Who's that?"

"I don't know exactly," Lucius replied "I met him a few days ago." *Surely this isn't about my curative,* he thought with an almost frantic fear. *Surely someone has not taken ill.*

"I came to talk to you," Mandrake said. He sunk his hands in the wide pockets of his trousers as he scrutinized the Professor.

"They don't want anything," Victoria interjected. "Don't ye be pesterin' my customers with yer homemade poisons!"

"Come now!" Mandrake cried indignantly. "That's hardly called for."

Victoria turned to Lucius and Foley. "He once tried to help with a headache I had," she told them, "and me throat hurt for two weeks after!"

The pair glanced at each other. Foley was trying very hard not to laugh, and Lucius could hardly blame him, but he was too tense to join in. He was still in the dark as to why the man might want him.

"I have come with a proposition, sir," Mandrake said as if in answer to the mental query. "I want to hire you on."

Lucius blinked. Confusion quickly overtook tension. "Onto what?"

"Why, to work for me." He drug a chair to their table and sat down heavily. "I sampled that remedy of yours, and I've never felt better."

"What'er you hiring him to do?" Foley questioned him.

"I sell curatives, son," Mandrake replied jovially. "Home remedies for every household. Sort of a traveling medicine man."

He winked. Victoria rolled her eyes and sneered.

"Your friend here," he went on to Foley, "has the know-how I need to create the product."

"He does?" Foley puzzled and then quickly changed his position. "I mean of course he does."

"What's your name, sir?"

"Wolgath."

"*Professor* Wolgath," Foley threw in.

Lucius shot him a glance. He knew almost nothing of this man, Robert Mandrake, and he was not at all sure about him.

"Professor, eh?" Mandrake grinned. "If I might ask, what's your background?"

Lucius sighed. "I graduated from Cambridge University in England."

Mandrake's face lit up.

"I studied botany and chemistry, which is why I knew how to correct your attempt."

"So what do you say, then?"

"Hold on there," Foley interrupted with a sly expression. "We haven't talked anything at all about a price here."

Lucius snapped toward him. "Foley!"

"I'll pay you five shillings a week."

This brought his attention back to Mandrake. That amount was three times the pay he was currently receiving.

"And I'll guarantee that for one month," the man added. "Whether I sell anything or not."

"I-" Lucius broke off. He searched frantically for some problem, some angle in the man's conversation that he might be missing.

"Now, it's not a stationary job," he went on. "I travel around a lot. All up and down the coast. Virginia, the Carolinas, Georgia. I don't know your family situation, but…"

"Actually, I-"

"I'll pay you three extra shillings a month for your trouble once we get going."

Lucius floundered. The deal was far too good to be true, but how could he refuse? The cameo necklace seemed to burn inside his breast pocket.

"He'll do it!" Foley exclaimed.

"*Stop* that!" Lucius barked and turned back to Mandrake. His mind was reeling, and at last he thought of the one large detail they had not yet discussed. And what if the man refused? As Lucius studied his hopeful expression, he suddenly knew that a refusal was not probable. He needed him.

"I will not go," he began slowly, "unless my two friends are allowed to come along if they chose."

Mandrake appeared lost, but it was Foley who asked, "Who's that?"

Lucius continued to speak only to the man opposite him. "Foley Conrad Princeton III and Victoria Smythers."

The sound of glass shattering brought all eyes in the room to Victoria. She had been standing quietly at the bar behind them polishing dishes. Now the rag hung limply from her hand and a spray of shattered glass was scattered about her feet. She stared at them all, her eyes darting from one to the other and lingering on Lucius.

"I'll pay you each a shilling a week if you accept," Lucius told them.

Victoria's pretty mouth all but fell open. "But you can't just-"

Mandrake thumped the table with his fist. "Agreed! You have yourself a job, Professor."

Lucius shook his hand and studied the young lady. Foley was on board, there was no questioning that. It was Victoria who was struggling with the decision. She twisted the rag in her fists. Her lips pursed so hard that the skin around them faded white. He hoped against hope that she would understand his offering. He had been given a chance to help her escape. Surely she would see that. In contrast the girl seemed utterly frightened.

"The decision is yours, you know," he told her. "You needn't come at all if you do not wish it."

Her wide eyes remained trained on him and then dropped to her hands in thought.

"Vicky!"

She cringed visibly as her uncle appeared in the doorway.

"What are you doin' standin' there girl, you-"

"I've asked ye not to call me Vicky." Her voice was dark and low.

"Scuse me, then," he mocked. "I'd be happy to call you something different, but right now I want you on the floor cleanin' up that glass. I'll call you names later."

"No."

The burly man crossed his arms and squinted one eye. "I done told you about that attitude. Now shut it."

"No," Victoria was smiling as she spoke then. "I donna think I will."

The man loomed over her, stretching to his full height. "I tol' you to *clean that mess!*"

She did not reply immediately, but began folding the cloth into a neat little square. This she tucked into the crease of her uncle's elbow.

"Why don't you do it instead?"

Lucius leaned toward Mandrake, though he kept his eyes on the little scene. "Would it be possible to depart sooner rather than later?"

"Any time."

"If it's all right with ye boys," Victoria commented, "I'll meet ye out front in half an hour."

Lucius got to his feet. "Foley, go and retrieve our things, please."

The boy scurried away as Lucius and Robert moved toward the door. He heard some gruff arguing behind them as they went, and considered turning around, but he also heard Victoria speaking calmly enough and decided against it.

The colorful cart was parked just in front of the inn. The pair stood beside it to wait.

"This'll be perfect," Mandrake declared. "You'll concoct it, and I'll sell it. I'll wager that little friend of yours is a mighty fine salesman as well. And of course, Ms. Smythers puts together a fine pot of stew. It's perfect!"

He went on in this vein for some time. Foley soon appeared with the bag the clerk had left for them, and he was more than happy to discuss strategy with their new employer. Lucius stood to one side leaning against the cart. He drew the cameo necklace from his pocket and stroked its fading ribbon. He could not help but think of the money. If he kept it carefully, he would have enough for a passage in just short of a year, and he would be able to *write* her. Since they would be traveling constantly, it would be impossible for her to respond. Still, at least it was something, and, God willing, it was a way out of this mess.

He tucked the keepsake back into his pocket just as Victoria appeared on the steps of the inn carrying a large satchel. Her uncle was following close on her hem.

"You'll be sorry! You'll never make it without someone to jerk you back in line when you get sore!"

"Maybe without you around I won't get so sore."

The hulking man glared at her placid expression before turning on

Lucius. "You did this ya good-for-nuthin' dandy!" he shouted. "You're stealin' my help away!"

Lucius shrugged. "Victoria was given a choice and she made it."

Mandrake helped the lady up into the driver's seat before climbing up himself and taking hold of the reins. Foley hopped up into the back and Lucius moved to follow him.

"Fine! Get goin'!" the man called from the doorway. "You just don't expect to have a room tonight!"

Lucius looked to him incredulously. "I'm going anyway!"

Surprise and extreme aggravation flashed across the man's face. Lucius pulled himself up to sit beside Foley in the floor of the cart. They trundled away and the pair watched as the man stalked back inside.

"Was that like a good deed, Professor?" Foley wondered curiously.

"I wanted it to be," Lucius replied.

The boy gave a sage nod. "Hm. Well, that was really extra good. You helped Victoria escape!"

Lucius was facing the boy and he could just see Victoria from the corner of his eye through the opening in the front of the cart. Her head snapped around in reaction to Foley's statement.

"She escaped herself," Lucius said. "I merely presented her with the opportunity."

Foley nodded again in agreement. "You did good, Professor."

Victoria moved to face forward once again. Lucius was suddenly leery. He was not at all regretful of what he had done in helping her, but what did he truly know of this girl he had just invited along with them? *She has a renown temper…what if she were to betray us and steal us all blind?* These musings lasted a mere minute before Lucius shoved them forcefully away. Why should he suspect Victoria anymore than Foley or Mandrake? He was surrounded by strangers.

But at least I know there is One I can trust. That is always my greatest comfort.

"Down the road we go, riding fearlessly into the future that lies ahead!"

Lucius cocked an eyebrow at the dark head of the boy. "You say that as if it's some grand adventure story."

Foley beamed up at him in return. "Isn't it?"

"Not quite."

It was interesting to watch the expressions cross Foley's upturned face as he digested this answer. "Well… If it can't be a grand adventure, maybe it'll at least be an amusing one."

"Be careful what you hope for," Lucius cautioned him. "It may turn out to be some sort of tragic calamity."

"Comedy?"

"No. Calamity."

The boy was silent for the span of some minutes. Then he faced the road with a decisive twitch of his chin. "All right, Professor. I'll be more serious about this business, but can I ask you one thing?"

"Certainly, Foley."

"What's a calamatty?"

Chapter 8

June 9, 1765

"Please, can we stop here?"

They were not even outside the limits of Bath when Victoria spoke thus. Her words seemed urgent, and Mandrake obligingly jerked his mule to a halt. Lucius and Foley, still seated in the rear, turned to peer at the driver through the small opening in the cover. Victoria was already alighting from her seat. The group had made one stop already so that Lucius could explain to the gentleman who had been giving him work that he would not be returning. He assumed that this would be a similar stop for Victoria; a last farewell to a friend or a cousin or an aunt. He never expected to see the jail rising before them when he leapt from the back of the wagon.

Victoria stood, tying a faded kerchief over her hair, staring at the building. "Professor Wolgath?" she said. "Would ye come with me, please?"

"Certainly." Lucius bowed and fell in step with the young lady. Still he watched the building with apprehension. The stone was dark and foreboding beyond the cracks of his ruined glasses.

Inside the front door was a wide office and reception area. Aside from a few scant chairs, the only piece of furniture in the place was a dominating oak desk, where a reedy man sat scribbling away. A pair of redcoat soldiers stood guard by an open hallway that lead into the dark recesses of the jail.

Lucius studied the room and the men warily. He had no experience being anywhere near a jail, and he could guess why Victoria might want him around, but somehow the lithe, near-sighted professor did not feel well equipped to deal with the various situations that might arise here.

The man at the desk glanced up when Victoria approached him. "Your name, ma'am?" he asked blandly.

"Victoria Smythers."

He drew a ledger from the corner of his desk and recorded her name in a long list there.

"And your business here?"

"I'd like a word with me dad," she replied. "Sean Grady Smythers."

The man scribbled something more before passing her the pen and asking for her mark. Lucius stood slightly behind her all the while, a silent and curious observer.

The man snapped at one of the soldiers. "Follow him."

Lucius expected that they would try to stop him, or at the very least require his name, but they allowed him to follow without even a second look. They walked down the short corridor behind the officer. Doors lined each side, designating a total of five different rooms before the hall ended in another that stretched to the left and right. The soldier opened the door of the last room and motioned for them to enter, but a commotion in the hall drew their attention.

Another redcoat appeared passed the corner. He was struggling to handle a man who was shorter than himself. He was clothed in foul, ragged garments with chains about his scrawny ankles and wrists. He was making it difficult for the soldier, refusing to move and pulling back against him, all the while with a ridiculous, toothless grin on his face.

"Give me a hand with this one, will you?"

The soldier bowed to Lucius and Victoria and turned to help his comrade. The man they were escorting lashed out, lunging toward the two visitors. Lucius grabbed Victoria's shoulders, and forcibly jerked her backward into the room. The insane man gnashed what few teeth he had and laughed in their faces before the soldiers were able to drag him away. Victoria slammed the door, but the demented image remained in Lucius' memory long afterward. A twisted picture of a wandering soul taking pleasure in darkness.

Victoria's shoulders were a taught line beneath his hands. Lucius dropped them quickly and stepped away from her.

"I apologize."

She shrugged and stepped around him. "Sometimes it's good to have a man around." Then she chuckled mirthlessly. "My, but I sound like a woman scorned now, don't I?"

Two chairs were positioned on opposite sides of a crooked table in the center of the room. Victoria took the one facing the door while Lucius moved into a corner. Vague light came from two narrow windows in the far wall. They spoke not a word to one another, but both watched the door. Lucius was too busy imagining the lunatic in chains coming in to talk. He was glad to see someone different walk into the room.

The man was calm, stiff, and gruff. He was escorted in by an armed redcoat who stood to one side of the door and pretended not to notice them all. Victoria's father was not scowling and he was not in chains, but Lucius remained very much aware of the fact that he was a prisoner.

"So it's you," he grumbled. "Victoria."

The girl made no reply and her father slumped down across from her.

"I was expecting someone different, though that's probably natural. You haven't come to see me once since I've been here."

"I've been a bit busy."

"An' you've brought a man with you, eh?"

He half-grinned at Lucius.

"Have you come for my blessing then?"

"No," Victoria answered flatly.

Her father grunted and shifted around in the chair. "Could a' brought me a plug at least. Been a year almost since I had any, you know."

"That's what happens when ye amass enough debt to buy the farm," Victoria sneered and crossed her arms. "Tobacco should be the least of yer worries."

He smacked the table with his thick hands. Lucius hated himself for flinching.

"Right you are!" Sean Smythers was saying. "I've got my daughter before my eyes for the first time in ages, so someone must be dead or dyin'. Out with it, now. Who's got the plague?"

Victoria scrutinized him for a long second. "No one is dying. I came to say goodbye to ye."

This was evidently a surprise. Lucius watched with an almost morbid fascination as a combination of emotions splayed across Smythers' face.

"Goodbye?"

"I've been offered a job that will take me away from here," Victoria explained dully.

"That's all?"

It was Wolgath's turn to be shocked then. He could not imagine that even this hardened prisoner would be so unfeeling at the knowledge that he would be parted-perhaps forever-from his only child. Even given their history, she had chosen to come and speak with him before she walked out, and this was how the man treated her? It would have been inconceivable had he not seen it firsthand.

Victoria was glaring in restrained outrage. "Yes. That's all." She spoke each word with distinct finality. She stood and moved for the door with Lucius walking after her.

"Wait!" Smythers leapt to his feet as well, holding his hands out to them. "That's not what I meant!"

"Oh!" Victoria propped her fists on her hips.

Smythers seemed fearful, his hands still raised in a pleading gesture. "I only meant is that all you were gonna say to me? Not that I should get more. I treated your mam like I treated you, and she walked out without a word."

"What do ye want, then?" the girl mumbled.

"I'll say I'm sorry," Smythers answered, "and you'll say that if you ever happen back here, you'll come and see your old dad. Even if you don't mean it."

She hesitated, tapping her foot and biting her lip. "If I happen back, I'll come and see ye," she finally repeated. "The trouble with me is that I do mean it."

Smythers dropped back into the chair and nodded. "That's fine then, isn't it?"

Victoria's features seemed frozen, as though she were fighting the tears. "Bye, Da."

She whirled around to storm from the room, nearly slamming the door on Lucius as he followed. She spoke not a word at first, and Lucius could not come up with a single thing to say to her. He had never seen an argument of that sort between such close relatives. Come to think of it, he had never before seen a family so broken apart. He had no means of comfort to offer the young woman, and so he too was silent.

"After all that's happened, and of all the rotten things he's done," Victoria murmured when they were still several feet from the cart. She halted her stiff footsteps, sighed, and snarled, "This is the lowest!"

"I-ahem-" This confused Lucius even more, and he stammered heavily over his words. "I'm... sorry."

Victoria crossed her skinny arms and glared at nothing in particular. "After all o' that, I would have been glad to leave 'im be! I would have been glad to let 'im have his cake and eat it too without ever havin' to share it with me. All that I would'a done for him, and he says that he *wants* to see me."

Lucius watched her cautiously throughout this passionate tirade, in complete quandary as to how he might help her. One of his large hands was half-outstretched to her.

Victoria glanced up at him. "And so? What's the matter with ye now?

Ye look ill, sure enough."

"Uh-" Lucius was struggling within himself. He dropped his hand and looked away for an instant. He had endured enough cursed problems of his own since he left England, he wondered if he had any words of encouragement left in him. The Bible weighed heavily in his pocket. It was suddenly stark clear that every single thing he might come up with to say to her that was of any worth at all, would come from there anyway. Goodness knows that's where he found his own comfort and reassurance these days. Perhaps if Victoria stayed with them long enough, she would see that as well.

"You needn't ever return here, you know," he began slowly. "At least you know that he would have wanted you to."

Victoria turned her glare on him. He felt that the scowl was not directed at him but that it was simply in his direction.

"Hey, Professor!" Foley called out from the direction of the wagon.

Victoria looked away and moved toward the others. Lucius followed, praying inwardly that the girl would be able to relinquish her anger some day, and that she would take the opportunity to let go when it came.

Chapter 9

June 10, 1765

Alexcena had always been somewhat of a patient lady, but the last day and a half had sorely tried her on the matter.

They had not gone far the first day before making camp. Commodore seemed to have remained fairly alert, circling the three humans every so often and always watching for movements around them. She caught a glimpse of Leo tucking a pistol beneath his blanket as he lay down. He had not meant for her to see it, and she could easily guess why, as the sight was somewhat unsettling. Tabitha lay down beside her and rolled onto her right side. Then she rolled to the left, and back to the right. Three times Alexcena awoke to her thrashing. She wondered how she would ever become accustomed to that, but on the morrow it was apparent that whatever sleep she had lost, Tabitha had missed much more.

They walked all the next day as well, pausing only twice for a short time to rest and to eat. Tabitha all but fell to her rump on the ground the second time they stopped. Leo watched her with a skeptical glance.

"Are you feeling all right, Tabitha?"

The girl calmed her heavy breaths and pulled herself up straight, though she kept her eyes on the ground. "Just fine, thank you."

Leo turned his head, but Alexcena saw him swallow a chuckle. She pursed her lips and hoped that Tabitha had not seen him. "How much farther to Smithfield, do you think?" she asked.

"Well, I was told it would be about a day's walk if we hurried. My guess is that we'll be there sometime tomorrow morning."

"But we've been walking all day already!" Tabitha exclaimed.

Leo scowled sardonically down at her. "We are not *hurrying*. The man didn't account for a frilly blond and all three of us already being exhausted from sailing when he spoke."

They said nothing else about it, but Alexcena could not keep their destination from her thoughts. *We made it to Williamsburg, we can certainly make it to Smithfield.* Selfish though it was, she hoped more for her own sake than anyone else's that they reached the settlement when Leo predicted they would. She did not realize that she was already expecting Lucius to be there waiting for her, just as she had done with the idea of Williamsburg.

That night was better in a way. Tabitha was so exhausted that she practically fell onto the blanket and never moved the entire night. Leo had not kept them at a hard pace by any means, but the distance was enough to wind both ladies. Alexcena found that she had no trouble falling asleep and not one dream throughout the night.

She awoke to the smell of smoke and the crackle of fire. She opened her eyes and saw that it was an hour or so since dawn. When she sat up, Commodore trotted around the fire to sit beside her. He struck the obvious pose of a good and faithful guard dog seeking praise. She obliged by scratching behind his ear.

Tabitha, who slept close by her, was rousing too. Leo sat on the opposite side of the fire working something she could not see. His eyes and hands were focused near the ground. He glanced up to smile his good morning at her and then returned to it. A few subtle, though curiously moist sounds reached her, and she could not overcome her curiosity, though she suspected that it might be in her best interest to do so. She rose up onto her knees to sidle around the fire so as to have a view of what he was at.

There on a flat rock in front of his lap was the carcass of a little, long-eared bunny. She could tell that it must have been a bunny by the cotton tail on the skin which was lying to one side. She could tell it was long-eared because of the head lying in the grass by the skin. Her stomach tightened as she watched Leopold's long knife slide through the creature's bare belly.

Blood stained the stone that was his table.

Up until that point, the diet of the three travelers had consisted of some bread, some cheese, dried nuts, and jerked meat. This was all provided by Leo from his large satchel. She had wondered what they would do once the store ran low, but she had not considered so far as-

"Felt like it was time for some fresh meat," Leo commented easily when he sensed her gaze.

Alexcena managed to swallow and looked discretely away. "Er-yes. Good idea. I was-am-hungry, too."

She moved back to her blankets. She had no quarrel with the hunter for killing his prey, but she had never actually witnessed the process. She was confident that she could eat the meat without consequence once it was actually cooked. Tabitha was a different matter.

She came fully awake barely a minute later and got to her feet. From that height she had a full, clear view of Leo's activity.

"What is that?" she asked in confusion.

Leo swallowed a sigh. "That is blood," he responded flatly.

Tabitha's eyes roved toward the lumps of fur. Her hands flew to her neck. "That's a bunny!?" she cried in a soft, high-pitched gasp.

"No, that's a skin." Leo pointed to the carcass with the scarlet blade of the knife. "*This* is a bunny."

"But you've, you've-"

The girl seemed to be fighting for words. Alexcena hung her head. Commodore groaned slightly.

"*Maimed* him!" Tabitha spluttered at last. "How could you?"

"For an educated rich girl you're not all that quick are you?" Leo snapped. "I haven't *maimed* him. I hunted and killed him, skinned him and gutted him. In another few minutes I'll have roasted him. And by the way, he's a she."

"Augh!" Tabitha fell to the ground, her young face buried in her palms. "That's…hideous!"

"It's not hideous. You've had meat before haven't you? Like veal or quail?"

Tabitha scowled pitifully at him. She resembled a traveler in a strange country having no knowledge of the language.

Alexcena looked to Leo. He happened to glance at her just then, and she made a small gesture with her hand, hoping to encourage him. She mentally pleaded with him to understand. Her cousin was incredibly naive and needed to hear an explanation. He looked to the girl reluctantly.

"Well, you know this was an act of mercy."

Suddenly Alexcena did not like his tone.

"These poor creatures are just plagued by sickness and frailty on a regular basis. These pitiful little folks suffer fiercely. This one here has probably been fighting off ails for years and I just saved her from a painful, lengthy death. Now are you ready for a taste?"

"Why must you be so cruel about it?" Tabitha snapped. "One might imagine there are calluses on your heart to match those on your hands."

Though her voice was enraged, her eyes remained teary and mournful. Alexcena was busy watching Leopold. The very air around him seemed to change. His expression softened, though his eyebrows remained low over his shrewd gaze.

"I do not enjoy the killing by any means," he told her blandly. "This was a living creation once, and it saddens me every time to think that they must die to sustain others, man or beast. But it has fallen to me to care for you while we're here, and you need meat to keep you as vibrant as you are. Nevertheless, I cannot force you to eat it, but rest assured that he will not have died in vain even if you never raise a bite to your lips. I'll see to that myself."

That all said, Leo returned to his task. None spoke a word the whole rest of the morning. In half an hour the meat was cooked through, and all three travelers partook of their portion. Even Commodore was given a mouthful or two. He eyed his masters as he chewed and grunted once in consternation at their silence. *Don't know why you all are so glum,* he seemed to convey. *Those cotton-tailed runts are quite delicious when roasted properly.*

Chapter 10

June 11, 1765

Leo shifted the strap of the bag on his shoulder as he walked. He kept the pace light for the sake of the ladies, but fast enough that they might cover decent ground. Even still, the little group was only moving half as quickly as he would if he were on his own. He tried to keep a careful eye on the others. Commodore periodically ran out ahead of them only to dash back. Alexcena trudged along at Leo's left. She was keeping up well enough, but her arms sagged, and she misstepped every so often. He glanced over his shoulder to see Tabitha stumbling along behind them. Her breaths puffed in and out of her chest audibly, even from a good seven feet away.

Leo flexed his jaw half for annoyance and half for pity. She so resembled the helpless youth she was. "Shall we stop, Tabitha?" he offered. A measure of concern leaked into his words.

The girl stopped short and blinked at him. "No. Why should we do that?" She raised an eyebrow, as though challenging him to say more.

Leo all but rolled his eyes. "Very well, ma'mzelle."

He looked forward once more and heard Alexcena sigh beside him. He lifted the strap of the oiled water sack over his head in order to pass it to her.

"Thank you."

"Don't mention it." He pointed ahead at the road they were on. "This path Commodore found for us should take us straight into Smithfield, I reckon. If not, it will at the very least lead us to someone who will direct us there. Shouldn't be long at all."

Alexcena nodded and wiped her mouth on her sleeve as she passed the sack back to him. He was dimly aware of the fact that Tabitha's huffing had grown closer, her footsteps more harried. When he looked to his right she was there, watching the water sack as it moved from Alexcena's hand to his. He held it out to her.

"Thirsty, ma'mzelle?"

She accepted the drink eagerly, but kept one eye on him as she turned it up. "Why is it that you keep calling me that?" she asked between sips.

"You remind me of an acquaintance of mine in Versailles."

"Thank you," she said and handed the water back to him.

He smirked roguishly. "That wasn't a compliment."

"I was thanking you for the drink," she replied hotly. She flipped her hair around as she faced forward again. "What was she like, your lady in Versailles?"

"Whoever said she was my lady?"

"Am I wrong?"

Leo shook his head and buried his hands in his pockets as they walked. "She was the sister of a friend. She knew almost no English, and she used to shoo me away with her frilly hem."

"You seem to have a horrible habit of pursuing women who want nothing to do with you."

"I never pursued Louisette," he replied casually.

Tabitha *tsked* in disbelief.

"She was seven," Leo told her. He took great delight in the fact that his remark stilled her sharp tongue. Her pale cheeks flushed pink. He saw this from the corner of his eye and vaguely wondered that she didn't acquire more color while on board the *Liberator. Shame,* he mused, *the affect might have been nice with that fair hair of hers.*

Commodore's thick barks from up ahead drew their attention. Leo refocused his eyes, but the dog was nowhere to be seen. Resting a hand on the butt of the pistol beneath his coat, he hurried forward. The barking ceased, and Leo's entire body tensed, only to relax when he caught sight of the animal in the trees just off the path. He was sitting beside a boy no older than twelve. The lad was smiling and scratching Commodore's massive ears, while the dog's tail swished from side to side.

Leo was somewhat startled by the sight of a child amidst the wild wood. He instantly dropped his hand from the weapon. The boy did not appear to notice him until the two ladies hastened to his side. When he saw them, the child leapt to his feet.

"I'm sorry, sir," he insisted. "I found your dog." He pointed to Commodore unnecessarily.

Leo concentrated on relaxing his stance. He crossed his arms and cocked his head to one side with a kind grin. "He's a huge one, isn't he?"

The boy smiled back and nodded, his features bright with excitement.

Leo knelt down. Commodore twisted his head around, as if to see why Leo was so bound and determined to distract his admirer. The boy put his hands in his pockets and watched them all. Everyone seemed unsure; the boy of strangers, and they of the child in the woods. It was Alexcena who moved next. She stood over the boy, looking down on his blond head.

"We are searching for a town called Smithfield. Do you know it?"

"We live there."

"You and your parents?"

The boy made a face. "And my baby brother. Charlie."

"Do you think you could take us there?" Leo asked him.

The boy nodded again. "Yes, sir, but I bet you could find it yourself. It's just that direction beyond the trees."

"We're looking for an office there," Alexcena told him. "A shipping business."

"There are a lot of those, but they're all next door to one another. Would you like me to show you, ma'am?"

Alexcena looked happily at Leo. He smiled and came to his feet. "I think that would be perfect."

The boy had spoken truthfully when he said the settlement was close, and it was not ten minutes later that the travelers found themselves at the door of the first of three shipping offices. Tabitha seemed leery of every building and passerby. It was clear she felt out of place. English ladies of her status did not often find themselves in the company of so many rough individuals, though some of them, especially in Williamsburg, had appeared every bit as well dressed and well-bred as she was. It was ironic to see some of the more haughty settlers looking down on her as a bedraggled stranger. Alexcena seemed far more nervous than her younger cousin. Her features were drawn and her arms remained wrapped about her small waist. Her wide hazel eyes darted in all directions, studying the face of everyone that passed. It was no mystery who she was looking for. Leo might have cautioned her against such hopes, except that he found himself doing the very same thing.

Calm down! He chided himself. *You kept your head in Williamsburg, you can keep it here.*

"Sir?"

Leo blinked down at the boy. "Sorry."

"We're here, sir," the boy told him. "The offices are there, there, and there." He pointed to each in succession.

Leo managed another friendly smile as he fumbled in his pocket. "Much obliged. You saved me looking foolish with the owner of the local mercantile," he said as he handed the lad a coin. "I'm hopeless with directions. We surely would have had to stop again if not for you."

The boy lit up as bright as the copper coin he'd been given. "Thank you, sir!" He bowed and scampered away.

"Helpless with directions?" Alexcena queried from behind him. He was astonished to see a faint smile crossing her lips. "That would have been wonderful to know before we began this venture."

He gave a casual shrug. "It was half true. I'm hopeless with counties and road names, but I'm amazing with a compass. If I ever lose that, one of you ladies will have to take over navigation."

"Or buy you a new compass."

Alexcena was trying very hard to be light, but her voice was tremulous and she seemed to shiver as she moved through the door of the office despite the summer air. Leo did his level best to swallow his own anxieties and eagerness. He was accustomed to being a leader; someone strong when all around him were weaker. The trouble was that the perils he had faced concerning his brother had all been few and far between, and none of them had ever been very serious.

After asking some questions of a few petulant clerks, they managed to find what should be the correct building. Leo entered first with the ladies close behind him. It was awkward, like having a pair of living shadows. Commodore was very discreet and merely remained outside, sitting contentedly by the stoop.

Inside the office was musty and bland. Dark wood paneled the walls, ceiling, and floor, making the place seem more cramped than it was already. There was an enormous desk close at one wall where a frazzled clerk sat scribbling away. A bewigged gentleman stood over him muttering instructions. Dingy smoke wafted and swirled from the pipe he held aloft in one hand. Neither man looked at the three strangers when they entered, and it was horrible waiting for them to conclude their business. Leo inched forward a few steps, willing them to finish.

It was only a minute or so before the gentleman straightened and bowed in their direction with a polite smile. He then said something else to his clerk and started toward the hall.

The clerk adjusted his glasses and looked to Leo. "Good day, sir. What can I do for you?"

"We're looking for information concerning a ship. We're told it belongs to your company. The *Scarlet Pride*."

The clerk hesitated. "We do own the vessel you seek," he said carefully, "but I'm not permitted to tell you much else about it, I'm afraid. What is it you wish to know?"

Leo cleared his constricting throat before answering. "We're looking for a passenger who was on board her some weeks ago."

"The *Scarlet Pride* docked in Smithfield upon its arrival, but I'm afraid I can't-"

"I'll speak with them, Neville."

Leo was surprised to see the gentleman treading back towards them.

"I believe I may be able to assist you. I'm Thomas Gibbs."

Leo nodded curtly, and felt the smallest measure of tension begin to ease inside him. "We'd be much obliged. This is Ms. Alexcena Condreve and Ms. Tabitha Winslett."

"Ladies." Gibbs bowed low.

"And I'm Leo Wolgath."

Gibbs paused mid-rise. "Wolgath?"

That could be good, Leo couldn't help thinking when he saw the man's quizzical expression.

"Did you say that your name is actually Wolgath?"

Getting better.

"Wolgath."

Alexcena's voice was a mere breath beside him. She moved forward before anyone could stop her.

"You know Lucius!" she gasped. "You know him!"

Her entire body trembled, and for an instant, Leo was certain she would burst into tears. Gibbs floundered, surprised by her reaction and unsure how to express his own. Luckily Tabitha was there to take her arm.

"Ah-yes," Gibbs finally said. "Yes, I knew Professor Wolgath."

"Knew!" Alexcena's voice could only be described as a gasp of terror.

"On the crossing, that is," Gibbs amended hurriedly. "We knew each other on board the *Scarlet Pride*."

In one fluid motion, Leo swept the ladies to the side and looked the man in the eye.

"You were with my brother on that ship?"

"I was, but I haven't seen him since he…disembarked."

"Here in Smithfield?" Leo no longer cared that his anxiety got the better of him. He allowed his eyes to bore into the other man, waiting for the blow or the happiness to come.

Gibbs frowned and gave the merest shake of his head.

Leo felt his skin grow cold. What before had been a scowl of concentration and sobriety now became a blank stare akin to utter surprise. He suddenly considered what he had not thus far. He knew it would be difficult to find Lucius, but his cursed optimistic nature had kept him from considering the ultimate possibility. What if they would never find him because he had not survived the journey as they had? Leo stared blankly at the man now and wondered how in the world he would stand it. Lucius had always been his opposite. Where he had been a roamer, his brother was stable. Whenever he thought of returning "home" he thought of Luc. What if Luc had gone where he could not follow?

Gibbs looked him up and down, watching as all of these things crossed his face, and his shoulders slumped as he debated how best to help them. "Let us take the ladies down the hall where they may have a seat in my office. Then I will explain to you what has happened."

Leo could only nod. Tabitha tugged Alexcena in step behind Mr. Gibbs. She was clearly distraught, but Leo was of no help to her. He could not even be a help to himself. For once Tabitha had kept her head and seemed to be effectively soothing her.

Gibbs led the ladies into his office, leaving the double doors open while Leo remained in the hall. He murmured kindly and poured them each a glass of water while they sat on a plush settee. Leo was left with his thoughts for a moment, and they threatened to topple him.

"My Lord," he moaned with barely a sound. "I have been as the worst fool to take this all for granted, haven't I?"

When Gibbs stepped through the door, Leo's head was dipped in silent supplication. The man seemed to realize some of what the other was thinking, and he waited patiently for Leo to notice him.

"I did not know your brother well," he began uncertainly, "but we all knew of his situation."

"You knew he was not where he was supposed to be?"

"Indeed. The problem was that he was struck with a crippling case of seasickness. No one, not even the Professor himself, knew what had befallen him until we were weeks into the voyage."

Leo nodded. "Then you know why we're here."

"Yes, I believe I do." Gibbs dropped his voice and turned his back on the office where the ladies remained. "But I must warn you that your search will prove quite difficult."

Leo felt his shoulders droop and his gaze begin to wander. "I gathered as much. Would you mind explaining to me precisely what has happened?"

"When we sighted land, we were caught in a grave storm. We were some two miles out when your brother was lost over the side."

Leo's stomach flipped and his knees buckled. His eyes jumped back to the face of the man before him. The stream of thought in his mind seemed to dry up; becoming as meaningless as dust.

Kindness radiated from Gibbs' stare. He clutched Leo's shoulder. "Steady, man."

Even as he spoke, he made a furtive glance toward the women again. Leo glared, briefly wondering why he should be interested in the ladies during such a conversation. Surely he did not fancy that he might be able to secure one of them!

"Steady," Gibbs voice rumbled again.

Leo closed his tired eyes, clenching them until they ached. He tried desperately to force his mind into motion. He felt his consciousness tilting crazily. Focusing on a single thread of calm, intelligent thought seemed an impossible task.

"You see what I am at," Gibbs breathed. "I did not feel it right to tell the ladies of this so swiftly. It would be better, I think, for them to hear it from a man they have known. A man of their own family."

Their family...

Leopold groaned aloud. With Lucius gone, Alexcena would never have reason to become a part of the Wolgath family. He would never become a connection to the Condreve family. All the expectations of the last year were undone by what he had just been told. Lucius had been claimed by the treacherous sea just two miles from life-sustaining land.

"It was all for nothing?" Leo's voice echoed from his throat as a mere croak, only just audible. "My brother is gone?"

"No one realized until the next morning that Professor Wolgath had fallen over the side. One of the sailors saw him fall, but in the confusion nothing could be done."

He could envision it. The figure of Lucius, blurred by rain and wind, standing tall on the deck of a heaving ship on the slope of a wave. He could imagine the man falling backward over the railing as the ship was thrown to one side. He could hear his last gulp for air as the final wave covered him, and all the while a mountain of shore was clear and distinct on the horizon. But then the imagining wore on as if of its own accord. The figure that was his brother lifted one arm, making a powerful stroke through the water. Then another. The creation of his mind kicked furiously, propelling himself away from the ship and toward the land.

Leo put a hand over his eyes, then opened them wide to take in a fresh view of the room. This helped to clear the dream from his head, and it was then that he realized Gibbs was speaking.

"It is for you to decide how you must explain all of this to them. I presume the three of you were close to Professor Wolgath?"

"I, um…" Leo struggled to answer. "Ms. Condreve is to be his wife."

Gibbs gave a sorrowed cluck of his tongue. "It is a tragic business to be sure. I shall help the three of you find lodgings for the night-or longer if you wish-and you can speak to the women in private. Is this agreeable to you?"

A sudden thought took hold. Like a spark to kindling, it flamed hot in Leo's soul.

"No. This is not agreeable."

Gibbs was taken aback, but inclined to comfort him. "Very well. What would you do?"

Leo's brow was dark, betraying his hidden flame of determination. "I will go to the coast, and the ladies with me."

"The coast?"

"Yes," Leo answered through gritted teeth. "I will search the coast for my brother."

"Brother? B-but he is most surely dead!"

"Two miles is nothing in a swift tide."

Gibbs started. "You cannot think he made it to shore. Think of the women, sir! They seem frail, indeed, as it is."

"They are not so frail as you think them," Leo replied. "We will go to the coast, and we will find my brother. Or we will honor his death."

Gibbs raised an eyebrow, but it was clear he could find nothing to say.

"I will give my brother this much," Leo continued. "We did not come this far to falter at the last."

Gibbs looked back toward the office. Alexcena's head was buried deep in her cousin's shoulder. The man sighed as he watched them. "If it were my love, my wife, I would want to go farther, to be sure."

Leo ran a hand through his hair and considered. "But I'll not tell her yet."

He saw from the corner of his eye that the other man was shocked by him again, but it mattered little. As Leo gazed at the women, his heart suffered all the more.

"How could I bear to crush her last hope when I have next to none left myself?"

Chapter 11

June 13, 1765

"Take this out and toss it, will you, Foley?" Lucius asked as he passed him a small basket of leaves and twigs.

"Sure, Professor."

Lucius paused to sit back for a moment. In the shade of the covered wagon he mopped his brow and polished his broken lenses as best he could.

He had very carefully explained to his employer that morning that he simply could not work with the set up inside the wagon. He delicately suggested that some sorting and straightening would do them a world of good, and Mandrake agreed.

"Yea, make it neat like. Then you'll know where everything is for sure!"

He had then hobbled into the woods in search of water and firewood, leaving Lucius, Foley, and Victoria to the task.

Now Lucius was crouched inside the sizable, stuffy wagon trying to take stock of everything. He had removed one three-tiered shelf to make more space temporarily. He had come across five or six small baskets of sticks, grass, and he-knew-not-what. There were countless bottles and paper packets. Those that contained substances he could identify he separated accordingly. Those he could not identify were set outside in a miscellaneous group. He found several stacks of papers, both personal and nonsense, which Mandrake would need to go through himself. There were three large jugs in one corner which contained different base mixtures. And of course there was plenty of dust and dirt to go around.

While Foley assisted Lucius, Victoria had independently discovered what few cooking utensils and pots there were. She sat perched on a fallen log for all the world like a squirrel and cleaning them as best she could with a fresh towel. Lucius had to admit that they were all making progress as he surveyed the neat piles all around the wagon.

Foley came back into view just as Lucius was brushing some loose leaves into a mound on the table top with a sheaf of scratch paper. Mandrake was right behind him.

"Hand me that basket again, Foley," Lucius murmured.

The boy jumped up into the wagon. Mandrake, meanwhile, was peering in after him with something akin to wonder on his face, a bundle of dry sticks clutched in his meaty arms. "You were really serious weren't you?"

"Indeed." Lucius raked the leaves into the basket and passed it back to Foley. "Throw those out too."

Mandrake barred the boy's way so as to glance down at the leaves. "What are you throwing those away for? That's some of my best mulberry leaves!"

Lucius quirked an eyebrow. "It's poison ivy."

Mandrake scratched his chin. "That explains a few things."

"I'm almost through cleaning out all these drawers," Lucius went on. "Then we can sweep this place out and move everything back in."

"Maybe you shoulda left it 'in' in the first place," Mandrake muttered.

Foley shot him an odd look as he went to toss the foliage.

Lucius gave the last full drawer in the place a mighty tug and let out an audible groan.

"What is it, Professor?" Foley knelt down beside him.

Lucius pulled out a bottle of pale, thick liquid. He turned it to show the label to Foley.

"Dah-day-"

"Daffy's Elixir."

"Yes, sir," Mandrake confirmed proudly. "Sent for that all the way from England. I like to keep a few proprietary blends so to speak."

Lucius yanked the cork from the bottle and took an experimental sniff. It was not merely the atrocious smell which caused him to wrinkle his nose. He was going to have to try and convince Mandrake to break several habits if they were going to be successful.

"Well?" Mandrake asked from behind. "What do you think of the inventory?"

"My estimate is that we are going to need to build it up a bit."

Mandrake cocked a pensive eyebrow up. "Somethin' tells me you found more in there than poison ivy."

Lucius faced the man and braced himself. Inwardly he prayed that Mandrake would hear him out on this score.

As if in reply to these very thoughts, Mandrake said, "That's precisely what I'm paying you to do, Professor! You point out to me where I've gone wrong in this business, and I'll change course. You mix'em, and I'll sell'em. You need it; we'll get it."

Lucius hesitated waiting for the man to laugh or resend what he had just said. Nothing happened, and so Lucius made his suggestions.

"It is my opinion that you should rid yourself of Daffy's Elixir, Sir Walter Raleigh's Cordial, and any other such patent remedies."

He gauged Mandrake's reaction. He could only guess at the investment the man had made in purchasing such so-called curatives in the first place. Astonishment crossed his features, closely followed by determination.

"Right."

"Victoria?" Lucius queried, and the young woman looked up. "Might I ask you to boil the bottles after we've emptied them?"

"Sure enough, sir."

"See that they're thoroughly cleaned, remove the labels, and then we can reuse them. Foley, will you start bringing them out?"

"You got it, Professor!"

"Mr. Mandrake, we are going to need some sort of a guide to the local plants and shrubs," Lucius went on. "I am no expert on the abundance of foreign foliage we find ourselves in."

Mandrake's face pinched with consternation. He rubbed his rough, round chin. "Wish you'd mentioned that back in Bath. Not exactly any shops right around the corner, ya know."

Lucius nodded, resolving to do as best he could. "Of course."

"I do have my old granny's journal, though. She knew all sorts of remedies and such."

Lucius immediately perked up. "That might prove even better."

Mandrake moved around to the front of the buggy and disappeared from sight. He patted the old mule as he passed. After some slight banging and a thud, he emerged carrying a weathered blue book, which he presented to Lucius.

"There you go. It's all her own drawings mind, but she made lots of notes."

Lucius opened to the middle to pass over a few pages. Inside he found detailed diagrams and some appalling spelling techniques.

"*Arder's Tung. Gud for plag, the fawling siknis, and al maner uf dezees.*"

"You see why I've had trouble with it," Mandrake sighed. "I can only read so much as it is."

Lucius nodded. "I see my work is cut out for me. If you don't mind, I think I'll try to make a few notes of my own about all this."

"Help yourself to anything in the desk," Mandrake replied with a flippant motion. "Make all the notes you need to make that book work for you, Wolgath."

Lucius put one foot up on the cart and stopped short. He looked down at the faded book in his hand and then back at Mandrake. "Might I ask you a question, sir?"

His employer waited expectantly.

"Why do you trust me like this?"

Victoria and Foley both paused and looked up at the question. Mandrake lightly chuckled.

"You think I hired you on without askin' around? I am affronted at that! I may not be much of a herbologist, but I am a man of business. I watched you for a few days. If you were going to cheat anyone, it would have been poor Victoria here, and obviously *that* hasn't happened. It's plain that you are not accustomed to physical work, but it is equally plain that you are accustomed to integrity and decency, and *that's* what I banked on, sir!"

Lucius felt his countenance soften. He could not help but feel moved by Mandrake's opinion of him by a mere two days observation.

"Besides," the man went on, "I don't keep any of my true valuables in the back of the wagon."

With that he turned and strode away, whistling. Foley sniggered, and Victoria shot him a glare.

Lucius felt the fabric of the book in his hand. The weight of responsibility in that moment seemed balanced with the calm of hope. He moved back into the shade of the cart. He found a few sheets of paper, ink, and quill pen and sat with his back to the side of the buggy. Opening to the first page of the book, he submerged the tip of the pen. He read the first few lines three times before finally allowing his thoughts to slip away to tenderer places. Then he took up a page and wrote.

"My dear lady, Alexcena…"

Chapter 12
June 13, 1765

Alexcena trudged along, her steps pounding as dully as her heart. She eyed Leo as he slowed his pace to match her shorter strides, but what she felt was far from gratitude at his thoughtfulness. She could not see beyond a new frustration.

Aside from her thoughts of Lucius, another concern had entered her life. It had come two days before when she and her companions had left Smithfield to journey on. She knew not exactly why, but Leo and Tabitha were both behaving strangely. Leopold had grown withdrawn, subdued, and worst of all, evasive. She had tried to ask him several questions about his conversation with the man, Thomas Gibbs. Each time he employed a different reply to tell her the same thing; neither Lucius nor the ship was in Smithfield. After a number of unanswered inquiries, she gave up trying to talk to him, but he stayed close at her side, often touching her arm or even her hand. She had an odd impression that he was attempting to apologize without allowing himself to speak. As frightening as this seemed, Tabitha's behavior was almost worse. For the first time since she had learned to cry, Tabitha was silent. Her bow lips were pursed so tightly that the skin around them was snow white, and her eyes kept flitting toward Leo. Occasionally she would glare, as though she was angry with him. Was that it? Did she realize that Leo was hiding something? Did she know it already and think it was something Alexcena ought to know?

It was a very quiet walk. At least it was until Tabitha hurt herself. There was a clear *snap* when she tripped on a thick oak root at the edge of the path.

"Ou-" She clamped her mouth shut, smothering her yelp.

The heads of the others whipped about to see her bending down to slip a hand under her hem. To Alexcena's surprise, Leo moved forward before she could, and so she remained still. He dropped his heavy bag to one side and knelt in front of her cousin.

"Did you hurt yourself?" he asked kindly and reached out his hand.

Tabitha slapped it away. "A gentleman would never touch a lady's hem!" she declared. "And you're certainly not going to look at my feet!"

Leo rolled his eyes. "Oh! Forgive my ignorance, ma'mzelle! I should know better than to offer assistance to an injured woman."

"I do not need your assistance," Tabitha grunted as she nearly lost her balance removing her shoe.

Alexcena remained silent, though she was amazed that her cousin was able to pull off her shoe while keeping the length of her skirt in a position to completely hide her feet from Leo the entire time.

"You have made it abundantly clear that you want no more burdens on this excursion," the girl went on, "and I am doing my best to fulfill that request and take care of myself."

Leo got to his feet. "That's your highfalutin arrogance talking. You're too young to care for yourself, but you can't stand the thought of accepting help from anyone who's not paid regularly to do it."

"Do you deny telling me that I was to be responsible for any consequences I face for being here?"

Leo looked her up and down as he considered. For a moment even Alexcena was curious as to what his answer might be.

He suddenly snatched the shoe and the subject from Tabitha's hands. "Have you really been traipsing through this wilderness in these?"

He held up the offending boot. It was of soft, pale leather with a hard sole and modest heel. One seam in the side had popped when she tripped, and a swath of leather now hung at an odd angle.

Tabitha looked nearly repentant. "I'm caring for my feet well enough. If there's one thing I've learned since my coming out in society, it's how to avoid sores, even when I'm forced to dance with a full card of boys who mistake my shoes for the dance floor."

He handed the thing back to her. "This ain't a dance floor. I suggest the next time we come across a shop you see about finding some decent shoes."

"I will if I choose!"

"But conveniently enough the decision's got to be yours without any help from anybody else!"

The conversation continued in a bickering fashion. It was odd that Leo was stooping to that, but Alexcena was in no mood to contemplate the lack of sense her companions were exhibiting. She turned her back on them both to see Commodore cutting a trail through the trees. His nose was low, almost pressed to the ground as he went. He moved several yards away, sniffing loudly. She thought to call him back, but curiosity won out, and she decided to follow. Leo and Tabitha were soon lost to sight behind her, but she could still hear them arguing.

"Commodore, what are you doing?"

The animal grunted in reply and darted ahead. Alexcena hesitated, looking back in the direction of her friends' voices and then forward where her Commodore had gone.

"Commodore! Come back!"

She blundered forward, crashing through bushes and grasping tree limbs to steady herself.

"Come back, dog!"

She had been so busy being afraid of the animal when she was with Lucius that she had not devoted much attention to the explanations of his training. Now when she was beginning to fear he would run off, she could not recall the commands, and Leo was not close enough to assist.

"Get back, boy!"

She had the vague impression that she could hear him scrambling in front of her, but it was difficult to hear anything over the noise she was making herself. Then there came a very distinct *gruff* off to her right. She slipped beneath a low hanging branch and saw him at last.

The dog was standing with his nose low and his shoulders hunched. He was pointing to a man. Alexcena's gaze slowly traveled along the animal's line of sight. She stared at the man, too startled to say anything. The stranger had his back to a large tree trunk. His eyes flitted up to Alexcena and then back to the dog.

"How do, ma'am." His tone was not at all cheerful. Alexcena was still too leery to answer, so he continued. "Do you think you could call back your dog, ma'am? I don't think he's taking too kindly to me."

At the man's words, she looked down at her friend. Commodore's floppy lip was hitched up in a snarl. She had never seen such an expression of hostility in him, and suddenly she was not at all certain that she wanted to call him back.

"Please, ma'am?" the man asked with clear strain in his voice. "I didn't find him, he found me. I mean you no harm."

Commodore sneezed.

Alexcena heard thrashing behind her, but she did not have to turn around to know who it was. So she was still watching the man when Leo appeared at Commodore's side. The stranger balked, and his eyes grew wide as he took in Leo's formidable appearance.

"Peace, man!" he exclaimed.

Leo blinked and rocked back. "You too."

"I was just telling your missus here," the man babbled, "I don't mean for no trouble. I was just walking through here homeward bound when your dog found me. I ain't touched him. I just want to go my way."

They all stood frozen for a moment. Alexcena felt her confusion beginning to ebb, but still she looked to see how Leo would react. Tabitha was just behind her now. Commodore sat back on his haunches looking at

Alexcena with something akin to pleasure. *Look, I found someone!*

"I think there's been a misunderstanding here," Leo said slowly. "Commodore, hike."

The dog turned and scampered into the trees with a soft moan.

"I'm Leo Wolgath. My friends and I are passing through too. You must have scared our dog."

The stranger visibly relaxed and the men shook hands. "I think you're wrong there. I'm man enough to admit that one scared the daylights out of me!"

"I wouldn't worry too much about him, he's too lazy to cause any real harm."

"Glad to hear it. I'm Matthew Hatchens. Pleasure to meet you."

Now that Alexcena was calmed, she took a moment to study Mr. Hatchens. He was of medium build and round around the middle with plain clothes and a long beard. Tufts of hair stuck out at odd angles beneath the old hat he wore. His smile was easy and his manner humble. As he exchanged pleasantries with Leo they discovered that he was a farmer and dwelt close by with his family.

"Ena?" Tabitha murmured from behind her. "Are you quite well? You look pale."

Her cousin passed a hand over her brow, worrying her hair. She was suddenly very aware that the men's eyes had turned to her, as if to see whether Tabitha's comment were true.

"How could I be pale?" she answered as happily as she could manage. "It's sweltering hot out here."

The statement was not altogether untrue, though it might have been an exaggeration. She could feel days of traveling on foot beginning to weigh on her, but she couldn't stand the thought of Leo slowing them down any more than they already were. Especially not for her. She was determined to reach Lucius as soon as possible, even if it meant fainting at his feet. So it was that she smiled meekly as Leo watched her.

"Scuse me, Mr. Wolgath-"

"Leo."

Matthew nodded. "You said you all are traveling through? Just the three of you?"

"We are."

"Well, I notice it's getting on in the day and the ladies do look terribly tired." He paused to tip his hat and smile in their direction. "If you'd like, I'd be glad to set you up for the night on my stead. I know my wife and daughter would be tickled to meet your missus and her friend."

Leo seemed apprehensive until Hatchens mentioned his wife and daughter. Then he grinned and dipped his head. "I believe Ms. Alexcena and Ms. Tabitha would appreciate that very much."

"Except that she's not his wife!" Tabitha blurted.

Hatchens looked to her and the girl blushed a deep red.

"I'm not either!"

Alexcena pursed her lips. *I don't believe that makes the situation look much better. In fact it makes it seem worse; two unmarried women traveling with a man!*

Leo groaned out a sigh. "None of us is married, but there is an acceptable explanation as to how we came to be traveling together."

Hatchens considered and nodded once. "I'll take your word on that. You look like the most reliable bet I've come across in a long time."

Alexcena suppressed a chuckle at that. *I agree with that. Leo is the most reliable one I've ever come across.*

Chapter 13
June 13, 1765

There was nothing grand or impressive about Matthew Hatchen's farm. He had mentioned that he was just starting out, and she could well believe it. The barn was rough hewn, like every other structure on the property. The house seemed nice enough, though. A wide one-story affair with a porch wrapping all the way around it. Flowers lined the front of the place and seemed to wave at them in the late afternoon breeze. Puffs of smoke drifted up from the stove pipe in the roof. The front windows were open, and the edges of plain white curtains could be seen fluttering there. The more Alexcena looked, the more she liked the place.

"My wife just arrived recently," Hatchens told them. "My eldest son and I came over a year ago to get started on the homestead. She stayed behind with our two youngest. I sent for her when she had something to come home to."

"You have a sturdy home, Matthew," Leo smiled and the other man seemed pleased.

Sturdy? Alexcena could not help giving a small shake of her head. 'Sturdy' hardly did the humble place justice. It was like coming across an exquisite, rolling garden and proclaiming it to be green. The scene was perfect in its simplicity. A cottage straight from the pages of a storybook. She could see herself in it. She could see Lucius waving to her from the porch as she headed home.

A child laughed and raced around the corner, chasing after a flop-eared dog. For an instant Alexcena was petrified that she had allowed her imagination to take over her sanity. Then she realized that the animal was not Commodore.

"Hold up there, Matty!" Hatchens called.

The boy looked up and beamed at the man. "Dad!" In a dash he was across the yard with his arms flung around his father's leg.

"Careful, there!" Hatchens chuckled. "I do have to walk, you know, and you must say hello to these here travelers."

The boy reluctantly released his father and looked to the other three with curious eyes, as though noticing them for the first time. "Hello."

Leo offered his hand and the boy shook it. "Pleasure to meet you."

A few raucous barks took everyone's attention back to the dog Matty had been chasing. He bounded passed them all right to Commodore. Tail wagging like mad, he jumped at the larger dog and then flitted back. The ridiculous puppy stretched his front paws forward and dipped his head, waiting for the other to pounce at him. All the while his tail beat and his tongue lulled to one side.

Commodore sat heavily and turned an almost forlorn gaze to Alexcena. *Do I have to?*

She ruffled his ears and hid a giggle.

"Momma says supper's almost ready," Matty piped up.

"Good!" Hatchens replied. "My Martha lays a splendid fare."

"I wish we could give her more warning," Alexcena admitted worriedly. "She won't be prepared…"

"You don't know my wife," Hatchens chuckled. "She's probably cooked enough for five extra mouths already. Come on inside now. Ladies first."

Matthew's daughter, Delilah, met them at the door. Her eyes grew round when she saw the ladies' bedraggled appearance and rounder still when she caught sight of Leo.

"Who is this, Father?"

"Our guests for the evening. Martha!"

A soft, smiling woman appeared. "Did you say guests, Matthew dear?"

"Indeed I did, sweet one." He took his wife's hand and pulled her forward, pressing a kiss to her smooth cheek. "I have brought travelers to stay the night here. This is my wife, Martha," he said to them. "This is Mr. Leopold W-"

"Just Leo." He bowed audaciously. "Your acquaintance is an enchantment, madam. May I introduce Ms. Tabitha Winslett-"

"How do you do?"

"And Ms. Alexcena Condreve."

Alexcena dropped a small, polite curtsy as Tabitha had done, but when she straightened the lady was staring at her strangely. "Pleasure to meet you."

Martha Hatchens' smile faltered and she almost seemed to squint at Alexcena. "I beg your pardon, but have we met before?"

Alexcena frowned. She didn't *think* she recognized her. How could she? "I do not believe so. May I ask why?"

Martha shook her head. "Forgive me. It's a silly thing. Your name sounded familiar, that's all."

"Delilah," Matthew ordered, "call your brother Andrew in." To his wife he teasingly added, "Woman, I'm famished."

"Well we can't eat now!" Martha exclaimed as if the fact were obvious. "These poor people just got here, and after coming a long way by the looks of them. They need time to clean up and catch their breath."

"We won't ruin your supper if we do that?" Leo asked humbly.

"Heavens, no!" Martha replied even as she tucked Alexcena's hand around her arm. "If there's one thing I know about cooking it's how to keep a meal hot without spoiling it! Matthew, you take care of Mr. Leo. Come along, Ms. Winslett."

The ladies were led to a small bedroom where Mrs. Hatchens offered them soap and wash cloths. Fresh, clear water was provided in a pitcher at the wash stand. They splashed away the grit and grime of the road as quickly as they could, though both were tempted to linger about it. In the privacy of the bedroom they changed their clothes and emerged to find Leo at table with the family. He rose along with Mr. Hatchens and his two sons as they came into the room.

Alexcena bobbed her head in acknowledgement. "Thank you all for waiting for us."

Leo withdrew the empty seat beside himself for her. This put her directly across from Delilah Hatchens. Matty-the youngest Hatchens-comically mimicked Leo by pulling out the chair to Alexcena's left for Tabitha. She caught his older brother, Andrew, hiding a chuckle from him as they sat. Mr. Hatchens was at the head of the table with Leo on one side and his wife on the other.

The meal consisted of a sumptuous roast with all manner of vegetables to accompany it. Tabitha eyed the dishes with round eyes and took up her silverware.

"Shall we ask a blessing on this fine food?" Matthew beamed.

Tabitha blushed a deep red as they joined hands. Alexcena raised an eyebrow to her at first, but she could feel her own stomach rumbling mightily as Hatchens prayed. Meals on the road had been light thus far and mostly cold. When the prayer was done, she was one of the first to spoon a helping onto her plate.

Everyone took their portions in relative silence. The three children watched the visitors with evident curiosity. Only Andrew was brave enough to ask the first question. Though granted he was no longer a child, for he was much older than the other two.

"Where is it that you all have come from, sir?"

"We come from England."

"That's a long way off," Andrew replied with humor. "Do you have much farther to go?"

"We don't know really. We're searching for someone."

Alexcena caught a subtle hesitation in his words which she could not make sense of. Was it regret? Worry? Suspicion?

"Oh, I forgot the bread!" Martha breathed and hurried away into the kitchen.

"-dreadfully ill on the voyage here," Delilah was saying. "Did you fare well on your trip, Mr.-"

Leo raised an eyebrow, though his casual expression remained in place. It was easy enough to guess why he was not allowing himself to smile overly much. Delilah was batting her eyes shamelessly at him.

"Wolgath," he answered. "My surname is Wolgath."

Alexcena never did forget the moments that followed that. Until her dying day they remained some of the worst of her life.

Martha Hatchens was just returning with a plate of thickly sliced bread. At Leo's words she let the plate fall the last few inches to the table. The sharp clatter nearly stopped Alexcena's heart. Martha was staring at Leopold.

"Wolgath!"

Matthew and Leo both rose slowly. Hatchens gently gripped his wife's elbow. "Martha? You're pale as a sheet."

"That name," she murmured, clutching her husband's sleeve. "It's the same as the Professor's. The one I told you about!"

"You've met my brother?" Leo implored her.

There was a clear edge of fear to his voice, but Alexcena missed it. She was gazing, silent and still. She seemed to be watching the scene unfold from afar, as though she had no part in it at all, despite the fact that it had everything to do with her… and him.

Martha glanced at her often as she spoke. "I was on the ship with him," the woman declared. "That's why I knew your name," she said to Alexcena. "He told me of you!"

"Calm down now, Martha."

"But don't you see?" the poor woman exclaimed. "I told you he claimed he was never meant to come to this land. He didn't know how he was to return, and they've come for him! But they don't know!"

"Where is he?" Tabitha demanded. "You must tell us where he's gone!"

"Tabitha, be quiet!" Leo barked.

"But what if she knows?" the girl went on. "We must find him. Don't you want to find him?"

Silence reigned as suddenly as the noise had broken out. Delilah and Matty watched the strangers with unmitigated horror. Andrew and Matthew appeared concerned and confused. Leo looked as though pain was physically tearing through some vital part of him. Tabitha was bewildered and indignant to the point of anger. Martha and Alexcena merely watched one another. Martha's cheeks glistened with tears while Alexcena's remained dry.

"What's become of him?" Tabitha demanded again.

Martha's next words fell like stones on Alexcena's heart. Her pulse roared in her ears and seemed to slow with each syllable.

"He was lost to us at sea. Just before we reached the shoreline."

The woman turned to hide her face in her husband's shirt. Tabitha clamped a hand over her mouth, though it did nothing to quiet her sobs. Alexcena could not fathom what to do. It was as though she had suddenly been covered by a layer of ice. The room was freezing. She looked dumbly down at the fork in her hand just as it was beginning to shake.

"Matty," Andrew said from somewhere distant, "go and get some water for the ladies."

Alexcena looked up mechanically at his words, wondering how water could make her warm.

"Do you need something else, ma'am?" he asked her.

"I can't have what I need just now," she managed to say before her teeth began to chatter.

She rose and left the room. She dared not excuse herself for fear that someone else would notice her trembling mouth. In an instant she was standing beneath a night sky scattered with stars. The air was close and warm, but her skin remained cold. She shook violently.

Lucius, lost? The thought did not make sense. He had never been lost as long as she'd known him. Though she knew very well that was not quite what Mrs. Hatchens had meant, she still could not make herself understand it. She could picture it, she even tried to imagine it, but the white hot pain that she should have felt seemed to dissolve as it reached her heart. *Something's wrong with me,* she thought frantically. *What's* wrong *with me?*

A breeze gently wrapped about her form where she stood in the middle of the yard. Her trembling began to calm and abate. She looked down at herself with wide, frightened eyes. She *should* be trembling. She should be crying and screaming and falling to the ground.

"Ena?"

At his voice she knew it was Leo behind her, but she did not turn. "What did she say?"

He paused, uncertain. "She said that Lucius was lost. He fell overboard."

Again, nothing. "I cannot feel it," she murmured. Perhaps if she heard it again the meaning would come through. "How did it happen?"

"In a storm not far from shore," he answered. "They sighted land that day and he fell overboard that night."

"Where?"

"Off the Virginia coast. South of Williamsburg."

Alexcena's brow furrowed with a new thought. When she left the room, Martha had seemed in no condition to talk further. She could not have shared that much.

"You knew this already?"

"Since Smithfield."

Now she turned on him, her face a mask of hurt. "Why did you not tell me?"

He had no answer. He was watching her as though she might shatter before his very eyes.

"You must never keep anything from me about Lucius. Never again!"

"You were nearly hysterical sitting in that office," he reminded her. "Should I have told you then?"

She paused, her forehead puckering again. "I don't know," she admitted. "My mind can't grasp this. It doesn't even hurt! It's-" She stopped mid-sentence as something else occurred to her. Something which probably ought to have been obvious at the start of it all. She gaped at Leo in shock.

"What is it?" He stepped forward with his arm out, ready to catch her if she fell.

"If you knew he was gone, then why on earth did you allow us to keep coming? Why didn't you turn us back around toward England?"

The lines of his chiseled face hardened. "I could not. Not after coming this far after him. The slightest chance of his survival was more than enough to keep me here."

All at once she saw his tight shoulders sag a little. His grim look softened into an expression of defeat.

"I ask your forgiveness," he said.

This confused her. "Why?"

He kept his eyes averted as he gave his answer. It was the first time Alexcena had ever seen this powerful man look helpless. "I did not tell you all that I knew, because I did not want to give you a reason to give up on Luc. I was fearful. I worried that if you gave up, you would want to go back. I had no right to keep you from that. If it is what you wish, I will see it done, but know that regardless of your choice to do so, I will stay."

As Alexcena listened, her stare became a scowl. A bile of anger swelled within her. When he was done, she shook her head at him. "Why is it that you Wolgaths have such a low opinion of my character?"

Leo's jaw dropped at that, though he uttered not a sound.

"That is why you didn't tell me, isn't it?" she snapped. "You were afraid that if you told me and my last hope was dashed I would run right back home. I traversed an entire ocean to find him, but I wouldn't be willing to go a few days more on foot to be certain?"

"I couldn't bare the possibility of destroying your hope in this," Leo admitted sheepishly. "It is all that sustains me now. What would I do if you fell apart?"

Suddenly she understood what it was he was not saying and hot tears pooled in her eyes. "You don't expect to find him."

Leo could only bring himself to shake his head.

Alexcena turned her face up to the sky. She felt the breeze cool her tears. Stars sparked high above, mirrored a thousand times in the water that clouded her vision. Her mind recalled all that Leo had just told her, and her matter-of-fact nature took hold once again.

"You're looking to the wrong source, Leopold!"

"What do you mean?"

She looked down from the stars to face him. "I have faith in my Lord who strengthens me!" she declared. "By that faith I tell you I am strong enough for this! You would be too if you'd just remember it. Now please leave me be. I'd like a moment to calm down before I join you inside."

Her words were vicious as she dismissed him. It was obvious that he was doubtful, even apprehensive, at the thought of leaving her, but he obeyed without pause.

Alexcena felt dizzy. Her head spun with all that she had just heard and said. She stumbled backward until she bumped into a nearby tree and slumped to the ground at its base. Hugging herself tightly about the ribs, she drew her legs in close, and tried not to think for several minutes. It was entirely possible that if she allowed her thoughts to continue to spin, as they had begun to do, she might swoon and remain confused, deaf, and dumb for days on end. There were two possibilities at hand where Lucius was concerned, and she knew she must steel herself for the both of them. True, the one would bring her great elation, but the other was certain to bring her crashing down. The higher she built herself up, the worse the fall would be. Still she knew that it would not destroy her if it were so.

We were made for this world as it was made for us. Surely we are able to withstand the horrors of it.

No matter how she ached, the pain would not overcome her. Her soul would live with the hope of light, and that was proof enough that she was not forsaken. She clutched her arms closer around herself, nearly smiling with the comfort brought by those thoughts.

That was when she felt it. The oblong lump inside her bodice that was the packet her father had given her just before they left. In an instant her hand slipped beneath its edge and withdrew the oilskin pouch. The outside was unmarked, but inside she knew was a letter for her Lucius. By the thickness, it must have been several pages.

For three long minutes she stared at it. Twice her fingers twitched toward the flap. How could she open it? It was for Lucius! Opening it meant conceding that she might never have the chance to deliver it to him. But had she not just admitted that she was strong enough to face that?

She turned up the flap. *Maybe I won't actually read it,* she thought oddly. *I just need to… see it, I suppose.*

Inside was a small, thinner letter sealed with wax. Lucius' name was elegantly inscribed there. Obviously this had not made the pouch so thick.

She dropped her hand inside again and pulled out a fistful of paper script currency.

Chapter 14
June 13, 1765

"For no, for new-"

"That's 'now'," Lucius corrected gently. He could see by the light of the fire that Foley's brow was puckering as he stared down at the page.

"For now-uh-"

"Recognize the shape. It's a *W*."

"Wah-weh-we?"

"Precisely."

"For now we see-" He appeared inordinately pleased with himself for recognizing one word on his own only to be flummoxed by the next. "Tr-tro-trug."

"It's a *T-H*, Foley. Together they make one sound."

The boy pursed his lips for a moment before bursting into a bright grin. "Oh, right! Thhhh! Througg!"

Mandrake chuckled around the stem of his pipe. Lucius was just wondering whether or not he should set his own work aside and help the boy when Victoria got to her feet. She crossed the camp to kneel beside Foley.

"This *G* is silent," she explained, pointing a long finger at the page. "Through."

"Through," Foley pronounced triumphantly. "I see it, but why is the *G* silent?"

"Because the *H* told it to hush."

Foley seemed confused, but when he did comprehend the jest he waved it off as childish.

Mandrake pulled his pipe from his lips and raised an eyebrow at the girl. "You know how to read, Victoria?"

She stood and put her hands casually on her hips. "When ye're runnin' a business, ye've got to know yer ins and outs on paper or ye'll get taken for every last cent ye're makin'. Now if ye gents don't mind, I believe I'll turn in." With that she walked the short distance to the cart, rummaged around for her quilt, and spread it on the ground.

The men turned their attention back to their musings; Mandrake to his smoke, Foley to his reading, and Lucius to the journal he was trying desperately to decipher.

This entire account ought to be a lesson to Foley on the importance of spelling words correctly... Who could honestly think that there exists four completely different spellings of the word herb, *and then use them all in the same paragraph!*

"She probably has the right idea, you know," Mandrake commented after several minutes. "We're neigh on close to Kinston. If we can make good time tomorrow, we might just reach it by nightfall. Best not stay awake too late."

As they spread their blankets away from Victoria's chosen spot, Foley had a sudden thought.

"Professor?"

"Yes, Foley?"

"How is it that you knew what the words were without looking? When I was trying to read, I mean."

"I'm teaching you from the Bible," Lucius replied simply. "That was a Bible verse I memorized some time ago."

The boy wrinkled his nose. "What was the rest of it?"

"Now we see through a glass darkly, but then-then-" Lucius spluttered and blinked. "Uh-"

"Go on," Foley urged. "I think there's more than that, Professor."

"I'm sure of it," Lucius affirmed, "but I can't remember it."

Mandrake chuckled as he tapped out his pipe on a log. "You folks are really something!" he said. "Ain't a fellow on this earth that could learn that whole Book. It's ludicrous, but you keep on trying."

Lucius worked to keep his face placid. "Just because something can't be done doesn't mean that it doesn't deserve effort. I've never actually tried to memorize any of it, but I've been a Christian so long that over the years certain things have stayed with me."

Mandrake sobered slightly, but still seemed amused. Then he snorted and shook his head.

Lucius vaguely wondered if this would become a problem for him. If nothing else it had thrown into shock a different problem, one that he had not considered overly much since his arrival on the continent. His studies were sorely lacking. He could feel it weighing heavily on his heart. The first day that he realized he would not be returning to England easily, he had witnessed his own downfall and confessed what he had done a few days later. He had asked forgiveness, and what had he offered since then in return? His praise was nonexistent and his devotion lacking. *A slothful beast be I.*

He fell asleep that night examining himself. With his background of science, it was an odd perspective to feel that he was under the magnifying glass. What with all that had happened to him in the last six months, all of the abrasions and heartache, his body and mind seemed to be covered by a tough callous. His heart thrummed with thoughts of all that he had not done. *This will not do.*

Chapter 15

June 14, 1765

Foley awoke to a strange bubbling sound somewhere close by. He sniffed and drew in a welcome scent. Butter!

Instantly the boy was wide awake. He sat up to see Victoria at the fire, stirring a large pot of oatmeal. He jumped up to stand nearer the pot and smelled again.

"Umm! When do we get to eat?"

"Soon," Victoria assured him. "Maybe he'll be awake by then, too."

Foley looked over to see Mandrake still snoring beneath his quilt. Once he heard it, he was surprised that the sound of his hideous snorts had not woken him before. He wrinkled his nose in disgust. *At least he could close his mouth!*

"All his talk of wanting to make time today, and he's the last one left asleep," Victoria went on. "Want some coffee, Foley?"

Victoria held a tin mug out to him. The pot sat to the side of the fire on a bed of coals. Foley considered. He had never tried coffee before. That was an adult's drink, like bourbon or wassail. But he was on his own now. By his reckoning that made him an honorary adult.

"Yes, thanks."

She wrapped her pot holder around the handle and began to pour. "I should've warned ye, there's not a drop a' milk."

Foley set his hat firmly on his head. "I'm a real man. I take it black!"

Victoria raised an eyebrow, but her amusement was obvious. "I take mine black on occasion, too, ye know. Does that make me a real man?"

"Nah! That just makes you tough," Foley replied easily. "You'd better be careful, though. I hear there's some kinds of coffee that'll put hair on your chest."

Victoria's lips pressed together to hide her laughter as she passed the boy his mug. "I'll watch out for that, sure enough."

Foley nodded gravely, satisfied that she understood the seriousness of such a situation. He lifted the cup and took a loud sip. He couldn't spit the stuff out fast enough. His mouth fell open instantly and the wretched liquid streamed back down into the cup. It burned his chin, but not nearly as much as it had burned his tongue. It was like swallowing a bitter fire.

"Hot enough for ye?" Victoria asked casually.

Foley gasped, choked, and carefully set the cup aside. "How do you drink that stuff?" he wondered as he glared at the mug.

"I'm tough, remember?" Victoria teased. "I also put in a bit o' sugar." She produced three lumps from her pocket and leaned over to drop them in Foley's cup. "Ye can try it again in a few minutes when it's cooled."

The boy doubted the sugar would help, but he would drink it when it was cool, just to know that he could. "I wonder how the Professor drinks his," he thought aloud.

"Search me," Victoria shrugged. "I haven't paid attention when he fixes it."

"Where is he?"

She jerked a thumb towards the trees to their left. "Headed off that way. Said he'd be back in a bit. Ye want to go let him know the coffee's done now?"

"All right."

"Don't go too far if you can't find him right off. He doesn't strike me as the type to have a fair sense of direction."

"All right."

Maybe when Lucius drinks his coffee, I can pour a little of mine in it when he's not looking, Foley thought as he trudged through the brush and trees. *Then I could show Victoria my empty cup without having to drink that stuff myself… But that would be lying. What if the Professor catches me lying?* Even he was smart enough to admit that the best way to keep from being caught doing something was to not do it at all. Somehow he knew there was no getting around that fact, but maybe he could come up with something.

He stopped his musing when he caught sight of Lucius a short distance off. He started to call out to him, but something made him take a closer look. The Professor looked *odd*. He was on bended knee with his head bowed and his hands held up even with his shoulders. Though Foley couldn't hear a sound, he suspected that he saw Lucius' lips moving. The boy watched, unsure of what to do and too afraid to interrupt, until Lucius came to his feet. He dusted off his breeches and turned, smiling toward the bush where Foley was crouched.

"Good morning, Foley."

The boy straightened and dashed forward. "Hey, Professor!" he shouted. "How'd you know it was me?"

"I heard you," Lucius replied, "and neither of our other friends would have fit behind that little bush."

"Yea, but what if it was a badger or a coon or something?"

"Then I would have said good morning to him too."

"Oh." That hadn't occurred to Foley. "Victoria almost has breakfast ready."

"Then we best go back."

They had not gone five steps before Foley's curiosity overcame him. "What were you doing back there, Professor?"

"I was speaking to my Lord," Lucius replied.

"But why were you on the ground?"

"Sometimes my Lord overwhelms me," Lucius explained simply.

"Oh." Foley nodded as though he understood, but he didn't. It was difficult for him to imagine someone being overwhelmed by God when they couldn't even see him. *Maybe Lucius can see him.* He watched the man with wide, astonished eyes.

Lucius noticed. "What is it?"

"Nothing!" Foley croaked too loudly.

The boy blushed and Lucius decided not to question him. When they arrived back at the campsite, Mandrake was awake and Victoria was spooning out bowls of the breakfast. Foley continued to watch him as they ate, letting his sweetened coffee grow cold in the process. He noticed that Lucius bowed his head for a moment before he ate. There was something different it seemed in his manner. He was talking and joking with the other two. He would have made Foley laugh too if he was not so intent on figuring him out. *Why would anyone smile if they could see God? Unless they were daft… He is a little strange, so maybe he is daft. He does it well, though if that's what he is.*

After everyone was finished, Lucius mentioned that he would like to discuss inventory with Robert. Victoria recruited Foley to help her carry the dishes down to the creek. The oatmeal was all gone, so they set everything inside the large pot and each lifted one side.

"Does the Professor seem different to you?" Foley asked her as they went. He spoke with all the tact a young boy can muster.

"Different how?"

"Different crazy."

Victoria blinked. "Well, he's always seemed 'different,' but never crazy."

"Yea."

"Ye know him better than me. Why d'ye ask such a thing?"

Foley sighed. "When I found him this morning he was on the ground. I thought he was praying, but he said he was talking."

"What else do ye think a prayin' man is doin'?"

Foley's brow wrinkled as he struggled to comprehend. It took him a minute to succeed. "Oh."

He suddenly felt better. *Of course* Lucius was praying. *Of course* he was religious. He had known that about him all along.

"Hey, Victoria, how'd you know that?"

The woman's face grew serious and her bottom lip nearly pouted out. "My momma took me to church sometimes."

"So how come she quit comin' around?"

Victoria huffed out a breath and dropped her side of the pot to the ground. "How should I know? Now get started washin'. I forgot the towel!" With that she stormed off into the brush.

Foley picked up a bowl and shook his head. "Wonder what's botherin' her."

Lucius ground the leaves in the mortar and pestle for all he was worth. As his arm moved, his eyes darted across the pages before him. The journal lay open to one side. Several sheets of notes were set beside it, weighted down by a rock. He had spent the majority of the morning collecting plant samples as they walked. Mandrake led his mule along, whistling as he went, and not seeming to pay one bit of attention to what Lucius was doing. Foley, however, was extremely interested, and Victoria was willing to help any time he requested it. Mandrake's mule, Wendy, was not eager to move, so Lucius was able to linger often over the specimens he found in the edges of the woods and catch up with ease when he was done. He was leery of many of the wild plants, for they were very different from the ones he had encountered in England. When he did come across something useful and altogether familiar, he took as much as he could. Even still, after a day of travel, he knew that the curatives he would be able to offer would be few and limited. He didn't have the slightest notion what Mandrake was expecting of him aside from viable product. He was slightly concerned that his abilities would prove to be a disappointment, and the man would end their engagement after the promised month. This worry remained at the back of his mind, but it was more of a passing thought that came now and then. The subject of worry itself was becoming a unique and yet familiar thing for him. Whether it was for Mandrake, or himself, or-most of all-Alexcena, the feeling passed as soon as it would come, and he would continue with his work. This was surely the kindest of blessings. There had been days not so long gone when his worry had nearly driven him insane. It pained him more to think of that than of all that he had lost. After all he did have the hope of regaining his former life. If he had lost his mind and soul, all might have truly been gone for ever.

He paused and pressed a hand to his side where a letter was tucked securely at his waist beneath his shirt. Unlike the ones he had written before in his mind, this one could be sent, and he had every intention of doing so when they came upon a settlement.

"Is everything all right, Professor?"

In a flash his hand went back to the pestle. "Just fine, Victoria," he replied. "Please be certain you're dividing those evenly."

"Sure enough, Professor."

He had set Victoria and Foley to preparing individual portions of herbal teas. Mandrake had provided an old muslin table cloth as material for the bundles. After Victoria had washed it, Lucius had cut it into meticulously even squares. Now he watched as Victoria placed four different leaves in the center of a square, twisted the corners together, and passed it to Foley, who tied a small bit of thread tightly around the twist. As he tied, the boy watched Lucius's work surreptitiously until at last he grew too interested to keep silent.

"How will these things work, Professor?"

"What things, Foley?"

He held up the bundle he had just tied. "These little bags."

Lucius felt his shoulders twitch with amusement. "I'd say you've just answered your own question. They simply act as a bag to transfer the leaves. When the customer is ready to brew the tea, they simply cut the string and everything they need is right there."

"Oooh," he intoned. "I thought they were some sort of special thing. You know, like an invention. What's that you're mixin', Professor?"

"Milkweed, sulfur, and camphor," Lucius explained. "It works wonders for gout."

"Smells awful."

"Gout's a painful thing. So much so that sometimes the smell makes no difference."

Foley blanched a little at that. He cut his eyes to Lucius and asked, "How do you catch the gut?"

Lucius knew he must have misunderstood the boy, but there passed a long moment before he could figure out how. Victoria burst out laughing in an instant.

"Well, I'm glad you're all in such a pleasant mood!"

Lucius eyed Mandrake as he ambled along toward them. It was Victoria who voiced his thoughts.

"I hope ye don't mind me askin', sir," she began, "but where'd ye disappear to that's got ye all cheery?"

"Hold up, now," the man answered. "I know what you're thinkin'. 'He's been gone neigh on two hours while we've been here working hard.' Well, so have I, and I got a surprise for you."

Lucius got to his feet and watched the man blandly. He wasn't sure that he cared for the inordinately pleased look on Mandrake's face. It was rather similar to that of a child who just found an unguarded pie on a neighbor's window sill.

"Now I know that we've been set off schedule a day or so," Mandrake said, "what with you pointing out that our inventory was still a mite low. That makes good sense, of course, but I thought that while you all worked on that, I should get busy on the tactics."

"Tactics?"

Mandrake turned to the wall of trees behind him and blew out a low whistle. "Come on out, Wendy!" A short pause later, he stepped into the trees and emerged tugging his mule along by her rope. "Come on now, Wendy. Don't fuss."

Victoria and Foley moved up beside Lucius to watch, drawn by their curiosity. Mandrake led Wendy around until they were looking at her side. Draped over her back was a length of faded canvas cunningly knotted on the corners so as to make it somewhat decorative and appealing. Painted across the canvas in rusty red was a slogan. *Not your doc's medicine.*

Lucius could do nothing but sigh. Victoria snickered and pursed her lips. Foley wrinkled his nose.

"What's that say?"

"Not your doc's medicine." Mandrake pulled the lapels of his coat and grinned like a proud papa. "Came up with it myself. What I figure is this; we stick to the small towns along the way. You go to a big town you'll find business, but you'll also find doctors who don't take kindly to the likes of us. Head for the quieter settlements, you'll find folks more in need, without doctors around to argue. You see?"

"I told you before," Lucius insisted, "I'm not a physician."

"That's why the sign says *not.*"

Lucius rubbed at a wrinkle on his forehead. "This is pressing the borders of my ethics."

"What ethic?" Mandrake pshawed. "You're supposed to manufacture the stuff, and I'm supposed to sell it. You don't worry about how the selling's done, and I won't worry about how the mixin's done. Get it?"

The men stared at one another. Mandrake was not agitated-yet-but it was clear that he was laying down the statute and would suffer little argument on the subject. If there was one thing Lucius could not stand, it was being told that his morals would need to change to accommodate someone else's immorality. Perhaps the situation was not quite so serious, but Lucius was feeling especially firm on such grounds. The implication that his mixtures were in fact medicine was far from the truth. The real problem was that he needed the job if he was ever going to make it back to Alexcena before she was forced to move on without him. Lucius could feel the eyes of Foley and Victoria on him. Their employments might be affected just as much as his if he were to press Mandrake too far. In the end, the need was greater than the stand, and he knew he could not afford to contest it.

"Of course not, sir," he said at last. "You are my employer. I will do as you say, but I would ask one stipulation if you are willing to consider it."

"And that is?"

"I would ask that you never refer to me as a doctor or physician of any sort. I will answer any question as to my qualifications, but I am not willing to confirm or create any falsehood about them."

Mandrake spread his arms wide. "And I wouldn't ask you to! Perish the thought. But I'm glad you brought it up. I don't ever want any of you to feel uneasy about our business endeavors together. Come, Wendy!"

He effectively ended the conversation by turning away with his mule. Lucius stared after him. He was beginning to realize that he did not appreciate the way Mandrake conducted himself in business. Or in general.

Foley wandered away, but Victoria remained, her eyes on Lucius. "Why did ye start that wi' him?"

Lucius turned to her. "He's being manipulative. What would you have had me say?"

The girl eyed him up and down. Lucius kept his stance nonchalant. He was not overly worried about Victoria's opinions, but he was not in the mood to explain his point again.

Victoria finally shrugged and gave him a grin. "I don't know. I s'pose we'll all get used to one another eventually."

"You think so?"

"Either that or we'll go our separate ways and all end up poor and miserable again."

Lucius shook his head. "I'd find something else. I have to if I'm ever to make it back."

"To England?" she mused, the grin still playing across her face. "You still have hope of that?"

"Yes." He didn't even pause to consider before answering. He knew it and felt it without a measure of doubt. "Yes. Even if I return to find her gone, I must go."

Chapter 16

June 14, 1765

The wagon jostled over a rut in the road, and Alexcena pressed a hand to her waist where she knew the packet of money remained tucked inside her bodice. Leo's concerned voice sounded close in her ear once more, like an ever-present buzzing in her mind.

"Are you all right, Ena?"

"Fine," she replied for the fourth time that day. "Do not worry about me."

For once she had to work to keep her voice kind. Leo had done nothing but fuss over her since the previous evening when the grievous news had fallen. Her own flitting thoughts were running almost wild and agitating enough without him asking whether she was all right every time she moved.

Questions presented themselves in her mind's eye with every other breath. Where is he? Is he hurt? Is he alive? Is he frightened? No matter the natural wanderings of her mind, she knew without hesitation that she would not leave the continent until she found someone who could give her the answers she needed, even if it meant that she would never again venture home.

She reminded herself constantly that her Lord would never require anything of her that she could not give, and this helped to quiet her racing thoughts. She had thought on this concept long into the night. She could well recall more than one time of mourning and sorrow when she had heard another person question God's purpose in a tragedy. But the way she saw it, it did not seem that it was so that God necessarily caused detriment or sorrow, but that He expects His people to face such things with sobriety, understanding, and wisdom, never wavering from that which is good and right. So it was that she was perfectly capable of pulling herself up and returning into the house the night before.

The fact that she was handling her sorrow did nothing to allay her confusion concerning her father's packet to Lucius. If Lawrence had intended the money to pay for their return trip, why had he not simply given it to Alexcena or Leo in the first place? (Leo carried more than enough coin in his bag, she knew, to see them home, but it could only help.) Not only that, but why had he sent so much? She had not counted it out, but she had seen enough to guess that it was far more than they would require for passage. Perplexed and indeed frightened by the discovery, she had simply stuffed it all back into the packet and tucked it safely to her side.

She had not told Leo. If she didn't know him better, she would call his behavior since the past night skittish. She was not about to give him one more thing to worry about. The reason she kept it from Tabitha should have been obvious to anyone. It had to do with the girl's lips and the way they were always moving.

But she had to give her cousin credit on that score. Tabitha seemed to be making an effort to control her usual character. At least when Leo was present, and that was pretty much all the time. The poor girl had babbled herself to sleep with words of comfort for Alexcena when they were left alone.

Alexcena had wondered as she lay down how she might ever find slumber, but it came easily. She welcomed the oblivion. The opportunity to allow her mind to rest as well as her body was altogether too inviting to resist.

They had all risen much too early that morning, and Mr. Hatchens had offered to have Andrew drive them down to the town of Suffolk, Virginia. Leo had accepted, saying that they would all be grateful for the chance to ride rather than walk.

Suffolk was not nearly as large as Williamsburg, though it seemed every bit as busy. While Leo received further directions from Andrew, Alexcena observed the rushing townspeople. To and fro they went from offices and shops along the short stretch.

"I never believed I would think it," Tabitha declared suddenly at Alexcena's side.

She blinked at her cousin. "What is that? And where did you disappear to the last few minutes?"

Tabitha did not turn, but stared oddly at the passers-by. It was clear she was preoccupied by her own thoughts. "I don't like cities anymore. At least I don't think I do."

Alexcena felt her surprise streak across her face. "You?" she blurted.

Tabitha nodded. "They seem-constricting. When I think of Penn or Cambridge back home, I see them the same way. I cannot fathom why, except that-"

"Yes?"

"Well, maybe it's because…" Tabitha turned her large green eyes to her. "Because I had never truly seen anyplace so open until we came here."

Alexcena was not altogether certain how she should respond to that beyond a smile. She was saved the trouble of it when Leo and Andrew came around the wagon to join them.

"We should be all set," Leo declared, rubbing his hands together. "Andrew has pointed the way and the Hatchens were kind enough to send some fresh supplies for us. I don't know how far we can get with so much of the day gone, but we should be on our way."

"You must thank your parents for us again," Alexcena insisted to Andrew. "You have all been so very generous to us."

The young man blushed and tried to hide it by ducking his head. "It was nothing. You heard my mother. She kept saying she felt as though she knew you."

Alexcena smiled to herself. "It is so like Lucius to befriend a gentle lady like your mother."

She felt Leo touch her shoulder. "And so like him to speak often of you." Then he turned to Andrew and offered his hand to him. "Safe journey, Hatchens."

"And to all of you."

When Alexcena turned around, she found that Tabitha was watching Leo, and there was something not right in her expression. It was as though she had eaten something distasteful and despaired of it. At first she assumed it was because he had interrupted her conversation before, or because he insisted that they continue on. More likely that, because it would inevitably mean that they would be sleeping another night on the woodland floor. These thoughts vanished when Tabitha spun the same unwavering look to her. What on earth should make Tabitha turn such an expression to her?

In the end she had no time to ponder it. Leo started toward the southeast edge of the town, ushering the women ahead of him until they were at its end. Then he took the lead, and Alexcena measured her strides to his. She needed to keep up if she was going to be able to talk to him, and she was very anxious for information.

"Will it be very long before we come to where we are going?" she asked.

"I'm afraid so," he responded cheerfully. "Several days at least. Hatchens was kind enough to give us a good start."

"Where will we be then?"

"Currituck, North Carolina."

She hesitated midstride. "Carolina? I thought we were going to the Virginia coast."

"False Cape, Virginia is a stretch of sea famous for storms and shipwrecks," he explained. "That's where the storm caught the *Scarlet Pride*. It's a terribly small settlement right on the border of North Carolina. Currituck is the closest settlement of any size. It's likely that Luc would have gone there looking for assistance. If we find no trace of him there, we will work our way north. It may take us a while to find anything out."

She nodded once in acknowledgment. "All right."

Leo nearly drew up short. His voice did not sound so carefree the next time he spoke. "We may never find anything, Ena."

She turned her head to look him in the eye. "All right, Leo."

He did not believe her. This she knew the moment she spoke the words. She only hoped that Leo would see that it was true. Until he did, she would simply follow his direction in silence.

They walked side by side along the dusty road with Commodore dashing ahead of them and Tabitha several steps behind. Leo held back his stride at times, and Alexcena was grateful for it. Her body was gradually growing more accustomed to the walking, although it was still trying to her muscles. Her bag, small though it was, pressed hard into her shoulder, and she was forced to shift it often. Leo's pack was easily three times the size of hers, and she couldn't help but notice that it never changed position. His hard shoulders were more than a match for it.

What with her pensiveness and Tabitha's odd mood, the afternoon's walk was practically silent. Leo, as always, seemed happy to remain quiet as long as the ladies were. Occasionally Commodore would trot back and press his large head up under her hand, as if to say, 'Despite the fact that I am utterly preoccupied with all these wonderful new smells, I still love you and require attention.' This she freely gave. The love she felt in return for Commodore now made it seem ridiculous that she had once feared him.

They came to a place along the road at the edge of the trees where a cluster of boulders provided shelter from any night winds. The sun was just beginning to set, but Leo declared that they could not find any place better for a night's rest. The ladies did not argue.

Leo set about gathering wood from the tree line and starting a fire. (They had found that even in these warm, new summer days, the flame was a special comfort in the night.) Alexcena pulled a few mugs and a kettle from her bag, and began to prepare a pot of coffee. Commodore pressed his nose to the ground and walked the perimeter. Tabitha plopped down at the base of one boulder and began fanning herself almost furiously. Alexcena glanced at her with some apprehension. Her cousin's cheeks were red. The fan was a mere bit of lace on sticks, and couldn't do much good to cool her. Still the girl kept her back straight and her gaze fixed away from the others, so Alexcena said nothing of it.

It was not until the fire was dancing strongly on its own that Leo noticed her. He was not so apt to keep his comments to himself. By that time Tabitha was rubbing a muscle in one of her legs absently. His eyes narrowed, and Alexcena was instantly put on edge by it. He rose and moved to kneel before the girl. She faced him, ruffled by his sudden nearness.

"Let me see your feet," he began bluntly.

The fan paused mid-wave. Even Alexcena was shocked by the statement. Tabitha paled perceptibly.

"I will not!" She twisted her legs away from him to emphasize the point. "I cannot believe you would ask such a thing!"

All at once Leo seemed to realize his blunder. He ran an exasperated hand through his hair, but the scowl remained. "This has nothing to do with manners or propriety. This is about your safety."

"I fail to see how you-"

"You've spent more time walking in the last several days than you've had to do in your entire life. I need to know if you have any sores that need attention before they contract infection, and you're too stubborn and smug to tell me if you're hurting. Now do as I say!"

"I refuse!" Tabitha exclaimed. "No man alive has ever laid eyes on my feet!"

This begged the question, *how many dead men have?* Before Alexcena had time to find that humorous, Tabitha blushed a deep red and went off again.

"Now do you see what you did? I said the word 'feet,' and to a man no less! Mother would swoon. Why must you always put me in such compromising positions?"

"I have never put you anywhere, lady," Leo growled, "but if I hear one more word of defiance out of you, I'll toss you on a ship for home at the next port and leave you to worry about how it's paid for."

Tabitha pursed her lips into a hard line. Glowering like an angry school girl, she thrust both legs forward, thus exposing her shoes. Tabitha Winslett was wearing the ugliest, clunkiest boots ever to be seen. Despite other unflattering attributes, they were polished to a high sheen with barely a trace of dust from the road. The contrast was peculiar. Alexcena had to smother a snicker at the sight of them. Leo gaped openly at her.

"What in all creation do you have on your feet?" he finally stammered.

"You told me to find some sensible shoes at the next good shop we came to," the girl explained unsteadily. "So I have. I purchased these in Suffolk."

"They're-they're-" Leo crossed his arms over his chest and tried again. "Do they fit you well enough?"

She nodded regally. "Well enough. They're hideous, of course, but the gentleman who sold them to me assured me that they were some of the best."

Leo harrumphed and got to his feet. "Just so long as they get the job done. See to it that if you do get a blister or a sore or something you tell me right off."

"Rest assured I shall," she sighed.

"Sure you will," he grumbled. "I suppose you'd keep us up half the night caterwaulin' if you did have any pains."

Alexcena bit her lip. As she listened to this hostile banter, a steady stream of guilt and embarrassment began to run inside of her. Leo had turned his back on Tabitha then and was moving by her. She reached up to touch his wrist.

"Leopold?"

He stopped at once to look down at her, softness replacing the stern glare. "Yes?"

Alexcena swallowed and dropped her gaze. "I have one."

"One what?"

"A sore...on my foot."

The fire snapped and crackled, filling the silence. She knew the eyes of the others were on her, and she felt like the worst fool. "I didn't think to say anything. It never occurred to me that it might become infected. I just wrapped it up and kept walking."

When she looked up, she saw that Leo was grinning almost amusedly. "I'm going to have more trouble out of you about this than I am out of her, aren't I?" he chuckled. He knelt down and began rummaging through his bag. "How long have you had it?"

"A few days. I think it may already have toughened up a little, though."

"Here." He drew out a small, battered tin and laughed again when Alexcena shrank back instinctively. "Don't worry. I'll never make the mistake of asking to see anything below a hemline again." He cut a sly look at Tabitha before explaining. "Just rub some of this salve on it, and tell me if it becomes any worse. You both may want to apply a bit of it at your collars too. I've just recently discovered that it's wonderful for keeping the gnats and such away."

With that he excused himself to gather more wood amongst the trees. Tabitha moved away from her chosen boulder and scooted towards Alexcena.

"May I see it? The sore, that is."

She obligingly removed her left shoe and stocking, and slowly unwound the white bandage she had tied around her foot. The blister was not terribly red or grotesque, but it was sizeable. The air burned on the exposed layers of skin. Alexcena sucked in a slight breath at the sensation. Without a word, Tabitha swiped the tin from her, removed the lid, and began to apply the pale balm. Alexcena had expected it to hurt more at first, but it didn't. The salve had a cooling affect that soothed her pain immediately. Tabitha, as always, talked idly while she dabbed.

"Can you believe what he asked? That cavalier chuckle… Men can be so boorish about sensitive things!"

Alexcena smiled in spite of herself. "He is only trying to look out for us."

"I deserve to be treated as a child for some of the decisions I've made," the girl remarked. "I know that, but my pride will not allow me to completely agree with it."

"Therefore you make the best of every opportunity to annoy him."

"Well, I don't do it on purpose!"

Alexcena's smile merely widened. "I know. What I don't know is whether or not that makes the situation pitiful or humorous."

It was a relief to share a small laugh with Tabitha after so many days of hard travel and listening to her companions bicker. When the moment had passed, she determined to ask her cousin about one of the chief grievances Leo had.

"Tabitha, back on the ship," she began slowly. "On the *Liberator*, well… May I ask you about Lieutenant Greyson?"

Tabitha hesitated, and a small smile flitted across her face. "What do you need to ask?"

"I don't suppose that I need to ask anything," Alexcena replied, "but I am somewhat curious."

Tabitha nodded. "He thought I was pretty and nice. He asked permission to write to me and I graciously declined."

"Was it the day we left the ship?"

Tabitha blinked in surprise. "As a matter of fact it was."

"We saw that conversation, Leo and I," Alexcena remembered. "He seemed unsettled by it."

Tabitha scoffed.

"By unsettled I mean furious. I believe he thought he was going to have to defend your honor."

Tabitha was completely surprised at that. "How could he think that I- that he-" she broke off and shook her head. "Men can be so insensitive about such things."

"Maybe you ought to have explained it to him."

"Maybe you ought to have told him about your sore."

Alexcena smiled sheepishly. The motivation which caused that was simple. "I was afraid."

"Why on earth would you be?"

"I can't give him a reason to stop," Alexcena explained. "If he chooses to fully believe that Lucius is gone, or that it's too dangerous to continue, he'll turn back. It scares me to think of continuing on without him."

Chapter 17

June 15, 1765

"Curatives and remedies! Get your curatives here, I say!"

Lucius glanced furtively at the faces of the passers-by in a vague attempt to catch their reaction. The town of Kinston was not at all crowded that day, and still Mandrake managed to attract a great deal of attention.

"What with all his howlin'," Victoria mumbled at Lucius' elbow, "we'll have half the cemetery up in arms!"

Lucius had to agree, but what was he to do? "This is his end of the bargain," he replied simply. "We must trust that he knows what he's doing."

Victoria quirked half a smile. "Trust and belief are very different things."

"We cure all, heal all! It's not your doc's medicine. Get your curatives here!"

Foley-at Lucius' other side-tugged at his sleeve. "How do we make money if no one wants to look at the stuff to buy it?"

Lucius leaned slightly toward him to answer. "Then we won't make any profit at all. That's how business works."

Foley wrinkled his nose. "All this work for days and days and we might not get anything?"

"Let us hope that does not become the pattern."

"Yea," Foley agreed. "We've only got this job for a month if it does."

Lucius cringed at the thought. He had lost far too much time already. This position had been a blessing beyond his deserving. If the situation did not change, he stood to lose not only a fair income and a job he could handle, but his only foreseeable chance at enough funds to sail home. This sparked a fear, and he immediately dipped his head.

Lord, I place my trust in You. Even so, if You are willing, I pray You would bless the endeavors of myself and my friends…Only if You are willing.

A breath of wind touched his face and brushed his hair.

Patience…

Lucius' eyes flew open. He wondered at once whether it was Foley or Victoria who had spoken. His gaze leapt from one to the other of them. He knew even before he took in their blank expressions that it had not been either one of them. The Voice was different somehow…

"Curatives! Get your remedies here!"

The looks they were drawing were swiftly changing to glares. Lucius suddenly realized something so astonishing that he spoke it aloud.

"I have never bought fruit from an obnoxious merchant."

Victoria raised an eyebrow. "All right."

Lucius ignored her and strode forward to place a hand on Mandrake's shoulder. "May I speak with you?"

"Hm?" Mandrake's head whipped around toward him.

"I think we should stop for the day."

"You do, eh?"

For an instant Lucius felt like an awful fool. Mandrake was not one to step back lightly when he had his mind set. Then he thought back to the near-lynching he had witnessed of the stamp collector's envoy, and he knew he had to try.

"These people do not seem so keen to purchase anything just now."

Mandrake suddenly began to notice the dark looks forming all around them. "Perhaps you're right there," he said. "This is a hostile crowd if ever I saw one."

Foley-ever ready for a swift gain-pshawed at their worries. "Aw, we've seen worse, Professor."

Mandrake looked beyond Lucius to address the boy. "Bein' a nuisance don't always bake the cake, son, and it surely will get you burned. We'll set camp here in the commons and try again tomorrow."

Lucius gave a sharp nod of agreement. Victoria did not seem worried one way or the other about it, but Foley squirmed as he tried to contain his disgruntlement. Lucius debated whether or not he should speak to the boy about it. He had to admit that Foley's more negative mannerisms seemed to have dissipated. Still the boy had a bad habit of always revealing his head, especially when he disagreed with something. It was odd to think of these things as a parent might, but he knew then that this was exactly how he felt about Foley. It would be difficult indeed to imagine a day in America without him.

On that thought he decided to leave the boy alone for the time being. He moved around the opposite side of the cart where he found Victoria seated with a needle and thread mending the hem of a skirt.

"No one in need of a cure today, then?" she said when she saw him.

"Not today," Lucius replied as he sat against the cart's wheel. "Or if they are they're not too concerned about it."

She shrugged. "S'the way it goes sometimes, ye know. I'm just glad old Rob quit that yellin'."

Lucius smiled and Victoria turned her attention back to her mending. He became dimly aware of the sounds of Mandrake and Foley inside. It was nice indeed to have a peaceful moment to himself. He absently reached for the cameo necklace in his pocket and began to stroke the silken ribbon.

"So is that the one ye're always writin' to?"

Lucius blinked at Victoria. "Pardon me?"

She lifted her chin toward his hand. "The lady. Every time you have yourself a moment, you're scribblin' away to someone."

"Oh." He looked stupidly down at the pearl cameo as he tried to recapture his train of thought. "No. This is just a-" he stuttered and blushed. Then, to regain his composure, he countered with, "How do you know it's just a lady I write to?"

Victoria made a show of indignance. "Ye mean to say there's more than one?" Lucius' mouth fell open and she had a small laugh at that. "I'm teasin' ye now. Ye never mentioned her, tis true, but I guessed. By the look of ye I think I'm right."

What could he do but nod? "She's back home in England," he explained awkwardly.

After a small pause, Victoria prompted him further. "Is that all ye know about her?"

He shook his head. "I beg your pardon. It just seems strange to speak of her outside of my own thoughts. I've said scarcely a word about her to anyone since I left."

He could pine for her all afternoon and throughout the evening to come, but his lips seemed to tremble at the thought of talking about her. They would so much rather talk *to* her. He wondered if he would even be able to explain. Everyone he had ever spoken to of her had known her already. Either that or they had not pressed him for the details. How could an accurate description be given?

"Brown hair," he said suddenly. "Not a common brown. It's rich and dark and the color of it seems to change when it shines in the light."

"And her eyes?" Victoria insisted.

Lucius chuckled bittersweet. "I couldn't tell you the color, but I remember just how they appear. They're so full of knowing. As though she already anticipates whatever it is you're about to say, and if she doesn't, she can't wait to hear it. Her family has done well, but she's never proud. None of them are. She's sweet as the tamest bird, and I would spend a happy lifetime waiting to see what she would do next at my windowsill. Being without her has been the most difficult experience of my life, to say the least. Sometimes the memory of her makes me ache more than the strain of anything else."

He took a breath and glanced at Victoria then. Her eyes were cloudy, and he felt anxious at that. These were all simply facts to him, and yet she seemed to be growing terribly emotional at hearing them.

"It will be a year-most likely more-before I can return. By that time I am certain to find her engaged or even married." He hesitated, his heart sinking mightily at the prospect. *It changes nothing.* "Return I must. I'll not say a word unless it's fitting, and then only to apologize."

He said this with finality, for it was what he had decided. He was surprised when he turned to Victoria and found her aghast. He raised an eyebrow and she swallowed. A scowl replaced her sorrowed look.

"Ye havena' said why it was that ye left her."

She narrowed one eye comically. Lucius was far too taken aback to find it amusing.

"Tis my own fault," he confessed with true feeling. "I was hoodwinked onto a vessel bound for this country. I was only supposed to be gone a few weeks. Now I've been gone for months."

"Hoodwinked?"

"In truth, yes."

Victoria rolled her eyes. "I meant what does the word mean, *Professor.*"

Lucius dipped his head meekly. "I mean that I was tricked."

"To say ye're tricked implies that it wasn't yer fault, so which is it?"

Lucius blinked. It seemed that she was deliberately attempting to confuse him. Or interrogate him. "It was my fault for believing the villains."

"And since ye've taken that guilt upon yerself, ye assume that the lady is gonna be blamin' ye for it. That is outrageous, sir!"

Lucius gave a small start, shaken by her view. "E-excuse me?"

The lady actually set a fist on her hip in earnest. "This woman must care for ye, and ye're obviously smitten with her, and yet ye donna trust her to believe yer story. That's a very low opinion ye have for the woman who's supposed to be the love of yer life!"

These were not new thoughts. How many times had he envisioned her responding in exactly the same way to his pleas? But wishful thinking is far from truth. He was no longer so naive as to think that a separation as distant and prolonged as this would not affect the relationship. Still he turned up a small smile at Victoria's protests.

"That is precisely what she would have said."

Chapter 18

June 16, 1765

The next day's dawning saw the travelers up bright and early breaking camp. Mandrake had arisen before the others-surprisingly enough-and had announced that they would press on quickly.

"This town would rather see us away than here. Just like a Tory town! Considering the differences twixt us and them, I see no reason to draw unnecessary hostility," he told them as they rubbed their bleary eyes and folded their blankets. "A successful merchant does his best to give his customers what they want, and in this case they want us to move on. So we shall. If we get going, we'll make Jacksonville around nightfall."

Wendy the mule twiddled her ears and showed her massive teeth to Mandrake. Lucius couldn't help but imagine her thinking, *I heard every word of that, and I know what that means for me!* He was thinking something quite similar himself.

Victoria wore a sour expression. "Ye keep quite a pace, don't ye?"

Mandrake merely grinned. "If there's one thing I've learned as a traveling peddler it's that you don't hang around where the money don't hang around."

"Yea!" Foley piped up.

Mandrake chuckled and patted Foley's shoulder. "There's a smart boy!"

Lucius pretended to ignore the pair as he readied his things and harnessed

Wendy. He spent the majority of his morning treading along behind the wagon as usual. (Often walking to one side, so as to avoid Wendy's indiscretions.) Midway through the day, as he was pausing to collect some useful roots, Foley dashed back to join him.

"Hey, Professor!"

Lucius calmly reached up to tilt his glasses on his ears, the better to see beyond the cracks in the lenses. "Yes, Foley?"

The boy slipped his hands into his pockets. One fingertip showed through a small hole there. "I wanted to walk with you for a bit."

Lucius lengthened his stride to catch up to the cart. He raised an eyebrow. "I'm astonished. I thought you had come to like walking near the front with Mandrake."

The lad pulled a face. "He's talking to Victoria. I think she likes being the driver."

"I would imagine so." The classic woman scorned. Lucius could well envision her enjoying the affect of talking down toward a man rather than up to one.

"I wanted to ask you about something, Professor."

"And I would be happy to answer you about something, Foley."

"Huh?"

Lucius chuckled. "Never mind."

"Why don't you like Mr. Mandrake all that much?"

"He is a fair employer." He glanced up in spite of himself to be sure that the man in question was still chattering with Victoria. "You seem to be taking quite an interest him."

Foley shrugged. "He talks about a lot of things I like to talk about."

"Like money?" Lucius remarked. "Don't turn your nose up at me for that, boy. I may not catch on to much, but the greed is plain on your face more often than not."

Foley crossed his arms uncomfortably. "Everyone's gotta have money. I just don't ever have any. My folks neither."

"You're making money now," Lucius pointed out patiently, "and yet that feeling remains in you."

"It's in Mr. Mandrake too," Foley replied adamantly, "and he told me he has a whole bundle his grandmother left him. He's using it to get his remedies sold and make more."

Lucius nodded, inwardly hoping the boy would understand. "That is a wonderful example. This is a lesson that is much more easily learned as a child. The love of money breeds evil and sorrow. Prosperity used wisely is not a wretched thing, but the control people give it over their existence is."

His prayers seemed to be answered as he watched Foley swallow and turn his countenance to the ground.

"Will you think on that for me, Foley?" he encouraged.

The boy hesitated and gave him a nod. "Sure, Professor."

Satisfied for the moment, Lucius decided to let the boy be on that subject for a time. After a few moments, he chose to broach a different topic.

"Now I have a question for you. Will you do your best to answer?"

Foley looked up, eager and curious. "Yea."

Lucius turned to him then. "What has happened to your family?"

The boy was openly startled by the inquiry and nearly became hostile. His steps changed to hard stomps. "They've got nothing to do with me. Why would you wanna talk about them?"

"I am attempting to take care of you. The story of your past is important to me."

He saw that Foley was battling confusion and frustration. He had told him before that he could speak of it all when he chose, but he had also grown somewhat concerned. If the boy was a runaway, there was a possibility that it was not justified, and how was he to handle that?

"I was telling the truth about…my mother."

Lucius nodded and waited for more.

Foley sighed, heavy and sharp. "Two years ago we came here on a ship. She got really sick and, er, only made it half way. My parents both had indenture contracts that paid their passage, but when the rich man found out mother wouldn't be there to work, he tore hers up. The captain wouldn't let us leave until her passage was paid for, and like I said, my father didn't have money. Prob'ly still doesn't."

The story had come out very fast, but Lucius was able to appreciate the full gravity of it all. "So what did he do?"

"He sold me!" Foley snapped, though not at Lucius. "He kept my baby brother and sister and he sold me to an old lady with a cane! Do you know the law about child indenture contracts?"

Lucius shook his head somewhat helplessly.

"They hold you 'til you're twenty-one. Half of my whole life sold!"

"So you broke the contract."

"I didn't sign nothing!" Foley defended. "I didn't agree to nothing. I might feel bad cause I miss my mother or my brother and sister, but I'll never feel bad for that, Professor!"

By then there was a stream of painful tears on each of Foley's flushed cheeks. He wiped them away derisively and stood still and defiant in the road, facing Lucius.

Lucius was filled with sympathy and regret. He laid a hand on the boy's shoulder. "It's all right now, Foley."

"You won't send me back?"

"No."

The boy rubbed his eyes again and sniffed. A measure of easiness returned to his voice when he said, "Good. I like staying with you, Professor."

"Ahoy, back there!" Mandrake called from ahead of them. "You men ready for a rest and a bite to eat?"

"Yes!" Foley dashed forward at that. Lucius did not know whether to chuckle or shake his head, but he tended toward the latter.

Victoria steered the cart to one side of the road and began pulling provisions from her bag. Lucius could not help but notice that Mandrake seemed to be looking for something in the wagon. He was not left wondering for long, since the man began talking to the others as he rummaged.

"It occurred to me," he grunted, his back to them all. "It occurred to me that our appearances might have something to do with our poor success in the last town. It doesn't matter how fine a peddler you are; if you've got dirt on your face and mud on your cuffs, people are going to wonder. So, along with refining our products-" He turned to face them then and bowed shortly to Lucius. "-I think we ought to polish up ourselves."

Foley was genuinely puzzled by the declaration. He held his thin arms up and began looking himself over. "Polish?"

"You know, fancy up our looks," Mandrake explained. "I hope you boys don't mind, but I took the liberty of purchasing a little something for the lady of the troupe to get things started."

Without further adieu, Mandrake threw his hands out from behind his back and tossed a large bundle to Victoria. She caught it easily and rose to her feet, allowing the bulk of it to fall straight in front of her.

It was a dress, plain, but quite pretty, all of blue stripes on white and gathers everywhere about it. It was made of gingham and lined with different fabric, which looked sure to be scratchy. Still, it was a far cry from the drab, maroon garb she normally wore.

The young woman stared at it in open astonishment. "But, but-this had to have come from a shop!"

"Of course it did," Mandrake replied with a sniff. "You'll probably have to work your poor fingers to the bone to stitch it up so's it fits you right."

While she seemed to struggle for a response, Mandrake considered the matter closed and turned to Foley and Lucius.

"Now, my boy," he said first to Foley, "you need to find you a good set of clothes to go with that plucky personality. You're a born peddler. It's time you looked like one. I'll be glad to help you find what you need in Jacksonville. Professor!"

Lucius hated to hear what the man was about to say. Whatever he asked of him was sure to be expensive, whether it be clothes or shoes or buckles or-

"Glasses!" Mandrake exclaimed. "You cannot be seen sporting broken spectacles. It makes the whole lot of us look like beggars. Have those lenses of yours fixed, and I'll wager it'll do you a world of good-not to mention us."

Without waiting for a reaction, Mandrake gave a sharp nod and moved toward Victoria, saying something about wanting to see her new frock. Lucius could only stare after him, a sinking feeling invading his chest.

"Glasses?" Lucius moaned to himself. "How will I ever afford that?"

"Don't worry, Professor," Foley said quite innocently. "It's only money."

Lucius choked back a grimace. Unsavory as it was, it seemed that money was the only earthly way he would ever return home. Without divine intervention the price remained the barrier.

"Yes," he replied huskily. "It's only money."

Chapter 19

June 18, 1765

What am I doing here? The question swirled, unanswered in her somewhat tortured mind.

Alexcena knew well where she *should* be. In a little house outside Cambridge somewhere. She could care less for the size so long as it was neat and comforting and nestled in a bed of flowers. Of course Lucius would be there too. She would keep his house and cook for him and remain at his side as often as she was able. The dream of it was a sweet intoxication that made it difficult for her to remember where she really was.

She was lying on her back on a dingy blanket, staring up at the last few night's stars with painful, hazy eyes. Commodore lay beside her, and she stroked his back absently with one hand.

It was hard for her to think of Lucius, and yet just as painful to try not to think of him. The possibilities and probabilities of his whereabouts were beyond number. Her problem did not seem to involve fearing the worst, but rather remembering and longing for the soul she loved best.

Musings such as this never could last very long. No matter how early her torn heart awoke her these days, Leopold was never far behind. Really that was all for the better. He had become all but her dearest friend, and it helped, she knew, to have a tangible reason to leave such melancholy behind. Even as she considered that, she heard him rise and yawn as he stretched. It was a now familiar beginning to a day she would not soon forget.

She heard Leo traipsing off through the trees. When she could hear him no more, she hastily got to her feet and slipped a fresh dress over her shift. Then she nudged Tabitha awake so that the younger girl could do the same. Commodore remained as he was, lying on his belly with his massive head between his paws. It was odd, but Alexcena had the impression that perhaps he missed his home and his master almost as much as she did.

Leo returned to the camp half an hour later with their day's portion of meat; two doves. Alexcena ate hers quickly so as not to think about it. Tabitha looked positively green. She took one, mincing little bite, swallowed audibly, and placed a hand over her lips as though she was astonished by her own action.

"Satisfied already, ma'amzelle?" Leo asked sardonically.

Tabitha smoothed her expression before giving her saucy reply. "Nearly. I happily possess the appetite of a bird, monsieur."

Alexcena was growing far too tired of this snide banter to find any of it amusing. She kept her thoughts to herself as they went on that morning, but as Tabitha began to lag behind, she felt compelled to act.

"Leopold?"

He slowed his stride and reached for the water bag at his side. "Are you thirsty, Ena?"

"No, but Tabitha must be." She glanced back as she spoke to see her cousin blundering through the underbrush several yards behind them. "We must let her rest for a moment."

All at once Leo's countenance grew hard and his legs quickened. "No," he grunted.

Alexcena's astonishment was near outrage, but she attempted to keep her voice low. "She's liable to faint in this heat!"

"When she's woman enough to ask me, I'll be happy to stop," he replied, undaunted. "She'll speak up when something's too much for her."

"She will not!"

"Then she'll learn from her own arrogance and benefit! Either that or she'll toughen up," he added as an afterthought. "However it works out we'll all be better off."

"What's that I hear?" Tabitha called from behind them. The haughtiness in her voice was made less affective by the stiff puffing of her strained breath. "You're speaking of me, aren't you?"

Alexcena and Leo hesitated just long enough for her to catch them.

"You were, weren't you?"

"You couldn't even hear us," Leo grumbled.

"I didn't have to. I could feel it! Now what is it?"

Leo shook his head incredulously. "Do you really think that way? That everyone is just as shallow as you that they don't know better than to sit around and gossip. Spout everyone else's business to your friends and then call yourself a good Christian lady for giving them forewarning!"

An appalled expression rose on her face then. "It's something awful. I knew it!"

Alexcena found herself once again an outsider witnessing a violent brawl of words and insults. As she stood there watching the two fighters, she realized that she was slowly growing accustomed to their bickering. In time it might even become easy for her to hold herself aloof to their arguments. Of course in time they would gradually return to their lives away from here and she would no longer need to ignore them. But there in lay the principal problem; *time*. How much time did they have before Lucius was unfindable? These spats had already cost them time in the past and were certain to cost them more. Was it possible that she could manage the journey to the coast without them? She would begin her search immediately once in town, allowing the pair at least two days to catch up. By then she might have turned over every leaf in the area, and they could set off together again. It seemed to be a fair plan, but she was not about to leave without giving them a clear image of the attitudes they had been displaying.

"-so arrogance is all right for you because you're a man," Tabitha was saying.

"Don't take up that torch with me!" Leo snapped. "I am filling my place as a man and a leader. You want to try it instead?"

"No! All I'm trying to do is keep up and keep out of your way, but you can't even allow me to do that without becoming angry with me."

Leo chuckled harshly. "Do you hear yourself?"

"Does either one of you hear yourself?" Alexcena spat without warning.

The eyes of both her companions, and even Commodore, jerked toward her in surprise. She held their gazes for an instant before she continued.

"I have listened to your spiteful, derisive comments to and about each other for days on end. No longer! Since you have each seen fit to give me such a clear view of the other's faults, I would like to make some suggestions, which I have contemplated at great length during the last fortnight." She looked first to Tabitha. "I would like you to stop behaving as though the world is your oyster and you have to put up with it." Then to Leo. "I would like you to stop assuming that my cousin is deliberately trying to offend you with her every breath. I think if you can find it within yourselves to try these methods, this country will become a happier place for all of us. That being said, I hope you both will excuse me."

She turned and headed straight along the vague path they were following. She soon became aware of Commodore's footfalls behind her, but no one else's. For all she knew the others were still standing as silently as she had left them. And so she found herself in the forest all alone.

Alone. Even the mere mention of the word caused an ache inside her chest. She had been surrounded by people ever since Lucius disappeared, and still she could not deny the loneliness that had grown day by day as he remained absent.

My Lord is with me, her mind whispered.

She paused in her walk and spoke the thought aloud. "My Lord is with me. And if my Lord is with me, who then can be against me?"

It was a disjointed concept, but the thought had brought the verse to mind, and it comforted her all the same.

So, with Commodore close behind, she continued on. Just as the sounds of burbling water reached her ears, the Great Dane dashed ahead and began happily lapping at the shallow brook. Alexcena had to admit that she felt every bit as glad as he seemed to be for the cool refreshment. She knelt close by him and drank cupfuls of water from her hands. She even thought it safe to unbutton the top few buttons of her dress and bathed her neck and face. Her eyes remained down as she refastened her collar, and so she did not notice until she was done that she was perhaps not as safe as she assumed. She lifted her face up in the direction of the opposite bank and her very blood halted inside her veins.

A woman no older than herself stood there. Her long hair fell in a thick braid over one shoulder. It was blacker than any raven she had ever seen. To Alexcena the woman seemed scantily clothed in a rough dress of pale hide, which merely covered her knees. On her feet she wore a pair of crude boots. A thick band of beads was wrapped close about her neck, serving as her only ornament. Over her shoulder was slung a strap to hold a sheathed dagger across her chest.

Alexcena's wide, startled eyes remained on the woman's face. Every aspect of her countenance was as smooth as a river rock, as though she had worn the same placid expression her entire life and never intended to change it. Her skin, Alexcena imagined, was nearly a match for the bark of the paler trees around them. For an instant she wondered if this girl was a clever carving, her feet forever rooted to one place.

The pair remained staring one another down for an instant which seemed more like an hour. Commodore at last looked up from his drink to see the newcomer. He flinched back at first, and seemed to sniff the air between them. Then he made a muffled groan and took two slow steps into the creek as if to say, 'I'm not so sure about this, but I am perfectly willing to go first.'

Alexcena remained on her knees, her hands still stretched down toward the water. She was suddenly aware of a sharp puffing sound. One full second passed before she realized the sound was her own now-shallow breathing. She clamped her mouth shut and swallowed. The woman across from her remained unmoved, seemingly unbothered, and silent.

Alexcena wondered how possible it was that they might both be thinking the same thing. *What do I do now?*

Chapter 20

June 18, 1765

Leopold crossed his arms as he watched Alexcena go. Inwardly he heaved a sigh of genuine grief. *Ena is in enough agony without me flying off at the handle, and here I've gone and done it again.*

He had been more concerned than ever for Alexcena ever since her discovery of Lucius' accident. He had even come to wonder if he should send her home and continue on his own, consequently removing Tabitha as well. But that would never do. He knew Alexcena well enough to know that he would not be able to convince her to return home.

This journey is too much…but she knew what she was at…

There was only one member of their trio who had no notion what she was doing when she left. He turned to face Tabitha directly. The girl was watching him with fearful eyes while she twirled a loose lock of her wild hair with two fingers. Leo was surprised to find that he was guilty for that as well. He had taken a heavy hand with the girl so that she would understand the gravity of her situation and respect his authority. Where exactly did the line between respectful apprehension and terror fall?

He half sighed to himself. His eyebrows drew low in consternation at the thought. Tabitha's hand fell to her side at that and she swallowed. He reflected that he must appear quite fierce in his frustration. The expression on her face was yet another example of just how high he could rise to the occasion of handling someone, whether they needed a guiding hand or a fist.

He tried to relax his features and dropped his arms. "Look here," he began, "if I've been harsh-"

"You needn't say that," Tabitha interrupted.

"I don't." Leo repeated flatly. Somewhere between the words 'look here' and 'if I've' Tabitha's features had grown soft in a most vulnerable way, and still her eyes remained as frightened as those of a trapped mouse. He was quite perplexed at this. "Why?"

"Because it's time that I admit to something," she said evenly. "You were about to say that you were sorry for having been harsh at times, and I appreciate that. What I need to say to you is that you have given me no less than I deserve."

She took a long breath, as though the conversation was taxing her wan strength. Leo cocked one eyebrow and set his thumbs in his belt.

"You really think so?"

She nodded slowly, every curl on her head bobbing with the motion.

"Because I was about to say that if I've been harsh it was only because you deserved it." He paused while she blushed and dropped her eyes. "But who among us truly ever gets what they deserve, eh? Our Lord Jesus knew exactly what we deserved and look at what He gave us instead."

She looked up at him again. The fear seemed to have abated to be replaced by traces of curiosity. Leo felt one corner of his mouth turn upwards in the smallest of grins.

"A servant who will not forgive his fellow servant is wicked as the parable goes."

He waited for her to speak. Tabitha hesitated. Then she licked her lips and said, "Do you know my Bible is the heaviest thing in my bag? It's because I know I'm not using it correctly. That's the thing I wanted to admit. The Word is full of love and grace and mercy and judgment. I have carried the sin of my pride for a very long time. I was so surrounded by riches and estates and servants waiting to do my will that it took me years to see it. When I did I ignored it." Her voice trailed into a forlorn little whisper.

Leo waited a moment, but when she did not continue he spoke his thoughts. "You are what you eat."

"What did you say?"

"You consort with high-born, high-and-mighty ladies of leisure and so you have become one."

She smiled then at his explanation. "Yes," she said with sincere agreement. "Yes, I have." Her shoulders drooped for a moment. Just when he expected her to fall to tears, she drew herself up straight and met his gaze. "I have thought that the love was a perpetual surety all my life, but if I don't change myself I may very well end up with the judgment."

Leo was speechless at first. It was the most intelligent homily he had ever heard her utter. Now she stood before him as a most comical representation of Joan of Arc, prepared to face any villain who fought against her, even her own flesh.

"So you must," he said finally.

She gave a stiff nod.

"I accept your admission and give you my word that I shall help you with this transition in any way you desire."

She nodded again and held her hand out to him. Leo took it delicately, but before he could lean in to kiss her knuckle, she gave his hand a rough shake. He nearly chuckled, realizing that a shake of the hand was what she had expected in the first place. *I'll keep my kisses to myself then.*

"Now let's try to catch up to your cousin, shall we?" he suggested to cover his own amusement. "I don't want her getting too far away."

They struck out into the trees. It was not difficult to tell which direction Alexcena had gone, even apart from her tracks on the narrow path. *Now if only we could pick up on some sign left by Lucius,* Leo mused. *His trail would probably look worse.*

"Where's Commodore, do you suppose?" Tabitha asked.

"Probably with Ena. It's amazing the bond that's come between those two."

"She used to be petrified of him."

"Yes," Leo chortled. "I had a few demonstrations of that in the past."

It was odd how effortless it seemed to be to talk casually with Tabitha. When he set his mind to it, that is. If she was true to her word and put away her snobbery, she might even be easy to get along with. Easy to befriend.

His thoughts changed the moment the sound caught his ear. There was water up ahead, but the sound that warranted his attention was higher off the ground than that. It was like a hush of wind, though not a single leaf moved around them. It was almost as if something was near them in the forest, moving just enough to disturb the air. Then his keen ears picked up a whimpering moan which could only come from Commodore.

By then he had come to a stop with Tabitha behind him. His eyes moved all around, seeing nothing peculiar. She placed a hand on his arm. He knew she must be frightened by his actions and hoped against hope that she did not choose to voice an opinion about it. He stretched his arm back, signaling for her to remain close behind him. She clung to it, so he assumed she understood. Then Leo drew one pistol from beneath his coat and stepped slowly forward.

As they came within sight of the creek, the first thing he saw was the native girl standing across from them. She captured his full attention, and it was only after that he realized that Alexcena was on her knees on the bank. Commodore was standing halfway in the brook between them. Tabitha knelt at Alexcena's side. Leo assumed that she must have been all right or Tabitha would have prodded him. She seemed just as spellbound by the girl as he was.

Despite the fact that she was a woman, Leo began to size her up. She appeared young and was very lean in build. He suddenly realized that whether she knew what a gun was or not, he must appear very menacing holding it up in front of himself. Still he was loath to holster it when she carried a dagger over her chest. He felt like an awful coward for holding a gun because of a woman. Had he only been concerned with himself he would have already put it away, but with Alexcena and Tabitha involved the matter was different.

The native girl moved first. She turned her head to one side and spoke a short phrase which Leo did not have a prayer of understanding. There was no answer to her call, but he heard again the strange, rushing wind noise. An instant later another figure appeared beside the girl. This was a man, obviously older and much stronger than she. He wore similar clothing and two feathers adorned his oddly cut hair. The pair stared almost blandly at the astonished travelers.

Leo remained as he was, the barrel of his pistol pointed straight up. He could not bring himself to move for fear that he would startle them, but neither could he speak. It was a silent, frightening impasse.

A minute or so after his arrival, the man raised his palm and spoke. "Put your weapon away. We need no bloodshed here."

Leo was so stunned at the sound of his own language coming from this dark-skinned man that several seconds passed before he realized he must be speaking to him. He stuck the gun into his belt and held his own hands out at his sides.

"You talk like us."

"My sister no, but I am learning." The man's voice was deep and rich, like thick coffee that soothes the senses. "There is a mission man and his wife in our village who use your words, but not your voice."

"Not our voice?"

It was Alexcena who answered him then. "The accent. He must mean our accents."

The man nodded somberly. "You have traveled long days to come here, no?"

"We have," Leo answered. "We are looking for someone who is lost."

"This is someone who wants to be found?"

For some reason the question hit Leo like a fist to the chest. He could only jerk his chin in the affirmative at first. When he spoke his voice was husky and low. "Yes he does."

The man did not reply right away. He seemed to be considering Leo's words and reaction in earnest. Then he widened his gaze to take in the ladies on their knees and the dog in the creek.

"You will come with us now."

Leo's mind immediately leapt back to the brace of pistols he carried.

"You will meet the missionary and his wife. They will help you if they can."

Before Leo could protest, Alexcena came to her feet. "But we must continue on!"

The tall man looked at her as though he was waiting for her to realize some error.

"We are traveling to the coast, where Virginia meets North Carolina," she explained fervently.

"And you are pointed in the wrong direction. Our village is in the right direction. You will come with us first." He turned to his sister then and spoke in swift, low tones. The girl dashed off and he said again, "You will come with us."

Leo came to himself enough to offer a pleasant smile. He crossed the creek, sloshing water halfway up his boots until he stood close to the man. He was nose to chest with him due to the small bank, but Leo suspected by the looks of him that it was not *entirely* because of it.

"I do usually like to know who I'm traveling with. I'm sure you feel the same way." He offered his hand. "Leopold Wolgath."

The man hesitated and accepted it in an iron grasp. "My Christian name is Joseph. I am Machapunga."

"Mashapuinja." Leo shook his head. "If that's your given name, I hope you won't mind if I stick with Joseph."

Joseph surprised them all by laughing out loud. "Machapunga is my tribe, my family. My born name you could not pronounce anyway, but it means Half Tall."

Leo's eyes roved from the man's boots to his feathers. "I think they were wrong about that. You look all tall from here."

Joseph laughed again, and Leo felt himself beginning to relax. Between the idle stories he had heard and the general look of the man, he had been very tense for the last few minutes. Now he turned to motion to the ladies to join them. Joseph moved back to make way for them on the bank. They were visibly apprehensive about such a meeting, so he gave them a wide berth.

"Joseph, this is Ms. Alexcena Condreve and her cousin Ms. Tabitha Winslett. Our escort is called Commodore."

Joseph dipped his head in salute to the ladies and stared down his nose at Commodore, who promptly plopped down at his feet with one ear cocked upward. The animal was obviously intrigued by the man. Joseph ignored the expression of interest and pointed upstream.

"The village is there. Not far."

He set off at a good pace, expecting them to follow. Alexcena glanced at Leo, offering a small smile to let him know that she was all right. *Because she knows by now that I will inevitably ask…*

She set off behind Joseph. Leo fell into step behind her. He placed a hand on Tabitha's arm to encourage her forward, but she stayed by him long enough to speak her thoughts.

"Do you trust him?"

Her whisper was so light that he had to rely on watching her lips to understand it. "So far," he answered honestly.

"Then why have you kept your gun in your belt and not its holster?"

Smart girl for once. "Because I've been ambushed before."

It was a plain truth. He wondered vaguely if allowing this high-strung dove of society to know that he held suspicions of their new guide was the smartest thing to do. But she had asked, and he had felt all along that it was best to hand her the truth so that she would know exactly what sort of situations her actions had brought her to. She looked on him then with eyes that seemed only half as frightened as they had half an hour ago when the fear had been of him. The dread was replaced swiftly enough by determination, and she stepped ahead of him in her cousin's wake.

Wonderful, he grumbled within himself. *She's more afraid of me than of a stranger she imagines to be a murderous heathen. Something seems to be wrong there.* He later reflected that this was not entirely true. After all she had not argued with the tall Machapunga.

The Machapunga village was not too far, as Joseph had said, but it was far enough. By the time they arrived Alexcena was more than ready for a rest and Tabitha looked as though she might fall over. Joseph had instructed his sister to go ahead of them and tell the villagers they were coming. This had made Alexcena wonder. It seemed to be a perfect way to lure three unsuspecting foreigners into a trap, but where she did not trust Joseph, she trusted Leopold.

They had no notion of what to expect save for the inaccurate imaginings of gossips in England and what little they had seen of Joseph and his sister. Alexcena spent the walk preparing herself for some sort of a wild scene involving war paint and drums and something akin to an enormous fire pit. She was all the more unsure when the forest gave way to a small clearing where there was nestled a quiet village of people.

The earth was hard and flat. Grass refused to grow where so many moccasins tread. There were only three buildings-huts of rough, dark wood and thatched roofs-though Alexcena suspected that there might be more because the main path followed a bend around these structures. The creek burbled right up beside the clearing. Stakes could be seen protruding from the water's surface, no doubt some clever way of trapping a passing fish. The village was not over crowded, but the population far outnumbered their troop. At first sight Alexcena estimated that there were twelve men, women, and children scattered about the area. All were dressed similarly, some in linen and some in hide, and all had black hair. It was the tones of their skin which varied the most, from rich brown to red clay to an almost olive hue. An elderly man sat close to the bank surrounded by three very young children. They laughed and smiled as the old man made noises and shapes with his hands. Everyone else was occupied with some task or other; weaving a mat, starting a cooking fire, stretching leather.

No one spoke a word. Joseph led them through the clearing toward the bend. Each of the people looked up to nod in acknowledgement of the newcomers. One woman even smiled as they passed her. Around the bend there were a few more buildings and one that was larger than all the rest on the far side. A racket drew their eyes to the left where they saw two young men carving a tree trunk into what seemed to be a narrow boat with a curious tool. Alexcena was thrown into astonishment because both were naked from the waist up. She looked away instantly and could well imagine Tabitha blushing furiously behind her.

"The mission home is here." Joseph gestured to the largest building. They were nearly upon it when the cloth that served as a door was pushed aside and a bewhiskered, middle-aged man stepped out to meet them. It was almost jarring to see someone dressed in clothes similar to their English style compared to the atmosphere of the rest of the village. He grinned jovially and spread his arms.

"Who are these friends you have found, Joseph?"

"Lost visitors walking in the wrong direction."

"Well, we're certainly glad that Joseph brought you here," the man said to them. He bowed low to the ground, sweeping his hat from his head. "I am Kent Dover, humble missionary at your service. How shall I call you?"

Leo bowed in return. "Call me Leo. Leo Wolgath."

Before another word was spoken, a lady burst from the hut, followed by Joseph's sister. This new lady was obviously Dover's wife. Unlike all around her, her locks were a brilliant blond. She wore them plaited into a long braid at her back. Her dress was of simple indigo linen. Her smile matched her husband's.

"Allow me to introduce my lovable wife, Elisabeth."

The lady glanced at Dover with a raised eyebrow and then returned her smile to the visitors.

"We're so happy to have you."

Alexcena could not help but notice that her eyes stayed with Tabitha and herself more than the men. It seemed that she was slightly desperate for companionship with ladies who spoke the same language.

"Thank you," she replied with a graceful bob of her head. "You're very kind."

Elisabeth made a happy sigh and nearly bounced in her excitement. "You all know my name, but who are all of you?"

"Oh!" Leo exclaimed. "Forgive me, ma'am. This is Ms. Alexcena and Ms. Tabitha, and I happen to be Leopold Wolgath."

"We're so happy to have you," Dover reiterated with an even broader smile.

"Yes, you've mentioned that," Leo replied.

The man realized his blunder and chuckled helplessly. "I'm sorry. It's just that we don't receive very many visitors this close to the Great and Dismal."

Alexcena's eyebrows furrowed. "The Great and Dismal?"

"Swamp."

"Sounds charming," Leo mumbled.

Dover waved the comment away. "It's not nearly so bad as it sounds this far north."

"They must call it that because it's so lonesome for the flowers in winter."

Dover laughed again, but it was Joseph who offered a bit of comfort.

"You have already passed by the top edge. You will have no need to cross where you are going."

"Ah, that's right! Joseph mentioned you were heading in the wrong direction."

Leo grinned. "My fault I'm afraid."

"Come into my office and we'll work on that," Dover said. "Meanwhile I'm sure my wife and Joseph's sister, Young Leaf, can find some way to divert the ladies."

With the men leading the way, they filed into the wide hut. The doorway was offset to the left and Alexcena was surprised to discover why. The structure was divided down the center with living quarters in one half and a chapel in the other. They passed the cloth door to see five rows of benches and a blackboard on the far wall. The doorway to Dover's office was in the far corner. Elisabeth took Alexcena's hand and pulled her to the right. The half that served as their home was one large room with a bed, table, chairs, bookshelf, and fire pit in the center of the floor.

"We can stay in here while the men talk," Elisabeth said with a giddy laugh. "I'm sure Young Leaf is dying to have a look at your hair, Ms. Tabitha. She was fascinated with mine when we first arrived." She then turned to the woman and spoke softly in the native tongue.

Tabitha meanwhile put a hand to her hair. "Why do you say that?"

"It's blond!" Elisabeth said cheerily. "I think you might be the only other person she's ever seen with yellow hair aside from myself, and yours is curly at that!" She said something else to Young Leaf and the woman finally cracked a smile.

"How long have you been here?" Alexcena wondered.

"Five years, which should explain why I'm so swift with the language," Elisabeth tittered. "How long have the two of you been traveling?"

"We left England on the first day of May," Alexcena answered. "We haven't stopped since."

"My goodness, you've come a long way!" she exclaimed with genuine sympathy.

"The ship landed in Williamsburg. We've come this far on foot."

Elisabeth pursed her lips and seemed to be considering something. The smile was quick to return. "I have just the thing for you ladies."

She dashed by Young Leaf to the bed. Once there, she dropped to her knees and began tugging something from underneath it. When she rose Alexcena couldn't help but put a hand to her mouth. Tears practically welled up in Tabitha's eyes as she exclaimed,

"It's a wash tub!"

Chapter 21

June 18 and 19, 1765

Alexcena was honestly content for the first time in a long time. Her injured heart would not allow her to be happy, this much was true. She did not imagine herself to be so. What she did know was that she was more comfortable than she had ever been in the great America.

They had stayed the night in the Machapunga village. At Elisabeth's urging both Alexcena and Tabitha had each taken a long, soothing bath with a thick-lathering soap and dried rose petals. Then Elisabeth had brushed and combed and smoothed Alexcena's hair while Young Leaf had done the same for Tabitha. (Tabitha was astonished that she was able to do anything with her wild mop.) Then they had assisted their hostess in preparing their meal for the evening, which was utterly delicious in the end.

The men had eventually emerged from their conclave; pulled, no doubt by the enticing scents from the next room. A thick bean stew flavored with onion and thyme and cooked with some other vegetables served as the centerpiece of the meal. To this the ladies added corn cakes, cooked greens, a pumpkin dish, and white corn.

Young Leaf and Joseph politely bowed out before dinner was served to return to their own home, leaving the three travelers and Commodore with the Dovers. As it turned out, Kent possessed quite a voice, and the evening was spent in joyous song. Alexcena found herself clapping and smiling at the duets and singing along with the hymns.

When the evening was over, Elisabeth strung a quilt across the living area so as to give Alexcena and Tabitha a more private place to lay their heads. Leo opted to move into the next room and sleep on one of the pews. Having seen the short benches before, Alexcena could not help but picture him lying across it with his arms falling down at either side and his legs hanging off the end at the knees.

The morning dawned far too early. Though she felt vastly refreshed, she would have dearly loved to lay lazily for an hour or so more. This feeling of comfort-brought on by a soft pillow and clean sheets-was quickly thwarted by guilt. Lucius was lost, and there she lay in bed wanting to wallow and doze the morning away.

Ought to be ashamed…and rebuked…What kind of woman am I?

With that she was eager to be awake. She could hear Elisabeth beyond the makeshift curtain. The smell of coffee was heavy in the air. The lady was humming a soft tune to herself as she moved about.

Tabitha, on the other hand, remained deep in sleep. Alexcena took care not to wake her as she rose from the pallet and slipped into her dress. Her hostess smiled at her as she moved past the curtain.

"Good morning. Do you take coffee?"

"Yes, thank you."

She glanced around while Elisabeth fetched a mug. She did not see either of the men, but her attention was drawn by something else. Across the Dover's bed was laid a blue striped dress and a maroon skirt. On top of them there was a pincushion, scissors, and a spool of thread.

"Here." Even as Elisabeth handed Alexcena the coffee and some sort of cake, she seemed to notice where Alexcena's eyes lay. She crossed the room to scoop up the sewing materials and put them away.

For some vague reason, this all appeared interesting to Alexcena, but she thought it best not to ask. Instead she sipped her coffee and bit into the round cake.

"Ummm!"

As happens with all truly delicious food, the exclamation escaped before it could be stopped. She looked questioningly to her new friend.

"Do you like it?" Elisabeth chuckled.

Alexcena nodded, taking another bite. "What *is* this?"

Elisabeth shrugged. "I just call them strawberry cakes. It's really just a simple cottage pudding with mashed strawberries ground into it."

"Did you invent these?" she asked and continued to chew slowly, savoring each burst of tart flavor in her mouth.

"Goodness, no. The ladies in the village taught me those. It's something of a traditional dish."

Alexcena was still in awe at the sweet cake when Tabitha joined them. With a bleary yawn, the girl stretched and asked, "What's that you're eating?"

Alexcena responded by breaking off a piece and offering it to her cousin. Tabitha's reaction was much the same as Alexcena's. She rounded on Elisabeth.

"You *must* give us the recipe!"

"Gladly," Elisabeth smiled, "and there is something else I should like to give you as well."

She moved to the bed, and Tabitha followed curiously. Elisabeth lifted the arm of the striped dress.

"I wondered if you would like to take these," she explained. "You seem to be struggling with the dress you're wearing. These are too short for me now, and linen breathes so much better than satin."

Her voice trailed away. It was obvious she was hoping that Tabitha was not offended by these observations. Alexcena's gaze flitted to her cousin, who was staring at the garments.

"But I can't just take them from you," she said after a moment.

"Feel! They're too short."

"I know!" With that Tabitha dashed away to retrieve her bag.

Alexcena was, at first, quite determined to mind her own business, but she directed a questioning glance at Elisabeth.

The other woman gave a twitch of her shoulders. "These clothes will serve your cousin in the wilderness far better than the ones she's wearing."

Alexcena was more grateful than she could say. All at once a weight of emotion covered her shoulders and she was tired. Amidst all of the travel and hardships it brought, there were her thoughts and feelings for Lucius. Then there was the sadness of being away from her parents and all that was familiar to her. Her shoulders began to sag, and for the first time she wondered just how much longer she would be able to withstand the search. The very thought scared her beyond words and even tears. How could she possibly wonder such a thing? What sort of hideous, heartless woman was she?

Elisabeth was watching her apprehensively. Alexcena noticed, but what could she say? The mix of emotions playing across her face must have been interesting, to be sure. After such a train of thought, she did not feel up to explaining. Tabitha rescued her from the burden of attempting to.

"Here!" the younger woman cried as she rejoined them. "I'll trade you this for the clothes." She held up a mother-of-pearl hair comb, set with no less than twenty blue beads along its edge.

Elisabeth would have refused, but it was quite clear what Tabitha would have said if she did. Instead she accepted the comb and held it toward the light of the window, pretending to consider. "You're sure?" she asked Tabitha.

"Quite." Without waiting for a reply, Tabitha gathered the clothes into her arms and flounced behind the curtain to change.

This little exchange had given Alexcena ample time to gather herself. She touched Elisabeth's arm and smiled. "Thank you for that."

"Are *you* all right though?"

Alexcena pondered the question and nodded. "As right as I can be. The circumstances of our journey were…less than pleasurable." She was surprised by the catch in her voice, and hoped that Elisabeth would not ask for a description.

The lady only smiled and squeezed her hand. "I shall pray that everything goes well for you. As it stands you have a nice surprise waiting outside. I hope it will be the first of many."

"Surprise?"

Alexcena enjoyed unexpected pleasantries, but she had endured more than enough shocks for one year.

Leo appeared in the doorway before she had time to worry. "Knock, knock, ladies. Time for you to come out and see what I've got for you." He turned his head, looking around the room for Tabitha. She stepped out from behind the curtain, and he gave a start as though he were frightened.

"Tabitha?"

She blinked. "Is something the matter?"

He stared oddly. "Is your hair braided?!"

The girl touched a hand to her head selfconsciously. Alexcena moved forward, hoping to prompt Leo to pull himself together. She had not the faintest idea what had gotten into him.

"Don't just stand there, Leo. You must show us the surprise. I'm dying to see it."

"You're dying to see *them*," he corrected as he led the way with a winning smile. It was clear what he meant as soon as they set foot outside.

Three horses stood there; one pale, one chestnut, and one dappled gray. Joseph stood close to them holding their leads. They were beautiful creatures, tall and muscular and silent-much like the Machapunga. They watched with uninterested, half-closed eyes as the ladies filed out of the cabin.

At first Alexcena could only stare. "Are these for us?"

"Yes, ma'am. Bit of trading with this and that, and now we won't have to be on our feet nearly as much," Leo answered. "My arsenal is a bit depleted and Ms. Winslett is short one fancy dress now, though."

Tabitha raised an eyebrow. "Yes, so I noticed."

"I am sorry about that," Leo scoffed, "but once a trade is given, it is very difficult to take it back. I'm sure the chief would happily keep the horse and your dress."

"Oh, no!" she said too quickly. "I'll not need it, thank you."

Alexcena was watching the animals throughout this banter, clearly dazzled by them. Commodore meandered into view. He paced back and forth before the horses as though considering them. Quite suddenly he plopped down before the gray mare and sneezed. The horse nodded sharply and pawed the ground once.

Alexcena could not help but smile.

"I'll have that one."

Chapter 22

June 20 and 21, 1765

"Anything you want here ladies and gentlemen. Home cures, remedies, and even a little of our famous sassafras tea!"

Inside the cart, Victoria leaned close to Lucius and said, "Famous, eh?"

Lucius grimaced. "It's a family recipe we found in his grandmother's journal," he explained. "He has cousins in Lexington, a brother in New York, and a great-uncle in Boston. By his logic, that tea is known in three colonies. More if he chooses to count all the colonies he's traveled through with it."

Victoria snickered lightly. Lucius couldn't join her, for he was in no mood to laugh. The first day in Jacksonville had gone well for them. Mandrake had subsequently predicted that the next day would be even more profitable. He therefore asked Lucius to give him a hand in the talking portion of the business. Lucius had so wanted to refuse, but all he could say was that if Mandrake somehow turned out to be correct, he would greet the crowd. Of course when he said 'crowd' he was counting on maybe ten all told. The cart was currently surrounded by at least fifty interested parties.

"As a special treat for you all," Mandrake went on, "I have convinced the man responsible for all these amazing concoctions to speak to you all here today. Ladies and gentlemen I humbly present the wonderful Professor Wolgath!"

"That'll be you, then," Victoria smirked.

Lucius planted something akin to a smile over his lips and tried to calm his nerves.

"Oh, don't forget these!" Victoria said, snatching the damaged glasses from Lucius' head and deftly slipping them into his waistcoat pocket.

The already dingy cart was transformed into a shadowy blur. Lucius suppressed a groan. *Just what I need.* He stepped through the flap to be met by what he assumed was a sea of faces. All he saw were fifty pale smudges.

"Don't be modest, Professor!" Mandrake declared. "Come on up here." The man grabbed the shoulder of his shirt and all but yanked him up into the driver's seat. "Tell the people about it!"

Lucius looked down at the gathering around them, doing his very best not to squint. "Hello. I'm Professor Wolgath," he began timidly. "I studied at Cambridge University in England."

"That's a rich man's school!" someone shouted from the crowd. "What're you doing here with the likes of Mr. Mandrake?"

Lucius wished he could see the expressions of the people. The man who had spoken sounded less than friendly. But perhaps his waistcoat was too tight…

Before Lucius could form a reply, Mandrake put an arm around his shoulders and took on an expression of woe most piteous. "A grave misfortune has brought this man to our shores nearly penniless. Tell 'em what you studied, Professor."

"Chemistry and Botany."

This declaration was met with a flurry of muttering from the people. Lucius caught just enough words to understand their reaction.

"-never heard of them."

"Know the first, but the other?"

"Who ever heard of Biminey and Cottany?"

"-some of that fancy learning. Don't know what it's got to do with us here."

Mandrake hurried to soothe the crowd. "Gentlemen! Ladies! You're looking at a bonefide scientist! This ain't one of your common every-day concoctors. He knows what he's doing!"

"But how do we know he knows what he's doing?"

"My Georgie!" a woman in the crowd defended. "Yesterday he could not speak for a sore throat. Today he's well thanks to them."

One of the men knelt close to the boy. "Is it true son?"

"Aye, sir!" the child squeaked as his mother tugged him the other way.

Mandrake grinned proudly. "There goes one satisfied customer. We would love the opportunity to make some more!"

A few members of the group seemed interested but there were others who still showed doubt. Among the former was a couple close to the front of the cart. The husband stepped forward, looking to Mandrake.

"Do you have any of Ward's Drops for my wife?"

"Ward's? Pha!" Mandrake chuckled. "I wouldn't give Ward's Drops to my mule. Step forward dear lady, and let the Professor help you."

Mandrake set a hand on Lucius' shoulder and shoved him down. Given that he couldn't see, it was a wonder he didn't land flat on his face. He tugged at his collar and offered a small bow.

"Sir, ma'am. How may I help you?"

A light tap landed on his sleeve. "Over here, Professor."

Lucius whirled around, dutifully ignoring the sniggering behind him and the blush creeping up his throat. "Sorry. Er-how may I help?"

The blur he assumed to be the lady rolled her sleeves almost up to the elbow and held out her forearms. Lucius saw nothing but a smear of pink.

"What do you assume is the cause of the…problem?"

"I thought it was poison ivy, but it's lasted too long and the balsam has done nothing for it."

"May I?" He was left no other option what with so many eyes upon him.

"All-all right."

Lucius gingerly took the lady's hand and leaned so low over her arm that he nearly brushed it with his nose. At last his vision came into focus. What he saw were pale red welts covered in white flecks as they peeled away. In his mind he began thumbing through all the remedies he could come up with that might be useful. The list was not long for something such as this, but he thought he had just the thing.

He straightened. "I believe I know what this needs. Just allow me to step into the cart-oaf!"

He turned only to ram his chest into the large wheel. The crowd at least seemed to enjoy it, and they were not short on laughter to prove it. *Who do I have the right to laugh at if I cannot laugh with those who are laughing at me?*

Lucius managed a chuckle as he rubbed the middle of his torso. "Better yet, why don't I have one of my assistants bring out what I need." *I certainly couldn't read the labels if I wanted to.* "Assistant?" he called and kicked the edge of the cart behind him with his heel.

Victoria's curly red head emerged from behind the patchwork cover. "Professor?"

"Victoria, would you bring me some dragon's arum, heather, and lemon oil please? Oh, and my mortar and pestle, and one of those squares we made for the tea leaves."

The husband stepped forward. "Now hold on there. I want my wife to have some relief, but this sounds mighty expensive. We may not be able-"

"I assure you that it will not be expensive. I'll explain exactly what I'm using so that you may find the ingredients for yourself in the future."

When Victoria returned with the necessary items, Lucius began grinding the leaves into a fine powder. He gradually added the lemon oil until he had a stiff paste. He invited the lady to dip her fingers in and smear some of it across her rash. The woman was delighted to find that her itching was stopped immediately. The husband was delighted to find that the fee was reasonable and that this was a cure they could make for themselves if need be.

"The only ingredient you might have trouble with would be the lemon oil. I merely used it because I had to have a liquid to bond the powder and the smell is pleasing."

"Thank you, indeed," the man said as he gave Lucius' hand a shake. "I really appreciate it, as I know my wife does."

After that almost everyone in the crowd had some ailment they wanted to share or some regimen they wanted to purchase. Fortunately none of the complaints were very serious. They stayed there for the remainder of the afternoon and sold much of the contents of their store. While Lucius was worrying that he wouldn't be able to keep up with the demand if they became any busier, Mandrake fingered the coins in his pocket and beamed. They had sold something to everyone there that day, even to the gentleman requesting a cure for his drastically thinned hair.

"Unfortunately," Lucius explained slowly, "I do not know of anyone in the world who has found a cure for baldness."

"Can't you give me something?"

Secure in the knowledge that it was the best he could do, Lucius handed him a tin of powder. "This will keep mites out of your wig."

The man paid for it with a shrug. "Maybe it'll get those mites outta my mattress too."

Lucius suppressed a cringe. "It certainly should."

After the man was gone, Mandrake was suddenly in front of Lucius, pumping his hand up and down with vigor. "I've never seen such skill with a crowd! I knew in my bones that you'd be a success. A great success!"

He trailed back around the side of the cart. Lucius had very little doubt that he was doing anything other than counting his money. Victoria soon jumped down from the wagon to join him.

"Today went well, didn't it though?"

"I should say so."

She flipped a lock of hair from her forehead. "Good thing too. I was starting to worry about us, sure enough."

"Well, where there's faith, there's a way."

She looked at him oddly then-though he could not tell it, for his glasses remained in his pocket. "You of all of us seem to have the most to be sad for, and yet you always manage to cheer right up."

"I take a powder for it," he teased.

Another couple approached as they were sharing a laugh at that. These two were slightly different from their previous customers in that they were very well-dressed. The man wore an immaculate wig while the lady was decked all in silk. In short they obviously had a great deal of money. Lucius, of course, did not notice as he rose to greet them.

"Good afternoon."

At first the pair was disjointed, paying almost no attention to Lucius and Victoria.

"I don't know why you insisted on coming here," the wife mumbled none-too softly.

"I'm interested!" the man replied. He was studying the cart as though fascinated by something crude and clever.

"But the physician does well. Why must we consort-*here?*"

The man ignored his wife and turned his attention to Lucius. "Good day. My wife and I heard snatches of your demonstrations as we went about town today. Very interesting suggestions you've made."

Lucius gave a slight bow. "Thank you, sir."

"I wonder if you might have anything you could recommend for a bad back. Mine has been giving me an awful time as of late."

"Certainly, sir. Victoria, will you fetch me the hawthorn root, please?"

She smiled and stepped up into the wagon. Lucius returned his attention to the patrons. He smiled, hoping that it was appropriate, since he could not see their expressions. Still they sounded pleasant enough.

"How long have you and your wife been married, Professor?" the lady asked presently.

Lucius was taken aback at first, and then chuckled at his own silliness. "To Victoria? I'm afraid you're mistaken, ma'am. We are not married."

"Ah, then she is your master's lovely bride?"

"Not at all, ma'am. Neither of us is married."

Victoria emerged then. The roots in her hand and her countenance stiff. She knew well where the conversation was headed, though Lucius remained unaware.

"*Oh*," the lady intoned heavily. "Oh, I *see*."

Lucius blinked first at her and then at her husband. "I beg your pardon?"

"I feel that my back is loosening up a bit," the husband said without warning. "Perhaps I won't be needing your roots and herbs after all. Come, dear." He took his wife's arm and they began to turn away.

"There must be some misunderstanding," Lucius said. Innocent confusion beamed from his eyes. "Are you certain, sir?"

The man sighed and half turned back to look Lucius in the eye. "We want nothing to do with your-your bawdy cart. Come, dear!"

Comprehension dawned, and Lucius felt a cold wave of anger wash over him. His hands curled into fists. He heard Victoria stomp back into the confines of the covered cart, but it made no difference. He was determined to speak.

"I was right, sir. There has been a grave mistake here," he began.

"I agree, there has."

"You have insulted my colleague in a most debase manner. I am only glad that you did so before we conducted our business together."

The wife, now frustrated, spoke up then. "She is a *woman*. An unattached woman traveling alone with two *men!* The implications are ghastly. Surely you must see that."

"You, madam, have no idea whether she is unaccompanied or not. Given that you are, I presume, a lady, I will not address that thought further." Lucius then directed his attention to the gentlemen. "Sir, when you speak of myself and my friends you imply faults in our honor and reputations. Reputations which you know nothing about. I will thank you not to make such assumptions in the future."

Lucius turned to enter the wagon, but the man stopped him again.

"Just a moment!" He waited until Lucius turned to give his tirade. "You have affronted me! You disgrace my opinion and my judgment, and you expect to turn away without hearing my say on the matter. I proclaim you a coward, sir!"

"A coward?"

"You have engaged me and offended my sensibilities. Now you are retreating into your pitiable little dwelling without facing your opponent. Yes, I deem you a coward!"

Lucius merely watched the man with something akin to a tired gaze. Then his eyes shifted toward the lady. "Ma'am, if I were you, I would be most concerned. Not once did your husband say that I had offended his wife. Good day to you both."

As he withdrew into the relative darkness of the cart, he vaguely wondered whether or not the man would force the issue. He might find himself engaged in a duel if he did, but Lucius seriously doubted that this would be the case. He knew the type well from his time at Cambridge. Pompous, overbearing men who felt entitled and even obliged to step on everyone else's toes as they blundered through life. Of course many such men that he had known had more than enough money to compensate for such faults. At least as far as society was concerned.

A strange puffing caught Lucius' attention, but in the failing light of the late afternoon, he could see nothing in the cover of the cart. He slipped the arms of his spectacles over his ears and saw Victoria dabbing at her eyes with a handkerchief. He assumed that she had not noticed him until she spoke.

"Why did ye do that?" she demanded.

Lucius hesitated, unsure of her meaning.

She looked to him with a tear-streaked face. "Why did ye bother to confront them?"

"They deserved it. Their manner was inexcusable."

"They were paying customers," she insisted.

Lucius shrugged. "In some ways they were right. I didn't consider your reputation when I invited you to come with us. The damage to you was not something I-"

"My reputation was in tatters long before ye saved me from there," Victoria interrupted carelessly. Then she brought the subject back around. "That's not the first time ye've come to my defense like that."

"It's not?"

"My uncle," she answered impatiently. "Ye keep doing this and I don't know why. I'm not worth it. Not like you."

Lucius' heart immediately softened toward the girl. This girl who had been turned so hard by years of harsh treatment.

"You can be, Victoria," he whispered thickly. "You just haven't figured that out yet."

She looked confused, and then her countenance was warmed by a small smile.

Lucius smiled back and then thought it best to look outside to be sure the offensive couple was gone. Instead of them he found Mandrake and Foley conversing with an elderly man with long, silver hair and a leather apron.

"Ah, Lucius. Come down, would you?" Mandrake requested when he saw him. "This is Mr. Harry Foster, and he's very keen to meet you."

Lucius bowed slightly. "How do you do, sir?"

"Well. Better than usual thanks to you."

"Oh?" Lucius glanced at Mandrake for some clue, but he gave nothing away. "Forgive me, but I don't remember having seen you before, Mr. Foster."

"That's because you haven't, though I don't see how you can see a bloomin' thing in those glasses anyway," Foster chuckled.

Lucius' gaze darted to Mandrake again. He had forgotten that he was still wearing the broken glasses.

"-did meet my daughter yesterday," Foster went on. "She and her mother were in town and they purchased some of your sassafras tea. Now my daughter, Lord bless her, has always been a bit unwell. She has a very delicate constitution and most food doesn't sit well with her, especially bread. She must be very careful what she eats. Last night, my wife brewed the tea for herself. It smelled so good that my daughter insisted on trying a bit. After an hour of her eyeing her mamma's mug, we allowed it. Now my girl says she's never felt better. She even woke up first this morning and had the coffee brewed before either of us was up. Says she hasn't felt so well since she was a child."

"That is wonderful news. I am so happy to hear that your daughter is better." Lucius said sincerely.

Mandrake's eyes were alight with greed. "And so you've come for more, eh?"

Foster did not answer right away. He was stroking his beard and scrutinizing Lucius. "I had," he said slowly, "and I will take a little with me. However-"

Lucius resisted the urge to squirm under his study. "Yes, sir?"

Foster set his hands on his hips. "I'd like to make a bargain with you. If you will give me the recipe for that tea and trade me those gold rims of yours, I will replace your glasses with new ones."

Lucius felt his mouth fall open. "My glasses?"

"That's right," Foster said. "That's what I do for a living. I'm partnered with the local doctor and we have an office a few streets away. I can provide you with a new set of spectacles to match your current lenses- without the corresponding cracks of course. I can have them to you by tomorrow evening."

A smile slowly began to spread over Lucius' lips. "That would be-"

"Hold on there!" Mandrake interrupted and stepped between the two men. "Just a minute, Mr. Foster. That tea has been a secret of *my* family for three decades. Any deals concerning it must be approved by me, and I dare say that I'm reluctant to part with it."

Foster's look was not hard, but determined. He crossed his arms as Mandrake had done. "Did you not just tell me that Professor Wolgath modified the recipe himself when you took him on, and that he's made it tenfold better than it was when your own granny made it?"

"Er-"

Foley joined the fray then. His pudgy hands balled into fists on his hips. "And aren't you the one who told the Professor his glasses gotta be fixed or he can't wear them?"

Mandrake was speechless. He had no argument and he knew it. Lucius leapt on the moment.

"Then, if it's all right with you Mandrake, I'll give Mr. Foster three portions of tea to take home." He removed his glasses and passed them around Mandrake. "I'll have the recipe written up for you when you return tomorrow," he told Foster.

The man folded the glasses and slipped them into his pocket. "Pleasure doing business with you."

When Foster was gone, Foley beamed up at Lucius and tugged at his sleeve. "I knew he could help you, Professor. I knew it! I met him on my way back and as soon as he told me his trade I knew he could help."

Lucius grinned. "You were right indeed, Foley." He tried to pat the boy's head, but being once again without his glasses, he missed.

"Owe!"

"Sorry."

"That's all right, Professor."

"Where have you been this afternoon anyway?"

"Victoria sent me for some cooking stuff." He held up a small bag for show. "Took me a while 'cause the shop keep at the mercantile is kinda old and we both wanted to make sure we got everything right. And he kept forgetting I was there."

"I see."

"Yea," Foley replied. "I better go make sure I got it right. It'll take me all day tomorrow if I have to take something back."

The boy scurried up into the cart with the goods while Lucius reluctantly faced Mandrake.

"I hope I haven't overstepped your authority, Robert," he said sincerely.

Mandrake shrugged and waved the comment away. "It was my own doing. Sometimes I really know how to set a trap for myself, don't I?"

The pair shook hands. Lucius was glad to see the day ending on a nice note. He would be even happier tomorrow when he could look at the blue sky above without having to ignore the enormous cracks running across it.

The next day dawned and proved to be every bit as busy as the day before. Lucius barely had time to anticipate his new spectacles. True to his word, Harry Foster returned at exactly five o'clock.

"I tell you, it took me twice as long as I thought it would, but here they are."

Lucius-expecting to receive glasses-was confused when Foster handed him a small wooden box. It was harshly carved, but all the edges were polished and smooth to the touch. Tiny hinges and a latch similar to those of a clock case held the lid shut. Curious, Lucius lifted it and found his new glasses nestled on a swatch of satin.

"My daughter makes those boxes for my customers. She was up half the night making that one for you."

Lucius was moved indeed by the thought. The wire framing was an unfamiliar metal, but the color was a shiny gray. Not unpleasing. He gingerly lifted the glasses and set them on his head. He blinked as his eyes began to relax behind them. The world seemed to sparkle anew and clear in his vision. There was not a smudge or a crack to be seen.

He smiled broadly. "I can see again!"

All around him chuckled, but he did not care. He reached into his pocket and withdrew a folded piece of paper to give to Foster.

"Your payment, sir. I cannot thank you enough."

Foster accepted the page and tipped his hat. "Likewise, Professor."

When the man had gone, Foley tugged at Lucius' sleeve. "I want to see, Professor!"

Lucius obligingly looked down at him.

"Whoa," Foley muttered. "Your eyes look bigger than the rest of your face."

"Whoa," Lucius mimicked in return.

"What?"

"I never realized what a filthy little boy you are."

Foley laughed unabashedly. "Very funny, Professor."

Victoria passed them then carrying a large pot. "He wasn't teasing."

"Huzah!"

The shout from inside the cart silenced them all and nearly made Victoria drop her pot. Mandrake dashed out and practically ran the short distance to them. Given his great girth, he was huffing and puffing by the time he stopped.

"Do you realize-" He wheezed, caught his breath, and started again. "Do you realize that the second day we were here we doubled the profits from the first? Then today we doubled the profits from the second day! That's more than I've ever made in one take, even when I was gambling!"

"Small wonder," Lucius said ryely.

Mandrake straightened his shoulders and looked at each of them proudly. "I knew we'd make a fine troop the moment I met all of you." With that he sauntered back to the wagon.

Victoria *humphed.* "As if it was his idea to bring Foley and me."

"Doesn't matter," Lucius smiled. "We're here now, and I think the three of us are better off. Even if we do have to live with Mandrake."

Chapter 23

June 22, 1765

Alexcena, being far from ignorant about horses, was completely aware of the fact that there would be a certain soreness involved in riding at great lengths. Still, even this discomfort was mild compared to the pain her feet and legs had been suffering as of late. Never before had she been so happy to sit atop even the finest of horses. She soon discovered that along with its appeal, the new circumstances of their travels also involved some awkwardness. As it turned out, the third horse had belonged to Joseph. Leo had only been able to procure two, and so she would share with Tabitha. It was not until they actually stepped forward to mount the animal that they realized something was missing. The horse was fitted with a bridle and a blanket; nothing more. Much to their horror, the only way for them to successfully ride without the aid of a sidesaddle was for them to straddle the horse.

Now, having been atop him for two days, Alexcena found that there was in fact a great advantage in balance when one was mounted in such a way. For every advantage there is an equal and opposite disadvantage. The disadvantage here was that her skirt was bunched up beneath her, allowing anyone who cared to look a clear view of the ankles of her boots.

It's just a good thing Mother is not here... She would be mortified indeed!

She was certain that Tabitha had thought the selfsame thing, though she had not said as much. Alexcena was very glad that she had not complained to Leo when the situation had arisen. The air between the pair had seemed to clear, and she could not have been more relieved. Even two days later they were still speaking amiably to one another.

"Why is it that you have traveled so much, Leo?"

Alexcena glanced at the man and saw him grinning at Tabitha's question.

"There are countless people in this world," Leo replied cryptically. "Thousands of them claim that they live in the most beautiful place on earth. I simply want to know who is telling the truth."

"But that's all a matter of opinion," Tabitha returned.

"True, but that's not really the end I'm after. I love the hunt and the sights and the sounds." Leo's expression took on a shine that Alexcena had rarely seen there before. "With every new place I visit there are so many new things to learn," he went on. "New questions, new trades, new roads. I can't get enough of it."

Alexcena swallowed a laugh and smiled good-naturedly at him. "I once thought that you and your brother were entirely different. Now I begin to think otherwise."

Leo bobbed his head in thanks. When he brought his face back up, he paused. His expression changed and he held out a hand for them to stop.

"Do you hear what I hear?"

Alexcena listened, and gradually she began to make out the sounds of something different from the woods surrounding them. She heard the stomp of hooves, the creak of wagon wheels, and the shouts of men.

"A town?" Tabitha wondered aloud.

Leo sniffed appreciatively, his eyes closed. "And salt. I'll bet you ladies my last bullet that we'll be in Currituck around the next bend!"

Commodore led the way into town, his head turning in every direction. His tail wagged as he plodded along in front of them, completely confident that they would follow.

"I see a mercantile there," Leo commented as they went, indicating the building he meant. "We'll stop in there for some supplies, and then we'll go on down to the docks."

"Do you really think anyone at the docks will know about Lucius?" Alexcena asked somewhat weakly.

Leo pursed his lips as though deciding whether or not to answer. "Joseph affirmed that Currituck was our best chance this far south of Williamsburg."

Alexcena's brow furrowed. She appreciated Leo's efforts to shield her, but firmly believed it was better that she knew the full measure of the dilemma.

They reigned in the horses at the rail before the mercantile. Leo hurried to help the ladies dismount, but Alexcena was not inclined to wait. She was eager to be on her way to the water's edge where she might hear some news and even more eager to have the conversations over with if it was not to be. She tried to pull her leg over the horse's neck while using both hands to keep her skirt from flipping up. The motions did not work well together and Tabitha did not notice soon enough to help. Alexcena slid from the horse sideways and fell back as soon as her left boot hit the ground. A pair of strong arms was close by to catch her.

"Thank you!" she exclaimed, assuming the arms belonged to Leo. She was quite shocked when an unfamiliar voice sounded in her ear.

"Not at all, love!"

She drew in a sharp breath and jerked away, twisting to see who it was that held her.

The man was a younger one. His blond hair was matted and filthy, much the same as his clothes. His features were grimy, though not unhandsome. When she pulled away, he buried his hands in his pockets and simply grinned at her.

"What's going on here!?" Leo demanded. He had come around the horse just as Alexcena was caught by the stranger. "Who are you?" even as he spoke, he helped Tabitha to the ground.

"Smith Darlum." The man bowed, his hands remaining in his pockets. "Resident rescuer of young beauties and sweet hearts."

Leo's eyes narrowed perceptibly. Darlum went on as though he didn't notice.

"And what do they call you?"

"Leo Wolgath," he growled with menace. "Defender of said beauties."

To everyone's surprise, Darlum broke out in a toothy smile.

"Ah! Splendid!" he exclaimed. "I know your brother, Lucius."

Lucius… Alexcena's ears began to roar. Before another thought could form in her mind, she swooned and felt herself falling again.

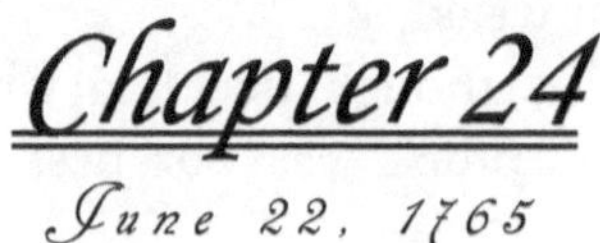

Chapter 24

June 22, 1765

Leopold watched in dismay as Alexcena's head fell back. For an instant he thought that she had fainted completely. Even as he caught her, it seemed that she was almost lifeless. Then her feet moved as he inclined her away from Darlum. The man was sniffing altogether too closely for Leo's liking. His mouth pulled into a hard line at the idea.

"To the stairs!" Tabitha exclaimed from somewhere behind him. "Take her to the stairs!"

Leo looked around to see the steps of the mercantile close behind them. He gently drew Alexcena around. Her eyes remained tightly closed, but her feet stumbled along, partially supporting her own weight. He helped her to sit on the second step, and she clung to the baluster of the railing.

"Are you well?" he asked.

She expelled a massive breath. "Yes."

"Are you hurting at all?"

Her eyes flickered open, much to his relief. "No." When Leo paused, she gave an order. "Ask him."

There was no need to explain. Leo knew exactly what she meant by her whispered words. He rose and Tabitha immediately took his seat. His full attention returned to Darlum.

The man was snickering easily at the women. "Do you feel better now, lady?"

"You tell me what you know of my brother," Leo said with a cold sneer.

Darlum was taken aback. "Sorry, old man. Didn't mean to startle anyone."

Leo crossed his arms. "Whether you meant to or not, you have. These ladies have been through enough without being antagonized further, so why don't you explain to us what you know."

He was trying to speak slowly and allow only a small measure of his anger to leech into his tone. This man could not have known what he had just done to them all, but Leo was keen to hear his story. The full implications of the claim were just beginning to dawn on him. Not only did this mean that Lucius had made it to shore alive; he might be found close by. In that very city!

Leo's nerves thrummed at the thought. His heart would have sung for joy, but Darlum was weighing heavily on his temper. Even then the man became distracted as Commodore approached and sat beside Leo, staring up at the stranger.

"Hello there my good fellow!" Darlum smiled as he leaned forward to pet the dog's head.

Commodore deftly jerked away while at once making a snap at the man's limb. Darlum barely made it back with his hand intact.

"Do keep your focus, Smith," Leo rumbled, unmoved by

Commodore's outburst. "Tell us about my brother."

He ground out the words, no longer caring about his temper. Smith took on an aloof expression. It seemed he was no longer in the mood to be quite so friendly either.

"Am I to understand that you know nothing of him? Since he came here, I would imagine."

Leo made no reply.

"And here I am. The one man better acquainted with him than anyone else around here, present company excepted. Amazing that we've run into one another, eh?"

Behind the men, Alexcena lifted her head from the railing. "Blessing," she said, briefly drawing their attention. "It's a blessing."

Smith bobbed his head respectfully in her direction before his eyes focused on Leo. His jaw jutted to one side. Leo recognized the look of a man who is considering something and expected what would come next.

"Tell you what, Wolgath," Smith began. "It's been a while since my last meal. You buy me a plate across the way and share a table with me. Then I'll tell you everything I know."

Leo briefly contemplated snatching the man up by his collar and forcing the words from him. In that instant his temper would have gladly superseded his Christian ethics. Alexcena spoke up before he could react.

"Of course," she replied calmly. "We will buy him a meal, and he will tell us of Lucius."

Darlum bowed in her direction. "Thank you indeed, ma'am."

Leo ground his teeth together. He had become uneasy with the situation. Given the glimmer in Darlum's sly eye, he could only guess what the man would ask for next, and they still had no idea how much he knew. Surely he would not be so stupid as to attempt to fleece them in exchange for a tiny piece of news-or none at all. Leo liked to think he was intimidating enough to deter that.

Smith led them around a corner to an eatery. They sat at a round table. Leo made certain he sat directly beside Smith. The ladies were not so keen to sit near him. They left the fifth chair vacant at his other side.

The plate was set before the man, and he tore into the meal with a gusto. Leo reached out, intending to grasp his wrist and stop his fork. Alexcena touched his arm to keep him from it. Leo obeyed begrudgingly, but he didn't think he would wait long. The slurping, smacking noises Smith was making as he ate were utterly nauseating.

All at once, halfway through his meal, Smith realized that the three travelers were staring at him. He grinned sloppily and rested his forearms on the table. "I know I'm handsome, but you folks are making me dreadfully selfconscious."

Leo glanced toward Alexcena, hoping for some signal that he could take charge of the situation. To his disappointment, she was watching Darlum.

"We are waiting for you to speak, sir," she told him.

"Are you?" Smith answered. "Well, that's flattering. Talking has always been one of my best suits. And it has been a while since I had good company to share it with. Why I can out-talk any one of my five sisters back in-"

"Mr. Darlum!" Alexcena interrupted. It was the first time since she nearly fainted that any emotion had shown in her voice. Leo stole another glance at her when he heard her sharp tone, but she remained focused on Smith.

"I'm afraid that my patience has been stretched beyond its limits throughout this ordeal," she went on. "I must ask you to come to the point. What do you know of Lucius?"

"Ah, right." Darlum wiped his mouth and set his utensils down. "Well, it's been a rough road, that much I can tell you."

So he began the tale, explaining that he was on board the *Scarlet Pride* with Lucius. He told them all that he knew of the voyage and the seasickness and the storm. Then he told them how he had traveled from Smithfield down to Currituck and there met Lucius again in the company of a boy.

"He was not injured when he came ashore?" Alexcena asked then.

"If he was, it wasn't much. He was fit as a fiddle when I saw him."

This was the part Leo was interested in. "How long were you with him?"

"Two, three days. We found work on a farm, but we had a minor disagreement with the farmer and his neighbors. We left town pretty quickly and I haven't seen him since then. I only just came back into town myself. Never really went too far after the bit with Lucius; just far enough to keep me head on my strong shoulders."

He winked and Alexcena easily ignored him. "When was that?"

"Around three weeks ago. Last I knew he was heading north. No! South. Definitely south."

Smith returned to his meal with just as much vigor as before. When he was finished, he rose, and tipped his hat to them as he left.

"Safe journeys all."

Leo, Alexcena, and Tabitha all remained seated and silent for some time. Leo kept his arms crossed and his eyes down on the table top. Eventually Darlum's words began to repeat themselves in his mind.

Fit as a fiddle…Fit as a fiddle…

The laughter rose up in him before he ever realized it was coming. It began as an almost silent chuckle that shook his shoulders and grew into a full, booming laugh.

"My brother has made it alive!" he cried. He faced Alexcena with a joyous smile. "You were right all along!"

In contrast to Leo, she appeared very serious. A single tear spilled from her eye. "Would that I could say I never doubted it."

Chapter 25
June 22 through 28, 1765

"Will you explain to me why we did this again, Professor?"

Lucius smiled down at his hands as he tied the strings of his shirt collar. He had his back to Foley, but he could well imagine the look on the boy's face by his tone. The boy stood behind him using his hands to knock the moisture from his brown hair. His shoes lay tossed to one side and his shirt was still thrown over a tree branch. His trousers bore splashes from the creek that ran beside them. The boy had his shoulders hunched over his bare chest. He did this so as to let everyone know he was sulking.

As amusing as it was to see this small person trying his best to appear ornery, Lucius knew he would need to drop his smile before he faced him. "You know very well why," he snapped.

"But I bathed last week."

"By the looks of you, no one would have known it," Lucius replied. "Let alone the smell."

"Nobody cares how clean I am," Foley grumbled as he jerked his shirt over his head.

"I care," Lucius said flatly. "And if I hear another word from you about it, I'll see to it that you bathe twice a week."

Foley pursed his lips before releasing a heavy sigh of defeat. "Sorry, Professor."

Lucius shook his head. "I pray your obstinacy will leave you someday. Until then I will try my best to weed it out of you."

Foley wrinkled his nose in confusion. "How?"

"You truly wish to know?"

Foley stopped quite suddenly, his eyes growing wide. "No, sir."

Lucius swallowed a chuckle and strode ahead. *Thought not.*

When they arrived back at the camp, they found Mandrake bending over something in the wagon and chortling gleefully to himself. Victoria was stringing a few pieces of clothing up to dry. She rolled her eyes and quite clearly conveyed that they should not bother asking without even opening her mouth. As was usual with Mandrake, there was no need to. He whirled to face them with a broad grin. "Well, Professor," he began cheerily, "you'll be happy to know that the rest of that Daffy's Elixir is good for something."

Lucius groaned. "Forgive me for saying so, Robert, but I do wish you'd get rid of it all."

"I know, I know," Mandrake answered almost sincerely. "But I just found a new use for some of it."

From behind his back, he drew a crude plank of wood for them to see. A dark stain had been applied to its pale grain. *Sandy Creek bound. Stops for no man.*

"What's Sandy Creek?" Lucius wondered.

"The next town we'll see. Ain't it clever? I figure I'll make a sign for each town we come upon. Makes the town folk feel special, see? Then I added the second part. This way if we do stop to sell a few things on the way, whoever we stop for will think they're getting a real treat, and they'll feel special just the same."

"And what does this have to do with Daffy's Elixir?"

"It's the paint, Professor. The paint!" Mandrake held the plank out at arm's length so that he could admire it. "This is definitely one of my better schemes. I'll be renown across the southern colonies one day, and I'll want everyone to say that I treat my customers special!"

Lucius crossed his arms. "You keep quite a pace for yourself."

"And us," Foley complained.

"How will you have enough signs?"

"Look all around!" Mandrake scoffed. "The woods are full of planks for the plucking. A few whacks with my hatchet, and that's all there is to it. Lord knows I have plenty of Elixir since you've been telling me not to sell it."

"It stains wood a dark maroon and you don't think it could harm a person's body?" Lucius exclaimed.

Mandrake jerked a thumb at his chest. "I been taking that Elixir for years and never had a bit of problem."

"I'll bet you've never had any help from it either," Lucius replied matter-of-factly. "And it has stained your tongue purple."

Surprise lit Mandrake's eyes, and he lowered his voice slightly. "You really think that's what did it?"

"Unless you've been eating blueberries every day since I've known you."

Mandrake relaxed into a bought of laughter. He thumped Lucius heartily on the shoulder. "I declare, Professor! You're always one for wit!"

Lucius was strangely unsettled by the comment. No one had ever mentioned that he was witty before. He could not recall ever being witty before. He had always been clever with books, that much was certain, but witty? All at once he realized that there were characteristics about him that were different. His journey was changing him, whether he chose to allow it or not. He was no longer as naive or indeed as meek as he had been in England. Perhaps the differences were somewhat for the better, but at what cost? Then too, he had not even realized up until now that anything was different about himself. All pride aside, it is frightening to think that one's personality might be shifting, and whither one cannot tell.

He found himself walking away from the others. He wanted some moments to himself to think of these things and to pray. Unfortunately, there wasn't time.

"Hurry, now, Professor!" Mandrake called. "We'll be on the move within the hour."

Lucius waved a hand to show his understanding. When he was alone in the shade of the trees, he fell to one knee, bowing his head low.

My Lord God, I have felt myself changing. It is hard to see and slow to hear, but I pray, Lord, that if You be willing You would open my eyes to it. I desire to be a good and faithful servant of You, Lord…

The others already had everything loaded into the wagon by the time he returned. Wendy was hitched and looking supremely aggravated.

"Come on, Professor!" Foley called. "We're waiting for you!"

I'm waiting for you…

It was Alexcena's voice. Those sweet tones were balm to a wounded man. How could he mistake it? Lucius halted, surprise and awe filling his head and clouding his vision. He had heard the voice. He knew it-and he knew he was not mad-but was it possible that his mind, overwrought with emotion, was tricking him? Even knowing it to be a mirage, Lucius hesitated. He wanted to hear more. He felt his world tilting crazily, thrown off balance by the sound. He allowed it, like a child leaning over some precipice. He stretched to follow the voice, but the illusion was already gone.

He straightened his shoulders and felt his senses returning. Something occurred to him then. It was a faint piece of his childhood. He remembered being told that if ever he should lose his way, he should stay put until he was found.

"Are you coming, Professor?" Mandrake chuckled. "We need to get a move on!"

Lucius' intensions shifted then. He felt that his feet were rooted deep into the ground by the embedded instinct to remain. This was coupled with an urge to return to the Virginia coast, where his journey in America began. Then that same feeling that had come on so strongly fled away as his agile intelligence overcame childish reverie.

You will be found much faster if you are not moving, he sighed inwardly. *But that is only true if there is someone coming to find you.*

He joined the others, walking alongside the cart with Foley.

In the span of one week they passed through Sandy Creek into South Carolina. From there they traveled through Little River, Georgetown, and Awendaw. Lucius eventually stopped asking where they were headed each day they set out. It mattered little so long as the business was working and coins were passing from hand to purse. He was mildly surprised, and quite relieved, to find that they were successful in each settlement. Mandrake insisted that they keep moving as much as possible. Since he 'had his wheels turning and a fistful of coin,' he wanted to make his name known all the way down the coast as far as Georgia and then travel back up.

Lucius was collecting specimens almost constantly as they went, but he was having difficulty keeping up with demand, so he enlisted Foley to be his official assistant. The boy was a fine helper when he could keep his mind focused. It was much the same with his lessons. Every night Lucius would endeavor to teach him using the only book he had; his Bible. Lucius strongly suspected that it would not matter what words he used to teach as he watched the boy struggle. The lad's mind was almost always elsewhere when it came to such work. He was proven correct the evening they camped outside Awendaw.

"Professor!" Foley moaned when he caught sight of the Book. "Words are too hard, and I'm tired."

Lucius scrutinized Foley for what seemed like a long moment. The boy squirmed attempting to keep the sheepish look from his face. His efforts were in vain. Lucius saw his motives clearly and already knew how he would combat them.

"All right."

Foley wrinkled his nose. "All right?"

"Yes, all right," Lucius reiterated easily. "You're too tired to study, so I shan't force you. Instead, I will read to you for a little while, and I'll keep the passage short so you will be satisfied."

Foley settled into a comfortable position. He still felt disgruntled by the Professor's decision, but at least he would not need to think during the new arrangement.

"Now, let me see," Lucius mumbled as he took up the Bible.

By this time Victoria had situated herself beside Foley. The knitting needles she held began to click furiously, though her emerald eyes remained on Lucius.

"Here it is. In the book of Judges. I nearly passed it."

Lucius began to read, telling the both of them the story of Samson. He read of his birth, how that he was born a Nazarite. He read of his sighting of the woman in Timnah. Then, of course, he came to Delilah.

"And Samson said unto her, if they bind me with seven green withs that were never dried then I shall be weak, and be as another man. Then the lords of the Philistines brought up to her seven green withs that were never dried, and she bound him with them. Now there were men lying in wait, abiding with her in the chamber. And she said unto him, 'The Philistines be upon thee, Samson.'"

Here he paused. He glanced at Foley, taking in his eager eyes and open mouth. Then he closed the Bible and turned as if to spread his quilt.

"What-but-Porfessor!" the boy stuttered.

"Yes, Foley?"

"The story's not finished yet. You stopped before the ending."

"I know, but those words are so big and I'm rather tired. It's too bad you're having such difficulty paying attention to your studies. You might have been able to continue on by yourself." He yawned audibly and rolled over. "Good night, Foley. Victoria."

Not so many minutes later, Lucius heard a boyish whisper.

"Victoria? Don't you want to know what happens to Samson?"

"Yes," she replied, "but I can read it any time I want to. Goodnight, Foley."

Lucius, being as tired as he was, only had time to smile at that before he was claimed by a deep sleep. This sleep, however needed, turned out to be restless indeed. Dark shapes formed in his mind's eye. They were tall, stalwart beings looming ominously over any human of normal height. Among them moved another figure who was pale as new cream. It was not long before the pale one came into focus, and he recognized Alexcena. She moved like a rolling fog through the trees, a stark contrast to the darkness surrounding her. Her face was drawn in an unmistakable look of concern and woe. He was astounded when she called his name, and then not once but several times.

"Lucius? Lucius?"

Then she was running. The branches pulled at her clothes and scratched her face. Twice they caught her rich hair as it streamed out behind her. He-the disembodied observer in all this-was powerless to save her. His heart thudded against the walls of his chest as she ran on.

"Lucius! Lucius! Lucius! "

His eyes opened in a snap. Before he knew what he was doing, he leapt to his feet, the faded quilt falling in a crumple on the ground. All was darkness and trees around him. His heart still raced, and he turned a full circle before he realized that he was looking for a vision that was not there. Tears began to fall then as his bruised heart began to slow.

Oh, Lord, he moaned inside, *how can I be content with what I have while I am so saddened by what I'm missing?*

Chapter 26
June 29, 1765

"Hey, Professor? Professor!"

"Hm?" Lucius blinked rapidly and looked down at his friend. "What is it, Foley?" he replied kindly.

The boy wrinkled his nose. "You've been acting funny again for two days. Now you don't even listen anymore." His chin rose with his ire. "I think something's happened that you're not letting me know about."

Lucius considered the statements. His gaze remained on his feet as he walked the dusty path. What could he say to the boy?

They had paused for a day outside of the settlement of Beaufort, one of the oldest towns in all of South Carolina. As usual Lucius found that he needed to collect more specimens, and Foley was ever at the ready to help him. Mandrake had been forced to purchase certain commodities over the course of their journey, but there were so many convenient ingredients in the feral forests around them that he insisted they forage as much as possible. Lucius agreed. This meant that he was constantly looking and hunting and plucking. Consequently, so was Foley.

"Look there, Professor!" The boy pointed and ran to a plant by the wayside. "Is this a good one?"

Lucius approached and bent to examine the plant further. "That's Valerian. Its most common use is to cure insomnia. Very good, Foley."

Foley wrinkled his brow. "What's somnia?"

"That's *in*somnia. It only means that it helps a person to sleep."

"Oh." The boy looked once more to the delicate flowers of the specimen. He took an experimental sniff of the sugary sweet scent, then fell to the ground, feigning a snore.

Lucius raised an eyebrow. "Nice try, but it doesn't work quite that quickly. Or by smell."

Foley shrugged, his jest thwarted. Leaping to his feet, he took the Valerian from the ground with an easy jerk.

"As to your question," Lucius began, knowing full well that he could have let the subject drop since Foley had forgotten it. "You have been wondering if something is wrong."

"Yes, sir," Foley replied as he handed the plant to Lucius.

Lucius dawdled at brushing the dirt from the roots. "I was frightened by something, Foley. A nightmare."

Foley was instantly taken in by the prospect of a good tall tale. "Was it a monster? A phantom? Oh no, Professor, were you some place scary like Louisiana? It's full of Frenchmen, y'know."

Lucius was forced to chuckle. "No, none of that. I don't know where it was, and I was not actually in it."

"Who was then?"

"Alexcena."

"The lady you loved in England?"

Lucius felt his throat grow thick. He fought to keep from clenching his teeth. "Yes. She was running through a dark wood somewhere as fast as she was able. Too fast really. Her breathing was uneven and the trees were hurting her, and she just kept calling for me."

Foley pshawed. "That's nothing to worry about, Professor. She's not really lost anywhere…probably."

"It prompted a new thought for me," Lucius went on. "I have been pained before by the idea that she would not need me, but what if she *does* need me? What if there is some possibility that she has come into difficulties and wants my help? Even if she has already given her heart to another, I would never deny her assistance. The thought that even that is impossible is maddening."

"Well-" Foley's face was comically pinched in concentration. "How long was it before she became your fiancé?"

"Twenty-seven years." Lucius shook his head. "Sorry. Ah… one year."

"See!" Foley proclaimed with a grin. "You haven't been gone that long. You'll probably have at least seven or eight months more before you *really* have to worry. Even then, whoever she falls for will help her with her problems and you won't have to worry about her!"

Lucius was profoundly disgusted by such unfeeling remarks. He had to try very hard to remember that the young boy was just that; a young boy.

"Thank you, Foley," he mumbled.

It's a shame there's not someone else around to hear this conversation, he thought. *Any other opinion could only cheer me up after that.*

He looked up to see that Foley had moved ahead of him and was standing at the base of a thick pine tree. The boy's head was tilted back and his arms were crossed.

"What about that tree is so fascinating to you?" Lucius called as he crossed the distance.

"This mark," Foley said over his shoulder. "Look."

He pointed to a spot on the truck some two feet above his head. The closer Lucius came, the better he could see the mark, and the more intrigued he was. Into the tree had been carved the head of an arrow and the line of its shaft. The image was wide and imperfect but distinguishable enough, formed by three simple strokes.

The carving was eye-level for Lucius. Despite his glasses, he stood very close to it, curious as to what it could mean. He lifted a hand to trace the deep cuts.

"I wonder what this could be for."

"Maybe it's from the Indians!"

"That is a very vulgar term, Foley," Lucius informed him dryly. "It only began because the Portuguese thought they had come to the east side of India. You ought to know better."

He returned to scrutinizing the arrow. His inquisitive brain became so intent that he did not perceive the approaching hoof beats until the horsemen were nearly upon them. Even though Foley was tugging at his shirt, he did not turn until he heard a furious cry from behind.

"Haaalt!"

Lucius leapt and turned a full around at that. He found himself face to face with two lines of some fifteen British soldiers on horseback. One officer in particular rode slightly ahead of the rest and was not five feet from the two travelers. It was he who had called for the company to halt.

Not a word was said beyond that. The noise of the horses puffing and snorting was enough to fill the silence. The set of the officer's jaw and the glare in his eyes conveyed to Lucius that speaking first might not be the best idea. Especially given the man's amount of support. *Strength in numbers…and musket balls.*

The officer was incredibly overweight, and Lucius was certain he saw the knees of the man's horse buckle as he dismounted. He snatched the tail of his tunic down flat over his girth and approached the pair in a rigid military march.

By the time he reached them, his moustache was all aquiver. He pointed the end of his riding whip directly at Lucius' chest. "In the name of the King's army, you will stand back from the trunk of a tree marked by the King's broad arrow or I shall have you thrashed by the King's men, so help me!"

The officer spoke loudly and rolled every *r* as far as possible. When he was done, he flipped the whip back under his arm. His face relaxed and he seemed to be expecting something from Lucius and Foley.

Lucius blinked and licked his lips. "I beg your pardon?"

The officer's glare almost returned. "These trees are marked for use as masts by the King's navy. Ergo, ye shall not touch any tree marked by the King's broad arrow or I *shall* have you *thrashed* in the name of the King by the King's men!"

"In the King's army," Foley mumbled.

Lucius tapped the back of the boy's heel with the toe of his shoe and prayed that he would keep his thoughts to himself. The officer's voice had risen to a sizeable volume once again. One meaty hand was wrapped around the grip of his riding crop as though it were the hilt of a sword. Neither of these things boded well for his being merciful if he thought the boy was being insolent.

Lucius' only desire at that moment was to diffuse the situation, and quickly at that. He bowed slightly. "My apologies, for myself and my young friend. We had no idea that we had committed any error."

"You have indeed, sir!" the officer snapped. "Do you mean to deny to a major of the King's army that you were in fact about to lay claim to a tree marked for use by the King's navy?!"

"I assure you, sir, I–"

"You call me, a major in the King's army, a liar?! I ought to have you thrashed in the name of the King's army! You ought to be summarily arrested for flagrant disrespect to the King's navy and an officer of the King's army!"

The man continued on in that vein for some minutes. After these first few sentences, the words seemed to smear together, but Lucius was quite certain he heard the phrase 'king's army' peppered throughout. In the meantime he was hastily trying to plan a way out of the situation. As the man was taking a breath, he seized his opportunity and placed a hand over his chest.

"I am grieved if my friend and I have done anything wrong. We are indebted to you for calling our attention to it. I pray you let us go in peace, and we shall never do it again."

The major squinted one eye at Lucius and sniffed mightily through his left nostril. Then he leaned back, his hands on his hips.

"Since it is impossible to fool me, I shall have to believe you, but you best hope that our paths never cross again you jack-a-nape. Elsewise I'll see you strapped to the highest yard arm in the King's navy in the name of the King's army! Maybe then you'll appreciate the importance of a good mast."

Having had his final word, the Major turned on his heel and marched back to his horse. The band rode away, leaving Lucius and Foley in a cover of dust.

"What was that about?" Foley wondered aloud.

Lucius shook his head in disgust as he began to dust himself off. "*That* is called turning the other cheek."

Chapter 27

June 30, 1765

Foley did his very best not to squirm and fidget on the hard pew that Sunday. He wanted to prove to the Professor that he could do it. He could sit through an entire sermon without moving if he tried. Alas, he tried too hard. Just before the preacher was done, a sudden cramp in his thigh caused the boy's leg to suffer some sort of spasm. His foot flew up and rammed into the underside of the pew directly in front of him. The gentleman sitting on that particular pew snorted and cleared his throat. Foley glanced at Lucius apprehensively. His friend was either ignoring the incident or truly focused on the preacher's words.

A movement in the pew in front of them drew Foley's attention. The woman seated to the man's right hissed something in his ear. She then turned her head slightly, her eye darting toward Lucius. She raised one eyebrow and then faced forward once more.

Foley grimaced. He saw at once that the lady had assumed that it was the Professor who had kicked her husband and probably thought that he had done so on purpose. Lucius remained impervious of it all, his attention being devoted to the sermon. Foley resolved to get him to leave the instant the service ended.

The preacher soon finished and the congregation was lead in one final song. A closing prayer was said, and Foley leapt to his feet. To his dismay Lucius remained seated.

"That was a lesson I needed to remember," he commented idly.

Foley noticed that the people in the pew before them were standing, but they were speaking to friends and had not turned around.

"Did you learn anything from it, Foley?" Lucius asked.

"I-er-"

Lucius lowered his brow as though suspecting a lie to follow. "Foley."

The boy huffed dejectedly. "To be honest, Professor, I had trouble listening completely today."

Lucius rose and placed a hand on the boy's shoulder. "It happens to all of us. We'll talk about it this afternoon."

"Yes, sir. Don't you think we ought to get back now?"

"Churches still make you uneasy, eh?"

"Er-yes."

Foley could not help darting another glance at the couple. They still had not looked back. Perhaps they would make it out before something was said. By the time they passed through the door to the churchyard, he was sure of it. Then he heard a reedy, feminine voice from behind them.

"There they are, dear. Excuse me, sir!"

Somehow he knew without even looking that this was not going to be a conversation he would enjoy. Lucius had already turned and so he followed suit. Two couples were moving swiftly towards them, the elder along with a much younger pair.

Foley grimaced, but Lucius smiled kindly.

"Were you speaking to me, madam?"

"I was!"

Her face betrayed no emotion, but Foley still cowered half behind Lucius.

"I am Muriel Faraday, and this is my husband, John Faraday."

"A pleasure to meet you both. I am Professor Lucius Wolgath."

Both men bowed and Mrs. Faraday curtsied.

"I want to speak to you about what happened during the service."

Lucius appeared much puzzled, his brows knitting together. "What happened?"

"Yes! You kicked my husband's pew from behind."

Foley gulped. It was worse than he feared. He saw Lucius open his mouth to reply. Then he hesitated and turned a knowing eye to the boy.

"Is this true?"

Foley grimaced again and scuffed the ground with his foot.

Lucius turned back to the couple. "Mr. Faraday, Mrs. Faraday, may I introduce Foley Princeton? I believe the quarrel is with him."

John Faraday spoke up then. "But there is no quarrel at all. We simply want to thank him."

Foley's head snapped up. "Thank him?!"

"Yes!" Mrs. Faraday intoned. "My husband has become notorious for sleeping at odd moments."

Faraday grinned a small grin. "Tis a consequence of being so old, I'm afraid. It seems that whenever I sit still for very long, I find myself snoring before I know what's happened."

"We've all been trying to help him with it," his wife went on. "Especially in public. It seems that you noticed it before the rest of us today, boy."

Foley breathed a deep breath of relief. Having dodged that trouble, he was not keen to try his hand at lying. (In fact he had learned not to try his hand at lying very often at all these days).

"Actually it was an accident, ma'am," he said. "I was sorry to have kicked you, sir, but I'm happy to be of help."

Faraday chuckled heartily. "That's all the better, my boy!"

"Well, we've met your son, now you must meet ours."

Foley started to reply to the lady, but found that he did not want to open his mouth. He felt Lucius looking down at him, but neither one said a word. Then the younger couple stepped forward.

"This is our son, Garret, and his wife, Lavinia."

"How do you do?"

"I could not help but overhear," Garret remarked. "You said that you are a Professor?"

"Yes," Lucius replied. "I am a graduate of Cambridge in England."

"Fascinating. Pray tell, what has brought you here from all the way over there?"

Foley glanced worriedly at Lucius. His smile was wan, but his tone was easy.

"I'm afraid that is a very long story, and much too dreary for a day as beautiful as this."

Garret laughed lightly. "I must say, Professor, that you have officially piqued my interest. I regret that my wife and I are leaving for home from here, else I would insist that you spend the afternoon relating the story to us."

"We are merely passing through as well," Lucius told them. "We are headed south."

"So are we," Garret said even as he glanced at his wife. "We are residents of Savannah in Georgia."

The name sparked a sudden memory in Foley. He tugged at Lucius' sleeve. "I think we might be heading that way next, Professor."

"Why do you say that, Foley?"

"I saw Mandrake painting a new sign. I couldn't read it, but Victoria was making me tell her the letters. I remember *s* and *v* and a lot of *a*'s."

"Sounds like Savannah all right," Garret said. "As soon as you're there, you must seek us out."

"It shouldn't be difficult for you to find Garret's office," Lavinia said. "He's a well-known lawyer."

"Now see how well this has all turned out?" Mrs. Faraday said with delight.

"I'll say!" Foley exclaimed.

Old Mr. Faraday chuckled at him. "Even so, young man, I would not recommend that you go about kicking anyone else's pew."

"Yes, sir."

They said their farewells, and Lucius and Foley headed for the town common where the cart was stationed.

"We are doubly blessed," Lucius declared happily as they walked. "Good company and a good sermon."

Foley nodded in unthinking agreement. He was still quite elated that he had not run into trouble for his misstep. He was trying so very hard to be good, after all.

"About that," Lucius continued. "You said you were not able to concentrate on the preacher's words."

"Yes, sir."

"The lesson had to do with remembering those less fortunate than yourself."

Foley thought on this for a moment, shoving his hands into his pockets. "I wonder who's remembering me."

He said this curiously, almost absently. He thought of his mother, whom he naturally assumed to be awaiting her journey to heaven. It was nice to think that maybe she remembered him. It was even nice to think that his younger siblings might remember him, but then the image of his father loomed in his mind. He shrugged the thoughts away. It did not matter, because who among them could reach him?

"I remember you, Foley."

"Huh?" He looked up at the Professor feeling almost confused by the statement. Lucius looked serious indeed with his brow furrowed over his spectacles.

"When we met you were destitute, aimless, and hungry. I did what I could for you, and when an opportunity was given me, I remembered you. I have brought you as far as I am able, and if the time comes that I can, I will take you further still. It is for you not to forget that you are no longer destitute and hungry while others around you might be."

Foley thought back on the beginning of their companionship. He could not deny what the Professor had said. The first thing the man had ever done for him, after all, was to give him his coat. He touched the sleeves on his arms (which Victoria had tailored to his small frame). There had been a mere two or three nights spent in the Professor's company that he had gone to bed without a bite to eat. Whenever he was able, the Professor had always seen to it that he had what he needed.

"I got one question, Professor," he said after all this thought.

"What is that?"

"What's *aimless?*"

"To be aimless is to be without purpose."

Foley gave a sure nod. "Our purpose is to get to England."

"Our purpose must be to serve God and Savior first." Lucius' answer was swift, but then his eyebrows knitted together in uncertainty. "Do you want to go to England with me, Foley?"

They were within sight of the cart then. The pair stopped and the boy turned to face him with a simple grin.

"I want to go where you go, Professor!"

"I noticed you didn't correct the Faradays when they assumed you were my son."

Foley dropped his eyes then, an embarrassed flush flooding his cheeks. "I didn't want to."

"I see."

Lucius smiled comfortingly, though the boy's eyes were still turned down. When Foley did look up, his expression was stern. There was a hint of defiance in his small face. "I'd just as soon not if somebody does it again."

Lucius might have laughed. His heart was warming with love for the boy; a love that had been growing steadily and quietly ever since he had come to know him. He knew without a doubt that he would care for him as a son. Still there was the matter of the pride to deal with…

Lucius crossed his arms. "I will accept that only if you will remove that disobedient scowl from your face. I will not have anyone thinking I am a no-account father, even if it means embarrassing you in public every time you over-step yourself. Is that quite clear?"

Foley's features came alive with happiness. He smiled, all discomfiture forgotten. Although he fully understood Lucius' short speech, his young brain moved beyond the discipline of it and latched onto the happier meaning. "Yes, sir! Thank you, Professor!"

Lucius allowed himself a smile then and shook his head. "There's hope yet for you, Foley."

Chapter 28
July 2, 1765

The travelers continued on, and two days later noble Wendy pulled the cart into the town of Savannah just inside the border of the colony of Georgia. It was a thriving, bustling area, full of business and motion and noise. Mandrake was the only one of the four that had ever before seen the place, and so he merely regarded it with a scrutinizing eye. His principle thought was to determine where best to situate his cart for the next several days. Foley and Victoria took in the scenery around them with equal measures of curiosity and interest. To Lucius it may as well have been just as quiet as the last several towns they had passed through. The travel had grown wearisome for him, and after all, there was really only one town in all Creation that was likely to hold his attention for long. It lay half a world away across the ocean.

The day began very slowly under the cover of a light rain. As it lifted they gradually began to see more customers. By late afternoon Mandrake was every bit as optimistic about Savannah as he had been about the other settlements.

"We're bound to do even better tomorrow!" he boasted. "So long as the doc in town doesn't take offense to us, that is. Our profits'll be as handsome as my square chin by the time we leave here."

Lucius was only partially paying heed to his employer's words. He had the infamous journal of remedies open before him. He was slowly turning the pages, searching for a particular method of preparing beet root, but he was having difficulty concentrating even on something as simple as that.

What's the matter with my head today?

Mandrake, affronted that Lucius did not seem as eager as he was, soon spoke up again. "Wouldn't you agree, Professor?"

"I think it's rather soon to say for certain," Lucius remarked begrudgingly.

"That's a poor excuse for enthusiasm," Mandrake huffed. "Look at how well we've done so far together. Don't you think we can pull it off again? And time and again at that. Ha ha!"

In spite of himself, Lucius did feel that he was smiling. "Yes. God above has blessed us, no doubt."

Mandrake waved a flippant hand. "Nonsense. Tis all thanks to you and your concoctions. Along with a little help from my old granny's notes, of course." He turned to Victoria then and continued his self-promoting speech.

A bitterness rose up in Lucius. He set the book aside and faced Mandrake. The expression he wore was enough to give the other man pause. In fact he stopped midsentence to ask,

"What's got into you, Lucius?" He chortled, and his wide girth shook. "You look like you just saw somebody die."

"Or someone dead." Regardless of his anger, Lucius worked to remain stoic. He crossed his arms before him. "I will not hear God and His works demeaned as nonsense by you or anyone else. I am a failure in truth if I have not proven that to you by now."

He kept his hard gaze aimed at Mandrake. His brows were low, and he hoped that in that instant he appeared as antagonized as he felt. His very insides seemed to twist at such a foolish jest. Mandrake, in his turn, seemed confused and then careless. "You take these things too seriously, Professor! I was only complimenting your diligent work after all."

There was a slight tightening of the man's eyes which impressed to Lucius that his words were not nearly so calm as they sounded. He took the observation in and was unmoved.

"Matters of respect to God are highly serious. Do try to remember that for your own sake."

Lucius turned to stalk away, but not quickly enough to miss hearing Mandrake's parting jibe.

"He must not be listening today! He hasn't struck me dead yet!"

Lucius bit his tongue and continued on without a backward look. An obvious glare marred his forehead. Anger left a vile taste inside his mouth. It was a wonder that he had not reacted more strongly. Stepping back and knowing that the Lord will take His vengeance in His own time is a hard lesson to keep when the errant child continues to cry out in mockery.

His feet carried him swiftly. Before long his temper cooled, but he continued to roam, not having any desire to return too soon and be provoked again. Being in a strange place, it was not too long before he realized that he was unsure of just how to return. This served his purpose well, and he slowed his pace to a stroll, content to study the buildings as he passed.

It was, without question, an attractive settlement. The streets were precise and even. He first passed a block of one-story homes. Then a block of shops. Then of two and three story homes. Then a common ground for livestock. There was no doubting the success of the people. Everywhere he turned people were working industriously at some task or other. The old men stood on the corners or in the shop doors talking of business or family. The very young chased one another through the yards, lending smiles to all who heard their merry laughter.

Lucius did not draw looks of curiosity from the passers-by as he had in the smaller towns thus far. This place was so large and so populated that he did not stand out at all. Instead most everyone greeted him with a cordial nod and a pleasant expression. This he enjoyed and happily returned. He still struggled with the attention that came with being considered a novelty. Being nearly ignored was a welcome change. He was quite surprised when, half an hour later, an unfamiliar voice called out to him.

"Professor Wolgath!"

He paused, so perplexed that he wondered if he had actually heard anything at all. But then a kindly hand landed on his shoulder.

"Is that you, sir?"

Lucius turned and knew the man at once, though his name escaped him. It was the lawyer from the church he had attended three days ago.

"-thought so," the man was saying. "I'm glad to see you made it into town. Garret Faraday."

"Of course, sir." Lucius bowed slightly. "It is good to see you again. I trust your lovely wife is well."

An odd look came over the man then. The corner of his mouth quirked up in near laughter.

Lucius blinked, puzzeled. "Have I said something out of place?"

"Not at all," Faraday murmured. The man seemed breathless with amusement. "It's just that two days ago my wife informed me that she is with child."

"Ah, huzzah!" Lucius exclaimed. "I congratulate you, sir."

Garret thanked him and they stood talking for a few minutes more before the man invited Lucius to his office.

"I was just heading back there myself," he explained.

Lucius fidgeted with the cuff of his left sleeve. "I should be happy to, but may I ask why it is that you wish to talk to me?"

Garret buried his hands in his pockets while his lips curled into an unobtrusive smile. "I told you when first we met that your situation piqued my interest. I am still hoping to coax you into revealing your story."

Lucius gave a small sigh. He had feared as much. He was not at all eager to begin that conversation. Garret Faraday would not-could not-turn out to be an addled man. If he were to hear the story, he would eventually ask how it was that Lucius landed on the dreadful voyage in the first place. How was he supposed to explain that he still did not *have* an explanation? He still had no idea how the entire ordeal began and he had not put much thought into it. All of his efforts had been focused on returning to England regardless. When he did take an instant to think back and wonder, it was difficult to recall all of the seemingly innocent events that occurred just before his departure.

All these things he considered during the short walk to Garret's office, even as he spoke lightly to the man. He followed him to one of the upper rooms in a two-story building, and his host called for tea as they went. Once he was seated before Garret's wide desk, the man wasted no time. He leaned back in his chair and clasped his hands over his belly.

"Now! Tell me how it is that a Professor of Cambridge came to play second fiddle to a tonic peddler."

"Funny you should say that… Second fiddle." Lucius had hoped for a much more subtle turn in the conversation; one that might be more easily avoided. "But Robert Mandrake does not treat any one of us with more favor than the others."

"You are reluctant to tell me?"

Lucius' glance, which had been wandering around the room, jumped to the face across from him. His look was placid and kindly and wholly unintimidating. Such a man of seeming honesty deserved an honest answer.

"I shouldn't like to tell you, no."

Garret considered and then leaned forward over his desk. "I think that perhaps if I were to explain to you my purpose here, you might be more forthcoming with your story. Are you willing to listen, Professor?"

Despite his own misgivings, Lucius' natural curiosity had arisen to the surface of his mind, as it was so wont to do. He nodded once.

"I myself was born here, in the Colonies, as was my wife. I attended Yale and apprenticed for several years in Connecticut before my wife and I decided to come back to the town we grew up in, which was in South Carolina. Then, a few years after that, I was offered a position here."

The door opened behind Lucius and a very young clerk entered bearing a tea service on a polished wooden tray.

"Yes, bring it here. Thank you, Bevins."

The clerk set the tray on the corner of the wide desk. He then poured from the steaming pot and managed to burn himself before handing each man a cup. When the clerk was gone, Lucius set to making his tea.

"As a lawyer, I serve many residents in town as well as some that live farther out," Faraday began. He paused and watched as Lucius meticulously added sugar and incredibly precise amounts of cream. When the Professor was satisfied, he lifted the cup to his lips and his eyes to Faraday. "Go on."

"I was one of the first lawyers to come to the settlement. In fact men of my occupation were banned from Savannah by law until just ten years ago. The colony of Georgia was first settled in this very city. General Oglethorpe and a group of trustees purchased the land for the colony and drew up a plan for Savannah."

"Oglethorpe," Lucius repeated. "Is that the same James Oglethorpe who served in Parliament all those years?"

"The very same. He oversaw an investigation long ago of gaols in England. Specifically those gaols that housed transgressors of politics or certain monetary crimes."

"Such as debt or embezzlement?"

"Exactly. What he found was that many of the wardens of these gaols were implementing torturous practices unbeknownst to the higher authorities. He, along with the committee conducting the investigation proposed that if many of these inmates were given the opportunity to separate themselves from their current situations, they could in fact become the industrious citizens of the Crown that they were before-or never were before as the case may be."

"I understand, but how does this concern you or me?"

Garret smiled and leaned back in his chair. "That, Professor, is precisely my point. The situation concerns everyone in the American Colonies. You see, when the idea of Georgia was first conceived, it was actually in response to pleas from the Carolinians. They were unsettled by the lack of settlements-if you'll pardon the pun-twixt them and the Spanish in Florida. No one much cared for the idea of sending prisoners to populate it, but then they had no choice when it came to that."

Lucius found that he would tend to agree. "Having convicts settled and free in the vicinity of honest colonists does sound unwise."

"Not convicts," the lawyer corrected him. "The people sent here were very carefully selected and had never been convicted of anything. They were those left with no options with which to better their circumstances. In the interest of appeasing the Carolinians and emptying a few more gaols to make way for murderers and the like, it was decided that people in such circumstances be sent here. Once a town was established and some comfort could be offered, the colony began attracting 'honest colonists' as you called them. Meanwhile, England continues to offer our port as an alternative to imprisonment for those who meet the requirements."

By this time Lucius was nearly finished with his tea. "This is a very interesting tale, but you still have not mentioned your purpose in all of this, sir."

"To the point then. My purpose is simple. I want to see to it that those who are sent here from England do what they came to do."

Lucius half shrugged at the man. "And what is it that they come to do?"

"Better their worth, Professor Wolgath."

A spark seemed to leap across Faraday's eye. It had been evident, if not obvious, throughout their entire discussion thus far that the subject was one he was passionate about. Until then, Lucius could not pinpoint what or why, but that single comment gave him a notion. Could it be that the man was so enthusiastic about helping people to improve themselves and their situations? Admirable indeed if it was true.

"Does that help you to understand, Professor?" he asked excitedly. When Lucius did not respond, he went on. "I want to offer something more than just a plot of land when their debt is paid, and I want every one of them to be able to prove that he has changed if he chooses. How can a man change the nature of his status if there are no means? I want them to have hope and confidence and purpose, and all of that through knowledge."

Notwithstanding all that he had just been told, Lucius was quite taken aback by the declaration.

"Knowledge?"

"Yes. That, and belief. Belief in the God and Savior that many of them have yet to truly see."

Lucius was astounded by the man's zeal. "And you want my help in this?"

"I am considering it strongly."

"You know almost nothing about me."

"I know that you seem to be a Christian brother, and-" he added with an easy grin, "I believe you are more than you appear to be."

"Why would you assume that?"

"Because you are the first professor I have ever met with patches in his shirt sleeves."

Lucius' eyes unconsciously darted down to take stock of his thin clothes. "Are there no other teachers in Savannah?"

"None willing to visit our prison."

"I ask that because I will be forced to turn you down." Faraday cocked an eyebrow, and so Lucius explained. "I have no other means of supporting myself than my employment with Robert Mandrake. The position requires me to travel constantly."

"I am not asking you to take up a charity with me, Professor," Faraday hurried to say. "If you are right for the part, it would be a paying occupation for you. I would personally see to it that you are given no less than what you are receiving now as payment."

Lucius could hardly believe what he was hearing. To teach, and for a Christian employer. Assisting those unfortunates who wanted-and needed-help. Even as he considered it, a measure of happy desire swelled within his heart.

"I must say," he murmured, "it is a most pleasing offer to behold."

Garret chuckled at Wolgath's serious expression. "Then take hold of it, man!"

Chapter 29
July 3, 1765

"Doesna seem that we did quite as well today as we usually do," Victoria remarked as she sliced a large, round potato into a small pot.

Mandrake nodded and pulled a pensive drag from his pipe. "I must admit that I wasn't trying as hard as I normally do, but then the Professor had me preoccupied." He cut a sly, almost amused glance at Wolgath.

Lucius and Foley were sitting to one side, deep in study together. Lucius had been following along over the boy's shoulder as he read a simple exercise. Then, when he noticed that he was the object of conversation between the others, he looked up.

"You thought I wouldn't catch on to what you were getting at, telling me that I should start reading through this book for myself." He held his grandmother's journal of remedies aloft.

Lucius remained almost deathly still. "Excuse me?"

"You thought I wouldn't know why you were pushing it at me, but I'm on to you, Professor."

Lucius cleared his throat, but made no reply. He had not wanted Mandrake to know about Faraday's offer. If he did not secure the position, and Mandrake somehow knew about it, it might jeopardize his current employment. Surely the man could not have known!

"A businessman is only as good as his knowledge," Mandrake prattled on. "There's no doubting that, but you're not the sort of man to just give a fellow the answer, are you?"

"I-"

"You want to make sure a lesson learned is learned well. Why I was worried sick when you left this morning trying to figure out what I would do if something happened to you. Then, as soon as you come back, you handed me the answer when you handed me ol' granny's book."

Lucius felt his squared shoulders relax at Mandrake's explanation. "You really think that?"

"It's only smart for the both of us to have a handle on these recipes. Even tried my hand at it earlier. Made that whole pot of sassafras tea by myself, and nobody was the wiser!"

Victoria's eyes grew wide with shock. "Really?" She gazed at the mug beside her with more than a small measure of suspicion and slowly pushed it away.

Mandrake simply laughed at her reaction. "Ah, come on, girlie! You didn't notice 'til just now. I mixed it up special for you and everything."

Victoria gave him a wry grin. "Allow me to return the favor."

From her other side she lifted a paper-wrapped bundle into view. Setting it on a wide rock, she unfolded the covering to reveal a modest-sized fish. Then she drew a long knife and began polishing it on her apron.

"My ma used to have a few remedies of her own, you see," she said conversationally. "She used to say that simmering fish eyes in a stew gave ya better eyesight and better hair."

She brought the knife down with vicious force and severed the fish's head.

Mandrake's expression was pinched and pale. "Truly?"

"Oh, yes. But look at ye, now! There's naught for ye to worry about. I'll ladle around them. Ma always said if ye ate the whole thing yer hair would fall out. Can't really remember what that's supposed to do to yer eyes. Oh well."

She brought the knife down again to cut off the creature's tail.

"Old wive's tale anyway."

Lucius shuddered. "Ah, V-Victoria? Did I mention I've been invited to eat somewhere else?"

She looked up, one eyebrow dropping low. "No, ye didn't."

"My apologies. I had intended to ask Foley, too. It's a couple we met at church, and they live here in Savannah, you see."

The girl *humphed* and looked down at her fish. "All right. I suppose I can keep these eyes good 'til tomorrow."

Mandrake laughed a hoarse laugh and threw a desperate glance at Lucius, who tried his best not to notice. Foley puffed out a breath of relief. Lucius was thankful that he was smart enough not to express his appreciation until later.

"Thank you for saving my neck, Professor," he breathed when they were two blocks away from their destination.

Lucius pursed his lips to hide his merriment. "I think it was your stomach I saved."

"That too!"

"You must remember to be very polite to this family," Lucius warned, his tone growing serious. "They never actually told me to invite anyone else, but I wanted to bring you anyway."

Foley turned a perplexed face up to him. "How come, Professor?"

Lucius sighed and clasped his hands behind his back. "I must tell you something in confidence, Foley."

The boy beamed at him. "Anything! I can keep a secret!"

"Mr. Faraday-" Lucius broke off, wondering if he should tell the boy at all. Resolute, though unsure, he began again. "Mr. Faraday is considering me for employment as a teacher of sorts."

"Really?"

Foley's voice betrayed no emotion, so Lucius continued to explain. "I am very interested in it. As a matter of fact, I have prayed that he accepts me for it. He has guaranteed me no less pay than what I receive now, so I would still be able to give the same to you."

Up until that point, Foley's energetic walk had deteriorated into a trudge. His hands were shoved deep into his pockets and his chin drooped toward his chest. To any eavesdropper on the conversation, it would have been obvious that Foley was convinced he was about to be sent away-again. When the affirmation came that he would be allowed to remain with Lucius, his gaze flew up to him. His voice filled with excitement.

"Really?"

Lucius was somewhat bemused by the boy's surprise. "Yes, of course, Foley."

"Good!" His pace picked up then. "Don't worry about a thing, Professor. I'll keep up my manners. I'll be just like a gentleman."

"And don't try to add your own input if they start asking me questions."

"Huh? What do you mean?"

"Be quiet."

"Oh. Right, Professor!"

Quicker than Lucius thought they should, they arrived at the lot. The house was larger than Garret's offices and magnificently crafted. Pale light filtered through the delicate curtains in most every window of the ground floor. Smoke puffed up from the chimney in easy clouds. A curving path of flat stones led to the porch steps. There was no mistaking the fact that the occupants of this house were well-off.

A maid gave them entrance, but Garret and his wife were not far from the door. Garret's smile was bright as he surveyed the pair.

"Good evening, Professor. I see you brought your boy too. Wonderful! You both remember Lavinia."

"How could we forget?" Lucius replied, bowing.

Foley made what he estimated to be an elegant gesture by lifting his arm high and then swinging it out behind his back as he bowed.

"M'lady!" he cried in an unnaturally deep tone.

Lucius felt the blood drain from his face, but the Faradays did not seem to notice either Foley's performance or his own discomfiture.

"We are so glad that you consented to join us," Garret told them. "Allow me to lead you to the dining room. I hope neither of you is half as hungry as I, or there shan't be enough to go around!"

The Faradays' home was rustically charming. Comprised entirely of cedar from the floorboards to the rafters, it was perfectly decorated in what Lucius thought was a very familiar style with traditional European furnishings and flourishes. The dishes and even the gleaming silverware had been imported. Lucius found himself wondering at the fact that two individuals who had been born colonists seemed to have developed a decided liking for the styles embraced abroad.

Garret saw his wife to her seat before taking his own at the head of the table. Lucius had the place across from Lavinia with Foley directly beside him. The maid hurried to provide another placement for the boy as they sat. Foley reached for his napkin and flipped it open with a *snap*.

Lucius longed for a moment alone so that he could berate the boy for putting on such an act-innocent though it be. Instead he looked to his host and hostess. "I do hope it's no trouble that I brought Foley along."

"Not at all!" Lavinia insisted. "You are both most welcome."

"Had I been thinking when I invited you," Garret added seriously, "I would have suggested that you bring him myself."

Even as they spoke, dishes of steaming stew were placed before each of them. A long platter of bread was set in the center of the table along with a dish of butter and another of thick cream.

"If I may ask, Professor," Garret continued as the meal was set, "I have not heard you speak of a wife. I presumed that you are not married. Is that correct?"

"I'm not married," Lucius replied. He had an odd feeling when he said it, as though his lips had gone numb with the words. "Not-not yet."

Garret gestured to Foley. "Then the two of you are all you have?"

Lucius hesitated for the briefest span of time, but when he spoke, he was certain of his reply. "We are each other's family now."

Garret took in the cryptic answer smoothly and went on. "A decision such as this is one that would affect your family. It is right that the boy hear of it now." He glanced beyond Lucius to Foley and a smile came to him. "I'll wager he is almost as eager to hear about all this as he is to eat that stew he is staring at so ravenously."

Foley's eyes were nearly as large as the bowl before him.

"Shall we say grace?"

Without waiting for an answer, Garret began the prayer, and when he was finished, Foley was the first to lift his spoon. The Faradays each took a piece of bread. Lucius pretended to carefully add cream to his stew, but he could not honestly have said that he was giving it much attention.

"If I may, Mr. Faraday," he began, "I am curious about the position. What would it entail?"

"Simple teaching, nothing more," he replied as he took up his own spoon. "Most of the prisoners here cannot read or write and many have no knowledge of arithmetic. There are many in prison to this day who welcome the opportunity to better themselves."

"So it would not be mandatory?"

"No." Garret took a massive bite of his bread and chewed slowly for a moment. "There will be but one stipulation on your curriculum. We would ask that you always have your Bible present so that the men may talk with you about it as well. Knowing you to be a fellow Christian, I have faith that you will handle that part of it admirably."

"You said we," Lucius remarked. "Who else will have authority over my situation?"

"Certain men who find it in the best interests of a community to offer just opportunity to all who will accept it. It is their generous donations throughout the year that will pay your salary. Being the commendable gentlemen that they are, they have chosen to remain anonymous in this endeavor. I, as their lawyer and friend, am not permitted to discuss them further."

"I understand. Are there any other regulations?"

"Just one. That you sign a binding contract for one year at this post."

Lucius felt his enthusiasm wan. *One year.* Well, what would that matter? It would take him that long to be able to make it back to England in any case. At least if he signed with Garret he would have guaranteed income for one year. *Still, one year is a very long time. One-seventieth of my existence. Roughly.*

"Now I'll take my turn then," Garret went on. "My curiosity is overwhelming me."

Lucius looked down at his dish. He could well guess the question.

"How did you come to be here?"

Lucius weighed his answers, and they were not good. None of the simple responses he would have preferred to give would satisfy Garret with the information he wanted. His hand was forced. Without looking up he parted his lips.

"I don't know."

Silence fell for several seconds. Lucius had no desire to meet the Faradays' stares. Foley covered his uncertainty well.

Garret was first to move, casually taking a drink from his cup before-

"I beg your pardon?"

Lucius was not certain if he had not heard his quiet words, or if that was simply his next question, so he continued.

"I do not know why I was sent here from England."

Lavinia tilted her head forward. "You mean to say that you do not know how you came to be on a ship?"

"I am painfully aware of that, Mrs. Faraday," he murmured as he looked up. "I walked aboard willingly. The problem was that I was told the ship was bound for an entirely different place. I never dreamed-"

Lucius broke off. He cast a sheepish glance down at his plate. He was more embarrassed than he cared to admit by the fact that his voice had cracked. Still no one else spoke.

"Whether it was all just a horrible accident or a calculated act is beyond me to say, but it matters little. This experience has tried me more than any other in my life. I hope and pray that I have come out the better for it and long to see its end."

When he had spoken thus, Lucius simply waited for a reply. He was not anxious, for he had no doubt that they thought him odd. His story was perplexing even to himself, but it was true. If the couple would not accept truth, then perhaps it was best that they turn him away in any case.

It was Garret's turn to perplex him. The man leaned back in his chair and crossed his arms. "Well, you have done it again, Professor!"

Lucius stared as though he could not quite make him out.

"You have piqued my interest," Garret told him. "I am going to have to insist that you accept my offer so that I can keep you close by. It would take at least a year to find you out it seems."

Lucius' forehead wrinkled as his eyebrows rose.

Lavinia seemed to stifle a chuckle and placed a hand on Garret's arm. "You will soon realize, Professor, that my husband has the gift of spontaneity."

Lucius-who was still attempting to cover his astonishment-looked to the lady. "Does he, ma'am?"

The corners of her eyes crinkled with merriment. "We were wed two weeks after we met."

"What say you, Professor?" Garret wondered as he lifted his glass. "Will you sign?"

There was nothing for it. Lucius raised his own cup. "I would like a look at the contract, but-yes, I believe I will."

Chapter 30
July 4, 1765

Mandrake's small eyes leapt from Lucius to Foley and back again. Then he gave them a crooked grin. "Awe, don't be teasin' me now, Professor." He waved them away as he bent to lift a satchel of supplies into the back of the wagon. "The morning's wearing," he grunted. "It's time for us to get a move on."

Lucius propped his hands on his hips and sighed. "I'm sorry, Robert, but I am quite serious. I have been offered a position here, and I accepted it."

From the corner of his vision, Lucius saw Foley cross his arms and give a stiff jerk of his head to silently emphasize his statement. Victoria was bustling about making sure everything was gathered into the cart. She gave no sign that she was aware of their conversation.

When Mandrake turned from the cart, he was truly serious. "You can't mean it!"

"I'm afraid I do," Lucius declared.

Anger flared in Mandrake's features. "And how are we s'posed to continue on without you?"

"You have the journal and you have my notes. I spent last night writing several pages of recommendations."

Mandrake looked away and grunted his thanks.

Lucius could not help but feel amused. Through the man's gruffness he could see him giving way to the idea. He wondered how much longer it would be before he realized that with Lucius gone from the equation, he would be entitled to a much larger portion of the profits.

"I have tarried with you one month and made no long-term agreements with you," Lucius went on. "You must admit that I am not breaking any word between us."

Mandrake rolled his eyes back to him and shrugged. "Your choice. I suppose those notes of yours will have to do. By the looks of the boy I reckon he aims to stay with you."

"Just so."

Mandrake stepped forward and took a knee before Foley, nearly falling over due to his wide weight. "You've made me sorta proud of you, lad. He ever cuts your wages, you come and see me." He winked and shook Foley's hand.

The boy mumbled his thanks and drew his arm back.

Mandrake rose and offered his hand. Lucius took it and placed his other on the man's shoulder. "I am grateful for the opportunity you gave me."

Mandrake shrugged again and pointed a finger at Lucius. "You gave me something more, eh?"

He was speaking of the remedies, of course. Lucius' smile was wane. "It wasn't the best that I might have shown you."

The older man shook his head. "Ah, Professor." With that he turned his back on him and would have gone to the cart, but Victoria caught his eye. "And what about you? You gonna stay with them?"

She gave Lucius the merest glance before addressing Mandrake. "Are ye willin' to pay me what he does now?"

Mandrake nodded. "I'll put up some extra if you'll promise not to cook fish ever again."

She cocked one hip to the side saucily and grinned. "Agreed."

While Mandrake went to see that Wendy was ready to depart, she approached Lucius and Foley to say her goodbyes.

"You're not staying, Victoria?" Foley piped up.

She regarded him in thought. "I think not." With that she reached out and rumpled his hat.

"Awe, come on, Victoria!"

She chuckled and looked to Lucius. "It's farewell then."

"Are you certain?" For his part he could not quite figure out why she should want to remain with Robert. Then again she had always gotten along with the man better than he had.

"I am," she said. "That is unless ye're willin' to make an honest woman outta me."

Lucius drew in a breath and his eyes widened in shock. In times to come when he looked back on the memory, he was never able to discern whether or not she was in earnest. Nevertheless he could only give one answer.

"I cannot."

The easy grin remained on her face and she hitched one shoulder. "Thought not. Be seein' ye then, Lucius."

They watched as she pulled herself up into the cart and it trundled away. They had no view of Mandrake in the driver's seat, but Victoria was clearly visible in the back. Once she turned around and gave them a cheery wave. Lucius bowed low. It was the last gesture he could offer her. He could not claim any great affection for the woman, but neither would he have minded her continued acquaintance. There was something almost resigned in her leaving that caused him some regret.

"Now what, Professor?"

Lucius looked officiously down at Foley. "What do you mean what?"

"I don' know."

"Weren't you paying attention at all last night? Were you too busy with your soup to listen to what was being said?"

At the mention of the delicious meal, Foley nodded his head without shame. "Yes, sir! It was the best I ever tasted."

Lucius could not hold his serious expression at that. "Well then I suppose you'll be glad to hear what was said while you were eating. There is a small cabin on the lot behind the Faradays' home. They offered to rent it to me for next to nothing. You'll be within sight of their kitchen, and I tell you here and now that if I catch you trying to sneak anything out at all, I'll make good on my threat to whip you sore."

He added the last part only because Foley's jaw had fallen at the thought. Lucius laughed and turned on his heel. "Let's go see if Garret is available to let us have a look at the place, shall we?"

After a few moments of walking in relative silence, Foley posed a question. "Will we have a cook, Professor?"

"Cook? Yes, we shall have to cook." He chuckled inside at his own joke.

"That wasn't what I meant."

"I know what you meant, and the answer is no. We can fend for ourselves, never fear."

Foley looked doubtful. "Maybe we should have tried harder to get Victoria to stay. What did she mean when she asked you that question?"

"Which one?"

"About making an honest woman out of her."

Lucius swallowed. "It's an expression. She was wondering if I might want to marry her some day."

"Oh. Well I can see why you said 'no,' Professor."

Lucius could only stare ahead as memories of Alexcena swam in his vision.

Foley was still chatting to himself. "Victoria can be awfully pushy."

"It wasn't just that," Lucius assured him. "I had someone else in mind."

Chapter 31
July 4, 1765

As usual, Tabitha was lagging behind. Her head drooped low and she stared at the ground, willing her feet to move. Sixteen years of privileged living did not an athletic woman make. The horses had given them all respite, but still she was stiff. So stiff, in fact, that it made little difference to her whether she was walking or riding. When Leo had suggested that they walk for an hour or so and lead the horses, she had not grumbled.

Despite all discomfort she found that she was fascinated by their surroundings regularly. This curiosity fueled her desire to press on and strive to become better at being a traveler. The wild romance of the forests in a young and unbridled country had captured her interest, and she was not concerned with having it back.

So she trudged, leading a mare on her right and with Commodore padding along on her left. She could hear the voices of the others, but the words were spoken so low that she could not distinguish them. She looked up-the better to hear-in time to see Alexcena stumble.

"Easy there!"

Leo caught her with ease, gripping her arm and one of her hands. Alexcena righted herself and tittered. Their fingers remained entwined.

"Why don't we stop for a while?" Leo said even as he looked back at Tabitha.

Tabitha blushed and looked away. She was embarrassed to have fallen so far behind when she was so desperate to prove herself.

"Seems I hear a stream," Leo declared as she approached. "You ladies wait here while I go have a look."

Did he just wink at her? No…

As Tabitha sat by the road she surveyed Alexcena. Her cousin's face was flushed. A pleasant smile graced her lips, but even as she watched it faded. Then Alexcena sank down beside her.

"I wish I knew where we are going!" she mumbled. "'South' is a very large direction to take."

She was speaking of the search for Lucius, of course. Tabitha could not help but wonder how often her cousin had thought of him lately. A nagging suspicion had grown in her young mind over the past month. She was vaguely ashamed of the speculation, but the possibility seemed so natural. So easy. Checking to see that Leo remained out of sight, she determined to voice her thoughts.

"Alexcena, may I ask you about something?"

A change crossed her face, wiping it clean of the fatigue that had settled there in those few still moments. "Yes?" she replied pleasantly.

"I was-well-thinking…wondering, um-Leopold."

If Alexcena had not been watching her so closely, she might have rolled her eyes. *I will be so glad when I leave these awkward years behind!*

"What about him?"

"Are you-" She struggled for words. "-closer with him than you let on?"

The change in Alexcena was immediate. Every bit of the weakness she had worn on her countenance a brief moment earlier returned with a vengeance. For the first time in her life, Tabitha thought her cousin appeared haggard indeed.

"No," Alexcena replied and a single tear slid down her pale cheek. "I am ashamed that you would wonder such a thing."

Suddenly Tabitha was ashamed herself. She had seen Alexcena in love.

She had been brought to tears by the sight of her with Lucius, and yet she had thought she saw enough evidence-vague though it be-to wonder. Not to mention Leopold. She respected him greatly, but apparently not enough to keep from considering that he might be capable of going after his own brother's fiancé.

"We are friends," Alexcena whimpered. "He is my dear friend, as you are, Tabitha." Without another word she drew her legs up and set her chin on her knees.

The younger girl felt her heart flutter as she fought within herself to find a way out of the conversation. "I am *sorry*, Alexcena!"

Her cousin said nothing. Tabitha pursed her lips and blushed. She had never been very adept at handling difficult silences. When she began to fidget, she decided perhaps it was time to move.

"I wonder what's keeping Leopold!"

She got to her feet and plunged into the forest, relieved to escape the tension she had brought to the air. She intended to find the man near the stream. She had forgotten to give him her waterbag anyway.

She followed the sound of trickling water. It grew louder, and she caught a glimpse of it sparkling ahead. Movement drew her attention to Leo. He was visible between the tree trunks to her left, a few feet further upstream than where she stood. His coat lay in a rumpled mound on the bank and his bag was open at his feet. Even with his back to her she could clearly see the blade he held as he drew it over the skin of his cheeks, cutting away the rough stubble there.

Tabitha gritted her teeth and ignored her fervent blush. She ought to have known. Leo only left them rarely. It only made sense that the man needed private moments just as they did. She was fortunate that she had not witnessed an even more personal scene.

All this she considered as she made her way back to the road. She had developed a habit of keeping her eyes on her feet when she walked. It prevented so much stumbling. But walking by herself, she did have a need to look up to check her direction. When she did her eyes grew wide, and she sniveled in her dread.

In the midst of the brush before her was a wolf, large and cinnamon brown. It stood not five feet away. Its eyes were pale and somber. To Tabitha he looked aggressive, but even as she watched he took one step back. Despite this show of uncertainty, a shiver of fear fluttered through her shoulders as she wondered what in the world she would do.

Something large began crashing through the undergrowth behind her. A horrified scream tore from her throat as whatever-it-was behind her burst through the leaves and sticks blocking it from view.

"*Yaaarrrggghhh!*"

Tabitha could hardly believe her eyes. Leopold had leapt from the bushes, arms raised, releasing a snarling, wordless shout. His face was a fearsome mask of anger directed at the wolf. The animal cowered back. One more growl from Leo sent him scurrying away westward.

Leo relaxed his stance. His eyes were alight with enjoyment and a boyish grin played across his countenance. "I guess we showed him, eh?"

Tabitha felt cold from head to toe. Her eyes were round as saucers. Her mouth hung open in shock. Her arms were wrapped around a tree at her back. Worst of all, there seemed to be nothing she could do about any of these things before Leo turned to look at her. The sight made him chuckle.

"Never fear, ma'amzelle," he said with great cheek. "I'll keep you safe."

He started away and Tabitha followed dumbly. She was more glad than she could say that her cousin was not falling for Leo after all.

Chapter 32

July 20, 1765

After a mere two weeks in his new post, Lucius had not only grown accustomed to it; he had grown to love it. The situation was wholly beneficial in multiple ways. He was able to work using his best skills and save a good portion of what he earned each month. This was due to the fact that the Faradays had extended their generosity by allowing him to live in the little cabin behind their home for a pittance. Foley was, naturally, staying there as well. While Lucius was away at the prison, Foley had the chance to attend a regular school. This he lamented with passion, but Lucius was fairly certain that his sour attitude was dwindling with each passing week.

Their evenings were happily spent together in their new dwelling. The cabin was comprised of an open living and kitchen area with a loft above where they both slept. Lucius was surprised by how adept Foley was at sharing the kitchen and cleaning work. That very morning he had awoken to the smell of weak coffee already brewing.

The cabin had been used for storage, though not overly much. It was mostly things that had once belonged to the Faradays. A few pots and bowls, a crooked table and two chairs, some random utensils, an old armchair, and a single chipped mug. They spent the first two nights in the loft sleeping on beds of hay. As soon as Lavinia Faraday had become aware of the fact, she had given them several blankets to use.

After the cabin was straightened and cleaned, the next order of business had been to fill it with food. The neighbors-who had proven to be kind-provided a few things by way of welcome. One gentleman had offered a small wheel of cheese. A couple across the way had given them a bucketful of milk, and one elderly lady had dropped off a rather odd-smelling pie. Fortunately it turned out to be delicious. Of course Lucius had purchased the usual necessities such as flour, coffee, sugar, jerked meat, and the like. It was the first occasion he had been given to cook in some time, and he had forgotten just how well he liked it.

"Cooking is the common man's form of chemistry," he told Foley cheerily that first night as he stirred a simple batter.

"What's chemistry?"

"It's a study of a specific type of science, Foley."

"Will I have to learn it in school?"

"I dare say not, but I will happily teach you in the evenings."

Foley held up his hands in surrender. "No thanks, Professor! I'm gonna have enough going on with everything I gotta learn at school as it is."

"Indeed you will."

Lucius had well expected such an answer from the boy, and it made him chuckle.

At last Lucius had found a small piece of the happiness he had lost when he discovered that he was going to be away from home for a very long time. Even the worrisome events of his first day's labor could not dampen his newfound contentment for long.

He was first unsettled by the sight of a rotund man in the foremost office of the jailhouse. It was none other than the excitable Major who had shouted at Foley and himself on the road one week before for examining a tree. For a moment he was optimistic that the man would not recognize him. This hope was dashed when the man shot a glare his way. It was felicitous indeed that Garret had accompanied him. The Major might well have locked him up on sight. Though the glare remained, the corners of his mouth rose with glee as he looked to Garret.

"What have you brought in today, Mr. Faraday? A vagrant, no doubt."

Garret's response was cheery. "Why should you say such a thing, Major? You can see for yourself that he is not in irons. Nor does he wear the red garb our local 'vagrants' are so wont to put on."

Lucius darted a peak at Garret, wondering if he had meant the comment the way it sounded. He kept his usual, pleasant expression.

The Major sniffed, ruffling his moustache as he did so. "What is it you have here then?"

"I believe you mean 'who.' This is Professor Lucius Wolgath."

The Major grunted superiorly.

"Professor," Garret went on, "this is Major Thomas Dunwhither. He and his detail have recently come to oversee our jailing facilities."

"And those who reside in them," Major Dunwhither added. "As I have reminded you time and again, *Mr. Faraday*, there are certain higher authorities who are rightfully concerned with the number of criminals here accused of political crimes. It is our duty to the King to see they are contained and punished to the furthest extent!"

"Well put," Garret said wryly, "though by your standards we should be locking up all of Parliament as well."

The Major had no reply to that, and his cheeks reddened to match his coat.

"But here we are bantering away about bureaucracy while the good Professor stands eager to begin his work," Garret continued with a suave gesture toward his friend.

"So he's the one you found for the job, eh?"

"Just so."

Dunwhither grunted again. "Well, he's got his work cut out for him, he does."

"Then I shall leave you to get him started, Major. I bid you good day, Lucius. We'll speak this evening."

Lucius watched his friend go before turning apprehensive eyes toward the Major. The man was tapping his foot and squinting at Lucius' with open dislike. He wondered if Dunwhither was weighing his options and deciding just how much trouble Faraday would cause him if he did lock the Professor up. If that theory were true, he chose not to test the man in the end. Presently his features relaxed and his tapping ceased.

"Right. I suppose we'll be seeing a good bit of each other for the foreseeable future, so I'll say what needs to be said now. If you lay one finger out of place while you're here, I'll make good on every threat I've ever thrown at you. Understood?"

"A-aye, sir," Lucius hurried to say. Part of him had already guessed that the man was nothing more than a pompous windbag. The problem was that by being an officer of England, he wielded a very real sword over Lucius' head; one he was certain he could not afford to cross. He had already seen that soldiers in this part of the world held much more authority over civilians than they seemed to in England.

"What party are you?" the Major then asked. "Whig or Tory?"

"Neither in truth, sir."

"A man without politics." Dunwhither rolled his eyes. "Well at least if you keep it that way we may not have as many problems as I thought. I'll have my lieutenant show you where you can do your teaching. Off with you."

Then Lucius, being summarily dismissed, had followed the obscure lieutenant into a small room at the far right corner of the building. It seemed that the foremost section of the jail was reserved for offices and a few visiting areas. The room was lit by a single lantern with only a table and two chairs to serve as furnishings.

"You'll be meeting with the men in here," the soldier explained. "There's always someone posted outside these quarters, so if no one is in here with you, you can always yell."

"Yell for what?" Lucius had asked innocently.

The soldier shook his head as he turned to leave. "I'll wager you'll know when the time comes. Someone'll bring your first *student* in directly."

When he had gone, Lucius sat himself down at the table with the books he had brought, his back facing the way he had come. Opposite him was another door. He stared at it for some minutes, occasionally straightening the small stack of books and shifting in his chair. Eventually some noise reached him, growing louder as it drew closer. Thumping and shouting and all manner of clatter became so thunderous that he was astonished not to find it in that very room. Then the door opened and the din rang louder. Lucius leapt to his feet as a redcoated soldier wrestled another man inside. The rough prisoner was not fighting so much as dragging his steps and lumbering around. All the while he sang a ditty, off key, and as strongly as he was able.

"-two mighty speakers, who rule in Parliament!"

"Shut your gob will you!"

"-mischief to event! Sorry, there, was that your toe?" the criminal paused to ask even as he trod on the soldier's boot. The soldier pummeled his neck and shoulders soundly, but the man only continued to sing.

"The horrid plan did lay, a mighty tax to gaaather, in North Amaricaaa!"

The soldier shoved him against the table and nimbly stepped back through the door. The lock turned and the man began to laugh. When the stranger faced Lucius, all laughter ceased. With his eyes on him, he yanked the chair out and plopped onto it.

Lucius followed suit. He surveyed the man, taking in his thick build, filthy clothes, and long beard, and wondering what in the world he had gotten himself into.

"Well?" the man said after a while. His glare deepened when Lucius did not respond right away.

Straightening his glasses, Lucius decided it was time to set to it.

"Right. My name is Wolgath. Professor Wolgath. I've been hired by certain citizens to visit this jail and apply my instructing skills to any of its inmates who choose to take advantage of my knowledge."

The man's brows knitted and then rose. "You mean you're gonna teach us? Outta those books?" He pointed with his left hand. His right moved in unison, pulled by the chain of the fetters binding his wrists. "What're you wantin' to teach?"

"Anything you wish to learn. Reading and writing, arithmetic, science. I even have my Bible if you would like to discuss that."

He waited for some reaction from the man, but he merely leaned his head to one side as though he were considering. Then the laughter returned.

"I'm too old to be learning that stuff," he scoffed.

Incredibly, the man began to get to his feet so as to leave. Lucius floundered, grasping for something to say.

"Exactly," he returned with a lame shrug. "You are too old to learn this *stuff*." He leaned back and crossed his arms. The pose did not make him appear as careless as he would have liked.

"How's that?"

"You should have learned these skills years ago as a boy, and you're probably trying to pull the wool over my eyes by implying you don't know them," Lucius went on. "Either way, I've got to be here now, so we can either brush up on what you may have forgotten or just converse. At least you're out of your cell."

This tact was a bit of a stretch. It was *possible* that the man had some education and it was *possible* that he simply did not want to be stuck in the room for an hour. At least that was how Lucius rationalized it within himself. He felt a compelling responsibility to convince the man to stay. Maybe he wouldn't accept his help now, but someday he might. The feeling came just as much from a Christian stand point as an employed stand point. True, he did not know if the man needed help, but he also had not gleaned enough to know that he did not.

"At least I'm outta my cell, eh?" he said as he slouched back down into his chair. "I don't happen to have a cell. They shove as many of us into one as they can fit, so I don't rightly see how I could call it 'mine.'" He eyed the walls darkly. "And all the rooms in this place look the same. Just bigger or smaller with more or less people inside them."

"No windows?"

"The only times I see daylight is when they let me out to work."

"Since they let you go to work, I suppose that means you were arrested for debts."

"A good lot o' those in here were. Ever since they started all these new taxes it's hard for any man to make a fair living. Then there's that Quartering Act. If a fellow can hardly feed his own family for the taxes he pays, how's he supposed to feed a few redcoats too?"

Lucius shifted his pose, leaning forward. "That is a question for a politician. I'm just a humble Professor."

"You're the one that said 'talk.' I'm just trying to oblige." He sat back and scrutinized Lucius. "How long have you been here?"

Lucius wished he could have gotten away with a simple reply. *I've been in Savannah one week...* Somehow he knew that was not what the man meant.

"I landed on American shores on the twenty-ninth of May."

The eyebrows rose and the man chuckled again. "Of this year? No wonder you don't want to talk governing."

Lucius expelled a heavy breath and looked the man in the eye. "I'm just here to do a job and to help if I can."

The expression slowly began to relax in some form of defeat.

"What work is it that you do?" Lucius asked.

The man took the prompt. "I tend horses some. Mostly I work in the cobbler's shop. The cobbler's my cousin, ya see. He helps me out from time to time. I used to work for a farmer outside of town, but once he found out why I was arrested, he wanted nothing more to do with me. Rotten Tory..."

The pair talked easily enough for twenty minutes more before a soldier came to escort the prisoner out.

"Nice talkin' to you, Professor," the man declared with a merry grin. "Next time drop your card first and I'll put the kettle on."

The interview had been difficult for Lucius. He was quite glad that it ended with a smile. The next two men to come in seemed much more timid. They were almost eager to learn what they had not in their formative years. While one struggled with numbers and wanted assistance, the other had a great interest in history and longed to be able to read of it for himself.

The fourth man was not so kind on him. The soldier led him to the chair and he sat staring at Lucius with eyes that seemed to focus on something beyond him. His expression was dull and fixed.

"Good day," Lucius said slowly. "I am Professor Wolgath."

"They said you're the new missionary."

Lucius blinked in puzzlement and concern over the man's toneless attitude. "The missionary will still come as usual. I'm here about a different matter, although I would be happy to-"

"Don't talk to the missionary. Why would I talk to you?" the man asked without really seeming to want to know.

Lucius sensed another trying visit, although this one seemed to be of a different caliber. "I apologize. I don't mean to be a nuisance, and we needn't talk at all. I'm a teacher you see. I'm here to offer my services to anyone who wishes to learn."

"A teacher?" His voice was edged with suspicion. His gaze narrowed. "What's this supposed to be about? You think we're not as smart as you because we're in prison?"

"Not at all," Lucius hurried to say.

"You think I'm a pitiable dog because I can't read and write like you?" The man got to his feet and lashed back with one leg. His chair skittered backward to clatter against the wall. His stone expression was nothing short of furious. "I don't need your charity!" he rumbled.

Rising to his feet, Lucius met his eye soberly. "I do not do this for charity. It is my job, and the opportunity is yours to refuse. But if you should change your mind, I'll be here."

Even as he spoke, a soldier burst through the door and took the man by his shoulders. As he was jerked away, the man spared Lucius one last glare.

Lucius mustered the integrity not to fall into his chair. He was troubled and shaken-to his shame-by the man's reaction. Knowing immediately what should be done, he went to the door and leaned out into the hall. The prisoner was still being pulled along farther down the way. Another soldier stood at attention directly across from him.

"What's this about?" Lucius snapped at him.

The soldier looked confused. He was a private and much younger than Lucius. His posture was cowering and almost fearful.

"That's the second man I've had who obviously did not want to be in here." Lucius' voice was much more forceful than he had intended, but the more he spoke, the more he realized the tone served his purpose. "I'm here to teach these men *if they want to be taught.* Tell them what I'm doing and stop bringing in prisoners who only want to argue with me."

"Yes, sir," the private murmured.

Lucius watched him hurry to meet his compatriot down the hall before withdrawing into the room. Crude and unplanned as it was, the order seemed to be followed perfectly well. The next man that came in looked positively ecstatic. He took his seat before Lucius could say a word and his gaze grew wide in wonder.

"You can really teach me to read?"

"Yes. I believe I can."

The old man rubbed his hands together with glee. "Let's get it done then! I just got me first letter from my missus and I can't wait to read it. I'd let the preacher read it to me, but being from my lady, it might get a little personal, ya see."

Lucius swallowed his embarrassment as well as a chuckle. "Well… I'm afraid it's a bit more complex than that, but I'll do my best if you will."

"Surely!"

"Then perhaps we'll both do well at this."

So it was that after two weeks, each of the men under his teaching did seem to be doing well in his studies. The amount of students he gained was fair. Garret was more confident than he that he would interest more still. The first man Lucius met-Mr. Timothy Corinth-made an appearance a few times a week to talk. The older man-Mr. Sheldon Cravats-had decided after two weeks that he did not have the patience to wait any longer to know what his wife had to say to him. Lucius was quite relieved to find that the note was as chaste and proper as could be. Sheldon was less satisfied.

"I waited all that time just to hear that the garden was flooded and the nag slipped her shoe again!?"

Lucius felt the astonishment cross his face and tried to clear it while comforting the man. "I'm certain if anything else had happened she would have told you."

Sheldon's brow darkened and his lip stiffened up. "Pha!" he scoffed. "Not once did she say she misses me. Not once did she say she cares. Whatever happened to absence making the heart grow fonder? Answer me that! I might as well be home with her for all the care she put into that letter. Waist o' good paper is all that was. I'll see ya, Professor."

"What's that? You just came in."

"If that's all she's gonna write to me about, it ain't worth the effort."

Lucius scrambled. "What about after you leave here? Literacy is a skill that stays with you once you have it… And you'll be able to write to your wife yourself."

Sheldon seemed to think on that for several seconds before returning to his seat. "You may have something there," he said with a grin most mischievous. "She'll never be expecting that."

Working with each man on his own had proven to be a wonderful strategy. Sheldon was a paradigm to some of the private conversations Lucius was beginning to have with the men. Such conversations, he was sure, would never have started in groups. Though he found deep and abiding encouragement in these moments, the conversations he treasured the most took place within his own thoughts.

It was in his mind that he was able to spend time with Alexcena. He wondered if he would ever grow weary of the ache such reminiscence brought to his heart. Somehow he could not imagine so. He even satisfied himself by calling it 'conditioning.' He would need all the resistance to such pain that he could get, since he faced the all-but-certain prospect of returning to England to find her married and gone.

Other thoughts and dialogues were much more pleasant and soothing. That of talking to his Lord, as he had done so often in the last few months. One-sided or otherwise, time spent in such contemplation gave balm to his soul.

And so he lived and breathed and found himself to be as comfortable and content as he could be.

Chapter 33

July 22, 1765

"Do you have any idea what town we'll come to next?"
Leo smiled and shrugged.
In truth Alexcena felt silly asking again. The question had become a regular one for her. She was routinely annoyed by the fact that there was no clear answer. She was very careful to rein in her anger, because she knew Leo had no way of knowing for certain. He in turn did his best to hide his laughter. She could see from the corner of her eye that he was looking towards her and gave an inward sigh. *At least one of us remains amused...*
"You might want to put a hand on your fellow rider."
At first Alexcena could not make sense of him. "I beg your pardon?"
Leo jerked his chin toward Tabitha, who was riding behind her atop

their horse. She glanced over her shoulder to see the girl's head bobbing to the side. Her eyelids fluttered in half-sleep.

Alexcena tried in vain to twist around in a comfortable way to hold Tabitha steady. As soon as she touched her arm, the girl gave a start and gripped Alexcena's shoulders in fear.

Leo's long laugh brought a blush to both ladies. "Why don't we stop for a rest," he suggested when he had caught his breath. "I would hate to have to pick ma'amzelle up if she were to fall from the horse."

Leo dismounted first and helped both ladies down. Alexcena shook a blanket out of her bag and spread it wide on the ground, inviting Tabitha to lie there. The girl obeyed and was soon fast asleep. Alexcena sat beside her while Leo tended the horses. She watched him but paid little attention. Her mind was wandering listlessly, and she thought she might be just as tired as Tabitha. It sounded nice to curl up beside Commodore, and-

She turned to Leo suddenly. He had flopped down under a tree with his Bible. He looked up at her sharp movement.

"What is it?"

"Where is Commodore?"

"He ran ahead a few minutes ago. Didn't you notice?"

She mutely shook her head.

Leo grinned a knowing grin. "I think you had better take a nap too. You're slipping, Ena."

Alexcena agreed. She leaned back and closed her eyes. Then she tried to fall asleep in her usual way.

Father in Heaven, You know all things. You know what is good and right in Your sight. I thank You for the hope You give us and for Your love and protection. I pray Lord, if it be Your will, that You would bless Lucius and keep him safe from the dangers abounding around him. I humbly ask that You would bless our long journey, that the effort would not be in vain. Though this is the desire of my heart, Your will be done before ours, Lord... Your will be done before ours...

She was nearly asleep when a sound invaded her thoughts. It was a simple sound; a whistle. At first she thought it must be Leo, but the melody was too far away. Shouldn't he be closer to them? Intrigued, she sat up, but saw nothing.

"Just a wagon comin' up the road."

Leo's tone was casual, but when she looked at him, his expression was stern. His gaze was focused on the grove of trees blocking the road from their view. Gradually the sounds of hoof beats and creaking wheels grew louder. The whistling became clearer, though the melody was disjointed. A woman's voice reached them then.

"Happy beast, idn't he?"

The whistling stopped, and a man's voice replied. "He's not wild... Must belong to somebody hereabouts."

"Poor thing might be lost!"

"Hmmm… You might be right there, Victoria."

Leo had come to his feet during all this banter. Alexcena wondered if he suspected the same thing she did. Sure enough, as soon as the cart passed the trees, Commodore plodded into view.

Leo hurried down the short embankment onto the road. "Commodore!"

Alexcena shook Tabitha's shoulder to rouse her. She had noticed right away that the cart was driven by a very large man. If he were to challenge Leo about the dog, there might be some trouble.

Commodore bounded past the trees to sit at Leo's feet. He was followed by a young woman with flashing red hair who stopped short by the wagon.

The large man rose to stand in the driver's box, one hand on his hip and the other holding the reins of the mule that pulled his conveyance. "I see you're familiar with our new friend."

Leo stood four feet ahead of the mule. His arms were crossed and his lips were curled up in a rakish, almost challenging, smirk. "I see you met my old one."

Commodore surprised everyone with a sharp bark. Tabitha sat up, fully awakened by it. Alexcena could only stare, perplexed, as Commodore let out another yelp and walked back toward the cart. He paraded around it in a circle. Every few steps he would emit an arrogant snort. When he was once again even with the mule, he sat and looked at Leo as if to say, 'There. That should explain everything. Now do you understand?'

But Leo did not understand. "Commodore, hither. Come on."

Oddly enough, the Great Dane whined and backed closer to the cart.

"Looks to me like maybe the doggy doesn't want to go with you," the driver remarked idly.

Alexcena rose and stepped down to Leo's side. She looked the man in the face. He gave her a lopsided smile, so she averted her gaze and surveyed the cart instead. Her eyes traveled over the patchwork cover down to the reedy woman before falling on Commodore. *What could be wrong with him?*

"Seems to me you folks are on your way somewhere," Leo said. "We'll just take our dog and you can be gone. No harm done."

Alexcena suppressed a shudder at the words. *No harm done.* Either Leo was overreacting, or the situation was much more volatile than she feared. Tension made the very air around them seem thick. Waves of anger and aggression were almost tangible around Leo's person.

The driver seemed unaware-or uncaring-of the reactions his attitude was provoking. He stroked his stubbly chin. "I don't know. The animal seems awful reluctant. Maybe I shouldn't give him to you."

"Oh, for heaven's sake, Robert!" the woman sighed with an impudent roll of her eyes. "Sure, an' ye know it's their dog."

Her voice was flippant, but when Alexcena met her eyes they were full of foreboding. She looked as if she sensed all the same things Alexcena felt.

The driver shrugged and ambled down from the cart. "S'pose you're right, Vicky. They did call him by name and all."

"I've asked ye not to call me that," the woman hissed.

"It's only right to turn him over," Robert went on. He had the nerve to lean down and tousle Commodore's ears. The dog made a low growl, and he drew himself up. "Course it's only fitting that when something is found there's a...*reward* for the finder, eh?"

Leo's glare tightened. "Is that right?"

The venom in his voice made Alexcena want to recoil. She tossed a glance at Tabitha, who sat pale-faced and staring. She flipped her fingers at their bags, hoping that Tabitha would understand. Somehow the girl did. She began hastily folding the blanket and gathering the satchels. Alexcena turned her attention back to Leo, by which time Robert was speaking again.

"Just a little thanks for finding your missing friend."

The wan smile fell from Leo's expression. "He wasn't missing and I have no intention of giving you anything. Now *step away from my dog.*"

His voice never rose, but the desired intimidation was accomplished nicely. Robert put a hand over his chest and backed away three steps. "I meant no offense, sir. None at all! I just thought you might like to know how such things are done."

"You strike me as someone who needs to do a lot more thinking before he decides to speak. Commodore, hike!"

The dog whimpered and looked mournfully back at the cart.

"*Commodore!*"

Leo's shout was enough to move him, and he dashed off passed the red-headed woman.

Alexcena turned on her heel to help Tabitha with the horses.

"We'll be heading out now," she heard Leo say as she took his horse's reins. "It was no pleasure at all talkin' to you."

He stalked by them with Alexcena, Tabitha, and two mounts in tow. The woman stepped back to allow them to pass easily.

"Need anything before you go?" Robert called after them. "We got everything for anything that ails you. We even got some of the comforting niceties for the ladies' toilette."

He failed to pronounce the word miserably, calling it instead 'toilet.' Still, Tabitha looked back.

"Oh no ya don't!" Leo exclaimed. He rushed back to take Tabitha by the arm, and glare at the man. "We are *not* interested!" He eyed the sign on the wagon with blatant disgust. *Not your doc's medicine.* Then he muttered almost to himself, "Lucius warned me about these traveling medicine mongers."

All at once the scene seemed to change. Alexcena was still walking away. She could hear the others coming behind her, but then she heard something else.

"Excuse me, sir. What was that ye said?"

Something about the woman's question struck Alexcena's attention. She turned back to listen closer.

"Ma'am?" The impatience was obvious in Leo's voice and in Robert's.

"Come on, Victoria!"

Victoria answered Leo first. "Who was it that warned you?"

"I said Lucius. My brother."

A soft smile brightened her lips. Alexcena felt as though she could not move, and, indeed, she could scarcely breathe waiting for the woman's next words.

Victoria turned to shout at Robert. "Ye go on. I'll catch ye."

He grunted and climbed into the driver's box. By the time the cart started away, Victoria was smiling at Leo again.

"I'm, ah… Victoria. Smythers. What would yer last name be, sir?"

Leo stiffened, his eyes growing round with realization. "Wolgath. My brother's name is Wolgath."

Victoria closed her eyes for a long moment. "I guessed as much. Ye smile jest like 'im."

"Do you know where he is?" Tabitha burst out. "Do you know where Professor Wolgath has gone?"

"I do."

Leo whirled around to smile at Alexcena. His expression was both elated and boyish at once. It was only then that Alexcena realized how she appeared. She did not remember feeling herself move, but somehow her hand had risen to cover her mouth. Tears were pouring down her cheeks. She was leaning her head against the horse's neck and her heart was swelling so that she wondered how she would contain it much longer. Then she felt herself smiling too.

Chapter 34
July 22, 1765

The horses pranced side by side. Tabitha sat behind Alexcena as always, but now Victoria was mounted behind Leo. She had insisted on traveling with them. In no time at all she had gathered her few belongings and told Robert of her intentions. Leo could not help but notice at the time that the man raised his voice at her. Since Victoria was not pursued when she came back to them and the cart started away again, he dismissed it. They were not two minutes down the road before Alexcena pointed out that the group was incomplete.

"Where's Commodore?"

"He's fine, Ena." Leo glanced at her and saw a doubtful look there, so he added, "Commodore, hither!"

Just as he expected the dog leapt through the trees to join them.

"Amazin', sure enough," Victoria said from behind him. "How did ye get him to do that for ye?"

Leo's grip on the reins tightened, an indication that he was more eager than he let on. "It's my brother's dog. Lucius trained him well."

From the corner of his eye, he saw a shiver run through Alexcena's shoulders. He ignored the concern in the corner of his mind. There was still much information yet to be gotten.

"I should like to know exactly where he is, Ms. Smythers."

"Last I knew of he had just been hired by a lawyer in Savannah, Georgia. That was goin' on three weeks ago."

"And you think he will still be there?"

"He told us he signed a contract with the man, though I dunno how long it was for."

Good. Maybe we have a chance this time. Leo's mind seemed to be in a state of numbness. Excitement thrummed through every fiber of him, but his mind had his body locked stiff. This he considered to be a good thing, since he might have hooted with laughter one moment and been reduced to tears the next.

"How do you know him?"

"He worked for Robert too," Victoria replied. "We all met in North Carolina. Lucius started makin' remedies for Robert, and we all traveled down to Georgia together."

"Is he well?"

Alexcena's words were so soft that Leo was not certain he had truly heard them until Victoria gave her answer.

"He's fine, dearie."

Alexcena gave one jerked nod in acknowledgement. Several times after that he caught her wiping her eyes and cheeks.

Being so late in the afternoon, the sun was nearly at the horizon. Leo knew they would need to stop soon, so he began to keep a lookout for a good place. All the while he asked more questions.

"How far is Savannah?"

"Several days at least."

"Where is Lucius staying?"

"He was offered a place in town by his new employer."

"Does he know anyone else in that town? Is there anyone who might be suspicious or dangerous?"

"There's Foley. He's a boy Lucius met long before he met me. That boy wouldn't try to hurt 'im or swindle 'im if his life depended on it. But you look like a man who knows as well as I do, there's always someone suspicious and dangerous about, whether ye see them or not."

Leo called for a halt shortly thereafter. The sun had just dipped out of sight and the trees had thinned out enough to allow them a decent area to camp. The three of them had developed a routine by then. Alexcena would begin clearing a wide area to put down blankets and Tabitha would start collecting small sticks to kindle a fire while Leo went in search of larger branches. He had picked up some beef in the last town they had passed through, and they would more than likely finish it off for their supper.

As Leo moved around the edges of the camp, he heard the ladies talking. Since the topic was Lucius-and he was within such good earshot-he couldn't help but listen.

"Victoria? We never properly introduced ourselves. This is Ms. Tabitha Winslett and I'm Alexcena Condreve."

"Nice to meet ya both."

"Have you heard my name before?"

"No."

Alexcena's voice had sounded desperate and strained. It was plain that she wanted to know if Lucius had spoken of her at all to the woman, and

Leo's heart sank to hear the answer. But Victoria was not finished speaking yet.

"I didn't have to know yer name to know ye're the one he writes to."

"He-he does?"

"He doesn't say much about ye because he keeps ye so close to his heart. He wants to protect yer mem'ry I always thought. I finally asked him about ye one day when I caught him writin'. May I ask ye ladies somethin'?"

"Of course."

"Lucius believes ye're in England. How did ye get here?"

"As soon as we knew what had happened to him, we chartered a ship to bring us here. We've been trying to find him ever since. We spoke to a man who had sailed with Lucius and he said he was heading south."

"He says he's going back to England as soon as he's able, but he expects to find ye married off."

"He what?" Tabitha blurted.

There was a long pause before Alexcena replied. "That's just what he would think. He underestimates his own value ceaselessly."

Leo took advantage of the conversation's end to make an unobtrusive re-entrance. He dropped the limbs and set to making a fire. When that was done, he gathered the water bags.

"I'm goin' to see if I can find us a bit more to drink and a place to wash up in the morning."

"We can do that when we wake, Leopold," Alexcena told him. "It's practically dark."

"Don't whine, Ena," he teased, attempting to lighten the mood. "This'll give you girls a chance to keep talkin' for a while."

Victoria surprised them by cocking a saucy eyebrow. "Afraid of the chatter, are ye?"

"All depends on who's chatting," Leo grinned, his white teeth reflecting the light of the fire. He ducked away and heard them start to talk immediately when he was gone.

Just my luck, he mused, *Alexcena's quiet enough, but what if this lady turns out to be just like Tabitha…or worse? Probably shouldn't think that… The girl is getting a mite better.*

By the time the voices had grown very faint, he still had not come across anything. The noises of the forest surrounded him. He listened hard but could not detect any sound of water. He did hear something odd, though. Something moving very near him.

"*Sssst.* Leo?"

Leo whirled around to see who had come up behind him. Had he realized the tree was so close, he would have turned the other way. As it was the upper right half of his body slammed into a cascade of low, leafy branches.

"Agh!"

Something sharp and fiery hot hit his forearm. His mind scrambled, wondering how a stick could have torn through his sleeves to stab his flesh. He clamped his other hand down over the spot, but something was very wrong. He did not feel the soft threads of his coat. Instead he felt smooth, oily scales over undulating muscle.

Snake.

There was just enough light-and just enough time-for him to have a look at his aggressor before he flung it away. The body was thin and incredibly long. More than half of it was solid black, but the tail was bone white. He did not recognize it, and that was cause for concern. He tossed it away and pressed his palm over the bite.

"Tabitha!" he snapped. "What did you come out here for?"

"I'm sorry-I didn't, I mean… Was that a snake?"

He could not see her face, but by the tone of her voice he guessed she was pale. *Why did she have to follow me? It coulda been her that was bitten!*

"Yes," he answered huffily. "Come on. You shouldn't be out here."

They began crashing through the brush together. *At least this noise might scare off anything else.*

"You were gone for several minutes," Tabitha tried to explain. "I just wanted to find you."

Leo clenched his fist and felt the injury begin to burn. "Good job," he muttered darkly.

When they stepped into the light of the campfire, Alexcena was already on her feet, her forehead creased with concern.

"What happened?"

Before he could warn her, Tabitha replied with the truth. "Leopold was bitten by a snake."

"What!? Are you all right?"

Alexcena started toward him, and Victoria stood up.

Great. Now I'll have all of them on me like mother hens.

Leo held up a hand to stop them. "It's fine. Not to worry." He sat down by his bag and pushed his sleeves up beyond his elbow. Tabitha blushed at the sight of his muscled forearm and looked away. Ordinarily, he would have found that funny. "I've been bitten before. This was just a small bucko. Black with a white tail. He wasn't venomous; I'm certain. You all just go on chatting and I'll take care of it."

He proceeded to treat himself, trying to remember every remedy he could think of. *Physician heal thyself, eh.* First he pinched the skin around the punctures to push more blood out. He was dimly aware of the ladies' voices and hoped that none of them was watching. Then he took up his water bag and splashed the area. He knew he had nothing with him that was good for such bites, so he simply drew a white strip of linen from his bag. This he wound several times around his arm to cover the injury. *Too bad I didn't hang on to that little fellow. I could have taken some of his fat to put on this. And snake meat is decent enough when cooked properly.*

After that he slouched out of his coat and lay down on his blanket. The ladies were still munching on the dried beef, but he found that he had lost his appetite. The skin of his forearm was hurting and seemed hot to the touch.

Just sore. It'll be better in the morning.

He rolled so that his back was to the women and drew a flask from the end of his bag. A few swallows of brandy helped him to fall asleep easily. His slumber was heavy and long.

Chapter 35
July 23, 1765

Leo awoke hours later to an odd sound. It was a light clicking, like the tapping of metal on porcelain. He could not make sense of it until he realized that his body was moving. He was still laying under his blanket-in the middle of summer no less-and yet he was trembling. His teeth were knocking together as he shivered. His head ached, and his skin was clammy. His heart seemed to beat against his ribs with frightful speed. That was the first moment he knew that he was in danger.

Voices reached him. It was morning and the women were stirring. He tried in desperation to open his eyes. They fluttered and he caught a glimpse of blue sky surrounded by treetops.

"Leopold!"

More than one pair of hands touched him. He worked to answer them. The palms ran over his face and down his arms.

"He's burning hot!"

"-my fault."

"What do we do? I don't-"

He tried to force his lips under control. "S'fine," he managed, and the effort made him dizzy.

"-got to get him up."

"Do you know what to do?"

"No. Know of a place though."

The hands seized his shoulders and pushed him up into a sitting position. The shivering subsided, but he felt his head falling loosely forward.

"Come on, Leo," someone said in his ear. "We've got to get you on the horse."

Sure thing, love. He could not tell if he had actually spoken the words or not. He wanted nothing more than to ease their fears. Somehow he didn't think he was doing very well at that. With a superhuman effort, he was able to stand. Someone was under each arm while someone else was behind him with her hands on his waist. He leaned on them heavily, despite his best efforts. They wobbled a few steps forward and raised his hands to the horse. By some miracle he was able to lift his leg while they pushed him up onto the animal's back. The horse stayed still even when he sagged forward on its neck.

He had time to mutter, "Good horse," before the world became dark again.

Part IV

The Unforeseen Rescue

Chapter 1

July 23, 1765

Merrybells.

The pale color of the soft petals against a backdrop of dark woodland brush caught his attention even in the nighttime shadows. He wandered closer, his chin falling to his chest as he stared at the drooping blossoms. He counted almost twenty in the cluster. As he watched a delicate hand that was not his own reached down to pluck a single stem.

"Strange to find them so late in summer," Lucius breathed. "Would that I could show them to you."

The small hand came away, clutching the flower. He allowed his gaze to follow it. Up the arm, shoulder, and neck his eyes traveled until they found the face of its owner. Though the straps of regret twisted around his heart, he was able to smile at Alexcena. She smiled back.

She studied the bloom while he took his time observing her. She appeared odd and not quite as familiar as she once had. He told himself that this was due to the unearthly light that caused her to glow in the dim evening.

"They look sad," she remarked of the limp merrybell. Then her eyes and eyebrows shifted upward. "They look like you."

Lucius tried to chuckle and managed a stiff croak. "They are meant to be so. Perhaps I am as well."

"Do not think that way."

She reached out to touch his wrist. He could almost convince himself that he felt it.

"Your happiness lies in things not of this world," she said, earnestly searching his face to see if he believed it. "Never forget that."

His head jerked in a brave nod. "I won't."

He knew what she said was true. He did his best to remind himself of the fact often in those days.

The corners of her mouth turned up for an instant. Then she withdrew her hand and made as if to back away.

Desperation seized Lucius. "I cannot keep you?" he called.

She looked back at him. "Not now, but you may keep this."

She offered the merrybell. Such a cheerful name for such a wilted thing…

"Professor Wolgath?"

Lucius started and looked to the rear door of the Faraday's home. The maid was leaning out and watching him with an odd look.

433

"The menfolk were wondering where you were."

"Oh!" Lucius cleared his throat twice. "I'll be in directly."

"Yes, sir."

When the girl was gone, he looked once more to the distant clump of merrybells at the edge of the Faraday's lot. Thoughts of the daydream still flickered in his mind.

He and Foley had been invited to dine with the Faradays and some friends. Lucius had agreed to take coffee with the gentlemen after seeing Foley back to the cottage so that he might work on his school studies. He had returned to the steps of the Faraday's back door only to pause at the sight of the late merrybells. He still stood with one foot on the first step.

A terse sigh pushed through his lips. His imaginings were strong on occasion, but never before had they stopped him in his tracks so. This was a worrisome thing; even a dangerous one. Was it possible for a man to undo his own mind? Knowing so little of the workings of insanity, Lucius could not offer himself a comforting answer. All he could do was determine within his heart that he would not allow such a thing to overtake him again. He would pray for strength of body and mind.

With deliberate motions he faced the door and entered the house. He joined the men in the parlor and the maid served coffee and dessert.

"By my boots, Faraday! Your cook serves the best pudding I have ever tasted."

"You say that every time you come, Gwinnett," Faraday replied to his friend. "Surely it is not perpetually true."

Garret was speaking to Button Gwinnett, a personal acquaintance of his who had come to Savannah some years before. The pair of them stood by the fireplace while Lucius remained on the settee. Garret had wanted Lucius to meet the man for some as yet unexplained reason. Lavinia, who was looking a bit rounder, had excused herself, saying that the baby had her fatigued.

"I regret that your wife could not join us," Garret commented to Gwinnett.

"So did she, but with our daughter Amelia not feeling well, she thought it best to stay home. Are you married, Professor?" he said to Lucius.

Wolgath had a flutter of nerves and an all too familiar cloud crossed his face. "Ah, no."

Gwinnett lifted his cup. "Someday then, hm? You know, I've been wed nearly ten years. We've had three daughters, and I find myself outnumbered in my own home."

"It's liable to happen to me next," Garret joked.

"You'll love it. It's a transcendent experience."

The pair moved to sit on the sofa across from Lucius. When the chuckling died down, Garret began speaking to the both of them.

"So, now to tell you both why I asked you here."

"Ah. The plot thickens," Gwinnett chortled.

"It's your own fault," Garret replied. "You've been here four years, and already you've engrossed yourself in politics. I thought between the two of us we could explain to the good Professor how the story goes over here."

"The story?" Lucius wondered aloud.

"Yes." Garret leaned back and crossed his arms. "You are working with men who are being punished by a system that is highly imperfect. Didn't you say to me recently that you should know better how it all works?"

Lucius raised a sardonic eyebrow. "Only because I've had so many men sneer at me when I tell them I have no political opinion to speak of."

Gwinnett slapped his knee. "Now that amazes me. A man who had the ambition to go through Cambridge, to earn *professorship*, and yet has no interest in his future."

The corners of Garret's eyes crinkled, unbeknownst to his friends.

"I never said that," Lucius declared.

"But you have not ever thought to wonder about those in power, is that right?"

"There was never much time for it in my life."

"The people might have a king," Garret said, "but we also have a parliamentary system and laws of governing which are not being followed, not here at least, by the people or their rulers."

"The problem is that in England, so often, matters concerning the colonies are considered simple diplomacy. Parliament says 'do this' and colonists are supposed to say 'how many times?' Over here tis different. Here it's money, life, and death. Laws are being passed that may very well strip honest citizens of their livings."

"Why should Parliament do such a thing?" Lucius asked. "England has debts of war to be sure, but-"

"But that's only one piece of the problem. England owns more property and more people than any other country in the world at present. Such an empire comes with consequences and costs," Gwinnett explained. "They have spread themselves far and wide defending their properties and fighting wars and regulating territories, and now they have realized that something must be done. More money is needed, and so they have gone after the most vulnerable of their assets to draw it."

"Most vulnerable? The colonies cover more ground than all of England. How can they be called vulnerable?"

"Lack of representation," Garret answered.

"I don't understand," Lucius admitted. "I thought the law was that no English shire could be taxed unless it was agreed upon by the shire's representative in Parliament."

"That's exactly what we colonists have said. There is no one in Parliament to stand for us. No one has been appointed and no one there seems concerned enough to speak up about it. They imply that we are lesser citizens simply because *we* live in the colonies *they* created. Taxes placed on our heads have been harsher than any that England has passed before, and they apply only to us. To make matters worse, the King has ignored all petitions sent to him; another right denied."

"Then, of course, there's the Admiralty Court," Gwinnett muttered.

"All right," Lucius sighed. "What's that?" He could feel his emotions churning. Did the powers that be in England truly think their subjects deserved lesser rights because they lived farther away from the King in his castle? In the back of his mind he was aware that ill-treatment was common enough. A poor man was not given the same recognition as a rich one. This he had always known, but never considered. He felt his loyalties waver. It was as though the entire purpose behind his coming to Savannah had been to bring him to this conversation.

Gwinnett steepled his fingers. "The King became aware that his colonies are growing increasingly... defiant. The argument is that the acts passed without colonial representation are unlawful, and therefore not binding. So our poor King has been forced to press his people harder. He has sent a vast portion of his military to America to see that laws are enforced. Then he saw to it that a court system was set up where any colonist had the legal right to a trial without a jury of his peers before a British officer. Such vast government operations only cause the debt to grow, and therefore more taxes must be passed on those who caused this whole mess for them."

Lucius could well guess who that might be. "The colonies."

Garret set his tea down and clasped his hands. "What with all the King's governors and all the King's men, there is much dissension among the citizens and much unrest in this part of the world. Abuses have been allowed to such an extent that I fear these people will not stand for it much longer. In the end, many of us would rather be called Americans than Englishmen. I know you intend to return to England as soon as possible, but I think it's important for you to understand all of this while you're here. The men and women who whittled civilization from wilderness on these shores did not do so to see her become a slave to an unwavering tyrant and his fellow corruptors. The ruling minority seeks to rebuild their wealth on the backs of the majority, but mark my words it will not be tolerated."

Six months ago, Lucius would never have believed that he might find himself in the midst of such a conversation. The words that passed were treason and dangerous indeed, still he was unshaken by the realization of it. Was it not also treacherous of the men in power to be so careless to the needs of the people?

"You think it has come to that?"

The flames of the fire flickered dully in Garret's eyes as he contemplated his answer. "Not yet."

Lucius nodded. "While there is time, there is hope."

A smile crossed Garret's lips. "And I believe there's time yet, Professor."

Chapter 2

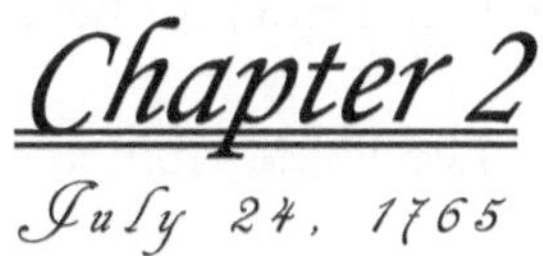

Leo's eyes opened, and he saw with stunning clarity a wooden ceiling above him. Befuddled, he let his gaze travel to the right and down the wall. There was a window there. Sunlight filtered in waves through the pale muslin curtains to fill the small room with light. He found that he was lying on a straw mattress that was altogether too short. Someone had graciously supplied a pillow for his feet as well as one for his head and a quilt for cover. This he pushed aside as he sat up.

Aside from thirst and a raging hunger, he felt like himself. He had no illusions about why he was there. The snake bite and the fever were still very much at the front of his mind. The only thing he could not recall was just how he had come to be where he was. Who had removed his coat and boots? Who had undone the strings of his collar? And where were his guns?

He listened, but heard no other stirrings in the house. Now the most important question of all; where were Alexcena and Tabitha? If anyone had intended to do them harm they would have simply left him to die in the woods. He could not make sense of his whereabouts, but he had most certainly not been left out in the open.

First things first.

Leo reached for his right arm and found a white bandage there. He began untying it-no easy task for a right-handed man using only his left. When it was removed he inspected the pair of punctures. The skin was tinged pink and still sore to the touch, but all and all, it did not feel so bad. He flexed his arm several times and felt only a bit of soreness in the muscle just at the bite.

Knew it wasn't venomous, he joked within himself.

He was still bending his arm when footfalls sounded and the door of the room was opened. Commodore trotted in, followed by a lanky man who smiled when he saw Leo.

"Hello!" He stepped forward and bent to offer his hand. "Glad to see you awake. I'm Marcus Braden."

Leo shook his hand. "It's good to be awake. I'm Leo Wolgath."

"Yes, I know. Your friends told us when they brought you here. Would you care for some coffee?"

"Uh, water, if that's all right."

"Say no more."

Braden disappeared and Commodore began inspecting Leo's arm for himself.

"None of that, please," Leo chided him and scratched his ears with his other hand.

Braden returned quickly with a full cup. "Here you are. How are you feeling?"

"Not too bad… Considering."

"The ladies were pretty worried when they came. You had a fever something fierce."

Leo stopped drinking to ask how long they had been there. He was nothing short of astonished by Braden's answer.

"Two days. Well, really a day and a half I reckon. It's nearly four just now. My wife's been havin' a time with the ladies. We don't live too close to town, you see." He winked cheerily.

Leo smiled. "I want to thank you, Braden. I'm much obliged to you for taking care of them and of me."

Braden grew serious then and looked Leo in the eye. "I like to think any decent man would do the same for me. Then, later, we found out you were a Christian brother, and that made it all the more important. I do have one bone to pick with you, though."

"What's that?"

Laughter lit Braden's eyes. "Now my boy is begging me for a dog.

Twixt him and his mamma, I'm gonna have to go around to every neighbor we got until I find one."

They shared a good chuckle and Leo said, "Well, I'm sorry to hear that. Where is everyone else?"

"The ladies are at the creek 'round back washing up. My boy's outside somewhere."

Leo's stomach chose that moment to enter the conversation with a growl. Braden hitched up a smile.

"Hungry, eh? I'll call the wife."

Smiling his gratitude, Leo waited patiently, all the while rubbing Commodore's neck and sending up prayers of thanks that his life was spared. *All good things do come down from above.*

When Mrs. Braden came in, the other three women were naturally close behind. Alexcena, Tabitha, and Victoria came into the little room to see how he was for themselves. It took much reassuring for them to believe that he was feeling so much better.

Alexcena placed her hands on her hips and looked at him in earnest. "You gave us all quite a fright, I'll have you know. I didn't know what we were to do that morning we found you all burnt up with fever."

Leo raised his eyebrows. "Burnt up with fever?"

"Thank heavens for Victoria," Alexcena went on as though she hadn't heard him.

"I met the Bradens about four days back with Robert, ye see," that woman explained. "I'm just thankful their house wasna too far away. I just knew they would help us!"

Before Leo could respond to any of this, a boy, no older than ten, rushed in between them to look Leo right in the face.

"Mister, you're alive!" he proclaimed with a deathly serious look.

Leo blinked. "I am."

The boy sat back and regarded him. "I was afraid you might die while you were sleeping in my bed."

"David!" exclaimed Mrs. Braden from the far corner. "What a thing to say."

David bowed his head. "Sorry, ma."

The lady-who was obviously Mrs. Braden-handed Leo a plate of cooked vegetables. "Eat slow now," she warned with a kindly look. "Don't want to make yourself sick again."

"I thank you very much, ma'am."

He accepted the plate and began to eat, forcing himself to move slowly. No easy task for a grown man with an empty belly. Everyone else began to trickle from the room. Alexcena and Tabitha were, in the end, the last to stay. Tabitha had been strangely silent, but Leo considered that in and of itself to be a blessing. He didn't suppose that perhaps she had something to say until they were alone.

"Finished?" Alexcena asked as she took the plate and left the room.

Leo, feeling satisfied and comfortable, leaned forward to balance his elbows on his knees. Since Tabitha was standing directly across from him, his eyes fell on her. It was then that he remembered how he had snapped at her that night in the woods. He had not meant to. It was just that he had been caught unawares. He was just about to express this when she opened her mouth.

"I'm sorry."

Her words were deliberate and slow, but her voice was so quiet he could not hear her. He knew what she said only by the shape of her lips. Then he felt like the worst cad.

"For this?" He held his right arm up and wiggled his fingers, hoping to ease her anxiety. "Don't be. It wasn't any fault of yours." Her lip trembled and he looked down at his hands. Why did she have to be so very delicate? "I'm sorry to you too, ma'amzelle. I never should have yelled at you that evening."

When he looked up, she was watching him in surprise. Then she nodded and dipped her head. Leo went back to examining his arm, expecting that to be the end of it.

"Do you remember what you said to us the next morning?"

"When I had the fever? Barely. I could hear you all, but I had an awful time trying to say anything."

She took a few timid steps forward. "You said something to me. You called me something different."

Leo chuckled, still unawares. "I was dizzy with fever. I'm sorry if I confused you for one of the others."

"It wasn't like that. It's just-" She broke off. Both her expression and her tone were somber. "You called me 'love.'"

She can't seriously think I was trying to insult her in that state!

"It's not the first time you've called me that. I just-"

"I was out of my mind with sickness," he replied somewhat sternly. "I didn't even know who I was speaking to."

Surprise crossed Tabitha's features, and she straightened up. "Oh," she said flatly. "Oh. Well, that's that then. I just wanted to be sure."

Her tone had changed. She sounded frightened, and he could not make sense of it given her haughty expression.

"I'm glad you're well."

Without another word she left him confused and speechless.

When Tabitha left Leopold she could think of nothing more than leaving the house. She needed a few minutes to steady her nerves. Already her emotions were ebbing up to show on her face. It was clear to Alexcena that something was amiss when the girl hurried by to rush out the door. She followed, concerned though she had no idea what had happened. By the time she made it outside, Tabitha was pacing near the trees. She stopped short.

"Tabitha?"

The girl did not answer at first. She paced a few more steps and then turned to Alexcena. "When you met Lucius, what was it like?"

Alexcena raised her eyebrows. The question stung, though it was not meant to. "I, um… I would say it was like finding the dearest friend I would ever know. Then it changed to something more. Something deeper."

"But it could be different than that," Tabitha remarked. "A relationship… a love… It could be different, could it not?"

"Of course." She stared at Tabitha, unable to make sense of her.

"You know, all those girls we know in England, I always heard them talking about finding the man who was different. Either wanting to find him or thinking they'd found him. I never heard any of them speak about finding the one who makes *you* different. They never spoke of a man who could make a change in you and make it easy for you to be better than you were."

Despite the girl's best efforts, tears began to fall and her face puckered in sorrow. By that time Alexcena was worried in truth.

"Tabitha, what's happened?"

"It's nothing. Nothing." She tried in vain to sound nonchalant.

"Is it Leo?" Alexcena had not meant to voice her guess so plainly, but the longer she stood there, the more it seemed to be true.

Tabitha's expression became utterly smooth and still. "Why would you say that?"

Alexcena remained silent, waiting for the girl to reveal more. She merely drew a handkerchief from her pocket. "I'll be inside in a minute, all right, Ena?"

How could she deny her a moment's privacy? She returned to the house to find that Mr. Braden and his son had gone to do some work in the shed. Victoria and Mrs. Braden were starting preparations for the evening meal. Mrs. Braden smiled when she saw her come in and suggested that she take more water in to Leo. She obeyed and found him lying back on the mattress again. Commodore lay lazily by his side.

"I can't believe I'm still so tired!" he groaned.

She passed him the cup and he sat up to drink. "But you are feeling better?"

"Another good night's rest and I'll be back to myself. Sorry about that." He winked as he teased her and she had to smile. "I'm also sorry about all of this."

She gave him a perplexed look.

"About spending two days here waiting for me to get passed the fever," he explained. "If I had been paying attention that night we would be much farther down the road by now."

"It was no one's fault you ran afoul of that snake."

Pain shot through his features. "But we're so close," he murmured.

She could not deny that she was impatient. Her heart had been beating faster ever since Victoria had told them what she knew, but she had also been terribly frightened for Leo. She placed her small hand on his larger one.

"What kind of a woman would I be if I didn't care enough about you to see that you were well? Lucius is doing fine. We know that now. You were not."

He said nothing in return, but kissed her knuckle by way of gratitude.

"I must ask one more night's rest of you and our new friends. We shall depart in the morning, and I will do everything in my power to see you to Savannah as soon as possible."

It was odd, but Alexcena felt encouraged by the mere word. "Soon…"

Leo leaned forward. "Sooner."

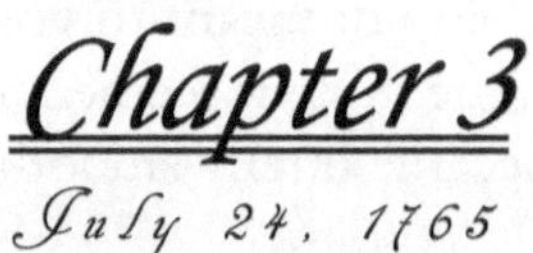

Chapter 3

July 24, 1765

Foley arrived home from school one day to find Lucius in his armchair staring at the window across from him. He did not look up as the boy ambled in and set his books on the table.

"Hey, Professor."

He moved then, reaching up to rub his eyes and crossing his legs. "Hello, Foley."

It was curious, though not unordinary, for the Professor to be home before Foley. The boy did not wonder much about that, but he did wonder about the way Lucius appeared; as though he had not slept in days, and much older than he had when he left that morning. So it seemed to Foley, at least.

Interested as ever, he sat on the floor by Lucius' chair. His chin jutted forward in thought. "You look like something's the matter, Professor."

Lucius removed his glasses and began tapping them against his knee. "I was just thinking about a conversation I had with Garret and a friend of his a few days ago."

"It must have been disgusting," Foley remarked with sympathy.

"Why do you say that?"

"Because you look sick, Professor."

Lucius almost laughed, but it faded fast. "It was about America and the manner in which she is governed. I was reminded of it because of something that happened today."

"What happened?"

The glasses paused and Lucius stared at nothing again. "His name was Timothy Corinth."

Foley's nose wrinkled. "Huh? Who's that?"

"He was one of the men I knew at the prison. He died today. He had been sick with a cold and he wasn't as healthy as he might have been. I didn't see him for a few days, and now-"

"So you taught him?"

"No. Not Timothy." A whisper of a smile came to him then. "He didn't care to learn, but he did care to talk. I saw him a few times a week and in the end we spent hours talking about nothing. I was just waiting for the opportunity to help him find truth and knowledge. And salvation too, if it was God's will to call to him. Now look what's happened. He's gone and I'm left wondering how I could have allowed myself to fail so miserably."

"How'd you fail?" Foley asked. "You're doing all right."

"I should have done more. I let him down."

"He was the one who didn't want to learn, wasn't he?" Foley said simply. This drew Lucius' eye, so he went on. "You said 'if it was God's will.' Maybe it just wasn't."

Lucius nodded and patted the boy's shoulder. "Thank you, Foley. I suppose I'm melancholy because I've been reminded of something else by this."

"What's that?"

"That I'm human."

Foley's mouth practically fell open. "You had to be reminded of that?"

"That's not exactly what I mean." He leaned forward and clasped his hands, as though carefully contemplating how he would explain. "I could die myself. Suddenly or with a few day's warning, it would make no difference. Even now death could be as close as breath and I would never know it until it was upon me. I've settled myself in to wait a year or more before I am able to go back to England. It sickens me to think I might not even accomplish that."

"I don't understand, Professor," Foley admitted when it seemed he was done. "Why should you be any more worried about that today than you were yesterday or the day before?"

For a long moment, he did not answer the boy. When he did speak, he seemed to be talking only to himself. "I once wanted to make so much of my life, and now here I sit, hoping only to survive that I might go to England again. And then only for one purpose."

Still jolly and wanting to be helpful, Foley nudged his arm. "Just don't think on it, Professor. Worry can't change one thing for you."

He watched as Lucius contemplated this. He looked horribly sad, and Foley tried to determine what game they might play that would cheer him up. In the end it was not necessary, for Lucius soon sat straighter in his chair.

"Take therefore no thought for the morrow, for the morrow shall take thought for the things of itself."

"What's that, Professor?"

"You don't recognize it?"

Foley shook his head, making Lucius chuckle.

"And here I thought you were beginning to retain all those Biblical lessons I've been having you learn."

"Not retaining? But I've learned them all." Foley was not defensive, but rather befuddled. Had he not shown the Professor that he could read all those passages? What could he have missed?

"There is a difference between reading something and understanding what it means. If you're simply repeating words without paying them any heed, what do you glean?"

Foley turned his head from side to side. "You confused me again, but by the sound of your voice, I think the answer is 'nothing.'"

"My point exactly. Now-" Lucius rose and rubbed his hands together. "Let us look to your schoolwork and I shall make certain that you grasp the concept completely."

Foley's shoulders slumped with dread. "Oh…"

Chapter 4

July 26, 1765

Alexcena awoke with a distinct shiver. The air around her was crisp and chilled with fog. The fire had died out hours earlier as the dew fell. The embers winked at her like so many burning stars. Commodore sensed her wakefulness and came to lay his head on her hand. In him she felt a kindred heart and wondered if it were possible that he could know what she knew. That today was the day. That they would reach Savannah by nightfall, and Alexcena believed anew with every breath she took that Lucius would be there.

The others were not awake yet she could tell. The noise of the wood did not quite cover Leo's deep breaths or Tabitha's light snores. Victoria lay deathly silent, her side rising as she inhaled. Alexcena savored the quiet minutes she would have to calm her nerves. Already they were beginning to roil, twisting her stomach and causing her hands to shake.

She sat up as silently as she was able and pushed the folded quilt back. Commodore followed her movements as she took a somewhat fresh dress from her satchel and slipped deeper into the shadows to don it. Then she drew a little cloth that she had over the thick leaves of a nearby bush to gather the dew. She scrubbed at her face and neck and hands. As she began to comb her fingers through her bedraggled hair, she saw the first pale hues of light appearing over the trees.

Never have I waited so long for the dawning of a day…

The more the sun rose, the better she felt. The fog had not helped the trembling of her hands, but it lifted quickly with the morning. Being in a grove of trees, she could not watch the sun rise, but she caught glimpses of it shining between the limbs. Golden rays warmed her face and comforted her heart.

Commodore did not wait long to nudge Leo's shoulder and sniff loudly at Tabitha's hair. The others rose and sooner than Alexcena realized, they were on their way. Hardly a word passed between them, and she was glad, for she had no way of knowing just how fragile her calm might be. Not a thing was said to her until they were atop their horses and on the road.

"It will be late afternoon before we get there, Ena," Leo said bluntly. He shifted with discomfiture and changed his hold on the reins before he continued. "You know…You know he may not be there."

In spite of herself, she smiled.

"Do you know it, Ena?"

"Yes."

Leo looked skeptical. "I hope so. It pains me to think what will happen if you do not."

"Then I am happy for both our sakes that it will not come to that."

He said nothing more, but she could sense his concern. She prayed that he would think back and remember how he should feel. Worry would neither put Lucius in Savannah, nor take him away. What would be would be, and in the end the worry would have served no purpose at all. Rather than fill herself with the fear, she chose to bring to mind the love. Her morning was spent in recollections of her days with Lucius. That year of her life that had been lined with gold and trimmed with a happiness she had not known. She remembered all that she could of their first meeting; their easy conversations; their first argument; their perfect companionship. They were one in the same, separated only by the years between them and a stretch of road. Her heart swelled with wonder at the relief to come when she would once again feel that she was her whole self.

They rode the horses side by side. Commodore marched before them at a quick trot. He did not dart away in search of a smell or a sound as he normally would. Alexcena wondered if it were possible that he might smell his master and know that he was near.

They did not stop along the way. None of them wanted to. Victoria was just as eager for Lucius to see all of them as they were to find him. They passed a bit of bread around at noon, but no one was very hungry. By then they had grown silent, each brooding in their own thoughts. So it was especially startling when three hours later, Victoria cried out.

"There!"

Commodore let out a bark and Alexcena felt Tabitha jump behind her. Victoria's arm was stretched out, pointing to a break in the trees.

"Those are some of the farmlands near town. We're close now."

For an instant everyone hesitated. The words sang through Alexcena's very soul. *We're close!*

Leo took up his reins. "Let's get to it then."

He tapped his mount's sides and sped off at a quick clip. Alexcena followed suit. She was hardly conscious of Victoria or Tabitha at all, despite the facts that Tabitha's hands were clutching her waist and Victoria's mad hair hid Leo's head from view. She was aware of the horses and keenly felt the thunder of every hoof beat. Her eyes were fixed on the road ahead, searching with vigor for the first glimpse she would have of Savannah. It was less than an hour before her desire was met, but even then her hunger only grew. It was not a city she was longing to find after all, but a man.

Leo held up a hand to halt them, and they dismounted just beside the first building they came to. People and wagons and livestock moved along the streets before them. While Alexcena's eyes searched each face, she kept one ear on what the others were saying.

"Where do we go from here?" Leo asked.

Victoria considered. "I don't know exactly. I don't know the man who hired him, or where he might be."

"Do you know where he was going to be working?"

"No. Just that he was gonna be teaching, though I don't think it woulda been at the school. Why would a lawyer be lookin' for a teacher for the school?"

Leo's jaw jutted forward in determination. "All right. Let's keep searching."

They began to move, up one street and down another. All the while Alexcena's gaze darted from man to man, face to face. Three times Leo asked passers-by if they knew of a Professor Wolgath. Three times the answer was 'no.'

"Look there," Leo said after a little while.

Alexcena's heart leapt-then sank when she saw that he was indicating a building.

"Postmaster's office," he explained. "If Lucius has been writing letters, that man should remember him." He gave Alexcena a smile of encouragement and passed the reins of his horse to Victoria. "I'll go find out. You ladies wait *right* here."

Alexcena watched him go. She felt Tabitha fidgeting behind her.

"This is maddening!" she whispered. "Shouldn't we have found him by now?"

"We've only been in town one hour, sure enough," Victoria replied blandly.

They kept talking, but Alexcena was no longer listening. For a time she watched the door of the Postmaster's office. Then her gaze slowly fell to the citizens of Savannah once more. The streets were not crowded, and it was relatively easy to look at each gentleman in turn. Long nose, no glasses, too short, too old, brown hair, black hair, powdered wig-

Blonde. Curly and blonde.

The man had passed while she was looking another way, and so she only saw his back. But could it be? Was it really so simple after all this time?

Without a word to Victoria and Tabitha, she moved across the road at

a quick walk. The man was moving slowly. It was easy for her to overtake him, to grasp his arm and shoulder.

"Lu-"

"I beg your pardon!"

Before her was not the beloved face she expected. Instead she saw the face of a haughty man years younger than she. He was well-dressed and recoiled in disgust at her touch.

Alexcena's lips parted in surprise. "I'm so sorry, I-"

The man shoved her hands away and glared, making her feel perfectly foolish. "What's this about?"

"I do apologize. I've made a mistake," she hurried to explain. Inside her mind raced. The man was angry. What would happen now?

He turned to call over his shoulder. "Captain!"

A soldier approached followed by two others. Alexcena immediately recognized the red coats. They came close and the man urged her forward. She shuddered as she all but fell against the Captain and hurried to right herself.

"Perhaps you should handle this woman," the young man said behind her. "She seems a bit disturbed."

He moved away, but Alexcena was hardly paying attention. Her focus was on the soldiers before her. The Captain looked her over in a most abrasive way.

"What's the matter here?"

A flicker of hope flared inside her. "Maybe you can help me," she said piteously.

Tabitha was suddenly at her side, gripping her hand. "Ena?"

A malicious grin stretched over the Captain's face. "Two of you, hm? Mayhap we can help you. What do ya think, gents?"

"Surely we can work something out."

They chuckled with dark glee. Panic began to rise as Alexcena realized what it was that they saw. Two young women, wearied by travel, poor in appearance, and seemingly alone.

She looked beyond them, straining to catch a glimpse of Leo coming out of the office. Across the way she saw Victoria holding the two horses and staring at the same building she was.

"We can help you," the Captain said, "but you should help us in return. Wouldn't you agree?"

He reached for her. Before Alexcena could move, he had one arm about her waist. His fingers clutched at the fabric of her cotton dress. She twisted around and slapped him. He was unflapped by the blow and even laughed as he released her. He allowed his hand to drag around her mid-drift as she spun away, and in that moment, Alexcena felt something pull loose beneath the fabric. A weight that she had forgotten she was carrying fell away. She was confused by it until she caught sight of the oilskin packet lying in the dirt between her and the soldiers.

"Hello, hello." The Captain bent to retrieve it and slowly unwound the string. "What's this you've dropped?"

"It's mine," was all she could think to say. She could feel Tabitha cowering behind her. She stood straight and unwavering. Her panic subsided now that she was a slight distance away from the man, and she knew just how she would proceed when he had the packet open. She waited for him to find what was hidden there.

"I don't believe-" The Captain's voice broke off as he fanned the thick bundle of bank notes out of the envelope. The other soldiers murmured low behind him. "There must be a few hundred pounds here," he murmured.

"At least," Alexcena assured him. "You can have it, all of it, if only-"

"Have it?" The Captain's face changed. His cool look became a contemptuous glare. "You, madam, are hereby under arrest."

Alexcena was befuddled. She tried to make sense of his words as she watched him shove the bills back into the envelope and tuck it away in his coat. It was Tabitha who protested aloud.

"What do you mean? She's done nothing!"

"She has been caught attempting to barter paper currency," the Captain responded. "Such currency is illegal in these colonies."

Cold fear rose like a crashing wave in Alexcena's chest as one of the other soldiers stepped forward and reached for her wrists. "B-but I had no idea!" She felt pathetic and childish, but she could not prevent the stutter in her voice. Nor could she stop her feet from digging into the ground as the man tried to jerk her forward.

The Captain waved an uncaring hand. "I am neither lawmaker nor judge. You can make your argument to the court."

The soldier tugged at her arms again, but her legs were locked, pushing her away from him. Tabitha shouted something unintelligible. The scene was beginning to attract the attention of the townsfolk. Had Alexcena felt able to look around, she would have seen a multitude of angry scowls falling on the redcoats. This interest increased all the more when Leo exploded into their midst.

"What is the meaning of this!" he thundered. An accusation rather than a question. He was suddenly quite close on her left, though she was unconscious as to which direction he had come from. He wrapped one arm about her shoulders and grasped her upper arm with his other hand, holding her steady. She felt his muscles bulge and knew he was preparing to rip her from the man's hold.

"Stand away, sir!" the soldier shouted at him. "This woman is under arrest and so shall *you* be if you continue to interfere."

Alexcena's eyes darted from the soldiers to Leo and all around them. A few of those people watching were moving forward. Several men and even one woman were approaching to stand behind them. The tense energy of the moment sparked against her very skin. She forced her mind to think, to find a way to end this before it culminated in an outburst of violence.

She looked to Leo and hissed, "Let me go!"

"Not on my life," he murmured without turning to her.

"Look around you," she insisted even as she began to wriggle free. "Let me *go*."

She escaped him to find herself thrust behind the soldiers. With the connection to her friends broken, she saw a stark line form between the redcoats and the colonists. Leo stood in front of all the rest, his eyes never leaving her. His voice came as a low growl and he took only one step forward before the point of a bayonet was put to his neck. The knife did not quite touch his skin, but still Alexcena began to shake at the possibility.

It was the Captain who held the knife, and so it was he who spoke. "Perhaps I should take the other little one as well to convince you? Stay back! The rest of you return to your business."

It was ended just that neatly. Alexcena found herself being pushed and prodded along with a soldier at each arm and nearly faint with fear. The last she heard from her companions in that hour was Leo's parting shout;

"We'll come for you!"

He said something more, but it was lost amongst a dozen other voices and footsteps. The sun still shone on her face, but her world was darkened and cold. She closed her eyes against it, hoping desperately that God above would hear her prayer.

Lord, remember me!

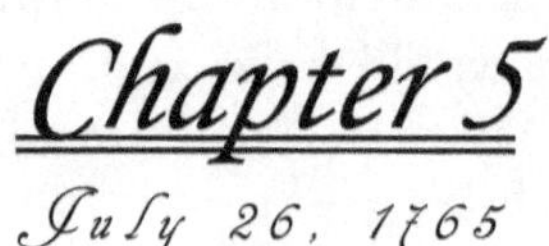

Chapter 5

July 26, 1765

"All done then, Faraday?"

Garret turned with a hint of a smile for the man who had spoken. "My business is concluded, Major Dunwhither. There's no need to say 'good day.' I can see myself out."

The Major *harrumphed* and set to fidgeting with some papers on his desk.

Garret resisted the urge to roll his eyes, but only just. He could not imagine a more turbulent man to serve as warden of the prison than Dunwhither. There were days when his work as a lawyer forced him to deal with the man, and he would be as complacent as his gruff manner would allow. Then there were days like this one when the man chose to clamp a ball and chain on Garret's ankle-so to speak-and saw to it that his work was doubly difficult. Either way, he was always superior and never pleasant, an attitude that Garret found insufferable. Therefore Garret, being who he was, made all the more efforts to be polite when he was in the man's presence. So it was that he smiled as he stepped aside to allow a cluster of soldiers to enter before he left. The smile fell from his face when he saw their purpose.

Major Dunwhither was unmoved. "Report, Captain."

"Major!" The soldier gave a stiff salute. "Prisoner, sir, arrested ten minutes passed in town."

Garret saw that their prisoner was a woman. She was almost frail in appearance. Her features were drawn, her eyes closed, and she seemed to be swaying slightly where she stood in the middle of the three men.

"What's your name, girl?"

The lady's eyes fluttered and her head bobbed. "Alexcena Condreve."

Her words were painfully slow, as though it took great effort for her to say them.

Dunwhither took note of it. "And your age?"

"*Lucius…*"

The word was so faint that Garret was certain he had not heard her properly. Even so, his heart beat faster.

"Excuse me?" Dunwhither asked, almost bored.

"Where…Lucius?" Alexcena managed. "Is he here?"

"She's hardly made sense since we came upon her, sir," the Captain explained. "We think she may be daft in truth."

"Very well," Dunwhither went on. "See her inside and report back to me, Captain."

"Yes, sir."

"Wait," Garret found himself saying. "Aren't you going to ask them what happened or why she was arrested?"

Dunwhither twitched his moustache to one side sternly. "In due course, Mr. Faraday."

The men were already propelling their catch toward the hall. He watched them go, knowing somehow that something important was occurring, though he could not say what. He had to be sure of one thing.

"This Lucius," he called out, "is his last name Wolgath?"

The lady only had time to look over her shoulder and nod.

It was a day to be remembered until the end of his age. A day to be held and caressed and savored, though Lucius spent his morning never knowing it. His wildest imaginings could not compare to the future that was coming to him.

He was outside when Garret arrived late that afternoon. He was inspecting a loose shudder on the cottage when his ears picked up the sound of clattering wheels. How could he not notice the racket his friend made rushing up at such a pace in his two-wheeled curricle. Lucius turned and would have smiled had Garret not looked so serious.

"Professor!" Garret called. He rose to his feet in the driver's box as the horse came to a stop. "I think you should come to the prison with me."

Lucius stepped closer to the carriage. "Has something happened?"

"A woman has been arrested," Garret told him, "though I don't know what for yet."

Lucius' brow furrowed. "That's not *all* that unusual."

"No, it's not. What is unusual is that she came into the prison asking for you."

"Me?" Lucius searched his recent memory, but he could not think of a single woman who might have reason to ask after him at the jail. Unless it was perhaps a relative of one of the men he knew. Still, why would any such woman need to see him?

The door of the cottage opened behind them, and Foley stepped out. "Hello, Mr. Faraday. Hey, Professor!"

Garret nodded and turned his attention back to Lucius. "I think we should hurry. The woman was quite desperate, and she did not seem well."

"Did she say who she was at all?"

Garret squinted, trying to remember.

"Because I can't think of-"

"Condreve. Alexcena Condreve."

Lucius Wolgath's world slowed almost to a complete stop. He looked at Garret as though he could not comprehend what he was seeing. In that moment he was not seeing him at all, but rather a vision of a dark-haired woman in irons. Try as he might, he could not mold her looks to match memory. He could not see her as Alexcena.

Calmly, as though disagreeing about a book or a painting, Lucius shook his head. "You heard wrong." His voice was hoarse even to his own ears. "It's not her."

As soon as he heard himself speak the theory out loud, he knew it was false. *He heard the name wrong…and it just happened to be the name that means the most to me alone on this earth?! But how could it be* her?! His face betrayed none of this, but his composure faltered.

"It's not-it's not possible!"

He gripped the wood of the curricle and leaned into it. His mind was suddenly too weak to contemplate the prospect and command his muscles at once.

Garret watched all of this in grave confusion. Then he lowered a hand toward him. "Come with me, Lucius."

Wolgath's mind took over the movements of his body and left off thinking then. He could not consider it after all-could not conceive of it. Only one word came to him after he climbed up to sit next to Garret.

"Faster."

This he said three times throughout their short journey. The sooner the dream ended, the better off he would be. That was certain, and most assuredly this was a dream. A grotesque fantasy he had chosen to torment himself with. Odd that he was unable to stop it all and return to sanity. He was grateful that Garret asked no questions. He did not have the words to answer the obvious ones.

Perhaps I'm ill…must be what has brought this on…What else? And there is the jail…And that dog, he looks just like my old friend…More evidence that this all lacks reality.

Despite his firm disbelief in all around him at that moment, he regarded the dog with something akin to a smile. The Great Dane stood beside two horses posted outside the prison. He watched the cart as it approached, and as soon as Lucius was on the ground, he trotted forward, his massive face turned upward. Lucius bent to rub both his ears.

"You know, you look just like Commodore."

In his mind he was delighting in a moment that was sure to end, so he was pleased when the dog nuzzled his hands and sat on his foot, waiting for more affection.

"Professor! *Finally!*"

A woman rushed forward and took his hands in her own.

"Victoria. What are you doing here?"

Her expression was a mixture of merriment and concern. She took hold of his arm and made as if to shove him forward. "Never mind me! Get in *there!*"

Lucius blinked. This was the first indication he perceived with clarity that perhaps this was not the illusion he thought it was. "If you tell me it's true, I shan't believe you."

"I'll let yer brother tell ye then."

"My brother?"

"Go!"

He turned away and all but fell through the door. *I'm going to come out of this feeling like a fool. Even if it is-*

His mind was suddenly still as a stone. His vision was filled by a tall figure with his back to him. He did not need to see his face to recognize those shoulders and that untamed hair. It was Leopold. His brother. Standing before Major Dunwhither's desk with his arms crossed. He could just picture the glare Leo must be wearing, and then he couldn't wait to see it for himself.

"Leopold!"

A smile spread over his face as he watched his brother turn and recognize him. He had expected him to grin, but Leo looked darkly serious as he stepped forward to throw his thick arms about Lucius' shoulders.

"We found you, Luc!"

Lucius felt a tremor run through him. His voice was barely a whisper when he answered. "You did."

He took on the full weight of his brother's embrace. The larger man was leaning on him, as though very tired and nearly spent. Lucius felt his shoulders drooping as he supported him. Even so, he would have stood thus for an hour without weakening, so bright was his gladness in that moment. In all the time he was in America, he had not considered that Leo might attempt to come for him. Might cross the span of a great ocean to search for him. His spirit cradled a newfound treasure in the debt of love he now owed his brother. He was honored and emboldened and grateful above all.

Then, in the space of a breath, he was aware of everyone else in the room. Dunwhither was on his feet behind the desk and demanding to know the meaning of all of this. Garret hurried to him and began speaking in low tones. A woman stood in the far corner. Her wild blonde hair shook as she wiped her eyes. Lucius' own widened when he saw her face.

"Tabitha Winslett!"

She sniffed and laughed a small laugh. "It's me, Professor."

It was true. It *was* her. Why would his mind imagine Tabitha Winslett of all people being there at such a moment? He could not entertain thoughts of denying it any longer. They had come, and they had come for him. The one factor holding his heart to the ground was one missing countenance.

Lucius gripped his brother's forearm. "Is it so?" he gasped.

"Yes."

"Then where is she?"

This time Dunwhither answered from across the room. "She is in her cell, under arrest by order of myself as an officer of the King's army!"

His harsh words effectively shattered the moment and brought Lucius back to his senses. He found that he was able to release his hold on Leo and be still, but he truly had no idea what to say.

"You still have not answered my question," Garret responded, speaking to Dunwhither. "We would like to know what the lady is being held for. She is a subject of the Crown and cannot be held without reason, so I ask you again, Major; what is she being held for?"

Lucius had never before heard Garret speak with such aggression. He was touched by his friend's desire to help them.

Dunwhither was silent for several moments. Then he seemed to find his anger once again. "I don't need to explain myself to you, Faraday!"

"No, you don't," Garret agreed, "but there is an entire township of citizens outside who do have the right to know what the army is up to. Especially when that army-which is meant to be protecting them-arrests a lady and is unwilling to say a word to her friends when they come to see about her."

Dunwhither considered. Then, as all windbags do in the end, he began to crumble. "This is all just-very simple!" he spluttered.

Garret crossed his arms and waited.

"My Captain will tell you. In the room, down there." With that he moved toward the hall and began shouting at a few soldiers of the King's army.

Garret gestured to the opposite corridor. "Lucius."

And so he was the first to walk down the short hallway, and the first to enter the room. The very room where he came to teach. He was followed by Leo and Garret. Tabitha mumbled something about staying out of the way and joined Victoria outside.

Lucius stared at the opposite door unblinkingly. "Lord, help me!" Leo put a hand on his shoulder, and he clutched it. "I can't begin to-"

Leo squeezed his shoulder and shook his head. "Time for that later, Luc."

Lucius nodded and returned his attention to the door while his brother moved toward Garret.

"I'm Leopold Wolgath. We're much obliged for your help, sir."

"Garret Faraday. Lawyer. I'm afraid you might be needing more of my help in the near future."

"I don't know how this could have happened to her."

"Who is she, this Ms. Condreve?"

Lucius was still watching the door, and so he heard rather than saw his brother smile.

"She needs no introduction."

The latch turned. The door opened.

"Bring her forward!" Dunwhither snapped from the shadows.

There she was. The first to step over the threshold. Lucius' eyes traveled up her figure. Her shoe, her skirt, her arms, her face. *Oh! That face!* Dirty and pale. She looked much like a frightened animal, teary-eyed and cringing. Her hair was bedraggled, falling loose over her shoulders. A leaf was even tangled in her locks. Then she caught sight of him and her features smoothed from a grimace into disbelief. A sigh fluttered from her full lips. In that moment, standing in his sight, she had never been more beautiful. Then, as if aiming to pierce the cover of his self-control entirely, she began to smile.

The emotion was a forceful one, bounding up from the depths of his soul, and not to be contained by the mere walls of his chest. He began to laugh in a low, husky tone. Two tears spilled fourth from each eye. He felt ridiculous for all of this and did his best to quell the reaction as the meeting went on. The conversation proved effective in reminding him that the situation was serious.

"Captain!" Dunwhither barked. "Explain yourself."

Lucius refocused his eyes to take in the entire scene. The Major and three other soldiers stood clustered around Alexcena. The only thing more stark than their red coats was the glint of the fetters holding her wrists. The Captain straightened his shoulders. "We found this woman attempting to peddle paper currency in town, sir."

"There you have it," Dunwhither declared. "An illegal act worthy of punishment."

"I had no idea it was so." Alexcena's eyes moved to the Major for but an instant while she spoke.

"Bank notes are common enough in England," Garret added. "Six months ago they were common enough here. Why should she have known being a stranger to these shores?"

"I did not know," Alexcena reiterated. "I had no intention of using the funds until I became desperate to get away from your Captain."

Lucius felt sorrowed anew at that insinuation. The tenderness had gone from her face. His concern must have shown, because her brow relaxed when she looked back at him. Then she extended a few fingers of one hand as if to smooth his concern away. He heard what she must be thinking clear as a brass bell.

I'm all right, Lucius. You needn't worry for me just yet.

The Captain sniffed. "I haven't the faintest idea what she means, sir. I found her lost and confused and offered my assistance. At that time she gave me the money."

"That is hardly how it happened," Alexcena interjected. "I dropped the bundle when I pulled away from you. You picked it up, and I, being frightened witless, offered it to you in the hopes that you would either help me or leave me alone."

"What stories!" the Captain sneered. "The woman is daft."

Garret stepped forward. "What's become of the money?"

Dunwhither chuckled dryly. "What for, Faraday?"

"It is evidence of the crime, as you call it. I should like to see it."

The Captain shrugged. He drew a handful of bills from within his coat and tossed them onto the table.

Alexcena raised a cool brow. "It was more than that."

The Captain glared, his cheeks growing red with anger.

Dunwhither lifted the bills and counted them. "There's thirty pounds here. Surely you do not believe that a woman such as this would have more. I'm surprised she carried this much."

"There was more," Alexcena insisted. "Much more."

Garret turned to the Captain with a measure of curiosity. "Surely you are not accepting a bribe, sir."

The Captain erupted. "Lies! All of it!"

Leo narrowed his eyes. "I would hope that if you had decided to pocket a few bank notes yourself, you were at least smart enough to give your friends their share." He indicated the two lesser soldiers standing closest to Alexcena. "Or did you think they would keep your secret for free?"

One of the men nudged his Captain, and it did not go unnoticed. Garret was standing close to them. To the astonishment of everyone his arm shot out, lightening quick, to slip into the Captain's coat and flip an oil skin packet onto the table. The Captain swallowed as Dunwhither reached for it. He took the briefest glance of its contents before rounding on the

Captain.

"What is this, then?" As if he didn't already know.

"I beg your pardon, sir. It slipped my mind."

"*Slipped your mind?!*"

Leo crossed his arms. "Embarrassment to the King's army, you are."

"Embarrassment to the commanders of your entire regiment, I'd say," Garret added.

"All of this will come out in a trial, mark my words," Leo went on.

"Whether by testimony or word-of-mouth," Garret finished.

"Don't be ridiculous," Dunwhither sneered.

He gathered the evidence from the table and took hold of Alexcena's arm, making as if to turn her back toward the bowels of the prison. Lucius' heart felt as though it might tear in two, and he had to do something.

"But you have no idea who she is, do you?!" he called.

The Major glanced back. "Is that supposed to scare me? Who cares for the reputation of a villain of a woman?"

"But you should care at least for the reputation of her father," Lucius replied. "He is well-known in the high societies of England. A prominent member of the Royal Society and a financier of the colleges of Cambridge."

"Imagine the humiliation," Garret sniffed. "All the eyes of London society upon you, only to watch you prove that you cannot even handle your own men."

Dunwhither's cheeks grew ruddy and then paled behind his bushy whiskers.

"Sergeant!" he barked.

"Sir?"

"Give me your keys."

Dunwhither bent and began to unlock the manacles that bound the dear wrists. Lucius held his breath.

When she was free, the Major straightened and cleared his throat. "I hereby pardon you, woman, by the mercy of King George. You are released, but! I shall keep these illegal currencies to ensure that they are not circulated on these shores."

"My letter!" Alexcena exclaimed. "There is a letter of a personal nature from my father in there. May I have it?"

Dunwhither fished the envelope out and passed it to her. He then moved from her path and nudged her forward. Lucius' hand was already outstretched, waiting to meet hers. When he had her, he tucked her swiftly away behind him. Garret and Leo closed in on either side, forming a human fortress around her.

Dunwhither said not another word to them. He sniffed loudly and herded the soldiers into the hallway, all but striking them as he went.

"Make me look the fool, will you? You're not fit to be toy soldiers!"

They wasted no time in leaving the room. With Leo in front of them and Garret behind, Lucius and Alexcena walked side by side. He kept her tucked tightly against himself, with one arm about her waist and one hand still grasping hers. His arms refused to let her go, now that they had her. Alexcena, for her part, seemed to feel the same way. Her free hand was knotted about the shoulder of his coat and showed no sign of loosening.

In just a few steps they were out the door, and Lucius' eyes closed against the brightness of the brilliant sun.

Chapter 6

July 26, 1765

Alexcena stumbled as they stepped out of the prison, but she did not fall. She was in the beloved arms and he would not allow her to fall. She turned her face into his side and breathed deeply, her eyes shut against the world.

All at once she felt something new. It was Lucius she was sure, pressing his cheek against her hair. When he spoke his voice was strained, almost wounded.

"Do you know what you've done?! You've left everything, Alexcena!"

"No," she found herself saying. "I came to find everything."

She had never stopped believing that Lucius would be found in Savannah from the moment she heard the name of the place. Still there was shock at first sight, which ebbed quickly. Lucius was still incredulous, and every so often a small noise would escape him to betray his emotions. She knew questions would come later, and so she savored those moments when no words were needed. She breathed in, feeling lightheaded with joy and fatigue and relief all at once. So much so that she barely noticed when he lifted her up because her legs had grown too weak to hold her.

Voices murmured all around. She distinguished none but his. He said only a few words to someone before lifting her higher. Then she felt that they were moving, and the ride was too smooth to be on a horse. *No matter. As long as I do not leave his side.*

She did not recall much about the journey but thought that it seemed short. Only when she felt herself being lowered and the arms retreating did she open her eyes. Lucius was staring down at her serious and pleading. He was passing her down to Leo from the seat of a carriage. She turned reluctantly to his brother.

"I can stand."

"Sure you can."

She swayed when he set her down, just as he had predicted. Lucius leapt from the cart to offer support around her shoulders. She closed her eyes and the corners of her mouth turned up as she put her head back on his arm.

"See? I'm balanced now."

Lucius murmured something she could not distinguish. Her mind was sliding towards sleep, and she could not seem to prevent it. *I came all this way to rescue you, and here you have rescued me,* she thought, although she must have spoken out loud, because Lucius replied.

"Don't talk now."

She obeyed. The voices began again, and this time she was able to gather the words.

"All of you, come inside. There's plenty of room."

"My goodness, Garret, what's happened?"

"-just needs a rest, I believe."

"Professor, I found a dog! Who's she?"

"Give us a moment please, Foley."

Alexcena dragged her eyes open when she felt boards beneath her feet. They had entered a lovely home, one that reminded her of the houses in England somewhat.

"Here," Lucius murmured. She let him guide her into a small sitting room down the hall, away from all the voices. Inside was a petite couch set before a wide fireplace, and he bade her lay down. As he helped her, he bent to kiss her cheek, all the while still pressing her hand with his own. When he sat back she saw that the pleading still covered his face.

"Are you hurt at all? Tell me what's wrong."

"No," she hurried to reassure him. "Only, I don't think I've eaten at all today. The soldiers did frighten me, but I'm unharmed. Seeing you has made my weak heart pound too."

"Seeing you," he repeated. "It is too much to believe."

"If it were it would not be true," she teased.

"I can't fathom how. Or what. Or why-" he broke off and seemed to be calming his thoughts as he stroked her fingers. She was glad, for she did not want to explain just then. She would much rather revel in his nearness.

"Do you need anything?" he asked.

"Yes," she breathed. "And I finally have it."

Soon after that-and much to her dismay-her eyes fell shut. Just before she fell prey to sleep, she felt Lucius moving, rising to his feet. He held her hand and looked upon her as she drifted off. Such a scene made for some very pleasant dreams.

Lucius knew she was asleep when her hold on his hand relaxed. His deft gaze traced her every feature. He was a starving man eating his fill and repairing all the flaws that time and distance had created in memory. Would that he could have watched her longer, but there was much explaining to be done.

He relinquished her hand, placing it gently at her side. For a moment he stared at it as well. Such a small, fragile thing. Petite, like the rest of her. How was it that this slip of a person had traveled all that distance and made it to him? He could not see it and yet he *was* seeing it. The contrast caused his mind to feel quite numb and useless. With an effort he turned to the door. There was a cluster of people he cared for beyond it, and all would be waiting for answers to some question or other. He had to speak to them all. But he was having difficulty focusing. Walking across the short room was prooving to be a challenge.

Pay attention, Luc. Right. Left. Right. Door.

"Perhaps we should leave them be," Garret was saying just outside.

Someone started to answer, but then Lucius pushed the door aside. All sounds ceased. Everyone watched him; some eagerly, some curiously, and all with a measure of concern. Commodore sat to one side with his tongue lulled out and an easy grin. All at once Lucius felt a great fatigue and wondered how he would ever be able to comprehend enough himself to explain.

He looked to each set of eyes individually. Garret and Lavinia. Leopold and Foley. Tabitha and Victoria. Then back over his shoulder into the salon. He was a man bewildered and surrounded.

"She is only sleeping," Leopold declared. He did not need to ask to know of whom he spoke. "She has not been injured, I am certain."

Somehow the voice of his brother managed to draw Lucius from his stupor. He grasped the handle of the door and pulled it shut. "Yes, of course."

When it was closed he found himself awash in an ocean of faces again.

"This hall is a bit close, isn't it?" Garret commented. "Perhaps we should all move onto the portico for some air, and I believe there are introductions to be made."

"Yes, of course," Lucius answered again. He wondered if it would be possible to answer every inquiry thus until he had sorted through the facts himself. He found the mathematical probability of such a conversation lasting any length of time to be impossible.

Once the gathering moved outside, Leopold took charge of introductions from the English side of things. For this-and many other things-Lucius was forever grateful.

"-Leopold Wolgath. A pleasure indeed, ma'am. May I also present Ms. Tabitha Winslett and Ms. Victoria Smythers. Ms. Alexcena Condreve, as you know, is laid up at the moment."

"How do you do, sir. Ladies. This is my wife, Lavina Faraday, and I am Garret Faraday."

"It is a great pleasure meeting you both," Tabitha nodded demurely.

Lucius could not help wondering if it was some sort of courteous reflex. The young lady looked rather pale herself. It made him worry as to what sort of ordeals his companions had traversed in order to find him. He shuddered away from that train of consciousness.

"And you lad?" Leo asked with a kindly smile at Foley.

Garret was taken off guard at that. "You do not know him?"

Foley had been standing to one side, half hidden behind Garret. He squirmed under everyone's scrutiny, his face growing dark with irritation and confusion.

Lucius swallowed and beckoned him forward. "Foley."

The boy moved around Garret to stand before Lucius, right in the middle of everyone. "Yes, Professor?"

"I'd like you to meet your Uncle Leo. Leopold, meet Foley Conrad Princeton III."

"I rather like that," Leo remarked. "It's regal without being drab."

Foley looked up at the large man. Lucius imagined that it must have seemed something like looking up at the top of a great tree. The boy swallowed and managed his discomfiture amdmirably. He touched the brim of his old hat and nodded with respect.

"Glad to meet you, sir."

Leo touched his forelock in return. "And you as well Mr. Third."

Foley grinned in thanks and seemed to relax a bit at that.

Lucius gestured to the ladies then. "This is Ms. Tabitha Winslett."

Foley bowed to her and then rounded on Lucius. "What about the lady inside, Professor?"

Lucius suppressed a thick lump in his throat so that he might answer.

"I'll explain later, Foley. Why don't you play with Commodore."

"Commodore?"

"My dog." Lucius found that his old companion was close at his side. He rubbed the top of his head affectionately.

"Commodore," Foley said again. He moved in front of the animal. The Great Dane lacked only a few inches being as tall as he was. The pair looked each other up and down, as though neither was sure what to make of the other. Then Commodore sneezed at Foley's feet.

"Eeegh. Come on boy, Commodore! Can't have you doing that again in front of the girls."

With that Foley led his new companion into the yard to play. Lucius watched them go and then caught Leo's gaze.

"I'm an uncle?"

"Yes."

Leo quirked an eyebrow. Lucius could sense that his brother was thinking of many comments he might make to tease him, but with new people about, he was unsure of himself. Lucius knew how he felt on that score.

"An orphan," Lucius explained. "He was an orphan. He is with me now. I met him in Virginia. At least I believe it was Virginia."

"So that explains why the pair of you did not know him," Garret said to Tabitha and Leopold. "But not how you know him, ma'am," he added to Victoria.

"Victoria worked for the same man I did when you met me, Garret. She knew Foley then."

"So the three of you-" Lavinia began, looking to Leo and Tabitha and then inside toward the salon. "It was the three of you who came to find Professor Wolgath?"

"Yes, ma'am," Leo replied.

"Then perhaps you can answer the riddle for us. Why was it that the Professor was sent here?"

Lucius, for his part, had forgotten that the fact was even a question. He had actually forgotten that he did not know. It was simply part of his life now that he had been sent to America. Now that it was brought to the front of his mind, he turned to Leo almost greedily. Leo looked to him once and then gave his answer directly.

"Rodney Dushaw."

Lucius exhaled a heavy breath and leaned back against the wall of the house.

"It was his plan, Luc," Leo went on apologetically, as though it were somehow his fault for passing on the information. "He wanted to be rid of you."

Garret blinked from one to the other of them. "But why on earth…"

Tabitha filled in the rest as delicately as she could. "Mr. Dushaw was a colleague of Lucius' at Cambridge. He held a certain affection for my cousin, Alexcena. He felt that the most effective way to win her was to remove Lucius. He also thought that he would be able to succeed Lucius in the standing that he held with the college. I imagine that it all went rather badly for him when Alexcena discovered his plot and followed Lucius shortly after his departure."

There were exclamations of horror and revoltion from the Faradays. Lucius barely heard a word as the voices all around him discussed the finer points of the plan that had sent him to America. He was watching Foley chase Commodore about the yard. The name Rodney Dushaw had been all but lost in his mind. It seemed odd to think of him even now, even knowing what he knew. It changed nothing. He was detached from all concern about the man. There was no possibility of confronting Dushaw, and perhaps there never would be. Anger did not enter his heart on hearing the truth. He determined then not to allow it on this matter. Vengeance was not his to take, and so he would not consider anger. Instead, he considered his friends.

"Leopold?"

Due to his silence of the last few minutes, the others broke off their conversation and looked at him as though they had forgotten he was there. His brother was standing closest to him.

"Luc?"

Lucius shook his head in his astonishment. "How did you all come here? How did you find me?"

"Alexcena found out everything shortly after you had gone," Leo told him. "It was she who first proposed chartering a vessel to come after you. Upon first hearing the tale, I only wanted to get my hands on Rodney, so I was a bit slower."

"But I came ashore in Virginia," Lucius insisted. "How did you ever decide to come down here?"

"You leave quite an impression on people in these parts and quite a trail I might add. Still I was astonished at how quickly we were able to find you out."

"The Lord above may have blessed your journey," Garret interjected.

Leo nodded with respect. "I believe so, sir."

"He must have," Lucius said. The passion in his voice betrayed his stoic expression. "How else could all of you have come to be here unhurt and well before my eyes?"

Leo cleared his throat and glanced at Tabitha, though Lucius did not see it. "Well… I did pick up a few new scars, but we can talk about that later."

Lucius held his forehead in one hand. The numbness of shock was fading for him. As he leaned against the house, it seemed as though his heart was hammering against the very boards. His beloved had come for him. His brother had delivered her.

"*How*, Leopold?"

The words were so strangled with emotion that Lucius did not recognize his own voice. He wanted his brother to explain so that it would make sense. He wanted to understand why he was feeling such upset in his being. He wanted his practical mind to realize the facts and calm his heart.

Leo stepped closer to him and put a heavy hand on his shoulder. "Baby brother," he chortled. "I already told you we knew what had befallen you. Do you think anything would stop me? Do you think anything or anyone could stop *her*?"

Lucius embraced his brother. He clung to him as a few emblazoned tears rolled down his hot cheeks. It made sense. They had come for him because they thought him worthy, even though he knew he certainly was not.

"Thank you," he murmured and patted Leo's back. "Thank you."

When the two men parted, the others were all looking elsewhere. Lavinia took opportunity of the silence then to fulfill the remainder of her duties as hostess.

"Can I offer anyone anything?" she asked, looking to Tabitha and Victoria. "Food, drink? A place to lie down?"

"Thank ye, ma'am," Victoria replied, "but there is something I need to pick up in town. I hope ye donna think me rude."

"Not at all," Lavinia smiled. "But do return. You're all most welcome to stay here."

"But-but you don't even know us," Tabitha stammered.

Lavinia's answer was easy. "No, but Professor Wolgath does."

Lucius nodded his appreciation to Garret. He was filled with gratitude for the kindness and affability the Faradays were offering his friends. Garret, in turn, was only too glad to be of service. It was plain to see that Lucius was not quite himself and unable to play host as one should to travelers.

"I'm sure Leopold is curious to know how you have been fairing,

Professor," he said. "Why not show him your new abode?"

"Oh," Lucius replied slowly. "All right."

Tabitha mumbled something Lucius did not hear and left them to join Victoria on the path in front of the house. Lavinia suppressed a yawn and declared that she would just slip back inside to rest if none of them needed her. So it was that the three men made their way around back to the cottage.

Leo eyed Tabitha and Victoria with a wrinkled brow as they went away. "Between the two of them, if they're not back in an hour, I'll be going to find them."

"Surely two ladies such as that haven't been difficult to travel with, Leopold," Garret teased gleefully.

Leopold held up a hand. "Leo, please."

"As you like."

"That's quite a nice place," Leo said when he surveyed Lucius' home.

"It belonged to my wife and I when we first came here," Garret explained. "We lived there while our own home was being built."

Just then Foley scampered around the back corner of the house, closely followed by Commodore. Again Lucius watched them. It was so much easier than trying to think or engage in conversation with the others. His emotions seemed to have temporarily worn themselves out and he chose not to prod them back into action for the time being. His agile, analytical, overly pensive mind, needed a rest.

Foley had stopped running and was petting the top of Commodore's head. The dog leaned on him as he would an adult, and Foley promptly fell under his weight. Commodore then set to licking his head all over. With weak efforts and long laughter, Foley attempted to push him away.

"Commodore," Lucius called even as he moved toward them. "Hike."

The dog whined a bit when he looked up at his master. Still he backed several steps away from Foley, who sat up at once. He struggled for breath between laughs. Lucius handed him a handkerchief and he began mopping his face and neck.

"That's disgusting," Leo chuckled.

Both he and Garret had come closer as well. Foley's laughter subsided when he took notice of them. It was obvious by the way he looked him up and down that he was still uncertain of Leo. Even so, he accepted the tall man's hand when he offered it and came to his feet.

"If you're my uncle," he began, "that must mean you're the Professor's older brother."

"I am Lucius' brother." To Garret, Leo added, "I feel like I've said that every day since I got to America. This whole country is gonna be calling me 'Lucius' brother' before this is over."

While Garret chuckled at that, Leo turned his attention back to the boy. "You're wondering about the ladies now, aren't you?"

Lucius was taken aback by his brother's question, but as soon as he took in Foley's expression, he realized that it must be true. The boy's brow had grown dark and his mouth grim. Even as he watched, his eyes strayed toward the big house. *He's thinking of Tabitha and Alexcena! He's wondering if having my family restored means I won't want him anymore! Or he's thinking that Alexcena may not want him.* Lucius applauded Leo's astuteness.

Foley shrugged. "All except for Victoria. I know her already."

"Ms. Winslett and Ms. Condreve are cousins," Leo explained. "They came with me to find Lucius."

Before Leo could say anything further, Lucius got down on one knee before Foley. "You remember me telling you of Alexcena Condreve, don't you Foley?"

"Yes, sir."

"You remember then that she is the lady I am engaged to?"

"Yes, sir." The boy's head drooped, though he kept his voice carefully nonchalant.

"You know I asked for Ms. Alexcena's hand after courting her for a whole year. That's three-hundred and sixty-five days that I saw her and spoke to her as much as I was able. In those days I grew to know her, and I know her well enough to know that you have no reason to worry, Foley." He waited for the boy to look at him and smiled. "You will always have a family with me."

Foley appeared marginally convinced, but there was nothing more Lucius could do about that. He could not blame him. The boy had already seen how easily a family can be torn asunder, and he had no idea what Alexcena was like. It was only a matter of course that he would be concerned. Lucius had every confidence that his mind would grow easier when he met Alexcena for the first time.

Foley straightened his hat and gave a stiff nod. "Yes, sir, Professor."

"What about you?" Leo asked Foley while Lucius rose to his feet. "How did you come to meet my brother?"

"I found him."

Leo burst out laughing and slapped his thigh. "I guess," he gasped, "that's as good an explanation as any!"

The corners of Foley's mouth slowly lifted in unison with his eyebrows.

"Why don't you show me inside," Leo said, patting the boy's shoulder.

"Been searching for Luc so long, I'm interested to see where he's been hiding out lately!"

Chapter 7
July 26, 1765

Tabitha put her hands on her hips and let her head fall to one side. "This is your errand? A coffee shop?"

Victoria turned back at the door and nodded. "I need to pick up some more beans. Are ye comin' in for a cup?"

What else have I to do? She grasped her skirt and stepped through the door behind Victoria. They took a table in a secluded corner by a large window. Victoria added a healthy amount of cream to her mug. Tabitha kept her coffee black.

"I'm surprised, ye know."

"Hm?" Tabitha set her mug down. She raised an eyebrow at Victoria, who was watching her with a knowing smirk.

"I thought ye'd stay behind with the others. Especially Lucius."

"Oh." The girl drummed her fingers and studied the wood grain of the table. She could not decide just how much she was willing to tell this woman she had known for less than a full week. "I thought they might like some privacy."

"And ye wanted some as well?"

Tabitha stiffened. Victoria reached across the table to pat her hand.

"Don't worry, dearie. I'm glad ye came. It's nice *not* to be alone sometimes." She shook her head. "I'll be honest with ye. I was not eager to stay back there at the moment."

Tabitha wrinkled her nose in confusion. "Why is that? If you don't mind I mean. You needn't tell me."

Victoria's gaze had drifted. The plains of her face had grown smooth and soft. She answered without hesitation. "I didna want to see Lucius with his lady. Not when they first came together. I thought it would hurt to watch."

A blush covered Tabitha's cheeks. It had not occurred to her that it might be a reason so personal. She swallowed another mouthful of coffee to avoid looking at Victoria, giving her a chance to recover herself if she wished. She was shocked when the lady went on.

"Lucius has played the hero for me twice. For a little while I wondered if he might wish to do it again. I knew he held love for someone else, but she was far away. I thought if I waited, he might begin to look my way a bit now and then."

A timid grin moved across her countenance. Tabitha recognized the pain behind it well. Too well. "Did he ever know?"

Victoria straightened. "He did. I told him meself. He was very gentlemanly when he let me know that he was not thinking the same thing. Then I met all of you. Once I realized who Alexcena was, I knew I had to lead ye all here. This way, at least I have repaid his kindness to me with one of my own."

"But you didn't want to watch it," Tabitha finished for her.

Victoria flourished an air of indignant arrogance, which was obviously false. "Just because I want him happy doesn't mean I want to scald meself with it! Heat and ice create an awful lot of steam, if ye get me."

They shared a laugh then, and Tabitha found herself relaxing. "I do," she giggled. "I've still got my own scars in here." She laid a hand over her chest.

"Do tell!" Victoria insisted.

Tabitha cleared her throat and lowered her voice. "Little more than six months ago, I was still in the midst of my own bout of affection for the Professor."

"I see."

"I was a foolish society flirt, and far less discrete than I ought to have been, so it was no secret. Then, in January, I was at Alexcena's birthday celebration, where they chose to announce their engagement."

Victoria winced.

"Did I mention that Alexcena is also my cousin?"

The older woman clucked her tongue and shook her head. "I knew ye knew the heartache from the minute I spoke to ye. But it's not as bad as they say, is it, dearie?"

Leopold's hard features fluttered through her mind. She swallowed and shrugged away from the vision. After a moment's pause, Tabitha felt she could smile and give an honest reply. "No. In the end, all things considered, it's really not." She was still hurting, and might continue to do so for a time, but this would pass. After its season it would pass.

"Ye must tell me, though. How did ye convince your cousin to bring ye along to search for him? Didn't she know about it all?"

"Yes, but she didn't know I had come along."

Tabitha explained her part of the long tale. How she had spirited herself aboard, paid for her own passage, and the arguments that ensued.

"Alexcena asked me about why I had come, naturally, and I didn't have an answer for her."

"It wasn't Lucius?"

She shook her head. "No. That much I knew."

When she didn't continue, Victoria leaned forward.

Tabitha fiddled with her coffee spoon. "I think it was more about... finding a way out. I had started to feel like a ridiculous doll in a tiny wooden house with no idea how to grow up. I was pampered, spoiled, and doted on. When no one was playing with me, I sat on the shelf gathering dust. Never changing, never maturing. I didn't know how to stop it all. So I left."

Victoria nodded and turned her cup in its saucer. Now *she* was giving *Tabitha* a moment to collect herself if she chose. It struck the girl funny. Three months ago she would not have been seen even looking at a woman such as Victoria. Now she was infinitely glad for her company.

"It's funny, ye might say," Victoria mused. "A way out was just what Lucius gave me. That was how he became my hero."

Chapter 8

July 26, 1765

Lucius found himself seated at the Faraday's dining room table that evening with almost no recollection as to how he had arrived there. The day had grown muddled for him, and in the hours that had followed the miraculous reunion, he had completely lost track of time. The realization concerned him for the state of his sanity. He therefore looked up from his half-eaten portion of food to take stock of the faces all around the table.

Garret was at the head as usual. Leopold was seated directly across from Lucius. Foley was at the corner of the table between Lucius and Garret. Lucius saw at once that none of the ladies were present. He then remembered that Victoria and Tabitha had returned saying that they had already eaten while they were out and were shown to a guest room upstairs. Lavinia had layed down for a nap earlier and had not yet risen. So the men had taken a quiet supper for themselves.

As Lucius came out of his stupor, he saw Garret rising to his feet. "I do hope you both will excuse me," he began, speaking to Leo and Lucius. "I have several letters to attend to. They've been waiting all day in my study and I simply cannot hold them up any longer."

"Of course," Lucius replied.

"Make yourselves at home. There's plenty of food left on the side board and in the kitchen."

"Foley, perhaps you ought to go on to bed," Lucius murmured.

"What for, Professor? I'm not-" An enormous yawn cut Foley's comment somewhat short.

"What? Tired? I say you are. Go on." He smiled as Foley trudged behind his chair toward the door. "And if you don't wash your face first, I'll see to it you sleep outside tomorrow."

Foley visibly brightened. "Really!?!"

Lucius turned to peer at him over his spectacles.

"Oh, right. Uh-washing, Professor!" This he hollered over his shoulder as he hurried out the back door.

When Lucius righted himself in his chair he found Leopold rubbing his eyes. "Surely you're not tired?"

Leo snorted. "I'm older than all of you. Of course I'm tired."

They chuckled quietly. Lucius was nearly put to tears again as he realized how good it felt to be joking with his brother. As was inevitable, his eyes roved back to the door of the salon across the hall. He sighed for pains past.

"She's all right, you know," Leo said gently. "She was just frightened today is all."

Lucius turned to look at him. "And Tabitha?"

"She's all right, too."

"That's not what I meant." Leo's brows rose, so Lucius amended swiftly. "Sorry. I mean I'm glad of that, but I was just wondering why it is that she came along."

"The girl is an enigma, and so I have no idea."

Mirth and amusement surged up within Lucius. He covered his mouth to muffle the sound. "Do you know," he gasped, "when you were helping me to get Alexcena down from the curricle...I saw Tabitha standing behind you..."

"And?"

"Well-" Lucius could hardly believe he was sharing such a thing with Leo. "The way she looked at you and I... And Alexcena in your arms... For one horrible moment I thought you might have taken Alexcena for yourself and brought Tabitha for me!"

Leo rolled his eyes and put a hand to his forehead. "Get some rest, Luc. I think you might need it more than me." With that he rose and moved toward the door. "I am going to go see if there's room in that cottage of yours for a man as tall as me. You coming, Luc?"

Lucius fought to keep his eyes away from the salon door, which could be seen just beyond Leo's shoulder. "No. I think I'll sit up a while. You're welcome to my half of the loft. I'm not-"

"What? Tired? I say you are," Leo smirked.

"I'll be there in a little while."

"Sure." Leo threw a look over his shoulder at the salon and grinned. "Just make sure you wash your face first."

Naturally, Lucius did not listen to his brother's advice about rest. He could not decide whether to look in on Alexcena or to find the maid to do it for him or to leave her be entirely. Thus undetermined he lingered in the dining room. The cook removed the dishes and brewed a pot of tea, which she served to him just before she went to bed. After that the house grew very still. Lucius let his legs stretch forward and leaned his head back over the top of the chair. Before he could blink he was fast asleep. Though he did not know it, he slept for exactly one half hour, until ten past ten. It was in that minute that he opened his eyes and saw the figure of Alexcena standing in the open door of the salon.

He could only watch her at first, stunned and sleep-clouded as he was. It seemed to him that she looked very much like a child, with an open face and curious eyes. Then-as she recalled the events of the day-a soft smile appeared on her lips.

Somehow as he slept his chair had tilted back three inches to lean against the wall. He intended to stand with demure, gentlemanly courtesy, but when he moved to do just that, the chair clattered to the floor, taking him with it. Lucius stood and set the chair up as quickly as he could. He then whirled around to find Alexcena looking just the same, still smiling.

He tried to return it, but an odd anxiety was rolling within him. He watched her closely and without blinking, as though she might shatter like so much thin glass before him. "Are you all right?"

She raised her thin eyebrows. "Are you?"

After a moment this struck them both as funny and they were able to laugh.

"Would you like something to eat? There's tea here." He gestured to one side so that she would see the tray set on the table. "It's sure to be cold now, I suppose."

Her eyes skipped toward it. "I'll have some of that."

Lucius moved to pull out a chair for her and she sat beside him. "Thank you."

The next half hour was destined to be a faded memory for Lucius. Even in the days to come, the words of that first conversation would vanish. What he did remember was the feeling. The happy, easy sensation of comfort. All worries were alleviated and all sorrows lifted for him in that tiny piece of time that they passed talking of nothing. It was as though they had never been separated. He could almost believe they were sitting in a drawing room of her parents' home and half expected Lawrence to join them.

Near the end of their interlude, Alexcena turned her head thoughtfully. "It's July."

"Yes." His answer was simple, but there was a clear question in his tone.

"When is your birthday, Lucius?"

"The eighteenth."

Alexcena's forehead puckered with regret. "Oh, dear. I've missed it again."

Lucius was confused. He searched his mind for the date and even glanced to the clock in the corner as though it would help him. "My goodness," he finally said. "I missed it too this time."

They laughed together again, a merry sound to fill the space still between them.

"I assumed I would cry when first I saw you."

Lucius gave the merest shake of his head. "You're too practical for that. Unless you're angry."

She snickered as she sipped from her cup. "Without cream this cold tea is actually quite good."

"Perhaps it will become the fashion one day," he returned. He did not want their moment to end. All too soon they must needs speak of much more complicated matters.

"Quite possible."

"Had I been thinking, I would have dashed into the kitchen and made you some fresh."

"Not at all. I'm enjoying this. Do you live here, Lucius?"

Whether due to spontaneity or design he could not say, but for whatever reason her hazel eyes deepened and intensified. Lucius swallowed.

"No. No, I live in a different house around back of this one."

"Will you show me?"

Clearing his throat, he rose. The simple part of the conversation was at its end. He led her by the hand through the house and out the back door.

All the while his heart pounded harder and harder. It was as though he was recognizing anew whose hand it was that he was holding. He was finally finding himself in the new realities of his life.

At the back door, they stepped down the short steps to the ground, and she bounded ahead a few paces. Lucius found himself frozen to the spot and released her hand so that she could go. The light of a full white moon spilled down, almost as bright as an early morning. It illuminated everything in the yard perfectly.

"Lucius, it's wonderful!" Alexcena breathed.

She was captivated by the sight of a plain cottage. He was captivated by the sight of her. His features grew rigid with determination. He marched toward her in no uncertain manner. When she turned around she was very startled by his stiff strides. He ignored her surprise, and when he was close enough, he drew her to him. He bent his tall frame around her, holding her for all his worth. She wasted no time in reacting, and he reveled in the feel of her embrace.

"I *love* you! Alexcena Condreve."

"I love you, Lucius."

A small laugh escaped him. He closed his eyes and held her tighter. "I know."

The moment was broken when she wriggled in his arms. He was by no means ready to let go, but he slackened his hold just enough for her to pull away. He was shocked to find her lovely countenance so twisted with evident sorrow.

"Then why haven't you trusted me?"

"What do you mean?"

"You didn't think I was waiting for you, did you?" she accused. "You thought I would find someone else to love that easily! I came all this way, and you weren't even expecting to find me at home waiting for you, were you?"

Tears fell from her cheeks. They were like tiny shards. Each one pierced his heart.

"I'm sorry. I never should have–"

"So it's true?" A sob shivered through her, and she bowed her head helplessly. "Why, Lucius? Was it because you began to feel that you didn't want me anymore? Did you start to grow away from me?"

He cupped her face in his hands. Still she refused to look at him. "How could you think it?"

"That's not an answer, Lucius," she said evenly. "After all that's happened, I've earned the truth."

At first he could think of nothing to say beyond 'I love you.' That was the very phrase she was doubting. He might have pointed out that she was doing the self-same thing by not trusting his love, but he knew it would not hold. This was the first time she had ever questioned while he had done so several times in their past together. *This should be a joyous night! It should not be marred by pain.*

Desperate to quell her hurt, he decided to follow the thought. He pulled her close again and chuckled in her ear. "My lady, you baffle me!"

When he leaned back, he saw that she was puzzled by his change of mood. He fervently hoped that she would not see beyond it to the trembling of his soul.

He led her to a fallen log at the edge of a thick cluster of trees and merrybells. They sat, hand in hand. He looked to her with an affectionate smile.

"Do you not see how we have changed?" he began. "For months you professed that I was doubting you and your commitment and your passion because I refused to whisk you away into heaven knows what sort of life until I had enough income to support you. Despite your sensibility, you declared in no uncertain terms that you did not care what we faced, so long as we did it as one. It took some time for you to convince me that your love would not wither. I surmise that this was due to the fact that I could hardly believe you had chosen to love me in the first place. Such blessings of goodness and light are difficult to comprehend. Undaunted by all of this, my heart grew to love you all the more. Now, here you sit, declaring that my love has been crushed by the weight of distance and a little time."

The truth dawned slowly. Her cheeks reddened by degree as he spoke.

"My entire life has been about returning to England ever since I realized where I was bound for," he went on. "I have thought of little else. The funniest part of it all is that I rarely considered more than one reason to return. It was not until I found Leo, Tabitha, and Commodore that I truly remembered all that I had forgotten. The stuff of my life, my home, everyone I love; all of that was stripped away until there was only you. There are those in this world who thrive when strife covers them, but I am sorry to say that I am not such a person. The very fabric of my faith was nearly torn by the horror I held for my situation, and I am deeply shamed by that. My soul was badly damaged by the idea that I might never again behold you. Now ask me again if I still want you."

Her lip merely trembled. Her eyes pooled, each reflecting a constellation of stars.

Lucius' worries ebbed. He fingered a rivulet of hair that had fallen over her shoulder. A half grin flickered across his mouth. "All this time I've been most horrified that I may never see you again, let alone be near you, speak to you. Now, impossibly, I have you to hold as my own, and you ask me to face the prospect of being without you again."

"No."

The word fluttered from her mouth amidst a shuddering breath. She reached forward to lay a hand on his arm. Her fingers smoothed his sleeve, and he felt the motion ripple across his skin beneath it. He watched the gentle movement, bowing his head.

"I have prayed to God time and again, apologizing for my weakness. I am humiliated by the fact that I could be so shaken. His Son suffered far more and still He loves us."

This confession became a silent prayer, bumbling and awkward. His reverence for God, Who had never left him in true need, rendered him speechless. His heart's longing to express a thanks that he could never hope to put into words became a surging force within him. It felt as though his very soul was stretching upward. The whole event was unplanned and instinctive, and almost the same second it had begun, it was over.

Lucius drew several deep breaths, trying to calm his beating heart. Unsure of himself, he lifted his gaze to find Alexcena watching him. He surveyed her figure slowly. Somehow looking at her had a comforting affect. Her clothes remained wrinkled and smudged. Her skin was pale and the strands of her hair were a tangled mass falling the length of her back. The complexion of her face was dull. She could almost be called frail, so weary was she from her journey. Lucius saw beyond all of this. He saw the moon shining on her wavy locks. He delighted in the blush coloring her high cheeks and the curve of her neck. A pair of wandering moths had chosen to land on her dress, one at her knee and the other on her shoulder. They waved their wings as if to heighten her graceful air. Her elegant lips were curled into the most exquisite of smiles.

"My lady."

She sighed a sigh of purest pleasure. Lucius leaned forward to place a fervent kiss on her forehead as he had the day he left her. In return she inched closer, encouraging his arms to encircle her. She turned her cheek for him to kiss and he did. Then she offered her lips. He could not find it within himself to resist just one more.

"Now do you know that I love you, Alexcena?" he whispered against her cheek.

"Yes."

Lucius had shut his eyes for the third kiss. He kept them shut as he drew in a slow breath for his next question.

"Then will you be mine for the rest of our days?"

His eyes still closed, he sensed the giddiness run through her.

"Yes, Lucius. I will marry you and love you all the rest of our days."

He opened his eyes then. A rakish grin came to him as he replied. "My dear heart. How I love to hear you say it!"

Chapter 9

July 27, 1765

Lucius awoke with a start. He was sitting in the armchair in the cabin. Pale sunlight was falling through the windows to reflect from his glasses. As soon as his eyes were opened, he stood up. Memories of the day before bombarded him. They mingled with recollections of the night's dreaming and times past enough to sufficiently confuse him.

How to tell what was real… Ah!

He had slept in the armchair that night because he did not want to wake Leo and Foley in the loft. Also because his brother's bulky frame alone had practically filled the space, leaving poor Foley curled up in a corner.

Lucius bounded to the ladder and looked up. His brother's arm and large hand were falling over the opening. Lucius nearly laughed with relief all over again. He stopped short when he noticed a pair of eyes shining down at him. He squinted up into the shadows.

"Commodore? How did you get up there?"

The eyes moved as the Great Dane rose onto all fours. Without warning he leapt, slid, and almost fell down the rungs of the ladder all at once. Lucius attempted to side-step disaster. Instead he managed to trip on his own heel and fall onto his back. Fortunately Commodore was there to slobber all over his face, giving him the necessary encouragement to sit up.

"That was hardly called for," Lucius grumbled as he cleaned his glasses on his cuff.

Commodore whimpered.

Lucius reached over to rub his ears. "I'm sorry. I should know by now to be more sensitive to your feelings."

Commodore *huffed,* as if to remark, 'I did travel all this way, after all.'

"Yes, you did. You're a good dog." He patted him on the back. As he stood, his attention moved toward the door of the cottage. "Now, let's go make certain I did not dream the rest of it."

He stepped outside and stared at the back of the Faradays' home, searching for the window of the guestroom. He found it easily. The light curtain was pulled to one side, and a face was illuminated there by the dawn. The curtain fell after allowing him only a glimpse, but it was more than enough for him to know.

It was little more than six hours ago that she had gone to that room after agreeing to marry him. He wondered how much of that time had been spent watching for him at the window. Would that he could have gone to her at once, but he needed a change of clothes. Telling himself repeatedly that she would still be there when he went in, he moved through the motions of freshening up. He even went so far as to trim his short beard and hair. All the while Commodore stayed at his heels. It was good to spend a few minutes talking to his dog as he once had.

Lucius had just finished up when he heard a loud thump somewhere above him. This was followed by a hoarse grunt and a child's laughter.

"Lucius!" Leo bellowed from the loft. "We're going to hafta have a talk about this low ceiling!"

Lucius grinned and crossed his arms. "Are you offering to remedy that?" he shouted.

Leo's feet appeared on the ladder. He climbed down with one palm pressed to his forehead. "No, but I'll gladly take up an axe and put in a new window for you up here."

Lucius gave him a small laugh. Then he turned toward the stove and reached for the tin pot. "Are you ready for some coffee?"

Leo hesitated and said, "I'll make it."

"It's no trouble." Lucius sounded less convincing that time, even to himself. He could not deny that he was eager to leave, despite his great efforts to suppress the feeling.

"Luc." Leo crossed the room to stand beside him with his hands on his hips and a knowing grin. "Go and let me make the coffee."

Lucius let out a breath. He touched his brother's arm. "I'm so very glad that you're here."

Leo took a playful swing at his shoulder before setting to the task of coffee. As Lucius was leaving he noticed Foley rubbing Commodore's head.

"Watch him for me, will you, Foley?"

"Sure thing, Professor."

Lucius could not cross the yard fast enough. He knocked and stepped inside just as Alexcena rounded the banister at the bottom of the stairs. Her joy was evident. Lucius stopped short, struck by the sight of her. If she had been beautiful the night before, she was nothing short of radiant then.

While he stood staring, she rushed forward to greet him. He was powerless to resist the fanatical urge to hold her. She came easily as he gathered her up, burying his hands in her rich hair.

"What is wrong with me?" Alexcena murmured with delight to herself. "I waited all that time to find you, and now I feel as if I've been suffocated by one night apart."

Lucius clamped his eyes shut. He knew just how she felt. "I thought I would wait another year for this. My sentence has dissolved, and my slumber is filled with fitful dreams of being away from you all over again."

They parted, both remembering that they were in someone else's home when a maid scurried by. Alexcena's gaze dropped from his eyes to his chest and she licked her lips.

"I'm worried about something, Lucius."

"What's that?" *Another excuse for me to pull you nearer?*

"My parents," she said. "I'm worried about marrying so far away from them. I'm worried about my family's reputation. What if people look badly on them?"

"Elopement. Is that what you mean?"

She nodded.

"But is it still considered elopement if you were given permission long ago?"

"*That* is not the part that everyone will know about. To them it will seem that you disappeared and I disappeared and then we reappeared married. I'm not thinking of what they'll say about us. I'm only afraid that my parents will be cast down for it."

"Knowing your parents, I would say they would tell us not to think of it."

"My father especially. Still, that doesn't make them any less vulnerable to society's gossips. One word can be most dangerous to families of position if uttered in the wrong ear."

After a moment's thought, Lucius had to agree with her. "I know. I wouldn't want them to bear such things either." He tried his best to look comforting, but inside he was floundering. The contract was signed, and he had promised to stay for one year. Did he dare leave to marry his love, thereby breaking the law and betraying his word to Garret? There was no denying that he was tempted.

"We'll talk about this later," he murmured and stroked her arm all the way down to her hand. "Let tomorrow take care of the things of itself. You're not to worry. Do you believe me?"

"Yes," she grinned, "and I believe Him too."

Lucius lifted her hand to kiss her knuckle. The motion served to calm him somewhat, and he returned his attention to his favorite subject.

"You look wonderful this morning."

Alexcena ducked her head, embarrassed. "Do you want to know my secret?" She lowered her voice to a light whisper. "I had a bath earlier."

Lucius could not help but laugh.

She smiled sheepishly. "Mrs. Faraday was up when I woke, and she insisted. The other girls are up there taking turns now. Stop laughing!" She gave him a small shove. "You know I'd never tell anyone but you."

"Glad to hear it," Lucius gasped when he was able. "You've met Mrs. Faraday then?"

"Yes, and Mr. Faraday, too. He's in the dining room now. I'm so very greatful to them both for all they have done."

"As am I." As he gave this answer, he offered his arm. "May I escort you to the dining room?"

"Just a moment. I have something for you." She reached into the pocket of her skirt and produced a battered envelope.

"This is the letter Major Dunwhither returned to you yesterday," Lucius declared as he studied it.

"Yes."

She pressed it into his hand. When he turned it over he found his own name written in a familiar script.

"It is from my father," Alexcena told him. "When I left England, he gave me a packet and told me it was for you. Along the way here, I learned that you had been lost off the coast in a storm…and I thought you might be dead… So I opened it." Her head hung low with the confession and the memory of her feelings then. "I found the money and this letter." She turned uncertain eyes to him then.

Lucius held her look and traced the side of her cheek. He gave his head a little shake. "We two are to be one. It might as well have been addressed to you in the first place."

She relaxed at that. The shadow of guilt left her.

Lucius slipped the letter into his coat and held out his arm once again. "I shall read the message this evening, when I have the time to read it slowly. For now, I would be most flattered if you would allow me to show you into the dining room."

"A wonderful idea."

They were halfway down the hall before she spoke again. Lucius felt his heart swell to hear the sound, no matter what she said.

"There is something different about you."

Lucius looked down at himself as though expecting to see some new trait. "There is?"

"Yes. Well, I mean there are a few things, but there's something in particular about your face." She regarded him for an instant before reaching up to touch the corner of his glasses. "These are new. What happened to your gold ones?"

"The Professor had gold-rimmed glasses?"

Lucius looked up to find that they had reached the dining room. Garret was sitting at the table.

"I did," he answered, "but I'm afraid the traveling was not good for them. I traded to acquire this new pair."

"They suit you," Alexcena said to him before turning to the other man. "Good morning again, Mr. Faraday."

Garret rose from his seat. "And to the two of you as well."

"I hope we are not intruding."

"Not at all. You'll stay for breakfast, won't you? Lavinia would be so disappointed if you did not."

Lucius endeavored to smile. "We wouldn't dream of missing it."

Garret seemed to be making a study of stirring his coffee, but Lucius had a feeling that he was also watching the two of them. Lucius led Alexcena to a chair beside the one Lavinia normally occupied on Garret's left. He held it out, and, after she had taken her seat, faltered over where to go. Gentility and true etiquette required that he sit across from her. He wondered if he could bend the rules and sit beside her instead. The decision was made for him when Garret gave Lavinia's usual chair a light kick.

Lucius cleared his throat and sat down.

"I did not have a chance to speak with you properly before, Mr. Faraday," Alexcena said, filling the awkward silence, "but I do hope that my friends and I have not caused a great inconvenience for you and your wife."

"Nothing of the sort!" Garret averred. "We are glad to have you. In fact, if I may confide, Lavinia grew up in a household of eighteen. I think she is uncomfortable if there is not some sort of bustle going on about."

A child's voice at the doorway startled them all.

"Professor, I'm-oh."

They all looked around to see Foley. He had stopped midstride-and mid sentence-on the threshold and was staring at Alexcena with unmitigated shock.

Lucius knew it was incumbent upon him to introduce Foley and Alexcena, but he thought it best to first prod the lad out of his nervous astonishment. "Yes, Foley, what is it?"

Foley shuffled and looked from one to the other of them before answering. "I'm ready to leave for school now, Professor."

Lucius looked him up and down with an upraised eyebrow. There stood Foley in a decent set of clothes. His face had been scrubbed, and his books were clasped under one arm. "So you are. The sight of you makes me all the more sorry to have to tell you that today is Saturday."

Foley's eyes grew round. His small mouth fell slack.

"Don't look so pitiful." By way of cheering the boy up, Lucius added, "It's sure to be a nice day. We can walk Commodore later. In the meantime come here and become acquainted with Ms. Condreve."

Foley took several slow steps to reach them.

"This is Alexcena. Alexcena, this is Foley."

She gave the boy one of her warmest smiles. "It's a pleasure to meet you, Foley."

Foley's mouth twitched. He seemed unsure of what to do under her gaze. "Um-me too-pleasure, I mean."

Lucius sympathized with Foley. She had quite a similar affect on him as well.

"How did you meet Lucius?" she asked easily.

For an instant Lucius wondered if the boy would be tempted to create one of his wild stories. He was astonished when he gave her the truth.

"He caught me picking his pocket."

"In truth?"

Foley nodded.

"And what did you find there?"

"That pink necklace he carries."

That stopped her at once. She looked to Lucius, who was already searching her face. Feeling sheepish, he wondered if he would find laughter in her eyes. Instead he saw a deep emotion he could not name, though he knew it well. It was a reflection of his own feeling. He drew the token from his pocket and held it up so that she might see.

"You still have it!" she breathed.

"Apparently this object carries a great deal of weight with Ms. Condreve," Garret remarked with a wink.

Lucius gestured toward her with it. "Put it on for you?"

She lifted her hair from her neck by way of an answer. Lucius soon had the length of ribbon tied at her throat. She reached up to touch the cameo.

"Thank you, Foley, for reminding me."

"And me," Lucius added.

Foley was at that moment backing toward the door. "Uh, I didn't do it on purpose or anything."

"Foley, where are you off to?"

"Well, I was gonna go join Uncle Leo in the cottage since I don't have school and all."

"Why don't you tell Leo to come in and we all shall have breakfast together," Garret suggested.

Foley nodded and bumped into the doorframe on his way out.

Alexcena sighed, still fiddeling with her necklace. "Do you think he's very afraid of me?"

"He doesn't know you, that's all."

"Who is he? How did he come to be staying with you?"

For a moment Lucius struggled to form his response. Foley had become so much of a fact in his life that it was difficult to remember that Alexcena knew nothing of him. "We just…came upon one another. He was on his own and so was I, and somehow we stuck together. He has grown to be as much a son to me as I could never have thought possible in so short a time."

"You've never had a son." Alexcena's expression remained placid, but he was certain he saw a teasing glint there as well.

He almost chuckled. "No. But I imagine this is what it feels like."

"What happened to his parents?"

Lucius considered carefully before answering. "It was some time before Foley was willing to divulge that information to me. I think he would feel better if I allow him to chose when it is told to you."

She gave a nod. "I shall endeavor to make him less afraid of me between now and then."

"There was never an easier job," Garret chortled. "I cannot imagine you harming even the tiniest flea, ma'am."

Lucius could not resist. "Perhaps not, but she did cause her mother to faint completely once."

Alexcena drew herself up. "I asked you never to repeat that story!"

"You said no such thing," he replied with a dignified air. "You only asked if I was shocked to hear it."

"Now I'm curious," Garret interrupted, his eyes wide. "What could you possibly have done, Ms. Condreve? If I may ask, that is."

"I set a wild animal loose in the house."

"Wild animal?" Garret looked from one to the other of them.

They both let him wonder for a few seconds before Alexcena burst into giggles and had to explain. "It was only a kitten, but to my mother it seemed to be a wild thing."

Soon enough the back door was heard opening, followed by Foley's light tread and a distinct clickling noise as well. When he appeared in the dining room, Commodore was right beside him.

"Foley, why did you bring him in here?" Lucius chided.

"I didn't mean to, Professor, he just pushed right passed me."

"Not to worry," Garret said. "If he jumps on anything we shall just show him out again."

Instinctively Lucius put a hand on Alexcena's arm. He remembered well how she had reacted to Commodore in the past. He began searching her face for any sign of fear, but he found none. His surprise at this was compounded when she held out her hand and commanded him.

"Commodore, hither."

Lucius watched as his dog approached and pressed the top of his head into her palm to be rubbed. Alexcena obliged.

"When did this happen?" Lucius wondered aloud. "You were petrified of him in England!"

"We grew quite close on the long voyage here," Alexcena told him. "I can't say that I wouldn't be frightened by any other dog that approached me, but at least I'm not afraid of him."

Garret mumbled something behind his napkin, which sounded suspiciously like, "Fortunate, since you will be in his presence so often in the future."

"Uncle Leo said that he would come in shortly," Foley explained. "And I met the other lady-"

"Ms. Winslett?" Garret supplied.

"Right, sir; Ms. Winslett. I saw her on the back porch. She said she would be in soon too."

"Very good. Why don't you have a seat then, my boy." As he spoke Garret gestured to the chairs on his right.

"Thank you, sir." Foley sat in the middle opposite Alexcena. He looked up at her and then swiftly down at the table. "May I ask a question, ma'am-Ms. Condreve-if it's not too much trouble?"

"Certainly, Foley."

"How did you get Commodore to come right up to you like that?"

"Commodore has several words that he has been taught to respond to.

If you like, I'll show you what they are after breakfast."

Foley shuffled. "I would like that, I mean if you would like that… ma'am."

Alexcena's expression softened even further, though Foley did not see it since he was still looking down. "I would be happy to, Foley."

Chapter 10
July 27, 1765

Leo stepped out the door of Lucius' cottage still holding a mug of coffee. He breathed deeply of its rich scent as he swallowed a gulp. It was not until he lowered the mug that he caught sight of Tabitha.

She was sitting on the steps of the Faraday's home directly across from him. Her head was bowed and her arms were propped on her knees. Her blonde hair fell in thick curtains on either side of her face, as though shielding her from her surroundings. The sight made him imagine a child attempting to hide. *I can't see you, so you can't see me.*

He crossed the yard at a leisurely pace, assuming she would notice him long before he reached her. She did not move until he was standing quite close. She was startled by the sight of his boots, and her head snapped up to his face at once.

"Leopold!"

She straightened her posture and folded her hands in prim fashion.

"Tabitha." He could not resist grinning as he moved to lean against the railing of the portico. Then, pretending to focus on his coffee, he remarked, "I don't believe I've ever seen you slouch before."

"I try not to do it. It's how I was trained."

Her voice was mild and even. He had expected haughty and saucy. This made him glance at her from the corner of his eye. She was staring at nothing in the distance.

"What are you thinking? Anything I can help with?" The concern came naturally before he thought to check it. *I've been bothering with her for so long it's becoming a habit.*

"I was thinking about myself, truth to tell."

Leo rolled his eyes. "Astonishing."

Ignoring his jibe, she began to explain. "I was thinking about all the reasons I felt I had for coming here."

"You mean Lucius." He felt guilty for being abrupt about the subject, but if she had not realized by then that it was not to be, then she needed a little abrasion to help her get rid of the notion.

"No. That's not it."

The words were uncaring, almost cheery. Leo turned directly to her, shocked by the answer.

"I felt smothered in my own home," she continued without looking his way. "I wanted a chance to grow up, and I was selfish enough to think I deserved what I wanted how I wanted it, no matter how it affected anyone else. I supposed that my actions were justified because I was entitled."

The curls trembled as she shook her head at the notion. It was clear by her expression that she did not feel so entitled anymore. Leopold was speechless. His lips parted, but he had not one word to say.

"I've been trying to decide what I should do, but I don't really know how to remedy the past just yet. I must go back. That much is at least clear."

She was still focused on something far off, and he wondered if she were talking more to herself than him. Then she turned to him, and her features came alive with laughter.

"Is your coffee too hot, Leopold?" she snickered.

"No!" He had answered too quickly and knew it. He clamped his hanging jaw shut.

He would have listened to her longer, curious as he had suddenly become. Before he could think of another question to ask, she rose and turned toward the door. Standing on the second step up, she was eye to eye with him for the first time.

"What will you do, Leo?"

He looked down into his mug for another swallow. "About what?"

"Will you return to England?"

He had known the answer to that for some time. "No. Took us long enough to get here, I think I'd like to see more of America first. I've never been to any place like it."

"Hm." Tabitha picked at the wood grain of the railing and was silent for a long moment. Then, just as she started toward the door, she exhaled a thick breath. "Too bad I'm not selfish enough to stay anymore."

"Stay?"

Leo could not make sense of the comment. He looked around to question her further, only to find the door already closing behind her. A part of him wondered if she had meant him to hear what she had said at all.

Chapter 11
July 27, 1765

The day was a bright one. It being a Saturday, Lucius was not obligated to go to work at the prison, and so he was free to spend his hours with his companions. He was glad of it indeed, for he was not certain he could have brought himself to do ought else under the circumstances. After breakfast he, Alexcena, and Foley went out of doors so that they might teach Foley the dog's commands. He was fascinated that Commodore followed every one without fail and delighted when he discovered the animal knew how to catch a stick he took to tossing. Tabitha and Victoria joined them, and eventually they decided to give Alexcena and Tabitha a tour of the city. Lucius was most animated and even excited as he pointed out various shops and streets. He described for them in detail his work at the prison and the stories of some of the men he had spoken to. His happiness grew with every step they took, for now he was able to share again with Alexcena the goings-on of his days. It was another forgotten element of his life coming alive in him again.

They followed several streets up and down and were close to the Faraday's neighborhood once again when a sudden summer shower struck. Foley offered to show Tabitha and Victoria back to the house, while Lucius and Alexcena ducked inside a coffee shop. Lucius watched through the window as Foley dashed ahead of them only to be outstripped by Commodore. The ladies followed not far behind.

In the relative quiet of the shop, Alexcena told Lucius all about her journey to find him. She explained how she came to know that he was missing and how she immediately contacted Leo. How she had been miserably ill at sea and how they traveled on shore. He was of course, most intrigued by her account of the Machapunga. Then she recounted their mutual acquaintances.

"We met so many people who remembered you that I would not have believed it myself if I had not lived it."

"Truly?"

"We met Victoria and that heavy-set gentleman, of course. Before that we met the Hatchens family, a Mr. Gibbs, and Mr. Darlum."

"Smith Darlum?"

Alexcena could only shudder.

"Yes," Lucius chuckled. "I know the feeling."

Lucius too had an account to give of his long journey. He recalled his landing during the dreadful storm and meeting Foley. He described his own travels with Smith and then with Robert Mandrake. When all was told between them, it was a relief for both. Each cared so much for the life of the other, that neither one wanted to miss knowing what was happening in the moments spent apart. The anxiety of separation had made them long for intelligence and closeness even more.

When the rain subsided, the pair thought it best to return to the house before another cloud could arrive. The July air became balmy and humid as the sun shone through the mists above, but a quick breeze served to make the temperature bearable.

By the time they arrived everyone was sitting down to some sandwiches on the portico in order to take advantage of the cooling wind. Leo in particular was about to take his first bite when Lucius hurried up the stairs and seized his right wrist. Leo remained calm enough.

"I don't keep my gold there anymore, sir. And if you look for it anywhere else, I think I'll knock you flat."

Lucius was busy shoving Leo's sleeve up and inspecting his arm. "I want to get a look at your injury."

Leo grinned. "She told you, didn't she?" Then, to Alexcena, "Worried about me still, eh?"

She suppressed a laugh and shook her head.

"What are you all talking about? Did something happen?" Lavinia wondered aloud with a searching glance at each of them.

Leo cleared his throat and averted his eyes. "I, um, had something of a run in with a, uh, snake several days ago."

Lavinia paled and laid a hand at her throat. Garret choked into his cup. Foley, who was sitting on the floor and rubbing Commodore, became puzzled. "How did you run into a snake without ever seeing it?"

"I see!" Lucius exclaimed triumphantly. "Here's where it got you."

Leo grimaced. "Arrogant little monster."

"It looks all right though," Lucius assured him and relinquished his arm. "You're fortunate it wasn't something more dangerous."

As he rolled down his sleeve, Leo shuddered. "Don't I know it. I still remember how sick I was that time in Spain." He made a face and reached for his sandwich.

No one cared to ruin their appetite by asking for the details of that particular tale.

Tabitha set down her plate and turned to Alexcena after a momentary silence. "Did anyone approach the two of you in the coffee shop?"

"No. Why should they?"

It was Garret who explained. "I'm afraid the story of your arrest and swift release has already traveled through much of town. We've had more than one caller here today wondering what happened."

A snicker trickled from Victoria. "In town two days and already gathering gossip, Ena."

Lucius raised an eyebrow. "Ena?" He glanced at Alexcena.

She blushed and nodded her head toward Leo. "He started it."

Lucius shrugged. "He would, but there is a bright side. He could have chosen to call you 'Ale.'"

Leo coughed and spluttered. He was able to laugh only after he had caught his breath. In fact everyone was laughing except Foley, who seemed to be distracted. When Lucius looked toward him, he saw the boy holding out a piece of meat from his sandwich. Commodore snapped it up.

"Foley," Lucius warned.

The boy looked up. "Sorry, Professor, but Uncle Leo said Commodore'd quit hitting my knees if I gave him something."

All eyes turned to Leo who became very interested in his plate. "We'll have to have a talk with that man," he said to no one in particular. "Handsome fellow, but he has no sense of manners at all sometimes."

After everyone had their fill-and twice as much for Lavinia-they dispersed again. Leo and Foley played with Commodore in the yard. Victoria and Tabitha disappeared somewhere. Lavinia declared that she was going to lie down, and Garret was not long after her to see if she might need anything. Normally each of these stalwart, resolute, and unique individuals would have found something more productive-or at least more interesting-to do on such a fine Saturday. As it was they each had their own excuses. The travelers were weary from walking and riding. Lucius was weary from shock. Lavina was weary from the child, and, what with her being in the family way, Garret was content to fuss over her.

So Lucius and Alexcena sat on the front steps and continued talking. So content were they in one another's company that they dared to hold hands, even in the open as they were.

"Tabitha has made some plans for herself," Alexcena mentioned.

"Indeed?"

"She's going back to England."

"England? How will she manage that?" To himself, Lucius couldn't help thinking, *'Tis a difficult thing to accomplish.*

"The ship that brought us here will be docking in Charleston in September. The Captain offered his services to us then if we should need them, so she plans to meet him there. Victoria has agreed to go along as her companion in exchange for the passage fee."

"How will she pay two fees?"

"Apparantly she gave Captain Loughdon something of an advance when she paid him originally and secured a return trip later, should she wish it. Knowing Tabitha and being aware of certain subtle hints she gave on the subject early this morning, I suspect she may have a bit more in the lining of some of her trunks on board the *Liberator*. The ship that is."

Lucius sat back and adjusted his glasses. "Well! It will be a shame to see her go so soon."

"Yes," Alexcena sighed. "She's growing into a lady more and more every day rather than a mere girl. I will not like to lose her."

"Who said anything of losing her?"

Her answering smile was faint indeed. "I know how it feels to have an ocean separating me from someone I love."

Lucius' heart was pricked with sympathy. He raised her hand to kiss it. "This will be different." She nodded and being well satisfied, he was able to grin. "It is different for us now, too."

Pink flew into her cheeks as she met his eyes. "Yes."

"Thanks to you. We would still be half a world apart if not for you, dear one."

Chapter 12

July 27, 1765

Dearest Alexcena,

Do not be startled by what you read here. A father knows when his daughter will need his comfort the most, and so here I am. You have taken your journey as you should have. It was clear to your mother and I that your heart would not rest nor your soul be quietted until you sought what you longed for. Were it not so your leaving would not have been borne. You have had a steady guide and a firm one to lead you. I assure you again that were those facts not so, such an endeavor never would have been allowed. I explain these things to you only to help you to understand the decision your mother and I have made in letting you go. I pray you will find forgiveness for us on that score and healing for the pain you must be feeling now.

Life is not a perfect thing. Our existence here is as much subject to chance as the trees to the weather or a grain of sand to the surf of the sea. Often times neither success nor failure play part in the happenings we face. Rather, we are disappointed for a time, just as in other days we might have been elated for a time. In circumstances that are left uncontrolled and found uncontrollable, all that is left to us is to find peace under Christ's yoke and continue on while there is still life remaining.

You have become a strong and a capable woman. Now it is for you to take comfort in knowing that you have done all that you could do amidst a storm that came into your lands. It is not failure; it is not defeat; it is not a call to revenge, which you know to be forbidden as well as I. It is instead shadowed days in which you must wait, for soon the healing sun will rise and bring to you warmth against your sorrow. Do not despair, dear daughter. Do not let the wind whip away your heart. If you can see no other reason to believe these words now, believe them simply because you trust and obey me. If you will obey me, then look to the Word for the truth of what I have said.

This life passes as a flower, and this time in it as a drop of water on its petal. Take care, daughter, that you are not early wilted when you return to us. Your Lucius could not have asked anything more of you than all that you have done for him.

The page waved in the breeze as it lay in Lucius' loose grasp. When first he had opened the letter Alexcena had presented to him from her father, he could not fathom the misunderstanding. He read only the greeting first, and that three times. Then he had looked to the name written on the back. Once he had truly confirmed that it was supposedly meant for him, he considered waiting until Alexcena could read it with him. This he was most thankful he had decided against after he read the missive for himself.

He was sitting in his armchair in the cabin. After a fourth reading of the letter, he had snuffed out his candle. Moonlight from the windows crept in, eventually giving him some sight of his surroundings, but he was not truly looking at anything. He was only pondering.

Lawrence Condreve, his mentor and companion, had not thought it likely that Alexcena would find him. Or at least, that she would find him alive. The idea grieved him. He could only thank the Lord God above that they had decided to allow the journey at all. He could well remember the anxieties and sorrows that had been his in the days that he spent wondering America and feeling so desolate for his beloved. Selfish though it was, he could not imagine being banished back to such days. But then he wondered if it were truly selfish at all. Had not Alexcena had similar thoughts and pains? The difference had been that she had been allowed to make use of resources that would take her to him. He merely had not been as fortunate. He had no doubt that he would have acted as she had.

At some point during his musing he heard a stirring in the loft above and Leopold descended the ladder to join him. He sat in one of the chairs at the table and looked at his brother, though he said not a word. Lucius was glad of it, but after some consideration he chose to talk.

"This is the letter Alexcena's father sent with her for me."

He handed over the letter, and Leo read it by the window that he might see. When he returned to his seat, he laid it on the table. "I would say it was more concerning you."

Lucius rubbed his forehead and swallowed to suppress the lump in his throat. "I was not expecting that."

Leo considered him briefly. "Doesn't matter in the end. He was just doing what he thought best. Trying to be there for his daughter if the worst should happen. The thing is that the worst did not happen. Don't trouble yourself about it."

"That is not so much what's troubling me."

Leo sat back in his chair. He cross his ankles and folded his arms over his stomach, waiting for Lucius to continue.

"I don't know where to go-how to proceed-" Lucius struggled to find words for his thoughts. "I wasn't prepared for all of this, all of you. Not that I mean that in an unfeeling way, it's just that now I don't know what to do next."

"I assume you'll be marrying her next won't you?"

"Yes. No, I-" Lucius cleared his throat and tugged at his collar. "I want to, believe me. I asked again and she said yes."

Leo ran a hand through his hair. "You thought you needed to ask again after all this?"

Lucius shifted in his embarrassment. "Well, no. It just seemed... polite."

In the blackness he felt rather than actually saw Leo rolling his eyes.

"We have both acknowledged now that there are some difficulties for us to face on that score," Lucius went on. "First of all there's Foley."

"You saw them together today just as well as I did, Luc. You know that won't be a problem when they come to know one another."

"It's a lot to ask of someone to suddenly take up raising a child."

"Did you hesitate?"

Lucius pressed that concern aside and went on. "I'm not anymore financially sound than I was in England. Even less so in fact. That was always a factor."

"A fair one, but more a concern of yours than hers."

"On that same topic there's my contract with Garret. I gave my word that I would stay here for one year. I can't feel right about returning to England to be married now."

"Why would you need to return to England?"

Lucius sighed. "That brings about the greatest concern for both of us. Alexcena's parents."

"I see. Being married here, they would not be able to attend the great occasion."

"It's not only that. If we did marry it would seem as though we had conspired to run away together. If people in their society derived the wrong impressions, the Condreves might face considerable scorn. Neither of us wants them subjected to that under any circumstance."

Lucius let his head fall forward under the weight of his thoughts. The more he voiced them aloud, the larger they seemed to become.

"What are you considering then?" Leo asked quietly.

"Sending Alexcena back to them."

"What!?"

Lucius glanced up at the ceiling, waiting to hear some noise from Foley after Leo's exclamation. The boy apparently slept on.

"How could you do that?" Leo whispered harshly.

"I don't want to do it," Lucius almost snapped. "I just wonder if it might be the best thing for them and for her. I could return after my year here as I had planned to. If the Condreves have managed to allay any questions as to Alexcena's whereabouts during all this time, her reputation and theirs will remain in tact."

"Such a radical solution after all she went through to come here."

A thread of anger tightened itself inside Lucius. He worked to calm his distraught mind. "What would you do," he asked slowly, "if you found yourself in such a position as I?"

"I would write to them."

No hesitation. No pensivity. Yet it seemed the simplest alternative in the world. Lucius was amazed that he had not thought of it sooner.

"Write to her parents," Leo urged. "Let them know that you are alive and well, as previously doubted. Then let them know that Alexcena has found you and that you intend to marry someday as you have all along. Find out their wishes and see to it that they know yours. They already love you, so the answer ought to be a favorable one, I should think."

He had added the last with a chuckle. Whether it was at his astonishment or his own teasing Lucius could not say. He began to laugh himself, and felt a great sense of relief.

"Wolgath, you astound me!"

"Not to worry, Luc," he replied, stretching his long arms high above his head. "You're not the first one to be astounded by my brilliance."

"I could even send the letter along with Tabitha," Lucius said, thinking out loud about this new and appealing plan. "It would save me having to buy postage for it and it would arrive so much safer."

"Tabitha?" Leo sat up straight with a sudden jolt. "What about Tabitha?"

"Alexcena told me she plans to return to England soon on board that ship."

"The *Liberator*? When it docks in Charleston?"

Lucius nodded. "Victoria will be going with her as a sort of ladies' maid I think."

Leo got to his feet and paced to the ladder, rubbing his chin as he went. "I'll go to Charleston with them," he declared as he reached for the first rung.

"Go with them? Have they asked you?"

"No, but it's not wise for two ladies such as them to be traveling alone such a long way."

Lucius had to admit that he was correct, but something in his brother's sudden change of demeanor made him wonder about his motives. "Is that the only reason?"

Leo paused half way up the ladder. "The only practicle one."

After Leo vanished into the loft, Lucius lit the candle and took out a pen, ink, and paper. In the most simple manner possible, he intimated all that had happened and all that he hoped for in a letter to Lawrence. The first light of dawn came to the horizon as he finished the last draft of his message. He smiled down at the words lining the page. His confidence had grown every time he read them. After breakfast he would give it to Alexcena. If she approved, they would send it on, and then all that would be left would be the waiting. At least this time they would be waiting together and not a world apart.

Chapter 13

September 2, 1765

Leo breathed deeply of the stinging salt air, hoping to clear his head with its sharpness. He had not wanted to leave Savannah. It was good to see his brother happy with his lady, and he had not wanted to miss seeing him again. As long as it had taken to find Lucius it was worrisome to think that he should leave so soon. But coming to Charleston had been his own idea. Then too, he had given his word, and he would not go back on that. September drew nearer and he, Tabitha, and Victoria had made plans to depart.

Depart they did, and he had grown more and more melancholy the farther they went. This bothered him to no end, mainly because he knew the reason why. Tabitha. Always Tabitha. When he slept, when he woke, as he walked, while he talked, he was always distracted by Tabitha. It had been so from the very beginning. That had seemed natural enough given that she had thrust herself into his care, albeit unwittingly. This time it was more than that. This time his concerns bordered on obsession. He could only blame himself for that and he knew all of those reasons as well.

Tabitha had not been her vibrant self since they had arrived in Savannah. She had grown withdrawn. It was as though a heavy curtain had been pulled over her visage. No longer was he able to discern her every attitude by voice or expression or movements, and he did not like it. He caught himself snapping at her on more than one occasion when she would not speak up. He blamed himself for this change in her, and he was guilty. So guilty that he kept catching himself becoming angry with her and wishing that she would come back to some semblance of herself so that he would be spared his guilt. This was not a line of thought he was proud of, but it was happening none the less. Try as he might to change his own mood, he could not affect it. He felt powerless. The closer they drew to Charleston the worse it became.

In the end the journey seemed longer than any other that he had taken in recent memory. Poor Victoria suffered the worst of it, he feared. With him behaving like a temperamental bear and Tabitha acting like an elusive young fox, she could not have enjoyed herself overly much. He was thankful that she had been blessed with a gift for knowing when to act and when to remain out of the way. He had also learned that she was far less defensive among friends rather than strangers, so his rising temper was not aggravated by hers.

At the end of it all, he found himself standing on a long wharf watching as the sailors on board the *Liberator* moved about the deck. Captain Loughdon descended the plank to greet them. The lines of his face were rigid as always, but something akin to curiosity peaked from the corners of his eyes. He nodded to each of them in turn before speaking to Leo.

"Did you find what you were looking for?"

"Yes. Our venture was quite successful."

Loughdon gave a tight, ascending smile. "And Ms. Condreve?"

"She is with Lucius, just as she should be."

Leo moved aside, allowing Tabitha to handle all of the arrangements with the Captain. Her dealings with Loughdon were none of his affair anyway. Besides, from his vantage point several feet back, he could keep an eye on Lieutenant Greyson.

Leo was not one to forget. He still remembered with keen clarity the attention the man had given Tabitha on their first voyage. He was more than a little unsure about the whole idea of this trip as it was. Greyson's presence was not helpful in soothing him.

"I'm glad I'm not standin' in front of ye."

"Hm?" Leo barely looked at Victoria before setting his sights back on Greyson.

"The fire in yer eyes is likely to burn straight through."

Leo ground his teeth and tried to force himself to relax. He uncrossed his arms and buried his hands in his pockets. Still he considered Greyson. He did not seem to be a dangerous sort of man. His demeanor had always been pleasant and meek whenever Leo had been around him. Aside from the bygone altercation that had passed between them when he had discovered Tabitha on board the *Liberator,* a cross word had not passed between them. Although Leo might have wanted to accuse the man of treating Tabitha inappropriately, even he had to admit that he had witnessed no true evidence of that. He had only been inflamed by the possibilities. Still it did not set well. Knowing what sort of man John Greyson was ought to have cured his apprehension on that point. Instead it had grown...

The truth came to Leopold as a wave comes to the shoreline. The truth of his irritations with Greyson could be explained in a single word; jealousy. Leo suddenly found that he was jealous of a man who had shown affection toward Tabitha.

He struggled to keep his inward thoughts from affecting the expression on his face. He was realizing several things at once and dared not allow anyone else to see his discomfiture until he had sorted himself out. In the mean time other things were happening around him as well. Loughdon looked to him then and dipped his head. As he and his lieutenant started away, Tabitha returned.

"They won't be departing until tomorrow morning due to the tides and cargo to unload," she said to Victoria, "but the Captain says we're welcome to come aboard now."

"We wouldn't have to worry about finding a place to stay tonight," Victoria thought aloud.

Tabitha nodded and looked to Leo with her large green eyes.

Leo gave a twitch of his shoulder. "Whatever you think. I can stay in town tonight if you like. In case something should happen."

The curtain fluttered and a hint of a smile crossed her lips. "I'm so accustomed to you being in charge, I fear I'm no longer certain about my own decisions."

So this is how she leaves, he thought bitterly. *A self-conscious shadow of her former self.*

But isn't this what you wanted from her? that annoying voice in the far corner of his mind crooned.

I wanted her to calm down and embrace wisdom, he thought back, *as much for her sake as anyone else's. I never wanted her to feel so accursedly embarrassed that she tucked herself away completely. Not only did she rid herself of all that was at first so very annoying about her character, now she has also suppressed all that was lovely about her. I did this to her and now there is no time to undo it. I'm sending her home damaged...*

All these thoughts came over the span of two minutes. All the while Tabitha and Victoria watched him, one with apprehension and the other with something akin to aggravation. When he realized that, he felt like a perfect idiot.

"Sorry. I'm holding you ladies up. I'll stay along the wharf here so you can send word if you need me for anything."

"Thank you," Tabitha murmured.

Victoria bobbed her head in respect. "I hope to see ye again, Leo."

"I'm pleased to have met you." He managed a smile. Victoria was after all amiable in her own coarse way.

Tabitha's good bye was not so encouraging. "Farewell, Leopold."

He nodded. "And you, Tabitha."

He could think of nothing else to say to her. It was odd that this would be the end of their relationship just as he was realizing that he might want something more. It was unlikely at best that they would ever see one another again once the ship was gone. She had become something of a fixture, and he felt a numb sensation knowing that she could be gone for good.

He watched them go and stood still for several moments even after they had disappeared on deck. There was nowhere he could think to go and nothing for him to do. He stared dumbly at sailors as they scuttled along ships and decks. There was a pressure building inside his chest. As he studied its coming he could well guess why it came. Soon it seemed as though all his body ached from the effort of standing still and his breaths grew short under the weight on his chest. With all the certainty a man can ever have, Leo Wolgath knew then that he could not watch that ship simply sail away.

<u>Chapter 14</u>

September 2, 1765

Tabitha was startled by a great ruckus above decks.

She had set to checking everything in her trunks. Since they had been left unattended on board the *Liberator* for months, she thought it only sensible to peruse them. She had only just run her hands over the first dress when the noise came. She leapt to her feet.

"What's happened?!" Victoria demanded.

Men's voices began to trickle down through the deck. Some were louder than others. Tabitha was uncertain, but one sounded distinctly familiar.

"I'll find out," she said.

When she stepped out of the door of the main deck into the pale light of the afternoon, she froze.

Halfway down the length of the ship stood Leopold Wolgath. He was speaking with the Captain, who looked nonetoo happy to see him. Loughdon had his hands on his hips, and his voice was raised the loudest of all. Leo looked defensive and determined, but he was speaking calmly.

How could he do this!?

The question thundered through Tabitha's mind. *He's been chipping away at my heart for weeks. Has he come to shatter it now? Why couldn't he just let me go?!*

She crossed the deck, anger flaring in her young face.

"-business being aboard, and I do not take kindly to unannounced passengers," Loughdon was saying.

Leo ignored his question when he saw her drawing close. "Tabitha!"

He looked relieved, but she was fearsome. "What are you *doing* here?!"

"I couldn't help myself."

Tabitha rocked back. She looked from Loughdon to Leo and back again. His answer confused her sufficiently enough to give her pause.

"-may not be a passenger at all," Leo was saying to the Captain, "if you'll just give me a moment." He looked meaningfully over Loughdon's shoulder.

All eyes turned to Tabitha. She flushed both from anger and embarrassment. She stood as straight as she was able and resented the fact that she still had to look a full foot up at him.

"I don't understand you!" she snapped.

"Yes, you do." He stepped around Loughdon to stand directly in front of her. "If you think about it hard enough you can probably even guess why I'm here."

"Why would I do that?" she fired back.

"Why are you so angry with me?"

She spoke through clenched teeth. "Because you're *here!* I don't want you to be. I want you to go!"

His voice was just a little smaller when he said, "Why?"

She closed her eyes. "You want me to say it out loud?"

The wind whipped her hair all around her face. The rush of it was the only noise she heard. Everyone else was still, waiting to hear what was said.

Leo swallowed. "You don't need to… I've been overbearing and hard with you ever since that first day at sea. If it was too much, I want you to know that I'm sorry."

"That's not it." Tabitha regretted her words the moment they left her mouth. He had so startled her with his apology that she had spoken out of turn. Then she knew she needed to explain. "You have taught me to be a better person than I was before," she said more softly. "I have never wanted you to apologize for that. I'm greatful for it!"

He was relieved, and then perplexed. "Then why are you upset that I'm here?"

"Because you don't want me." The admission took herculean effort to voice. Her eyes opened and she found him watching her with evident pain. "For months I've had to be near you and know it, waiting for the day I could escape you. Why couldn't you let me have that? Even that!"

"It's not true."

"It is true! Why else would I not have wanted you to come-"

"Not that." Leo shook his head at her. "It's not true that I don't want you. I came because I don't want to be without you."

"Stop it. You're not this cruel."

"You're right; I'm not," he insisted. "That's why you ought to be able to see that it's true."

Her eyes flashed with defiance. "What if it's not? I won't stand to be played with, Leo. I'm not the other women you've chased after."

"I have never chased after anyone. You're not like the others. You changed. For a time you were delightful, and I crushed it. I came to get you back."

He was right. She disagreed that it was his doing, but she did feel crushed. She had intended on putting the pieces back together while they crossed the sea, though she knew that there would be one piece missing. The piece she gave to Leo.

She hung her head, not knowing what to believe. He had not said a word all this time, and he chose now to come to her?

Strong hands encircled her arms. When she looked up she was not surprised to see him so close.

"I know this is hard now, but let me stay. I've made you forget that you can trust me. Let me show you again."

He was pleading with her. Her reserve would not have held up to less, to say nothing of all this. Shock and fear and longing and love all mingled inside her, making her small shoulders tremble.

Leo stroked her arms. "Let me show you."

She laid her head against his chest. It was so easy to lean into. She hoped that he was telling the truth, but the rational part of her knew that he was without question.

Chapter 15

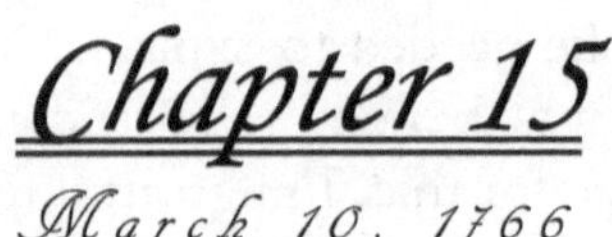

Lucius awoke to the feel of straw poking his back through the fabric of the mattress.

Normal now. Familiar… Reminds me I'm home…

After rising Lucius moved down the ladder to dress. He found Foley already slipping his good shirt on over his head.

"How did you get up without waking me?"

"You were tired, Professor," Foley answered stoically as his head popped through the opening of the collar. "You were at the Faradays' house really late, remember?"

Alexcena had accepted the Faradays' gracious offer to allow her to stay in one of the two spare bedrooms of their home. (The other was by then a nursery for the newborn child of Lavinia and Garret.) Lucius and Foley had been invited to dine with them all the evening before, and Lucius had stayed behind when Foley went off to bed. He thought back to the hour he spent talking with Alexcena when dinner was over.

"Yes, I do remember something like that."

He sat down at the table just as Commodore came inside. He ducked through the wooden slat Lucius had put over a cut out in the door with ease.

"Just like back at the Green isn't it, boy?"

Commodore sat close by his chair, and he rubbed his ears with vigor.

"I'm still amazed that he can fit through that hole," Foley remarked.

"He's tall, but he's sleek, aren't you, Commodore?"

The Great Dane gave a husky bark.

"Right."

Lucius left the cabin promptly at fifteen minutes to eight and found Alexcena on the Faradays' front porch.

"Waiting for me?"

She smiled coolly. "Aren't I always?"

"Usually."

Alexcena rose as early as he did every day. She had declared that she could not bare to sit idle while Lucius worked for hours so many days in the week, and so she had taken a position. She worked as a companion to an elderly widow who dwelt in one of the townhouses, her son having taken over the family estate and she being an independent woman. She had taken the position only three months prior. Her employer had proven to be a pleasant lady, though she was known to be somewhat strict. Alexcena had learned how to enjoy the work, and Lucius had seen that she was much happier to be helping him to secure their future rather than waiting for him to work for the whole of it.

Alexcena rocked back on her heels. He saw that she was toying with the strings of her apron and knew that something was on her mind. She did not waste time revealing her thoughts. "Lucius, do you ever mind that

I'm working?"

Lucius shook his head at her. "You have asked me this question at least ten different ways."

"I know, but I always feel that you're only allowing me to do it because I want to and not because you want me to."

He sobered. "I don't want you to feel as though you must work outside of home, but I know that it gives you great pleasure to help me in any way that you can. And you are helping me-and therefore us-by doing what you are doing. I admire you for it, my dear one."

She gave him a nod and another, warmer smile. "I do want to help."

"Don't I know it." He gave her a regal bow. "I bid you good day then, Ms. Condreve."

"Good day to you Lucius."

His heart beat lightly all the way to the prison. They had waited so long for word from Alexcena's parents that Lucius could not help thinking that it must not be long in coming now. His mind was filled with thoughts of his love and blessings, and so he was dreadfully ill prepared for what awaited him that day. The blow came to him quickly, like the fall of a blacksmith's hammer. In the end it was better and worse that way at the same time.

It all seemed so simple, so usual, when he went in. Two men were waiting for him in the customary room. A soldier and a prisoner.

"You're late, Professor," the soldier muttered.

"Home life."

The man sneered and turned to the door. "You've got your work cut out for you. This one was eager, soon as he heard your name."

The soldier slammed the heavy door behind him. The prisoner did not move. He sat as he had all along. His head was bowed over his manacled hands as they lay on the table. With his shoulders hunched and his forehead low, he seemed dormant. Like a sleeping volcano, he sat silent and smoldering.

Lucius watched him for but a moment before he sat down.

"The way the Private talked, it would seem that you know my name," he said cautiously. "What is yours?"

The man made no sign that he had heard the words. A cold shadow of suspicion crept into Lucius' mind. Still he tried again.

"Are you well, man?"

The thin, hunched shoulders trembled beneath the ragged shirt. A sound rose from him. It was a hoarse, scratching sound, hardly distinguishable as laughter. It was mirthless, contemptible.

"Thousands of miles from life and country, the wonderful Professor Wolgath asks if I am well."

The voice was a hollow rasp, and when the man had done speaking he coughed for several seconds. He raised his head then and wiped the corner of his mouth with his sleeve. Lucius couldn't help but notice that a pink smear was left there.

"A physician comes to the jail on occasion," the Professor told him. "If you're ill I can make arrangements to-"

"Why?" the prisoner demanded in a stronger voice. "Why would you of all people concern yourself with my health?"

Lucius was doubly confused. The man had asked to see him only to become hostile. He could not fathom it.

"Why do you say that?"

The man hesitated and turned his head to one side. His eyebrows rose as comprehension dawned. "You don't recognize me, at all?"

Lucius sat back, at a loss.

The prisoner leaned his head forward again, cradling his forehead in his hands and burying his fingers in his hair. "Just between the two of us, that may be the greatest revenge yet."

Lucius floundered, fumbling through his memory as fast as he was able. He stared, watching as the man raised his head and combed his long hair back, revealing a smooth forehead. For an instant Lucius had a clearer depiction of him. He wore a thick beard, but with his dull brown hair away from his face there was a glimmer of something familiar about his eyes. The high cheekbones and square jaw too reminded him of someone. When the recognition came, he felt a twinge in the back of his neck. He wondered if he wasn't truly beholding a ghost.

"Rodney."

"Very good, Lucius," Rodney jeered. "Now try to remember my last name, the worst half."

Lucius made no answer. Many thoughts and ideas were running all about his head, none of them pleasant. Until that moment he had not felt anger towards Rodney Dushaw. For months he had not been certain who was responsible for the disaster. He was so consumed by all the other concerns he faced, that eventually it had not even mattered to him. Even when Alexcena had explained all, and he knew, it had meant nothing. Now he was face to face with the man, and the knowledge was jarringly vital.

"I've always thought that goodness and evil were more than just characteristics," Rodney went on with ludicrous nonchalance. "I've always thought they were inherited in some degree. Do you suppose the same is true of stupidity, Lucius? I wonder, you see, because you have a gift for simplicity that is unmatched by anyone I have ever heard of. I've had hunting dogs more perceptive than you."

He broke off to cough again.

"Is this all you wanted?" Lucius asked. He was incredulous of the man before him and anxious for the interview to be over. "To sharpen your wit on me?"

"Nonsense," he choked. "You'd dull it."

"Do you not see yourself?" Lucius demanded. "Do you not see that your jibes do not matter?"

"Why?" Rodney snapped, his yellow-rimmed eyes blazing. "Because you're on that side of the table and I'm on this side? Because your wrists are free while mine are chained?"

"Because you serve a doomed master, and so you doom yourself."

"I am ten times the man you'll ever be!" Rodney shouted and leapt to his feet. "I would have had all that I wanted and more if you hadn't stumbled into my way!" All the while he paced.

Lucius sat still, endeavoring to remain calm. "How did you come to be here, Rodney?"

"I thought you would ask that. Wanting a good excuse for a laugh at me?" This he spoke more calmly.

Lucius shook his head. "That's not so."

"Don't lie to a liar, Lucius. Why else would you care to know?"

"Tell me, and I'll explain."

He chuckled dryly and took his seat once more. "Very well. It was debt. Mine and my father's. So much so in fact that I was told I would never be able to pay it off on a salary from the work house. I was sent here instead. I was at the work house in the first place because I lost my professorship!" He spat the word as though it were a heinous curse. "Do you care to know how I lost my professorship? It was that woman. *Elida!*"

The name was spoken in a feral growl. Lucius had to think hard to remember the woman. The one that Rodney had been courting on pretense in England.

"She ruined me. She made sure everyone knew all my darkest secrets and then she ran like a dog. Amazing how life's coincidences line up like a firing squad to shoot you in the back."

"Coincidences? Rodney, you have done this to yourself!" Lucius declared. "Consequences to your actions have come because you were deserving of them. You have not been the man that you could be. You chose to be the man you wanted to be. How could you have expected a different result than this?"

Rodney glared behind scraggly strands of brown hair. "And so with one fell swoop, you remove all guilt from yourself."

Lucius could only shake his head. The man had been thinking this way for a long time, he realized. It might be too late to convince him.

"You cannot blame me for any of this, and you cannot deny that your heart is blackened by the lies you've told to others and to yourself. Your own actions have brought you this low, not those of anyone else. How can you hope to rise from it on your own?"

Rodney swallowed and gave another small cough. Then he changed the subject.

"And Alexcena? How do you excuse yourself from that?"

"What do you mean?"

"I wanted her," Dushaw barked. "I had known her far longer than you. I had been trying to court her for weeks before you ever came into her life. How can you call yourself an honorable man when you stole the object of another man's affection?"

"Are you still capable of affection?" Lucius tossed back. He had not meant to say it and quickly continued. "You have forgotten one crucial factor in your story. *She* never wanted *you*."

"Do you even know where she is? What's befallen her, hm?"

Lucius recognized that Rodney just wanted to prick him. To draw blood to the surface and watch it spill. He knew that this was the last pleasure he might indulge in where Lucius was concerned, and he was giving in to it. Lucius might have put him in his place except for one thing; he did not want Rodney to know where Alexcena was.

"That is not who we should be discussing," he said after a suitable hesitation. "You are in far more danger. I can help you if only you will consent to listen to what I say."

"You, the simpleton, helping me. With that?"

Lucius had, not thinking, set his hand on his Bible atop the stack of books.

Rodney coughed. He tried to cover his mouth with his arm, and tiny dots of red fell there.

"What is it?" Lucius asked harshly. "Pneumonia? Cancer? Is it too much for you to believe that you might be close to death?"

"Good!" Dushaw spat. "I welcome it. The life I'm leading is no longer a life at all. I'm done. It'll be nice to sleep the long sleep and know that you remain here."

"Your life is more valuable than that," Lucius replied fervently. "Once it's over you won't have another chance at it."

He could not quell his concern for the man's soul. It sickened him to think that anyone might be so cavalier about eternity.

"I don't want anything from you," Rodney wheezed around his coughs. "Even if I did, I would never ask it."

Lucius sat back, defeated. "That's a shame," he breathed, "because if you asked the right question, I would give you all that I could."

Rodney turned his head to scowl at the door behind him, as though willing one of the soldiers to open it and drag him away. Lucius considered him for a time before deciding to speak again.

"There is one thing that I would know of you, Rodney."

Very slowly Dushaw faced him.

"You sent me here to get me out of your way. So that you could live the life you wanted. The one that you believe I stole."

Rodney's jaw flexed as he gritted his teeth.

"After I was gone," Lucius went on, "did you gain anything?"

The corner of one of Rodney's eyes twitched. He expelled a long, rattling breath, his gaze boring into Lucius.

"What a foolish question."

That was the end of it; the last word. For it was after that Rodney rose to his feet and moved to beat on the door. Lucius could only stare as he allowed the redcoats to manhandle him down the hall. He neither communicated with him nor saw him the rest of his days. A mere three weeks later, Rodney Dushaw was found dead in a prison cell.

Chapter 16

March 10, 1766

Lucius went home that afternoon as if entranced. When he arrived at the cottage, he could remember nothing of the walk. It was not until he had left the prison that he allowed himself to consider all that he had seen and heard. The conversation had been so unreal and so short-lived that he found it almost unbelievable. So distracted was he with recalling the event that Alexcena was obliged to walk right up to him before he acknowledged her.

"Lucius?"

"What? My goodness!" He grinned and his chuckle was only half forced. "I didn't see you."

She had walked to meet him on the path to the cabin. Now she stared up at him through a shade of long lashes. "Am I so unnoticeable?"

Being beside the Faradays' home, they were secluded for the most part. He took the opportunity to stroke her cheek. "Ridiculous. You can't help being noticeable." Leaning in, he kissed her forehead.

"What's the matter, Lucius?"

He debated within himself as he held her. This was not something he was about to keep from her. His only regret was that it had come on a day when they would have so many other, happier things to discuss. He would tell her, but he was not willing to do so that evening.

"Where are Foley and Commodore?" he asked into her hair.

"Out with one of Foley's friends."

"Capital!" In one swift movement, he took her by the hand and tugged her back toward the road. "I have something I want to show you."

"Lucius!" she laughed merrily. "What are we doing?"

"It is not far. Come with me, just for a little while."

He knew she would not refuse. For Alexcena's part, she could not resist that incandescent smile.

He led her two blocks down to where the road cut a corner around a large mercantile. From there they passed three well-kept homes and came to a vacant lot.

"This is it," Lucius breathed with evident pleasure.

Alexcena raised an eyebrow, looking for the joke. "This is what?"

"Ours."

He enjoyed watching as her mouth fell open and her cheeks drained of color. Then she raised a hand to cover her mouth and looked once more to the lot.

"Oh, my, Lucius!"

He laughed and wondered if she would swoon; but of course he knew that she would not. Making an elegant leg, he bowed.

"Would you fancy a tour, my heart? See here." He took her hand once again and guided her forward. "This will be the front walk."

He made a great show of opening the nonexistent front door. Alexcena could only smile as she watched. The color was fast returning to her cheeks, drawn by a spark of joy.

"This shall be the foyer, and I fully intend to carry you across the threshold."

Before she knew what was happening, Lucius lifted her up and did just that. He spun her through the parlor and the study, stopping at the line of trees at the back of the property. There, beneath a shelter of boughs, he set her on her feet. Though she kept her hold on his forearms.

"When did you do this?" she wondered, her cheeks flushed with merriment.

"Garret helped me to arrange it last week. I wasn't certain it would happen at all until two days ago. Then I was waiting for the right moment to show you."

"Today was right?"

"Yes. Today is perfect."

Lucius wound one hand into the hair that fell below her shoulders and kissed her, not caring if one person were to see. Alexcena sobered and gave in to the kiss he sought. Though it lasted for but a moment, the feeling of contentment it brought remained with each of them. Lucius' smile broadened as he watched her.

"I have walked miles and miles of this New World," Lucius said when the moment had ended.

"So have I."

"It is a plenteous, fascinating land," he went on in quiet regard, his eyes moving to the trees around them. "I believe we'll do well here."

Alexcena raised a teasing eyebrow. "I believe we *are* doing well here."

He gave her a sheepish smile of agreement, but remained serious. "I have to tell you I was barely able to afford the plot."

"*We* were barely able to afford the plot," she replied.

He studied her, the corners of his mouth creeping up again. "You should have more than a tiny room in a small cottage, but it will take some time-"

He broke off. She looked serene as ever. Even in the shadows of the trees-rather especially in the shadows of the great trees-she was radiant.

"I know it will take time, Lucius…but we'll get there."

He fingered a curl of hair at her temple. Then, leaning in, he sighed in her ear. "That is precisely what I thought you would say."

They walked more slowly than was necessarily appropriate along the way back to the house. They went hand in hand, perfectly at ease. When they arrived Alexcena went inside to see if Lavinia might need her help with the baby. Foley was just walking home with Commodore and Garret was standing in the doorway.

"You told her at last!" he said by way of greeting.

"I told you," Lucius reminded him, "I wanted the day to be just right. You may recall that it has rained the last few days."

"Yes, I suppose that would dampen the enthusiasm of anyone looking at a piece of land for the first time."

Then Lucius was dimly aware of the approaching clammer of hoof beats. Even hearing the sound, he paid it no mind until he heard Foley call,

"Post rider coming! Post rider coming!"

Lucius felt his pulse rush. He turned to watch the man coming. It seemed ages ago since he had sent his letter with Tabitha to be delivered to the Condreves. He had thought much of it as of late, wondering if something might have happened to the response. Wondering if they waited in vain. Every time a post rider came through, his hopes rose and fell again. This time he held his shoulders straight. This time he determined to remain impassive for Alexcena's sake more than his own. He had seen her on the verge of tears more than once when letters had been delivered and no answer was among them. This time he would be much stronger than he had been for her on such occasions. He would not allow his heart to be bruised.

The rider stopped in front of the house and walked up to the men. "Looking for Mr. Faraday, Mrs. Faraday, and Mr. Wolgath."

"Wolgath?" Garret cried. "You have post for Wolgath?"

"Yes, sir. Have I the correct house?"

Lucius held fast to his calm. This had happened to him once or twice before and had turned out to be disappointing. "Yes," he responded. "You have the correct house."

The rider held out a stack of five or so envelopes, touched his cap, and was gone again.

"Let's-uh-go on inside then," Lucius murmured. Ordinarily he would not have invited himself even into Garret's home, but his nerves were getting the better of him.

Garret stood to one side and allowed him to enter first. He heard Foley coming in as well and footsteps descending the stairs.

"What is going on, Garret?" Lavinia said from somewhere above.

"Post has arrived."

"Letters?" Alexcena's voice then. He both felt and heard her dash down the last few steps to draw close. "What is it, Lucius? Who has written?"

Lucius remained as he was, staring at the bundle in his hands. The letter on top was addressed to Garret from some business office or other. Lucius was afraid to look at the rest. Until his dying day he never understood why, but for some reason when he passed Alexcena the stack the last envelope remained in his grasp. As soon as he gave them to her he knew it was a cowardly thing to do. He had been afraid to look at them himself. She obviously was not as she began flipping through them quickly.

"Mr. Faraday, Mr. Faraday, Lavinia, and-" She stopped, breathless. "And-Leopold! Lucius it's a letter from Leopold to you!"

Lucius was no longer paying attention. He was looking down at the last envelope. It was addressed to him in a tailored, familiar script. He did not need to see the return address to know that the name there would be Condreve. For all the time that had passed for him to prepare, he was still entirely unprepared for that moment. He had talked of this day time and again with Alexcena. They knew what the answer would be. How could it be anything other than favorable when her parents were so enamored with Lucius and they were so in love? There was no doubting it. Lucius knew what would be written there without a moment's worry. They had only been waiting for the permission to arrive, and here it was at last. The final word that would truly set them free to be together.

"It's a letter from your father."

When Lucius spoke his voice was husky to his own ears. All talking in the room ceased. He lifted his eyes to Alexcena and saw no other. Wonderment clouded her features. Two tears spilled down her cheeks before she could check them.

Lucius Wolgath smiled at her, and with his thumb, he broke the seal of the letter.

The End